Catlorian:

Savon'el

by

R. L. Pool

DORRANCE
PUBLISHING CO
EST. 1920
PITTSBURGH, PENNSYLVANIA 15238

Dorrance Publishing Co
585 Alpha Drive
Suite 103
Pittsburgh, PA 15238
Visit our website at *www.dorrancebookstore.com*

ISBN: 978-1-4809-2410-9
eISBN: 978-1-4809-2939-5

Prologue

The large man in the shimmering black cloak sat in the glade on a fallen tree. His blond hair was tied back and his silver eyes gazed into the still forest. The head of a great puma rested upon his lap, as did two gray squirrel kits. He absently stroked the tawny fur between the great cat's ears as he pondered the old historian's question.

He had never desired to discuss the "whys" and "wherefores" of his actions. The only reason he thought to do so now was the old one who sat upon the ground before him.

Terillion was old. Those who were acquainted with him only remember the wrinkled old man with the whining voice and his senile eccentricities.

Maxim knew him better.

This was the oldest living sage in known existence. His prime purpose was the gathering of information, any information, and it mattered little how insignificant.

Well, the life and quest of Maxim Anteroe, "Wanderer," could be described as anything but insignificant.

"Please understand, I do not attempt to justify my actions or the reasons for them. I simply wish, as you say, to set the record straight. Therefore, let us begin at the beginning.

"I was alive long before this world entered into existence. How long? You would not believe me. If you must know, I have never really counted the passage of time, for to do so might cause me to slip into madness. Let it suffice to say that I have watched as two worlds prior to this one came into being and fell into destruction. I realize that, should these words be read beyond you, my friend, others might stare in disbelief, or—worse—scorn. Whatever the reception, it does not alter the truth of my statement. My age is greater than even the Lady Brea of Sylvan Sha'terra, for I watched her birth, death, and rebirth.

"I have watched throughout this world's history—its rise, decline, and rebirth—and am saddened. To my knowledge, I am the only true worshipper of those called 'Fates.' I serve the Three Sisters exclusively. This has been both a curse and a gift: a gift in that I have been granted immortality, and a curse for the same reason.

"The Sisters have an insatiable desire to study the universal constant of an entire world's lifecycle. I am the agent for that study in that I have the ability to recall any conversation, idea, anything I see or perceive. You cannot imagine what it is like to live through creation, feel the love, sorrow, pain, happiness, and joy of millions, and then stand by and watch as the entire creation disappears.

"After the second world turned to ash, as recorded through my tears, I could stand no more.

"'Why?' I asked. 'Have you no compassion? Are you so cold in your godhood that you could not lift a finger to stop the destruction long before it happened? How much death can you see before it is enough? Why must I be party to your disinterested entertainment?'

"One does not lightly question the actions of gods, but I, in my pain and remorse, transgressed all common sense and did so. What could they do to me that could possibly be worse than what I'd just witnessed? I was soon to learn, for their answer increased my burden tenfold.

"'You, yourself,' they replied, 'are immortal at our whim. Was that a mistake? We think not. We selected you for what you are, no more, no less. Until now, you've done well.

"'Perhaps, however, you are correct. We could simply remove man's ability to make choices. They would be incapable of doing anything we had not directed into their fate. Is that what you wish, Maxim? A world of toys, of playthings that have no mind, no direction or will short of godly intervention? No! This is the one rule the Creator will not allow to be broken! Man must make of his fate what he will and must care for the innocent life he was created to tend! But we are not without compassion. You, Maxim Anteroe, will witness and record but the next ten cycles of creation. Then you will be free to return to the dust, since that seems to be your wish.

"'Mark this well, Maxim. You are not to directly influence the worlds you encounter. This is our wish and your fate!'

"For centuries I wandered the realms of infinity, the horror of my reality fitting itself into the recesses of my overly active mind.

"That horror, you see, stems not from the lives of the 'intelligent' inhabitants of those worlds, though I do have a certain compassion for those who, by dint of talent, compassion, and loyalty, carry out the duties assigned by the Creator. It is for the very life and balance of nature, the trees, grass, the indigenous life that is always the first to appear and thrive and is, ultimately, the last to die, that I mourn. Those who may read this manuscript may see that there is a method to my madness after all.

"I was drawn to this world at its creation, stepping through a gate into serenity. The peaceful beauty of this world so closely resembled the one before I thought I had traveled back in time.

"My joy lasted only a short while, however, as I became aware of, first, the subtle differences between this world and the last. Then, when I felt the presence of humanity, I realized I had been sent to witness yet another cycle of pain.

"I turned my agile mind to the problem of prolonging this world. Being forbidden to actively participate in its development, I cannot take an active hand in guiding the inhabitants.

"However..."

Chapter One

The sphere hung in the eternity of breathless space, its face turning on its tilted axis toward the yellow sun so far distant. Its seas lapped at the shores of the landmasses that grew out of the throes of its creation.

Four of these rises were in relatively close proximity and, while the gods chuckled, the intelligent life upon them swore them to be all.

These lesser gods could well laugh for they had been here, watching, as the greater gods drew away. The races of men had formed violent alliances and had all but destroyed what the Creator had wrought. Those of the greater gods turned away in disgust.

Those of the lesser sphere stayed on, some to care for those who still believed, others to force belief in their evil intent. The Mage War had devastated much of what was beautiful in the land, resulting in the intense heat in that vast continent just below the equatorial center of the spinning globe. Then, the perpetual winter in that one far north and closest to the northern hub of that invisible axis.

The two great masses of land between those held most of what was left of the survivors: the living things of flora and fauna, and the last of the races of men.

The worst of the war had raged on the largest continent of Ta'el, Catlor, whose surface of ranges, mountains, and plains once teemed with harmony and whose creatures lived within the framework provided by the Creator. The greater gods provided mankind with the knowledge of healing and magic with which to care for the living things and with a greater intelligence to aid in that endeavor.

The fair Sha'terra, those we call "elves," held sway within the vast forests of that before time and lived in haughty harmony with the race of Cheal.

The Cheal were closest to the earth, their powers supplemented by the quirk of nature that allowed them to mind-bond, at the powerful change that puberty creates, to "called" beasts. It was not a random thing, this calling. In those days, a creature was known to travel hundreds of leagues to bond with the one that called in fever. Once the bond was made, this pact was unbreakable short of death, the living entity of that pact smaller with the loss. Thereafter, half a beast, man or animal, existed where once there was a whole.

Then the wide portals through the planes appeared and through them came the others. While the Sha'terra pulled back into their forests and allowed the strange ones to enter undisturbed, the Cheal watched the writhing curtains flow from world to world. The Cheal were used to freedom and, while they were welcomed or tolerated by the fair race, these others held them in fear, scorned them at every turn, and fought them to attain "ownership" of the lands freely given for their use by the very gods they proclaimed. The Cheal tried to aid and attempted to teach, but in the end they failed to reach these new men of strange race.

The wavering portal opened upon a world wild and green, and they walked through with their "saola" familiars.

Soon, in the time of the gods, these races of man—dwarf, the stout stone workers and miners of the minerals of the earth; human, the barbaric intellectual users of the plenty without return and possessing strength in adaptability; and the gray elves, called bright, who were joined by other races of elves, each the offspring of Sha'terra ventures to other worlds and the effect of years of inbreeding, yet each haughty in its own bloodline--each wanted more than his share.

The Elf-Dwarf War had begun, and humanity chose sides as it would. Those on the side of evil found the formula for the recreation of life. Gualu sprang into existence as the expendable slaves of the evil wizard's whim. These vile replications of humanity were never gifted with anything close to heart; thus, they were the perfect weapons in the evil hand.

Somewhere in the violence that rocked the entire planet, the original reason for the war was forgotten. Though the time of its origin was forgotten, the Mage War erupted into being and ravaged the planet.

The Sha'terra shook their sad mane and withdrew to elsewhere. The Triad, Lords of Light, the gods of that bright race, followed its chosen.

The powers of the arcane were learned and used to devastating effect, growing more and more powerful with each year. Deaths exceeded births after but a few centuries of the conflict. Birthing mothers cried, not in pain but in loss, as they knew the child that cried from their wombs would soon return to the dust.

In the end, the balance between what was good and what was evil was achieved in the final devastation, with many of the wielders of the magiks joined in a common goal. They were of both sides, sickened of death, sickened more of the privations of groups of vast evil that destroyed with no reason save the destruction itself.

With the crushing of that evil came a decision.

The magiks wielded were too powerful a temptation. It cost the practitioners nothing save the ministrations of spells spoken as objects were combined. The articles, or components, of the making of these more and more powerful spells rested in shoulder pouches slung from the shoulders of these Mages. Books of power in the forging of the spells littered libraries within their fortresses. The centuries-long war taught them all—all of the remaining Mages of power—that there could be no winner. There were only losers.

There was one among them, chosen by all, who was tasked with the answer. His name was stripped from him so no one could use it against him should they disagree with his final decision. He was to ask for no guidance as he pondered this.

His response was unique in its simplicity.

"I have thought on this well and, though you might think me mad, have found a solution. We all agree that the magiks of our world are just too easy, that the casting of spells bears only the cost of diction and the loss of a few cheap components. Therefore, the only answer is our magiks must change. The cost to those who would be practitioners must be high enough to prevent misuse. This *must* be done!"

"What of the evil?"

"That too must be taken into account. I have met with the Elders of each hall and they agree with my hypothesis. I have chosen from among you one who must be prepared to deal with the shift of Balance."

A man stepped forward then. In his eyes no fear could be found, nor was he overwhelmed with self. His robes were cast off with his name. He stood naked to the assembly and waited.

"Here, then, is he chosen for his self-soul and his non-judgmental intellect. Each must give unto him of our essence. I will be the focus of your chant and deliver it to this chosen vessel against that day."

The power of that combined chant flowed through the Decider into the body of the chosen. He fell to the rich green earth. The chant continued on, the vessel filling with thrown-off power as the assemblage gave of itself. The last words were spoken and the air about the throng ceased in its powerful reverberations.

"He sleeps," stated the Decider.

Six dwarves bore a coffin made of translucent green crystal and set it next to the motionless body. They lifted the smooth lid, laid it aside, and backed away.

The Decider gazed at the peacefully sleeping man, sighed as sadness touched his eyes, and began speaking the words of wind and air. Breezes, strange in their lack of direction and fragrance, stirred the gathering. As the body of the chosen one drifted from the ground, a cloak of green draped him as if pulled from the very air. He settled into the green crystal coffin, arms folded, to await the un-hoped for.

The Decider came forward and passed his hand above the coffin. A sword of brilliance materialized, as did a staff of wondrous proportions. The staff floated down to lay beside the figure within the crystal, but the sword stayed suspended. Its jeweled sheath shone multicolored light upon those closest—the light from the three moons of Ta'el.

The Decider retrieved pen and parchment from his pouch and wrote. His light chant could be heard but not understood by those close. Once finished, the pen went back into his pouch, but the parchment was rolled and placed into a small tube, then tucked into the sleeper's hand.

"Let the Lords of Light be witness..." spoke he, his hand raised to the three moons as they stood aligned with one another in the night sky.

"Let the Triad be the key," responded the others.

"May the Blade of Balance..."

"Be used only to return Balance."

"May he we name Warden of Ta'el..."

"Sleep for eternity."

The lid lifted as if on air and settled over the sleeping man. The sword hovered directly above. The Decider murmured words of power and, with a finger brilliant with that power, etched the lid of the coffin. The runes etched there glowed only for a moment.

The deeds necessary for safety were not yet done.

"I need copper from each of us," declared the Decider, his stormy blue eyes flashing. "There is but one more thing that must be forged against the un-hoped for."

Each Mage took what they could—a bangle, an eye from a boot, a coin minted in far places— but all contributed.

When the baskets of copper found their way to the Decider, he had them turned over to an aging dwarf whose smelter glowed with an arcane fire. Into this went the pieces of copper, and the gnarled hands of the small smith stirred until all was melted and combined. His tongs sought the form made months before and heated within the forge lest the result be cold and brittle.

Into the mold poured all from the smelter, even though normally all could never fit within that casting. When nearly cool, he turned the casting over and the rough form of a great sword fell smoldering to the ground. The smith's quick tongs grasped it and lifted it to the surface of the great anvil. His stature required that he stand upon a stump above that surface to work his magic of hammer and tong. He turned once to the faces of the throng, and then he waved them back. His strong right hand found the sheath of the hammer that rode his hip and slid it from its confinement.

Those of elfin descent backed away farther as the loathing crawled over their bodies and penetrated to their very souls.

"This ting mus' be tempered wit' arcane an' hammered wit' col' wrought," stated the dwarf as he lifted the hammer and dropped it to the waiting metal.

The Decider stood above the anvil and held his hands over the copper sword as the Mages began their chant.

The memory haunted him now. As the Decider, he had called upon the Mages of the world to join in the twisting of the magiks. What had been possible with the use of components in a spell was now only possible by the spending of one's own essence.

He had the choice, then, to destroy the evil but had not. A single tear of regret formed at the corner of one smoldering blue eye as his hand pulled at the neat white beard. His white hair and brows were the only announcement of his extreme age, the only exception to the extended lifetime afforded by the jewel that rested, hidden, against his breast.

"Master?" asked a voice from the door.

He turned from the portal that faced out over the walls of the great city to the youth who had called.

"Will you eat now, Myrlin?"

Why not? What else should he do that he hadn't? He'd felt the evil approach again and had no help for it. Even Warden had been secreted in safety by the elements against this day, yet of him there was no sign.

There was time yet, so he decided, for himself this time, to eat. Then he would make what preparations he could. Time was a precious commodity these days, but you know, haste makes...whatever.

"I'm coming, youngster. Be patient with an old man."

Chapter Two

Pain, despair, loathing. Silver dragon emblem on silver armor, engulfed in red screaming flame. Panic, smoke, monstrous figures wheel high over a burning city. One approaches, fear, panic, the maniacal laughter reaches down, entrapped in futility, panic, fear.

Water. A figure walks in...on...over water. Sunlight. Floating over water, someone carries... Wet sand. Pain...

He woke.

He lay motionless until his vision cleared and the shaking subsided. The sweat on his body was cold and clammy, and, try as he might, he couldn't remember the dream, if a dream it was.

He looked cautiously about this room. A lamp of fish oil on the small table beside the bed cast its flickering warmth about the room. All about was the feel of warmth, cleanliness, and comfort. The homespun coverlet had been quilted by hand. The dark sturdy wood of the chest, which sat against the wall between the door and the small hearth, showed the high polish of use and care. The stone of the walls kept the heat of the day away from this room, yet the high window above his head allowed the smell of the salt winds to enter. This room had a soul, a feeling of comfort and love. Home.

The door opened and the youth allowed his eyes to be drawn to it.

The cherubic face of a small woman peered through the doorway. She smiled in genuine relief and care at the sight of the young man now awake.

The smile seemed to brighten the room, the laugh lines of her face deep with constant use. This woman knew happiness and shared that happiness with all, including this young man who lay upon the handmade rope bed. She winked at the youth and turned her head away from the room.

"'E's woked, Culligan. Yer young'un is woked up," said she.

She bustled into the room, drying her hands on the sky-blue apron worn over her yellow dress. She was but five feet and plump. Not fat as one would expect, but rounded as a grandmother would be to young ones. The sparkle in her eyes and the youthful step made one argue with the silver in her hair.

"Now yo'dnt should be movin' too much, young'un," she said as she began fussing with the coverlet, smoothing it and tucking it about him. "The bump on yer 'ead prolly'll make yer 'ead spin a bit if ye does."

The young man reached tentative, shaking fingers to the bandage behind his left ear. The pain seemed to radiate from there and something else.

"'Tis a'right. Dinna bleed much 'tall."

"Now let th' bairn be, Megan. He'll be fine in a bit. Might ye be makin' some broth? Been too long wit'out vittles, I be thinkin'."

When the deep voice reached him from the doorway, the young man had been watching the small woman, Megan, move about the bed, her gentle concern causing a smile of trust and warmth to reach his lips. He turned his head toward the door instinctively to see who was there.

The pain ripped through his head and a low moan escaped his lips. His vision blurred anew and he closed his eyes against the pain and vertigo.

"Ye see, Cully? I canna leave ye to see after the bairn. Yer've gotta be kerful o' 'es 'ead."

"I'll mind it, lass," said the voice as the youth heard the man move toward the bed. "Now, do yer wanna starve this 'un what yer've only jist brought back to th' livin'? Aye, ye'd best be makin' tha' broth now. I'll look after the boy."

"A'right, Cully, but ye mind 'es 'ead," came the response as the youth felt the woman leave.

"I will, luv."

The youth felt the man's presence at the side of the bed and risked opening his eyes. They cleared after a moment and he got his first look at Culligan Vandergast.

He was big, six feet plus, and massive, all muscle and sinew. His homespun shirt, open at the collar, harnessed a massive chest matted with bright red hair speckled with gray. The hair that framed his squared-off face was of the same bright red, graying slightly at the temples. The clean smell of wind and salt was about him, his tanned leathery features told of life on the sea and his calloused hands spoke volumes on hard work. His icy gray eyes cast concern to the youth, a question unasked, a strange sense of joy, and a past of something else. There was power here, and tenderness. The youth felt the line between the two and the protectiveness that demanded answers.

"Well, me boyo, looks like ye'll live." he said as he sat on the edge of the bed and looked down at the youth. "Now, before the li'l woman comes back an' unleashes a tirade o' gentle curses upon me head fer botherin' ye, mayhap ye cin tell me how ye came ta be washin' up on th' tide like a bushel o' kelp."

Culligan frowned with concern as the youth's face became even paler, the fear a tangible thing.

"'Tis a'right, boyo. Jist tell me yer name. There must be some what is worried about ye, an' I've nothin' agin half elfs."

The boy's eyes grew large and his mouth opened slightly. No sound came forth and he began shaking with effort and fear. The sweat beaded on his lip as he looked up at the big redhead. The horror shown in his face caused Culligan to stand and grasp the youth by the shoulders.

"'Tis a'right, I say!"

"Wha'd ya do ta 'im, Cully?" came the stern voice of Megan.

She pulled Culligan away from the bed and pushed him back. Then she turned and sat on the bed and placed her cool hand on the youth's brow.

"Jes' loo' at 'im." she continued with a frown. "'E be scart spitless."

She leaned over the boy then and took his face in her hands.

"Wha' is it, laddy? C'mon. Yer cin tell ol' Megan."

The youth seemed to calm at the old woman's touch and she continued.

"Jes' take it slow."

He gazed into the soft blue of the woman's eyes and found a tear. He closed his own and swallowed. His throat was parched and his voice seemed to be useless, but the power of this woman's caring reached through and gave the youth the strength he needed.

"I don't..." he croaked, then swallowed again. "I don't know anything. Gods, I don't even know my own name."

He spent another two weeks in bed being mothered before Megan was finally convinced that he should be up and about. Then she allowed him to fetch for her around the house as long as he promised not to "'arm 'is self."

Culligan noticed the youth's restlessness of the past several days and decided that enough was enough.

"Would yer like ta go out wit' me in th' morn, boyo?" he asked as they sat down to the evening meal. "Th' ice be comin' an' we needs ta git as much fishin' in afore th' season end."

Megan placed a protective hand on the young man's arm and glared at the big redhead.

"Now, Cully, ye mus' le' th' lad 'eal."

"Megan, me luv, th' bairn has had eno' motherin'. Let 'im stretch hisself a bit."

"'E's jes' now movin' proper. If ye git 'im out on yer boat, ye'll work 'im ta death."

"Let's let th' boy make his own mind up on tha', lass." He grinned and then turned to the half elf. "Well, lad?"

The youth looked into the small woman's face and saw the concern. He knew that soon he'd have to move on, if for no other reason than to meet others whose faces or names would fight through the blackness around his memory. This wonderful woman had given him a home, a mother's love, though he knew not his own or if he even still had one, and had asked for no recompense. This lady had treated a total stranger as a son and he would do anything to keep from harming her. It would be better, he thought, to finish his healing away, but not too far away.

"Lady Megan," said he, as he placed his hand over the one she rested on his arm, "it would do me good to get out into the sunshine and do some honest, hard work to promote the healing that you have started. It's now up to me to see that you've not wasted your time."

He got a small smile and a light nod from the old woman. He turned back to Culligan. "When do I start?"

"We go on the dawn, lad. I'll fix ye up wi' a slicker 'n boots. Ye might check in the chest there in th' room ye been stayin'. Is our boy, Eton's. Me stuffs a bit large. His things would prolly fit ye better. He's away now an' I'm sure he wouldn't mind."

"You're sure it's all right?"

"Ah, ye'd like him, lad." The big redhead turned to his lady and added, "Now dinna worry, Megan. I'll make th' boy go slow. Honest, me luv."

Megan turned a stern look on Culligan and, as her blue eyes sparkled, said, "Culligan Vandergast. If ye 'arm 'im by over workin' 'im, ye'll 'ave me ta reckon wit'."

The half elf could see in her eyes that this was no idle threat.

The youth spent the next two months working with Culligan on his fishing boat named, appropriately, *Megan's Lament*. Culligan had suggested that he use "Boyo" as his name, but only "till ye git yer own back, lad."

He pulled his share of the work in drawing the nets, bailing, and, if becalmed, rowing the sleek fishing boat back to Seafoam. All of the residents of the village accepted him as if he'd lived there his entire life, and he was content. Though knowing that one day he'd have to leave, he knew he'd always be welcome here in this village.

His body hardened as it healed. The muscles in his powerful arms, legs, and massive chest bunched as he lifted the weight of the fishing tack. His skin tanned brown except for the scars on his arms, and his auburn hair bleached until it was a reddish blond. His elfish features and short stature, half a head over five feet, made him fair to look upon.

Culligan watched him closely through those first weeks and knew there was more to this young man than met the eye. On a day several weeks after the young man began working on the boat, a freak wind came up, churning the small bay into choppy soup. They couldn't go out in that so Culligan decided to take the half elf into his work room. Boyo stared in awe at the armor and weapons Culligan had made for himself.

"Ah, Boyo," the big redhead explained, "we wasn't always th' fishermen ye see here. We all was once fighters in the games at Seaborne. I was th' one called th' Red Avenger. The pretty people would come dun ta watch th' spillin' o' blood an' banquet their minds inta blackness fer days."

The sadness in the big man's eyes told the tale. He'd been a slave sold into the games. His prowess on the field of slaughter for entertainment had earned him the freedom he now held so precious. Only the gods knew how many men Culligan had slain to win free. Even Cully couldn't recall, but every soul weighed on his, a debt owed them for the wand he'd earned through their blood.

Then the moment was gone. In its place was a man who proudly displayed his hobby to an interested youngster.

"I come dun here when th' water's rough or th' ice be thick an' practice. It keeps me in shape an' tuned, jes' in case o' pirates an' marauders an' such. I haven't had many ta spar wit' lately, so would ye like ta go a round or so wit' me, lad?"

Boyo smiled and pulled at one of the practice swords. It was a bastard sword, four and a half feet long from pommel to tip, with a wide blade and an extended grip. It left the bracket with a song and, if it weren't for the dulled blade, one would believe this to be a weapon of quality from its balance and grip and the way it made itself but an extension of the wielder's body.

Culligan saw the light shine in the half elf's amber eyes and nodded. He'd watched the young man move as he worked on the boat, saw the calluses on his hands when he'd carried him from the beach, and thought he might help to jar some of those elusive memories loose in the practice ring.

After working in the ring for some two hours, Culligan decided that the only part of this young man that had no memory was his mind. The strokes and counterstrokes were superb and must have been taught from birth and by a master. Cully carefully drew the knowledge out, driving with ever increasing energy until the young man's body responded without thought, knew without knowing, and moved on instinct alone. As the last ring of steel echoed through the practice ring and the two stood grinning at each other, a pert, peeved voice cut across them.

"Yer've gone 'n got yerse'f all asweat, young'un. Culligan, ye promised not ta push 'im so."

Megan stood in the doorway, a stern look on her face and her tiny right foot patted the ground impatiently.

"Ah, but Megan, me luv," began the big redhead, looking somewhat like a child caught with his hand in the cookie jar, "loo' at 'im. He's tired, true, but wha' o' th' grin on his face, aye?"

She turned her stern gaze on the grinning half elf and the stern frown melted into a smile. Then, pointing a small finger at the both of them and trying to regain her stern composure, she said, "Ye'll no be settin' foot in me 'ouse drippin' sweat on me clean floors. Git washed, the both o' ye! Supper's 'most ready."

Then she turned and stalked back toward the house.

The two grinned at each other and followed her as she marched happily across her small lawn. The men went around to the pump to wash.

"Lad," said Cully as he dried a moment later, "yer've had trainin', an' from th' loo' o' it, a grand teacher. If ye'll let me, I'll help ye grind off some o' th' rough edges. I got some o' me old scale out in th' shop could be sized for ye, an' a good sword could be found in there ta yer likin', I'll bound. I dinna know who ye are any mor'n ye do, but yer've got good trainin' an' breedin'. I like ye, lad."

The old gladiator glanced over at the youth and continued. "I know we decided ta call ye Boyo, but we gotta find ye a proper name."

Boyo looked at Culligan soberly for a moment. Then the smell of stewed chicken caught his nose and he grinned.

"It doesn't really matter, Cully. Time will come when I'll know all. When that time is here, I'll be able to tell you everything there is to know about me. There is one thing, however, I refuse to be called."

"Wha's that, lad?"

"Late for Megan's stew." He laughed as he threw the cloth at Culligan and ran for the kitchen door.

After the supper dishes had been washed and put away, the two men sat in the small parlor with their feet stretched toward the fire. Megan was puttering about in the kitchen preparing dough for tomorrow's bread. Culligan smoked an old briar and the half elf gazed at the sword and the Freedom Wand crossed over the mantle.

Culligan saw the direction of the youth's gaze, got up, and took the sheathed sword from the wall.

"Th' wand yer've heard me speak of, but this here is me darlin'. She's th' one what won me my freedom. That's why she stays there wit' the symbol she won."

He pulled the blade from the lacquered leather sheath and handed it hilt first to Boyo.

The half elf had never seen such a beautiful sword. It had a silver filigreed pommel and a leather-wrapped grip that would allow the use of both hands. The cross pieces curved slightly downward and were made of the same dull alloy as the flawless blade.

"She's a beauty, aye? Ah, but she's like any good woman." he said softly. "She holds a secret."

The old gladiator grinned and took the sword back from the half elf. He held it out before him, one hand on the grip close to the pommel, the other hand about midway down the blade.

"She loo's like a normal blade, don't she? Well, watch."

When Culligan finished his demonstration, the young half elf stared in total astonishment. A sword wasn't supposed to do the things this one could do. His disbelief brought a proud grin to Culligan's lips, and he readily complied when Boyo asked to show him again.

The two of them sat up late that evening, a thing that caused Megan to cluck her tongue at as she made her way to bed. Culligan demonstrated the tricks the sword could do, and the half elf picked them up after only a bit of practice. Finally, after the young man demonstrated that he could make that amazing sword do some of the things it was designed to do, Culligan took it back and looked at the youth sternly.

"This here sword is special, lad. The man who carries it mus' be worthy. If not, she'll let ye know. She has a name too, but ye'll not learn that 'til ye prove ye kin handle 'er. Now, I think it's time ta git some sleep. It'll be a fair day tomorrow, an' we'll need ta be out at the crack o' dawn. Winter be comin' on strong this year an' we must be gittin' our share."

Boyo watched reluctantly as Cully returned the sword to its sheath and hung it back on the wall.

Throughout the long winter of working the tack and nets for the next season, the half elf spent many late evenings in the practice ring honing his skills. Finally, one late winter morning just before the melt, he was finally rewarded by being formally introduced to Culligan's "darlin'."

Chapter Three

"She'll do."

The large man leaned against the wall at the side of the street and watched the young girl gaze into the shop window.

She was but five foot four and slight of build. Her long black hair, interspersed with eight small braids, contrasted beautifully with her fair complexion and partially hid the "Pouncing Falcon" emblazoned on the back of the bright yellow cloak pulled tight about her against the chill.

Three weeks ago he'd seen her on the street, intent on an errand for her temple. Her purposeful stride, her black hair, and the fire in her manner drew him. He'd inquired through his considerable contacts within Catlorian and arranged this day to his liking.

He was Lord Cartellion, the "Unholy Saladin of Death," and "Right Hand of Death." These titles, given to him by the populace and, if the truth were known, enhanced by his own people, rode his almost seven foot frame as easily as his armor. He was completely encased in black plate steel that seemed to ripple with every movement of his well-proportioned physique, almost as if it were a component of the man rather than a protective covering. The only relief in the black was the bone white skull emblem staring with eyeless sockets from his left breast. This emblem was the talisman of his god, and his god was Death.

As he levered away from the wall and strolled toward the girl, the god-gifted "Soul Searing" blade strapped to his back moaned softly.

"Not today, my friend." he whispered softly from within his Y-slit helm. "Today we make life, as was willed by our god."

Oddly there was no rattle of armor as the big Saladin strolled panther quiet to stand behind the girl.

"Are you a cleric of the goddess Freya?"

The deep, melodic baritone, strangely devoid of emotion, broke through the girl's reverie. She tossed her black tresses and smiled as she turned toward the voice, but the smile vanished as her green eyes took in the black armor, the white skull, and the hilt of the great sword that rode the Saladin's back. A pool of fear began feeding on her insides as she realized who stood before her.

"Excuse me, m'lord?"

She couldn't move. Though there was traffic on the street, no one would penetrate the twenty-foot buffer all gave the Lord Saladin. Most tried desperately not to notice him and hoped not to be noticed in return. Melisande, however, had been noticed and had no such escape. Cartellion smiled within his helm.

"You are a member of the order of clerics who worship the goddess Freya, correct?" said the man as he casually leaned against the wall of the shop.

"Yes, m'lord, though I am but an acolyte."

"You believe in love and happiness and all that?"

"Of course, m'lord," she answered defensively. "These are things all have a right to."

Cartellion was pleased. Only this one would say what she felt with the fear he could smell welling up within her.

"I believe I could use some instruction in these concepts. Would you be available this evening to come to my apartments for private discussions?"

The young cleric's mouth opened slightly in surprise. Could she have heard correctly? Did Lord Cartellion actually say he wanted to learn of her goddess and "the Joy"?

"He cannot expect me to..." she thought as she glanced from the helm to his breastplate, to his crotch, then back to his helm. She shook her head a bit to regain her composure.

"Uh, m'lord, there are more qualified instructors than I, priestesses with more training. Anything I would do would have to be approved by the temple clergy. I have but recently entered the service of Lady Freya and, I'm afraid, haven't the experience, the...knowledge required. I have taken the required vow of chastity and, even were that not so, my…inexperience would but offend, I fear."

"The temple clergy would have to give permission, you say?"

"Yes, m'lord."

"To the temple then."

He turned on his heel and walked off in the direction of the temple district, leaving the girl in a quandary as to what to do.

Cartellion glanced back and, seeing that she still stood frozen with a surprised look on her face, shouted, "Come then!" without breaking stride. The young cleric had to run to catch up with the big Saladin and slowed to a quick walk when she arrived at a position two paces behind.

Cartellion removed his helm as he stepped through the door into the rectory. High Priestess Serena heard the girl as she came through the door and turned to welcome whoever was there. She gasped at the soft beauty of the Lord Saladin's features.

The girl, who had reached the Saladin's side and glanced up, was also taken aback. It was the High Priestess who broke the awkward silence.

"Yes, m'lord?" she said in her soft, throaty voice. "What brings Lord Cartellion within the gates of Love and Happiness, the gift of Our Lady Freya?"

Cartellion scowled at the priestess, his black eyes narrowing at the greeting. Then, as if rethinking his position, a smile came softly to his lips, a smile that could have made the virginal girl beside him swoon had it not been for the roiling fear in her belly.

"I desire instruction," said he, "and I wish this one to instruct."

"Melisande, Lord?" asked the High Priestess as she glanced at the black-haired girl.

Melisande's eyes met hers with a silent plea of "please no!"

Serena gave the young cleric a small smile and a nod that said, "Don't worry, child. I'll handle this."

"Wouldn't you prefer a more experienced teacher than this one, m'lord?"

Cartellion frowned and stepped over to the crystal offertory.

"She's been in training for only a very few months, and she'll need at least two years more before being ready to properly instruct…"

Cartellion smiled and dropped one hundred gold pieces into the crystal bowl.

"Perhaps in a few months then. She would be much better qualified to render you the instruction you desire in a few more months, but now you could speak with someone else..."

Two hundred more gold pieces sang into the crystal bowl.

"...Someone more..."

"I desire a child by this one."

He was no longer smiling. A string of two hundred and fifty platinum pieces fell into the chiming crystal bowl and the High Priestess's mouth dropped open.

"What?" Melisande exclaimed in open-mouthed astonishment. She shook her head and grinned to herself. How could this monster even think...

Then her eyes found those of Serena. The half smile and the look of sympathy told her everything. She was paralyzed in shock and only vaguely heard her High Priestess as she answered the Lord Saladin. "Of course, m'lord."

Melisande shook off the paralysis and stared at the priestess. "But, m'lady, what of my vow of chastity? I cannot forsake my—"

The High Priestess raised a hand, effectively cutting off Melisande's protest.

"There will be special dispensation given, Melisande. Now, go and make ready."

"But—"

"Shush!" said the High Priestess sternly. Then, to Cartellion, "We shall prepare her as best we can and send her to your apartments at six this evening if that is acceptable?"

Cartellion looked from Serena down into the green pools of the young girl's eyes.

"Very well," he stated, then he donned his helm and strode from the temple.

Melisande stared incredulously at Serena and screamed, "Why?"

This was a nightmare from which she knew she would never wake. She had just been sold to Lord Cartellion, and not just for a night of pleasure but to have his child! "What have you done, Serena? Why?"

The High Priestess placed a soft hand on the shaking girl's head and looked deep into her eyes.

"Do you believe in the power of the Lady to bring healing, happiness, and love to those less fortunate?"

"Yes, but that's—"

"Do you believe that those not knowing the blessings of our Lady are the least fortunate of all?"

"Yes, but—"

"It is, therefore, your duty to do what can be done to bring the joy of our Lady to those of the least, is it not?"

"Yes, but—"

"Can you name anyone knowing less than Lord Cartellion on the subject of love, peace, joy, and happiness?"

Melisande opened her mouth to protest again, but the logic, though just a bit strange, finally struck her. She felt childish, and a strange sense of humility entered her soul. She dropped her eyes to the floor.

"No, m'lady."

The goddess Freya had set an almost impossible task for her. Attempting to teach one such as the Lord Saladin on the subject of love would be a challenge for a High Priestess. Only a miracle could allow a virginal acolyte to accomplish this alone. She opened her heart and soul and silently prayed for guidance from her goddess.

"Go, now, Melisande, and make yourself ready. I shall come for you this evening."

Hours later the two priests escorted her to the door of the two-storied building in the elite section of Catlorian. Though the area was where the guild masters, rich merchants, and the Myrlin of Catlorian resided, this building was nondescript save the huge iron-bound oaken door. The iron knocker had been set high in the center of the door and there was no door handle.

Melisande lifted the heavy ring of the knocker and let it fall. Immediately a manservant opened the door and stood aside to usher the girl within. Melisande glanced once toward the departing backs of the two priests, took a deep breath, and entered.

"The master awaits you in the parlor," said the servant softly.

As he lead her down the hallway, the door behind her closed softly by itself. Melisande noted doors to the left and right and a stairway at the end of the hall that led, obviously, to the upper floor. The servant stopped at the last door on the left, knocked once, opened the door, and stood aside to allow Melisande to enter.

The parlor was large and masculine in its décor of dark wood and leather. Lord Cartellion leaned on the mantle of the large hearth at the far end of the room and held a crystal goblet filled with pale wine.

Melisande glanced quickly back at the door only to find the servant gone and the door closed. She shuddered and turned her attention to Cartellion.

He was dressed in black from his high leather boots and britches to his black silk shirt that was open to the waist. His belt was iron inlaid black leather, with the ever-present white skull as its buckle. His black eyes flashed at the sight of the nervous young cleric dressed in yellow gossamer. He sensed her fear, but there was something else. Beneath the almost palpable fear, he felt the question, the curiosity, and the strength of will. Yes, he'd chosen wisely.

"Sylvan wine, cleric?"

At her nervous nod, he moved to the sideboard, filled a pearl inlaid crystal goblet with the amber liquid, and brought it to her.

"Please, make yourself comfortable," he said as he crossed to a leather chair and sat.

She could not take her eyes from him. He seemed the same size as before, though he no longer wore his armor. His movements were cat-like and precise with no wasted motion. She felt clumsy as she sat in a wood-bound leather chair across the low table from him.

"What will you teach me, cleric?"

He leaned toward the girl to ask the question and grinned. She was having great difficulty thinking in the presence of this man. Serena and the others had crammed her full of thoughts and ideas through her bath and dressing and the priests had continued the priming the entire distance from the temple, but now, with him so close, she seemed to have forgotten everything.

"You have no thoughts on this subject?" Cartellion continued as he leaned back and swirled his wine in his glass. "Do you just spring love and caring upon an unsuspecting world?"

"No!" she exclaimed, shocked from her paralysis by his words. Then, calmer, "No, m'lord. Not in such a nonchalant fashion. We believe that everyone deserves as much happiness and love as they can get."

"Does that include me?"

"Everyone means everyone, m'lord."

"Even if my form of happiness does not meet with yours? If what truly makes me happy is to ride through a village slaying every man, woman, and child? I am entitled to my happiness, am I not?"

"Are you asking for my opinion or my teachings?"

"Are they not one in the same?" Cartellion was having fun, now that he thought on it, for the first time. "Now, I am entitled to my happiness, correct?"

"Only if it does not conflict with the happiness of others. This is what we are taught and this is what we protect."

"Really?"

"That is why we are taught to fight, only at need and only to protect those incapable of protecting themselves."

"You fight, too?"

"As I said, only at need."

"But caring and bringing happiness and...love for your fellows..." he mused as he leaned forward again. He placed an elbow on his knee to prop his chin on a fist. "How can such a thing be if the person you are attempting to show this love and caring for is, say, some poor misbegotten beggar, fallen on hard times, and in attempting to take his own life is...saved by one of you?"

These things are not taught in the course of instructing young acolytes first entered into the service, but Melisande was warming to the subject, though still a bit worried as to the correctness of her answers. She delved deep within and tapped her faith and emotions for the answers. Whether or not it was the correct answer by doctrine was irrelevant. He was asking *her*!

"Well, we'd probably take him in and care for him. We'd show him the value and blessings of love and try to ease his mind as much as possible. What help we could give, we would give and leave the rest to our faith in the Lady."

"So what you are saying is you'd take him in as he is. He'd be a drain on your manna, a drain on the coffers of the temple, and in the end he would more than probably kill himself anyway, once free of your tenderness?"

"Not exactly, but, if true, we would seek comfort in the attempt and accept the failure. Everyone fails from time to time, Lord Cartellion. Learning from one's failure, that is the important thing. Though, m'lord, in my limited experience, it is not the easiest."

"That is...interesting to say the least," he said softly.

Cartellion seemed to be caught up in his own thoughts for a moment. Then, with a slight shake of his head, he raised his glass and drank.

"Well," he said as he placed the empty goblet on the table and stood, all in one fluid motion, "enough of this."

Melisande stood slowly. She knew what was to come next, but she had no idea how to approach it.

The big Saladin glanced toward the door. An aging manservant opened it and stood as if called. Cartellion motioned toward the young cleric and the servant nodded, stepped aside, and extended a hand toward the girl, soundlessly asking her to follow.

Melisande left the parlor and followed the manservant down the hall to the stairway. She listened to the old one ramble on about how "good" his master was to his servants, how "nice," and on and on until Melisande couldn't help but wonder if they knew the same man.

The servant stopped at the base of the stairway and turned back to the girl. "I will send a servant to assist you before the master comes to you. Please, make yourself comfortable and at ease. You've nothing to fear from my master."

He patted her hand and disappeared through a door to the right of the stairway.

Melisande looked up the stairway, sighed, and began the climb slowly. She had that resolute feeling that she had no choices in this matter and steeled herself for what was to come. When she arrived at the top of the stairs, she found herself at one end of an incredibly large room. The entire second floor made up Lord Cartellion's training and bedroom.

The far end had the three walls lined with rack after rack of weapons of all shapes and sizes, shields, bucklers, and armor. Weighted rods stood in a special rack to the left of a huge oaken pillar, the worn places on the wood evidence of continuous pounding by someone training with the rods.

The center of the room was sand-filled and open, a pit for hand-to-hand training and, no doubt, sport. The question in her mind was, however, sport with whom?

Every six feet or so were small, shuttered windows close to the ceiling. Sconces held unlit torches between each window, and the dwindling sunlight made its way softly through the shutters.

Where Melisande stood was the area set aside for Lord Cartellion's sleeping quarters. The huge bed, flanked on either side by a large onyx, scale inlaid wardrobe, caused her to gasp. Its breathtaking, though heartrending, beauty held her.

The headboard was constructed of the largest scales from a golden dragon, and the heads of silver dragons served as bedposts. The tails of the silver dragons made the sideboards and—by curving around the end of the bed, intertwining, and curving back along its length—the footboard.

Melisande was both awestruck and sickened at the thought that Lord Cartellion may have personally killed these beautiful, intelligent creatures for pleasure and the trophy.

A soft touch at her elbow interrupted her thoughts.

"If there is anything you wish to do in preparation," said a small young female servant, "change, pray, or whatever, be informed that the master will attend you in but one quarter of an hour."

Melisande had not heard the girl arrive and watched as she moved noiselessly to one of the wardrobes. She opened it and withdrew a black silk robe with a silver sash and the ever-present white skull over the heart. She partially closed the door to the wardrobe and, with a small smile, disappeared down the stairs.

Whether by accident or design, the partially open door intrigued the young cleric. She moved cautiously to the wardrobe and, after a timid glance at the stairway, opened the door wide. She stepped back in astonishment at the number and luxury of the robes and scanty feminine articles, all white, displayed. A smile came to her lips as she ran her fingers through the material—so soft, so inviting. However, the smile fell abruptly when her green eyes found the items mounted on the inside of the door.

There were whips, some satin and some leather, bindings of material from silk to chain, and an assortment of other devices, the use of which could only be guessed at by the innocent young girl.

She slammed the door, stood with her back against it, and tried to regain some semblance of composure. All the training in the world would not be enough to squelch the icy fear that ran down her spine and massed in the pit of her stomach. She stumbled to the bed and fell to her knees. She clasped her shaking hands before her and, as she rested her head on them, prayed harder than she'd ever prayed before.

From somewhere deep in her tormented mind, her mother's sweet voice came through.

"Little one, you must always remember that to give pleasure, you must be willing to feel pleasure. There is no evil in enjoying the feelings accompanying the act of procreation. Revel in it, my sweet innocent. If you feel the sweet ecstasy and exhilaration, surely you are imparting the same. And don't worry about the games some men wish to play, for they are, generally, easy creatures to control and please. Just follow your feelings, little one. They will guide you."

Melisande took a deep breath and stood. She dried the tears from her face on the sleeves of her gown with still-shaking hands. She turned and stepped back to the wardrobe and, taking a firm grip on her determination, opened the door wide. She chose several garments, as many as propriety and good taste would allow, and donned them, consciously ignoring the paraphernalia mounted on the door. Then, after securely closing the door, she moved back to the side of the bed to await Lord Cartellion and her fate.

She was only a bit surprised when, after a few moments, Cartellion appeared at the top of the stairway with no noise to alert her of his coming.

He stopped there and gazed across the twenty or so feet that separated them. His black eyes danced as he devoured the girl with them. Then, with a secretive smile, he reached out a hand and made a casual lifting, flicking motion.

Melisande found herself deposited softly into the very middle of the bed.

He moved toward the same wardrobe Melisande had used and nodded. The door opened wide at his silent command and he removed a small stand and began to place certain items from the door upon it.

Cartellion glanced about the room and as his gaze passed each window, it would softly close the shutters with a small "click."

The room was suddenly thrown into darkness so deep that Melisande felt she would suffocate. Then, just as suddenly, a pale light enveloped her, building from the eye sockets of the two dragons until the bed was bathed in the cold soft pale of cloudless moonlight.

"Hmmm. Is there anything you wish to say before we begin?"

The deep soft voice of the Saladin enhanced the unfamiliar sensations that coursed through her young body. Desire, a feeling never before encountered in her short existence, flowed freely from every pore and dripped from the green pools that were her eyes. She drew a ragged breath.

"As this is your first time, I will endeavor to be...gentle."

A few hours later, Lord Cartellion lifted the satin coverlet up to her chin and left her in the fuzziness and cuddly warmth of her own afterglow, curled up with a sweet smile and tears trailing from those green eyes.

He stopped at the head of the stairs and after a moment turned to her.

"In the morning, the servants will arrive to see you properly freshened for the day. Whatever you need, you need only ask."

A strange faraway look came over his features then.

"You will see me again within the next ten months. Please, take good care of yourself."

He started down the stairs before he stopped suddenly and looked back at the girl.

"Thank you, cheesa," he said softly and disappeared down the stairs.

Melisande lay in the warmth of the bed, a look of rapture still upon her face. Suddenly she sat bolt upright.

"Did he say 'Thank you'?"

Chapter Four

Arantar had followed the small raiding party of gualu for the most part of three days and now watched as they made camp not more than fifty yards from his vantage point in this small clump of woods.

They sleep without fear, Arantar-sao.

The half elf Royal Huntsmaster felt the growling thought and the presence of the ruddy silver wolf off to his left about twenty feet or so.

We can report their position to the garrison, Fang, now that we are certain in which direction they go. Blacky, you and Fang must keep them in sight until my return.

Of course, Arantar-sao, came the sweet breezy thought, as if from far away. *Brother, watch from ground as I watch from sky.*

Arantar could barely make out the form of the raven perched on a limb high above the enemy's encampment.

I won't be long, my friends. Be careful. I haven't found the daku yet.

With that, the half elf slipped away with no more noise than a whisper. He mounted his horse, secreted deep in the forest, and rode for the garrison encampment some twelve miles away.

Arantar Adenedhel was part Cheal, though he knew neither the word nor what it represented. He was one of the few left in this world born with the capacity, the driven need, to mind-bond with animals, though in his case it was reduced by the addition of elfin blood.

Once there were many of human descent with the Cheal blood. Most left before the Mage War, but a very few survived to mingle, in self-preservation, with the other races of this world. This bloodline, though thinned through the centuries and mixed with the powerful elfin on his mother's side, flowed strong in the Huntsmaster's veins.

Arantar had heard the tales as a child growing up in an Elvin village within the eastern border of the Eldewood Forest. His mother would tell them as she took her young son into the forest to teach him to identify and use the healing herbs that were her trade. He heard them from the old men who came to his father's fire for counsel and entertainment. The stories told of the talents and magiks of that time before the Great War.

He, like others, believed them to be great stories with little truth or distortions meant to enhance a particularly exciting tale.

His father, Boer Highman, Warden of the Eastern Border, Commander of the Royal Border Guards under Prince LeMand, and sworn to the Queen Lady Galan, had also told of the wonders of the time before the freak creations, the gualu, had banded with the dark ones to push the bright elves from the Eldewood. He spoke of men who could become animals at a whim to help those in trouble, but who kept to themselves due to the superstitious prejudices of those they'd helped.

Arantar knew of prejudice for he'd had his share. The day a pompous young elf called him "half-breed" brought the meaning of that word home to him with a vengeance. To Arantar, that one's face looked much better a few moments later after he had forcibly removed the haughty smirk from it, along with several layers of skin. Time after time, the young half elf faced the bigotry of the elves in his community and had to prove, at least to himself, that he was as good as they. He felt kin to those spoken of in the stories, but it wasn't until later in his life that he actually believed.

In his twelfth year, as was the custom of the village, he underwent the local equivalent of the "Rites of Passage." These rites decreed that he must go forth, armed with spear, bow, and dagger, and range the forest until he knew every tree, the placement of every rock, and the voice of every brook and stream. He would have no aid and must live or die by his own wits, training and, if necessary, his will alone. He could return if he could do so as a man and no sooner.

He had been looked upon his entire life as inferior for being half elf. His enemies made bets, covered by his friends, that he would never return. They had no idea how strongly the Cheal blood ran in his veins.

He'd been out for but a week, reveling in the serenity of his surroundings, when the trap hit him. It was gualu-fashioned, but concealed as only an elf could conceal from another. The trap was simple, a warped sapling, spiked and bent so that, when tripped, it would strike an elfin hound in the chest.

How could he not have seen and avoided the trap? The one-word answer screamed from his lips the moment the pain erupted in his legs.

"Daku!"

The trap was old and, as he pulled the spikes painfully from his thighs, he knew he would need help and a place of safety. The spikes were dirty. If he could not get the wounds clean, they would become infected.

He cast about for shelter as his inherited Cheal will calmed him. His ice-blue eyes saw the game trail that led up the side of a hill, and the darkness etched near that could only be a cave. He hobbled and finally crawled to the small opening and all but fell inside. He cared not, at that moment, whether it was safe, but that it was dry, for he smelled the rain on the wind. The cave mouth was small, but it opened into a ten by twelve by six foot high cavern.

He set to work on his wounds, knowing that he did not have the right herbs to treat them, instead washing them with the watered wine he carried in his wineskin. The pain from his wounds and the added sting of the alcohol finally overwhelmed him and he fell unconscious.

When he woke, it was to delirium. He was sweating and freezing at the same time. The wounds were warm and puffy, but there was no pain.

"No pain. That's good." Then he shook his head and frowned. "No, that's not good. That's bad. Sweating, freezing, not good. Must have help. Must call. Must ca…"

He felt the warmth on his legs and opened his fevered eyes.

"No. Can't be. Wolf? Eating my leg? Can't move. Can't scream." Then, with a chuckle, "No. Just tasting, licking. Must be dream. Must be dr…"

Be still, saola.

The low growl threaded its way though his mind and, strangely, brought peace.

Must clean hurt. No hurt saola.

He slept.

When next he woke, he found another vision perched upon his chest. It was a large raven, and it was poking sweet grasses into his mouth with its long black beak.

He chewed, the sweet nectar cool to his parched throat, and recognized it as one of the herbs his mother recommended. He noticed the darkness at the entrance to the cave. It looked like a dog. No, a wolf. A ruddy silver wolf, young, but not a puppy.

He tried to laugh, but his throat was still too sore.

"I'm being tended to by a wolf and a raven. I'm in real fine shape!" he thought with a silent chuckle.

Sleep, saola. Earth brother watches. I tend. Sleep.

The soft breeze blew through his mind, and he smiled and slipped into a more peaceful slumber.

He woke with a start, sat up quickly, and looked about the cave. It was dark, but his bloodline gave him certain advantages. One such was his ability to see better than most in darkness. The fever had left him and so, obviously, had his visions. He laughed at his own weakness and the soreness in his legs and went back to sleep.

The light, which filtered through the brush at the entrance to the cave, woke him gently. He felt the warmth at his side. He opened his eyes and glanced down cautiously without moving anything but his eyes.

The wolf was back and lay close to him. The even rise and fall of the animal's chest told the half elf that it slept.

"What in all hells is happening?" he thought as he was careful not to move.

The breeze from his dream blew through his mind again.

Saola, you wake. Earth brother watch all night. Many ugly. Keep safe. I watch now.

The raven flew into the cave and lit on the floor next to the wolf. It cocked its head to the side and the sweet thought stole through Arantar's mind.

Trouble in mind, saola? Speak in mind. I know. Strange for you. Strange for me. But is. Is.

Arantar glanced at the wolf, then back to the raven. Could it be possible? The young half elf, not being burdened with the "logic" of adulthood, decided that if they could talk to him, he should be able to talk to them. He stared at the raven and concentrated as hard as he was able.

You can hear my thoughts?

He felt something stir in his mind. A changing, twisting of his thoughts. Then, as his talent leaped to full, he felt the power radiate from his mind.

The wolf stirred and a soft growl slid through the youth's mind.

Saola need no shout. Am tired. You still weak. Sleep. Talk better when well.

It wasn't a rebuke, but it was more like a friend asking another for rest after a long night.

Arantar reached out a timid hand to touch the ruddy silver coat. The wolf sighed but made no move to prevent the touch. The young half elf brushed gently at the stiff coat and was surprised at the changing colors that ran liquid through his mind. It was contentment he felt, the wolf's contentment.

The raven shifted from foot to foot, then flew up and out of the cave. That soft breeze blew back into the youth's mind.

I watch now, saola. You listen, earth brother. You sleep.

The wolf hunted and the raven brought the sweet grasses. Arantar soon became used to the comings and goings of the two and the feeling that he knew where they were when not in sight.

One night, after he'd mastered the art of thinking without "shouting," he asked the question uppermost in his mind.

How is it that I can talk to you two with my mind? I've heard the stories that it was possible, but I never believed. What brought you here and now?

The now familiar growl walked through his mind.

Not know, saola. Was hunting. Heard call. Came.

Call?

Yes. came the soft sweet thought from the doorway as the raven glided in to light on the youth's shoulder.

Was gliding high on wind. Heard call. Knew must come. Must come. Did. Found earth brother here. Never had earth brother. Now have earth brother and saola.

Saola. You both call me by that name. What does it mean?

The wolf raised his head and gazed wisely, or so it seemed to the young half elf, into those steel blue eyes.

Pack leaders tell of before time when saola many. Earth and sky brothers many. Say saola is. Just is. Saola friend, whelp mate, mind brother. You are saola. Sky brother same.

You mean that I am saola to you and you are saola to me?

No. You saola. Me earth brother.

I, sky brother. interjected the raven. *You only saola. We brother. You saola. See?*

Arantar didn't see at all. They were saying that he was something different, yet the same as they. It got terribly confusing for him at his young age.

It was many years later that he realized what they had meant. They were his brothers, true, but he was more. If the two animals held to their own life-cycles, the wolf would die of old age within the next twelve to fifteen years, and the raven maybe five years beyond that.

Now, however, they were linked, irrevocably, to the young half elf and as long as Arantar lived, they would live within his lifecycle, starting from their then-apparent age within their metabolism.

Arantar, the wolf he called Fang and the raven he called Blacky, roamed the woods for over a year before the youth felt the need to return home. Return he did, to awe, speculation, and a party paid for by the foolish bets of his enemies.

A few years later, the young half elf enlisted into the Prince's Own Royal Border Guard as a scout and tracker. It wasn't long before his nerve, skill, and secret talents earned him a reputation few could match.

Now, at twenty-eight, he was Huntsmaster, promoted just a year ago, and in great demand by the commanders within the region. His talent for reconnaissance and information gathering, as well as his prowess with bow and the great sword at his back, was well known. Few were the men who met him who didn't like him, though it was widely known that the young half elf would rather keep to himself than mingle. He was a loner who, strangely, kept company with a large black bird and a wolf.

I know not what it is, my friends, but something is calling. I can feel restlessness in my soul. I yearn to be away and it matters not in which direction. It is a yearning just to travel.

The twinge in his mind, now familiar with much use, sent the communication to the raven, perched upon the standard driven into the ground before the tent of the field commander, and the wolf at his feet. The skirmish of the night before had once again excited the yearning deep within his soul.

He sat cleaning and honing the great sword distractedly while the restlessness in his blood rode him. He could say nothing to the others in his unit, for they might not understand. Not even the small Huntsmaster who sat across the campfire from him, setting silver barbs to his white fletched arrows. Even Tao might not understand, though he too had expressed a desire to travel and would act on it within the next couple of months.

Is the blood yearn, Arantar-sao. came the growling thought as the wolf's yellow eyes sought his. *Same as others, savon must. Must go on savon if to find peace in self.*

His mother had warned that the elfin blood might one day cause him discomfort. He'd had his share of discomfort, most due to the bigotry he'd lived with day to day, but nothing to match the senseless yearning he now felt.

You go. We go.

The breezy communication from the raven asked nothing. It merely stated an accepted fact as far as these two were concerned.

I cannot ask you to forsake your home and friends to travel with me, I know not where. I could never do that to you, my friends.

Ask not, Arantar-sao. came the heavy growl as the wolf shifted to a more comfortable position at the Huntsmaster's feet. *Without you we are not. Must come, be whole. We are as you are.*

Blacky?

True as earth brother say. You go, we go. Yearning not hard now. Mother will know when time is. Sleep, Arantar-sao. Tomorrow soon. Time for savon not yet. Mother will know. Mother will know.

With that, the raven pushed its head beneath a wing and went to sleep.

There is much to see beyond these borders, my friends. thought the Huntsmaster softly. *We will see it all together.*

Then he rolled into his blanket and went to sleep.

Chapter Five

On this early spring day the catch was extraordinary. Culligan and Boyo had filled *Megan's Lament* to the gunwales. The others from the village were well on their way to doing the same when Culligan upped the sea anchor and hoisted the small sail.

"Hey, Barnak, me lad!" he called over the fifty or so yards separating his boat from Barnak's *Sandpiper*. "It'll be a surprise, fer sure, to me Megan tha' I be comin' in this early."

Barnak, Cully's neighbor in Seafoam and one of the original companions to found the village, was pulling his nets in full. His toothy smile was easy to see over the calm waters off Argentum Peak in the Gallius Sea. This day would go down in the record books for all the fisher folk of Seafoam.

"Culligan!" he yelled through cupped hands. "Ye'll be gittin' back afore the rest o' us. See Rachel has the pot on and the rest is ready ta celebrate. The fishies is beggin' ta jump in me net an' I'll be as full as ye in no time a'tall!"

"Aye, we'll ha' a time o' it t'night, fer sure. See ye when ye gets in." Then, to the half elf, "Put 'er hard over, Boyo. I cinna wait ta see th' cliffs o' White Bay an' the loo' on Megan's face. Take 'er in."

Culligan looked beyond Argentum Peak toward what he knew to be Seafoam as the half elf tacked the little fishing boat into the wind.

"'Er's a haze o'er home, lad. Loo's like the fog dinna burn off from this morn."

As they rounded the bend leading into White Bay, it became apparent that the haze came not from any natural occurrence but from the smoke rising above the cliffs. Fear clutched Cully's throat as his choked voice gave a name to that fear, deep and lethal.

"Raiders."

The word caused a wild sense of panic to grip the half elf as he guided the ship toward the pier. Culligan grabbed a seven-foot gaff from the bow of the boat and leaped as the half elf put the ship into its berth. The big man landed on the pier running and was halfway to the top of the carved steps by the time Boyo had managed to tie off the mooring lines and follow. He took his cue from the big redhead and grabbed the tiller arm. A quarter turn twist to the left and Boyo held a five-foot piece of seasoned wood, two inches in diameter. He leaped to the pier and ran for the steps up the cliff.

The steps, cut into the sheer face of the white cliff, became a path that ran through the center of the village. When he reached the path, the half elf could hear Cully, four houses down, calling for his Megan.

All about him were the remains of the fighting. The dead lay in grizzly disarray. They were all men, some old and some young, but all armed with pikes, gaffs, or staffs of seasoned wood. Boyo ran through the houses seeking any survivors.

When he arrived at the house he'd shared with Cully and Megan, he found the old gladiator standing on the porch staring out to sea. A black look of barely controlled rage had replaced the carefree visage of but a few moments before.

"They took me Megan, Boyo."

The words were low and lethal.

"They slaughtered all th' menfolk an' stole the women. I gotta wait here fer th' rest, lad, but ye mus' be away."

Boyo cast a dark glance at the big redhead as that one caught his eye. Cully found a strange cast to the half elf's eyes. They were normally amber, but now in his anger the half elf's eyes had gone molten. There was power here, such that Culligan had only seen once, but he could not remember where.

"I need ye ta fin' th' wood elves, lad. They ha' he'ped us in th' past, as we done fer them. We need th' he'p now. I cinna go fer the waitin', so I'm askin' ye ta go in me stead."

He laid a big hand on the half elf's shoulder and continued.

"I'll no wait fer ye, lad. I cinna. When th' others git in, we'll be armin' ourselves an' be goin' after 'em. I be thinkin' t'were a slave raid an' th' tracks say Seaborne, th' black city." He turned his gaze back to the sea and added, "When I fin' 'em, they'll be beggin' fer death 'ere I'm done."

"I'll go now."

Boyo turned, eager to find the wood elves and return, but found a restraining hand on his shoulder.

"Hold on, lad," said Cully as he held him fast. "Aye, there's need in haste, but ye dinna need ta go off li' this. Meg would have me arse if'n she saw this." He looked the half elf up and down, then continued, "Ye'd best be wearin' the scale. Ye dinna know wha' ye'll git inta e'er ye reach th' elves."

Cully pushed the boy gently back into the house. Boyo saw the blood on the floor and the broken furniture.

"Cully, is she...is this..."

"No, Boyo. It's likely tha' me Megan took a chunk outta one o' them blaggards what snatched her. Tha's her knife o'er there. Meg's a fighter, but I don' know whether or no she be gone, but the slavers don' carry dead wit' 'em, so..."

He moved his hand to the youth's back and gave him a gentle shove.

"Hurry, lad."

The half elf moved swiftly down the short hall to the room he'd been given for his use how long ago? Several months at least. He took a firm grip on the tiller arm and pushed the door open.

Nothing had been disturbed. The scale armor hung on the rack where he'd left it this morning.

It was full armor from the scale-covered sleeves to the leggings of leather-bound metal scale. Culligan had fitted it to him from his store of old armor. Inside the leather collar, the initials "R.A." had been burned. This was the armor that Culligan Vandergast the Red Avenger had worn as a young gladiator.

He donned the armor quickly, tightened the straps for fit and comfort as he'd been taught, slipped on his soft leather boots, and left the room to find Cully.

The big redhead stood on the porch and watched as the rest of the ships turned into port. He held the bastard sword from over the mantle in his big hands.

"We'll be away soon, lad." he said without looking away from the water. "Ye mus' be away, now. Here. Take this wit' ye."

He laid the sheathed sword into the half elf's hands, again without looking.

"They dinna know ye, Boyo, but they knows this. Use 'er as proof tha' Culligan sends ye. If'n ye ask 'em, they'll come. Aye, they'll come."

"Who do I ask for when I do find them?"

Cully turned then and looked into the young half elf's eyes. He saw them go from the familiar amber to molten and back again as the youth fought with his desire to stay with this big man, yet he knew the need to seek help.

"Any one o' th' elves o' this region'll know me, lad. No fear o' that. Take this wit' ye, jist in case." he added as he tossed a small leather backpack. "It's yer's, plus th' stuff inside. Don' know what it is, but ye had it wit' ye when we found ye. I packed ye a change o' clothes, some iron rations, and me own neck knife."

Boyo glanced up from the pack into the coldest icy blue eyes in creation.

"When ye fin' 'em, tell 'em. Then git ta Seaborne. Ask at th' wharf fer me. Anyone will know where I be by then. Fin' me, Boyo, an' we'll make th' blaggards pay 'till th' sea runs red."

The half elf felt then the sheer power of this redheaded mountain of a man. There was no doubt in his mind that, given the chance, Culligan would go alone against whomever had taken Megan and, in this mood, have a very good chance of killing every man. He nodded.

Boyo shrugged into the sword harness, centering it on his back, shouldered the pack, and, after a hand to the big gladiator's arm, turned and ran for the forest. His own anger fueled his legs as he ran.

"Gods help you bastards if you've hurt Megan." he whispered as he ran. "If Culligan doesn't kill you, I surely will."

He entered the woods at dusk and ran until fatigue began to set in. The armor would take some getting used to and tended to not only limit his movements but weigh him down. He had no idea in which way he should go to find those he'd been sent to find, but he knew he could not stop until he did.

What he did not know was that this forest presented its own separate set of problems. The predators of the woods were as nothing compared to the magical influence this forest had on time.

During the time of the Sha'terra, the Eldewood had been enchanted. The method used was old and caused layers of time distortion to radiate from the very center so that as one passed through each distinctive layer the distortion became more prevalent. Although no one, save those of the oldest Sha'terra, knew exactly how this distortion worked, basically each layer would cause time to slow.

The first, or Outer Forest, caused no distortion and was a buffer for those who knew and traveled the region. There were markers, for those who knew them, warning of the boundary into the Eldewood Vale.

The Vale caused time to exist at about a twenty to one ratio. One hour spent inside the Eldewood Vale would see about a day pass without. There was no discomfort, no obvious change, and one would never know the difference unless they knew that the boundary had been crossed.

Fifty or so miles into the Eldewood Vale, another time boundary existed: the Inner Vale. Here, again, time slowed. Here it could be obvious depending on the seasons, but even then one would have to know what they looked for. One could walk here for a day and two months would pass without.

The final vale, the Vale of Light, was the center of the forest. A sacred place blessed by the Mother of Creation. Its boundaries lie between one hundred and two hundred fifty miles within the Inner Vale. Here, the enchantment was still at its peak. Time all but stood still here. One day among the silver barked trees of the Vale of Light would see more than a century pass outside. The wards cast at each layer guaranteed that none could get this deep into the Vales that could possibly cause harm within.

The half elf was not aware that, as he rested, he sat within a mile of the boundary to the Eldewood Vale. He laid the sheathed sword on his lap, hilt to his left hand, an automatic precaution as if drilled into him from birth, and ate a small portion of the enriched trail bread packed by Culligan. He didn't know which way to go to find the help he sought. All of his hope centered on the wood elves finding him and recognizing the sword he carried. He reasoned that, for them to find him, he must keep moving.

Unfortunately for Boyo, the help he sought was watching him, though distractedly. When one wishes to be found by these inhabitants of the woods, one has to make it obvious that that is one's purpose. It became a game to the elves to watch without being seen. All Boyo had to do was speak a single word and the game would have ended in the help needed. Soon, however, the game became a bore and, though they recognized the sword, they left him alone.

The youth finished the bit of trail bread, strapped the sword back in place, and walked deeper into the forest.

Once within the Eldewood Vale, the trees began, subtly, to guide him. The path before him turned so gently that the youth didn't notice. The wards on the Vales compelled the trees, plants, and animals to aid in disorientation. By the middle of the third day, the half elf had traveled over forty miles, but he had penetrated only half of the distance through the Eldewood Vale.

By the end of the fourth day, Boyo knew he was lost. Even the position of the sun seemed to be in league with the power directing him astray. Though he tried to use the sun for navigation, it seemed to move when he wasn't paying attention.

He sat on a stone and tended his small fire, the snared coney just starting to brown. He was certain that he would never see Culligan, Megan, or anyone else again. He felt he had betrayed the trust Culligan had given him and the futility of his situation flooded him with sadness. He wept.

Suddenly fatigue, greater than any he'd known, settled into his mind and body. He shook his head to free himself from the creeping lethargy but failed. He barely had time to slide off of the stone before the blackness overtook him.

When morning came, he woke to find himself in a clearing with one path out. It came to him, as if from something outside speaking, that this path was his to follow, and if he should leave it for any reason he would be lost forever. This was the power of the Eldewood, the name coming to him from within, though he could not remember who told him or where he was at the time.

"Thank you." he whispered in the hope that those responsible for saving him would somehow hear his words and know how grateful he was. He shouldered his pack and sword and set out again.

On the morning of his tenth day since leaving Cully at Seafoam, he arrived at the border between the Eldewood Vale and the outer forest. The half elf, however, could not accept what his eyes saw.

On this side of the invisible boundary, the forest was green, vibrant, and alive. On the other, the multicolored hues of late autumn greeted him in preparation for winter.

"This cannot be!" he exclaimed.

The coolness of the season cut through his armor as he crossed the boundary into real time and brought the realization that not only could it be but it was. He'd gone into the forest in the early spring and it was now just a snow flurry from winter, a difference of at least eight months!

At dusk, he stepped out of the woods within twenty feet of the wide white smoothness of the "King's Way Road", that ran between Catlorian and Seaborne. The temperature dropped and the youth found some shelter in a small cove of brush to the side of the white road.

He lit a small fire and sat close in an attempt to stay warm. He had no cloak, since he had not needed one during a season that should have lasted for several months and should have gotten warmer with time. What had happened, his confused mind kept asking? Was Cully at Seaborne, even now, waiting for him to arrive? Somehow he knew that were he to mount that road in the morning and follow it east, he would eventually arrive at Seaborne. Then he would follow Cully until he caught up with him.

"That is the plan."

That being decided, and though he'd failed to contact the wood elves and, in the process, had lost several months of his life to the forest, he set his sword across his lap and hunched down to wait for morning.

He felt the man before he saw him. He glanced up to see the man as he stepped across the smooth expanse of white in the moonlight.

He was tall, this man, and dressed in black, save for the cloak. Though black as well, it seemed to ripple with a silver sheen as the man moved and the moonlight struck it. The half elf's right thumb pushed at the hilt of the sword, releasing it from the bind of the sheath.

The man stopped short of the fire and raised the hood of his cloak from his head. His blond hair caught the light as he stood with hands down, palms forward to show the half elf he had no weapons.

"May I sit and share your fire, youth?"

The voice was deep, musical, and soothing. The young half elf motioned to the stump next to the fire and the stranger came forward and sat. The sword stayed on the youth's lap, the blade loosened in its sheath.

"What do you fear, youth?" he asked. "You sit as tense as a cat awaiting attack before launching one of your own. I assure you, I mean you no harm."

"I'm sorry, sir, but you must realize that under the circumstances I have little choice. I don't know you, or what you intend, if anything. I mean no disrespect, but I must be cautious. I apologize in advance for any inadvertent misinterpretation. I too wish no harm to you."

"Good, then. May I make some tea?"

Without waiting for a response, the stranger reached into his bag and brought forth a small kettle and three small packages. He filled the kettle from his water skin and settled it on the fire. He began adding the contents of the packages to the water, very carefully it seemed.

Boyo recognized Adder's Tongue and Nightshade, two deadly poisons, but not the third. He figured, however, that given the other two ingredients to this strange man's tea, the third must be as deadly as the first. He shook his head.

Then, as the water began to boil, the aroma of that brew swept over him and, strangely, brought a peace and warmth.

"Where are you bound, youth?"

The half elf, strangely, smiled and tapped the pommel of the sword to reseat it. He laid it to the side and put his hands out toward the fire.

"I'm off to Seaborne to tell a friend that I failed him."

"Failed?"

"It matters not. I only know that I did not get the help he sent me for and I must get to him to render what aid I can. Something of value has been taken and I am obliged to help retrieve it."

"You mean 'them', don't you? You have a mission other than that. You must go to Catlorian. There you may find what you seek."

The half elf glanced quickly, yet found the stranger looking into his cup.

"There is a debt to be paid. My road goes to Seaborne and that payment, even if it is a payment in blood. Maybe you are correct in that what I've lost is in Catlorian. However, it will have to wait."

The stranger looked up from his cup and into the youth's eyes. The stranger's eyes were liquid silver and drew the youth to them.

"Look at me, young one."

The command was low and soft, but Boyo could not refuse. Quivering yellow fire began in the center of the stranger's eyes. Then red fire circled that. It enveloped the half elf's mind and held him for a moment. Then suddenly the half elf slumped to the ground next to the fire.

The stranger stood and finished his cup of tea. He moved the youth to a more comfortable position and sighed.

"I am sorry, youth, but your destiny lies in Catlorian."

He fished around in his bag, pulled a cloak from it, and laid it over the sleeping youth's form. Then he moved back to the White Way and disappeared.

The half elf woke next to a campfire and sat up. Twenty feet from him, an expanse of what seemed to be white granite went to his left and right toward what destinations he knew not. He pushed the cloak back and got to his feet. As he stretched, he saw, in the early morning light, a post on the other side of the road that proclaimed this the "Kings Way

Road". He shrugged, because he did not recognize the name, the road, or his place upon it.

The shock went straight to his soul and he sat down hard. He remembered nothing prior to awakening! He sat looking at the perfect expanse of white and knew he didn't even know his own name.

"Don't sit there, stupid!" came a commanding voice from inside. "What good is it to sit here bemoaning your loss when you haven't the first clue as to what it is you've lost? You could try to find answers, or you could just sit here like an ass!"

He saw then the pack and sword that lay next to him on the ground. He opened the pack and, though nothing miraculous happened to bring back his memory, some of the things tingled at his mind. The bundle of hair, for instance, seemed to mean something to him, but the other things meant nothing at all.

The five loaves of trail bread were welcome, though he had no memory of where they came from. He broke one open and took a bite. It was palatable, but not great.

He took the sword in hand, hefted it, and brought the great blade from its sheath. It was familiar, from the filigreed pommel, the down-turned hilts, and the dull metal blade, yet he couldn't place it. The dull sheen of this blade seemed to call and beckon him to remember. He sheathed it and reached for the cloak. It had no memory for him at all. He stood and tossed it on and, while fastening the catch at his throat, found it to be a bit longer than his size, but it was functional. Then, while looking both ways up and down the white expanse of road, he absently slung the sword to his back and strapped it in place, the hilt over his left shoulder. When he realized what he'd done, he grinned.

"So, it is mine, then."

He'd be patient. He had the feeling that he'd been in worse situations, and it made no difference whether he'd been able to extract himself from them or this was the result of failure. Today was now. He knew he must decide what to do now and where to go. Left or right?

He shouldered the pack and stepped out onto the white roadway, noting as he did that the surface seemed to give under his feet; yet when he stepped off, it slowly returned to its original smoothness.

As he stood and marveled at the engineering genius that must have gone into the making of this material, he felt the pull, the gossamer strands that seemed to direct him to the left and west. He didn't fight the pull but went with it.

"What have I to lose?" he thought. "What course have I? Besides, I have everything to gain. For every moment I spend going in this direction, I've gained a moment of memory."

His reasoning calmed him and a small smile played at his lips. He set out toward the city in the center of the world, though he knew it not. He was headed for Catlorian.

Chapter Six

The large man knelt next to one of the mounds that lined the path at the southern end of the village. Though most of these people couldn't write, the signs were there for those who could read them.

Here were the flaming daggers of old Gortex, the old man who had told the stories of the old days in the arena, while the man sweated in the training ring. Next were three mounds side by side, each marked with the headbands of his friends, the triplets, and the mace sigil of their father, Segren. On and on they rose, the mounds of the old and young men who had befriended him and helped to raise him. They were murdered here in defense of this his village, and he was here to bring retribution.

He stood and moved, quiet as the great tawny puma before him, into the village.

He was six foot tall and massive. The full arm gauntlet, which covered his left arm, seemed a part of his body rather than a cumbersome piece of steel and leather. His steel-studded vest and high boots held a magic he was not aware of, yet they were worn, again, as an extension of his existence. His right arm was bare, save for the bracer that encircled both wrist and thumb.

His practiced eye read the signs of the violence as if it had happened yesterday. The fishermen were out on the bay when the attack came. All the men and boys left behind were butchered and the women were taken.

"Slavers."

The curse whispered through the ruined throat of this powerful man, the old scar across his larynx evidence of the failed attempt to remove his life.

That had been over eighteen years ago in Seaborne. The gang leader of the street gang "White Dove" had found out that it had been he who had returned the small dog to the rich but loving owner and had ruined the extortion attempt. He'd told the owner who had stolen the dog and where they could be found. The mercenaries the owner hired reduced the numbers of the street gangs by twenty percent before they were called off.

He still bore the scars of the infinity, burned into each cheekbone, that named him traitor for life. Tret sliced his throat and threw him into the bay.

The sting of the salt water brought him out of the shock at having his throat cut, but it seemed to take him straight into delirium.

He was sinking into a cold, calm, and peaceful place when he felt the nudge.

"Water beasts." he thought.

That thought brought with it a strange humor. He couldn't feel them eating him, but maybe, he reckoned, he was just too cold. Maybe they'd eat everything but his head and he'd watch them toss him back and forth like a ball.

These thoughts, though grizzly, came normal to this child of five. He'd survived the streets of Seaborne only through his maturity and cunning. A child surviving those streets was worth many a man at twenty.

He laughed and instantly got his lungs full of salt water. That shocked him into a calm panic, if there were such a thing, and, though he knew he was drowning, he also knew he was being nudged swiftly to the surface.

His head broke the surface and a stiff nose struck him in the stomach. As the Sha'el held him above the surface, he retched, coughed, took a deep ragged breath, and passed out.

When he woke, three gray, wet, warm bodies with blunt noses and playful smiles supported him. To his right he saw the shoreline churning by and reasoned that he was being transported south. Seaborne was lost behind him and the boy had no way to know how long he'd been unconscious. He relaxed and watched the shoreline pass and the Sha'el jump and chatter all about him.

They seemed happy that he was awake, and they seemed to revel in his laugh as they sailed over him to dive, splashing into the water on the other side.

Laugh? More of a croak. His throat was swollen and he couldn't talk. The gash across his throat was numb. The knife had missed his jugular by the width of a single layer of skin, but it still tore through his larynx, rendering it totally useless. The shock returned with the memory and he began choking.

As if they understood, the Sha'el swerved and sped for the shoreline. Once there, they nudged the boy to shore just as he passed out again.

There, watching from the ridge above, stood a yearling mountain cat, a puma. The Sha'el chattered at the cat for a moment and turned back out to sea.

The tawny puma moved silently down the incline, sunk his teeth into the boy's shirt, and, with stubborn determination, dragged the boy away from the shore, up the incline, and into the forest over one hundred yards away. There the cat lay next to the boy, giving warmth, until he stirred. Before the boy's eyes opened, the puma melted back into the forest.

This strange behavior did not go unnoticed.

The wood elves had watched the puma move through the forest. They called him "Fleet Fur" and marveled at the one-mindedness of this animal. Their curiosity demanded that they follow and watch.

Mountain cats were known to inhabit the Coastal Mountains far to the southwest of the Crystal Ranges. There had never been one seen within the Eldewood, and this one was relentless. It seemed to know where the boundaries to the Vales were and skirted them. It had come into the forest directly east of Catlorian and had walked completely around the forest, just at the boundary to the Eldewood Vale, until he arrived here, at this time, on this ridge, seemingly for this reason.

When the cat slipped away, they smiled, secure in the knowledge that some power was behind these strange actions and, their curiosity slaked, they too slipped away.

The puma growled from the porch of the house the young man knew well. This was the house the woman had brought him to after she found him wandering from the forest.

She was kind and gentle and spoke softly to him. When she saw the jagged slash across his throat, her face paled and her anger flared.

"Cully, Ge' 're quick!" she yelled in her strange accent.

By the way she'd scanned the wood line, the youngster knew that were they there, those responsible would pay dearly at the sure hands of the small angry woman.

"Tis a wee bairn wha's got cut foully!" she added, still watching the wood line.

A shadow fell over him and, as he looked up, he saw the largest mass of human being he'd ever seen. The bright red hair swept in the breeze as the giant reached down and gently lifted the boy into his arms.

"Aye, Megan. Tis a dark day when some would cut th' throat o' a child an' brand 'im so."

The big hand gently felt the puckered burns on his cheeks as he spoke, then those same huge hands wrapped themselves about the boy protectively and held him safely while the big man moved back toward the village.

"Bring 'im ta th' 'ouse, Cully. Them cuts needs loo'in' after."

Now the young man pointed a gauntleted finger up the main path toward the north.

<Search.> he growled in cat speech.

The big puma jumped from the porch and moved silently through the paths of the village, looking for any sign that would help his friend.

The gauntleted hand went to the spiked basket of the "Bourjon Blade", which rode at the small of his back. The two feet of single-edged steel slid noiselessly from the lacquered sheath and settled familiarly into the strong left hand.

His right hand pulled the long dagger from the sheath strapped to his bare leg. The long sword, strapped securely to his broad back, was all but useless in the confines of the small house, should he need it. The dagger would have to do, as it had in the past.

He entered the house at a crouch, the dagger flat along the inside of his right forearm and the Bourjon Blade flicking side to side. All signs said that nothing was left here, but years of battle and experience had taught him to always expect the worst.

He found the overturned table and broken dishes. The chairs before the hearth were overturned as well. The hearth was cold. Above the mantle, Cully's "Freedom Wand" still hung. The dim outline of the great bastard sword, which once hung across it, could still be seen.

"If Cully's taken Mole," he thought to himself, "war must have been declared!"

With that thought, he moved toward the hall. His feet softly avoided the knife in the entry to the hall. It was Megan's blood-encrusted butcher knife.

"At least Meg hurt one of those bastards."

He looked into the master bedroom only to find old signs of hurried packing. Cully had wasted no time stuffing necessities into his old knapsack. He left the door open and turned to the other door, the door to his own room.

He could still hear Cully's voice as the old gladiator fitted the door in place.

"Aye, boy, me Megan's been after me ta build another room on th' house. Wha' better reason than fer a room fer a small boyo wha' needs it?"

Cully came to the pallet where the boy had lain for the past four days, alternately sleeping and listening to the sounds of building from that room. Neighbors had come and gone, some to help with the building, some to touch the boy's hair softly and coo to him that "everthin' will be a'right, chil'."

The swelling had receded due to Megan's patient care and the stitches in his throat had stopped hurting. The boy was able to eat some broth and a bit of porridge from time to time. The big man leaned down and lifted the boy, pallet and all, and carried him through the door into his new room. Megan stood and turned from making the bed and wiped at the tears that welled up in the boy's eyes.

Cully laid him onto the soft clean bed and stroked his hair.

"Ah, me boyo, tis happiness or sadness wha' brings th' tears?"

The boy grinned up at the two of them.

"Tha's me boy!"

"Now don' dote on 'im so, Cully," said the small woman softly, but with a smile. "'Tis a wee bairn what's lost. Yer've got yer own name too, don't ye, wee lad?"

She fussed with the coverlet and smoothed the boy's hair from his face.

"Well, soon's yer t'roat 'eals, ye'll be tellin' us, so's we kin fin' yer fambly."

The tears came now. He wanted to tell them that he'd never had a family, that his name was Nethan DeBurge', late of the White Doves of Seaborne, for which he would be forever damned. He opened his mouth to speak, but only croaking sounds escaped his ruined throat.

"Easy, Boyo. Time will 'elp. Gi' yerself some time."

The deep, gentle voice of Culligan Vandergast caused the boy to stop struggling. He looked from the small loving woman to the massive redhead, pointed a small finger to his chest and, using sheer will, managed one word through his tears.

"Eton." he whispered.

Eton pushed the door open and found his boots and slicker discarded on the floor, as if someone had thrown them off hastily.

"This is where they let the stranger stay." he thought.

Megan had written about the stranger, the half elf, who had washed up on the shore just south of White Bay. She'd said he had no memory but was courteous to a fault.

"Just like them," his thought continued, "to take in strays just as they did me. He was probably on the boat with Cully, ran in here, changed, and left with the rest of the men."

He sheathed the dagger and left the room, closing the door behind him. He slid the Bourjon Blade back into its sheath as he strode through the front room for the front door.

<Not.> came the cat growl as Eton stepped out onto the porch. <Mother?>

The cat's question hurt. If Megan had taken a knife to one of them, they might have killed her. Yet of that there was no sign. No mound was raised and no pool of blood in here to say what had happened. If they had killed her, the slavers would not have taken her body. If not, they may kill her later on.

Yet something scratched at the back of his mind. Megan was strong and commanding. It is possible that the raiders offered her a deal, say the blood of the innocent women, if she cooperated. Megan would have gone for that for two reasons: one, she could help keep the women and young girls from harm by being there to control the abuse, and two, she *knew* that Cully and the others would be along, though it might take a while. Yes, her Cully would be along and then…

<Not.> he growled, though reluctantly.

He looked north up the path that led to Clamshell. South led to Dragon's Teeth, some seventeen hundred or so miles. In past times, the common practice for slavers in Dragon's Teeth was an excruciating death and all slaves set free to either stay within the realm or return, with the ruler's help, to the place where they were taken.

Eton had been hearing rumors, however, that caused him to think that things had changed south of Seafoam. But still, the tracks and wheel marks, still embedded in the dirt of the path after so many months, said that they came in that way but left another. That was the mystery. Possibly they had carried the captives to Seaborne. Slavery was not frowned upon there and a good price could be had for recalcitrant slaves. He'd have to check the sign at the other end of the village. But first...

<Search trail.> he growled as he pointed north up the path.

The puma bounded off of the porch to search that path to a point beyond the known border of the village. He knew that his saola would feel him, and the big cat did not wish to be far from him while the questions in his mind were so confused.

Eton stepped off of the porch, moved right, and started around the house toward Culligan's training pavilion and shop. He looked out toward the forest, which loomed but a half mile away, and sighed. His boot nudged a small stack of firewood and dislodged two or three pieces. He squatted to pick them up and restack them on the pile, but as his eyes went to the open field between here and the forest, once more he remembered.

He was eight and big for his age. He'd been working with Cully on *Megan's Lament* for over a year, and that morning he'd left the house early to check on the nets they'd hung behind the house. As he rounded the corner of the house, he heard the screams. He broke into a run for the backfield without a thought and, at full sprint, grabbed two pieces of the seasoned firewood from the pile there.

He saw the triplets running frantically for the safety of the village and the dark blurs of the beasts that chased them. They were wild dogs and thought that the three small boys would be a good snack.

Eton passed the triplets as they ran, stopped at a crouch with hard wood in each hand, and growled.

The dogs were on him in a second, or so thought Culligan and Barnak as the two men ran toward him from between the houses. Culligan had his staff and old Barnak had a shark knife in each hand. Before they'd gotten within twenty yards of the fight, however, Barnak grabbed Cully's arm and dragged him to a stop.

"What in the bloody blue blazes ya doin', Barnak!" yelled the gladiator as Barnak held his arm firm. "Eton's bein' et alive by them dogs! Le' me go!"

"Lo' ag'in, Cully," said the graying fisherman. "Them dogs got Eton right where *he* wants 'em."

Cully glanced at Barnak's crooked grin and swore him insane. Then he turned to look to his boy and stopped fighting. He couldn't believe what he saw.

A half-dozen starving dogs were attacking the boy and he was smiling.

His hands and arms worked independently, yet in harmony, as he alternately blocked an attack of one dog while the other hand laid solid wood soundly on the head or flanks of another. He moved through them and back again and again, wreaking havoc on the frustrated hounds.

Finally, as if they all decided at the same moment that this was not the easy meal they'd been after and that the wood this little whirling dervish wailed at them with hurt, the dogs turned and ran for the relative safety of the forest.

Eton laughed his hoarse laugh and flung the wood after them, scoring hits with both his left and right hand. Then he turned his back on them and skipped back toward the two men, beaming.

The noise from the wood line caused him to stop, and the three of them looked in that direction. The sound of growling hate and pain-filled dogs floated back to them. Barnak smiled.

"Lo's like sumpin' dinna like wha' them dogs had in mind."

Later that day, some of the men would track those dogs only to find their carcasses just within the tree line. The tracks of a large cat were found throughout the carnage.

"Ah, lad!" Cully sighed after he grabbed the boy up and hugged him tight, then put him back on his feet. "Ye gave ol' Cully a scare. Tell me, where'd ye larn ta do that' wit' yer two hands?"

"Didn't." he whispered. "Just felt right."

Barnak squatted next to the youngster and looked deep into his eyes.

"Eton, ye ha' th' talent fer two-handed fightin'. If th' ol' man here an' Meg says it's a'right, I could teach ye wha' I knows."

He turned his crooked smile on the old gladiator and got his nod.

"I was oncet th' arena master o' the twin blades, aye Cully? Ne'er kin tell when tha' skill will be useful."

"Aye, friend, I remember, but we'll speak ta Megan this e'en 'bout it." Then, to the boy, "Wha' she says goes, 'kay Eton?"

The boy nodded his head with a smile. He knew he could crawl up in the little woman's lap and get her to allow just about anything, but he tried never to abuse her love for him.

Eton replaced the wood on the stack, stood, and took a deep breath. He ignored the tear that ran down his right cheek. He walked through the overgrown weeds between the houses to the training pavilion and stepped inside. He'd spent many hours here through the years learning the skills of old Barnak.

"Use yer speed, Eton lad. Tis yer best weapon." he'd said time and again. "Don' be fooled by th' deceptive safety o' more'n ye ha' now."

Old Barnak had pushed him to the limits of his skill and beyond every free day after the boats came in and all the chores were done. Every day, that is, except for the one week period just after he'd turned twelve.

He'd never been sick, not even a cold, and that was the main reason Megan and Cully were so worried. A freak storm came up from the east and stayed the entire week while the boy was ill. He laid in a feverish, semiconscious delirium, alternately hot and then cold. The women in the village took turns helping Megan tend him, but the little woman would not leave the boy's side.

They'd shooed Cully and Barnak out into the storm, and the two men ended up in the community house with Cully pacing and Barnak frowning into his mug.

"Culligan, ye ol' worry wart," mumbled Barnak irritably as he stared into his warmed rum, "sit dun a'fore ye wears frazzles in me narves!"

Culligan stopped his pacing, his huge hands clinching, and glared at his old friend.

"Sure, Barnak, an' I s'pose yer no worried 'tall 'bout th' boy, eh?"

"Aye, friend, I'm worried, but he be a strong 'un. I cinna do nothin' ta 'elp but sit an' implore me gods."

Culligan reached out a strong hand to the old gladiator's shoulder. Then, as the door flew open, his eyes jerked toward the sound. He looked away and sighed as Turan and Chakar entered from the driving rain.

"'Ey, Barnak. Cully. 'Ow's th' boy?"

Turan asked the question as he and Chakar shook out their heavy slickers, hung them, and crossed to the fireplace.

"'Bout th' same, I s'pose," came the surly response. "Ye'd t'ink we cinna help wit' th' fetchin' an' carryin'. We been sent out like bairns what's got underfoot."

Turan chuckled at that. Watching Culligan Vandergast in this state was much like watching tigers pace at a zoo two hours after feeding time and someone forgot.

"Ye shoulda been wit' me an' Chakar a li'l while ago. Seen th' strangest thing I e'er seen!"

"Strange, hells, Turan!" interjected Chakar. "I'm still a'quakin' from th' strangeness o' tha' one!"

Chakar pushed his hands toward the fire as if the warmth would rid his body of the cold of fear.

"I don' know, Chakar," said Turan. "T'weren't tha' a'feared o' th' cat. He dinna wan' us, I swear."

Culligan stopped his pacing and turned a quizzical look on the pair.

"A cat?" he asked.

"Aye, Cully. No cat like we seen in th' forest a'fore. This 'un were light brown an', I swear ta ye, Cully, he only took notice o' us when this oaf of a Chakar snapped a twig wit' his big foot! Th' cat stopped pacin'—"

"Pacin'?"

"Yeah, Cully." Turan continued. "The cat paced back an' forth in th' lee o' the wood line wit' his eyes only fer th' village. Anyways, th' cat stopped an' looked at us—"

"I still say 'e loo'ed 'ungry, Turan!"

"Nonsense! Cully, I swear tha' th' cat looked...well...concerned. Worried, ye might say. I thought I got it wrong, but when we finally decided to leave—"

"As ye decided, Turan. No' me. I dinna wan' ta leave no big cat on me tail an' jus' leave!"

"Chakar, think 'bout it! Did th' cat make any moves to us?"

"No, but—"

"Did it move from where 'e were?"

"No!" stated Chakar, his arms folded akimbo and a stubborn look on his face.

"Then wha' did 'e do, pray tell?"

"Nothin'!" grated the old fisherman. "But tha' don' mean 'e woonta if'n 'e got th' chancet!"

"I keep tellin' this idiot," said Turan to the room at large, a thumb gesturing at the stubborn fisherman, "tha' th' cat dinna mean us no harm. 'Course, Chakar is convinced tha' th' brown beauty wan's 'im fer supper!"

They all laughed, even the surly Chakar. After a bit of jovial poking, it was Barnak who brought the subject back around.

"Well? Wha' 'appened ta th' cat?"

"It were strange, Barnak." Turan said as he took a sip from his mug and his face went serious. "I could almost feel tha' tha' cat were waitin'. Som'pin' were s'pose ta happen an' tha' cat were a part o' it. It jist went back ta pacin' an' ignored us. Ever oncet in a while, it'd lay dun facin' th' village an' lay its head on its paws, its ears flickin' this way an' tha'. Then, it'd git up an' pace some more. Ne'er seen nothin' like it, I swear."

"Aye, Turan," stated Chakar, a bit more calmly this time, "an' I ne'er wish ta see it a'gin. Now I think on it, ye mighta been right. Though I still t'ink maybe, given another day, we'd a been et, tha' cat di'nt really care if'n we was there or not. 'E jes' kep' pacin' like ol' Cully."

Cully stopped his pacing and glared at the two men.

"Aye, Chakar, they both paces when they's worried 'bout som'pin'"

Cully let only one thought of the legends cross his mind before he shook them away, then he went back to pacing.

Turan kept an eye on the puma throughout that week and reported its movements every evening at the community house. All he ever reported, however, was that the cat "jus' paces."

Then one day, as the storm seemed to recede, the cat's head jerked up, he yawned, stretched, and bounded back into the forest.

"At least I kin tell 'em som'pin' differ'nt t'night." Turan thought as he gathered his gear and made toward the village.

He heard the commotion long before he got back to the village and he walked quickly to Cully's. Fear that the boy had gotten worse gnawed at his insides as he ran to join the others there. Then he saw Megan's smiling but tired face on the porch.

"Eton'll be jes' fine now." she said in a tired voice. "'E says 'e's sorry ta 'ave made ever'body worry so, 'n 'e promised ne'er ta do it a'gin."

Everyone laughed and Culligan gathered the small woman into his massive arms.

"Drinks are on me at the community house." he said to one and all.

"Drinks, me arse, Culligan Vandergast!" said one of the women. "Us wimmen'll cook up a quick dish an' we'll ha' us a celebration party! Meanwhile, some o' us is gonna rescue poor ol' Meg so's she kin git some rest."

Megan smiled down at the small woman.

"Thanks, Tilly. Yer a angel, I swears." she said, then turned to go back inside.

"'Ey, Cully!" yelled Turan as Cully turned to follow the little woman through the door.

"Be there in a minute, lass." Cully said as he usher Megan through the door and turned back to Turan.

Turan walked up to the porch and Cully leaned over the banister.

"Thought ye'd like ta know. Th' cat's gone."

"Gone? When?"

"Jes' now. 'E sat up an' loo'd on th' village, stretched a bit, and left. I don' know, Cully. T'was strange, fer sure."

"Yeah, strange," replied the redhead as he rubbed his chin with one of his big hands. "Tha's 'bout th' same time me Eton come outta th' fever."

He thought about it just a few moments then, with a shake of his head, turned his attention back to Turan.

"Thanks, Turan, an' ye'd bes' be gittin' dun ta th' community house a'-fore Chakar drinks up all th' rum an' eats all th' food! I'll see ta th' boy, then meet ya there."

It was a full week before Megan would let the boy out of her sight, and only because he promised to "go easy." He'd gone out with the triplets to gather windfall for the fires. These villagers never cut living wood, but they depended on windfall and peat for their cooking and heating.

Something called to the young boy. Something drew him to the edge of the forest. The triplets had moved off to the south along the forest edge and left Eton alone. Eton had moved into the forest just under the branches of the tree line.

That's when he saw the puma, its tawny coat glistening in the forest fil-tered sunlight. It padded slowly toward him, and Eton carefully slid the long dagger out of the sheath on his leg and spun it up to lay flat against his right forearm. His left hand still held a short piece of seasoned wood he'd just picked up. He took a firmer grip on it and slipped into the comfort of the fighters crouch. He was prepared for anything, except for what hap-pened next.

The cat approached within three feet, slowly, and abruptly lay down.

"What's this?" he thought for a moment.

He knew then what was missing. There was no feeling of threat, no feel-ing of danger. He'd moved into the defensive stance, but inside he knew.

"This cat means me no harm." Then he added, "I hope."

Eton carefully sheathed the dagger and knelt slowly next to the great head. He kept a tight grip on the wood as he reached out with his right hand to rub the tawny fur between the cat's ears. He heard and felt the rumbling of contentment as the cat closed its eyes and licked its nose.

He also felt something more. Something strange. Colors rippled in waves through his mind, waves of peaceful satisfaction.

Eton let the wood drop as he slid closer to use both hands to scratch the big cat's ears.

"This guy likes me!" came the joyous thought to the boy's mind.

The big cat's purr deepened as if in response, and it rolled over on its side with its head on Eton's leg. Eton's hand went there to scratch at the lighter fur under the big cat's jaw.

"Eton? Eton, where are ye?"

The cat straightened up at the sound of two of the triplets, Larn and Garn, and looked in the direction from which the voices had come. The big cat's eyes sought Eton's, its tongue snapped out to the boy's hand, and then it rose silently and disappeared into the forest.

Eton stood and looked but couldn't see where the big cat had gone. However, he found that, deep within, he could feel the puma as it moved through the forest. Eton knew where the big cat was, even without seeing it. The beat of its heart seemed to throb in the young boy's mind.

Finally Eton looked toward where the two boys should be and whistled. With a last look toward the forest, he moved to join them.

"Eton, where were you?" said Larn breathlessly as he and his brother ran up. "Ol' Meg would skin us if anythin' happened to you out here after bein' so sick an' all."

"You'd never believe me," whispered the youth as he shook his head. "You'd just never believe."

The young warrior noted the signs of fevered activity about the pavilion. There were sharpening stones discarded on the floor, leather and metal pieces used to quickly upgrade old armor, racks empty of shields and lances. He also noticed that the anvil was out of place. He smiled.

He stepped to it, wrapped massive arms about it, lifted, and pushed. A section of the floor slid away and revealed a short stairway down into the dark. He moved to the bottom of that stairway, found the tinderbox in the niche, as always, lit the short candle he found there, and entered the old gladiator's "weapons room."

He remembered this room from the time Cully brought him down soon after he began training with Barnak. Here, the gladiators stored most of their "special" weapons. Now the racks were empty and the only thing left was the stuffed head of a one-eyed grizzly bear.

Eton's hand came up to trace the three scars that appeared under the leather headband he wore. One traveled straight up from the middle of his forehead to just beyond the crown of his head. Another paralleled the first, yet lower and to the left. The last was lower still and, under his hair, a piece of his ear was missing. He shivered at the remembrance.

After his first encounter with the puma, he'd spent many days running through the woods, testing the companionship of the tawny cat. He always seemed to know where the cat was without knowing how or why.

A few months after that first meeting, while moving swiftly toward the feeling, Eton ran right into the path of a maddened grizzly bear. He'd had no time to react as the bear's great paw ripped gouges in the boy's head, dazing him and throwing him to the ground. He stared up into over a thousand pounds of angry death and knew, full well, that momentarily he would be quite dead. A strange calm settled over him at the thought and he smiled.

A light brown blur hit the grizzly, its jaws locked tight to the bear's throat, great claws gripped the monster's back, and the rear claws ripped large pieces of hide, muscle, and entrails from the thing's belly. The puma was totally enraged.

With his left eye swollen shut and the blood streaming down the side of his head, the boy gripped his dagger with both hands. He screamed and, literally running up the side of the great beast, plunged the dagger up to the hilt in the beast's eye. The bear convulsed as it died, and the boy was thrown into a tree.

Megan told him later that she'd been drawn out of the house by a "soul-rendin' caterwaulin'." The cat had dragged the boy from the woods to the pavilion, as close as he could get before his strength gave out. Then, when Megan saw Eton, the cat turned and limped back into the forest.

She said that after regaining consciousness he'd whispered, "Fleet. He's hurt." Then he slipped back into a fitful unconsciousness.

Megan left the boy in the hands of two of the wise women of the village. Cully had watched as the little woman drew water, bundled clean linen, and walked stiffly out of the backdoor and toward the woods. She said not one word, but the look on her face was one the old gladiator knew well. It said that she would brook no interference so Culligan, wisely, did not interfere. He returned instead to the boy's bedside.

The scalp wounds were deep, but his skull was hard and in one piece. The wounds were tended, cleaned, and bandaged, yet the boy still writhed in pain, moaning. Suddenly the moaning ceased and a smile spread over the boy's face as he slipped into healing sleep.

Moments later, Megan reentered the house with a pail of bloody bandages to be burned. She slipped into Eton's room, saw the peaceful smile, grinned, and turned to deal with the bandages in the pail.

"Megan?"

"No' now, Cully," she whispered. "Ye wouldna believe it nohow. I tell ye later." Then, with a sidelong glance at the boy, added, "Maybe."

Eton moved back up the stairway and closed the secret door. He stepped out of the pavilion into the sunlight of late afternoon. Only a few of his questions had been answered after looking through the village. Megan's last letter was received a full nine or ten months before, and that was just about the time they'd heard rumors of marauders moving up the coast from Dragon's Teeth.

The stories told that these slavers were killing all males and capturing all females of the villages they'd encountered. Seafoam was just one of the victims. Now, through all of the signs he could read, Cully and the other retired gladiators were giving chase with blood on their minds.

Just as Eton decided that he would have to trail them to Clamshell and beyond, the puma appeared next to him.

<Man. Man-den, next.>

The cat speech told the young warrior that Culligan, at least, had been able to reach Clamshell to alert the fishermen there. It also meant that Clamshell, out of respect and self-preservation, was keeping watch over Seafoam for the pursuing Cully and crew.

<I talk. Fleet fade.> he growled as he moved between the houses toward the main path. Fleet slipped into the tall grass that now grew between the houses and disappeared.

"Stand or die!"

The challenge reached Eton as he stepped out onto the path. The challenger was a huge man with an eight-foot pike. From the look of him, he knew how to use it.

Eton knew him. He'd traded with Seafoam from time to time and was considered a friend. He also knew the two men flanking the big one. Eton smiled and held both hands out from his sides, palms up.

"Eton, is that you?" asked the one on the big man's right as they drew closer. Eton's grin turned into a smile.

"'Ey, boys, it be Cully's boy, Eton."

The big one grounded his pike, ran up to the youth, and grabbed him in a bear hug.

"Cully said ye'd be along," he growled as he put the warrior down and grabbed Eton's shoulders. "He dinna ha' time, 'e said, ta git somebody ta write, but 'e knew ye'd come, an' we was ta watch fer ya."

"The signs say almost a year, Grizell. What happened, and is Megan with you?"

"No, boyo." The big man sighed. "Aye, t'was 'bout ten month ago, I'd say, when th' raiders come. Took th' wimmen an' slaughtered the menfolk an' younguns what was there. Woonta done it 'cept Cully an' th' rest was on th' water at th' time."

"And Cully?"

"Cully were seein' blood, an' th' rest t'weren't much better. Kep' cursin' unholy curses while he honed that bloody cutlass o' his."

"Cutlass?" whispered the youth in disbelief. "You mean his sword, right? A big, beautiful bastard sword?"

"No, boyo. I said cutlass an' I mean cutlass. I knows th' dif'ernce!"

Eton knew he'd hit a nerve and changed the subject.

"What about the half elf?"

"What half elf?"

"Meg wrote me about a young half elf that Cully had fished—"

"Yeah! I 'member now. Aye, I met 'im a coupla times when Cully'd pull in ta port up at Clamshell. No, boy, 'e wasna wit' th' crew what follered Cully. I don' know where 'e went, but I weren't gonna question Cully, if ya know what I mean. Th' raiders musta learnt tha' Cully was ahind 'em an' they bypast us entire. Cully said if'n you or anyone else wants ta know, 'e were goin' ta Seaborne first. I thinks 'e said some'at 'bout takin' ship, if'n 'e don' fin' th' wimmen in Seaborne."

The big man looked out toward the falling sun.

"We gots maybe two, three hour afore sunset, Eton. Ya needs ta come back wit' us ta Clamshell."

Eton was in somewhat of a quandary. Did the raiders take Cully's sword? Maybe. The half elf was probably with Cully on the water, otherwise there would have been a mound for him as well. Unless...

If he had been in league with the raiders, he might have come in with Cully and, while the big gladiator waited for the other boats, could have taken the sword as his booty and run. But where? Toward Clamshell? Probably not. Back the way they'd come, toward Dragon's Teeth? No, the signs didn't tell him that. Besides, he'd have heard something about it if the half elf had gone that way. Every elf in the region knew Cully and the great sword Mole by sight and would have told him.

The young warrior looked off toward the forest. The Eldewood? Maybe.

"No, Grizell," he whispered to the big fisherman, "I have some checking around to do yet. If I'm not there by nightfall, I won't be coming." Then, with a glance about the village, he added, "Thanks for watching after the place. I am in your debt."

"No, boyo, 'tis I who's in yer father's debt. We'll watch 'til either 'e come back, or we hears tha' he ain't comin. Now, if'n yer goin' inta th' woods, be extry kerful. They's some strange thin's what goes on in thar."

Eton smiled. He, after all, was one of the strange things. He clasped the big man's arm, nodded, and headed for the wood line. Grizell shook his head and, with the other two men in tow, turned back toward Clamshell. He took one last look over his shoulder at the young warrior as he disappeared into the fabled Eldewood with the cat-like grace with which he moved. Then he saw the tawny puma following. He'd heard the stories but until then had given them no credence. He smiled.

"Them two's on th' hunt," he mumbled. "Glad it ain't me they's huntin'."

Chapter Seven

Melisande Dorn, cleric of Freya, the goddess of love and fertility, bringer of joy, harmony, and happiness, was angry.

Not the testy anger most fall into from time to time, but the potent rage that can only come to a mother betrayed. The anger that comes when you find that the child you've carried within you, whom you've suffered in joyful pain to bring into the world, has been taken from you. Taken just three days after its birth and before you've been allowed to see it, hold it, or kiss it. Then you find out that it was handed over to its father, who just so happens to be Lord Cartellion, the Right Hand of Death.

Almost ten months ago she'd been an acolyte doing her service for the goddess Freya. She'd served in the houses of healing, participated in the ceremonies of blessings for the shepherds and farmers of the region, and simply basked in the light of her faith.

Then Lord Cartellion had come to temple asking for a vessel for his progeny and, specifically, for Melisande.

She had, as he had told her, conceived that very night. A life grew within her womb that was the union of his incredible evil and her naïve goodness. She continued her duties for as long as she was able and ended each day in prayer to the Lady, thanking her for the magic of motherhood.

During the last month of her pregnancy, she spent most of her time walking in the gardens talking to her unborn son, studying the healing spells that made her cleric, and praying to her goddess. When the life inside her moved, the wonder of it sent wave upon wave of joy, expectation, and fulfillment through the young girl.

The thought that her son would grow up surrounded by all the love a mother could give, and the unlimited love of the goddess Freya, filled the girl with more happiness than she thought she could possibly bear. Through her training, she knew that it was better to bring girl children to the Lady Freya, but it mattered little to Melisande. This was *her* child. The life in her belly was something *she'd* done. Though she knew it to be a boy, it mattered not which gender it would have been. She was his mother and she loved him.

Thunder rolled in the Crystal Ranges the night Melisande went into labor. She radiated the glow of impending motherhood, that special glow that women have when about to bring life into the world. She heard the first cries through her joyful pain, and then the fatigue engulfed her. The clerics in attendance administered a light sedative and shushed her gently when she asked of her child. They all smiled and told her that the beautiful boy had the features of his father and the smile of his mother. She smiled at the reference and succumbed to the fatigue of the birth and the lethargy of the sedative. She slept.

She awoke refreshed, her soul challenging the gods in her joy. She whispered a gentle "good morn" to the old cleric as she entered with a platter of food.

Melisande realized that she was ravenous. She attempted to carry on a conversation with this old one as she ate, but something in the old cleric's demeanor confused her. Melisande shrugged and decided that she would not let anything dampen her joy this day.

"How is my baby, m'lady?"

"'Tis well. 'Tis well," was the only response she could get.

"I will see him now," she said as she pushed the platter away.

"Talk to the High Priestess, child."

The old cleric said this as she lifted the platter and turned to the door. Melisande was put out by the attitude. Did not this one know of the miracle of birth that had happened here just...?

"How long have I slept, m'lady? I must see that my child doesn't go hungry due to my lethargy."

"You've slept three days, child," and, as she saw the shocked look on the girl's face, "but worry not for the child. He's been well cared for. Sleep a bit and I will send for your mother, the High Priestess."

"What do you mean?" she began with a slight waver in her voice.

"Hush, child. Don't read more into what's said than is there. Your mother will answer all of your questions to your satisfaction, I'm sure. For now, sleep."

The old cleric walked back to the bed, laid a gentle hand on the girl's forehead and Melisande drifted into dreamless sleep.

Melisande woke to a gentle hand shaking her and a familiar voice.

"Melisande? It is your mother. Wake, child. 'Tis a new day. Awaken to the joy of a new day."

The girl opened her eyes to her mother's beautiful face and the warm fuzzy feeling one gets when one has slept long and peacefully.

"Hello, Mother. Have you seen my child, my son?"

She did not want to lose the warmth of the moment, but she needed to know that her mother was proud of her. Strangely, her mother's words seemed to come from far away.

"I've seen him, my little one, a strong and beautiful boy. You've done well."

Melisande sighed and her mother's smile calmed her insides.

"I want to see him, Mother. When may I?"

"Not just now, little one. Now you must wake and eat. We will speak later of your beautiful boy."

Her mother's voice wavered a bit at that last, but Melisande thought that it must have been the deep emotions running free. Her mother was proud of her and would help her daughter to raise the boy in the path of love and happiness. Her mother smiled as she left the room and it was enough.

Two weeks passed and, though they treated her as eggshell, none would take her to the nursery or speak to her of her baby boy. She wanted to see, hold, cuddle, and nurse her own child. This constant "later" was making her uneasy and, strangely, angry.

On this day, Melisande rose, dressed, and went to find her mother. Enough was enough! She knocked on the oaken doors that lead to her mother's study.

"Enter," came the soft response from within.

Melisande pushed the door open and entered the study of the High Priestess of the goddess Freya. Books of healing, husbandry, rights, and related tomes lined the walls from floor to ceiling. A small desk, covered with manuscripts and writing utensils, was placed below the single window. Her mother, Ester Dorn, sat upon the reclining couch in the center of the room.

"Mother, where is my baby?" Melisande blurted without preamble. "I've asked but get no answers. Are all so cruel as to not let me see him when they all know how desperately I wish to hold him?"

"Come. Sit with me, little one, and we will talk."

"No, Mother. I want to see my son. I want to see him *now!*"

"You cannot see him, child."

Melisande's heart stopped. Her mother's words were spoken with so much finality.

"Is he ill? Is that it? Is he sick? I must go to him, then, Mother. He needs me now. He needs—"

"His father."

The words came from her mother's mouth, but they were all wrong. Maybe she'd heard wrong. Maybe...

"The boy's father came on the third day, as was agreed upon, and collected his son."

"What?!"

"You must have known, child. You cannot have thought..."

The shocked look on her daughter's face spoke otherwise.

"But you did, didn't you?"

This was not her mother. This was a stranger in her mother's study. Her mother would never allow her child to be taken. All clerics of Freya are taught to fight as a deterrent to more harm. Her mother would have fought to the death to keep her grandchild. No, this was not her mother, not as she remembered her.

"Where is he, Mother? What have you done?"

The last question stung her mother's ears as it came through Melisande's controlled hysteria.

"Lord Cartellion contracted with the temple to father a son. He has done that, with our blessing, with you as vessel. He came and collected what his seed brought forth. That is all."

Melisande was angry, outraged, confused, and disoriented.

"He came and took my baby and you allowed it? He can't do that. I won't let him get away with it. I'll—"

"You will do nothing."

The steel in her mother's voice left no doubt as to the truth. Lord Cartellion had come, gathered her son, and left, all with the blessing of the temple, as well as this woman who claimed to be her mother!

"You, Melisande," continued this stranger who could not be her mother, "will go to temple sanctuary now and pray to Our Lady Freya for enlightenment and guidance, since you will not accept it from me. A child was born to you. That is your purpose. Its life is not yours to own! It is for its family to teach, raise, and care for. Not you!"

The black anger was beginning to well up inside the girl and she fought it, but the panic she felt mixed with the anger and it seeped into her soul and her words.

"How many children have you given up, Mother?"

High Priestess Ester Dorn, of the Goddess Freya, looked deep into her daughter's eyes, smiled, and replied.

"Twelve."

A day later, Melisande walked softly to the door to the Hall of Records. She felt as an intruder and had to continually remind herself that the records kept here were public domain.

"Anyone can read them, so why not me?"

The question was asked, and answered, for the twelfth or thirteenth time and she pushed the door open.

A large black book rested on a heavy stand in the center of the room surrounded by other books of births that occurred throughout this continent. The walls were lined with these books, floor to ceiling, encompassing every birth and death ever to take place in this plane of existence. There were genealogies, books of titles, coats of arms, and land rights, but these had very little interest to the young cleric.

Melisande went straight to the massive book on the stand. Closed, it was thirty-four inches long, twenty-four inches wide, and eighteen inches deep. It was the book of births to the priestesses of Freya, the genealogy complete. This was the book that would tell Melisande the names of all of those who'd come to the temple for progeny.

It was open to a page with but three entries. The last read, "Mother: Melisande Dorn, Father: Lord Cartellion, Child: male, unnamed, Date: ER1832, third of the Serpent."

The two others mattered little to the girl, as they were for two other girls in the temple not related to her as far as she knew. She wanted to know of the twelve others who were her brothers and sisters. She turned the pages back, back to the time of her birth.

"Mother: Ester Dorn, Father: Lord Belmont, Child: girl, Melisande."

"Lord Belmont?" she thought. "But what of my father here at temple?"

She went to one of the cases along the wall, searched, and found the book she needed and opened it. It opened, as if intended to do so, to the page with Lord Belmont's name at the top of the page. The cleric's eyes widened in shock as she read the entry.

"Lord Belmont, High Lord of the Guild of Saladin and brother to…"

Melisande slammed the book closed. It couldn't be true. She was the daughter of the highest ranked evil in this world, the complete opposite of all that she'd been taught. Pain and confusion engulfed her and she ran from the room, down the corridors she thought she'd known so well, and into the gardens. The loss to her soul enveloped her and she thought she might strangle on the blackness that engulfed her. She gathered herself up to confront her mother. Her mother must explain this. She *must*!

"He is my *uncle*, Mother. Brother to Lord Belmont! You knew, didn't you? And you didn't stop this! Why, Mother?"

The young cleric was close to tears. Not the tears of sadness or hurt, but the angry tears of rage and betrayal.

"It matters not, child, that he is your uncle. It matters only that the child was born healthy and male. You are but a vessel for the next generation, this you must understand. You must adjust to this that you may continue serving the Lady Freya."

"I am no longer certain that I wish to, Mother." The words were tinged in darkness. "You've let him take my child from me, without allowing me to hold, love, or even see him. If this is what it means to 'serve,' maybe I'm just not cut out for it!"

"The goddess protect you, daughter, for your faith has fallen. You seek answers? Ask the Lady. If she won't hear you and you persist, the answer will become evident in the loss of your power to heal. Think hard, child. Pray for guidance. Don't let your doubts destroy you."

"Doubts? You say doubts, Mother? I have no doubts. I know what you have done and I will put it right!"

Melisande glared at this woman who'd been her mother forever, but was now this stranger. How could anyone give up a part of themselves, another life to another without the pain? Did her mother feel the loss of her children, or was she so callous in her faith as to simply believe her own words?

Melisande wanted to see her son and, by the goddess or without, she would do just that.

"I will see Cartellion."

Ester Dorn shook her head sadly as the terse words rang in her ears, and she watched her daughter storm from the room and slam the door behind her.

Melisande spent the rest of the day trying to locate the Saladin. From his apartments, she was directed to his stable. From there, to another place and still another until she was quite sure she was being run in circles. At every place, she'd left messages for Cartellion to get in touch with her.

It was becoming evident, from the locations to which she had been directed and the information she'd gathered on the big Saladin's activities, that he was settling his affairs prior to leaving the city for awhile. She returned to his apartments only to find that he'd just left for the Banke of Catlorian.

She ran.

He was moving away from her toward the business district when she saw him. There was no mistaking the black-plate armor, the gait, and the sheer size of the Lord Saladin. Where he strode, there was emptiness. None would stand before Lord Cartellion as he walked the streets of Catlorian. None save one angry cleric of the goddess Freya.

"Cartellion!" she yelled. "We must talk!"

He stopped and turned. All she could see were his eyes through the Y slits of his helmet.

"What is it, cheesa?"

The deep resonance of his voice came as from a distance and carried with it the absolute absence of emotion.

Cartellion, his valet, and his stableman had referred to Melisande as "cheesa." When she'd asked the valet the word's meaning, he'd smiled and stated that it was Wurmish with several different meanings. "Wife," "mistress," and "child" were the meanings he knew, but he insisted that she ask his master if she found him.

"Cheesa, m'lord?" she asked as she came before him. "In what way do you use the word?"

"Does it matter?" came the offhanded reply.

"I've searched for you all over this city. Didn't you get my messages?"

"Yes."

The big Saladin crossed his arms over his chest as he gazed at this girl, her anger a palpable thing to his senses.

"Well? Why didn't you answer?"

"Why should I, woman?"

He felt the rage building and it brought a small smile to his lips. He glanced about and noted that, though none would look at them, they were drawing a certain amount of attention.

"I believe it would be better if we moved out of the traffic for this discussion, don't you, cheesa?"

Traffic? There wasn't a soul within twenty feet of them. People avoided the area, averted their eyes, and went to great lengths to avoid being noticed by the large messenger of Death. Cartellion turned toward the side of the street and the people parted as if some force were keeping the buffer between them and him. The force had a name and its name was fear. Stark, bright, enveloping fear.

Melisande, however, was beyond fear and, some might say, good sense. She was wrapped in black anger and it tinged every word that came from her mouth. She wanted answers and she wanted them now. Her voice was kept low, barely controlled and dripped with malice.

"Where is my son, Cartellion?"

Cartellion turned, folded his arms again, and leaned on a wall at the side of the street. His title had been thrown away as he became a target for her malice and anger. The smile within his helm disappeared at the question.

"You meant to say, cheesa, 'Where is *my* son?' didn't you? He is yours by birth only. He is *mine*! A woman, a *cleric*," the word spat out as distasteful, "should know their place. Obviously you do not!"

"I will see him, Cartellion. He is of my body and I have a right—"

"You have *no* rights in this matter, woman. You were merely a convenience, a temporary housing for the man-child I craved. Nothing more! Accept it, cheesa, your purpose has been fulfilled!"

There was no attempt to hide her anger and contempt. Civility had been thrown to the wind. The concept that she should be used as a baby factory for such as he—and should like it—sent wave after wave of black, seething anger through her soul.

The smile returned beneath the helm as Cartellion felt the transformation. He was amused. This one had fire, by the gods! Hopefully his son would inherit this, without the outrageous concept this woman holds in equal importance.

"You wanted a son for what purpose, Cartellion?"

His smile grew. "Why, to follow in my footsteps, of course."

"And if he doesn't? If he finds that life is precious and love a thing to strive toward? If he inherits my love of life?"

The eyes within the helm glowed red.

"Then he will die and I will try again."

Shocked, Melisande knew that this monster meant every word. He would kill his own son if he did not live up to expectation.

The glow receded and the big Saladin shrugged.

"He is being well cared for, cheesa. When he reaches the age to be trained, he will take the vows of Saladin. Until that time, he remains my son and the honorary title of Saladin is his. He will come to no harm and, until he proves a disappointment, he is safe. That, cheesa, is my promise to you."

For now, she thought, his promise would do. His title as well as his claim to it demanded strict honor. He hadn't lied. He could not! Her child was safe for the moment.

"I wish to see him." she said, her voice soft yet undefeated.

He looked down into her eyes. He felt the anger still there, but she held the reins tight. Something inside softened. Not much, but enough.

"You may see him in a few months. I will bring him here to my apartments. Graisson will contact you with my return date, for I have no knowledge of when that will be. When I return, you will be allowed to see your son. I'll not stand in your way."

She knew Graisson as Lord Cartellion's lieutenant and right hand. She nodded.

"I'll be here."

A sharp malicious laugh came from deep within the helm as she turned on her heel to walk away.

"If you live."

"Demon spawn son of a bitch!" she spat back.

"Thank you, cheesa."

He tasted the black anger that once again filled her being.

"Evil-tainted bastard." she tossed back as she continued to stride away.

"Down to the depths of my soul," came the retort, "and not just a taint."

She turned the first corner she came to and ran. Tears of anger, frustration, and pain ran freely down her cheeks. She ran through the northeastern gate of the city and on until she could run no more. She fell to her knees and let the tears come.

She was in a clearing within the edge of the forest. She was alone.

"Why, Lady, why?" she screamed as she threw her head back and let the tears stream.

There was no answer.

She ripped her surgical pouch open and, through her tears, found the small knife she kept there. She slashed her hand and the blood welled up. She called on that part of her that was healer and touched her wound. The bleeding stopped, the edges of the slash sealed, and the pain ceased.

"What have I done to displease you?" she gasped as her head fell forward. "If I have done something so wrong to have my child ripped from me, please tell me. I have tried to do the best I am able and to be worthy. If I am not, please, I beseech you, enlighten me so that I may do better. Please, don't leave me here in this blackness."

Still no answer.

Her anger turned to despair and the despair to self-pity. She wept.

A vortex of swirling light and unknown depth developed behind the girl. The swirling displacement of air lifted leaves, twigs, and flowers from the earth in a dance few have witnessed and none would forget. The power of the incredible forces required moved and shifted with nature.

The swirling of the air whipped the girl's dark hair about and brought her up from the blackness. She turned slowly as the gate collapsed with a snap. A stranger stood there, over six foot tall, his features covered by a shimmering black cloak. He tossed back the hood to reveal his handsome face topped by sun-blond hair held loosely at the nape of his neck. His eyes drew her as the young cleric caught them. They were mirrored silver.

"Greetings, Melisande Dorn, daughter of Freya."

His deep, melodic voice filled the clearing with soft, friendly vibrations.

"Greetings, m'lord." she replied breathlessly. She wiped her tear-stained cheeks on her sleeve and added, "You seem to have me at a disadvantage."

The stranger smiled and bowed.

"I am called Anteroe. Maxim Anteroe. A wanderer by trade, though I have been called by many names."

"I have heard of you, sir, and I know the other names. 'Meddler' is one, yet 'friend' is another. I have heard many...stories of you, m'lord."

"Do not believe over half of them, child." he laughed.

"I am learning not to believe half of what I hear and to withhold judgment on the other half."

Her cynicism caused him to pause. Then he nodded.

"The lessons of wisdom are both painful and hard to understand. Not all of the world is a garden of roses."

"No." She laughed bitterly. "It seems rather filled with thorns at the moment."

With solemn tenderness, Wanderer lifted the girl's chin with a gentle finger and looked deep into those pain-filled eyes of green. He saw the pain and betrayal and the soul in danger of darkness.

"There is still beauty in this world. One needs only to look."

His hand dropped as she continued to look into the mirrored silver of his eyes. His voice took on a tone used in dealing with a sad child.

"What you have done will be recorded in the books of history and, when the change is noted, you, by bearing a son for Cartellion, will be remembered as she who placed a seed within his cold, black heart."

A blossom of hope came to the young cleric. If only...

"Is there any way I may help that seed to grow?"

"Only time, and the Fates, can tell, and they are not saying. When the Sisters speak, their voices do not bring relief. Not to mortal hearts."

Melisande saw his eyes seem, at that moment, to lose some of their luster. For just a moment she saw, revealed, a soul of uncounted lifetimes filled with images best forgotten, yet unforgettable. She saw the pain of the unspeakable horrors he'd seen.

The moment passed quickly and once again his eyes were mirrors to the world.

"Dear one," he said softly, "if, in the future, you wish to speak to one who will not judge, come here to this place and I will hear. Even if I am not present, I will hear you."

Melisande felt the power gather as this man stretched a hand out to his side. Nature and time quickened under his hand and a rose grew and blossomed white as she watched. He turned slowly and walked away from the girl, his hand tracing lines of power in the air before him. The swirling vortex began again as the portal to elsewhere opened and, as he stepped through the dance of wind, flowers, and grass, he turned back to her.

"Remember, daughter of Freya, there is still beauty in this world. Go out and look. You will find it, and I know you will appreciate it."

The gate collapsed about him and, in a blink, he was gone and she was alone again.

"No, not alone." she thought as she looked at the rose of purest white. "Never again alone."

She resisted the urge to touch the rose. It belonged here and she belonged with humanity, doing what she could to help end the suffering. She would remember this clearing, this place that had reached out to a soul black with self-doubt and misery, touched it and helped it to begin the road to healing. Even if the need to return never occurred, she would remember.

Melisande Dorn, cleric of Freya, stood on her feet and began the long walk back to the city.

By the time she'd made the gate, she'd made up her mind and turned toward the temple district.

High Priestess Ester noted the change in her daughter immediately.

"Well, little one, I see you've found answers."

"Yes, Mother, I have, but not from the source I asked." Then her eyebrows knitted as she frowned and added, "At least, I don't think…"

She shook her head to clear it. Could it be that…? She smiled.

"No matter, Mother. I've come to ask permission to leave Catlorian for a time. It has become important for me to see the rest of the world, for I've lived my life for too long in relatively protected bliss. This I can no longer endure."

Ester heard no pleading in her daughter's voice but the request for understanding. She remembered a time when she'd asked her mother the same question in the same way.

"In two weeks, your Coming of Power ceremony will be held. At that time you will be anointed Priestess of Our Lady Freya, if this is your wish?"

"Yes, Mother," she replied, "it is my wish."

"Then you will be allowed, with my blessing, to go into the world, fully armed to heal, love, and care for others. I am very proud, my little one."

Melisande spent some of her leisure time over the next several days making plans of her own. Once a priestess, she'd sign on to go with a group of adventurers and aid them in whatever endeavor was presented. She could not bear sitting about waiting for Cartellion to bring her son home. Between returning to her studies and her duties at the house of healing, there was only enough time to prepare for her ceremony.

Yet, just a few days prior to her anointment, as she went about some errand, she found the flier posted by Sage Terillion.

"This is just what I've been looking for." she thought as she tucked the flier into one of her pouches and continued on her way.

Chapter Eight

He ran.

Not as a man would, but with the ground-eating lope of a wolf and in total silence. He was large, over six feet tall, and rangy. His well-proportioned muscles rippled with every move. An aura of intense, untapped power surrounded him.

He wore a gray wolf pelt as loincloth and as a cloak the pelt of a wolf of an unusual color: bright red. The head of the red wolf served as a hood and had fallen back to rest in the middle of the large man's back. His braided red hair disappeared under the red pelt and continued down to the small of his back.

A burnished brown chain mail vest strained against the man's chest and knee-length doeskin boots covered his powerful calves and swift feet. The hilt of a knife protruded from the top of each boot. The hilts showed wear, but they were well cared for as were the razor sharp blades sheathed below them.

A bastard sword was harnessed to his back, but it wouldn't draw as much attention as the two-handed club that rode at his wide leather belt. A quiver of white fletched arrows rode opposite the sword and a small, strange-looking crossbow hung from his left hip.

He carried the powerful elfin bow in his left hand, parallel to the earth as he ran. It had been made specifically for him and was tuned to his strength, talent, and being. He was positively deadly with it.

He ran, but "he" was not there.

Knowing that he would be running this way for the bulk of three days, the young man had set his senses flaring and had mentally retreated to his place of solitude, trusting his well-honed senses to direct his feet southwest toward Catlorian.

Here, in his place of peace, he found his link to his god, the Great One. Here, inside this man's mind, a huge red wolf lived.

<*Well Come, name-brother.*> growled the wolf in the singsong of wolf speech. <*Come me here to bring wish of Great One.*>

<*Well Come, Red Wolf. What wish?*>

<*First, must you remember. Remember…*>

His mind drifted back to the time of his youth, back to the womb of the Clan of the Wolf. Back to the Northern Mountain Ranges beyond the Crystal Ranges and the village that sat in the mountains above abandoned Ravagar.

He was ten summers again in the shelter provided for the Shaman of the clan, Gray-Fang. The yearning for the hunt was strong, as it was then. He had no understanding of the purpose behind his study with the Shaman. It was boring to have to sit day after day and listen to the withered old man recite the history of the clan over and over again. Then he'd have to repeat it back over and over again.

Boring, that is, unless it occurred at night over an open fire, for then the histories unfolded in visions in the fire. He loved studying the old stories at night, but the Shaman thought it important to go over them daily. He had the youth repeating the old stories to the young ones when he wasn't hunting or studying.

The Shaman stopped his recitation abruptly and snarled at the youth.

"You, fire hair, must pay attention! What you learn here is important and you must learn it well! Those things you wish to do now in your youth, you will do, but you have a higher destiny before you. This you must remember!"

"I wish only to do my part for the clan, Shaman. Hunt the meat, learn the healing ways, and share the sorrows and joys of my brothers. I see no need for all of this. You shall remain Shaman forever. Why am I trained as your replacement?"

The old man smiled. Did this one not notice the age that weighed heavy on the Shaman's body and soul, or was this a youth's attempt at complementary release from "imprisonment"?

No. It was an honest question from this fire haired youth. How much, then, to tell him to make him understand? Just enough would not be enough, nor would it be prudent to lie to this one.

The old Shaman looked into those smoldering green eyes and knew, of a certainty, nothing short of total honesty would do. This one's talent in memory, arms, tracking, hunting, and anything else one could name were deemed uncanny. Some would even say "magical," but not to this youth's face, for to accuse him of "demon trafficking" was always a painful path.

Yes, the time had come. The Shaman shifted on the fur of his pallet and spoke to the youth in a very low and serious voice.

"Listen well, young one, for I will now tell of your birth. Ten summers and days ago, you were born to a seventh son and the most renowned warrior of this clan, Gold Spear, and your mother, the greatest herb mistress and healer in the clan's history, Nightshade."

"These things I know, Shaman."

"Patience, youth. I must tell this in my time in my own way."

"Forgive me, Shaman. Please, go on."

The old man paused and looked directly into those eyes. What he would say next was important and, despite this one's uncanny memory, he must make sure that every word is taken in.

"What you do not know, my young friend, is this. The 'Fire-Hair' with which you've been born has not been seen in seven generations. You, should you live beyond your naming, might well be the 'GRRIRR GYA' foretold in the old legends.

"He who would be GRRIRR GYA is destined to wear the furs of Clan Leader, War Chief and Shaman, all at once. This is the destiny that is yours to follow. If you be the one, the destiny of this, your clan, rests within *you*!"

The boy understood then why he had been singled out by the warriors for training, why the Shaman sought him for teaching, and why his mother used what little time he had left for training in herb lore and healing. He understood why his father gave no quarter in combat training and why the War Chief asked him his opinion about every little security problem.

He knew now that his destiny was tied to the survival of his clan. To fail could mean the destruction of a way of life. The Clan of the Wolf lived close to the earth, taking only that needed to survive and maintain it. It was in his hands to see that this way of life continued.

"I am sorry for my earlier impatience, my Shaman. Teach me, that I do honor for the clan, be I the one or no. Teach me, Shaman, that I may do what I must."

The old Shaman smiled. This one could be the one foretold, or the father of the one. He gazed again into those green eyes and saw the intelligence, wisdom, and power of ages gone. Yes, this could truly be the one he had waited for his entire life. He closed his eyes for a moment and asked the Great One for enough time to teach this one all that he had garnered in his one hundred and twenty three years.

He opened his eyes and smiled.

"Now, fire hair, as I was saying…"

Three summers more found the youth seated at the council fire between his father and mother. The Shaman sat across the fire to his right, the War Chief to his left, and the Clan Leader sat directly across the fire from him.

The Clan Leader had heard all that he needed to hear. He looked the youth over with a practiced eye in a futile search for the weakness that could mean death for this one. He stifled a smile.

"I've heard the herb mistress say that there is naught left she can teach. Yes, and that you have taught her still more than she herself knew."

Nightshade sat stoically while inside her pride in her son threatened to burst her asunder.

"From the Shaman, you have learned more than he was able to teach. He says that you have committed all of our history to memory and have come to understand things better than even he could."

The Shaman nodded to the Clan Leader and turned a quick grin on the boy.

"From your father," and here the first smile, "that you have bested him in the training battles. A decisive victory, I might add."

Gold Spear beamed. There was no dishonor at being bested in combat—if you were truly bested. The large veteran had never gone into training with his son with less than full power. To have done less could mean death at the hands of the first foe faced. Yes, this warrior was proud of his son. Very proud indeed.

"We have discussed your accomplishments in council and have determined that you are ready to discover your man-name. This is the greatest challenge a boy must face for, if he returns, he is boy no longer."

He raised the staff of Clan Leader and held it in both hands horizontal to the ground and out toward the fire and beyond to the boy.

"Do you accept the challenge, fire hair?"

The formal query was made and there was no hesitation in the boy's answer. His right fist came to his chest sharply and his eyes met the Clan Leader's over the staff he might have to protect one day.

"Yes, Clan Leader, I accept. May I bring honor to my clan, my house, and myself, or die in the attempt."

"DONE!"

For six suns he'd traveled following game trails and getting a feel for the soft solitude that surrounded him. He smelled the wind for water and weather as he'd been taught and found the berries that would sustain him should he need the energy.

Then there was something else on the wind. It was the unmistakable scent of human blood. He followed the invisible trail cautiously until he found the old man in the underbrush.

The little man had obviously crawled there to die, a feat of incredible magnitude considering the number and seriousness of the wounds covering his body. The smell of death was also in the air, but it was coming from a way off from where he found the old one. The youth vowed to solve this riddle once he had cared for the old one's healing, if possible.

He licked the many wounds clean and bound them using one or more of the healing poultices he'd learned from his mother. Then he built a crude lean-to and carefully laid the old man within.

Seeing that he could do no more for the old one, he turned his attention to the death smell. He followed the scent to a path between two low cliffs. From the signs, someone had stood upon the cliff and cast down stone. The scent of death was stronger here and he followed it.

He came upon the bodies no more than twelve man-lengths away. There were four, and they had been dead for at least half of the day. He looked closer and read the signs that told of something, or someone, being dragged away.

This was a riddle. He'd found the blood spoor that lead to where he'd found the old one, yet these drag marks led in the opposite direction.

Wait! No, not dragged. Someone *crawled* away!

The riddle was this: The old one had been beaten almost to death, these were dead, and, it seems, another had crawled away in the opposite direction, possibly to die, but where is the one who had done all of this? Where is the warrior who had killed, crippled, and all but buried these men?

He shrugged. A great battle had been fought here, but there were no answers. He had no more time for the dead. The riddle would wait and the forest would care for the carrion. He returned to the old one.

The old man seemed to breathe easier now and the youth studied him. He'd never seen the slanted eyes, the slight, slim smallness of his build, and the strange, wise calm that surrounded the old one even in sleep. The youth picked the twigs from the wispy beard and went to hunt the meat, roots, and herbs he would need to return this one to health.

Three days passed before the old man stirred. The youth had improved the shelter and hunted, though never venturing far from the camp and his charge.

The young man noted the stirrings and brought a bowl of broth and a slice of meat he'd roasted to the old one as the latter's eyes fluttered open.

The old one eyed the youth with some suspicion as he drank from the bowl, but he refused the meat. The youth offered a small cup of his "Ravagar Wine" to the old one and, though still suspicious, the old one brought it to his lips.

The old man almost reopened all of his wounds with the retching. It took a moment to get his body back under control and, once there, he eyed the youth with an angry glare.

"Why do you go through all of this trouble to save my pitiful life only to poison me?"

"I am sorry, old one," said the boy softly as he backed away, his head down. "This is a healthful mixture of herbs, spices, and fermented goat's blood that is a staple of my village for generations. It never occurred to me that there were those who could not drink the medicine and were actually repulsed by it. Please, I meant you no ill."

"Save your medicine for yourself then, youth," said he, a bit softer than a moment before. "I shall heal now from within."

"From within? But, what does that…"

The old man slipped into a sleep that, if he were other than he was, the youth would have thought was close to death. He watched.

The old man awoke the next morning with a new strength and, over the next few days, regained his health rapidly. The youth watched this with ever increasing curiosity.

Then came the day when the old one decided to tell the youth his story.

He was Pak Chu-So. He'd come here from a land far to the east and over the sea. The dead, he said, were his doing.

He'd been driven from his ancestral home for his dealings with outsiders. Some of the more courageous had followed him here and lain in ambush. They'd showered him with stones and thought him dead. When they'd come down to check, though beaten and bleeding, the old one slew four and had seen that the fifth would no longer have the use of his legs.

The youth smiled and voiced his doubts as to the truth of this story.

The old man moved toward the youth with the grace of a cat, his hands blurring in a pattern the youth had never seen and, to the boy's quick mind, one impossible to defend. A slender finger snapped out and drove into the boy's shoulder.

The blinding pain dropped the youth to his knees. He'd felt pain before, great pain, but this was indescribable! When the red haze lifted from his eyes, he felt Pak Chu-So massaging his shoulder. The pain slipped away and the old one leaned away.

"Do not let outward appearances fool you, youth. Your eyes can trick you. Do not trust them."

"How is it that you, with a mere touch, can cause such pain? My father has put me to my knees before with blows in the training pits, but never have I felt such pain!"

The old one stood and, as the youth too stood, Pak looked the boy over.

"If you are willing," he said finally, "I can teach this to you, but you must be willing to learn."

Never before had Pak Chu-So had such a willing student. For two and one half seasons, the youth stayed with the old one, improved the shelter to a small hut near a spring, learned the skills as the old man taught them, and hunted. It was on an occasion of the latter that the youth genuinely impressed the old master.

The day was chilly but clear. Pak Chu-So and the youth stood before the hut as the boy prepared to hunt. The youth stopped mid-sentence, cocked his head, and sniffed the air.

A moment later, they both heard the low growl from the wood line. Nine wolves stalked from the woods and formed a semicircle before them with a great gray in the center. Pak assumed a defensive posture, his mind and body tuned to the coming conflict, and hoped his student had done the same. He was shocked when he heard the singsong growls of wolf-speech coming from the throat of his student.

The gray's ears came forward and he too took up the growling melody. Finally the youth growled a short sound and relaxed. He turned to the old one and smiled at the open-mouthed astonishment he saw there.

"I've apologized for hunting his area without permission. He understands that there was need and has granted permission and protection."

Pak closed his mouth, swallowed, and nodded.

"However, there is a problem. Hunters have wounded his whelp, and it is beyond his kind to help. Finding one of my clan, to him, is a stroke of fortune. I must go with him now to help as I may."

"Bring that one here, my friend, that I may assist."

As the youth shouldered his pack and stepped off toward the wood line, he stopped and turned to the old one.

"You do realize that should the pup die, we may have to fight for our lives?"

"Then, let us not fail," said the old one as he waved a hand to send the youth after the wounded pup.

The youth returned a moment later with the limp form of the yearling wolf in his arms. A quarrel from a crossbow protruded from the animal's side, but it did not come through to the other side.

Pak had brought a table from the hut and placed several silk rolls of instruments to one side and a clean cloth over the rest.

"Place him here, youth." he said as he helped the boy toward the table. "This is something I know of and you may wish to learn."

As the youth gently laid the pup upon the cloth, Pak heard the weak whimper.

"Tell them that, though what I do may seem strange, it is necessary. Tell them also that they should not interfere or all may be lost. The missile is close to this one's life source. I will do what I can."

The old one did not wait. While the youth spoke in the wolf-speech, Pak unrolled one of the silken bundles. Arranged in neat rows were silver needles of different lengths, all very thin. The old one placed a gentle hand on the pup's head and inserted a three-inch needle just behind its left ear. The whimpering stopped, though the pup's eyes were open and alert.

"I have stopped the pain and the flow of energy to this one's body. He cannot move until I remove the needle. Now, youth, it is imperative that you explain that I must open this one to save its life."

The old one did not wait for the youth to growl the translation. He gently began to separate the skin from the quarrel with his fingers, coaxing it apart as if in answer to a soft request. When there was room, Pak slipped a slender hand into the pup's body, cupped the barbed tip in his hand, and withdrew the quarrel.

"It is to you I turn, youth," said the old one as he gently began coaxing the skin back together. "You know the healing of his kind as I do not."

The youth watched as the skin bonded, though not permanently without time, and was in awe.

"How did you—"

"This I will teach if time permits. Now you must do what you can. When I remove the needle, this one will be in pain. What will you do?"

The youth grinned and brought out his skin of Ravagar Wine. Pak frowned as the boy pulled the stopper and poured a trickle into the pup's mouth and was rewarded as the pup began to lick the brew into its throat and stomach. After a bit, he felt that the pup had had enough, and he placed the stopper back into the wineskin.

"He no longer needs your needle, Master."

When Pak removed the needle, the wolf jerked once and then sighed. The youth applied a poultice to the wound and wrapped clean linen about the wolf's chest to hold it in place.

Two weeks later, the youth shouldered his pack again, this time bidding farewell to Pak Chu-So and the young wolf that had become the old man's constant companion.

The gray had promised to protect this place and the old man for as long as his pack endured. Pak had never known such peace since the days of his youth. He stroked the brown fur between the wolf pup's ears and looked into the youth's green eyes.

"I shall return, friend Pak, when I may to learn more from you. There is a challenge I must face that I've put off for too long. I must be about it. Be well, Master."

"I shall, my young friend, thanks to your skill and care. I shall be here when you have need. Travel safe, fire hair."

The skills the old one had already taught to the youth were considerable, though he knew that he had just brushed the surface of the ancient's knowledge. He had not, however, earned his man-name, and he knew he would not be whole until he did.

Twelve sunrises later he topped a rise and came face to face with his destiny.

A prince of the lupine stood in a bright beam of sunlight. The smell of fear had never touched his coat, and he would easily have outweighed all but the largest of the warriors in the youth's clan.

His color? A magnificent color, yet rare for a wolf: a bright, coppery red-gold.

<*Well Come, fire hair.*> came the deep wolf-speech. <*Wait long for you. Now you come, good.*>

<*Why do you wait for me, brother?*>

The red showed his beautiful, yet deadly fangs.

<*You are GRRIRR GYA or not. My task, find which. You die, not. I die, am."*>

<*I do not wish to fight you, my brother.*>

<*Must, or die.*>

The great wolf leaped, but the youth moved too quickly. The battle seemed to last for hours, with neither combatant using anything but what nature supplied. Hand and claw, teeth and fangs, sinew, bone, and muscle. The dance between the two looked even, though the youth was a good deal smaller than the wolf.

Suddenly the wolf snapped at an arm that seemed to disappear. Even in the lust of battle, the teachings of Pak Chu-So came through. The youth had used one of Pak's blurred feints to draw the wolf to it. Then he drove his hand up and in, penetrating the chest of the great red wolf. He grasped the still-beating heart and ripped it from the wolf's chest. As the wolf died, the youth held the heart high and howled.

The battle was over, the bloodlust slackened, and the youth never felt the ground when he hit it.

He found himself in spirit, hovering between life and death, lost it seemed in a world of limbo.

Then he saw the great white wolf, as tall as his shoulders and exuding limitless power. He was power, this wolf, for he was, it came to the youth, the very deity that guided and protected the Clan of the Wolf. This was the Great Wolf Spirit who stood before this youth to pass judgment.

The youth hung his head and waited.

The Great One came to a stop in front of the boy and, with his muzzle, lifted the boy's face. The wolf locked the boy's green eyes to his yellow ones and knowledge began to touch the youth's mind.

The youth knew, without knowing how, what he must become. His name would be Red Wolf, and he would roam for many turns of the seasons from his clan to learn all he can from those outside. His destiny was to hold all of the positions of power at once and bring his people out of darkness back into the light. This was his destiny, his calling, and his fate. All he had to do was believe and it would be so. Red Wolf believed and...Awoke.

He found himself on his back with the still-warm heart of the red wolf in his hand. Every wound he had received in the battle was healed, and the fatigue he should have felt was gone. He stood, looked down at the huge red wolf, and said a quiet prayer to his god for this one. Then he ate the raw heart, as was the custom of his clan, skinned the wolf, and gave all but the skinned head to the carrion beasts of the forest.

In respect for the teachings of Pak Chu-So, whose lessons helped to win through his test, he built a small fire and burned the head as an offering to Pak's god, Huan-Ti.

He stayed that evening in that sacred place of battle and left at first light for his village. Before he could take his man-name, he had to abide with the ceremonies.

Four days later, he walked into his village and presented the wolf pelt to the Shaman, along with the tale of how it was won. In due course, the ceremonies were held and the pelt was returned to him along with his new name. That evening, Red Wolf spoke long with the Shaman and his mother, wrestled and pinned his father, and ate and drank with his friends until late evening.

The next morning, the youth packed his belongings, donned the red wolf pelt, and left the village behind. Few were awake to see the red wolf pelt ride the broad shoulders out of the village into the world.

His mother was one of those few. She'd been told that he would return every two to three years to council with the three leaders of the clan, to share what experiences and knowledge he had gained, and to assess whether Red Wolf could cease his wanderings and don the three pelts of power.

<...Remember.>

Red Wolf returned to his name-brother within his place of peace.

<I have remembered, my brother. I have remembered all.>

<Then, message.>

The great wolf paused.

<Southeast, brother.>

Red Wolf snapped to awareness and the run. He could feel that all but a bit of three suns had passed, and he could see by that same sun that he was now running southeast.

Chapter Nine

The blond half elf sat with his back to the tree and tended the small fire. His gaze drifted to his surroundings, surroundings not only strange but totally unknown to him. He knew he was lost.

He grinned.

"No, not lost. I just don't have any idea where I am." he thought to himself.

The grin broadened.

"Hells! I don't have any idea *who* I am!"

His memory was gone, his life ripped from him by what, or who, he knew not. All he had were memories of his present, say less than a week now, and strange waking dreams.

Yet something kept drawing him toward the city whose lights burned in the far distance just visible over the horizon in the darkness.

His history was a mystery, as were the things he had with him when he woke. A hand-and-half bastard sword lay across his knee, the hilt toward his left hand, and a dagger rested in a sheath at the nape of his neck beneath the collar of the scale mailed shirt he wore over a broadcloth shirt. The armor fit him perfectly and was adjusted to his comfort. How he knew this was another mystery, but the half elf had taken a position that stated that anything that didn't kill him...

Something was missing, however. Something other than, or possibly linked to, his missing memory. Something he should—must—remember, yet could not.

The darkness had settled in quickly where he sat, but he took no notice. He wasn't surprised, as he might have been under different circumstances, that he could see his surroundings, in detail, in the darkness out to three score feet from where he sat. He just marked it as another talent from unknown parents.

The coney he'd been roasting was almost ready, yet the many pairs of red eyes that watched from the darkness caused him to wait and made his movements slow and small. The wolf smell on the breeze told him what they were. Slowly and casually with his left hand, he lay another fagot of wood on the fire while, with his right thumb, he released the hilt of that sword from the bind of the sheath.

He hated killing, except to live, a sense that seemed to have been taught as well as felt. There was no need to entice the pack to attack when it could be prevented somehow. The low growling just on the breeze was unnerving, but he held his movements to a minimum.

The growling ceased and, as he looked up casually without making an attempt to make eye contact with the beasts, noticed that they were looking to his left. He moved his gaze in that direction, again slowly and deliberately.

A young man stepped from the woods as silently as death. He was clothed in gray wolf pelt loincloth and a cloak of a red wolf skin across broad shoulders. His hair was braided and long. A bright red shine came from it as the firelight struck it.

His six-foot frame rippled relaxed sinew and slim muscle and, though his frame seemed slight, there was an aura of power, unseen yet obvious. It came from within the man, this power. It spoke of strength and speed of incredible proportions, not with bravado but with its presence alone.

"May I share your fire in exchange for some wine?"

The deep voice left no doubt that, should he wish it, the man could take what he wished and leave the half elf as fodder for the wolves still in the darkness. Yet the youth felt that this one's pride and honor would not allow this to one who had caused him no harm.

The half elf slowly moved his right hand from the sheathed sword to his right knee and extended his left to the stone across the fire from him.

The man stepped toward the fire but abruptly stopped. One of the wolves had growled a strangely inflected tone, more or less singsong. The man glanced toward the growl and growled himself in much the same manner. The larger wolves disappeared into the woods as three young pups toddled into the firelight, sat, and watched the two men.

"They hunt."

The man sat on the proffered stone and sliced a bit of meat from the roasting coney. As he chewed, he offered the half elf his wineskin. The youth took the skin, unstopped it, and took a mouthful of the warm liquid.

His eyes watered and his guts felt as if filled with molten lead, but he smiled and handed the wineskin back to the red headed barbarian. The man took the skin, drank deep, stopped the skin, and wiped his mouth on the back of his hand.

"The pups must stay with me until the others return and they are hungry."

The fire in the half elf's throat allowed for no words, so he pointed to the two coneys he'd hung in a tree, out of reach of scavengers, ten paces away.

The wolf man nodded, grinned, and spun. With a speed too quick to follow, he plucked the knives that protruded from the top of each of his boots and, with each hand, threw them.

One of the blades sliced through one of the strings that held one of the coneys and it dropped to the ground. The other nicked the string, yet didn't cut it through. Both knives were imbedded deep into the wood.

The pups watched the man and never moved to where the coney lay. The red head grinned at the half elf and shrugged.

The half elf smiled slightly as his left hand flashed for the blade at the nape of his neck. In one motion, he sent it straight and true to slice the remaining coney from the tree and it joined the other on the ground.

The wolf man raised an eyebrow slightly and grinned, then frowned when he heard the pups whimper. The three young wolves looked at the two coneys on the ground, yet would not move to them.

The half elf knew, somehow, that the young wolves were asking permission and, as the wolf man growled softly, he knew it had been given.

The pups leaped on the coneys and were soon chewing in delight.

The man grinned at the half elf and, after retrieving the knives from the tree, he glanced toward the glow that was the lights of Catlorian. He returned the neck knife to the half elf and extended a hand.

"I am known as Red Wolf."

The half elf took the strong hand in his, a sure, strong grip.

"I wish I could tell you who I am, but I cannot. He said in a somewhat choked voice. "I have no memory save from the past few days. I'm sorry."

He released the barbarian's strong grip and shrugged. Red Wolf, however, grinned.

"It's of no concern, pup. A name must be earned. Let us see what name you will earn."

The half elf grinned in return and turned his gaze to the glow in the distance. Maybe there he would find the life he'd lost, the memories that sat so close to the surface yet so far away.

Red Wolf cast a sidelong glance at the half elf and thought.

"This one bears a tale that could be interesting if told."

His appraisal took in the efficiency of movement, the calluses on his hands, the fingers of his left, and the calluses across the forefinger of his right. There were also calluses on both hands that told of work yet matched the hilt of the bastard sword that sat on this one's lap. The instrument that caused the wear on the fingers of this one's left and right hands was not in evidence, but this one did not look to be one who would leave it on purpose.

Ah, well. The tale would be told or not. This one would definitely bear watching.

This scrutiny was not noticed by the half elf. He was busy with thoughts of his own. The city in the distance was Catlorian, the center of this part of the world in which he found himself. How he knew this, and not much else, was irrelevant. He just knew that those lights drew him and he would go.

"We must rest." stated the barbarian. "The wolves will watch and protect. Tomorrow will be a long day, I fear."

"Yes," thought the half elf, "but it will be another day."

He rolled into his cloak and slept.

The blond half elf woke from his dream with a start. He was drenched in cold sweat and only his inner strength kept his body from shaking.

As if from long practice, he didn't move until he took in his surroundings. He felt that it was a short time before sunrise from the smell of the air around him and a sense from some forgotten place within his mind.

Red Wolf sat near the fire, a look of strange concentration on his face. It looked as if he were listening to the woods themselves. Two coneys were spitted above the small fire and two more lay next to the barbarian.

Then the youth felt the small warm bodies next to him. The wolf pups had taken up with him for his body warmth.

Red Wolf glanced toward him and grinned.

"From the sound of it, your demons have chased you all night. A bit of breakfast might be a good thing for you. Join me."

The half elf moved to get up and the pups jumped up and moved away. Red Wolf growled something low and soft, and one of them minced back toward the youth and licked his hand. Red Wolf growled again and, as they moved to the edge of the small clearing, threw the two raw coneys to them.

The blond youth wrapped the cloak about him and found a place next to the fire to sit. He took a slice of one of the coneys and, as he chewed, let his senses pierce the early morning.

"So, traveler, how is it that someone with obviously elfin blood finds himself without his bow?"

Red Wolf had watched the young half elf for a while and, as the coneys disappeared and the wolf pups lay satisfied, sat and sipped from his wineskin.

The blond youth drank from his wineskin and pondered the question. This barbarian seemed to exude trust. There seemed no reason not to tell this one everything. Besides, what was there to tell? He'd come awake beside a white road and, though he knew not where it led, had followed it. Something kept drawing him toward that city in the distance. Something deeply hidden also told him that there was something more, something important, then nothing.

Red Wolf listened until the short tale was finished and nodded.

"Try this." he said as he handed the half elf his long bow.

While the barbarian watched his every move, the half elf took the bow.

It felt strangely familiar, yet the half elf knew with a certainty that this bow had been made specifically for the barbarian. How he knew this, he didn't know, but the feeling was there, as was the knowledge. He held the elfin-crafted bow in his hands and as he recognized, somehow, the craftsmanship, the flashes of memory began.

Someone was explaining or showing, or both, how to use a bow. Someone he should know, but someone without a face. The half elf shook his head and reluctantly returned the bow.

Red Wolf's head snapped up suddenly and, with a glance at the blond youth, melted noiselessly into the woods. The half elf felt something as well and within a fraction of a second followed the barbarian's lead. He slid into the brush and took up a vantage point where he could see without being seen.

A tall figure in a shimmering black cloak stepped into the camp and sat down by the fire. He pulled a small kettle from a bag, poured water into it, and sat it on the fire. He reached into another pouch and removed three smaller pouches and, as the water came to a boil, added a little from each to the water.

The half elf recognized the ingredients, but he could not place the familiarity. There was a nagging at the back of his brain that this was not the first time he'd seen this mixture. An ache began just behind his eyes, a product of the conflict within his mind.

A flash of lightning from the west of their camp brought the half elf's head up. The thunder promised a storm that may or may not reach here. It was still far away, and the blond seemed to have other worries right now.

He watched as Red Wolf stepped into the clearing, dropped the strange club, and sat down across from the stranger. The youth was tempted to follow suit, yet his dreams and caution warned him not to move until he was certain. Certain of what, he could not say, but he slipped silently to the right to get a better look at this strange man.

The stranger's head snapped up and, from beneath the hood, the half elf knew, *knew*, that he was seen.

"Someone is clumping about in the woods." he said softly.

"Not your concern, Wanderer, but you may have made him a bit nervous."

"Of what? Me?"

Red Wolf grinned and he too seemed to look directly to where the half elf crouched in the darkness.

"Of everything at this point in time. He has some… problems for which there seem to be no answers, so he's a bit cautious. If I didn't know you, I'd be a bit cautious as well."

"Problems?" asked the man a bit petulantly from within his hood, "For one born to move in the forest, it seems his biggest problem is moving quietly!"

The man threw back his hood and, as the firelight danced on his sun-blond hair, cast the gaze of his mirrored silver eyes directly at the half elf.

"Wouldn't you rather be by the fire?"

The question came from behind the half elf but in the voice of the man in the cloak. Yet the blond youth had never seen the man's mouth move.

He knew then that he was in the presence of power that could not be hidden from. He stood and walked slowly back to the fire and sat, cautious and alert, but reconciled to the fact that he was in the presence of someone of consequence.

The man watched as the half elf came out of the wood line, his hands well away from his weapons, and smiled.

"Will you join me?" he asked as he motioned toward his teapot.

The deep timbre of the stranger's voice bespoke politeness, but the half elf had watched the ingredients go into that brew and wanted none of it.

"Thank you, but no." he replied softly with a curt nod. "I think I will stick to my wine."

Wanderer shrugged and sipped from his cup. After a moment he looked back at the half elf, his head cocked to one side.

"Are you bound for Catlorian?"

"Yes, m'lord, I seem to be drawn in that direction."

"Hmmm." responded the man. Then, "Are you sure you won't join me in a spot of tea? It would frankly be the cordial thing to do, you know, and I assure you it will do you no harm."

"I would really rather not, if you please. I'm a bit cautious as to what I put into my body, not knowing what I can or cannot withstand and, to be as frank, I'm not sure about the ingredients you've brewed there."

"I have told you that it will do you no harm."

"Yes, but caution tells me otherwise."

"Caution? Impertinence is more like it!"

The half elf glanced at the barbarian, but found that one grinning.

"I'm sorry, sir, but I did not mean—"

"I've offered you my tea and not only have you turned me down, you've managed to insult my attempt at being sociable!"

"I'm sorry, sir. Please, allow me." he said as he reached for a cup.

The smell from that brew was quite good and seemed to hang in the air about the camp. He took a small sip and, though tart to the tongue, found it settled his stomach.

Wanderer watched the half elf for a moment, nodded, and turned his attention to the young barbarian.

"Red Wolf, I've a message from a sage in Catlorian."

Red Wolf glanced at the half elf and, after a small frown crossed his face, grunted at the stranger.

"It seems he's learned of you somehow. He knows you wander about and see things that might be of value for a collector of information. He believes you may have some information that he needs that you'd be willing to share. He mentioned a reward for pertinent information. He sent this along to explain."

Wanderer handed the barbarian a scroll and after Red Wolf sniffed it, broke the seal, and opened it, Wanderer shook his head and took it back.

Unfortunately, though a few of the "word pictures" were familiar, nothing else was. Red Wolf could neither read nor write. A female half elf ranger had been teaching him the rudiments of reading, but she had been called back to Catlorian just recently. Greenleaf was a shape-changer and though she loved him, she knew his destiny and would under no circumstances stand in his way. Quite the contrary, she would walk through fire to see his path fulfilled.

"Sorry, my friend."

Wanderer read the scroll to the barbarian, which contained some information that may or may not be within a keep that stood many leagues to the northeast of Catlorian. Then the two spoke of past acquaintances and occurrences while the half elf listened with the mug of tea warming his hands.

Wanderer turned his attention back to the half elf and noticed that the tea was still untouched.

"Aren't you going to drink your tea?"

"Thank you, but no. Though I am sure that it may be good for you, I'm not as certain it would be as good for me."

The half elf started to hand the mug back to the stranger when a strange yet familiar red flame began to outline Wanderer's eyes, a yellow quivering fire at its center. The young blond froze as if transfixed.

"You really should finish your tea."

The voice seemed to come from far away, yet, to the half elf, it was as if it came from within. Of course he would finish this tea. Besides, not only was it the polite thing to do, it was very wholesome tea at that.

He took a long drink from the mug and smiled at the stranger.

Immediately the world became intensely clear. The trees moved to the left and right, the eyes of the fire looked at him, and the barbarian's bow got up and walked into the wood line.

He grinned and went stiff. He fell backward and lay sprawled on the grass.

Red Wolf looked at the half elf and then at Wanderer and growled.

"Don't worry, my friend. He'll be fine in a moment. Now, about the lands east of Ravagar..."

The half elf was no longer aware of them. He was running. It was night, but his shadow stood out before him as if a great fire burned behind him. His breath tore in gasps from his lungs. Fear, disgust, despair.

He glanced back in his headlong flight to see an entire city on fire as dark creatures turned and wheeled above it. The feelings of pain, anger, and sorrow tore at him. He plunged down a steep grade and slid to a stop. He looked down over the cliff into the darkness beyond and heard the waves smash into the rocks below.

He heard a cold maniacal laugh that set ice into his veins with its sheer malevolence. He turned and a blast of red fire roared toward him. He screamed and stepped back.

He fell into oblivion.

Pain, despair, cold, wet sand, Cully...

Red Wolf kept a glancing vigil over the half elf as he thrashed about on the ground.

"That wasn't nice." he growled softly. "That was not a nice thing to do to the pup, pushing him like that."

Wanderer paused in the middle of his sip from his cup and looked from the barbarian to the half elf. He shrugged. "It will work its way out. You'll see."

"That is why I didn't interfere." Then, with each word measured and laced with feral intent, "Just remember to never do that again."

The tone was not lost on Wanderer. He looked deep into the eyes of the powerful barbarian and saw the feral gleam. It said, "Don't touch what is under my care."

"Not to worry, my friend." he replied. "He'll not remember what he sees, nor that I was ever here. I just aided him to place some memories where they will be more...accessible."

With that, Wanderer replaced his pot and pouches into his bag, rose, and stretched.

"Ah, well, I guess I must be going. Don't forget to check in with Terillion when you get into Catlorian."

"Travel far, Wanderer."

The feral growl said more than the cordial farewell. Wanderer looked again into the cold green eyes of that barbarian and studied what he found there. Then, as if he reached some conclusion, he smiled and raised his hand in farewell.

"One more thing." he said as he turned toward the white expanse before him. "The evil that haunts this youth's passage has its sights on you as well."

He turned those silver eyes on the barbarian again and Red Wolf could sense the concern.

"Be careful, my friend. Travel safe, fire hair."

He was gone.

The half elf woke sitting upright with a startled look on his face and cold sweat trickling down his spine. The last thing he remembered was drinking from the barbarian's wineskin. There was something else, however, that he could not quite grasp, lingering images that sparkled in his mind just out of reach.

"How do you feel?"

The half elf held his head in both hands in a vain hope to reduce the throbbing. The tone of the barbarian's question struck him as strange, however.

"I feel terrible." he replied. "Just remind me never to drink from your wineskin again."

Red Wolf smiled as he picked up his club, bow, and knapsack.

"It is an hour before sunrise and I must go to Catlorian. Someone there needs to talk to me about what I may or may not know. If you wish to accompany me, let us go."

"Since I must go that way anyway and if you don't mind the company?"

"Just try to keep up."

"I'll do my best."

Red Wolf glanced at the young "pup."

"He probably will." he thought. Then, "Come on."

Chapter Ten

He needed information and supplies. This was the only reason he would consider going into this border town: information and people.

At six feet and well-muscled, Arantar Adenedhel was an impressive man, though his size was muted as he squatted at the edge of the forest. He'd resigned his commission as Huntsmaster a bit over a month ago because of the driving need to travel. The "savon" had taken hold on his elfish side and would not let him have a moment's peace. He sighed as he gazed down on the caravan that had pulled up outside of the only tavern in the squalid little place.

Your spirit yearns, Arantar-sao?

The growling thought broke through his revelry. He didn't have to see the feral yellow of the wolf's eyes to feel them on him.

Aye, Fang. I know not where my fate leads me, but 'tis good not to face it alone.

The thoughts directed at the ruddy silver wolf were as common to him as speech, yet more rewarding at times than speech with men.

Go now, Arantar-sao. came the light, breezy thought from where the raven perched. *We will be here if need.*

As will I, my friends.

With that the half elf stood, tightened the straps that held the great sword to his back, and remounted his roan warhorse. He applied pressure with his knees and the horse started down the hill at a trot. He guided the mount to the tie rail in front of the tavern and dismounted. As was his practice and the training of his roan, he did not tie it to the rail. The warhorse snorted as he took his place beside a big ebony stallion decked out in chain mail barding. It too was not tied.

Arantar noted the barding and the breeding of the powerful black, but he could not tell, from the tack or the shield that hung on the cantle, from where the rider might have come.

He shrugged and stepped to the porch that ran the length of the front of the tavern and glanced back at the array of impromptu booths set up by traveling merchants in the caravan. The scent of herbs and spices, oils, and leather filled the yard. He would need to get supplies before leaving but first, food cooked by hands other than his own.

The young elf leaned back in his chair, looking as bored as he felt. He was bored to tears to be living in his father's town, on his father's land, with his father's friends. Bonaire needed a change, some excitement, before he, gods forbid, began to like it here in Borderlend.

He glanced at his new acquaintance and thought that this fellow might be what he needed. The pale gray of this dark-haired knight's skin darkened under his moody hazel eyes. Bonaire had watched him arrive a short while ago on a big black warhorse. He'd asked about directions to Catlorian. When he'd asked for the knight's reason for traveling so far, he first received a stony stare that seemed to cut right through him. Then a rather long and boring story followed.

The fellow's name was Solothon Calendera and, until recently, he'd lived in a real castle about a couple of hundred or so miles southeast of Borderlend. He was on his way, he'd said, to Catlorian to inquire about a pair of black crystal shirakens he'd found stuck in his dead dogs, or something like that. What intrigued Bonaire most about "Sol" was the way he rubbed his left shoulder as his mood swung black, like now. Bonaire didn't care much to know the full story behind Solothon's need to visit the fabled city and showed it, but that shouldn't have been enough to irritate this knight nor invite that black look of hate.

Sir Solothon Calendera, son of Mage Sneog Marande, Duke of Laranthia, knight errant of the New Order of the Knights of the Laurel, dedicated to the protection of the secrets of the mystical Eldewood, was once known for his easy nature, his love of life and living things, and his patience under the most difficult of conditions. He was courageous, courteous, gallant, and so dedicated to the code of chivalry that he was looked upon as the probable captain of the Order in the future. This possibility filled the young knight with dreams of glory, of returned nobility and honor to the disbanded organization from which he and his fellows took their name.

Then he found his kooshies, Balak and Anaka, dead.

He'd gone hunting that morning, as was his custom, to escape the boredom of castle life. He'd expected Balak, Anaka, and Alderon to meet him, as they always did, and accompany him. When they didn't show up, Solothon turned his mount toward the river thinking the kooshies were off somewhere and would return to the place beside the waterfall to find him.

The great warhorse felt the wrongness before they reached the glade. On the far side of the clearing, Alderon stood over the dead bodies of his brother and sister. The sad eyes of the great elfin hound filled Solothon with pain and sorrow and its muted whine, filled with despair, cut through the elf's heart like a dagger. The silent question was there for any sensitive soul to hear.

"Why?"

Solothon slipped from his saddle and walked slowly to where Balak lay, his tongue hanging black from the side of his mouth and his great black eyes open and staring into eternity.

The knight gently closed the kooshie's eyes and stroked its neck. That is when he noticed the black shiraken embedded deep into the hound's throat. It was of black crystal and only the points of two blades remained outside of the hound's skin.

As Solothon's hand closed on the weapon in an effort to remove it, he felt a shock travel up his arm and burn into his brain. His sorrow was suddenly gone, replaced by incoherent anger. He felt something oily on his fingers and knew it for what it was.

"Poison."

The word sounded as if from someone else's mouth, so lethally was it uttered. He reached again for the embedded weapon and pulled it from the hound's throat, oblivious to the red film flowing over and then receding from his vision. He stood and looked at the shiraken for a moment, caught up in the feelings of hate and frustration that should not have been there.

The weapon was embossed with the likeness of a dragon pierced through with a lance. Even in his angered state, Solothon knew that this was not right. He could not, however, concentrate on that question.

He moved to Anaka's dead body and closed her eyes as well. Though it too gave him a shock like the first one, he pulled the shiraken from her throat.

He was now fully enraged. A red film shadowed his vision and his face contorted into a grimace of pure undirected hate. He thought he saw a dark figure in the tree line and started to move toward it, his hand to the hilt of his sword. He wanted those responsible. No power on Ta'el would save them. He would destroy them and their friends and family and anyone else who stood in his way. There was no rock they could crawl under to save them from his wrath. There was no place for them to hide from...

Alderon bayed his death lament.

Suddenly Solothon was normal again, his anger gone and the strange compunction to destroy gone. All he felt was a drain to his spirit and a burning sensation in his left shoulder. Beneath the chain mail and padding he wore, the pentagram birthmark, his father's hereditary gift, was enflamed.

When Solothon told his story before the Duke's council, and displayed the shirakens, they advised him to make this journey to Catlorian. The embossing was unfamiliar to them, though the poison was not. "Purple Worm" poison was lethal enough to kill even the hardy kooshie, and someone had used liberal amounts of the stuff.

The answers, they said, could come only from the center of wisdom and weaponry that was Catlorian.

As he'd sat his mount, provisions for the first leg of his journey securely fastened behind his saddle, his mother touched his boot.

"Be careful, my son." she'd cautioned. "Trust no one but he you would die for, and then take care."

He'd leaned down to kiss her cheek and rode from the only home he'd ever known.

Now, however, he sat opposite this loafing, spoiled elf and listened to his pathetic little stories of boredom at the hands of his doting mother and rich father. Then he noted the entrance of the warrior in the livery of the Royal Border Guards.

Arantar stepped through the door to the tavern and was struck by the familiarity. It seemed that no matter where one went, a tavern was a tavern. The noise, banter, and the smell of passable food, spilt drink, and unwashed bodies were the same.

Here the Western Border Guards came to release the tensions of the day, the hawkers moved from table to table extolling the virtues of their wares, the wenches went about their duties with an experienced dodge when a hand got too close, and the loafers came to see it all.

Arantar glanced about for an empty table but found none. Then a young elf, who sat at a table close to the bar at the center of the room and leaned back in his chair, hailed him.

"Join us, Guardsman. I'm certain my surly friend here won't mind."

Arantar noted the black look the knight shot the youth and the ambivalence with which it was received, but since there were no other tables he nodded his acceptance. The youth started in as soon as Arantar was seated.

"I am Bonaire Blackabar, son of the noble owner of this pesthole called Borderlend, and this is my new friend, Sir Solothon Calendera, a noble knight in the service of...some order or another. He is on his way to Catlorian, on some business or another, and I may join him. I have not yet decided. Now, what brings a Royal Border Guard this far from his tramping grounds?"

Arantar could see that Solothon cared little whether this one came with him or not. Judging by the looks of disgust on the faces of the clientele as they glanced at the boisterous young elf, he could see that Bonaire would probably not be missed if he did go.

This one's flippancy with the order to which the knight belonged didn't set well with the Huntsmaster either, and his response was short because of it.

"I am no longer with the Prince's Own, as you can see by the absence of crest. I am on my way northwest to see what I may. I am called Arantar."

The knight's head came up and his hazel eyes came to rest on the Huntsmaster.

"You are Arantar Adenedhel?"

"Yes, sir knight. You've heard of me?"

"Indeed, Huntsmaster. We of the Order of the Knights of the Laurel like to keep up with those whose prowess in the field and honor in battle have brought honor to them and those about them. I am pleased to make your acquaintance."

"And I you, sir. I believe that I heard that you were on your way to Catlorian?"

"Yes. I need to see someone there about some...artifacts that have come into my possession."

"I am heading in that direction and could, if you are willing, use the company. With talk of gualu bandits and uprisings, safety in numbers..."

"I would be honored, Huntsmaster."

"Well, that's just wonderful," interjected Bonaire, "but I see that you have no drink. Innkeeper! Where is that peasant when you need him? *Innkeeper!*"

A small balding man wearing a wine-stained apron over his ample belly appeared at the table. He glared at Bonaire for a moment before he looked at the other two men at the table.

"Wha' kin ah be gittin' fer ye, sirs?"

The fact that he seemed to be addressing all at the table but Bonaire rankled the young elf.

"You can get us some food and be quick. Don't you see my friends are hungry? And see that you put it on my tab!"

"Augh, Bonaire. Dinna ye know ye cinna be insultin' folk li' that?"

"Insulting? What do you mean insulting?"

"A man mus' ne'er be forced ta be beholden."

"Innkeeper?" said Arantar, drawing the small man's attention away from what might have been a long and involved description of what a man should and should not, ought and ought not, can and cannot do for another unbidden. Besides, he was hungry.

"What have you to eat?" he said to the innkeeper. Then, aside to Bonaire, "Thanks, but I pay my own way."

The little man straightened up with a smile that said, "See?"

"We ha' a tasty mackerel, served wi' fresh bread, all fer a silver, if ye please."

"I do, and a glass of white wine. Thank you."

"Aye. Will be as ye request, sir." Then, to Solothon, "And ye, sir knight?"

"The same." the response snapped from tightened lips.

The innkeeper looked down at Bonaire with a smile, making the young elf even less happy than he was.

"Just bring me another beer, you old woman."

The innkeeper snorted and headed for his kitchen, while Bonaire turned his attention to Arantar.

"What made you leave your post to go rambling off?"

"Nothing that could possibly interest you."

The response was quickly delivered and as quickly regretted. There was just something in the elf's demeanor that brought out the…

"It just got a bit too quiet." he added as if to change the sting.

A big man in the livery of the Western Border Guard turned toward the table and, as his calloused hand caressed his half-filled wine cup, snorted.

"Ye oughta be out on the west side border, pal."

"You get incursions often then?" Arantar asked, always the soldier.

"Well, the gualu is startin' ta rise up ag'in. Nobody know why, but I guess it be the season fer it. Heared they been raidin' supply caravans fer Heartstone, too. If yer goin' outta town, be watchful."

"I'll do that, and thanks."

"Ye'd do the same fer me, Huntsmaster."

The burly man nodded and turned back to his wine and reflections.

The innkeeper brought Arantar's food and the food for the surly knight and set it carefully on the table. The wineglasses he set without spilling a drop, but he slammed the elf's tankard to the table with a frown and watched with a slight grin as Bonaire dodged back to avoid the splashing fluid.

Half an hour later, Arantar rose, paid for his meal, and moved toward the door. He stopped by the burly guardsman and pointed back to where Bonaire sat in surly silence.

"Nice lad there. Looks like he'd make a fine recruit."

The man grinned at the sarcasm and scowled in the direction noted.

"We've tried, but his dad owns th' bloody village. You know how that goes."

Soldiers knew something about other men, something that is trained into their souls. A soldier must trust his back to his comrades. The old soldier sighed, a comment on that trust from one soldier to another, of the attempt made yet refused. The old soldier glanced back at Bonaire and shrugged.

"Give me a year with that 'un in the guard and he'd either be a man or dead. Either way'd be better'n the way he be now. Damn, what a waste o' flesh!"

"You'll get no argument from me on that, my friend. This one will probably have to learn the hard way, if at all."

With a comradely slap on the old soldier's back, Arantar bade him well and moved toward the door. The big guardsman smiled, comrades in arms no matter the front.

Arantar wrapped his cloak about himself, stepped into the sunlight, and toward the merchant's booths. Solothon and Bonaire came out of the tavern just behind him and, as Solothon turned toward the section set up for horse-trading and feed, Bonaire set off down the street.

The young elf had made up his mind. He would leave this town and never return. Though his mother and father would beg him to stay, he would tell them and be away with his newfound friend, Solothon.

He turned a corner and, after stopping to gather himself, walked up to the front door. He practiced in his mind how he would wave off all complaints, shake his father's hand, and kiss his mother's tear-stained cheek. It would be sad, but...

His father stepped through the door before he got to it. The older elf stopped for a minute and looked his son up and down with a shake of his head and a sigh. "Father," stated Bonaire solemnly, "I am leaving."

"Good-bye," said his father as he stepped off of the porch in a brisk stride toward the tavern.

"What about money?" called a somewhat flustered Bonaire. "I may need some in my travels and you might never have the chance to gift me again!"

His father turned to the youth with a look of impatience, dug deep into his pocket, and threw three gold coins toward the startled youth.

"Don't spend them all in one place." he called over his shoulder as he turned and strode off down the street, the off-key strains of an old drinking song whistling through his lips.

"The pain of my sudden departure must be buried deep, such is the sorrow of my father." thought the young elf as he shook his head and steeled himself for the telling of his mother.

She greeted him at the door with a smile.

"Ah, Bonaire, my boy, you're home." Then, with a frown, "What do you want now?"

"Dear, dear Mother, I leave today to make my own way in the world and, although I know that you would rather that I stay, there is naught that you can do to dissuade me."

"Dissuade you, my son? Now why ever would I wish to do that?"

Bonaire's mouth moved and nothing came out. His mother stood in the doorway with her hands on her hips as if waiting for something.

"Let me make it easier, Bonaire." she said after a tense minute with her smile turning to a frown. "That is not the answer I expected, therefore, I will ask again: what do you want?"

She was taking his news too bravely, he thought as he tried to regain control of his mouth. Finally he stammered out an answer. "Uh, well, uh, I will need some capital to start with, sort of an investment really."

"As I expected!" she snapped as she loosed five platinum coins from a string about her neck and tossed them to the youth. "That's all you get! Now I'm busy. Go away."

Bonaire caught the coins and moved as if to kiss his mother good-bye, but she stopped him with a hand on his chest and a smile.

"Have a good time, Bonaire, and don't forget to write. Yes, write. Don't bother coming home until you can do so on your own and in your own prosperity. Now, shoo!"

She pushed Bonaire out of the front door, closed it, and went back to her embroidery.

Bonaire stood outside the door for a moment and wondered whether or not to go to her.

"No, it's better this way." he thought. "Less pain."

With a sigh and a hand to his chest, he turned and walked back toward the caravan with a new step. Off on adventure, excitement, and the promise of treasure untold.

Arantar was sizing up the different booths as Bonaire returned. He needed provisions, and there seemed to be a wide assortment of wares to be had and most were of good quality. He stopped at one booth where the main merchandise seemed to be copper, glass, and porcelain vials filled with alchemy condiments. He noted that on a back shelf, partially covered by a scrap of cloth, was a kit of some kind with small vials and carefully protected strips of paper. The merchant noted the Huntsmaster's interest and quickly moved toward him.

"That, my friend," said he, "is a test kit for analyzing substances and mixtures. It can be used to detect poison or contamination in your day-to-day travels. Meat, water, feed, whatever needs testing—this kit will be proof positive of its wholesome nature. It will even detect, if you will, rabies in meat! There is a book of instruction included that will explain, in detail, the many benefits and uses of this amazing kit."

Knowing that rampaging gualu and their daku masters sometimes poison what they cannot carry away, Arantar thought a kit of this sort could prove useful. He nodded and counted out the gold pieces required.

Meanwhile, Solothon, having finished looking over the available tack and horses in the caravan, made his way to the Huntsmaster's side. He tried several times, politely, to gain the merchant's attention, but to no avail. So, as the merchant passed close, the knight reached out and grasped the man's sleeve.

For a moment, the merchant's dark weathered face took on the expression of annoyance. Then, as he quickly noted the carriage and armor of the young elf and the fine quality of his cloak, his look changed to that of the appeasing merchant, willing to please his "superiors."

"Yes, kind sir. What may this humble servant possess that may be of interest to a knight such as yourself?"

The words dripped honey from the smooth tongue of the professional salesman.

"Have you anything other than this displayed here?"

"Anything...? Yes, sir. I have an abundance of anything and everything! I have..."

Quickly the merchant realized that this tact was wrong, for the young knight was not biting and was more than a bit of a challenge.

"Ahhh! Yes! I see that you are a knight in good standing, though, I apologize to say, I do not recognize the order. Please forgive me, sir knight."

A short bow and the knight's attention seemed to return. A challenge indeed!

"You, as a knight, could be in need of a sword as befits your station and, yes, dear sir, I have a wonderfully vast selection that you may choose from, if you will."

The merchant waved the knight to the side of the booth where, under a drape, there were racked an abundance of swords. He'd bought them in Seaborne for such a low price that he could sell them all at a copper apiece and still turn a nice tidy profit. Frankly he'd had hopes of unloading them here in the outback prior to reaching Catlorian, because most were of such poor quality that no one within that great city would buy them and, should he attempt to sell them to the merchants there...well, it would be better to melt them down before insulting the quality of that clientele.

He put on his very best "you can trust me" look and desperately hoped that this elf would not notice, but he failed.

"No, merchant." stated the surly knight. "I seek for something else."

Immediately the look on the merchant's face went from pleasant to one reserved for those not wishing to buy but "peruse." It said, "I have better things to do than entertain a loafer." Solothon, however, either did not notice or ignored the look entirely.

"I seek magical devices, used in the study and performance of same. I am a student of those arts, though not as a profession, and would wish to purchase items for my own enlightenment."

Magically the merchant transformed back into the sweet salesman of a moment ago.

"Yes, sir!" he exclaimed as he began pulling small cases from boxes and settling them on the counter, careful to present them in good light.

"I have talisman, catalysts, brimstone, and the like. Look through these, I pray you, good sir, and see if something touches your fancy. If not, please speak but a word and I will bring even more. I am at your disposal."

Solothon, however, could not find anything displayed here that he could not find in his own possessions. He glanced at the Huntsmaster.

"Find anything interesting?"

Arantar glanced up from his perusal of the booklet, which had come with the detection kit, and found the look in the knight's eyes a bit troubling.

"Some possibilities. You?"

Solothon shrugged.

The surly knight had become somewhat of a challenge to the merchant. To be the best, one must swing with the mood of one's clientele, but this elf would not hold his moods still long enough to get a fix on them!

"Magical...magical..." Then, "Ahhh!"

He pulled an overly ornate silver dagger from a red wood case and laid it on the counter.

"Maybe this will be of some use, sir?"

"What's that?" asked the knight as he turned back to the merchant.

"It is a dagger, sir, and a very interesting one at that, I might add!"

The merchant noted the mood swing again to annoyed disinterest and redoubled his efforts and speed in his delivery.

"As you can see, sir, it seems to be a gaudy bit of silver done up into a dagger. However..."

The merchant slipped a heavy glove on his hand, drew the blade from its sheath, and softly spoke the word "on." Instantly the entire dagger, both hilt and blade, erupted into bright yellow fire. The merchant whispered, "Off," and the blade returned to its previous state. As it did so, the merchant took it in his other hand and slipped it into its sheath.

"This dagger, made of elfin silver by the bye, is a product of the school of magic in Catlorian. It has no curse and no necessary incantations. It seems that a student of that school made this after attaining his Rune of the Element of Fire."

He drew the dagger again with the gloved hand.

"It is, quite literally, on..."—the dagger burst into flame—"or off..." The blade returned to cold. "It will start a fire, no matter how wet the wood, and if you've a mind, you could cook your meat from the inside out. You must always remember, however, to turn it off prior to returning it to its sheath. Once there, it is quite safe. I would say that in the right hand, this weapon could be very useful for the insignificant sum of two hundred fifty gold?"

To the merchant's dismay, Solothon was not impressed and, as that knight renewed his interest in other items on the counter, the merchant shrugged and noted, while he arranged the sheathed dagger on a red cloth on the counter, the knight had not left. He still had a chance, but decided to turn his attention to the Huntsmaster for a breath.

He eyed the hilt of the Huntsmaster's sword as it peered over that one's shoulder. From the hilt, he could see that it was a standard issue greater two-handed sword that had seen much use. He knew he would have to approach this carefully, for those who deal in arms must remember that those who know arms best are those who use them. A lot of information can be gleaned from just looking over the sword of a fighting man.

"Please, sir," he said softly, "may I see your sword?"

Arantar looked the merchant over from head to toe before sliding the great blade from its clamshell sheath. The merchant noted the caution and the look he received and knew to tread lightly. This man was no ordinary fighter, given to handing over the things that serve and save his everyday life. He knew he had to be careful and his timing had to be impeccable.

He pursed his lips and shook his head.

"This will never do."

He waited for but a moment for the look on Arantar's face to change.

"Oh," he interjected quickly, "it's a fine and decent sword, sir. I meant no offense. However, even after the care you've given it, and I see that it has been very well cared for indeed, it has seen better days, and if you've noticed the metal fatigue close to the hilt, you must admit that a newer sword should be to your interest."

He handed the sword back carefully, at the same time honoring the sword and the man who wielded it, but as if it would break if dropped, so "old" was it.

"I have a very good assortment of blades that t'would serve, I think, sir. May I show them to you?"

Arantar looked at his great blade. It had served him well and he'd worked long with it to make it his own, but it was, as the merchant had stated, a standard blade. Though he did not think that the stress on the blade was as protracted as the merchant intimated, it wouldn't hurt to look.

At the Huntsmaster's nod, the merchant stepped to a long chest, until now unopened.

"I have two great swords, sir, one reputed to have been owned by a paladin as he started his travels into the world. It is a sword of excellence and, if you know the ranking, is quite well made. In fact, the man who crafted it has stated that if it were to ever break he would take his own life!"

As he spoke, he removed a great sword from the case wrapped in black cloth. He lifted the cloth and displayed a sword of exceptional workmanship. The five feet of blade was obviously an alloy of some type, for it did not shine. The color was a strange flat gray. The hilts were of the same alloy and curved down slightly from the handle, which was of some type of bone, wrapped carefully and tightly with an equally different type of leather. Upon the alloy blade close to the hilt, a perfect black rose was embossed.

"The story goes that the smnith was a member of some order that prided themselves as makers of exceptional arms. I would say, sir, that displayed here is evidence that their pride is well founded."

Arantar lifted the great blade, for the merchant had presented it hilt first on the counter. The merchant's slight smile was all that gave him away.

Arantar, however, hadn't noticed. The handle slipped into his hands as if fitted there by a master. The balance seemed to shift until it was perfect for him and him alone. The sword called to him, sang for him. The leather and bone of the grip caressed his hands as if it were a lover.

The merchant grinned. He knew he had a sale and he was going to get his worth. He would ask for five hundred gold and this one would pay it. He could have laughed. Though this sale was not easy, it was a stone in his crown!

"How much?" breathed the Huntsmaster. He could not take his eyes from the blade.

"Two hundred seventy-five."

The words came out, but they were wrong! The merchant cleared his throat and smiled.

"I'm sorry, sir. I've misspoken. I should have said two hundred and seventy-five..."

There it was again! No matter how he tried, he could not say what he wished!

"I'll take it," said the Huntsmaster breathlessly.

The merchant took the gold in numb hands. This was wrong! Not only that, but...

"The one who crafted this blade named it."

Arantar glanced up from the blade to see a strange look on the merchant's face. It was as if the man had no control of his mouth, for the words seemed to come from far away.

"Its name is 'Gray Wolf.' I believe that may mean something to you?"

Arantar smiled and caressed the blade with his fingertips. He took the lacquered leather, clamshell sheath from the merchant and stood back to admire his purchase.

Solothon noted the workmanship in that blade and turned his attention once more on the merchant.

"Excuse me?"

The merchant turn his eyes slowly from the Huntsmaster to the knight and in an instant whatever had controlled him left him. He shuddered and glanced back at the Huntsmaster.

"Excuse me!" stated the knight once more.

"Oh, sorry, sir!" stated the merchant as he turned his attention to the task that the knight represented.

"Do you have long swords, such as the one I wield, of that quality in your inventory. I warn you, do not show me the garbage you showed me before!"

The merchant smiled. Though he was still shaken by the strangeness of the last transaction, he knew the tricks.

Find one who could afford a well-made item, wave it about—though demurely—so that others close could see the quality to be the very best, then sell it at a price that is within the bounds of profit. Those watching could not help but to think that a good sale is to be had.

Problem is, the last sale had not gone as planned and he would be very careful about the next.

He looked the elfin knight over again and nodded. He should have known that the armor, though chain mail, was of exceptional make, and the barding was well-loomed linen. He should have seen that straight off.

"I have these, good sir, if you've a mind for a pair?"

The swords were a matched set. The merchant drew each from its sheath and laid them on the counter, crossing the blades in his presentation. They were identical, from the leather wrapped handles and the strange triangle just below the hilts to the filigreed "blood groove" that went the length of the blade.

"These were crafted in Seaborne for a gladiator who followed the order of Udin. The man contracted their forging, but he never returned to claim them. After many years of waiting, the smith sold them to me for a song, considering their obvious quality."

He turned the blades, hilts first, toward the knight.

"Try them, good sir." As Solothon lifted each by the handle, "Feel how they settle into the hand, the balance and the ease at which they move in concert with the wielder."

They felt good in the knight's hands, though his left was never intended to wield such a blade.

"I will part with them for a mere one hundred twenty-five gold per blade. I couldn't possibly sell them so cheap to anyone but a knight of your obvious stature."

The smile came easily now that the price he intended actually came out of his mouth.

Solothon, however, was not yet satisfied. He was never the one to buy at first glance, no matter the quality.

"Have you any others of equal or greater quality?"

The merchant frowned. He looked the knight over again and felt the strangeness of the moods again. He would not give up or give in!

"I do have one other that might be of some interest." he stated as he lifted a leather case from the box under the counter and set it gently on the counter.

He opened the case and removed a long sword wrapped in gray cloth and laid it on top of the closed case. As he removed the cloth from the blade, all conversation stopped in the area. The green blade shone brightly in the afternoon sunlight.

It was a long sword crafted of green crystal, the handle wrapped in white dragon hide, and the hilts and pommel of elfin silver. It was a weapon crafted, not forged, by a master with patience and love.

Bonaire was startled by the flash and, after a moment, realized that he had not taken a breath. His intake of air seemed to break the spell on all but himself.

"This is the prize of my collection." stated the merchant a bit louder than necessary, for he'd seen the look on Bonaire's face. "Only one craftsman could have made it, a gnome whose name I am not at liberty to divulge. The price for this weapon of perfection? A paltry three hundred twenty five gold."

Solothon knew that this was not his weapon and never would be, despite the price. The twin long swords, however...

"Though anyone of right mind would want to own this wonderful weapon, I am afraid that the twin blades you showed earlier would be of more service to me at this time. One hundred twenty apiece, did you say?"

"One twenty-five, sir, and, may I say, a good choice!"

"I have no need for three swords, however, and a matched set is more to my liking. Would you care to give me a price for the one I carry?"

The merchant took the sword from the knight's hand and examined it. He looked it over with a hawker's flourish, and he carefully hid his surprise at the fine quality of the elfin-made sword. It was not made at the quality of these others, yet he could see that it was not cheaply crafted.

"Hmmm." he said as he turned the blade over in his hand. "I could give you both blades, the matching sheaths, and the sharpening kit for...two hundred and your old sword. Deal?"

The knight looked at the twin blades, then his own, and nodded sharply. "Done!"

The merchant smiled his best smile as he took the elf's gold. As Solothon returned the blades to their sheaths and lifted them and the accessories in preparation to leave, the merchant gave him a shallow bow.

"May these 'Song Swords', for such was the name given, protect you from all wishing you harm."

The effect on the bystanders was his main concern and, it seemed, it worked.

Bonaire could not take his eyes from the green crystal sword. As the merchant made a show of covering it with the gray cloth, Bonaire moved closer.

"Excuse me, sir." he said breathlessly. "May I touch it?"

"Why, of course, good sir."

The merchant, pleased that the desired effect had been achieved, uncovered the blade and slid the handle toward the elf.

Bonaire gripped the dragon hide and lifted. The sheer weightlessness of the blade almost caused him to drop the sword. His smile widened as he turned the sword over in his hand, noting the depth of the blade—a good quarter inch—and the delicate stitching of the dragon skin to conform to the hand.

The merchant smiled. It was time.

"The blade need never be sharpened, for it was crafted perpetually sharp." Then, lower, "I sense an aura of power about you, young sir. Are you not a power wielder, of Mage Born?"

Bonaire liked the sound of that! "Mage Born." Oh, he'd semi-apprenticed for his mother, a minor mage before she'd met and married his father. He'd learned the basic spells and showed a talent, but his attention span was always a bit short.

The merchant was a master in his chosen field. He would never lie about his merchandise. He might embellish a bit upon its virtues, but never lie. In this case, he didn't have to. The green crystal sword would sell itself to the right purchaser. The challenge was in the pursuit of the purchaser. He knew this elf to be a novice in the usage of magic, and he really hadn't said directly that he thought Bonaire *was* "Mage Born". It was merely a question posed in such a way as to have a desired effect. He smiled his merchant's smile.

"You must know that the green crystal, or any other color crystal item if cut precisely, can be used to channel magical power, or so I've heard."

He waited for Bonaire to acknowledge this as a fact all Mages would know. At the young elf's stern nod, the merchant's grin widened.

"This sword was cut in that fashion and with a small amount of preparation, I've been led to believe, it could most definitely be used to channel yours. Besides, green crystal can't turn on an elfin mage and bite as a steel sword could."

The last was perfect! True elf kind could not use cold-wrought iron for it burned, though steel wouldn't. So what if he got his facts mixed up? He could be forgiven, for did not his "elfin Mage" nod his agreement?

Bonaire was quite taken with both the sword and with the salesman. He was quite convinced that this sword was the only one an up-and-coming wielder of magic would use.

"I wish to purchase this sword, but I have limited capital and wish to purchase a dagger as well."

The merchant could have kissed himself! He produced a small box from among his other wares.

"I have twin crystal daggers here, sir." he said as he opened the box. "One such as you would of course know the special properties of black crystal."

He had the young elf. Bonaire was totally entranced.

"Watch this, young sir."

He placed the points of the daggers together and, holding the hilt of the one in his right hand, released the left. The daggers seemed bonded at their points.

"No matter how you hold this one," he stated as he moved the daggers through some very intricate maneuvers, "the other will not stray. They will stay bonded until you physically grasp the other and part them."

He grasped the other handle and they became two again. Then he slid them into their steel-lined sheaths mounted on a special harness.

"I will sell all three of these magnificent weapons to you, but only to you, sir, for a mere four hundred twenty-five in gold. For no one else could I possible go this low and, dear sir," he added with a bit of sorrow in his voice, "I am sorry that I cannot go lower for you, for I have children...."

Bonaire was pleased with himself. He did not even realize, as he handed over the five coins of platinum, that what he would receive in change would be very little.

The merchant knew, of course, and counted out gold pieces until he had the seventy-five. He handed this change, the sheath for the sword, and the box containing the daggers to the young elf with a slight bow.

"May these weapons protect you, young master, in your travels."

The wording was perfect, the inflection immaculate, and the desired response self-evident. Bonaire nodded sternly as he accepted the title.

"I thank you, good sir." he stated with a slight nod of his head. "Now, have you something one could use in his travels to keep out the chill?"

"Why, of course, young sir!"

If he worked this just right, this popinjay would spend every last ounce of his gold right here! He began pulling out some of his best cloaks to display for the elf, mentally adding two hundred percent to the price.

Arantar caught the merchant's attention, who, after making sure that the elf was deep into his selection, stepped over to the Huntsmaster.

"The dagger you showed earlier. May I see it?"

Arantar had noted the glove the merchant had worn and knew that not only the blade but the whole dagger burned after the command. The Huntsmaster also knew that if this dagger were purchased in Catlorian, this merchant wished to unload it before returning there because no one there would buy it!

Arantar said one hundred; the merchant, two. The Huntsmaster said one twenty; the merchant, one fifty. Arantar counted out the coins and the merchant sighed.

Solothon had moved to Bonaire's side when the daggers were displayed and waited until the merchant left.

"Excuse me, Bonaire," he asked softly. "might I see one of your daggers?"

Bonaire, the "young master," was a bit put off with this interruption and waved the knight away without looking up.

"One thing at a time, please! I am trying to conduct some business here!"

The knight felt the blackness rise and, though he tried hard to control it, it tainted his words.

"This is very important to me. I must see one of your daggers, *now!*"

The words were low and not a request. Bonaire looked up into those hazel eyes with a retort on his lips, but he swallowed it. Something in there prompted him to hand over one of the daggers as quickly as he could without another word.

Solothon held the dagger in the sunlight, the black anger suddenly gone. The workmanship was remarkably akin to the shirakens secreted in his pouch. He pulled one from that pouch to compare them, but, as the sunlight bathed the weapon, the pentagram birthmark felt like it had erupted in flame. The black anger, which plagued him often now, blazed with the fire in his left arm. He handed the dagger back to Bonaire, who took it and backed away, then turned on the merchant.

"I need information, merchant, and you, in your travels, may have what I need."

The merchant had finished his negotiations with the Huntsmaster and had turned back to young Bonaire, only to find that one backing slowly from the knight. He turned to the knight and lost his professional smile. The mood change here was clear as day to those who make a profession of reading them. Danger was exposed. Tread lightly.

"Of course, sir. My business moves me from place to place, selling what I might for the meager profit I take in. I help those who cannot travel to the mainstream of commerce, selling them convenience, comfort..."

He stopped. The knight was looking at him, not only with ill-concealed loathing, but also with barely controlled rage. The merchant's prattling had so angered Solothon that he was finding it very difficult to maintain.

"Have you ever seen anything like this?" Solothon asked tightly as he handed the shiraken to the merchant.

The merchant took the weapon gently in a shaking hand and turned it over carefully. Dealing with crystal as much as he had, he recognized the workmanship, if not the craftsman, and that this weapon was incredibly sharp. He also knew the worth of such a weapon, especially to a certain assassin he knew in Catlorian. He studied the embossing carefully.

"I've seen this symbol before." he said softly. "Now where was that? I believe someone was wearing it. Oh yes! Yes! I remember now! In Catlorian, last year when we were there, a man was wearing a design much like this. I'm not sure it was exact, but it was very much like it.

"Now, for the weapon itself, only one man makes weapons of this type and out of crystal."

He'd slipped back into his delivery system and paused for effect. That pause almost cost his life. The merchant's eyes drifted up to the knight's dark ones and he realized his mistake at the same time Solothon prompted.

"And who might that be?"

The words were laced with black malice and a promise of pain should the merchant pause again.

"Ydra, a little gnomish fellow who owns a specialty shop in Catlorian. From the design, I can tell that this," pointing to the shiraken, "and that," gesturing at the dagger, "will return to the caster if thrown and not impeded. If you wish to use them that way, I'd suggest fast hands or Elvin silver gloves! Once thrown, these weapons don't slow down. If anything, they increase in speed. I could give you a real good price for this if you're willing to part with it, say two hundred-fifty gold?"

Solothon reached out and took the weapon from the merchant. His black look made the man lean backward from him. As he replaced the shiraken into the pouch, it seemed that the malice he'd felt dropped to irritation and then it was gone.

Arantar had watched the moody knight during this discourse and had watched the irrational anger build and then fall. He found the point where intervention was acceptable and stepped in.

"Thank you, kind sir." he said, accentuating the need for ending. "You have been a great help to myself and companions. May you travel safe."

The merchant smiled his thanks to the Huntsmaster and, as he bowed and backed away from the counter, said, "Travel far." He then disappeared into the tent at the rear of the booth.

As the three men,—for Bonaire had followed, his mind on his new "toys"—made their way to the horses, it came to Arantar that he knew nothing of these others, save that the one seemed of proud bearing and good breeding, while the other... Well, only time would tell if the youth, who mounted the smallish black adorned with too many vestments, would prove their undoing.

The Huntsmaster checked the belly strap on his roan and again cast his attention on the knight.

The young knight was retightening his cinch, yet his thoughts seemed elsewhere as evidenced in the far-away look and the knitted brow. After a moment, however, he shook his head as if to remove some random thought, patted his animal's neck, smiled, and mounted, once again in control.

"There is something strange in the air." grinned the Huntsmaster to himself. "This knight, though of seeming fine character, will bear watching, but this Bonaire fellow will need a keeper! Mother, what have I gotten myself into?"

Arantar glanced toward the young elf and smiled. The poor pony had all the vestments of a warhorse, yet none of the training or the size to carry it. The Huntsmaster made a quick mental note to discuss with that one the necessities required, as well as those not required, for a life on the trail.

The three cantered toward the western trail from the village, the Huntsmaster, of long practice, taking the lead while the knight, as well with trained response, took the trailing position. Bonaire had finally gotten his pony to move with the rest when the high wheedling voice reached them.

"Remember, cavalier, it takes more than friends and a good horse to prove your worth."

Arantar's sharp eyes could not tell where the voice's owner stood in the crowd behind them. He frowned. Then, with a subtle motion, he brought his companions forward and touched his mount's flanks softly.

Solothon followed and kept a sharp eye to their rear until the forest blocked their view.

"Who said that?" asked Bonaire nervously. "What did he mean? Hey!"

Arantar and the knight had things to worry about other than the gaudily dressed youth on the noisy horse.

The Huntsmaster had no time to explain the "sixth sense" he'd learned through training and battles with all types of foes. Something about this whole thing smelled...funny. He knew he'd have to be especially on his guard to bring these inexperienced youths to Catlorian unharmed.

As they rounded a sharp turn in the trail, the black raven floated down softly to the Huntsmaster's shoulder.

Information found, Arantar-sao?

Not much. he replied to the soft breeze in his mind. *But I did find a new sword, and these.* The last was accentuated with a nod toward the two in tow.

The quick indrawn breath warned Arantar that the silver-gray wolf had broken cover to take up an easy pace beside the roan.

It took Bonaire a moment to regain control of the small black, but that wasn't what bothered Arantar. His attention was on the knight.

Solothon's hand snatched the lance from its boot the moment the wolf broke cover, and he settled his trained mount with a word.

Arantar turned in his saddle.

"These are my companions and mean you no harm. Trust me."

Solothon nodded and allowed the lance to return to the boot at his stirrup, while Bonaire mumbled something harsh to his pony and pulled at the reins.

Arantar-sao finds new tooth. Finds iron elf with head trouble. And other?

The colors that broke into Arantar's mind caused him to chuckle. When a wolf laughs in mind-speech, it is always colorful.

The three companions rode northwest from Borderlend through the early afternoon. Fang, the ruddy silver wolf, took his normal position out in front. Of long practice, the wolf sent a short growl back to his saola periodically to let Arantar know where and how the wolf fared. The raven flew high above the three with a wary eye to the surroundings. The day was warm, bright, and quiet.

It felt wrong. The Huntsmaster's ingrained battle senses noted the difference in the feel of the woods about them and the wolf had missed his check-in.

Fang?

No answer. The blankness in his mind told him that his friend was in trouble and they were riding right into it themselves. He could not even feel his friend in his mind.

"Watch yourselves!" he stated sharply as his hands found the hilt of his great sword.

Blacky! What is there?

Uglies! Arantar-sao! Many uglies! No fly-kill! No fly-kill! Front, back, side! Many ugly!

Gualu without bows. Arantar motioned the two following to move up into a wedge of the three horses to better negotiate an attack. In the back of his mind, he hoped that his friend had not died for him, but his sharp battle honed senses were searching.

"'Ware the flanks." he breathed as the two obeyed his demands and brought their mounts to either side of his, but back a half of a horse-length.

"Waggagoon combagya!"

The great sword swept out of the sheath on the Huntsmaster's back and filled his hands as he stood in his stirrups.

Bonaire was all but unseated by the unreasoning fear that swept through him, while Solothon watched, as if a spectator, as the gualu broke from the woods about them. Neither youth had been here, where to think is to die. They had not the wisdom and experience of the Huntsmaster of the Royal Border Guard.

"Wake up, or die!" he shouted as he drove his mount toward the nearest two attackers.

One of the gualu brought its bastard sword up in a slash intended to unseat the Huntsmaster only to find a stiff boot that stopped its cut in mid-swing. The heavy sword, of its own, continued its swing and buried itself in its wielder's throat. Arantar kneed his war mount to the right and into another gualu, as the first strangled on its own blood. That beast swung its sword at the Huntsmaster as the shoulder of the trained war mount forced it away. Arantar's back swing rang heavily against the smaller sword.

Bonaire was finding life very difficult to maintain. When the gualu broke cover, the black pony went into hysterics. Its eyes grew large and it shied left and right, spoiling the stroke from the first gualu to reach him. Bonaire couldn't control the pony and unsheathe his new green sword. All he could do was hold on to the reins and pray for a miracle. Two more gualu broke toward him as his prayer went unanswered.

Solothon's hesitation nearly cost him his life. Were it not for the superbly trained warhorse, the slashing swords in the hands of the slobbering gualu would have unhorsed and killed him. The mount felt the danger and, though its mind knew that its master should be doing something, moved to sidestep one blow and drove its shoulder into another. Even with that, the blow that had been intended to unseat the knight sliced through the mail at the knight's right calf.

The pain caused instant retaliation. The years of training came to the fore as the knight of the Order of the Laurel drew his sword. The skill, courage, and something more came forward into the battle. A red haze appeared around the edges of the knight's vision.

The sword he drew sang softly as it cleared the sheath and, without pause, was blooded as it sang through the gualu from collar to crotch. The red haze grew, as did the song from the sword. A grin of pure battle lust formed behind the visor of the young knight's helm. He spurred his mount forward to meet his attackers.

Arantar was once again in his element. His thoughts, his sinews, his very being were caught up in the battle song that coursed through his veins. He grasped the great sword with both hands and, as he guided his mount with his knees, carried the battle to his sworn enemies. The gualu, though pushed away a moment before, saw the great sword only as it passed through its right shoulder and down. The passage of the blade saw the gualu's head, left shoulder, and arm removed as one piece.

Arantar swung the sword through and over, deflecting the blow aimed to unseat him by the gualu on his left. The backstroke of the great blade in the hands of the Huntsmaster removed the head of that gualu and carried through the neck of the one that had scurried forward to help its compatriot. Both crumpled as black blood gushed from the severed stumps.

The gleaming sword in the hand of the elfin knight sang the sweet song of death. The gualu had thought him easy prey from the outset, yet now attacked in sheer desperation. Here was a warrior totally caught up in battle mania, as the melody of the sword flowed in his veins. The sword danced effortlessly through the skull of the first gualu he reached, then back to split another through the abdomen, spilling blood and bile onto the killing ground. The screams of the dying fueled the savagery of the young knight's attack. The blind rage all but encompassed his being, held back by the sweet song of the very instrument of death that should have driven him over. His grin was broader now as he spurred his war mount into two more of the slobbering beasts.

One of those unlucky gualu heard the song of death just as the sword laid its head open. Its companion stepped in brain as the young knight's backstroke sliced deeply through its chest. The blood sprayed freely and in a curious arc as the gualu spun to the ground.

Bonaire finally got the frightened pony under some control and drew the green sword. All of his young life he'd been pushed to train in the fighting arts. Though he tried to avoid the training as much as possible, his father, though indulgent in most things, refused to allow this. All of the hours of training, the repetitive thrusts and parries, and all of the knowledge forced into him while he whined came through to him at that moment.

As the two gualu moved toward him, the green crystal sword moved softly in his hand. The balance, the edge, the energy incumbent to that blade seemed to reach into his soul and draw forth that part that was the fighter. Suddenly the pony stopped its fidgeting under the total control of a new fighter who now grinned at the on-coming enemy.

The first gualu to reach him slashed with his sword in an effort to bring the brightly robed Bonaire from the horse's back. The green sparked off of the metal sword then flashed back to cleave the gualu's skull, ear to ear, spraying blood and brain into the air.

At another time, the young elf would have retched at this sight, but some power had reached out from inside his spirit to take control. He turned in his saddle to find the other.

That one brought its sword up and over the saddle again in the hope of unseating the young Bonaire, but found green crystal instead. The sword, in the hands of the seemingly unskilled elf, seemed to direct itself as it parried the stroke and then carried through the attacker's chest severing arteries and slicing its heart in two. The follow-through caught that gualu's companion just under the armpit and stopped only as it emerged at its opposite shoulder. That luckless soldier felt its head and shoulder, arm still attached, fall across its back before it crumpled and died.

Still another leapt at the young elf with a stroke aimed at Bonaire's arm. Bonaire seemed possessed as the green crystal wrapped the attacker's sword into a spin. When the elf disengaged, the gualu had lost its left arm at the shoulder. As its life stream sprayed the bushes, the gualu dropped to its knees and screamed. Bonaire's sword ended the scream permanently.

Then Bonaire looked up into the glowing eyes of a gualu easily half again the size of these others. The hate dripped from its fangs as it growled foul curses in its own tongue. Bonaire smiled, still caught up in the adrenaline rush of battle.

"Come then, bastard!" he rasped softly. "It's your turn to die!"

Then he spurred the pony forward.

Arantar had but one more gualu to care for with the loving caress of his Gray Wolf. The gualu had thought to get in close and strike before the half elf could reverse the path of that great sword. As it charged, it stumbled. When it regained its footing, it also gained the dull gray blade as it passed through its body. Such was that stroke that the gualu looked down at the red line drawn through its midsection just before it fell. When it struck the ground, the top half of its body rolled away from the bottom half.

The Huntsmaster made a quick scan of the trees and brush in a practiced glance to check for more or hidden enemies. Seeing none and getting no report from the raven, he turned his attention to his companions.

The last of those attacking the elfin knight thought to land a stroke on the knight's unprotected back. However, the superbly trained warhorse felt the enemy and sidestepped over to deflect the blow. The gualu's sword dislodged from its hands as it collided with the black mount's rump and it fell with a clatter a few feet away. The gualu raced to retrieve the bastard sword and, as it turned to renew its attack, it heard the soft moan close to its ear.

The knight's sword played through that one's neck and lifted the head straight into the air in a geyser of blood. The decapitated body stood for a moment then, as if realizing the futility of the situation, spun slowly to the ground.

As the gualu died, so died the song of the sword. The red receded from the young knight's vision and he looked down upon the blood that dripped from the now-quiet sword, then at the carnage he had wreaked. He took a deep, ragged breath, blew it out, spun the sword in a short arc to remove the blood, sheathed it, and slumped in the saddle.

Arantar watched the final stroke, saw the knight sheath his sword, and watched the energy drain from his body. Then he saw the blood that dripped from his boot.

The Huntsmaster rode quickly to the knight's side and leaped from his horse. He grabbed a handful of bandaging from his own stocks and wrapped it about the knight's thigh to staunch the flow of blood. He tied it as tight as was necessary, received a nod from the knight, then looked to where Bonaire had squared off with the great gualu.

Bonaire had dismounted as soon as he was close and attacked without preamble. The Habuk-ha was good, not like the others here, but still not good enough to penetrate the guard spun in green crystal.

All of Bonaire's senses were at peak now. His training returned to his limbs and the sword moved as a part of that training as quickly as if it were an extension of his soul. The strokes, parries, and counterstrokes were too quick to follow. The sound of crystal on steel, steel on crystal, set up a ringing in the forest that silenced all creatures within a league.

The great gualu parried one stroke and returned for the slashing counterstroke but found, to its dismay, the length of the crystal sword imbedded into its chest to the hilt.

Arantar nodded as the sword slid through the gualu body. A classic feint, then a duck under the counter to drive the blade home. He nodded in approval again as Bonaire spun on his toes, twisted the sword one-quarter turn, withdrew the blade over his shoulder, stepped away, and turned at the ready, sword up and cradled on the back of his other hand.

The Habuk-ha looked down at the gaping hole in his chest and the life fluids as they pumped to the ground. It looked up at the young elf, raised its sword in salute, and crumpled to the ground dead.

Bonaire looked down at the fallen gualu in some confusion. Then he looked about his killing ground. The smell of blood and bile hung in the air and the corpses lay in disarray where they fell. He looked over at the Huntsmaster, his face gone ashen.

Arantar knew the look. First kill. You either accept the inevitability of death, or you die a little each day until it claims you. Many years before he'd been where Bonaire now stood, and he did for this youth what was done for him.

He grasped his great sword in one hand and brought it up and out before him toward the young elf. He held a grim look on his face as he held the heavy sword, point up, and waited.

Bonaire was sick and confused, but somewhere inside he knew what was expected. He raised the green crystal sword in a shaky hand and mimicked Arantar's pose, sword out toward the Huntsmaster, point up.

Arantar brought the hilt to his chest with a snap, the blade flat across his body.

Bonaire did the same.

Arantar snapped the great sword back to its original position, blade up and out toward the young elf, and smiled.

As Bonaire repeated this movement, he also smiled. Then he sheathed his sword and, as his color began to return, began checking the bodies of the fallen.

Arantar knew that there were many ways to tell a newly blooded warrior that it was all right to be afraid, to feel sick at the killing, and to feel the pain at removing another's life, even the lives of these. The "Soldier's Salute", from one warrior to another, almost always made the point easier to understand. It said, "I'm alive, you're alive! Better them than me! Now let's get on with it!"

Besides, though Bonaire might be a pain in the arse on most days, he'd been trained well and deserved the benefit of the doubt and a few well-placed pointers from a seasoned veteran, not as special attention, but for the preservation of the group. Any soldier will tell you that a fighting group is only as good as its worst member. It is in the best interest of that group to ensure that its worst member is as good as is possible.

The Huntsmaster turned again to the knight and helped him from his mount. He half led, half carried the knight from the killing ground and sat him down with his back against a tree. Bonaire ran over to take the reins of the knight's prancing war mount, but neither he nor the Huntsmaster's roan would allow him to take their reins. As he tied his horse to the makeshift picket, he heard the soft whine deep in the brush. He drew his sword and moved toward the sound.

He used the sword to push away the brush and found the wolf, Fang, entrapped in netting with a strange dart in its shoulder.

Though afraid, the young elf sheathed his sword and moved deeper into the brush to retrieve the wolf. Fang growled softly, not with menace, as Bonaire noticed, but with a drugged acknowledgement of the elf, as opposed to an enemy. Carefully the youth cut the netting away and removed the dart. Then, as he whispered soothingly to the wolf, he picked the animal up and carried it awkwardly back to the Huntsmaster.

"Arantar, I found the wolf! It looks like he might have been poisoned!"

Arantar's head snapped around at the sound of the straining elf's words and ran to help. He took the wolf from the winded Bonaire, laid him next to the knight and turned to the young elf. Bonaire laid the dart in his hand.

"This was stuck in his shoulder, but I don't know what was in it."

Arantar laid a strong hand on Bonaire's shoulder and gripped it. The look in his eyes was something Bonaire had never seen. It was pride.

"Thank you, my young friend. I'd thought I'd lost him after being together for a very long time. I thank you from the bottom of my heart and am forever in your debt."

Bonaire's chest expanded visibly at this and he nodded his acceptance. Although he would not have admitted it at the time, praise from a true warrior of Arantar's prestige was praise indeed! The young elf moved off into the brush, a strange lightness to his step, to search for their attacker's camp with a new courage. After encircling the immediate area out thirty or forty yards and finding nothing, he returned to the picket to check his horse for wounds.

Arantar ran his hands over the wolf's body, but found no other wounds. The wolf's eyes were glassy and, though there was an attempt at mind-touch, it was more of a far away growl. The Huntsmaster examined the dart, a reusable type with a small sack of rubbery material into which poison or drugs could be drawn. He remembered his new test kit and fetched it from his knapsack.

After reading the instructions carefully and testing the residue in the sack, it showed to be nothing more than a tranquilizer. With rest, his friend would be up and running in no time at all.

That, however, was the strange thing. Why the drug and not poison? He was happy for the good tidings, but it just didn't make sense. He shook his head and, with a quick thank you to the Mother, he returned the kit to his knapsack and turned his attention to the wound on Solothon's thigh.

Bonaire took the packs the gualu had worn and rummaged through them. Along with strange foodstuff and dirty clothing, he found several coppers in each. He shrugged, made a mental note to tell someone of the finding if they asked, placed the accumulated ninety or so coppers in his pouch, and threw the packs into the brush. Then he looked at the dead gualu and grinned.

Arantar decided against using one of his few potions to heal the knight's wound, for it wasn't deep or life threatening. Instead, he used his own knowledge of field medicine, a few herbs and dry moss, though he knew that it was probably the incredible amount of adrenaline in a newly blooded warrior that sapped his strength. After a few hours of rest, they would all feel much better.

Bonaire had heard the old stories told at his father's tavern about how to treat gualu after battle. One train of thought was to stack their bodies one on top of the other, head to toe, as a humorous insult. Another was to remove their heads and place them on the hilt of their own swords, driven into the earth, as a warning of the savagery dealt out by those sworn to defend.

The latter intrigued the young elf and he began the grizzly work of removing those heads. After the fifth head fell away from the green crystal, Bonaire's arm began to ache, but, to his credit, his resolve to "do this thing right" pushed him to complete his self-appointed task.

Arantar leaned back against the tree next to the knight and closed his eyes. His left hand was buried in the coarse fur of the wolf at his side and his body relaxed. The raven fluttered its wings as it sat high in the tree above him and, as the Huntsmaster raised his eyes to find it, the sweet breeze blew through his mind.

Arantar-sao, earth brother be good soon. No worry. He strong. No more uglies here now. No dangerous I see now.

Thanks, Blacky. I'll rest now. Keep watch over the robed one and wake me if you think he might be in trouble.

Will, Arantar-sao. You rest. I watch.

The Huntsmaster closed his eyes again, knowing that the raven would wake him quickly through the mind touch if there was need.

It was some two hours later and well into the afternoon when the companions remounted their horses. The ruddy silver wolf was still a bit weak but was healing from the drug quickly. Moving would only allow the drug to leave its system the quicker.

Solothon's thigh had stopped bleeding and, due to the knight's strange constitution, had already begun to heal. His limp was barely noticeable as he moved about his warhorse checking all ties and straps.

Arantar had finally convinced Bonaire that the gaudy barding was too much for his pony and the young elf reluctantly rolled it up and tied it to the cantle of his saddle.

Arantar turned in his saddle and surveyed his companions once more. Then, with a nod to the knight, he put his roan into a fast walk. He felt an unease all about this place, as if there was something he'd forgotten. With all of the attention he'd trained on these two, he felt that he'd let something slide and that was not like him.

They'd taken to the game trails, the Huntsmaster's training taking him to a more defendable locale and the unease guiding him to cover their tracks. Bonaire seemed a bit perturbed and the knight surlier.

Fang, stay no sword side, far but close. Blacky, what do you see?

The breeze blew through his thoughts as the wolf moved into the forest on Arantar's left, "no-sword side."

I go far in front and see nothing, Arantar-sao, but feel not good.

Before the Huntsmaster could determine whether the bird's uneasy feelings were a product of his own unease, transmitted somehow through the mind bond, or whether the raven felt the same uneasy sensation, a small, cloaked figure stepped out from the trees in front of him.

The Huntsmaster moved forward while the two elves reined in to wait. At least, he thought, they'd learned something.

The cloaked man, a bit over five feet, held the silver-gray cloak closer about him and turned toward the small clearing to the Huntsmaster's front.

"Greetings, sir."

The Huntsmaster's words seemed to fall on deaf ears as the man continued to walk toward the other side of the clearing. Arantar entered the clearing and, as he glanced back, found that the others had followed him into the clearing. Before he could wave the two elves back into the tree line, the guttural tones of Daku ripped at his ears.

"Allaga swargta!"

Arantar's hands filled with gray sword as he turned back to the man who now faced them. The daku lifted his arms and the cloak fell away from bone-white flesh stretched over fine bones.

"Damn." breathed the Huntsmaster as he tried to turn toward his companions. "Take cov—"

He never finished his warning. The daku had moved quickly into the spell and, as it muttered softly in the guttural language of the dark elves, the three warriors stiffened in their saddles. As the horses moved under the onslaught of magiks, the riders fell heavily to the ground.

The ruddy silver wolf was a blur as it streaked from the wood line straight for the albino daku. The daku, however, was faster and, as its hands came together smartly, three darts of red light flew from its fingertips to strike the wolf full in the chest.

The wolf crumpled to the ground and, in pain, slipped back into the forest. It knew, somehow, that the daku had not meant to kill it, though this was foreign to the wolf's mind, and decided that, as long as Arantar was not being attacked directly, his best bet was to stay close and, though it rankled, watch.

The daku, meanwhile, had moved to the three horses murmuring to them in what Arantar believed to be ancient "equine", the language of horses. The mounts calmed at the man's approach and seemed to converse with him. A white hand appeared from within the cloak with a small knife as the daku moved to Arantar's roan. Arantar struggled in his paralysis in fear for his mount, but he could have saved his strength. His efforts were futile and the knife was used only to cut the straps to the packs tied to the saddle.

The daku went through each pack and saddlebag carefully, discarding anything it did not find useful and pocketing anything it found valuable. The gold and platinum went quickly into its pouch while the coppers were tossed away with distain. The food was scattered about as not worth bothering with. It gathered the four wineskins and two waterskins and spent a little longer with them tasting each and pouring some of the contents on the piles of debris it had made. It removed the saddles from the horses and stacked them neatly to one side with the bridles.

Then, after it stood and stretched from its labors, the daku turned and surveyed the three prone figures one at a time. With a bone-white finger, it pointed to each, as if reciting some child's riddle, and after the finger ended its bouncing motion on Bonaire, the daku clapped his hands and moved quickly to the young elf's paralyzed body.

The first thing it saw where the twin daggers. It hummed to itself as it removed the harness from the fuming Bonaire and examined each dagger individually. It giggled as the daggers and harness disappeared into its cloak. Then it went about the business of methodically stripping the young elf.

Strangely, as the daku picked up Bonaire's green blade, the sword began to hum in a distinctively menacing manner, so much so that the daku dropped it quickly and gave it a wide berth on its way to Solothon.

Solothon fumed in angry silence as the daku stripped him of armor, clothing, and weapons. When the daku found the shirakens, it became very excited. It murmured to itself as it held the weapons into the fading sunlight and glanced at the grimace on the knight's face. He dropped the crystal weapons into his pouch and grabbed the hilt of one of the knight's swords.

Instantly the pain ripped at the dark elf to his very soul. The touch of Elvin silver to a daku was like taking a brand to your skin. The hilt bit the hand, the daku dropped the sword, and, as with Bonaire's, the daku gave it a wide berth.

Arantar had managed, somehow, to move his head just enough to follow the daku's progress and, as the dark one came to his side, Arantar was finally able to see within the cowl. The pinkish eyes stared malevolence as it rubbed at the burn on its hand. The Huntsmaster fared no better than his companions and in short order he too was stripped. Anything of value went into the daku's pouch, while everything else, including the great swords, where discarded. However, when it saw the flame dagger, it giggled with glee. It grabbed the handle and once again screamed. The Elvin silver bit deep and brought many guttural curses down on the Huntsmaster's head.

The albino said something in the horse language and the three horses moved to the edge of the clearing. Then the daku reached into a pocket inside its robe and removed a piece of gray cloth folded into a very small square. It began unfolding the material until it became a very large bag of strangely light cloth.

Arantar was able to move his head just enough to see the albino place all three saddles into the bag along with the bridles and saddle blankets. It took the Huntsmaster a moment to realize what this thing was. He'd read about them in old books and heard about them around campfires and in kitchens all over Catlor. This was an ancient "bag of holding". The old soldiers and scholars he'd spoken to on the subject had tried to explain how they worked, but Arantar still couldn't understand. You put an object into the bag and, as long as you didn't pierce the material, the object would disappear into a void until you reached into the bag to retrieve it.

The Huntsmaster watched the daku fold the bag back into its original small square and place it back into the folds of its cloak. He could also see that Bonaire's hand inched slowly toward the hilt of the green crystal sword.

Bonaire's brows creased as he called on his every will to move his hand. He just knew that if he could grip the amazing sword once more, he could do something about this evil thing. He almost had it when the boot came down on the hand and ground it into the rough dirt.

The daku stood over him and, with a pale grin, wagged a gaunt white finger at him.

Solothon was in terrible burning pain. From the moment the spell was cast, the birthmark on his left arm had all but burst into flame. He could do nothing to remove the pain or help his companions. He was helpless and that, above all else, he could not endure. The rage in his mind burst forth in the blood crimson of killing lust. This creature had dared to rummage his belongings, take the evidence of his friend's deaths, and treated them all evilly. As the madness threatened to take total control, it still was no match for the spell.

Finally the daku stood next to the Huntsmaster and grinned at him from within the cowl of his cloak.

"You do not understand, Huntsmaster?" it asked with a thick accent to his high-pitched voice. "You have picked the wrong cavalier to companion with.

"I serve the one power who will give the Eldewood back to us, the one who will return our power, the one who is the power behind this spider. It is my pleasurable duty to remove any potential threats to that eventuality."

Arantar saw then the red spider embroidered on the daku's elfin cloak and grimaced.

The dark elf lost its grin and spit in the Huntsmaster's face. Then it reached into another pouch and retrieved three small stones, all about the same size and all the same dull shade of gray. Red flecks of demon fire danced about the daku's face as it placed one stone on each man's chest.

"It was nice doing business to you, sirs."

The daku turned and, as it strolled away, waved a white hand and disappeared.

The stone on the Huntsmaster's bare chest began to hum, crackle, and burn as it turned a dull red. The half elf knew then what was to come. The final payment from the daku was to be death in the grizzliest fashion imaginable and there seemed to be nothing he could do about it.

The thought fueled a deep-seated anger as Arantar struggled against the invisible fetters. His mind, his very will, blazed to full at that moment and the gift of his mother's blood came to his aid.

The stone had gone through a bright pink and was turning white, the heat increasing with the change of shades of the stone. The burning pain was the catalyst and the life of his companions his drive.

The power of the Huntsmaster's mind rolled his body and allowed the stone to fall to the ground. As the stone set fire to the grass where it fell, Arantar called on his power to roll him away, all the while beating at the spell that held him frozen. After the second roll, his power of will and of mind shattered the spell.

In one swift movement, the Huntsmaster was on his feet, slapped the stones from his companion's chests, and dragged them well away from where the stones landed.

The stones passed through a blinding white and exploded in screaming, wailing demon-fire. Everything within two paces of the stones was cinder, and nothing would ever grow where the demon fire had touched.

Bonaire, strangely enough, was first to shake off the effects of the spell.

"See what may be salvaged from that mess." was the Huntsmaster's order.

The wine, Bonaire found, had been poisoned. He shrugged and gathered up what was usable of his possessions and stowed them in his knapsack.

Solothon, however, was livid, and the pentagram birthmark still burned at his soul. He muttered to himself as he dug into the mess in his saddlebag for the vial of holy water he carried with him at all times. He uncorked one of the containers and poured it over the birthmark in an effort to cool the painful burning with the sanctified liquid. However, where the liquid touched skin, blisters erupted as the acidic properties of the tainted water burned into the elf.

The Huntsmaster had been going through his belongings and was stowing the items into a saddlebag when the knight's scream set him in motion. He saw the blisters rise and break and knew that, if left alone, the knight would suffer a certainly debilitating or—worse—fatal wound from the acid. He uncorked his wineskin on the run. As the contents washed over the open and bleeding blisters, the Elvin knight stiffened. The Huntsmaster looked into the elf's eyes and saw it then.

There was a soft red glow in those eyes and a madness that raged behind the bars of the knight's own control. The Huntsmaster felt it as it radiated from the young knight's body. He ripped clean linen from a stash untouched by the daku and wrapped it tightly about the ugly wound while Solothon muttered strange curses.

"'Tis a cowardly way to fight, striking from stealth, an abomination in the guise of elf-kind. A blight even upon its own race—"

"Solothon, listen to me!" growled the Huntsmaster through gritted teeth. "We must move quickly. T'will be dark soon and we must be well away from here."

The young knight turned his eyes toward the Huntsmaster and, as he seemed to regain his reason, nodded. The rage, which moments before consumed him, was gone and with it a good bit of strength. Though he was once more in control, he was weak. He grinned as Arantar slapped his shoulder, and he began to repair and don his armor one piece at a time.

Bonaire picked that instant to address them.

"Say, you're not thinking of riding dressed in your armor, are you, Sol? Don't you have any other clothes? You know, something comfortable?"

Arantar felt the rage building and wondered at it.

"Try to lighten up a bit, will you, Sol?"

That was it. The Huntsmaster felt the hate snap and crackle from the knight.

"You haughty little bastard!" roared the knight as he spun, sword in hand.

Bonaire's backpedaling would not save him and the sword was in motion.

Arantar gripped the knight by the sword arm and spun him around. Then he locked his arms about Solothon, pinning the knight's arms to his sides, and screamed into the knight's face.

"Control it, sir knight! Concentrate, dammit! We are your friends! Think, man. Think! Look at me, Solothon!"

Arantar had had dealings with berserkers before, and this one showed all the signs. If it were not for the Huntsmaster's strength, Bonaire would have been spitted then and there. All Arantar could do was hold on until the fit passed. Should he lose his grip or release him too soon…

The knight sagged in Arantar's arms and the Huntsmaster released him. He placed a hand on the elf's shoulder and, as the dark eyes met his, he gripped the shoulder.

"Look, Solothon, I know not what curse is upon you, but we need each other to survive. We must put as much distance between this place and us as quickly as is possible. I know it is not easy, but I too must walk to save the back of my friend and companion. I need to know that I can count on you, friend. I need your help."

Solothon nodded and turned sad eyes on the Huntsmaster.

"I am sorry, friend. I know not what devil fills my soul and I fear it will come to no good. I will try to control this demon. I will try…"

His head fell, as did his voice. Arantar's grip on the young knight's shoulder never wavered.

"I know, my friend, and I will be here to help. Come then. I'll help you, you'll help me, and we'll all reach safety together." Then, as he turned to the wide-eyed Bonaire, "You keep your smart mouth shut! Now, get up on that horse and lead the way! Find us safety for the night. The wolf will help. We will follow as best we can, but don't get too far ahead for we may have need of you."

Bonaire leaped to the bare back of his pony and, after a quick look at the Elvin knight, followed the wolf into the woods to the right.

Arantar helped the knight into his armor and then offered his shoulder. The knight shook his head and set off under his own power in the direction the young elf had taken, his black war mount trailing behind.

The Huntsmaster followed the limping knight warily. He knew that they could come under attack at any time, or the berserker rage trapped within this one could flare up more brightly than before. Should that be the case, he steeled himself to do whatever had to be done, even though it might have to be drastic and more permanent than he wished.

The miles passed slowly as more and more the Huntsmaster watched as the knight's limp became more pronounced. Here the proud elf swerved as if drunk, but after a shake of his head he limped on.

The day decayed into twilight and still no sign of safe haven. The raven flew above them but had not seen anything out of the ordinary. Finally the knight swerved into a tree and stopped.

Fang?

Yes, Arantar-sao. came the immediate reply from some distance ahead.

Bring the other back. We stop here.

The Huntsmaster came up to the knight's back and placed a hand on his shoulder.

"Solothon, we—"

The knight turned on him. His eyes were sunken and his face was contorted in rage, a baseless anger that no logic could prevail against.

"You! It's all your fault!" he screamed as his wavering hand tried to find the hilt of his sword. "You don't want me to make it to Catlorian, do you? Well, I know you now, sir! You and that other dung are in league with the beast that did the deed, but I won't quit! Do you here? I will not quit until you and all others die by my—"

With that, his hand found his sword and, with it half drawn, he collapsed.

Arantar caught him as he sunk to the ground and, as he propped him against the tree, he heard the pony.

"What happened to him?"

"I don't know," replied the Huntsmaster as he checked the knight's pulse and looked into his eyes. "He seemed to go into delirium and collapse."

"Well, maybe some wine would help, but you'll have to use yours. Mine is poison since that albino touched it."

Poison?

"Damn! I used that garbage on his bleeding arm."

He grabbed his wineskin, thankful that he'd had no need to sip from it, unstopped it, and smelled. Yes, the smell was wrong, but he would check it more thoroughly later.

"Bonaire, help me!" he shouted as he grabbed the knight under his arms and lifted. "I heard moving water over there beyond the wood line! We must get him to it if he is to survive!"

It was not an easy task, even with the two of them. Solothon thrashed about in his delirium and caused them to stumble many times before they reached the little brook. They laid him at the edge of the watercourse with his left arm submerged.

Arantar leaped into the water and, after removing the arm piece from the knight's mail, began scrubbing at the wound feverishly, if somewhat mercilessly. When he felt that the wound must surely be clean, Arantar pushed Solothon away from the water, stepped out, and dried the wound with the little reserve of clean linen he had left, saving a small amount to bind the wound.

Together, Arantar and Bonaire dragged the knight a bit farther from the brook and, while Bonaire was sent to gather some kindling for a fire, Arantar checked the knight's condition. The elf's skin was very hot, but he no longer thrashed about. The Huntsmaster thought about removing the rest of the knight's armor, but discarded that idea immediately. There was no way to know when the next assault would come, if at all. To leave the knight totally unprotected was not an option. He drew some water from the brook in his small tin bowl and used it to cool the knight's brow.

Setting a fire now was dangerous, but the Huntsmaster knew he had to make a broth for the knight and a field potion to help him heal. He had the poison test kit, but all of his healing potions were gone. He'd have to rely on his knowledge of the woodlands to make it to civilization.

As he went about making the small fire with the wood Bonaire had provided, the Huntsmaster explained what was to be done with all of the tainted provisions. Then Arantar glanced at the wolf and a heartbeat later the wolf disappeared into the woods.

Bonaire gathered up the wineskins and packs of food and went into the forest far away from the brook. He found a large stump of a long-dead tree and, as he'd been instructed, began chopping a large hole deep into the rotted wood at its center. Once it was deep and wide enough, he gathered up the packs and dumped the contents into the hole. The tainted wine and water was poured over that and the acid on top of that.

Arantar had explained that normally the whole mess would be burned where it lay, but a fire that large would probably draw unwelcome company. The young elf began stacking rock about the trunk until he'd built what looked to be a small cairn. The Huntsmaster had said that this would be a sign to other rangers of the poison buried here and, if the situation permitted, they would finish the task.

Bonaire stood back to admire his handiwork and caught the movement out of the corner of his eye.

A doe grazed but forty yards away. He reached slowly for the bow and quiver of arrows he'd brought. The doe moved slowly behind a clump of brush and Bonaire nocked an arrow. Soon the deer reappeared beyond the brush.

Bonaire drew the arrow slowly to his ear, took a deep breath, sighted along the shaft of the arrow, and released it. The arrow sped faster than the elf could follow.

The doe's head came up abruptly. It coughed, took two quick steps forward, and stopped. Bonaire still held the breath until the deer turned and bolted back into the tree line. He blew the air out in disgust.

He began the trek to where he'd shot his arrow at the deer to retrieve it. He could have sworn that he'd hit the beast, but...

He found the drops of blood where they trailed off into the woods in the direction the deer had gone. Bonaire followed the blood trail and twenty feet inside the wood line he found the doe in a quickly formed pool of blood. Bonaire's arrow protruded from the animal's side where it had penetrated and stopped her heart.

The young elf had to wait for the shaking in his hands to stop before tending to the deer. He felt he'd done something right here. He'd brought food to the table, a huntsman he was. He gutted it and left the entrails to be rendered by the forest creatures. Then he tied a loop of rope about the deer's neck and began the tedious task of dragging it back to the small camp.

Just outside of camp, however, he smelled the delicious flavor of roasting meat. As he dragged his trophy into camp, he saw the two coneys on the spit and the pot boiling with what looked to be potatoes within.

"Come and sit, Bonaire," said the Huntsmaster without turning. "Pull your kill to the tree and I will help you butcher it in a moment. First," he continued as he turned toward the startled elf, "you must learn how to survive at savon. Come, my friend, and sit."

Bonaire obeyed, in total awe of the Huntsmaster. He found a seat just across the fire from Arantar and sat down heavily, a rapt look on his face.

"How did you know it was me?" he asked softly. "And the deer?"

"That, my dear Bonaire, is a secret I will not reveal. Suffice it to say that years of training aided me, as well as some small talents I hold."

At that the wolf snorted and, as it rose and paced toward the deer carcass, the colors broke into Arantar's mind. The Huntsmaster smiled.

"When on the trail, my young friend, kill only what you can carry and only that which will not spoil as you travel, as many have fallen prey to bad food as gualu arrows. Now we need haste, for our companion is poisoned and needs speed for his healing."

Solothon picked that instant to mutter and turn in his uneasy sleep.

"The thought was good, Bonaire, and the skill commendable. However, more thought would have accented smaller game, as the wolf brought, and the tuber you see boiling in the pot. The forest will supply all that is necessary to survive, but you must learn to take only that needed. We will smoke what we can of your kill in the time we have allotted, but the rest is waste. I do not know this forest, nor of any living here that may have need of the bulk of this deer."

Bonaire sighed and hung his head.

"I do not condemn you, Bonaire." stated the Huntsmaster quickly. "I thank you for it. You attempted to help with your talents and you are to be commended. I, of us all, have no right to condemn after my failure of this day!"

Bonaire's head jerked up and he saw the anger on the Huntsmaster's face.

"What?" he exclaimed. "If you had not been here, we would have been killed, charred and forgotten by now. Where have you failed?"

"If I had been using my experience and talents properly, I would have known that a dark elf would have to have been commanding those gualu, especially with a Habuk-Ha present. I should have been on my guard. I should have known!"

"Now," he continued angrily, "our companion lay in mortal danger, we are without provisions to aid his healing, and we are still many days from Catlorian and his deliverance."

The Royal Huntsmaster sighed and looked down at his boots. Then he sighed again and his eyes came up to meet those of the elf.

"It is now too late. The lesson taught. I will not belabor nor belittle my shortfalls. I will learn from them that I might never make the same mistake a second time. Remember, my young friend, a failure one manages to live through becomes a lesson only if one admits the failure."

Bonaire heard the words and, strangely, they seeped into his mind. He held a deep respect for the stern Huntsmaster and more of what the experienced warrior was teaching slipped into the youth's brain, though tucked away for later study perhaps.

"Come, Bonaire," said the Huntsmaster with somewhat renewed vigor. "A new day will be here soon and we must make ready to meet it!"

He handed a spitted coney to the young elf and, as Bonaire bit tenderly at the hot meat, smiled.

"'Tis always better to face a new day rested and fed. Tomorrow we shall take stock of what must be done, but for now we will see to ourselves."

Later, after they had eaten, the Huntsmaster made the knight, whose fever seemed to hang on but who slept less fitfully than before, as comfortable as he could. While he cooled the knight's brow with damp cloths, he fed seasoned wood to the fire to dry the strips of venison.

Bonaire dragged the remainder of the carcass deeper into the woods where the forest would render it and moved about the camp in a restless and random manner. Suddenly he stopped.

"Arantar!" he whispered excitedly.

Arantar's hand snapped to the hilt of the large sword that lay but a thought away, and turned toward the sound of the youth's voice. His hand slipped away from the hilt and back to the wet cloths as the excited youth came over and dropped to his knees.

"What is it, Bonaire?"

"Well, although it is true that I paid less attention to my mother's teachings than I should have, maybe I do remember some stuff!"

"What?"

"Okay! Okay, I remember her telling me about the Devil's pentagales, or something, and they were made to move us quickly from place to place."

"Yes, Bonaire. I've seen them, and they are called 'Druid's Pentacles', but I've never had the occasion nor the desire to use one."

"But that's it!"

"What's it? Make sense, man!"

"Listen, if we could find one, you could make it work, right?"

"Yes. So? Bonaire, I have no idea in which direction to go, save in a direct coarse to Catlorian. We have no time to search about for a Pentacle, even if one should be in this area."

"Yeah, I know, but that's just it! My mother taught me how to divine such things, if I can just remember how."

"Then, my friend, you shall attempt this 'divining' first thing in the morning. For now, sleep. The rest may aid your memory. I shall take the first watch then wake you for the next."

Bonaire nodded and lay close to the fire wrapped in his gaudy cloak. Soon, and strangely for an elf, he was fast asleep.

Next lesson is awake-sleep, Arantar-sao.

The growling thought brought a smile to the Huntsmaster's lips.

It seems we must help this one grow quickly, my friends. While he does hold promise, I just hope he survives long enough to learn the necessities.

He let the colors and breeze walk softly though his mind and sighed.

Me sleep much, Arantar-sao. came the growled thought. *You sleep, I watch. Air brother watch, too. Safe all.*

I will watch until the meat is finished then. Wake me when the fast white ball goes behind the mountain.

He figured that it would take the moon of Paladin about six hours to fall behind the mountain range. Plenty of time for "awake-sleep".

An hour or so later he was at rest, each fiber of his being attuned to his surroundings. He could be fully awake in a second should the need arise.

A soft growl brought him out of his warrior's trance, the growl a wake-up call and nothing more. Three hours later, he awoke the sleepy-headed Bonaire and waited long enough to be sure the elf would not return to sleep. He warned Bonaire to wake him at daybreak and slipped back into the "sleep-awake" state of the warrior's trance.

It was still dark, the horizon just warning of the light soon to spring upon the day. Arantar slid smoothly from the trance to wide-awake. Bonaire squatted before him, waiting.

"Are you awake?" whispered the elf softly as the Huntsmaster's eyes came open.

"Yes. What is it?"

"It'll be daylight soon and I wanted to tell you that I remembered how my Mom taught me to find things."

"Good!" Arantar stated as he turned to check on Solothon.

The knight's fever was gone, it seemed, but he was in a very deep sleep. The Huntsmaster shifted the knight's head to a more comfortable position and turned to the young elf.

"First, you must help me pack up the camp. Then you can try it, okay?"

They built a travois for the knight and, though the black warhorse did not seem to like the idea of pulling his master behind him, a few soft words from the Huntsmaster calmed him. Then the experienced warrior turned his attention to the campsite.

He showed Bonaire how to dispose of any sign that would give an indication that anyone had been there. If they were being followed, he did not want to make it easy, and time was running out for them. He weighed his efforts against throwing a tracker off long enough to get Solothon to a safe haven for healing.

When he felt that there was no more to be done, he placed a strong hand on Bonaire's shoulder.

"Now, Bonaire, try what you will to locate a Pentacle. Solothon rests at more peace now, but I don't know whether he heals or dies."

The young elf nodded and walked to the center of the clearing. He went back over his mother's words carefully and acted on them as they became clear.

"Now, my son, close your eyes and blank your mind, as you would a chalkboard with a wet cloth. In that blankness, picture that object you wish to find. Now slowly raise your arms out to your sides and extend them as far as you can reach, your palms forward and your second and third fingers held to your palms by your thumbs. Now turn until you feel the tug. It will be slight, but you should feel it."

Bonaire turned slowly and, excitement racing through him, he felt the tug.

"Once felt, bring both hands to center, arms straight and extended before you. Touch your forefingers together and bring them to your brow. Concentrate now, my son, for now you must keep a clear picture of that you wish to find, for this is the crucial time!"

The young elf strained to picture each detail of the picture he'd seen in his mother's house of a Druid's Pentacle. He felt that to fail now was to fail everything. He must not fail!

"Now point the joined forefingers straight out before you and turn slightly left and right until you feel the greatest pull. That is the direction to the object for which you seek!"

At that point, Bonaire was almost pulled onto his face, so strong was the pull. He turned slightly and the force slackened, turned back, and it peaked.

"It's that way, Arantar, and I think quite close. I think I did it!"

"Good work, my friend!" he exclaimed. Then, soberly, "Bonaire, it is possible that your talents will save our friend. If, however, after all we have done, he does not survive, know that to have tried and failed is always better than not to have tried at all. There is no dishonor in that failure."

Then the big half elf smiled and slapped the elf on the shoulder.

"But let us not think of failure, my friend. Go ahead of us and break a trail. I will follow with the knight as quickly as I can. You are the only one who may ride for us, so you must scout and be wary for us all. The wolf will help. Should he growl at you, return to me quickly, for we will have need. He will know if we are in peril. He will also render you what aid he can give, should you have need. Remember, Bonaire, the wolf is a valuable friend to have out here. A friend, but never a pet."

Chapter Eleven

Iaprene' Anolin rode the great golden palomino mare along the trail made for her by the trees of the Eldewood Vale. The flowing mane of the well-muscled horse and its proud carriage matched that of its rider.

The girl's long blonde tresses fell over the shimmering Elvin cloak to her waist. As the horse cantered along the path, the cloak billowed, displaying not only the faultless midnight blue of the cloaks lining but the golden gown that covered every curve of her perfect small body.

Iaprene'—Rene' to her friends—was one of the most talented and beautiful of the fair race that lived within the Vales of the Eldewood, and she knew it. The horse's saddle, bridle, and blanket were all designed by Rene', for Rene'...side-saddle of course. She was, after all, a lady.

When but a child, despite her doting mother and father, she had learned that vanity, and the temperament that was associated with the conceit it brings, were the crutch of those who could do no more than exist. She had, with the insistence of her mother, taken up the worship of the Elvin goddess Celeste, the goddess of Romance and Beauty. She felt, at that time, that it was but fitting that one as beautiful as herself should worship the only goddess who deified beauty, such was the height of her vanity.

Then came the ranger.

She was basking in the spring sunlight that filtered through the trees when the strangest feeling fluttered through her. The silent call for help reached that place within that had been locked away by her vanity. She walked stiffly on, following the call until she found him.

He was near death as he leaned against the tree and slid down to his knees, a pool of his own blood quickly forming from the gualu arrow that pierced his chest. He knew that every minute he lived was a miracle, and he'd asked the gods for help he knew would never come.

Then he saw her, a little girl of no more than eight years. Her golden eyes were filled with pain and, as she walked toward him in her little golden playsuit, he knew that the pain she felt was his.

Rene' had no choice. The soul-deep caring that this man's pain brought to her being changed the little girl forever. As he watched, unable to move, she came to him and placed a small timid hand to the ranger's forehead and, with tears that fell unnoticed from her golden eyes, she prayed.

Such was the depth of the small girl's true caring for the life of a stranger, and the all-consuming need she felt to aid, no matter the cost, could only have been because the goddess, herself, heard. Such power flowed from the child into the ranger that she collapsed.

Had not the huntsman realized what the girl was doing, she would surely have given her own life force to him in total. As it was, he pushed her hand away before the drain from her small constitution was complete.

With the arrow still protruding from his body, he whistled a feathered guide and carried the girl to the Elvin settlement.

After the arrow was removed, the healing done, and the story told, he was directed to the small elaborate cottage wherein lay the child in a deep sleep.

The girl's mother paced the porch and wrung her hands at the thought of her "baby" in peril.

"M'lady," said he, "t'would have been better to give the child more training in the healing arts before allowing her to practice them. The power she gave to me almost cost her life. I owe this little one my life and more, for she all but gave hers to the gods for mine."

"Healing arts?" she said softly, a confused look on her face. "Iaprene' has never been trained in the healing arts. She is far above those things. She is beautiful, talented and—"

"And filled with such love and caring for others as to drain her very life-force to aid a stranger!" he finished for the astonished lady.

"I care not whatever else you do, woman," he continued as he stepped onto the porch, the rage barely concealed within his breast, "but should you, or anyone else discourage this child from training the power she holds naturally, controlling it, that power, untrained, could be the death of her. I hold you responsible. I owe her my life, and by all the gods I'll not see her harmed through your vain negligence!"

Rene's father, a portly elf of some great stature within the village, had hurried to the cottage upon hearing that his "little darling" had fallen ill. He'd come up the path at the same time the ranger had lashed out at Rene's mother.

"Now see here, young man," he began.

"And who are you?" the still-angry ranger asked as he turned on him.

"I am Elfinoe Anolin, Rene's father, and I will have you to know—"

His pompous tirade was stopped by the ranger's finger as it tapped stiffly against his chest, keeping time with every word the angry ranger spoke.

"I will have *you* know, sir, that, unless this child is allowed the training she needs, I will hold you personally responsible for any suffering she endures!"

The ranger looked closer at the stricken face of the small rotund man and sighed. In a softer tone, he continued.

"This child has touched me and saved me from certain death. She did not have to, but her loving and caring nature would not let my life leave me, even at the cost of her own. She, and the rest of the world through her, needs the training she should have. There is a special bond between that child and I that only death may sever. I, and those of my profession, will never allow harm to befall this one without massive retribution. She is now, and forever, ranger protected. I, Cashme're, have so declared."

The two parents looked into the eyes of the Lord Ranger and knew then the truth. This was Lord Cashme're, a name known to many in the Eldewood as a follower of the Mother, protector of the woodlands, and a warrior of no mean accomplishment. His last breath would be given to protect their little girl, even from herself.

The call would go out to all Ranger Lords, and to the High Ranger himself, that Iaprene' Anolin was ranger protected. Any causing her harm of any kind was in danger of a ranger's sure and accurate wrath.

Rene's mother recovered first and said, in a small voice, "I will speak with our local priestess as soon as I may, I promise. She will get all of the training that is necessary. I will see to it."

The father nodded and asked, somewhat softly, "Please forgive us and tell us what happened."

"By your leave," Cashme're replied, "I would first see the little one. Then I will relate the story in total."

Elfinoe nodded and stepped away from the door. The ranger waved the nurse back to her chair as he entered and stood beside the girl's bed. He looked down at her sleeping face, kissed her softly on the forehead, and left the room. When he stepped back to the porch, Rene's parents saw the tears and a gentle smile. He sat and began the story.

Priestess Sl'everin heard the light knock at the door of the Temple of Celeste. She'd been with the temple for several years here in Catlorian and a knock usually meant a soul in deep trouble. She sent her talent out and immediately opened the door.

The girl's eyes were red-rimmed, her face tear stained, and her small body shook with the shock of myriad emotions: love, hate, sadness, pain, death, and all the ranges thereof emanating from the massed populace of Catlorian.

Sl'everin knew the problem because she too had this "gift." She held the child close, enveloping her within the safety of her own aura and effectively shielding her from the seemingly insurmountable emotions. It had taken the priestess many years to develop the talent, to control it, to direct the empathy, while blotting out the emotions attempting to control and overpower her.

After that first night, Sl'everin became Rene's constant companion and confidant. She taught the child a little at a time to build and control the barriers necessary to her well-being and independence. Rene', in turn, clung to every word the priestess uttered and emulated the grace and poise in the priestess's every movement.

Rene' found, after a time, that she could direct her talent and control it to a point that she could reach out to one individual without being drowned by the emotions of all the others. She also found that she could better reach the ills of the sufferer and would know instinctively where the pain existed to create a cure.

Her natural caring nature accelerated her in her studies and power, along with her need to know more and more to help others. She took the vows of the clergy and continued to consume every scrap of knowledge available and beg for more. On her tenth year anniversary, Rene' got the call for an audience with the High Priestess.

Rene' appeared at the door to the priestess's study exactly at the time required, as was her habit, dressed in the clothing she knew would enhance her natural beauty.

Though still a bit vain and temperamental, Rene' was also convinced of her own capabilities, and rightly so. Rene' was exactly what she seemed: a lady, a skilled cleric, and a studied scholar. The door opened.

"Come in, child, and sit," came the soft voice from the divan. "We will talk for a while, if you have no pressing engagements?"

The High Priestess was one of those whose beauty was immortal without the need for trappings. She sat, her long legs drawn up under her, upon the divan and smiled as Rene' swept into the room. The lithe girl draped herself over the cushion on the chair offered and, after a nod, the High Priestess smiled.

"Rene', it has become obvious to those teaching you that you have more hunger for knowledge than we have food for your mind. We are afraid that if we keep you only to the study and practice of the healing arts, you will someday lose interest or, far worse, stunt the natural power retained within you. Are these observations correct? Have we read the signs rightly?"

The girl bared her heart to the High Priestess. She'd been meaning, for months, to seek permission to return home to rest in the forest she loved and search her soul for what she felt was missing. The High Priestess smiled and granted her all the time she wished and explained that, no matter where she ended up, there would always be a place there at the temple for her.

She left that afternoon for the Druid's Pentacle and home.

Just outside of the East Gate and just within the forest of the Eldewood, the first Druid's Pentacle sat. At each point of the star, carved into the silvery surface by forgotten builders, a pillar rose. Each pillar was covered with runes of power and was used to negotiate the magical transport from one Pentacle to another. Those who had the knowledge of their use could travel great distances in the blink of an eye.

Rene' left the East Gate and rode directly toward the Pentacle. There, in the eave of the forest, she saw Cashme're.

"Well, little one," he said as she leapt from her horse and hugged him tightly, "I thought you'd never be allowed to return to us. We've missed you for too long."

He still insisted on calling her "little one," though, at five feet and two inches tall, she was as tall as he.

"I've missed you, too, my ranger." she said gleefully.

Now that she was away from Catlorian, the need to get home wasn't as driven as it once was, especially since her very special ranger was there to meet her. She sat with Cashme're and told him everything: her wants, her needs, her wishes, and her hunger for more of what she did not know.

He nodded and smiled. He thought he knew what would fill the gap in her incredibly sharp and active intellect and told her.

"Magic? Are you serious?"

"Think about it, little one. You have the power and the intellect and the drive needed. You cannot be contained in one sphere of study. There are many that I know who've gone far in the field of magiks, and not one of them have your desire and drive to excel."

"But I don't wish to give up the priesthood to study the arcane arts. I just couldn't, my ranger!"

"I would never suggest that, little one. On the contrary, there are those who hold both disciplines and are very good at both. You, my sweet Rene', could be great. The skills you have now are akin to and use the same power inherent in the magiks of this world. I do not ask that you give up anything. The contrary is true! I ask that you check into adding the arcane to your realm of study while continuing to pursue your clerical studies. The two could work hand-in-hand and fill the need that you now feel you have to fill."

He held her by the shoulders and looked into her eyes. He could see the indecision there and the worry that she might have to lose something to gain something else.

"Listen to me, little one. You needn't decide now. I have an acquaintance with whom I wish you to speak. After you've talked with him, you may make your decision with more information. Okay?"

She grinned and hugged him.

"Now, my little priestess, I will be seeing you to the fourth Pentacle where I must leave you. Something has come up that needs my attention, but I will see you again just as soon as I can."

Cashme're walked beside her, his hand firmly on the bridle to her palomino, to the center of the Druid's Pentacle. Rene' felt the worry in the ranger's aura but pulled back to keep from intruding. If he wished her to know...

The runes faded and they were once again at the boundary of the Elde-wood Vale. Rene' stepped off of the silver surface and the ranger aided her in remounting her mare. He placed a soft hand on her knee as she looked down into his troubled eyes.

"Once home, little one, ask your father to find one known as Yarda, Master Mage. Tell your father to use the name Cashme're and tell of a debt to be paid. He will come. Speak with him, Rene', and I believe your needs will be answered."

He stepped to one of the pillars, touched three runes, and stepped to the center of the pentagram. She saw him smile a sad smile and disappear.

Yarda came as the ranger had said.

Rene' apprenticed with the Master Mage for several years while keeping up a steady correspondence with her temple in Catlorian. She absorbed the knowledge of the arcane like a sponge and practiced the intricate patterns of spell casting. Her natural grace and demand for perfection imbued each spell with a power unrivaled by the Master Mage himself.

Then one day Yarda called her to his study. The room was, as always, untidy with books and scrolls stacked and scattered throughout. The old mage smiled as the golden lady swept into the room.

"Rene', my girl, you have been one of the best, if not *the* best, student I've ever had the pleasure to teach. I thank my friend Cashme're for allowing me to pay my debt to him as your tutor. Now it seems I've all but run out of more to teach you. I've sent word to friends and colleagues in Catlorian, and they've allowed that you may go to them for further study. I hope you never lose the fervor with which you approach your studies, as few of my colleagues have retained the energy necessary to take them beyond the levels of competence they now hold. It was recommended that you seek out the Myrlin. He has heard of you and, for reasons I cannot fathom, he has shown an interest in your accomplishments."

The old Mage sighed and smiled at the young girl.

"Go to Catlorian, Rene', for therein lies your future."

A week later, she found the old mage dead in his bed. She mourned for him, as a good friend would, then set out for Catlorian.

As she rode for the fourth Pentacle, her hand found the tiny golden heart on a fine golden chain about her delicate throat. It was a gift from Cashme're and she cherished it. This day would be perfect, she thought, if she found her ranger waiting beside the silver surface.

Instead she found a knight standing stiffly beside one of the pentacle pillars. As she approached, he removed his gleaming silver helm and bowed low.

"Fair lady, have I the honor of addressing Lady Iaprene' Anolin, protected of Rangers and the fairest mage in the realm?"

"I don't know about all of that, sir knight," she giggled, "but I am Iaprene' Anolin, though my friends call me Rene'."

"Ah, yes, then, Lady Rene'. Therefore, you must now know that I, Sir Jake of Pentecost, first in the service of the Lords of Light, have been chosen by one known as Cashme're, a friend and great warrior, for the delightful privilege of escorting you this very day to the gates of Catlorian and beyond, if you please."

He finished with another bow and the jet-black warhorse, which stood in full battle dress behind him, nudged him with its nose.

"Ah! Excuse me, dear Lady, but I've failed to introduce my friend and long time companion of many endeavors, Midnight."

The warhorse snorted and, with a bent foreleg, bowed in regal fashion. As the horse straightened up slowly, Rene' could have sworn it winked at her.

"How beautiful he is, Sir Jake," she giggled, "and, yes, I would be pleased to be escorted by such a noble knight and his valiant and trusted friend."

Sir Jake leaned close to the girl's stirrup and said quietly, "Careful, my lady. He is a notorious flirt."

The knight shot a scathing look at the black warhorse, yet he was met with a turned head as if not to notice.

"Harrumph!" snorted the knight. Then, "Shall we depart, my lady?"

"In a moment, Sir Jake," she responded, her eyes seeking for the source of the feeling. "I believe we have company."

Sir Jake looked toward the lady's concern and, sure enough, there came an elf youth, all in leather and riding a black pony. He saw no saddle, but he did see the elegant hilt of a sword that appeared over the youth's shoulder.

Rene' felt that the object of this one's concern was somewhere behind him. Somewhere…

"'Ware, Midnight. T'would seem the company you mention comes bearing arms. Stay behind me, dear Lady. If they be friend, all is well. If they be foe…"

Arantar and his roan led the fidgety warhorse bearing the travois, yet kept his battle honed senses at peak as he followed the young mage through the forest. Occasionally he'd stop to check on the knight, but he found that that one slept calmly, if a bit pale. The worry the ranger had that this was a stage before death hastened his way.

They traveled a bit slowly for several hours until Bonaire saw the pillars through the trees. He glanced back at Arantar, pointed, and nudged the pony into a trot.

Hoping that the Huntsmaster, at least, could make the thing work, Bonaire's eyes were for the pillars covered with runes and the smooth silver surface of the Pentacle. He tried to remember what his mother had told him about them, that each pillar carried a different set of runes describing class, race, occupation, and destination. Her description was exact in every detail, and he realized that even he could make it work. He had to tell Arantar! As he pulled at the makeshift reins to turn the pony about, a loud voice boomed out.

"WHO GOES THERE?"

Bonaire saw the large and incredibly tall knight in shining full plate armor stride purposefully toward him.

The youth caught the shimmer of gold behind the knight and chanced a glance. His jaw dropped.

She sat sidesaddle upon a well-muscled palomino mare. Bonaire had never seen such beauty. The gold of her form-fitting dress fell from beneath her immaculate cloak of Elvin gray. Her golden-blonde hair billowed in the slight breeze and was as fine as silk. The young mage could get lost in that hair...

"BRIGAND, BEWARE!"

The booming voice brought the elf back to reality. The knight came on.

"State your name and business, sir! Lie not, for your doom is before you!"

"Uh, what?" was all the young mage could get out.

Sir Jake stopped but ten feet away, planted his feet, and placed one hand to the hilt of the great sword that rode his broad back. The other hand was reserved to point an armored finger toward the young elf.

"Your name and business, I say!"

"Uh, Bonaire Blackabar, and I'm—"

"BLACKGUARD, ARE YOU?!!" The sword swept from the sheath. "Well! We shall do battle here and now!"

"Uh, *halt*!" The youth shouted as the knight dropped his visor and took a step toward him.

The knight's hand went to his visor and snapped it up.

"Halt?"

"Yes, halt!"

Bonaire needed time and this big guy wasn't listening at all! He hoped that the Huntsmaster would get here before this big knight turned him into dog food!

"Look, sir, have I drawn sword on you? Have I threatened you in any way?"

"Hmmm, no," said the knight as his left hand came up to scratch at his chin guard and his brows knitted in deep concentration. Then, as if coming to the only logical explanation, he looked up at the youth with a slight smile, his brow drawing down again in a frown.

"Being a 'blackguard' makes you a brigand and, as such, you are a liar and a fool!"

Again he reached for his visor to snap it down but stopped.

"Wait! You are ahorse! I shall mount as well that we might fight on an even footing, so to speak."

With that, the big knight returned his sword without a glance to the sheath at his back, turned on his heel, and strode toward the black warhorse. The horse shook its head with what, to Bonaire, seemed a sad look in its eyes.

"Wait, sir!" cried the bewildered Bonaire.

The great sword flicked out of the sheath again as the knight turned as to combat.

"What?"

"I have come seeking the Druid's—"

"A druid?" interrupted the knight. "I'm no druid, sir." Then turning to an equally bewildered Rene', "Do you know of any druids about, dear Lady?"

"No, Sir Jake," she all but giggled, "but there may—"

"No druids here, liar!" came the booming voice as the knight turned again toward Bonaire. "Prepare to meet your doom, sir!"

The knight took one purposeful step toward the young elf, stopped, knitted his brow, and suddenly grinned.

"Oh, yes!" he boomed, an up-thrust forefinger for punctuation. "My mount!"

He turned again toward the big black warhorse. It had taken a step toward one of the pillars, leaned a shoulder against it, and crossed its forelegs. It looked anywhere but at Sir Jake, seemingly embarrassed at the knight's antics and bored with the whole goings on.

"Sir Jake?"

The girl's sweet voice stopped the knight in mid-stride and turned him sharply toward the voice.

"Yes, dear Lady?"

"It would seem to me that since there are trees here, a druid could not be too far away. However," she continued as the knight's brows again knitted in deep concentration, "if you would stop long enough, without interruption, to hear the boy's explanation, you might find that those coming up the path behind him are the objects of his concern."

Indeed, at that moment, Arantar appeared through the trees just behind the young elf. He sent a mental request for Fang to stay with the travois as he stopped next to the worried Bonaire.

"Arantar, I tried—"

The Huntsmaster's raised hand cut him off and motioned for the youth to dismount. Arantar surveyed the scene and accurately denoted that Bonaire had once again gotten in over his head.

Rene' set her empathic talent toward the Huntsmaster and felt the worry and fear he had for the one in deep sleep upon the travois.

Arantar whispered, "Stay here."

Protocol was stiff in most orders of knights, and the approach you take is as important as the words you chose. He approached to within fifteen feet of the large knight and, with a courtly bow, announced himself.

"Good day to you, sir knight. I am Arantar Adenedhel, late of the Prince's Own Royal Border Guards, where I held some small measure of station as Huntsmaster. Please forgive the impetuosity of youth."

He displayed a hand, palm up, toward the bristling Bonaire.

"He is in my charge and is but learning the protocol of those of your grand station."

The tall knight straightened at the comment and, folding his arms akimbo, tried to look stern. The look in the knight's eye and the slight upturn at the corners of his mouth told Arantar that this approach was working. He continued.

"We have recently been set upon by gualu and the magiks of a black elf. My friend and noble companion," he took a step toward the travois with another palm-up flourish, "a young and honorable knight in the service of the New Order of the Laurel within the Eldewood Vale has been sorely wounded and poisoned. We haste for the succor of healing for our friend."

The last was said with drooped shoulders and bowed head.

"Well! Harrumph!" stated the big knight. "I would be sorely remiss if I, ah, through zealousness, allowed another honorable knight and his retinue to come to unnecessary harm."

Then, as if realizing he was behind in this discussion, he slid the sword into the sheath at his back and bowed.

"Oh, please pardon my rudeness, most noble Huntsmaster. I am Sir Jake of Pentecost, first in the service of the Lords of Light, and I am at your service."

The knight then turned a palm-up flourish toward the girl on the golden mare.

"This dear lady is the Priestess Mage Iaprene' Anolin."

Arantar again bowed low and tapped Bonaire on the leg. Bonaire copied the bow, though somewhat awkwardly.

"If you gentlemen have quite finished with your pleasantries," said the girl softly, "I should like to administer what aid I might to the wounded one."

She extended a tiny hand toward Jake and, as that worthy fairly leapt to her assistance, she slid gracefully from the palomino's back.

As she swept past Arantar, she whispered, "Well done, Huntsmaster."

"The blessings of the rangers to you, Lady Rene'." he replied.

She grinned and stepped lightly past the enamored Bonaire to the travois. She brushed an errant lock of hair from the young knight's brow and felt the sheen of magiks there. She frowned and laid a dainty hand on his brow, felt the knight's own healing power as it strove with the poison and won, and sent peace through that touch from her soul.

The color began to return to the knight's face as the girl bent to check the bandages on his arm and leg. She nodded and rose.

"You've done well, Huntsmaster. Your bindings and his strength have healed him far better than I could. He should rest the day. A light meal upon waking would be advisable, followed by more rest. Within two days, at the rate he heals, he should be back to normal."

"I thank you, Lady Rene'."

"We travel by Pentacle to Catlorian," she continued. "Will you join us?"

Arantar looked askance of the large knight and received an apologetic smile and nod.

"T'would be our pleasure to have you join us, good sir!" he boomed.

Arantar again bowed low, Bonaire just a fraction of a second behind him. Then he spoke to Solothon's mount and his own and moved, with both mounts following, to the center of the silver pentagram.

Sir Jake offered his arm to the golden cleric and led her mount onto the silver surface as an awed Bonaire followed.

The knight glanced back at his black stallion and grimaced.

"Well, Midnight, are you coming?"

The black shrugged away from the pillar and fairly minced to the knight's side.

"One day, Midnight..." he muttered sternly. "Are we all here?" Then he turned to Lady Rene' and asked, "Shall I do the honors, m'lady?"

"Please do, Sir Jake."

The knight stepped to one of the silver pillars, touched three runes in succession, returned to the center of the pentagram, and placed his sword before him, point down.

"TO CATLORIAN!" he boomed.

The group vanished from within the pentagram with only the tracks about the apron to give evidence that anyone had been there at all.

The Pentacle sat waiting for the next traveler to approach.

Chapter Twelve

Eton ran through the Outer Forest on a direct path to the Eldewood Vale. The puma moved silently beside him like a light brown smoke through the trees. Soon the markers to the Vale came into view, and the big warrior stopped short of the border to make camp while the puma slipped off to chase down a pair of rabbits.

They had run through the night to get to this place, a place Eton remembered as a boy. Here he'd whistled the call of the wood folk. The elves who lived within the wild woods held Eton as one of their own and always answered.

They were a curious sort, though they never seemed inclined to meddle in the affairs of those outside their woods. They'd watch and follow until the subject of their curiosity ceased to amuse them. Then they'd find something else to be curious about.

Eton sat close to the fire with his cloak wrapped about him against the evening chill. He stroked the Bourjon Blade across the stone he held as the coneys roasted. The puma had curled up across the fire from him and was seemingly asleep. The big cat felt the eyes before the warrior did.

Eton carefully laid the stone on the ground and slid the long dagger into his right hand, spun up softly to rest the blade against his arm. He held very still, every fiber of his being alive with energy, his speed to be called on at a heartbeat.

Then the whistle, soft and trilling, sifted through the trees. The cat laid his big head down and relaxed the coiled muscles bunched for attack. Eton sheathed the dagger and returned the trilling tones. The three figures seemed to materialize from the trees. Eton's hands moved.

<Welcome to my fire, brothers.>

These three knew Eton from years gone by. They read the signing, for it was theirs, used for silent communication within the forest. The language was Elvin at its basest form, but these knew that the youth before them had not the vocal capacity to speak the trilling tones of elf speech. In deference, they too signed.

<The blessings of the Mother upon you and yours, brother.>

Eton passed his wineskin to one of the three and came right to the point.

<I search for one traveling the Vale with the Red One's sword on his back. Has he drawn your attention?>

The three spoke quietly to each other for a moment before the one appointed spokesman signed.

<Yes.>

<Do you know his destination?>

<Yes.>

Eton was used to the direct, clipped way the elves signed. He knew it was an unconscious jab at his inability to carry on a conversation in their spoken tongue. Usually it wouldn't bother him, but now it annoyed.

He leaned forward and told the story of the village deserted, the signs of struggle, the graves of many, the meeting with Grizel, and the news of the half elf. He added his opinion that the half elf was probably in league with the slavers as well.

<If he were in league with those body thieves, why would the Red One gift him his blade?>

<I know not, brother. That is why I ask.>

<He ran into the forest without a word. We thought him on an errand for the Red One. The trees of the Vale played a pretty trick and lost him to their bosom. He cried out for aid and we helped him to the White Way. He arrived two...three suns, your time. We sent a message to the Red One, but he was gone. Now we watch for you and his return.>

<You saw the half elf to the White Way?>

<Yes, but he found the Meddler there and went to sleep. We know no more.>

They rose and made the sign for swift peaceful travel and slipped silently into the forest. A moment later, the spokesman returned.

<Do you wish the Green Way?>

<Yes, brother. I need haste and would be thankful for the Green Way.>

<Sleep now, brother. On the morrow the Green Way will open for you. Farewell, my brother.>

Sleep came softly for the man and cat. The Eldewood granted sweet rest before the long, hard trail upon waking. Eton's last days in Seafoam came as a dream on the heels of this gifting.

He was eighteen and large. He'd heard the stories of the slavers and the gualu in the southern reaches and, after long discussion with his father and Barnak, decided to venture down to the southern border and see for himself. Barnak called him away from the community house on the night before his departure.

"Come wit' me, Eton. I've somethin' ta show ye," said he as he led the youth to his cottage.

When the two entered the big front room, Barnak went straight to the large chest nestled against the wall and lifted the oil lamp and coverlet from it. The old gladiator pulled a small golden chain from his neck and, as it cleared his tunic, Eton saw the tiny key. Barnak knelt before the chest to unlock it, but before he opened the chest, his eyes turned to the youth.

"Eton, wha's in here be me whole treasure. T'were all I had when I come here many year ago. T'is me own secret." As he opened the lid to the chest, he continued, "Now I be sharin' wit' me fav'rite."

Inside the chest was armor. Most of it was too gaudy to wear anywhere but in the arena, but, for its gaudiness, it was excellent armor. Barnak carefully moved these pieces out of the way and found what he wanted. He lifted the studded leather from the chest and handed it to Eton. Then, as the startled youth looked from the soft leather to the grizzled warrior, Barnak reached back into the chest for the matching boots. As he turned to the young warrior, Barnak saw the awe in the boy's eyes and the way he held the leather in his arms.

"Don' jist stan' there, Eton! Put it on! 'N these too," he added as he set the boots on the floor. "They seen me t'rew hard times, boyo. It's time they was used by one what has th' talent 'n skill they was made ta perteck!"

The old fighter turned back to the chest and Eton unfolded the soft steel-studded garment.

Just looking at it, the lad knew it was just too small for his large frame, but, to make this man happy, Eton would try to squeeze into it. If he could get into it, he could take it off later after he'd left and he wouldn't hurt this great man's feelings.

He barely squeezed it over his head and was about to call for Barnak to help when the leather began to stretch. No, grow. As the youth slipped it onto his body and hooked the catches, the vest of steel-studded leather seemed to pull in and conform to every muscle it encountered. It became as if a second skin and moved as he moved with no restriction at all. He pulled the boots on and they too conformed to his every measurement.

Barnak turned from the chest with a wide leather belt and smiled.

"Good! They fit. I figgered they would. Now," he said as he handed the belt to the lad, "put this on tight. Ye'll fin' there's strappin's 'n rings on it t'will serve well fer yer possessions, 'n fer this."

Barnak handed the sheathed weapon to the startled youth. Eton slipped his left hand into the basket hilt and drew the short blade from the oiled sheath. He felt the balance and the way it seemed to seat itself into his left hand.

"Tha's where it b'longs," stated the gladiator as he took the sheath and strapped it across the back of the belt.

"Tha' blade were a gift from me last master. He said it come from a land called Bourj. Tha's why I calls it a Bourjon Blade. I ne'er used it, but I kep' it case me own son might fin' a need. I ne'er had me no son 'cept you, Eton. Ye are the closest I'll e'er have."

The old campaigner looked old for a moment. Then with a shake of his head he grinned.

"Ye'll notice, Boyo, tha' the sheath are where I been teachin' ye. Tha' blade fit in th' sheath at yer back an' are designed fer the left han' only. Though I taught ye ta fight with any blade in either han', this one be special. It'll make yer left hand a shield an' a weapon both. Now, one more t'ing."

The old gladiator turned, once more, to the chest. When he turned back, Eton gasped.

In the old warriors hands was a single arm gauntlet. It covered each of the fingers in scaled leather and was layered all the way to the shoulder, where the turned-up collar rose a good two inches to protect the neck on that side.

Again the youth slipped it on and it conformed to his size and shape and was as light as the skin on his left arm. Barnak showed him where it connected across his back to the belt and clipped into the rings on the vest.

"Barnak," he whispered, "I cannot take your treasure."

"If'n ye doesn't use 'em, who will? I luv's ye, boyo. I started teachin' ye early on ta use this, an' I'll be burned if'n ye doesn't! I ain't a son of me own an' no time left ta be trainin' another. Yer it!"

The old warrior grabbed the boy and drew him into a bear hug. When he released him, the warrior slapped the boy on the armored shoulder and glared into his eyes.

"'Member, Eton, use yer speed. Ye'll fin' tha' wha' I give ye will suffice as armor fer wha' ye cain't defend against." Then, as the old man's eyes filled with tears, he added, "This be yer home, boy! Don' ferget it!"

"I won't, Uncle," he whispered.

Eton left the next morning amid tears and happiness from his friends and a gentle kiss on each scarred cheek from Megan.

"Now don't ye be fergittin' where ye come from, Eton," she said as she smiled through her tears. "This be yer 'ome, an' it'll be 'ere whene'er ye return."

Then she pushed him toward the trail into the Eldewood.

He traveled with the wood elves for several years and served with the border guards as scout for a few more. He learned the quiet sign from his elf friends and cat speech from a druid with whom he wintered.

He also learned bear speech just in case.

Wherever he traveled, the tawny puma was never far away. Eton called him "Fleet" after the Elvin name "Flerret." He was on the western border when he'd received his last letter from Megan, and it had taken seven months to get to him. He decided to come home.

He woke. Fleet inspected the green path that seemed to go directly north for miles. Eton shouldered his pack, stretched, and grinned. It was a clear morning. He began his run.

The pace was one he knew well, one referred to as a "warrior's pace". It had been developed over many years to allow a man or group of men to travel quickly from one place to another without a stop, yet not tire them beyond their means. Armies could keep this pace for half a day and then storm into battle at journey's end.

The Green Way passed silently under Eton's feet for two days, with brief stops for rest late at night. On the morning of the third day, he saw the King's Way Road, the "White Way" the wood elves spoke of. The Green Way had led him to the half elf's day old camp beside the White Way, such was Eton's desire and the magic of the Green Way.

"Well, Fleet," he whispered, "It looks like we are not that far behind him now."

The young warrior stepped up on the expanse of white and looked toward Seaborne. A grimace crossed his face as he thought of having to return to that city after this prey. One day perhaps, but...

He turned his gaze the other way, toward Catlorian. If this half elf were smart, and he had taken Cully's sword and was in league with the slaving bastards, he might have gone toward the white city and not toward the city he knew Cully would march to—Seaborne.

"He came up here on the road, I'm betting, and went west toward Catlorian."

He followed the King's Road for several miles until the signs told him that his prey went into the wood line. He grinned and followed.

Chapter Thirteen

"What shall we call you, pup?"

"I have no name that I can remember. It never occurred that I would need one, yet 'hey, you' does seem a bit impersonal."

The big man in wolf pelt looked down at the youth as that one settled his pack and sword on his back.

"I see you as a wanderer in search of something stolen or lost. I shall call you Savon'el."

The youth nodded at the use of the Elvin word for wanderer. It was a name as good as any so he grinned at the barbarian and nodded his assent.

"It is a long way, pup, and it won't get closer standing here."

At that, the big man turned and started off at a run. Savon'el had but a moment to realize that, if he were going, he'd better start now. He broke into a run that would allow him to catch the barbarian without using excess energy.

He glanced at Red Wolf more than once during that run and noticed that, though the pace seemed fast for him, the barbarian seemed to be loping along, taking it easy, as if he, at a moment, could simply leave the half elf in his wake. He also noted that though he could run with the lightness and quiet whisper of his Elvin half, the big barbarian moved like smoke in the wind with no evidence of his passing.

Savon'el noticed also, with some apprehension, that the wolf pack had joined them in this run. With Red Wolf at the head, the half elf in the center, and wolves at both flanks and taking up rear guard, it seemed more of a tactical arrangement than a pack moving silently through the woods.

Red Wolf kept his pace slow intentionally, though the wolves growled and chaffed at being held at what would be considered a walking pace. He needed time, first to acclimate the youth to the run and then time to study his new pup. His curiosity was piqued by the demeanor the youth displayed but mostly by the attention paid him by Wanderer. The enigma of Ta'el had popped into and out of Red Wolf's life many times in the past, and most of those ended in knowledge or experience the young barbarian needed in his path. However, this youth…

Red Wolf watched subtly as the young half elf ran. The youth's gait settled in and after a small amount of minor shifting of equipment and armor, the half elf seemed to run in relative comfort. The barbarian was rewarded in his musings as the half elf's right arm, as if of long habit, was held down and straight at his side, the hand closed on something only remembered by the body.

A covey of quail shot up from the path and instantly that right arm rose and the left hand went to the half elf's shoulder. As his hand closed on the hilt of the sword at his back, a troubled look slipped across Savon'el's face. He shrugged, dropped the right arm, and settled back into the run.

"Yes," thought the barbarian, "this one will need help this day."

They ran throughout the morning, past sunrise and into the late morning hours. Red Wolf, as of long custom, allowed his senses to flair beyond the normal that he might more easily watch the half elf.

His senses snapped. They were being watched.

He growled and two wolves broke from the pack, backtracking to pick up on any that might be following. They returned shortly, growling that they'd found nothing, no scent, and no movement.

Red Wolf knew his senses. If the wolves found nothing, the observer was obviously in league with "Demon Traffickers".

The barbarian had been raised to distrust all practitioners of magiks, though he tolerated some of them out of a grudging respect but nothing more. He allowed his mind to drift, his body maintained by his well-honed senses. He stretched that mind into his surroundings to find the unease that lurked there. He found it!

It was cold, malevolent, and malignant, and it tracked not only him but the savon'el! The evil sought the savon'el and, in seeking, came close. The barbarian felt that the half elf, in his strange condition of mind, was defenseless, so with a mental grin he reached out with his mind to the pursuer, diverting it with an ever-so-subtle tap on the shoulder. Then he dove to his "center," the place wherein dwelt his soul.

As he arrived there he felt another, not his name brother and not the evil without but just a curious mind. A mental growl and whoever or whatever was gone. With a mental note to search out this newest interloper, Red Wolf returned to the run and glanced at the savon'el.

"This one has more trouble than he realizes." Then, with a grin, "Anyone who can anger a high level Demon Trafficker as this one has must be all right."

Red Wolf slowed the run just a bit and after they rounded a stand of elms they entered a small clearing that seemed to have been set up as a rest camp. Wood had been stacked neatly to one side of a fire pit, and a long leather pouch lie next to it on the ground. It was as if this place had been prepared for them, yet there was no sign of the preparers.

The barbarian noted that though the youth seemed to be in excellent condition, the events of the day were beginning to show. He took a nut from one of the small pouches at his waist and tossed it.

"Here," he said. "Chew on this. It will help."

Savon'el had seen "battle nut" before, though he could not remember when or where. He knew that he did not like narcotics, yet without some aid at this time he would collapse soon. He popped the nut into his mouth and, as if from practice or some remembrance of others, ground the nut between his teeth and, after depositing it between his cheek and gum, allowed the sweet juices to roll into his throat. He felt the narcotic relax the stretched muscles, wash the pain from his head, and give him, though temporarily, a much-needed infusion of energy.

Red Wolf waited until he could see the nut take effect and tossed the leather pouch to Savon'el.

"Take that and see if you can get us some fresh meat."

The pouch rattled a bit as the half elf caught it, and it took him a moment to realize what this was. The pouch was narrow and twice as long as a man's arm. He opened the tie at the end of the bag and gasped.

Inside the bag was an Elvin-made composite war bow, intricately designed for strength and speed, with over a dozen white-fletched arrows tipped with silver barbs.

The half elf carefully removed the bow and ran his hands over it, as of a lover to the one he loved. His mind may have forgotten, but his hands and body remembered. It took but second for the bow to be strung, and the sure hands and eyes checked each shaft for balance and straightness. He strummed the string and listened to the balanced hum that ran the length of the string.

Suddenly he stopped and, with a look of confusion and question, he stared at the barbarian.

"Don't beat it to death, pup. Accept what you learn or relearn. Don't question, just accept."

Red Wolf settled kindling in the fire pit and grinned.

"It was made by an old friend, Taofey Eth'nerhan, a fletcher of some experience and a Huntsmaster by trade. Those arrows are his trademark and, as your hands have already noticed, they are as perfect as the bow."

Red Wolf struck the tinderbox and, as the dried moss caught, held it below the dry kindling. It caught fire quickly, and after he removed, closed, and put away the tinderbox, he added more kindling and small branches. He glanced up from his chore and grinned at the half elf.

"I am hungry!" he stated sharply enough to awaken the half elf from the dream state he'd entered.

He watched as Savon'el ran toward a field that opened toward the south, his right hand holding the riser level with the ground and his right arm straight and solid. The barbarian growled softly and two wolves disappeared after the young half elf to "watch and protect".

To Savon'el, it was pure joy. The feel of the bow in his hand, the arrows at his back within the pouch that, once folded down onto itself, became a quiver for the beautiful arrows that rested at his left shoulder just below the sword, and the wind in his face made the emptiness in his mind just a bit less empty.

He flushed a rabbit from a brush pile some twenty meters to his left. His left hand, of its own doing, swept an arrow from the quiver, nocked it as the arm bearing the bow brought it up, drew, and fired. One watching would have seen but a blur in one single movement, and it took the rabbit cleanly through its heart, killing it instantly.

Savon'el was amazed at himself until the vision of that old man came to him. He seemed to remember many hours of repetitive teachings of "Do it again! Do it again!" He knew that the old man was his teacher, though he didn't know where or when. He smiled and silently thanked the old man for his patience.

As he went to retrieve the first coney, a second broke from the brush. The same fluid motion netted the same result. The arrow penetrated the neck and severed the spine.

Savon'el collected the coneys, found, cleaned, checked, and restored the two arrows to the quiver, and started back toward the camp. His step was light as was his heart. He'd found a part of himself with a great deal of help from the amazing man who now sat tending the small fire.

He was not prepared for the red demon fire that blazed suddenly from the brush before him. He stood mesmerized by the flame, unable to move, speak, or breathe.

"So, my little bird, you sought escape? Not so! My bounty will ride you to your death! My curse upon you for a year and a day!"

The maniacal laughter sliced through the half elf and cold crept into his soul. Then the brush exploded and sent hot sparks all about him.

Red Wolf had come to his feet when he saw the demon fire and had to watch as the youth stood as still as stone. When the brush exploded, however, Savon'el went into action beating some of the small fires with a handful of brush and stomping on others. He watched as the half elf kicked dirt over the last of the fires and stomped them to death, all the while holding the coneys high above it all. Then, with a glance about, the savon'el continued his way toward the camp as if nothing had happened.

There would be a time, Red Wolf thought, when this one would need his help, and he knew he might not be there when the time came. He knew, however, that now was not that time.

"Not yet, at any rate."

Chapter Fourteen

Melisande pulled the leaflet from her pouch again and read it. The flowing script was familiar to anyone who had the need to read the histories as she had. It read:

WANTED: PERSONS OF SKILL AND DARING TO UNDERTAKE, FOR GAIN AND ADVENTURE, A QUEST FOR KNOWLEDGE.
Seek information at Terillion's apartments, Catlorian.

She'd used the two weeks wisely. She'd thrown herself into the combat training, pushing her known limits and then beyond. She knew she had to know her capabilities in a real situation and that she could, and would, carry her own weight.

She had also spent many late hours poring over books in the clerical library in the temple. She'd convinced herself that to be selected for any adventure, you must prove yourself to be the best or else you'd be left behind as a hindrance. She'd queried her mother, all of her teachers, and her fellows, wringing every drop of clerical information she could possibly garner. She was relentless in her thirst.

Maxim Anteroe had told her to see the world. She determined that she would, yet not as someone's baggage. She would be a companion, a good right arm, and an adventurer in her own right, or nothing!

She needed the action, the adventure, and the experience it would bring. Most of all, she needed the diversion. She would have to fill her time well until Cartellion brought her son to Catlorian.

On the day prior to her Coming to Power ceremony, Melisande found herself outside of the old sage's apartment.

Terillion was the oldest living sage on this continent, perhaps the world. He was said to have, within the walls of his apartments, the collective history of this world dating back to the creation. No one knew where the old man got his information, but its veracity had always proven true.

Melisande paused, took a deep breath, and knocked.

"Yes? Yes? Well, what is it?"

The cracked, wheedling voice from within made Melisande think of the poor man always pestered by naughty little children.

"Young pups always bothering me when I need to be working."

Melisande heard the mumbling, punctuated by each step as the man made his way to the door. The bolt snapped back and the small man's head, sparsely covered with wispy white hair, popped around the doorjamb as the door came open.

"Yes? Yes? I haven't all day you know. What is it?"

"Are you the sage who wishes to hire adventurers?"

"What? What? Adventurers, you say? Whatever for?"

Melisande smiled her sweetest smile at the old man and sighed.

"You've placed notices up all over Catlorian that state that you seek people to retrieve information for you. Remember?"

"Of course I remember!" the ancient snapped. Then, "Uh...remember what?"

Melisande sighed again, but before she could explain, a light seemed to go off in the old man's eyes.

"Oh, yes indeed! I remember now! Yes. Yes. Oh, do come in."

Then he closed the door in her face.

The young cleric shook her head and smiled. "This will not be easy," she thought as she again knocked.

"Yes? Yes? What is it?"

The little man's head popped back around the door.

"All of these interruptions! How's a man supposed to get any work done around here?" As he noticed the girl, "Yes? May I help you?"

"You asked me in, then closed the door in my face."

The old man looked genuinely confused. "Do I know you?"

"I just spoke to you about the notices you have posted all over the city!"

"Notices? What notices?"

Melisande was not known for her patience, though she had been working on it. However, this little man stood very close to the edge of what patience she still maintained. She closed her eyes, took a deep breath, and tried again.

"According to the advertisement you placed, the mission was to retrieve information or knowledge and return it to you for just payment."

"Information? Knowledge? Oh! Yes! Please, do come in!"

When the door was again thrust closed, Melisande was ready. She reached out a strong hand and stopped the door short of closing and slipped her booted foot in to keep it open. She pushed the door ajar.

"Do you wish me in or out?"

The old man turned from his slow walk down the hall, a strange look on his face.

"Come in? Whatever for?"

That was it! Melisande no longer stood on the cliff, but dove over the side!

"To get information, from *you*, for this excursion *you* are putting together and hiring adventurers to fulfill! To 'Quest for knowledge,' as you put it! Now do you remember?"

"Well," he said softly, "you needn't get all hot about it! Come in! Come in!"

He tried to push the door closed, looked, and then backed up. "Oh! Excuse me! Do come in and, if you please, close the door."

Melisande closed the door behind her and followed the little man through the dimly lit hallway into a room that resembled more of a warehouse than the massive library the cleric had thought to find. There were boxes of odds and ends, books stacked five feet high, books and papers stacked haphazardly on shelves and tables, and a large black sword that dripped blackness from its blade into the wood of the floor where it leaned, as a seeming afterthought, against the far wall in the corner.

The old man went directly to a little desk, which sat in the middle of the vast jumble, and sat. He picked a pen from the dozen in a holder, dipped it in his inkwell, and began copying, quite efficiently, from one book into what seemed to be a journal.

The young cleric made her way to the small stool that sat across the desk from him and sat. She waited for quite awhile until she finally decided that the man had forgotten her, and she just here in front of him!

"Well?"

At that, the old man threw his quill straight up into the air, fell backward off of his stool, and looked up at Melisande in what could only be described as fear. After a moment, the man took a ragged breath and rose, righting his stool as he did so.

"What are you doing in here? What do you mean by sneaking up on an old man and scaring him half to death? Well?!"

"I have been sitting here the entire time, sir," she bit off slowly.

"You have? Well, who let you in?"

"YOU DID!" Melisande all but screamed as she came to her feet.

"I did? But why?"

The puzzled look on the old man's face finally pushed her beyond her patience. This was Terillion, a name synonymous with great wisdom, knowledge, and intelligence. She was not about to sit here and be run in merry little circles by this man for his sport!

"Look, friend," she stated through clinched teeth, "I think you are smarter than you are trying to make me believe. You could not possibly be this scatter-brained, yet still be the great Terillion, the greatest sage in all of Catlor!"

"My dear girl," he replied as he pulled his stool back to the desk and sat, "A man can attain the name of 'great' simply by reading something and writing it at the same time. I don't remember all of the information I transcribe! There is far too much of it, as you can see if you just look about this place!"

"Then you don't need adventurers?"

"Oh, yes. I do, indeed. I may be a bit distracted at times, but I do remember some things, if only eventually."

His quirky smile caused the girl to grin.

"Then, good sir, please tell me what it's all about."

"Well…" said he, as he scratched at his wispy beard. His notes were ignored as he studied the girl in the bright yellow cloak. "I need a group to go to a specific location. An ancient sorcerer's tower, so called 'Black Tower,' up close to the source of the Lost Souls River. There are some writings there, I believe, and some ancient books. Plus, if they are found, human teeth, and no, you cannot have a reason for my wanting them. The teeth must be human, not human-*oid*!"

"Human teeth?" muttered the girl in distaste.

"Purely reference, my dear. There have long been references to teeth and magic, but human teeth are somewhat of the necessity. Otherwise the entire study is a waste of time and, as you see, I haven't much of that left!"

His chuckle brought her grin back.

"The keep was once, I believe, the center of the old death god cult with all of those Saladins and such like hanging about. Why, I believe if my memory has not totally deserted me, the Lords Belmont and Cartellion both started there many years ago, though I'm not certain why they left."

He slipped from the stool and stepped to a pile of books close to the black sword. Starting from the top, he began to first, look in each and then, when it obviously did not hold the information sought, he tossed it aside with a mumbled "No!" Finally, close to the bottom of the second stack, he found a tome that must have been at least ten inches thick. He thumbed through it quickly and ran his finger down a list he found on one of the pages.

"Hah!" he shouted, startling the girl just a bit. "Here it is! Cartellion was just a young buck of a Saladin when he was brought here by Belmont."

"I wonder why he was here?" the girl mused, more to herself than aloud.

"Why, it seems that the old keep was the original temple of Death himself! That's where the whole thing started!"

"Where is the temple now?"

"Why, right here in Catlorian. Cartellion built the cult to such a large concern that it could no longer be contained within that tower. He moved the whole mess here. It is said that he moved in such a hurry that a lot of references and such were left. Cartellion took only the latest editions of any reference material left in the tower."

"Do you think that there may be any information left by him of any value?"

"That I'm not sure of. However, the tower was there when Belmont and his cronies moved in, ancient in its construction. It has been intimated that it was there *before* the Mage War! If that is so..."

"Then, maybe we *will* find something of value!"

"The original owner, that 'Sorcerer', left it many, many years before Belmont and his cult found it. Now it stands vacant, as far as I have been able to ascertain."

"So anything is possible?"

"Oh, quite! Quite! The tower itself is supposed to be in good repair, but it is said that some of the sorcerer's magic is loose within. For that reason alone those who go must be of staunch character and under no illusions."

Melisande fell quiet for a moment. Then she asked the question she really wanted to ask.

"May I come back later to research more into Cartellion? I have some questions that need answers. Would you mind?"

"Of course not, dear girl."

His business was selling information. If this pretty young thing wished information, he'd provide—at a cost, naturally.

"What would you like to know, my dear?"

"Part of it deals with some lost temple records. That, if you like, we will look into at some later time."

"Tell me what temple and I will start compiling information as early as tomorrow, if that is correct?"

"That would be wonderful! The Temple of Freya. We've had some dealings with Cartellion's family and—"

"Of course! Cartellion chose that temple some months ago for a child. I remember now. He contracted with some lass at the temple for a son. Nice young man, now that I remember it."

"Cartellion?"

The question came out as incredulous, but Melisande quickly changed her look of shock to one of slight interest. The old man's response, however, sent her looking for support.

"No! No! The lad. His son!"

"Beg your pardon?" she choked out.

"Oh, yes. I was on a plane Cartellion called… uh…Shadow, I think. I was there to pick up some other references when I met them."

"Them?" she responded in a choked whisper. "Them who?"

"Why, the boy and his father. Cartellion had the boy taken there for his early training. He seems a strong and intelligent boy, much like his father."

Melisande was dumbfounded. Cartellion had whisked the baby to another plane and one, it seemed, with a quicker time line than this one. If what she now suspected was true, it would not be too much of a stretch to have her meet her thirteen to sixteen-year-old son, less than six months after he was actually born! Her anger was starting again, and she knew she would have to learn to control it.

"How would one get there, to Shadow, I mean, should the desire present itself?"

"Well, if you could not find a gate, then die. Either will put you there in one form or another."

Melisande had no intention of being the one to die. Just after the thought was formed, the implication struck her that she had had the thought without a qualm. Her anger fueled the deadly intent.

"No, the boy is a strapping youth, built much like his father. His name is... Let's see, what was it? Begins with a 'V', I think. Vegnor? Vagelin? Veknes?" The old man sighed and shook his head. "It was something like that. A name only Cartellion would choose."

Suddenly he sat up straight on his stool, a grin of wonder on his lips.

"Oh, yes! They called him Vrek! Named after some demon his father knows, no doubt."

"So my son's name is Vrek," she mumbled. Then, aloud, "That's a horrible name!"

"Maybe so, but it fits. The boy has a terrible temper. Even his father cannot control him when the anger strikes."

"Well, I would not have chosen it. What does he look like?"

"Oh, he's a strapping big fellow, for a boy. A bit over five feet already, with brown hair and black eyes."

That old anger was back. Black eyes. His father's eyes. There would be time enough, still, to see what Cartellion had done to her son and, hopefully, undo when she returned. For now...

"Are there any other volunteers?"

"Yes. There is a wolf and a half elf. Kind of forgetful, or so I'm told, but perfectly suited for this."

"Did you say a wolf?"

"Yes. Yes. A wolf. You must go to the Adventurer's Guild in two days when it reopens—"

"The new tavern? Why there and not—"

"Just listen! A wolf will come for you. Yes, he'll come for you at the Adventurer's Guild. Yes. Yes. A red wolf."

Chapter Fifteen

Red Wolf tried, with the power of his will, to break through the wall that guarded the youth's memory. After the half elf stomped out the strange fire, he came back into camp as if nothing out of the ordinary had transpired and began the process of cleaning and spitting the coneys. After but a very few minutes, the barbarian had to stop. The block was too strong. He silently cursed Wanderer and vowed to stay on his guard.

"Catlorian may hold the key to this mystery," he thought. "Maybe Brea can help."

With a mental nod, he tossed another branch onto the small fire. The half elf returned the arrows and war bow to the pouch with gentle hands and tied the flap down securely. Then, reluctantly, he held it out to the barbarian.

"Thank you, my friend, for the loan of this weapon. It is truly a work of art and love. That much I read in the feel and balance. That same feeling has allowed my body to remind me that I have the skill to use it. For that, and other things, I thank you."

"Keep it," came the reply as the barbarian waved the offering away. "I have no use for it and it seems that it fits you better anyway."

"But—"

"No buts, pup."

Red Wolf leaned toward the half elf and held him with his eyes. Such was the barbarian's power that the savon'el could not extricate himself from that gaze.

"If you must know, I am a student of the art of perception. You, you must admit, are a bit of a puzzle. I love a challenge. I will not tell you how or why, but I sent for this bow specifically because of the way you move and because I hate to be wrong." The last was said with a slight grin.

The youth looked down at the case, then at the barbarian, and opened his mouth to say something, but he ended with his eyes on the case again.

"No, pup, don't thank me. It could have just as easily been a mistake. It may still prove wrong, but I do not believe so. I have a belief that all warriors should have the weapons they are familiar with, and that makes the group stronger. That sword, for instance."

The youth glanced at the strange sword that now rested in his lap.

"That may or may not be yours in truth. However, it fits you and I choose to believe the former. Now, let us roast some rabbit, rest, and sleep. Tomorrow will be a hard day, no doubt."

The conversation fell to Red Wolf's tales of his travels and friends he'd made. They ate and finally the savon'el rolled into the too-large cloak and drifted into tired slumber.

Red Wolf sniffed the night air and growled to his friends to keep a light sleep. His senses sharp, he felt the danger that would come with the dawn. He set himself into "lotus," brought his talents to bear, and slipped into trance. This would allow him the rest he needed, yet would allow his senses to flare. He rested.

It was early morning before sunrise and the smell brought him to full awake as nothing else could. It was the stench of death, of rotting corpses, of deteriorated human meat. He growled and felt the wolves retreat into the woods. Their sense of smell was totally overpowered by the smell that got stronger and stronger with each passing second.

He nudged the savon'el but found that one wide-awake. The half elf lay still, a habit of long practice, though he did not know when that practice may have begun, and allowed his senses to reconnoiter the darkness.

Then the sound of trudging steps and clanking armor reached them, and the smell grew unbearable.

Savon'el came to his feet as the first of the rotting corpses broke toward him from the woods. Suddenly his sword was in his hand.

Red Wolf growled deep in his throat for two reasons. One, to let the wolves know that they were to stay away. Two, because he was angry. A demon trafficker had raised men of honor from their eternal slumber and set them to destruction. His two-handed war club found his hands and he leapt toward the two death-knights that, at that same moment, broke from the wood line.

Savon'el had but a moment to survey the attacker, the red spider on the rusted breastplate, and the red glow from the eye sockets of the skull within the helmet. His mind remembered the emblem, though from where was lost in the tangled mess of his memories. All of this took less than a second and the half elf was fighting for his life.

The warrior that Savon'el faced at one time was skilled, but now his movements were stiff, as if a marionette in the hands of a bizarre puppeteer. As the half elf brought an under-hand slash across the body of the attacker, that one spun and brought his sword down, hilt first, into the scale armor that covered the half elf's shoulder. Then it was a nightmare of slash and parry, strike and counterstrike, until the undead knight brought his sword down toward Savon'el's head in an over-hand slash, only to have it parried at the last moment by the half elf's flashing counter.

What happened next was strange.

As the swords came together, the cross-guards locked. The stench from the decomposed body gave the savon'el all the strength he needed to wrench his sword free. At the same moment, the death-knight yanked on his with all of his supernatural strength.

When the swords came free, the unnatural forces exerted threw the half elf to the ground with his sword embedded deep into the ground next to him. Without a thought, he leapt back to his feet, but as his hand found the hilt of his sword, his eyes snapped back to his foe. He froze.

The death-knight stood and seemed to gaze at the sword that protruded from his chest. How his sword came to rest, up to the hilt, through the red spider emblem on his breastplate would be a mystery forever, but the result was stranger. The undead warrior, who could not be killed because he was already dead, fell with a clatter and never moved again.

Savon'el knew.

He turned quickly toward the barbarian and found, to his horror, the barbarian's club lay discarded on the ground. Then he saw the skill of the warrior of the Wolf Clan as he parried the swords of both death knights with but the flat of his hands.

Savon'el knew he could not help, for somewhere in the back of his mind he realized that there, about the barbarian, was his killing ground. To set foot there was to invite death. But he could help in a different way.

"Red Wolf," he yelled, "kill the red spider!"

The big warrior was enraged. His trusted weapon had failed him and, after bashing one of these demons in the chest with it, he had simply released it. Now he used every bit of his skill to keep these rusted weapons from his body until he could find a target. As the half elf's words snapped into his awareness, his right hand curled into a claw. His left parried the sword that came for his head and his right shattered the armor at the death knight's chest as if made of glass. The hand passed through thick metal, and dead meat and shards flew from the hole as he withdrew the hand.

Savon'el remembered something about an old man and the "claws of the eagle" as the death knight flew backward a good six feet and shattered as he struck the ground.

As if in a single motion, the barbarian pivoted, intercepted the second attacker, brushed away the sword, and drove his left, now in the same claw as the right, through the breastplate with such force as to shatter it into several small pieces. The death knight crumpled to the ground as if a rag doll.

The big barbarian tossed back his head and let out a howl of triumph and contempt that brought chills up the spine of his half elf companion. Red Wolf glanced over at the savon'el and grinned a grin of draining adrenalin and chuckled. Then he took the helms of each of the two death knights and dumped what was left of their heads into the fire. He sat in lotus with his hands raised upward until the skulls were burned to dust. It didn't take long, for the skulls were very old indeed. Then he glanced back at the savon'el.

The half elf stood, the hand-and-a-half sword held limply in his left hand while the seven-inch gash in his right bicep bled through the hole in his armor. The stench, loathing, exertion, and the nightmare result of this encounter took its toll. He vomited.

Red Wolf waited. He knew he could help, but he also knew that there was a time for it. That time was not now.

The savon'el wiped his lips on the back of his hand and looked from the corpse to the barbarian. At the big warrior's nod, the young half elf trudged toward the fire.

The barbarian removed the sleeve from the half elf's armored right arm and, with ointments and herbs from his pouch, bound the wound. Then the warrior handed the savon'el a small flask.

If the contents had been Ravagar Wine, the youth would have drunk it nonetheless. Though it was not that potent wine and he did not recognize the taste, it soon rejuvenated him.

Red Wolf grinned as the draught took effect in the pup. Then a cackling laugh drifted up from the armor of the one Savon'el had battled. He went to it and growled. He yanked the rusted sword from the breastplate and drove his hand down toward the red spider emblem. He came away with the emblem in his hand, and the breastplate shattered on the ground. He wrapped the emblem with a piece of cloth from another pouch and handed it to Savon'el.

"We might be able to get some information on this emblem in Catlorian. Whatever, or whoever, tracks us may find us there as they found us here. In Catlorian we may find some of the answers that are missing from your mind."

The big barbarian stepped back to one of the bodies and lifted a pouch he'd noticed earlier. Inside were two of the most perfect rubies he'd seen, easily worth two hundred gold apiece.

The savon'el looked from the grin on the barbarian's face to the pile of armor that was the death knight he'd faced. No pouch. Nothing.

"Just my luck," he thought with a grin. "No memory, no warning, a vanquished foe that shouldn't have existed, and nothing to show for it but pain and a hole in my memory."

Then he glanced back at the big barbarian and the war bow that lay in its pouch by the fire and smiled. Okay, maybe "nothing" was a bit too strong.

Red Wolf returned to his place by the fire and dropped into lotus.

"Watch for me, friend," he said to the astonished savon'el. "I need a little time to heal."

Then he drifted into a trance.

Savon'el was astonished. Here this amazing warrior had taken on two of these undead knights bare-handed and suffered only a few minor cuts and bruises, yet he trusted a stranger with watching out for him as he drifted into a trance, unprotected. Then this man, this wolf brother, warrior, and denizen of the woods, called him "friend." Damn right he'd watch and fight the King of Hades if necessary!

Red Wolf dove to his "place" and the strangeness of before was back, but this time he knew what it was. The tendrils of telepathy followed whomever out when Red Wolf's sharp growl roared into existence. The taste of this one was not of an enemy, thought the barbarian, but whatever the reason he did not like the intrusion and vowed to find the one responsible.

It was full morning before the two were ready to start again. Red Wolf checked and rebound Savon'el's wounds, they settled their packs, and they were off.

This last camp was but a few miles east of Catlorian, and Red Wolf had consciously paralleled the King's Way in his haste to get the savon'el to Catlorian. They broke from the trees a bit over fifteen miles from the Eastern Gate, and Savon'el got his first glimpse of the fabled hub of an entire civilization.

The city of Catlorian was built with a precision long forgotten by the present inhabitants. Though some dwarves claimed to have seen the workmanship of some of their ancestors in the stone of the hundred-foot high walls, none were sure of the city's origin. No seam marred the surface, nor would stains form on the stone. The walls stood in the middle of a great plain, a white beacon for the traveler, a place of refuge for the homeless, and the center of trade on the continent of Catlor.

The walls, five of them in all, stood thirty miles to a side and formed, if viewed from above, a perfect pentagon. The main streets of the city added to the design by forming a perfect star with the Mage's Tower, one hundred and twenty feet tall, at the very center of the city. The gates opened to each corner, and for all intents and purposes the city made a perfect pentagram.

The King's Constables, the law for the entire city, guarded these gates with five men each and carried out the rules with no mercy and with no prejudice. The King of Catlorian, Jon DeLonge, ruled the city and the region with a strong, fair hand and with an eye for continued trade and justice. All, if not loved, respected him.

Red Wolf glanced back at the savon'el and grinned. Then with a howl of pure delight, freedom, and animal abandon, he stretched his pace to his normal running speed.

Savon'el, who ran at a good pace—a pace his Elvin half would have considered fast—could not keep pace with the man born to run the wild woods with the wolves. The young half elf was resigned to arrive when he arrived and watched as the barbarian's form quickly and silently crossed the bridge and diminished in size.

Three outside and two inside guards, with a captain for each, guarded the gates. One of the guards saw the barbarian coming and called for the captain, while the other two joined him and leveled their halberds to bar the way.

The captain came out of the gatehouse wiping the ale from his lips with the back of his sleeve. He squinted toward the oncoming Red Wolf and then grinned. He placed his hands on his hips and waited.

"Hey, Wolf!" he yelled when the barbarian came into earshot. "What's the hurry? You late for a party?"

Then he laughed.

The guards raised their weapons and stepped out of the barbarian's path as he came to a walk and then a stop next to the captain and, with a strong handshake, joined the laugh. He glanced back the way he'd come and saw that the savon'el hadn't slowed down or stopped, but was coming on with sheer stubbornness.

"Just showing a young pup of a half elf what running is all about."

"Yeah," said the big captain with a grin. "Looks like yer showin' off is all. Kinda like the time ya burned down th' brothel, eh?"

"*Me*? That wasn't me! It wasn't me who fell out of the upstairs window and..."

The conversation degenerated into pleasant jabs from one to another.

The other guards listened to this banter until Savon'el arrived and leveled their weapons at his approach. The captain slapped his friend on the shoulder and moved to his men.

"Hey, Jake, he's with me."

Jake glanced back at the barbarian and grinned. He waved the guards back and said "Welcome," to the out of breath half elf. Then he turned back to Red Wolf.

"Wolf, there's supposed ta be some big doin's down at the new tavern tonight."

"Where?" came the question as the big captain laid a massive hand on the barbarian's shoulder.

"The place is called 'The Adventurer's Guild' and Brea will prob'ly be playin'. Knowin' you, that's where you'll be, but do me a favor. Don't start nothin' tonight. I got the duty 'til daylight, and I'd just as soon have a quiet tour as have ta come down there an' clean up your mess. What do ya say? Please?"

"What? Me cause trouble?" said Red Wolf incredulously. "I wouldn't dream of doing anything of the sort!"

"Now, Wolf. I know ya from way back. Me an' you have been known ta cause a ruckus from time ta time. Just try an' give me a break t'night. Huh?"

"I'll try," said the resigned barbarian, "if everyone else does."

The poor guardsman gazed skyward. He knew, just as surely as dawn turns to dusk, that before the evening came to full circle something would happen that would ruin his night of duty, and the man called Red Wolf would have had something to do with it.

"Just give me the coppers an go on in, me boyo."

Red Wolf drew the coins from his pouch and tossed them to his friend. Then he glanced at the half elf. Something whipped across the youth's face. A remembrance, it seemed. Savon'el stared at the burly guard with a question in his eyes.

"What is it, pup?"

The half elf shook his head. Why could he not place that memory, and what had triggered it? He knew he should ask something, but he could not remember what. It was so damned frustrating!

"Nothing, I guess. It's just that…" Then, with a sigh, "Nothing."

The guardsman took the offered silver piece and counted back the change.

"That's three coppers for entrance an' a copper for money changin'." Then, quietly, "Stick with the Wolf, boyo. He'll show ya a good time an' take care you ain't damaged much ta boot."

The streets of Catlorian were alive with people of all shapes and sizes, each going from one place to another or nowhere in particular. This is ever the curse, and blessing, of any large city. There is so much to offer with space at a premium.

The press of people didn't bother the savon'el as much as he thought it would. Though he felt more at home in the open, he found a strange familiarity in the hustle and bustle. As they passed a fish market, the smell caused him to draw up short. Where was the smell he should remember? The salt of the sea? What memory or memories were these that were making his head hurt again?

Then he remembered his new friend's advice.

"Don't question, just accept."

The big barbarian headed straight for Sage Terillion's apartments. It was the sage who had penned the message brought by Wanderer, and it was Terillion who, for some reason, needed Red Wolf's help. That would be his first stop, then on to the fun.

On the way, they passed the slave market. Red Wolf stopped for a moment to admire the three females chained to the post in the center of the raised stage.

"What say ye, good sirs?" came the wheedling voice of the barker. "This one's but seventeen years and a virgin, by the gods. She'll be good for the trainin' for the lucky man that purchase this fine specimen. I do, by law, gotta warn ya that she been judged a thief, so watch yourself."

The banter went on that way while the men, and a few women, bid on the girls. Savon'el turned away in anger.

"What's wrong, pup?"

"These slavers sell their wares with impunity here. I thought you said that this was the hub of civilization?"

"It is, pup. Didn't you hear the man say she'd been judged a thief? Bet on it! The man is not a 'slaver,' as you put it. He's an official of the city government."

He laid a hand on the savon'el's shoulder and turned him around.

"Listen, pup. If every thief were sentenced to death, that would be wrong. Some steal because they must eat. I'm not saying it's right, but there is a reason. Now, they could lock them up, charge everybody a healthy tax, and keep them in a style for which they have not earned, but is that fair?

"That young lady will be sold to someone, maybe as a whore or as a helper for someone's wife. Whatever! But she will be cared for, one way or another. She won't be a burden to the taxpayers, and she, I believe, will have a punishment to fit her crime. These people are not like the dealers in flesh at Seaborne. There are laws that govern how these 'slaves' are to be treated and for how long! This is more humane if you think about it."

At the mention of Seaborne, a thread of memory slipped through, but it was gone just as quickly.

"I can see the point, but I still don't like it."

Red Wolf led the way to the door at the end of the alley and knocked.

"Wait a minute! Wait a minute! I'm coming! I'm coming!"

The high-pitched, cracked voice came from somewhere beyond the closed door. After several catches were released, the door was cracked enough for the old man's head to pop through.

"Well? What is it? I haven't all day, you know! Young pups always bothering a poor old man. Yes? What is it?"

Savon'el heard the low growl start in the depths of the barbarian's chest at the word "pups" and laid a hand on warrior's arm. Red Wolf glanced at the young half elf, grinned, and turned his attention on the old sage.

"You sent a message to me, old one, by way of Anteroe."

"A message? Let's see now." Then, his finger on his scraggly chin, he glanced back at the barbarian and added, "Who are you?"

"I am called Red Wolf."

"Red Wolf? Oh, yes! Red Wolf! Yes! Yes, I did, didn't I! Oh, please, do come in and bring your friend. He is with you, is he not? Maxim said something about a half elf, but it seems I've forgotten... Wait! That's it! It seems that *he's* forgotten! Please, do come in."

"Yes, sage," said the barbarian as he and Savon'el entered the apartment and closed the door. "He is a friend and good companion. You may be able to help him, if you will."

"Yes. Yes," said the old man petulantly, waving a hand to ward off distractions. "Later. Later. Down to business. I need someone to lead a party of adventurers on a quest. Yes, a quest for information. You will travel to the source of the River of Souls to the Black Keep of Radagast. Inside you will find some rare books, publications, papers, and possibly artifacts I should like to study. Among those artifacts may be found human teeth. I should like to have as many of these teeth as you and your party can find. However, I will not pay for them unless they are *human*. I'll not pay for any other sort."

Red Wolf scratched his chin and glanced at the savon'el. The half elf shrugged and the barbarian grinned.

"I will think on this mission, sage. However, you could speed my decision with a little information, if you please?"

"What is it?"

"What image does a red spider bring to mind?"

"Red spider? Red spider. Where did you see a red spider?"

"On the armor of three men sent to attack us, only the men in the armor were dead already. All that is left of them is a piece of armor bearing the likeness of a red spider."

"You have it with you?" asked the old man excitedly.

Red Wolf nodded to the half elf, who removed the piece of steel from his pack.

"Well, what do you know?" stated the sage as he took the piece of metal from Savon'el and turned it over in his hands. "This is not of the Black Sorcerer's Tower, as Radagast is sometimes called, but you never know. I would be surprised if you did not find some information on these devils within, being undead and all."

He handed the piece of steel back to the half elf and turned to the barbarian.

"Well, will you take the job?"

Red Wolf rubbed his chin and glanced at the half elf.

"What's in it for me?"

"Hmmmm."

The old sage looked the barbarian over while he pulled at his scraggly beard. He decided that haggling with this one would be counterproductive and came out with his bottom line.

"You will be paid, as leader of this quest, at a somewhat higher rate. Let's say one hundred thirty-five gold and one thousand gold for every human tooth recovered. All expenses for preparation, the mission, and return will be included. Each member of your party will receive one hundred gold and a ten percent share of the teeth. Agreed?"

"Let's say that all members share in the recovered teeth equally. I will not take a share, as I want nothing to do with these teeth at all. I would, however, like to replenish my stock of herbs and poultices from your stock at your expense."

"Done!"

The old one grinned and led Red Wolf to his pantry. As the barbarian walked through the extensive storehouse, pausing at this or that container, he questioned the sage.

"Who else?"

Savon'el dropped into a chair and let the weariness wash over him. The rigors of the night, the run, and this constant pounding headache finally caught up with him.

Red Wolf felt the half elf sag and, as he glanced back, saw the bone weariness drag him down. He watched as the half elf leaned forward and, with his elbows on his knees, held his head in both hands.

"I've a cleric," said the old man as he kept mental track of what the barbarian took for a final tally later. "She's asked to go. Strange, that. I've never felt so much raw anger from a cleric of her order before. Not for me, of course, but someone has made a deadly enemy."

"Is she competent?"

The old sage placed a thoughtful finger to his pursed lips.

"I believe she will do. She seems to have been hurt or betrayed, and the anger seems to ride on her sleeve, but I believe she will do. Yes, she'll do."

The barbarian closed his pouches and the two returned to the old sage's sitting room. Terillion looked down at the half elf and asked the barbarian the question softly.

"Is he going with you?"

"I don't know as yet."

The barbarian knelt before the savon'el and tapped him on the knee. Savon'el raised blood-shot eyes to the barbarian, though the grin came as well. Red Wolf placed a berry, blue in color but with red stripes throughout, in his hand.

"Chew it, pup. Swallow the juices but not the pulp. It will help. Just chew."

The half elf popped the berry into his mouth without a thought. After but a few moments of chewing the bitter fruit, the weariness slipped away. He knew it still lingered out there beyond the effects of the berry, but he was, for now, refreshed. He nodded his thanks and stood.

"Do you want to join me on this little jaunt, friend?" asked the barbarian as he rose to his feet as well.

"Why not?" he thought to himself. Then, aloud, "If you don't mind the company, I might find more of myself as the days go, as long as you don't feel that I may put the party at risk. I fear that the powers that track me wish me ill and will go through anyone to reach me. I fear that my demons may put the party at jeopardy."

"We will deal with that when the time comes, pup. For now, you are counted as companion and member in full standing."

The last was said as the barbarian laid a strong hand on the half elf's shoulder. He grinned and turned back to Terillion.

"Old one, I would ask to cast the fates before I go."

"Certainly, friend."

Red Wolf carefully removed the small velvet bag from his pouch, emptied the carved tokens into his hand, and sat on the floor. His body slipped quietly into lotus and he cleared his mind. He began to shake the tokens in his cupped hands softly and gently as his mind slipped deeper into the softness of trance. When the moment arrived, his hands parted and the tokens fell to the floor. Red Wolf came out of his trance quickly at the startled inflow of breath from the wise old sage. He glanced at the sage, then at the tokens, and then back to the old man.

"The Rites of Manhood have been stolen from him and must be fulfilled," stated the old one. "I know that you cast the fates for yourself, friend, and I have never seen this before, but these tokens have fallen for him, not you!"

Terillion looked into the barbarian's troubled eyes and knew that the fear was not for himself, but the "pup" he'd taken as his friend. Then he glanced toward the savon'el.

"Look," he said softly.

Red Wolf followed the old one's gaze and found the half elf transfixed, his eyes for the token on the floor before the barbarian. Red Wolf let his eyes fall to the floor before him. The only token standing was one in the shape of a white wolf, and it faced the savon'el. The barbarian raked the tokens up and placed them back into his bag, then glanced back at the savon'el.

The half elf had been drawn to the figure of the white wolf; for some reason his mind locked on that figure as if his life depended on it. As the barbarian's hand took the tokens from view, it seemed that something in the half elf's mind snapped as well and he raised his eyes to his friend.

"Come, pup," said the barbarian as he pushed the half elf to the door. "I think a healer, a few drinks, some food, and an early bed will do you good."

Terillion let the half elf out first, but as the barbarian went to follow, the old man grabbed his arm.

"I believe Brea may be able to help this one, if she will. She has been rather distracted of late and may not be reachable. However, she is playing at the new tavern. The 'Adventurer's Guild' it's called. I have a feeling that... No. Never mind."

Then the old one let the barbarian out and closed the door behind him.

"Hold up, pup," said Red Wolf softly.

Savon'el stopped and turned back to his friend as that one removed the red wolf pelt from his shoulders and, after folding it reverently, placed it into his pack. Then he took a light gray cloak out of the pack and let it straighten itself before he draped it over his shoulders. At the half elf's questioning look, he grinned.

"The pelt of Red Wolf is known throughout Catlorian, and I am no stranger to...ah...strife within the walls of this city. I do not wish to endanger my traveling cloak through some...inadvertent accident."

At the half elf's strange look, the barbarian laughed loud and long. Before long, the half elf joined in and they both headed for the main street.

Catlorian had its main thoroughfares and side streets. The side streets were generally sparsely populated with traffic, but the main avenues were packed.

The barbarian moved with grace through the crush of bodies hurriedly trying to get from point "A" to point "B" in as little time as possible. However, the half elf had to push his way through like a man walking through knee-deep mud.

Suddenly the crowd surged away and the half elf slammed into black plate armor.

"You club-footed oaf," came the soft yet angry tones from within the black helm. "You insult me with your jostling. Stand and give me satisfaction."

The man in black armor did not hurry. His hand found the hilt of the great black sword at his back. The eyes behind the helm glowed red as the hand slowly began to draw the black sword from its sheath.

Strangely, Savon'el recognized the sword for what it was. It was a "Soul Reaver". It fed on the souls it set free and could only be wielded by a High Saladin. How did he know this? That would have to wait, for he knew he was in trouble.

"Well, coward, I see you have no stomach for apologies. Will you fight for your honor or no?"

The half elf had backed away from the big black clad knight, but at the word "coward" he stopped, narrowed his eyes, and his left hand reached for the sword at his back.

The Saladin smiled a deadly smile behind his helm and resumed pulling the dark, dripping blade slowly from its sheath.

Suddenly a huge hand fell on the half elf's shoulder and a cheerful, though gravelly, voice cut through the tension.

"Say, Wolf, who's yer friend?"

The black armored knight obviously did not like whoever was standing behind him, but the savon'el could have kissed him at that point.

"You have no business interfering here, Stone."

The voice was soft and clear, though filled with menace.

Savon'el had not taken his eyes from the Saladin or his sword. However, when that knight looked far above his own head, he had to put a face to the graveled voice.

The man was huge. His hand felt like it weighed a ton, yet it seemed small for the man. He was dressed all in green, steel-studded leathers, and his eyes held contempt for the black armored Saladin before him.

"Take your ungodly sword elsewhere, Cartellion. It will not feed easily here today. You know the rules."

The High Saladin nodded and his helm tilted toward the savon'el. The red glow within dissipated as the black sword was once again seated in its sheath. Something drew Savon'el's eyes to the slits in the black helm.

"Our business is not finished, coward," said the Saladin softly. "I shall have satisfaction. One day you and I will meet in Honor Combat, but for now I will wait. It seems you have friends who crave your presence for a little while longer. Savor the time, half elf. You have very little left you."

He turned and, where he walked, all parted before him and none touched him in passing.

"Nasty attitude of late, that Cartellion." stated the big ranger. "Been that way for a while. Not much of a welcome, what?"

With his hand still on the half elf's shoulder, he extended his other to the barbarian.

"Where have ya been, friend?" he asked as his large hand enveloped that of the barbarian.

"I've been around. How long has he been here?"

"Don't really know, but Ah hear he's off again soon. Ah say good riddance." Then, to the half elf, "Try to steer clear of him, bud. He's been lookin' for a fight for a bit now, and Ah wouldn't want to be the one he picked today."

Savon'el nodded as the big man squeezed the shoulder and lifted his hand. Red Wolf nodded and looked down the street.

"We're off to the new tavern."

"The Adventurer's Guild?"

"Yeah, that's it. You coming?"

"Not now, Wolf. Ah'm off on an errand, though Ah might see ya there later."

"I'll watch for you and keep a pint cold just in case."

"You do that."

With that, the big ranger slid through the crowd with the same grace as Red Wolf: all expedient motion.

"Well, pup, I hear a brew calling me and you look like you need one."

Savon'el didn't need to be asked twice. He needed a drink all right. Several.

The Adventurer's Guild was the newest establishment in Catlorian, refurbished recently by an adventurer for other adventurers. The furnishings had been induced to repair themselves overnight if broken, the very best kind of insurance a proprietor could have for a business of this sort. If you fill a room the size of a city block with all types of adventurous beings bored with inactivity, fights are bound to erupt. Fredrick, the cleric, had done well in asking for help from the Mage's Guild.

As with everything else in the new tavern, the method of payment was innovative. The half-ogre, Grek, or Grouch as most called him, dispensed the liquor and food, but you were on your honor to pay for your order by throwing the cost into several large casks placed strategically throughout the tavern. The type of people likely to frequent the establishment would frown on anyone disrupting the possibility of good food, drink, and fun by stealing the profits. The place might have to close and then where would they be? If Grouch didn't get you, one of these surely would. Few would maintain the thought to leave without paying.

Savon'el saw all types of people as they entered the tavern: elves, dwarves, knights of both persuasions, clerics, druids, and fighters of all races. These were adventurers, all. He took in the sight and smell of the tavern and, somewhere in the back of his mind, knew he'd been in a place like this before, only...

The sound of a lyre strummed softly from the small stage caught his attention and he was immediately transfixed.

She was a small, lithe Elvin woman, beautiful beyond imagination and dressed in shimmering black silk. Lovely as life, light as dew and as fragile as gossamer, both old and young, she was one of the last of the immortal Sha'terra. She was...

Landra Brea looked from the stage to the audience below. Her music flowed with, around, and through those there. When she played, none spoke above a whisper; such was the power of the music, and such was the power of the musician.

She saw the half elf in her power and knew all of his past and present for her power was at the source of Life and in league with the Fates. She knew also that the time was not right for past knowledge to return to this one. However...

Savon'el stood with his mouth half open and gazed at the beautiful Brea. It was more than beauty that held him entranced, but the sure knowledge that he'd seen her before at court.

"At court? What court? Where?"

The questions screamed through his mind and made his head pound worse than before, but he could not escape it, rooted as he was by her presence. He couldn't take his eyes from the Elvin beauty.

Red Wolf was halfway to the bar when he felt the loss of the savon'el. He looked back, grinned, and knew what had transpired.

"Another one for Brea," he sighed as he took the young half elf's arm and led him to a table close to the bar.

Chapter Sixteen

The trees completely encircled the silver, rune-carved platform as it glinted in the early afternoon sunlight. Those five pillars awaited the touch of a hand to release the magiks set within. This was a guarded place, a place unnoticed by the humanity that moved along the road leading to the eastern gate of the city seven miles away. The dust, noise, and confusion never reached here where the air held the scent of green found only in a forest at peace.

The air at the center of the pentacle shimmered, stretched, and then warped. Five figures, one unconscious upon a crudely built travois, faded into existence. The reins to five mounts were held loosely in three hands: a Huntsmaster in the chain mail and livery, minus the signet, of the Royal Border Guards; a young elf dressed in leather jerkin and trousers; and a knight in polished silver armor who held the reins of a magnificent black war mount and a slightly smaller golden palomino.

Upon this golden mount sat, on a special sidesaddle, the golden magecleric, Iaprene' Anolin. A great ruddy silver wolf lay unconcerned at the feet of the Huntsmaster and a huge raven perched on the crosspiece of the travois.

"That was great!" exploded the young elf, Bonaire.

The explosion of childlike glee shook Arantar from his disorientation. He watched as the wolf rose, stretched, and padded to the edge of the pentagram, then he took in his surroundings.

"Sir Jake," he growled, "where in the seven hells are we!"

"Excuse me, sir," replied the knight indignantly, "but you must have forgotten that you are in the presence of a lady of some breeding! Do apologize!"

"Of course, good sir. Excuse my ignorance, please, m'lady. It was an unfortunate slip of the tongue, prompted by the rigors of wounded travel and the strangeness of this mode of transportation. Please accept my deepest apologies for my vulgar tongue."

"I understand, Huntsmaster," the girl replied with a tiny grin, "and consider your apology accepted."

"I thank you, m'lady. Now," said he, turning back to the large knight, as that worthy made to lead the lady's horse from the Pentacle, "I ask again, where are we?"

"Why, at the Catlorian Druid's Pentacle, of course!" he replied haughtily in a tone that meant that everyone who *was* anyone knew this.

He continued to lead the lady's horse through the trees and glanced back toward the Huntsmaster. Then he noticed his own war mount lagging about the Pentacle, obviously not in any hurry to follow his "master."

"Dammit, Midnight!" he boomed. "Are you coming?"

"Sir Jake!"

The sharpness in the girl's voice drew the big knight's eyes quickly.

"Yes, Lady Rene'?" At her stern look of disapproval, he added, "I've erred, dear lady?"

"I should say that you have!" she replied in a soft yet stern voice. "You have corrected one of these downtrodden gentlemen for using profanity accidentally, yet with the very next breath you have the audacity to swear like a commoner, and at that sweet animal there!"

The dainty wave of her hand in the general direction of the big warhorse only added fuel to the insubordinate attitude. The horse stopped in midstride and, looking for all the world like one hurt by the words of a friend, turned its great head away.

"You should be ashamed, sir!" concluded the golden mage girl.

"Oh, but I am, m'lady! I am!" the knight stated as he dropped to one knee, head bowed and one gauntleted hand to his brow. "I am humbled by my own callousness, dear lady. Is there naught I might do? Say, slay a red dragon, punish a band of brigands, anything that might be worthy penance for my wrong?"

Arantar had never, in all of his years at court, seen this much manure piled in one place! To make matters worse, this knight believed every word he spouted! The big black warhorse snorted to get the Huntsmaster's attention, shook his head, and stamped.

"His bloody horse has more sense than he!" he thought.

He started to say something in the big fellow's defense when he caught the sidelong glance from Rene'. She placed a dainty finger to her lips and shook her head. Though he thought she was having too much fun at the knight's expense, he kept his silence and watched.

"Sir Jake?"

The sound of the lady's voice brought the knight's head up in total attention.

"I believe you could best divest yourself of any effrontery by simply suggesting an adequate lodging where I might stay during my visit, good food and comfort, of course, being the primary concern."

The knight seemed deep in thought, his brows furrowed and he was, possibly, in pain at the necessity.

"You might also consider assisting these gentlemen in the same vein," she added. "You may remember that they've just recently been set upon by bandits."

Sir Jake came to his feet swiftly, for all of his seeming bulk, and kissed the girl's offered hand.

"Of course, dear lady!"

He strode back to the travois just as Solothon regained consciousness. The raven hopped from one side of the travois to the other, away from the oncoming knight.

"First things first!" he boomed as he removed a small vial filled with a bluish liquid from a leather pouch at his hip.

"Here, sir knight!" he boomed as he handed the vial to the bleary eyed and thoroughly confused Solothon. "Drink this! T'is unseemly for a knight and obvious leader of his valiant companions to enter Catlorian flat of his back! This potion will aid you to health as only this and time have the power to do!"

Solothon took the vial with a nod and drank its contents. It tasted of sunshine, blue skies, and the green of open fields. It was as sweet as nectar to parched lips. The weakness of poisoned exhaustion flowed from his body as the potion chased it. The wounds on arm and leg knitted and were healed beneath the bandages as the liquid did its work.

The Elvin knight rose from the travois with a new energy. He removed the gauntlet from his right hand and offered it to the big knight.

"Thank you, Sir...?"

"Jake of Pentacost, First in the service of the Lords of Light!" boomed the knight proudly as he took the proffered hand. "But you have been robbed by villainous forces. Have you the wherewithal to pay the gate fee and find lodging and food for you and your companions?"

Jake took the downcast demeanor and the futile anger that rose in the young knight as answer.

"I thought not, but no matter, I have aplenty! Fear not, noble sir, for I would not dream of offering you charity, for I myself would take such an offer as insult to my capabilities. No, sir, let us call this what it is! A loan, a favor intended to be returned in good time, if you will, from one noble knight to the other."

While Jake spoke, he retrieved a small pouch from beneath his cloak and handed it ceremoniously to the young knight. Solothon took the pouch from the big knight and tucked it away without looking,—something one would do only if one wished to insult the gift. He was a bit irritated at the necessity, but he kept a tight rein on his building anger.

"I thank you, Sir Jake of Pentecost, as I am sure my companions agree. I am Solothon Calendera, knight errant to the Dukedom of Laranthia, in the service of the New Order of the Laurel, an order dedicated to the protection of the Vales of Light within the Eldewood Forest and to returning the order to its previous honor and glory. I formally acknowledge this...loan," the last word accented, "and the honorable favor you have bestowed. Upon my word-bond, this loan will be repaid in kind, and I am at your service."

The big knight responded to the curt nod with one of his own.

"And I at yours, sir. Be not in a rush to repay until you come into your own. If our fates show rightly, we shall meet again and the debt shall indeed be repaid. Now, good companions of this good knight," said he, turning toward Arantar and Bonaire, "for, mark my words well, as the Lords of Light deem myself worthy, so do I deem him as such, and he will one day take up the fight for right and honor and will truly acquit his honorable quest, no doubt with full knowledge of the foul dangers lurking unknown and evil behind every bush and tree, and will prove himself, at peril for his own life, and without batting an eye..."

"Sir Jake?"

The lady's voice interrupted the knight's single-sentence dissertation, given with one forefinger pointed skyward, head tossed back, and the other gauntleted hand flat against the small of his back. It took him a moment to realize that the voice belonged to the Lady Rene', but once that realization took, he pulled the finger into his fist and placed it with the other at his back. Then he turned to the lady with a cock of his head.

"Yes, dear lady?"

"You were going to, I believe, suggest adequate lodging and dining arrangements?"

"Ah, yes! An adequate abode for these honorable gentlemen and for your delightful personage in Catlorian. Yes, I'm sorry. I do tend to run on a bit, don't I? Well!" His brow furrowed once again. "There is a new establishment in the city run by some poor fellow who used to be somewhat of a campaigner himself. From what I've heard, it may well be a fine place to stay for those who go forth from time to time upon adventure, dealing with brigands and such. I believe it could be adequate to your needs, m'lady, and the food, they say, is quite palatable. I've come, as an added bonus to escorting you, m'lady, to see the place and evaluate it for myself. Professional courtesy, you understand. I believe the old campaigner's name is Frederick, a priest in good standing but to a strange unknown god, Udin. The priest doesn't venture out any more. I can't remember why, though I hear he hails from another land, one unheard of in my circles, I can tell you, and from what I have been privy to..."

"Thank you, Sir Jake," said the mage girl with a sweet smile, effectively cutting off another long and rambling oration. "I shall surely take your advice, as I am certain these gentlemen will. I'm sorry to interrupt what must truly be an interesting tale, but I am a bit tired and still have some very important errands to pursue before I may think of rest and sustenance."

"My apologies, m'lady, I wasn't thinking." He again picked up the lead for Rene's mare and began to follow the narrow trail north through the trees, adding, "Come then, gentlemen, to the city at the center of the world—Catlorian."

Solothon quickly dropped the travois from his warhorse and followed.

"Come along, Midnight, and please do not embarrass me further in front of this lovely lady!" he boomed with a glance back at his black war mount. "Sometimes I don't believe Midnight has the proper attitude, yet he is an impressive fighter nonetheless! Why, I remember a time..."

And he would have, had not Arantar picked that moment to catch up with him and call out.

"You spoke of the Lords of Light. I hate admitting limited knowledge, and I mean no disrespect, but just who are the Lords of Light?"

The Huntsmaster could not have picked a better subject for a discourse with the large knight. Sir Jake's eyes sparkled as he spoke and his free hand gestured sharply as he made point after point.

It seemed that sometime during the conflict called the Mage Wars, the three gods that made up the triad Lords of Light found themselves divest of followers. The Sha'terra, the triad's chosen, had taken great losses while defending the Eldewood from the onslaught of the dark elves and their evil leaders, and they had withdrawn to elsewhere. That is, save two: the Lady Brea, "Lady of Life" and Master Bard, and her husband, Tensor, Time Strider.

The lady had, for reasons unknown, removed herself from the conflict early on, but she had returned to help with the rebuilding.

Lord Tensor, believing her killed, brought sharp retribution to the dwarf race. In his attempt to kill them all, he also killed those of his own who dared to stand in his way. Thus, Lord Tensor, Time Strider, was forever cursed as "Kin Slayer."

The Lords of Light, each powerful in their own right within the bounds of their individual realms of Knowledge, War and Law, together made a power that no single deity, save the Creator himself, could withstand.

"However," continued the knight, "there is an old saying that goes 'Do the gods exist because men believe, or do men believe because the gods exist?' I prefer the latter.

"When the Lords of Light found that their followers were no more, they withdrew. I've kept the faith, though not Elvin myself, alone against the day when they will return, and, mark me well, that day will come, and not too far in the future, when the Lords of Light, in all of their terrible power, will return to find me, Sir Jake of Pentecost, lighting the way as I've done, lo, these many years, and with humble piety, and remarkable deeds...HOLD!"

The knight brought Rene's mare to a quick halt and the three companions walked up beside him. They gazed out over a vast plain with the high walls of the city of Catlorian at its very center less than six miles from where they stood. From their vantage point, they could see the Great Eastern Gate, one of five in the pentagon shaped city. The wide beaten-earth road that led to that gate was filled with wagons of all shapes and sizes, men on horseback or afoot, with their women and children in tow. Then the knight saw the caravan of smallish wagons that rolled slowly toward the city.

"Stand back, dear lady!" he boomed. "Those dwarven wagons are bringing up a great deal of dust, and unfortunately I've nothing with which to protect you. I travel light, you see, so that I might easily deal with brigands and their ilk!" Then his eyes narrowed. "Some of those dwarves look to be brigands!"

He quickly placed one hand on the cantle of his saddle, Midnight having instinctively come to his side, and lifted himself straight into the saddle without the use of his stirrups as if his own weight were nothing. Bonaire's jaw dropped at this display of awesome strength and he backed slowly away.

"Wait here!" he boomed as he tapped heels to the big war mount. "I'll check!"

"Wait, sir..." But the rest trailed off at the big knight's back as the girl's outstretched hand slowly returned to her lap.

Arantar shook his head with a small grin. Then, as he led his horse to the girl's side, he cautioned his saola-friends.

It would be better for you to stay in the forest. We've had very few dealings with large cities and I'm afraid...

Yes, Arantar-sao, came the growling reply to his mind, *I stay, but close. Call, I come.*

I fly to tall stone. came the breeze to his mind. *You call, I call earth-brother. We come. Not alone, Arantar-sao. We watch. We come.*

Then, as the wolf slipped silently back into the forest, the big black bird lifted toward the walls of the great city. Arantar placed his hand on the girl's saddle to draw her attention. She glanced at him and then to the big knight, who had taken up an animated argument with no less than thirty of the small fellows, each with either a short, double-bitted axe or heavy cudgel.

"My friends and I will take our leave of you here, m'lady. I wish to thank you again for your assistance in getting us here." Then, with a glance at Sir Jake, "Will you be safe from here?"

The young woman slapped her tiny hand to her ornate saddle in frustration as her eyes followed the argument that raged below.

"Safe? Why, of course! Sir Jake will see that I'm protected from everything, whether the protection is necessary or not!"

She turned her angry gaze on the Huntsmaster, noted the small grin that played at the edges of his lips, and her frown softened.

"Truly, sir, I shall be quite safe. He means well, but..." she trailed off with a sigh.

"I was rather hoping to catch a ride with that caravan, but," Arantar grinned in the direction of the ongoing angry discussion, "it seems that they may no longer be disposed to anyone joining them above their own stature. Well, no matter. We shall no doubt arrive shortly after you. Farewell, and thank you again."

Rene' watched Arantar move off at an angle toward the road, away from the argument, and panicked.

"Huntsmaster, please!"

The ranger stopped and turned back to find the girl looking toward the big knight with genuine concern on her face. Sir Jake seemed to have settled the discussion, though, from the looks directed at his back, and at those to whom he was returning, probably not amiably.

"Would you mind terribly accompanying Sir Jake and me to Catlorian?" she asked quickly. She looked on the glowering faces below and added, "I believe strongly in safety in numbers." Then, as Sir Jake reined his mount in next to her, "Sir Jake, would you mind the company of these gentlemen to the gates?"

Arantar saw the look in her beautiful eyes that said, though she knew herself to be in good hands, the pompous Sir Jake had a dangerous knack of getting himself into situations without trying. With the Huntsmaster and his companions along, she reasoned, Sir Jake might not unwittingly endanger the girl out of hand. Arantar nodded and turned to the big knight.

"If you would not mind, sir, we are new to the city and may need your council."

The knight cast an approving glance at the Huntsmaster as the mage girl mouthed her thank you from behind him. Then he set an appraising scowl on the three of them.

"Well, m'lady, the Huntsmaster's calling is most honorable, and at their head stands a valiant knight of a noble order. He, of course, stands on his own merit, as you well know, so therefore I shall put my faith and trust in them as good companions! Please, join us!"

Arantar nodded his acceptance but glared at the young elf when he placed both hands on his hips and snapped at the knight. "Hey! What about me?"

Bonaire received a steely glare from the knight.

"You? What about you? I have nothing upon which to place my trust, other than you are an accepted companion of these good men. As for trusting in you on your own, I have nothing with which to pass judgment."

Arantar's hand came down on the young elf's shoulder as gloom threatened to settle over him and his self-worth began to plummet.

"I stand by him, good sir, and have seen him acquit himself on the field of battle against great odds. He is still young, true, and in need of training in some ways, but I would and have trusted him with my own life and the life of my good and trusted friend, Sir Solothon, and I have not found him wanting."

Rene' felt the change in the young elf at these words. Somehow Bonaire believed in the Huntsmaster and hung on every word the ranger uttered. She watched as the elf's chest came up and his lips grew firm.

Then she felt the seething power from the Elvin knight. He intrigued her. Why the anger and the perpetual frown?

"I may have erred in my assessment, young sir," stated the big knight to Bonaire. "If I have offended a noble and blooded companion of these true warriors, I apologize." He nodded a stern head toward the young elf and, at Arantar's insistent motioning, it was returned. "Shall we?"

The small party moved along the road to the city with Arantar, Rene', and Sir Jake locked in idle conversation. Bonaire listened from his self-appointed position as rearguard while Solothon seethed in ever building anger.

He fought, with every step, to gain control of that anger, but the situation kept nagging. His mail was heavy and hot in the early autumn sunlight and he would be more comfortable riding, as he should as a knight. Yet his steel mail would cut his mount because he had no saddle, so he couldn't ride. He wouldn't—*couldn't*—defrock himself of any honorable armor just to ride, yet he still had to drag this damned horse along because, as a knight, he needed a mount to ride into battle, but *he could not ride!*

The anger built with every step. As fast as he reasoned away one level of anger, another replaced it, and by the time the party reached the gates his control was worn thin.

"Hey, Sir Jake!" came the shout from the friendly guard who met them at the gate. "How's me namesake?"

He was a burly man dressed in the livery of the Royal House of Catlorian. He gripped the knight's outstretched hand in a strong grasp.

"Haven't seen ya 'round lately. Where ya been?"

"Oh, hither and yon, you know, Jake. Always out to serve with my good right arm, the cause of justice, chivalry..."

"Yeah, yeah, I know, but what about the rest of these?" he said as he gestured toward the big knight's companions.

"The lady is with me, but I vouchsafe the others as good companions. Here, my friend," said the knight as he laid five gold pieces into the burly guard's hand. "Allow them the hospitality of the great city of Catlorian, the hub of civilization, and the loins from whence spring…"

"Sir Jake?"

The knight, again with a forefinger thrust skyward, turned to look toward the girl.

"I am tired and hungry," she said softly but with controlled fury in her voice, "and if we stay here much longer, I shall get all dusty. If you please, Sir Jake, can we go now?"

"Of course!" he responded quickly as he began to lead her mount through the gate. Then he stopped and turned to his other companions. "For your own safety, good sirs, read yonder sign." He gestured toward a huge, old but recently repainted placard beside the gate. "There are few rules in Catlorian, yet each will be followed on pain of major punishment."

The placard read:

LAWS GOVERNING COMPORTMENT WITHIN THE
CONFINES OF THE GREAT CITY OF CATLORIAN

1. Mounted personnel will ride at a walk. Those moving at greater speed will be subject to fine (5GP minimum) and their animal will be confiscated.
2. NO LITTERING!
3. Duels, tournaments, and Honor Combat will be fought only in the Warrior's or Ranger's Guild training areas.
4. No drunkenness, disorderliness, or disturbances to the peace of the city.

Those responsible for any of the above will be subject to incarceration for one month (minimum) and/or fined up to 500 GP.

"Bonaire," said the Huntsmaster quietly over his shoulder to the mounted elf, "I think it to be in your best interest to dismount."

"But why? I can control…" The horse shied violently at the rumbling wagons of the dwarven caravan.

"That is why, my friend," sighed the Huntsmaster at the quickly dismounting elf. "You can walk your mount like the rest of us and help with the lady, if you will."

Sir Jake led Rene's palomino through the gates for a little way, away from the stream of traffic, and he stopped and spoke quietly to Rene' for a moment before turning to Arantar and the others.

"Sir Solothon, Huntsmaster and..."—for want of another title—"my good elf, I have some business to dispense with the Myrlin and cannot take the Lady Rene' with me. If you would be so kind as to assist her in her endeavors, I should be ever so thankful."

Arantar caught the strained look on Solothon's face, but the Elvin knight's nod of acceptance showed he was still in control. Acting as the knight's second, Arantar answered for him.

"Of course, Sir Jake. Sir Solothon, myself, and good Bonaire would be most pleased to assist and will ensure that the lady reaches her destination safely."

"My thanks, good sirs!" boomed the big knight. "I shall endeavor to meet you at the Adventurer's Guild this evening."

Sir Jake turned to the lady and, with a courtly bow and a curt "M'lady," turned to leave.

"One question, Sir Jake, if you please," said the Huntsmaster.

The big knight stopped and glanced askance over his shoulder. "Yes?"

"Just where is the Adventurer's Guild?"

Chapter Seventeen

The short, portly barman saw the two as they came near the bar, the bar towel making yet another vain attempt at keeping the bar dry.

"C'mon in, ya'll. We're havin' ourselves a grand reopenin' party. Booze 'n stuff's on the house fer the nex' hour. If'n you be hungry, go on inna kitchen." Then, with a glance at the large barbarian, "'Ceptin' fer you! You stay outta the kitchen! We'll fin' what you need 'n bring it to ya."

Melisande sat close to the bar. She'd put together that the "red wolf" Terillion had mentioned must be the notorious Red Wolf himself, and she had come to this opening with the sole purpose of finding him.

She'd heard the lyre upon entering and saw the way all eyes locked to the beauty on stage.

"Brea is at it again," she'd murmured as she made her way to her table.

She glanced around the tavern of mostly familiar faces and then at Red Wolf, who stood at the bar in close conversation with the barman. At a table close by sat a half elf, probably a fighter from his dress and weapons. Red Wolf glanced his way from time to time, seemingly keeping an eye on him, if she didn't miss her guess.

This half elf, probably the one mentioned by Terillion earlier, was reasonably handsome, though the cleric noted that she had seen better. She wouldn't have given him a second look had it not been for the enraptured look he held for the Elvin bard on stage. It made the cleric's blood boil. The decision was made, one way or another, that look would fade. She decided to bide her time and watch, but she stood and moved to a table closer to the bar, her bright yellow cloak billowing with the movement. She sat close enough to hear what was been said without being noticed.

Red Wolf was notorious for his drinking escapades and was offered a small cask of wine.

"No, friend. I've been away from your civilized people too long. I think a mug of your best ale and a haunch of venison, spit roasted, will do me fine."

The barman committed the order to memory, grinned, and turned to the half elf.

"And you, mate?"

Savon'el could not take his eyes from the Elvin bard, her beauty, yet something more, holding him captive to her music. The barman followed the half elf's amber eyes to the stage and shook his head with a grin.

"Yo, bud!" he yelled as he clapped his hands. "Quit gawkin'! You can talk to 'er later."

Though the words shook Savon'el from his trance, the beauty and the haunting melody still had him.

"Oh, ah, a glass of wine, if you please."

"What kind?"

Savon'el frowned. He was spellbound by the timeless bard and had no time for this. He was tired and bruised, and the wound on his arm, though healing, was very sore. As long as he listened, all that had happened was washed clean from his being.

The barman knew the signs well, for he too had been a traveler in the realms of adventure and the music still held him. He reached beneath the bar and brought forth a small silver bound cask. He poured a delicate porcelain goblet half full and brought it to the table.

"Tell ya what, bud," he said. "Brea brought some o' this stuff up special, 'n seein' as how you're new here, I got a deal for ya. I don't reco'nize ya, 'n I been in the city for over two year." He placed the goblet on the table before the half elf and continued, "If ya can tell me that ya ever drunk this afore, I'll gi' ya two hunnerd gold pieces." Then, he added, "This on yer word, bud!"

"On my word?" he asked as he cradled the fragile glass in his cupped hands.

"On yer word o' honor, bud, if ya got any."

The barman ignored the flared look of insult from the half elf and turned to Red Wolf.

"'Bout as much as you do, I 'spose." At the barbarian's glare, he chuckled and added, "Don't be lookin' at me like that, 'n drink yer damned drink!"

"You were good enough to offer me a drink." The barbarian grinned. "Now, I offer you one."

"Whoa, bud! You can jist keep that stuff!"

"You liked it well enough the last time I was in the city. Of course, you were a few cups in, but..."

"Yeah, right," retorted the barman with a grimace. Then, "There's a couple o' fellas from the Bear Clan right over there. Don't they drink the same stuff you do?"

Red Wolf glanced toward the two barbarians and a low growl escaped his throat. The wolf and bear clans had been at each other's throats longer than anyone could remember. Only his pledge to Jake, the guard, kept him from attacking them right here and right now.

"Go an' talk to 'em," the barman continued with a grin. "They prob'ly got some with 'em. They got me with it jist three day ago."

"They still use bear sweat in the makings, from what I hear, and have no talent for the brewing process. They're not smart enough to use proper ingredients, but that is not unusual for them. Have you ever seen a smart bear?"

"Yeah. Where do ya think I got these scars?"

The barman opened his tunic to reveal four long scars across his body diagonally, from his left shoulder to his right hip. Melisande moved to the bar next to the barbarian to get a better look at the damage.

"He mustn't have been too smart," she commented, "to have left you alive."

"Naw, it thunked I were dead. I can pertend real good when I have to, missy."

Melisande smiled and turned toward the half elf as that one sat and gazed into the golden depths of the rich amber wine.

He lifted the goblet to his nose. Rich, delicate, but strong, the aroma was intoxicating alone. It smelled of rain, sunshine, and earth. Everything that was pleasant, happy, and soft in life was there in that porcelain goblet.

He took a sip and, as the amber sweetness fell across his tongue, it brought fleeting images and feelings close to the wall of his mind. The name broke through to slide across his thoughts as the liquid cascaded, welcome, down his throat.

"T'is Sylvan Wine of a vintage I knew, but I have since forgotten."

The barman's jaw dropped.

"Yer've drunk it a'fore?"

"I must have," the half elf replied as a small grin played at the corners of his mouth. "I just cannot remember when."

Red Wolf leaned closer to Blegral and whispered, "Notice the scar? He must have taken a good shot to the head and his memories are, at present, displaced."

"Well, he got th' name anyways, so I guess he wins the bet!"

Melisande had moved to Savon'el's table and sat. She looked into his face and saw peace as he sipped the delicate wine and watched the Elvin woman on stage. He didn't even acknowledge the two perfect gemstones the barman held as payment for the wager.

Red Wolf took them, placed them on the table, and tapped Savon'el lightly on the shoulder.

"These are yours," he said. "You want them, don't you?"

The half elf turned his head dreamily toward his companion and then down at the gems. He picked up one and tossed it back to the barman.

"I should be paying you, friend," he said. "There is a memory here, though I know it not. At least I can now savor a part that was missing. Thank you."

The barman looked at the gem, at Savon'el, whose attention had returned to the bard on stage, and then at the barbarian. Red Wolf simply shook his head and shrugged his shoulders at this folly.

"Ya oughta bring 'im by more often, Wolf," said the barman as he returned the gem to an apron pocket.

"I just don't get it," replied the barbarian. "You lost the bet and paid off. He got the drink and the gems free. Even though, to his mind, it was worth it, it just doesn't make sense." Then he shook his head again. "I just don't get it."

"If he be hangin' aroun' you fer long, he done lost what good sense he had." Then, to the Savon'el, "He get ya inta any trouble yet?"

"Wha...?" The young half elf was once again distracted. "No. Actually he's kept me out of a good bit as of late."

"Well, if'n he says som'pin 'bout goin' downtown ta see what's shakin', stay in yer room an' lock the door. Let 'im go off by hisself. B'lieve me, he don't need no help!"

Red Wolf's ears pricked up, his retort filled with humor and mischief.

"What? You don't enjoy the hunt, short of falling out of windows of course?"

"Naw! That weren't me, bud. You be thinkin' o' yerself there…"

Savon'el sipped again at his wine and let the good-natured banter filter through his mind. He gazed at the beautiful bard. She'd finished playing and, as she spoke to those close to her in passing, she made her way toward the bar. Savon'el stood as she approached, but he sat again as the days of rough travel and the wine came upon him.

"Pup?" asked the barbarian. "Are you all right?"

"Sorry, my friend. It seems I'm just a bit off tonight."

"That's what I thought."

The half elf's eyes followed the Elvin bard as she made her way toward them.

"Ye'd think he ain't never see'd a woman afore," said the barman with a shake of his head.

"No, friend," replied the barbarian, "there is more here that I haven't seen."

"What say we fix 'im up with one o' them girls what jist come back from the alchemist?"

"They would show him a good time, I suppose, but…"

Melisande was furious. Here was this young man who, from what she'd gathered, had been put through evil times. He was caught in the web spun by that Elvin witch, and now they were thinking of "fixing him up"? Were all men this compassionate, the races would have died out long ago! She slipped over to a chair close to Savon'el.

"Tell ya what, bud," said the barman to Savon'el, "I be seein' ya stare that way ever since ya been in the place. I think I'll do ya a favor." Then he moved out from behind the bar and headed toward Brea.

"Who is he, Red Wolf?"

"His name is Blegral, pup. He's good at keeping the conversation going and the wine flowing. He's an old campaigner who just got tired of the life we live. Now he adventures through tales brought by the rest of us."

"And the lady?"

"That would be Brea," came the soft reply from the chair next to him.

His glance was caught and held by the sparkling green eyes of the young cleric. She seemed to look directly into his soul, and at that point he was willing, should she find something there upon which to hang a memory.

"WOLFIE!"

The melodic voice, touched with the innocence of the little girl, caused the young half elf to turn about sharply. He rose quickly from his chair and stood rooted in awe.

Brea, she named Lady of Life and Master Bard, the last of the Sylvan Sha'terra, that is to say immortal Elvin females, ran lightly to where Red Wolf stood at the bar. A low growl of contentment came from the barbarian's throat as the Elvin beauty wrapped her arms about his neck and slipped between him and the bar. She settled in close as the young barbarian turned in that embrace to smile down at her.

"Greetings to thee, Brea, Daughter of Light. May the Lords shine their blessings upon thee."

Melisande recognized the language as ancient Elvin, the soft sounds of the Sylvan sliding through the air with its hidden power seemed at odds with the voice that spoke it.

"And for thee as well, friend," the Bard responded softly. Then, in the common, "Now what have you been up to?"

As if the answer, that was not offered, was inconsequential, she turned sideways in his embrace and looked directly at Savon'el.

"And who are you?"

Somewhere in the half elf's mind, amid his total awe of the beauty before him, something quietly snapped into his memory: a vision of this woman, Brea, playing her harp at court, as seen from a small hidden place behind a tapestry. All other figures were shadow except her, and all much larger than he who watched.

His head throbbed as he tried to remember, then he sighed. He, as before, tucked the information away for future reference. Right now, the bluest eyes in creation locked her gaze with his and he could not move or speak.

"Brea, he knows not his name or his past," stated the barbarian softly, recognizing the power that flowed toward the young half elf. "I've named him Savon'el, for he is, indeed, a wanderer in search of his past to guarantee his future. The scar is but an inkling to the original cause, though meddlers may share the burden. There is more, but it is not mine to tell."

The blue in the eyes of that beauty became deeper as the half elf watched. Then without warning her eyes dropped. She closed her eyes and stood very still. When her eyelids fluttered open again, the blue was filled with sadness.

"The Fates say he shouldn't know his answers yet, and to tell him now would place the weight and danger of his life too soon upon him. I'm truly sorry, Red Wolf."

The barbarian raised her head with a gentle finger and looked into those sad eyes.

"*You* know, Brea, and for now that is enough."

"He will need your aid for a time, my friend, though I am afraid your paths will too soon diverge. He will need friends, true friends, soon. For now, he needs rest and distraction."

She moved from the barbarian's embrace and approached the half elf. She placed one small hand on his chest and pushed him back into his chair, then slid her lithe body into his lap.

Melisande was livid. How could she treat him so? From what she'd overheard, the whole of his life had been ripped from him, and she dares to dally with him with a distracted "oh, well"?

The ancient blue eyes met those smoldering green, and the Bard's power locked with the young cleric's anger. Melisande's anger turned to sadness as she somehow understood that gaze. It said this one needs diversion and some measure of peace, if only for a short while. Melisande was still irritated, but she now understood the game for what and why it was. She sat next to the savon'el and ran a finger about the rim of the porcelain goblet.

"Will you be in Catlorian for a while, Savon'el?" Brea asked with an impish grin as she wrapped her arms about his neck and looked deep into his eyes.

The Elvin word for "wanderer" rippled off of her tongue softly and sent a chill of delight up the half elf's spine.

"I've no idea, my lady," he replied softly as he glanced at the big barbarian.

"Finally got your tongue, pup?"

"If you travel with the likes of him," stated the Bard softly, a thumb jerked toward Red Wolf, "you'll be deep into trouble before nightfall."

"Why do all insinuate this?" cried the barbarian, a feigned look of hurt on his face. "I merely attempt to have a good time and all I get is abuse!"

"But, Wolfie, it seems that Catlorian is the beneficiary of your...uh... good times."

"I have been blamed for everything that happens in Catlorian whether I'm here or not! At this point, it would seem that your luck is with you. Were it not a 'Grand Reopening' of this tavern and the furniture expensive to replace, I would show you just how something could be started!"

"That has been taken care of by the Myrlin and others, I believe," stated Brea. "Don't let that excuse stand in your way."

"Truly?" The barbarian's grin was evil as he added, "Where are those bear teat suckers?"

"Do you think you can handle them, Wolfie? I've heard that you've gotten a bit...soft."

Red Wolf soft? The thought ran through Savon'el's wine- and hardship-inhibited mind and centered on this unlikely fact. This man who could, and has, driven his hands through plate steel, soft? The half elf shook his head and drank from the goblet. His smile broadened as the wine took hold.

Brea, meanwhile, had snuggled deeper into Savon'el's lap, his arm loose about her small waist. Her little-girl demeanor said, "Protect me from this awful barbarian."

Unfortunately, Savon'el had had enough wine, atop the rigors of his travels, to convince him that maybe...

Red Wolf knew this game well.

"Brea, where is Tensor?"

"Oh, he's around somewhere. You know him," she answered with a wave of her tiny hand. "Probably chasing one of *those* clerics about, I'd wager. I caught one making advances earlier and had to put her in her place."

"I'm sure you acted...appropriately," grinned the barbarian. "Careful, pup. Tensor is her husband and he doesn't believe in sharing. He is also extremely good with a bow."

"Oh, he thinks he is," retorted the Elvin Bard.

Savon'el was not, at this point, totally coherent. As far as he could tell, he had successfully defended this beautiful Elvin goddess from the wrath of Red Wolf. Therefore, how bad could this Tensor fellow be? He laid a hand on the Bard's soft shoulder and glanced at the barbarian with a bleary gaze.

"Shounds like a challenge to me!"

Melisande looked dumbfounded at the tipsy half elf, then at the empty goblet. Had this one lost all of his wits? If he knew...

"But he doesn't," she reminded herself, "and he's drunk."

She glanced up angrily at the barbarian only to have her heart skip a beat as the elf writhed into existence next to Red Wolf.

Clipped to a silver belt fashioned as a silver dragon biting its tail was a forest green quiver. The monogram of a stylized "T" with an hourglass as its base shimmered from the catch. A shift of the elf's head sent cascades of motion through his silver hair. He shifted the light wooden harp he carried to the bar and smiled at his bride.

"Well, my love, what fool have you gotten into trouble this time? I seem to recall the word 'challenge'?"

His amber eyes glinted with mischief and an amused smile played at his lips.

"Why, Tensor!" replied the beauty as she began to rise from Savon'el's lap. Then she stopped, turned, and administered a lingering kiss that seemed to reach deep into the half elf's soul.

"Hey, Tensor," said Red Wolf helpfully, "my friend here wishes to challenge you to an archery competition."

"Oh?"

The Sylvan turned his amused gaze on the inebriated half elf.

"Would, say, a platinum piece at...oh...a half a mile be acceptable?"

"Tensor!"

The soft yet firm voice of the Elvin girl who warmed the savon'el's lap reached out and softly slapped her husband.

"Then a hundred paces at the same platinum piece? Acceptable?"

"Shounds a'right ta me."

Savon'el attempted to rise, then remembered the girl on his lap.

"Uh...if you pleash, m'lady?"

She stood with a giggle, but her glance at her husband told him all he needed to know. Here was one in dire straits, and though she could help, she was bound not to. He'd seen his share and more of this, and he would play along with his love for her sake. She offered diversion from the pain and danger, nothing more. His smile was for her alone.

Red Wolf looked skyward, a grin on his face, and shook his head.

The green-eyed cleric had had enough. This cruelty had gone past good sense and, were it not for her need to accompany this barbarian on his errand, she'd...she'd...

What?

Then she remembered something from her studies, a spell of healing that would, at times of need, slow the effects of poisons. The casting didn't appear to be especially difficult, though she's been warned that the book wherein the spell was found was, for a time, outside of her abilities.

"Can't hurt," she thought as she reached out and caught the half elf's hand.

Savon'el's bleary gaze came around to fall into the cool green pools.

"You don't really want to go through with this, do you?" she asked softly as she attempted to harness the spell and channel it through the medium of touch.

There was a twinge in that touch that, to her, didn't feel right. Savon'el glanced down at her, shook off her hand, took the last sip from the goblet, stood unsteadily and turned to the amused Tensor.

"At your pleasure, sir," he stated with a courtly wave of his hand, and fell face-first to the floor.

Melisande was quickly at his side, turning him over and cradling his head on her lap. She trained a scowl of anger toward the grinning barbarian.

Red Wolf looked down at the small woman, at the angry look she gave him, and at the blissful smile on the young half elf's lips. He could contain it no longer. His laughter filled the great hall.

"Daughter of Freya," sighed the soft voice at Melisande's elbow. The cleric turned, instantly riveted by those timeless blue eyes, as the Bard continued, "do not direct your rage in such a way. I, and few others, know what drives you. Beware that, in your anger, you misjudge those around you and their intentions. The one you hold has a destiny that, if known too soon, might not come to fruition. We have but given him respite from his demons. They shall return on the morrow, but for now they rest.

"You wish to leave the city in hope of escaping *your* demons. This one, and his overlarge companion there, are your best hope.

"Besides, you have a destiny of your own, though you may not know it now, and for a time it coincides with theirs. Let not the actions of a few, or one, encourage preconceived notions of how the rest of the world acts."

Then, with a mischievous grin, "Besides, a well-schooled cleric should know her limitations."

"How did you…" the young cleric blurted. Then, she lowered her head and sighed. "Yes, m'lady."

Melisande scooped up the unconscious half elf and, taking the key from Blegral, proceeded up the stairs to the rooms above.

Brea followed the girl's progress up the stairway with a sad look. Then she turned her attention to the door at the far end of the tavern. She saw the rather large young human with the full arm gauntlet covering his left arm step through the door and watched as his eyes followed the yellow-cloaked cleric and her burden up the stairway. He glanced around the room until his eyes met hers. Then, with a smile, he slipped over to a vacant table close to the door and sat.

"Grek," she called softly, "I see more customers entering. Be a good boy and see to them."

The huge half-ogre ducked his head as he came out of the kitchen and with a gentle "Yeth, ma'am," proceeded through the throng.

Chapter Eighteen

Bonaire led the palomino, upon which rested Lady Rene', as he followed his companions down to the second street and turned right. The children surrounded them there, crying and begging for a handout, so many that the companions had to either stop or push through them.

"Please, sir," begged one young girl of maybe twelve years as she pointed to a boy of eight with a bandaged head and foot, "My brother's been hit by a wagon, my mother's sick, and my father has left town. We need money for my mother and brother. Can you help, please?"

"Me li'l brother, Tim, 'zat home, sick wit' th' purge, doncha know. I hasn't the coin fer th' healin'…"

"I haven't had no food fer three day…"

Arantar tried to explain that there was nothing they could do for them, as they had nothing to spare. As he spoke softly from one child to another, the Huntsmaster noticed the obvious strain on the knight, and as he watched, Solothon's lips pulled away from his teeth and a red glow burned in his eyes. Arantar tried in vain to reach the young knight, but there were too many children pawing at him.

From somewhere in the bowels of the earth came the words, the malignant power ripping from between tightly clinched teeth.

"GO AWAY!"

It was not a shout, but all on the street heard and were chilled to the bone. Most of the children ran away screaming, and didn't stop until many streets were between them and the demon. The rest backed away slowly in shock, their eyes big and their mouths agape, and some spoke prayers while others signed quick, ineffectual wards.

Arantar looked upon the panic, finally controlled the shaking in his hands, and turned to the young knight only to find calm confusion on his face.

"Cute children," the knight murmured softly, as if nothing had transpired. "I wonder why their parents allow them to run in the streets? Dangerous, you know?"

Then he turned and continued toward the big building on the right on the next block, leaving Arantar, Bonaire, and Lady Rene' staring after him.

"Huntsmaster?"

"Yes, m'lady?"

"What happened? What did he do? What *is* he?"

"That, Lady Rene', is a good question. He's what we in the realms call a 'Berserker.' However, I've never seen one this erratic before. It's as if something is driving him, something outside of himself. I just don't know."

"I think I might," she replied, her hand to her chin as they began to follow in the wake of the young knight. "Back at the Pentacle I felt something… something magical surrounding his body. It may be some type of spell causing this, but I feel that there is something more. I don't know how to explain it. I just feel…"

She sighed and looked at the Huntsmaster.

"I will look into this as soon as I can get to the Guild. I will try to find out what is going on with our unhappy friend, I promise."

"I hope so, m'lady. He's just too damned dangerous this way for friend or foe."

Rene' didn't reprimand Arantar for his choice of words, for she too felt him to be "damned."

"I will check with some colleagues I know and see what I can do. In the meanwhile, do all you can to see that he stays calm."

"I will try, m'lady. I'll try."

"Well, I won't!" exclaimed Bonaire. "The guy's nuts, if you ask me, and I'm staying well clear of him!"

"Good idea, my young friend," replied the Huntsmaster. "You do that."

Then, to himself, "Besides, that saves me from having to suggest that very same thing."

Two teenage boys came out of the stable to greet them as the three joined Solothon at the front of what could only be the Adventurer's Guild Inn and Tavern.

"Hoy! Take care o' yer horses, Gov?"

Arantar looked the lads over, noting the insincere smiles and casual respect. "How much?"

"Oh, a copper apiece. Right, John?"

"Uh, yeah, Sammy. A copper fer sure."

"Right. A copper per."

"How about this," Arantar stated, a low tone in his voice. "I give you two gold, one for each of you, and you see to it that they are well cared for. Don't touch the reins to the roan or large black. They will follow you on their own. Do you understand?"

"Oh, sure, Gov," replied the one called Sammy. "We'll take real good care o' 'em fer ya. Right, John?"

Arantar didn't wait for John's answer but nodded at Solothon. The knight retrieved the two gold pieces from the loaned pouch and, after tossing them to Sammy, handed the pouch to the Huntsmaster.

"Here, you handle this."

The gold pieces disappeared into Sammy's pocket and he turned to Rene'.

"You gittin' down, sweet cheeks, or do ya wanna join me an' John in the stable for a while?"

"Watch your mouth, young man!" she answered tightly. "Now, come here and help me down."

"Screw that, honeysuckle. Git down yerself!"

Arantar's strong hand on the knight's chest stopped him. Bonaire walked to the lady's stirrup, pushed the boy aside, and raised a hand for the lady. As Rene' dismounted, her eyes caught Sammy's, but her reprimand of "You should learn some manners, young man" fell on deaf ears.

Bonaire removed her bags from her cantle and threw them over his shoulder atop his own. Arantar watched as the two boys laughed and led two of the horses away while the roan and big black followed them through the stable doors.

"Something's wrong, m'lady," he said softly. "I shall come back out once we've settled you in relative comfort and check on the welfare of our mounts. Something is amiss, I feel."

After glancing at the stable door, Rene' lay a gentle hand on the Huntsmaster's arm.

"I'm not certain I disagree with you, but if you do go, bring someone you trust with you."

Then, with the slight pressure of her hand on his arm for comfort, Arantar led her up the steps to the double doors.

The noise was a constant, unintelligible hum out on the porch where they stood. All of the shutters were open to the street and, after seeing objects sailing out through the windows, the fact that there was no glass in the panes, and the reason for it, became obvious. This was an establishment designed as an "unwinding place" for people who made their living in the world of the rough and tumble.

Arantar grabbed a handful of bright cloak and forced Bonaire to read the sign next to the door. It read:

THE ADVENTURER'S GUILD RULES:

NO BARED WEAPONS ALLOWED INSIDE.

RULE NUMBER ONE IS THE ONLY RULE.

If you forget Rule 1 or 2, come back out here and
READ THIS AGAIN!

"I believe it to be in your best interest to heed the rules here," he said softly into the elf's ear. "This is not your father's tavern."

"Nice place," quipped the girl as she stepped through the door, one hand on the Huntsmaster's arm and the other on the small golden heart at her throat.

"Now *this* is more like it!"

The Huntsmaster saw Bonaire's face light up and knew his warning had fallen on deaf ears.

"Be careful, Bonaire."

"Heck, Arantar, this is just my speed! You might think this is not like my father's tavern, but it's close enough. I'm going to get a beer and mingle!"

"Do that, but first help us to seat the lady."

"Oh, sure! Sorry, I just...you know."

"I know, Bonaire, but look around you first. What do you see?"

"Well, people drinking and having a good time. See? Everybody is here. Knights, rangers, daku... *Daku*?!"

"Shhh! Not so loud!" answered the Huntsmaster in a low voice. "Keep to your manners, Bonaire. Stay out of trouble and keep your eyes open for he who robbed us."

As the elf wandered toward the bar at the far end of the tavern, the Huntsmaster led the girl close to a table occupied by two men in chain mail, obviously deep into their drink. As he looked about for an empty table, one of the men reached clumsily for the girl's arm.

"Hi, sweets! C'mere an' sit on me lap. We'll talk 'bout the first thing what comes up."

His companion thought this was the funniest joke he'd heard, his guffaw ringing into the din about them and fueled his friend to new heights of forwardness.

Rene' pulled back before the hand reached her and stepped quickly behind Arantar.

"Oh ho! I see!" exclaimed the first man to his friend, his bleary gaze never leaving the golden-garbed cleric. "I guess we'll jist hafta whip her boyfriend here, 'less he uses his wits an' leaves!"

With that, the two stood and, as Arantar backed slowly forcing the girl away from them, they each took a stumbling step toward him and stopped. Arantar noticed the smug looks had vanished, and they were no longer looking at Rene' but over and past them. As the Huntsmaster attempted to rebuke the two for their behavior, someone very large pushed him and Rene' aside. Arantar had to look up to see the face atop the mass of muscled flesh in leather.

The face was ugly! The mottled skin of his massive body was covered with scars, and his hands were the size of a man's head. He was half ogre and he was displeased.

"You fellowth have cauthed enough trouble. Now, *move!*"

"An' jest who's gonna make—"

Huge hands took a man's head in each and brought them together with a resounding *crack!* Men came from other tables and dragged the two to a wall and propped them up. Then, they returned to their revelry.

"Thorry 'bout that," stated the big bouncer, "but they been athkin' fer that all day. Here," he continued with a wave of his hand to the now-vacant table, "will thith do?"

Rene' stepped out from behind the Huntsmaster and, as she lay a tiny hand on the half ogre's arm, said, "Yes, thank you..."

"It'th Grouch, ma'am. That'th not my name, but it'th what everbody callth me. My real name'th Grek."

"Well, then thank you, Grek."

"Thank you, mith." He beamed.

Bonaire had moved up behind the lady as Solothon, who'd stopped at the entrance to check the notices, joined them.

Grouch looked at them, the table, and then back to the lady in gold.

"Are thoth fellowth with you?"

"Yes, Grek. They are. Is there a problem?"

"Well, thereth four o' you and only two chairth."

He lumbered toward an adjacent table and several of the men there left their chairs at his approach. He calmly picked up two of the vacated chairs and brought them back.

"There we go," he stated as he placed the chairs about the table.

He stood back as Solothon seated the girl and the men took their seats.

"Now, ith there thomething you'd like to drink, ma'am?"

"Yes, Grek, some white wine, if you please."

"Thertainly. Thertainly. An' you thirth?"

"Wine," said Arantar.

"Ale," from the knight.

"A beer, please," replied Bonaire.

"Right," stated the half ogre as he committed the order to memory. "We have thome venithon, taterth, and freth bread inna kitchen. Can I bring you thome?"

"Yes, please, Grek. You're a wonder, and thank you."

The pretty smile and attentive manner of the golden cleric had Grouch flustered.

"My pleathure, mith," he stated as he gave her a rough bow and started for the kitchen.

"Grek?"

The big half ogre turned back at her voice and cocked his head to one side.

"We left our horses in the care of two boys in the stable, but even after leaving two gold pieces to care for them, we are a bit concerned for their well-being."

"You *paid* thothe boyth? I warned 'em, I did. Never fear, ma'am. Nothin' bad will happen to your hortheth. I will thee to that!"

He turned back toward the kitchen and bellowed, "Hey, Blegral! Four wineth here." before heading for the side door.

Rene' followed his progress and noted that the elfin bard she knew as Brea was gone. Then she saw her in the arms of the big redheaded barbarian at the bar. Rene' saw the bard extract herself from the brawny arms to sit on the lap of an obviously drunk half elf sitting at a table close to the bar. She watched as Tensor appeared at the bar and grinned as the half elf stood and promptly passed out. A black-haired cleric, of Freya obviously, stepped around the table to kneel at the half elf's side. Moments later the barbarian's laughter reached her.

The cleric picked up the prone figure and, taking keys from the barman, climbed the stairs to the rooms above.

"So much for decorum," she thought sarcastically.

Then that something else that was a part of her felt it. Something else was at work here, something that pushed hard at her empathic shielding, an anger that seemed to boil up and recede.

"What is it, m'lady?"

Arantar's voice shook the girl from her musings.

"Uh, nothing." Then, a bit more sheepishly, "Mostly feminine curiosity."

"Well, if you will allow, I'd like to see if I can get some information on the daku who robbed us."

"Me too!"

Arantar turned to see the ill-concealed excitement on Bonaire's face and had just enough time to grab the youth's sleeve as that one stood to move toward the main throng of rowdies.

"Be very careful, my friend," he said. "This is not your father's town, nor his tavern. These people are not accustomed to being questioned. Be discrete."

"I will! I will! Don't you trust me?"

"Of course, my friend. I just don't trust them."

"Oh!" stated the youth thoughtfully. "Okay, I'll be careful. If I find anything, I'll come and get you first. Okay?"

At Arantar's nod, Bonaire wandered toward a small group of young elves and, before long, was engaged in conversation with a beer in his hand.

Arantar watched him until a soft touch on his arm brought his attention back to the mage girl. Rene's concerned look toward the brightly cloaked elf caused Arantar to cover her hand with his.

"Will he be all right, Huntsmaster?"

"I hope so, m'lady. He needs to learn his limits. I just hope he doesn't reach them here and now."

He patted the hand and turned to her.

"Now I must see to that information. Sir Solothon," he asked with a glance at the moody knight, "will you be here for a bit while I'm gone?"

"And just where else would I be?" he replied a bit too shortly.

Arantar saw the flicker of red in the knight's eyes and felt the battle for control that raged within. Finally the flicker faded.

"Sorry, Arantar. I don't know why, but all of this noise and jostling has me all keyed up. Don't mind me. I'll stay with the lady until you return. Then I'll go up to our rooms if you'll arrange for them." He sighed. "That potion healed my body, but I'm afraid that only time will heal my soul."

"I won't be long, friend," he stated as he rose. "M'lady?"

He received a nod from Rene', slipped the straps to his two great swords over his shoulder, and stepped through the throng toward the bar.

As he came closer to the bar, the barman's voice rose over the din.

"You know how those Freya clerics are."

As Blegral noticed the approach of the Huntsmaster, he moved to that portion of the bar.

"Hold that thought, Wolf. Yes, sir, what kin I do fer ya?"

"I'm looking for information," stated the Huntsmaster as he leaned the swords against the bar.

"Information about what?"

"About a thief."

"Inside or outside Catlorian?"

"Inside."

"Wait a moment," stated the barman as he looked about the large room, a thoughtful expression on his face.

"Grouch!" he yelled when he found the face he was looking for.

The half ogre came out of the kitchen drying his hands on a bit of grimy cloth and responded to Blegral's wave for him to come. The barman whispered something and pointed into the throng. Grouch nodded and crossed the room to a man easily six and a half feet tall in green steel-studded leather. The well-worn hilt of a great sword peeked over his right shoulder and through the black hair that was held loosely in a leather thong. His brown eyes held amusement as he listened for a moment, looked toward the Huntsmaster, and nodded. His smile grew as he said something to the half ogre and turned back to his conversation and the tankard of ale he held.

"He thaid he'd be here in a bit, okay?" said the half ogre as he lumbered passed toward the kitchen.

"There ya go," said the barman. "That's the guy ya wanna talk to. Now, is there anythin' else I can do for ya? Maybe somethin' ta drink while ya wait?"

"No, thanks." Then, as he looked about the throng, "Well, maybe. My companions and I need a place to stay, as does Lady Rene'. Have you accommodations?"

"Sure! I still got a coupla rooms. Ya could fit four in one if'n yer friendly, if ya know what I mean."

"Yes, I do, and I don't appreciate the reference. Lady Rene' is in my care for her safety and well-being, nothing more."

The Huntsmaster's voice was low, but the deadly meaning was there.

Blegral simply shrugged. "Suit yerself. That's two gold apiece in advance."

Arantar tossed the gold on the bar. The coins disappeared into the barman's apron before they finished ringing.

"Sure ya don't wanna drink?"

"My wine waits at my table," said Arantar. Then he added, "I hope."

"Okay, jist holler if ya need anythin'."

The barman turned back to his conversation with the redheaded barbarian while Arantar leaned his back on the bar and waited. The big man in green finished his conversation and tankard, laughed, and strode toward him.

"Yeah?" he asked as he leaned on the bar next to the Huntsmaster. "Name's Stone. What kin ah do fer ya?"

"I am Arantar Adenedhel and I have need of information concerning a thief."

"I have no knowledge of thieves, though there's a bunch—"

"Please, hear me out," interrupted the Huntsmaster.

As Stone listened, Arantar recounted the attack by the gualu and the albino daku. Stone stood with a grave visage as the tale was told, nodding at this point or that.

"We have heard that the shirakens and daggers could be sold here, and if so my companions and I wish to claim them. The thief has made an error in judgment in that he left us alive. I will not give the same quarter should I meet him here."

"Tell me," queried the ranger, "does this albino daku happen ta have a red spider symbol here?" Stone tapped his left breast.

Red Wolf heard this and his attention went to the conversation. Though Blegral continued talking, the barbarian heard little of what the barman said.

"Yes!" stated the Huntsmaster. "Have you seen him?"

"He was in here earlier tryin' ta sell yer stuff, but nobody was buyin'. Ah told him ta try the Monk's Guild or one of the martial arts schools. Other than that, ah don't know. He called hisself Arendel. May not mean much if he's yer thief, but..."

The big ranger shrugged. Arantar nodded and thanked the ranger for his help, then started back to his table. Before he took a second step, he turned back.

"Do you know of any employment opportunities for one of my talents?"

"Ex-Huntsmaster?" replied the ranger. "Sure! Go on down to the Guild and check. Pay's kinda low right now, but the work's steady. Or ya might keep yer eyes on the board by the door. Sometimes there's a well payin' job posted there. Matter o' fact, there was somebody in here lookin' fer people ta go up Lost Souls River. I think it's still posted, but ah ain't sure."

Arantar extended a hand to the big ranger, and it was instantly engulfed in an iron grip.

"Thanks, Stone. Would you join us at our table for a moment?"

Stone looked toward the distant table, caught the golden glimmer, grinned, and nodded. "Blegral, send a tankard to this gentleman's table fer me, will ya?"

"Sure, Stone, no problem. GROUCH!"

Stone followed the Huntsmaster to the table and, as Arantar began to introduce Rene', the big ranger bowed low, took her hand, and kissed it.

"Lady Rene', you're lookin' well."

"Thank you, Stone," she replied demurely. "How have you been?"

"Jus' fine, m'lady, and as always Ah'm at yer disposal."

Arantar hadn't thought that the story of the golden priestess had reached this far, but Stone was, after all, the Guild Master for such as he. Why should he not pay his blessings upon she named by the legendary Cashme're as "protected"? Besides, she'd spent much of her young life here in this city.

"If you could see me to the Myrlin's quarters, I would appreciate it."

The big ranger glanced out of a window before replying. "He's generally at table at this time of evenin', but Ah'll be goin' that way later if you can wait?"

"That will be fine. It will give me a bit of time to freshen up and become presentable."

"You are always 'presentable,' m'lady. However, rooms are at a premium fer some reason. Lots o' folks have come to Catlorian this week and nobody knows why. There's a rumor of some bad things goin' on down south, but Ah didn't get no particulars."

Then, with a grin, he added, "Red Wolf's even here, so I know there will be at least one fight tonight."

"Red Wolf?" asked Arantar.

"Yeah. He's the fellow with the braided red hair talkin' ta Blegral an' Tensor. He's s'pose ta be leadin' that excursion I told ya about. Matter o' fact, yer daku left in a big hurry when he caught sight of Wolf and his friend."

Grouch arrived at their table with a tray bearing four glasses of wine and a tankard of stout. He'd forced his way through the throng, leaving over-turned chairs and tables in his wake, but not one drop of wine was lost.

"Thank you Gro...Grek," said the Huntsmaster, but as he dug into the pouch for payment, Grouch interrupted.

"Uh, wait a minute."

He reached into the pocket of his dirty apron and brought out two gold pieces and laid them on the table.

"Thothe fellath inna thtableth thaid they'd be more'n happy ta take ek-thra care o' yer hortheth, thpethially thinthe I exthplained the conthequen-theth. Bethideth, it'th only one thilver fer the drinkth."

He dug into his pocket again and retrieved ten silver coins while pock-eting one of the gold. He laid the silver on the table before Lady Rene'.

"Now," he continued, "jutht toth it inna barrel over there."

"That one?" asked the Huntsmaster as he made to rise.

"No, no!" interrupted the half ogre. "Toth it! Here, lemme thyow ya."

Grek took a silver coin in his massive hand and, with his tongue between his teeth like a child aiming a stone at a rabbit, brought the hand back to throw. He took a deep breath and threw the coin.

It sang as it left the half ogre's hard fingers, ricocheted off of a steel stud in one of the tables, and shattered a mug on its way to imbed itself into the wood of the barrel.

"Darn!" Grek exclaimed dejectedly. "No matter how much I practith, I jitht can't get it inna barrel."

"Maybe if you use less force," came the golden mage's soft voice.

Rene' rose and took one of the coins gently between her thumb and forefinger. She flipped it with a small arc toward the barrel and, though its forward momentum decayed rapidly, it struck three helmed heads to carry it the rest of the way. It seemed that it was destined to strike the barrel in the same location as the embedded coin, but a young ranger picked that moment to raise his mug to his lips. The coin rang as it bounced off the mug, cleared the top of the barrel, and settled at the very center of the coins within.

"Softness works every time," she said softly with a grin as she returned to her seat.

The men at the table looked at her, the barrel, at her, and then at Grouch. The poor fellow was still trying to figure out how she'd done that. He scratched his head and ambled away toward the kitchen, tipping over chairs and people on the way.

Stone chuckled as he stood.

"You always keep 'em guessin, don't ya, Rene'? Well, Ah gotta be gettin' back over there with them rowdies." Then, "Ah'll come get ya when it's time to go, all right, m'lady?"

Rene' smiled and nodded. Stone moved gracefully through the crowd with his tankard until he was swallowed up in the masses.

Bonaire returned to the table, weaving his way through the people without spilling his beer. He took the chair recently vacated and sat panting.

"Hey! Look...found...guy selling...stuff!"

"Slow down, Bonaire," said the Huntsmaster as he laid a hand on the young elf's shoulder. "Take a breath."

Bonaire slumped down and took a long breath, followed by a long pull at his beer.

"Whew! Okay! I'm okay," he said excitedly as he looked into his mug. "Okay. I talked to some fellows who said they saw our daku in here earlier trying to sell our stuff, right?"

He cast a gaze at the moody knight and continued.

"You know, Sol? My daggers? Your shirakens?" At Solothon's frown, he continued, "Well, anyway, these guys, friends of mine now, told me that the guy we're looking for is at the Platinum Dragon trying to sell our stuff right now!"

Bonaire looked from one member of the group to the others at the table, scarcely able to contain his excitement.

"Well?"

Rene' had been listening while watching the big barbarian at the bar, the one with the flaming red hair. She knew him from somewhere, but she couldn't place him. Then she saw the other barbarian in tiger skin move to the bar. The red-haired man slipped over to him and said something that made the man jerk up his head and look at the redhead. Then he looked toward a table where two other barbarians in bearskin were drinking.

"Well?" prompted Bonaire again.

Whatever response could have been made was drowned out by a loud, deep voice.

"*What?!*"

The Huntsmaster's attention was snapped toward the bar some fifty yards away. He saw the red-haired barbarian hop up on the bar to sit grinning, while another barbarian, one in tiger skin and at least twice as large, stalked to the table where the Bear Clan barbarians sat.

The tiger-skinned barbarian brought both hands down on their table, shattering it and forcing the two who sat there into tables to the side and behind them.

"I'LL TAKE YA ALL ON!"

Chapter Nineteen

Arantar had seen these things before. A fight breaks out in one part of a tavern and ripples its way throughout. As chairs and tables are overturned, those at those tables attack the people closest, who in turn overturn other tables and chairs whose occupants, and so forth.

He had less than a second to react. He scooped up the small mage girl in his arms and ran for the money barrel.

"'Ware the brawl, Bonaire," he yelled as he moved.

He tossed the golden mage into the barrel with a "Stay close to this side, m'lady" and turned to see the fight heading his way. He spared a quick glance at Solothon.

The moody knight sat with his wineglass as if unaware of what was coming his way. As the brawl overtook him, he tried to ignore the jostling, but when some poor fellow was thrown onto his table and spilled his drink, he snapped.

Arantar knew he couldn't leave the girl, nor could he have made it to the knight before the obvious happened.

The knight rose—slowly, it seemed to the Huntsmaster—and his hand went for the hilt of the sword at his hip. The red glow of pure hatred radiated from his eyes and his lips pulled back over his teeth in a horrid grin.

"You *dare*?" he said in a voice as cold as death as his sword slowly slipped from the sheath.

Suddenly, a huge, mottled fist caught him on the side of the head and sent him hard into the wall where he slumped into a heap, sword half-drawn.

"The ruleth ith no weaponth!"

The half ogre shook his head and walked through the mayhem toward the bar, sending bodies flying in his wake.

The Huntsmaster had but a moment to sigh in relief. The fight was all around him, and it took everything he had to keep it away from the lady in the money barrel.

"Need a hand?"

The voice was one Arantar knew and, as the body of some poor soul flew past him, he grinned.

"Glad you could make it, Tao!"

The smaller Huntsmaster grinned as he allowed the fist aimed at his head to continue on its journey, along with its owner, into a post. A quick sidekick sent the man over a table and into two other fighters.

Upstairs, Melisande heard the fighting and made to rise from the savon'el's bed. A strong hand gripped her arm and she turned back quickly, her anger flaring, only to find a fitful half elf in the throes of a nightmare. Her anger left quickly and she lay back next to this strange man, a soft hand brushing the blond hair from his eyes. The half elf's frown softened and he slept.

"Who's the lady?"

Back downstairs, Arantar risked a quick look at the small half elf and grinned. There were none better than this small Huntsmaster in a fight, whether it was in a tavern or a pitched battle. The small man's body harnessed great speed and strength, as well as a precise mind. Here was Taofey Eth'nerhan, Master Fletcher, Huntsmaster, and friend. His grin broadened.

"Don't you recognize her? Cashme're's little one."

"The Ranger's blest?"

"The very same."

A large man charged the small Huntsmaster, and Arantar took the moment to watch. Tao waited and at the last moment went into the air, wrapped his legs about the man's neck, spun, and sent the man, upside down, into a post ten feet away. Tao landed on his feet and grinned, awaiting the next foolhardy soul to come his way.

"ARE YOU FINISHED?"

At the booming voice, the fighting stopped, and every open eye went to the balcony above the bar.

There stood Fredrick the Cleric, his staff held loosely in his left hand while his right gripped the banister before him. He surveyed the damage and shook his head, though one could see a small grin play at the edges of his mouth if one looked closely.

"Now, if you're all quite finished, please help the one next to you. There are clerics here? Good! See to those who have had more damage than their due. Good night."

All eyes watched as the old cleric turned and stepped back into his rooms.

"Tao, could you help Lady Rene' out of the barrel? I have to see about someone."

Without waiting for response, Arantar moved quickly toward the knight. Grek met him there with a sad look, if there was such a thing on a half-ogre.

"Thorry, friend. He gi' me no choithe."

"He'll understand, Grek, though I think he'll be a bit sore for the experience. I think you just saved him from a nasty fate. Thanks."

The half-ogre nodded and moved toward the bar, the chairs and tables already beginning to slowly mend themselves. Bonaire pulled himself from under a broken table and stood with a frightened look about him.

"Bonaire, help me with him!" As the young elf ran to help, he added, "Let's get him to our room."

"Is he all right?"

Arantar turned to the golden mage girl and nodded. Her frown told him she didn't believe him.

"He'll be okay after a good night's rest, m'lady."

"I'm not as certain as you on that score," she responded.

"Nor am I," came a soft voice from behind her.

Brea stepped to the Huntsmaster and touched his arm. "Put him on this chair, Huntsmaster."

As he did so, she laid a hand on the knight's brow and closed her eyes. After a moment, the moody knight began to breathe easier and she sighed.

"There is much going on here. I've removed a spell that was placed upon him sometime earlier, but there is something else at play here. Something I can't put my finger on. Huntsmaster, is he a friend?"

"For my part, m'lady, yes."

"Good. I think that, before too long, he will need your friendship and help. I will do what I can, but the rest is up to him and," she added, a meaningful look at Arantar, "you as well."

The Elvin immortal looked long into the Huntsmaster's eyes before she continued. "There are a great many things at work here, the least being your friend's condition. My help comes with a cost. Are you willing to pay it?"

The Huntsmaster looked down for a moment and then back into those blue eyes. "Whatever I must do, I shall."

"Then hear me, Huntsmaster," she said softly. "I don't know how or why you've been brought into this, but you've stumbled into a destiny from which you may not be able to extricate yourself. This one and another are linked, for good or ill, into a destiny that has many tendrils running from it. I cannot tell you what you must do or what is coming. To do so would remove your choices—one thing I am not allowed to do. Whatever you choose to do, or not do, is for you alone. However, I can say that to do nothing carries a far greater danger."

"For me or others?"

"Both, my friend."

"You spoke of another?"

"Yes, a wanderer, a savon'el whose life has been ripped from him, but whose destiny holds a promise of peace. His name is what he is, a wanderer in search of his destiny. His destiny, Sir Solothon's, and yours, for you may no longer have a choice in that matter, are entwined. From here on, the choices you make may well mean life or death. They will need your strength, but they must lead. Do you understand?"

"Not really. You know I will stand with Sir Solothon, but—"

"His fate is tied with the savon'el's. They are no longer a separate thing. If you stand with this one, you must stand with the other. There is great evil at work here and you must choose to stand against it."

"If that be my fate, then who am I to turn from it?"

"You still don't understand, Huntsmaster," sighed the beautiful bard, her eyes searching the Huntsmaster's. "It is not your fate to lay down your life or desires for them. It is, however, your fate that you *choose* whether or not to lay it down. There is no destiny, no writing in the stars. There is only your choice and what you make of it. Stay or go, it is your choice and no one else's. The others may or may not survive their fate should you decide the former or the latter, but they must follow the path that has, for now, been lain at their feet. You, should you decide to leave now, may still be a target of the evil that seeks them, though you are no longer involved. As I said, you may not be able to withdraw. I just don't know."

"Then, m'lady, my choice is made. I know not what I've, as you say, stumbled into, but I'm not one to turn my back on friends and good companions. I will see this to the end, whatever that might be." Then, with a grin, "Besides, I have a debt to pay."

The grin was returned. "That you have and not just to me." Then, the grin was gone. "See the savon'el and his friend Solothon through to the end, whatever that may be, and your debt shall be paid. Just be aware that you have placed yourself into a game that you do not control."

"Then let us hope that the gamesman is good at his trade."

"Rene', are you all right?"

Arantar turned from those ageless blue eyes to see Stone approach through the broken furniture. He glanced over at Tao as that one shook his head with a smile, raised a hand in farewell, and left.

"Yes, Stone, I'm fine, though I think the tavern is a bit worse for wear."

Stone saw the Elvin bard and the unconscious knight and frowned.

"Is there anythin' Ah can do, Landra Brea?"

"No, my friend, and, before you ask, there is naught to be done for this one that a good night's rest wouldn't help."

The big ranger grinned and turned to the Huntsmaster.

"Welcome to Catlorian, Arantar."

"Thanks," he returned, a grin beginning to form at the corners of his mouth. "This is the norm here?"

"Only when..." began the ranger, his eyes gazing about the debris. "Well, never mind. Ah guess Ah cain't blame everythin' on him." Then, as his eyes returned to the Huntsmaster, "Ah think you'd better get 'im to your room before the furniture swallers 'im up."

Arantar nodded at Bonaire and, together, they lifted the knight onto the Huntsmaster's shoulders. He glanced at Rene' as his burden settled itself.

"M'lady?"

"You go ahead," she replied. "The Guild Master is taking me to see the Myrlin, but I should return shortly."

"Please be careful, m'lady. It is turning dark and I fear—"

"Don't worry, Huntsmaster," came the voice of the Guild Master of Rangers. "There are none to challenge the Ranger's Blest this night."

Arantar nodded, saw the smile on the mage girl's lips, and turned with his burden toward the stairs with Bonaire taking up the rear.

Rene' watched until they made the stairs, then turned back to Stone.

"He waits, m'lady. He seemed more serious than Ah've ever seen him. What is it?"

"Let us go and find out, my friend."

As they left, two pair of eyes followed. The mirrored silver eyes of Maxim Anteroe watched from the shadow of the stairway. His gaze saw them out and then turned to the owner of the second set of eyes.

Eton had watched all of this with curiosity and, though he heard naught of what passed between them, he could sense that these were somehow linked to his prey. He turned his eyes back toward the stairs and caught the glint of silver and something else. He shook his head and sat back down on the newly repaired chair as he waited for the table to do the same.

Bonaire fumbled with the key and finally got it into the lock. Arantar picked the rope bed next to the door to deposit the unconscious knight. As he turned toward the room, the lamplight filtering in through the window was blocked out.

"So, half elf, you do not die as required!"

The dark shape at the window hovered as if floating, and the voice was one the Huntsmaster knew well. From the corner of his eye, he saw Bonaire had taken refuge behind the bed, his bow in hand. A quick glance and slight nod told the elf to wait.

"Not from the lack of trying though I'd wager," answered the Huntsmaster. As he moved slowly to his right, away from the crouching Bonaire, he asked, "Tell me, Arendel, what could I have done to anger you so much?"

"Well, for one thing, you've placed yourself between me and my prey. If that weren't enough, you made a pact with that Elvin bitch to protect him, yes?"

"I see your mouth moving, daku, but see only bile flowing from it."

At that, Bonaire snapped to one knee and fired. The arrow ricocheted off the window frame and lodged into the wall across the street. The darkness quickly disappeared as Arantar sprinted to the window, his hands filled with steel. A quick look up and down the street and a glancing look above and below the window told him the daku had fled. The question was, for how long?

"Long enough to get a good night's sleep, Huntsmaster."

Arantar turned quickly at the words and saw Bonaire stumble back from the cloaked figure, then the man casually brushed his hood from his head.

He knew this man, though not to speak with him. This man had visited many campfires and spoken to his commanders within their closed tents. There was something about him that Arantar could not quite...

"Arendel will not return this night, but I don't think he is quite finished with you yet."

"What do you know of this, Anteroe?"

The silver eyes took in the stance of the trained warrior. Though the sword was held slightly lowered and the Huntsmaster seemed to stand just a bit relaxed, Maxim Anteroe knew this one. He knew that any move he made on the others would draw an immediate attack and, though he knew the warrior's attack would be fruitless, the wanderer needed this one to not distrust him.

"I know that that daku was contracted to dispatch your knight and another and has failed, as of yet, to complete his mission. I also know you, Arantar Adenedhel, Huntsmaster to the Prince's Own and sworn, even in retirement, to the Lady Galen. You have naught to fear from me, Huntsmaster, and I may be able to help you."

"How?" asked Arantar, the sword point falling until it touched the floor with his hands resting on the pommel.

"There are…events unfolding, events of far-reaching effect, that will be decided by the choices we make. You were not destined to take a hand in this, yet you intervened and are now caught in it. You, by dent of your character, will stand by this knight, though you know him not, and give your all in service as friend, will you not?"

Arantar glanced at the unconscious form on the bed and then turned his eyes back to those silver ones.

"You know that I will. I know what I need to know of him; he is a good and true companion and a good hand on the field. I know he has a warrant on his head, a contract as you say, and…other things that I may be able to aid him with, but that is all. I do know, however, that he would not abandon me. His honor would not allow it, and neither will mine."

"I thought as much, yet there is another…"

"The savon'el?"

"So you've been warned."

"Only that the Landra Brea said that Sir Solothon has a friend he's never met who is a wanderer. She said I'd need to take a stand with them both e'er this game has ended."

"Yes, my namesake will need your arm as well before all is finished, but I was referring to one of your party."

"Who?"

"Lady Rene', Huntsmaster. What she must choose to do will be very difficult, and before this, how you said, 'game is ended,' she will have to make other difficult choices as well. I know you, Huntsmaster, and I know you are very good at what you do. However, you must pay close attention to know when to help and when not to. Choices will be made, and some may not be to your liking. You can only help if you don't stand in the way of those whose choices are the most important."

"You speak in riddles, Anteroe. Brea said I must follow and not lead, and you say I must not 'stand in the way.' Suppose I see a choice they've made, or are willing to make, is a bad one. Am I to stand idle and watch it fail?"

"That would be your choice. Choose wisely, friend."

With that, Wanderer walked to the door and opened it.

"Wait! How am I to know?"

"You will," he stated as he glanced back. "Know this, Huntsmaster. Though the savon'el is in danger for his life, this young knight's soul is as well. By the way, I believe Lady Rene' will be returning in a very few moments. She will have been asked to accompany one known as Red Wolf to the source of the Lost Souls River, and she must not go alone! If you choose to help her and your knight, you must follow them and aid them where you may. Now, she will need a key to her room and possibly some moral support."

Then the door closed behind him.

Arantar stood with his eyes on the closed door, trying to digest and decipher what had transpired, until Bonaire breached the moment.

"What in the bloody hell just happened?"

Arantar could see that the elf was scared all but witless, the blood drained from his visage.

"Where'd that guy come from, and is that daku coming back with friends?"

"Calm yourself, Bonaire. We should be all right for the night, but we must remain on our guard nonetheless."

As the Huntsmaster moved to the elf's side, he continued.

"That 'guy' is Maxim Anteroe and, if he says we have naught to fear this night, I believe him. Yet I would be stupid to think that our position is secure. I must return to the tavern to wait for Lady Rene', but I ask you, my friend, to watch over our companion until I return. Can you do that?"

"Sure. Sure. Just don't be too long, okay?"

"I won't. Just watch the window and stay alert."

With that, he shouldered the straps to his swords and went through the door. He surveyed the tavern as he came to the bottom of the stairs and found that most of the patrons had left for the evening. There were only a few adventurers at tables throughout the great hall, one lone warrior at a table by the door, and the barbarian he'd watched earlier standing at the bar. He moved to the bar and, after leaning his swords against it, turned to Red Wolf.

"You are Red Wolf?" At the barbarian's nod, "One of my companions will ask to accompany you up the Lost Souls River, and if that happens I would ask to join as well."

"Do you speak for this companion, Huntsmaster?"

"No. I've been approached by…someone to ensure this companion does not go without me. That is to say, me and my other companions."

"How many are you?"

"Three, though one may or may not wish to join this excursion. So, let us say two and a possibility of a third. There is also a possibility of a fourth."

"Who are these three you speak of?"

"The companion who will ask to join you is the Lady Rene', mage and cleric. Then there is a knight errant in good standing, a young warrior whom I will vouch for should he desire to attend, and myself."

"The fourth?"

"That one I have no answer for. I was told that he, like myself, is on savon and will need my aid at some point for reasons that were not explained. It seems that he is a friend to my Sir Solothon, though they have never met, and their fates have become intertwined somehow for good or ill."

"It seems, Huntsmaster, this 'someone' would have to be the one known as Wanderer, yes?"

A reluctant nod from the Huntsmaster brought a sigh and grin to the barbarian.

"Only Wanderer could possibly make a simple explanation so convoluted."

"Then you know this savon'el?"

"There are many in this city now. We will have to see. Just to make certain that I have this correct, you wish to join me and my retinue on this adventure?"

"As do I!" stated the mage girl as she made her way to the bar. "You are leading this excursion, aren't you, Red Wolf?"

Chapter Twenty

Arantar returned to his room late. Rene' was strangely distracted upon her return to the tavern and, after her discussion with the barbarian, said only that she would discuss everything in the morning. As the Huntsmaster entered his room, the light from the flagging lamp showed the raven perched on the sill below the window.

Arantar-sao, bad gone. I watch. You rest.

Thank you, my friend, but I'll sleep against the door this night.

Saola tired. Must rest. Soon, rest not. Trust air brother. Earth brother say bad in forest now.

Perhaps you're right, Blacky, but...

No but, saola. Sleep.

All right, my friend. sent the Huntsmaster with a trill of colors. *You've kept me alive this long. I trust you.*

Good.

The raven hopped twice and took flight out of the window.

A few minutes before dawn, the Huntsmaster came awake. Someone walked down the hallway, someone light but sure. Arantar listened until he heard the soft footfalls move down the stairs.

"Arantar?"

"Yes, Bonaire?"

"Can we talk?"

"Later. Sleep now."

He had to have time to think this through, and dealing with Bonaire was not conducive to good concentration.

"I can't, Arantar. I don't even know why I slept last night. My race, as you know, has no real need for sleep, yet last night I slept. Why?"

The Huntsmaster stifled a comment about the properties of too much drink and sighed.

"Sometimes the old saying 'sleep on it' carries more wisdom than was intended."

"But I can't...I'm not supposed to...What is going on, Arantar?"

The Huntsmaster sighed again as he sat up and scooted his back against the headboard. The chances of thinking through this situation alone evaporated as he realized that Bonaire was essentially correct. All of their decisions from here on would have to be discussed. He tried to put everything into perspective, but he found the exercise created an even more confusing atmosphere.

So now he thought the best thing might be to get everything out then sort it.

"Tell me, Bonaire, what did you think of the events of last night?"

The young elf sat up in the darkness, felt for his boots, and began drawing them on. "There are some really strange things going on around here. The daku, for instance."

Bonaire felt his way to the Huntsmaster's cot and sat at the foot end.

"Why did it try so hard to kill us? He...she...it had us cold. We were helpless. It took all of our stuff," he stated as he ticked the points off on his fingers, "*and* used demon fire, *and* poisoned our food and wine, *and* turned Sol's holy water to acid. He was serious! What'd we ever do to him...her... damn! It?

"Now," he said a bit quieter, "it's back and *still* wants to kill us! For what? And what about that guy last night...uh...Wanderer? What was he on about?"

"I don't know, Bonaire," he answered with a sigh. "Somehow we've been targeted, for reasons we don't yet know, to share the fate of someone we've never met. However," he continued as he felt the confusion from the young elf, "I met a fellow last night who might shed some light on the subject."

"Who?"

"You remember the big red-headed barbarian at the bar last night? Well, his name is Red Wolf. He was with Lady Brea last night, remember? After she took that curse off Sir Solothon here, she told me the same thing Anteroe basically said, yet she added a bit more. Then, Anteroe said that Lady Rene' would be going with Red Wolf on his mission and I should not let her go alone. I met with Red Wolf last night while waiting for Rene' and told him that if Rene' asked to go, I would volunteer as well. Now, I think Red Wolf and his companion are part of this thing we've stumbled into and, frankly, Bonaire, I'm not sure we could extract ourselves from our present course if we tried. This savon'el—"

"Savon'el?"

"Yes. That's the name Lady Brea gave him, and the name Anteroe alluded to last night. She said he was Solothon's friend, though I doubt our knight knows of it. Anyway, this fellow has some powerful friends and, from what I've gathered, some equally powerful enemies. I suggest we find this savon'el and share what information we have. Maybe ask him to join us on this mission to at least get out of the city into familiar surroundings to better protect ourselves. Maybe we will be better able to render a decision that will give us back our choices."

"Join *us?*" interjected the young elf. "Wait a minute, Arantar. I never agreed to—"

"And I never locked you in. I told the barbarian that you might wish to go. Maybe pursue some experience in the field along with any treasure afforded?"

"Treasure?" The pause was short. "Okay, but what about him?"

"Him? You mean the savon'el?"

"No, I mean Sol."

"What about him?" asked the Huntsmaster. "What do we need to know, other than we are linked for good or ill and for whatever purpose the Fates have decided? We know now that a curse was placed upon him with the express purpose of causing his death and destroying his honor. The question is: how did 'they' know to cast a curse that would send him into a berserker rage in such a way as to have it peak here? He would have been killed, dishonored, and discredited last night save for circumstances. Though he may not agree, having been knocked unconscious was far better than dishonorably murdering innocents and being killed like a mad dog."

"I do agree," came the deep voice from the cot next to the Huntsmaster.

As the soft light of the false dawn fell through the window, Arantar watched the knight slowly sit up and place his feet on the cold floor.

"Sol!" exclaimed the young elf. "You're awake!"

"An astute observation," he replied dryly. He held his head in both hands as he moaned. "Gods! I feel like the left wheel of a fully laden dwarven wagon! I remember most of what happened, but there are things that seem a bit…fuzzy. Tell me, did we get visitors through here all night last night?"

"You might think that," replied the Huntsmaster. As the light continued to grow with the coming day, Arantar went on to tell the knight of the events of the past evening, including Brea's gift and the daku's visit, adding, "You must remember Wanderer?"

"I seem to remember something about my soul being in danger?"

"You remember rightly, friend. Did you hear our discussion just now?"

"Yes, and I can answer your unasked question. I feel the burden I've carried from Laranthia is gone, yet something is still not right. However, to add my voice and perspective, I offer this opinion: Somehow, and for some reason, some force has brought us together. I must repay my debt to the Lady Brea. Though you say that you made the bargain, it was for my health and is therefore my burden. That debt calls for us to find this savon'el and, though it may be like leaping from the cauldron into the coals, join him. Whoever this savon'el is, we are as much a part of his destiny as he is ours."

Arantar glanced at the knight in the light that now streamed through the open window and saw something cross his face. It was as if a shadow of doubt or fear, or maybe a bit of both, slid though the knight's mind.

"What is it, Solothon?"

"Nothing, my friend. Nothing but…no," he said with a sigh and a shake of his head. "Nothing."

"Come now, friend," prompted the Huntsmaster. "We're all in this together. Tell us."

"It's just that…" He sighed again and leaned his elbows on his knees. "I was aware earlier, but not because I wished to be. It was either a dream or a premonition…"

He had found himself standing in full armor beside his battle-dressed warhorse in an open field. A hundred yards away another man stood, also in full armor, but his was as black as midnight. He'd watched as the man mounted his horse… No. A nightmare steed whose gleaming red eyes and flaming hooves seemed to show a distinct dislike for inactivity. The man mounted with an alarming grace, what with the supposed bulk of steel weighing him down.

Solothon too mounted and felt the muscles of his great steed bunch and shake, its nostrils flared and its dance just barely controllable by its master.

The man reached out a hand and, from the very shadows, a lance formed: black and dripping with blackness.

Solothon slipped the lance from the boot at his stirrup and, noting the sharp barb at its tip, brought it up and rested the butt on his saddle, its point up in salute.

Without a word, the man lowered his lance and spurred his mount. Blood dripped from the monster's fangs as its hooves set small fires with its passage.

Solothon remembered that he had shouted, "For Laranthia and the Laurel!" and, lowering his lance, unleashed the fury in his warhorse's heart.

They came together quickly. Solothon saw his lance deflected by the dark shield and watched as the black lance burned, as if in slow motion, through his body. Then...

"I woke. I've been lying here pondering that dream, if a dream it was. Is this to be my fate? I believe that, given our circumstance and if I allow it, it shall."

Then, as he stood and stretched, "However, the gods give us the choice that we may more easily make our own mistakes. Let us hope that this, if it happens, will be the result of a mistake on my part or in my judgment. That way I may guard against it."

"Well said, sir," stated Arantar as he stood and slapped the knight softly on the shoulder. "Now, who's for breakfast?"

"Me!" shouted Bonaire as he headed for the door, not waiting for Solothon to get into his armor.

"Wait," said the Huntsmaster. "I know that I shall need a few things this day, as I know you both will. I suggest we divide what we have in this pouch." He pulled Sir Jake's loaned pouch from his saddlebag and continued. "Then each of us will be responsible for repayment, as well as for our provisioning."

He counted out the gold coins, sixty-five to a pile, and held the two extra gold pieces in his hand.

"Since this is a joint venture, I shall use these to pay for our room tonight, if need be. Now, I suggest after breakfast we set about locking in our employment with Red Wolf, finding this savon'el, and our black-elf friend, in that order."

Solothon's brows were knitted. "I would rather take care of that daku first."

"I know, Solothon," said the Huntsmaster, "but we must see to the immediate problems first. We need to know where we will be getting our next meal. Besides, we owe a debt of honor to Brea and, indirectly, to this savon'el."

"Granted," answered the Knight reluctantly. "You're right. First things first."

"Yeah!" said the young elf. "First things first. First, breakfast!"

Arantar watched the young elf scoop up one of the small piles of gold and leave. He shook his head with a smile and turned back to Solothon. "Would that it will be easy for us, that we might claim the simplicity with which that one accepts situations."

Solothon looked up from his buckles and, for the first time since Arantar met him, smiled.

"I'll meet you downstairs, Solothon. I'll even try to save some food for you from our young friend, but please hurry!"

Then he too picked up his share of gold and left the room.

The Huntsmaster found many of the revelers from the night before sitting at the tables quietly. They were bruised, hung over, and more subdued in the light of the new day.

He stepped up to the bar where meats, cheeses, flagons of ale, and a huge pot of steaming Kaff awaited the boarders. He filled one of the plates, lifted a mug of the hot brew, and turned to the common room. Bonaire sat at a table close to the bar writing on a scrap of parchment while sipping on a mug of beer. The barbarian, Red Wolf, sat at the next table from him.

Arantar walked over to the barbarian's table and noted the bowl of eggs, the wineskin, and a mug.

"May I join you?"

Red Wolf looked up from his mug and recognized Arantar from the night before. "Sure." Then, as he lifted his wineskin from the table, "Join me?"

"What is it?"

"It's just my breakfast drink. Some wine with a couple of things added for extra protein."

"No thanks," said the Huntsmaster with a slight shake of his head as he sat his plate on the table and took a seat. "I'll stick to meats and cheeses this morning."

"Your loss," said the barbarian. Then he took a long drink from his mug and wiped his mouth with the back of his hand.

"Tell me," said the Huntsmaster. "Do you know where I might find the lady Brea this morning?"

"No, but if you leave a note on the bulletin board she'll find you. Why do you want her?"

"Last night a great deal happened, as you know. I have many questions for her, besides the debt I owe."

"What debt?" asked the barbarian as he reached over to take a bit of meat from Arantar's plate.

"Help yourself."

He was used to this from his years in the service and took no affront. He took a drink from his mug and felt the steaming Kaff reach down and dispel the restlessness of the night. He put the mug on the table and, while he rolled some meat and cheese into a piece of bread, answered the barbarian's question.

"She removed a curse from my friend. She said she did it as a favor for a friend of a friend, but I don't believe my friend has met this fellow. I asked you about him last night, remember? She said his name was Savon'el. A strange name, but she seemed serious. Do you know of anyone by that name?"

Red Wolf remembered the fellow in black asking about the pup and, being naturally cautious, decided that until he had more information no one would get any information out of him where it concerned his charge.

"Savon'el?" he responded innocently. "Isn't that the elfish word for wanderer?"

"Yes, it is. Someone of that name visited us last night in our room and he said something about our destinies being tied to his, and—"

"Wanderer. Yes, you said as much last night," stated the barbarian rather quickly.

"Yes. He appeared in our room and told us our lives were in danger. We figure it has something to do with this Savon'el, but I haven't the foggiest idea where to look."

Red Wolf looked up appraisingly at the Huntsmaster, but something beyond Arantar drew his attention. He lifted his hand.

"Hey, pup! Over here!"

Arantar turned in the direction Red Wolf's attention had been drawn and saw first the yellow robe and black hair of the cleric of Freya he'd seen last night. Behind her, holding to her shoulder as if for support, was the blond half elf she'd carried upstairs.

Melisande guided Savon'el to the table, sat him down, and stepped over to the bar for some food and Kaff for her patient. She'd seen the mischief in the barbarian's eyes and was not going to have more of the same this morning! She poured a large mug of Kaff for the half elf and set it before him, caressing his hair lightly as she did so.

Red Wolf leaned forward in his chair with a grin, but before he could get a word out, the cleric's hand fell hard on the table before him.

"Red Wolf," she said quietly, but with a bit more anger than she intended, "don't start with him this morning."

The grin broadened as the barbarian glanced into the cleric's eyes. The gleam of fun vied with the innocence of his words.

"Start with him? But whatever do you mean?"

The words were spoken a good deal louder than necessary and ripped through the half elf's throbbing head like a claw. His head held in both hands in an attempt to keep it from exploding, he looked up at his friend through pain-filled eyes.

"Shhhh!"

Arantar stood when the cleric came to the table and remained on his feet as he addressed her.

"Excuse me, m'lady. I am Arantar Adenedhel."

"Melisande Dorn," she replied with a small smile and nod, "Priestess to the Lady Freya and this," she continued as she laid a soft hand on the blond half elf's shoulder, "is…"

"Pup," interrupted the still-grinning barbarian. "Just call him Pup. He's a good companion with whom I've traveled many miles."

"Gods, Red Wolf!" said the half elf through clenched teeth. "Do you have to talk so loud? I think I drank half of the Sylvan wine in captivity last night, and it's paying me back for its extinction!"

"Well, I've got just the thing for you," the barbarian responded with a grin as he slid his mug across the table until it sat under Savon'el's nose.

The half elf's head came up slowly and a look of green revulsion tinged his cheeks.

Melisande reached out quickly and, with the back of her hand, slid the mug forcefully back at the barbarian. She placed one cool hand on the half elf's forehead and pointed a finger at the redheaded barbarian.

"Wasn't last night enough for you?" she accused. The anger in her voice seemed to increase the gleam in the barbarian's eye. "I think you'd better leave him alone to recover from your last bout of helpfulness!"

Arantar saw Solothon making his way down the stairs and over to the pot of Kaff. When the knight saw him, the Huntsmaster motioned him over.

"May I present Sir Solothon Calendera," said Arantar as the knight brought his Kaff to the table, "knight errant of Laranthia and my trusted companion."

Solothon bowed slightly as the Huntsmaster continued.

"This," he motioned to the barbarian, "is Red Wolf, the leader of our excursion. We met last night after you...went to bed. And this," he motioned to the black-haired cleric, "is Melisande Dorn, priestess of Freya."

When Arantar motioned toward Savon'el, Red Wolf took over.

"This stanch and hardy warrior is a comrade of mine I call Pup. He is trustworthy and steadfast in battle, though," he added with a grin, "for some reason he seems to be a bit under the weather this morning."

"Please, Sir Solothon, won't you join us?" asked the cleric.

"As you wish, m'lady," he replied as he pulled a chair from Bonaire's table and sat. Then, to Red Wolf, "The Huntsmaster has offered his services as do I, if you will accept them."

The barbarian nodded and turned the topic to the one they were interested in.

"Before going any farther, I will need to know more of you. You understand that this is not merely a casual walk through the forest. There are dangers before and behind us and I must know if I can trust you in a pinch."

"Understood," stated the Huntsmaster. "If you will allow it, I will relate—"

"Arantar, see what I did!"

Bonaire pulled his chair to their table without asking and handed the Huntsmaster the parchment he'd been working on. Arantar took the scrap of paper and read it.

"'Arendel, you bitch, I'll get even. Bonaire Blackabar.'"

"I'm gonna tack it up on the board where that—"

"Bonaire!" said Arantar quickly, nodding toward the lady.

"Uh... daku will see it."

"If all you seek is a daku, there are many in town, though I don't see—"

"Lady Melisande," interrupted the Huntsmaster, "I believe there are few albino daku who wear the silver grey of the Elvin race with a red spider embroidered on the left breast."

At the mention of the spider, Savon'el's head came up and Red Wolf leaned forward in his chair. Melisande, having remembered some of what the blond half elf had muttered in his sleep, stepped behind Savon'el and rested a hand on each shoulder.

"A red spider?" growled the barbarian.

"Yes," replied Arantar. "Does that mean anything to you?"

"Maybe. Go on with your story."

Arantar frowned but continued.

"This daku, Arendel by name, spent a great deal of time and energy to ensure we would part with our souls. Now, because all of his efforts came, obviously, to no avail, he toys with us. He wants us dead, though I cannot fathom a reason. This is not just a simple clash of races, such as has been going on for ages. He wants us *dead*!"

Then the Huntsmaster turned his gaze on the barbarian, who sat casually spinning some type of silver star in his fingers.

"From what I've been able to ascertain, our enemy and all that has occurred is linked, somehow, with the fellow I asked you about, this Savon'el."

Savon'el glanced quickly at Red Wolf, but that one never blinked.

"How do you figure—?"

"Excuse me," interrupted Solothon. "What do you have there?"

Red Wolf glanced down at his fingers, which were absently spinning the shiraken.

"Oh, Pup, someone left this for you. Do you recognize it?"

Savon'el took the proffered weapon, turned it in his fingers, and gazed at the embossed dragon. Disturbing thoughts, friend and foe, intermixed yet separate, went through his thoughts, causing the pain to increase and his vision to blur.

"Ask me about this later, please," he said as he handed the shiraken back with one hand and cradled his head with the other.

"May I see that?" asked the knight.

Red Wolf reluctantly placed the shiraken in the knight's hand. Solothon looked at the dragon emblem.

"Would you know of anyone who uses black crystal weapons of this type, but with the dragon pierced with a lance?"

Red Wolf looked askance of the knight. These strangers seemed to know far more than was healthy about too many things. Was it coincidence, or were they as they seemed? Caution counseled, "Wait," and he held the look until the knight shook his head, handed the shiraken back to the barbarian, and sipped at his Kaff. After a moment he stood and turned to the barbarian.

"For the purpose of this excursion, I know there will be payment, but what of expenses? We find we are without the wherewithal to purchase the things we will need, such as saddles, provisions, and so forth."

"Our employer has stated that he will pay expenses. Your tack and provisions will fall under that heading, though your weapons and such are your responsibility. If that is acceptable, we are now six."

"Seven," stated the cleric. "You will have need of me, and I understand the risks."

"Then seven it is."

Solothon nodded and then asked, "Where can I find a shop that sells weapons such as I've described?"

"You might try the Shoppe Arcane, next to the Platinum Dragon Restaurant. Just go out the door and turn right…"

As the knight committed the directions to memory, Bonaire stood and moved to his side.

"Mind if I join you?" he asked.

"Not at all," answered the knight as he turned toward the door. "Maybe between us we can find our property."

Arantar watched as they turned to leave, happy that they decided to go together. It seemed prudent, in light of the events of the past few days, to move about the city in pairs or a group rather than alone.

"Wait!"

The soft lilting voice brought both elves to a stop and brought all eyes to the foot of the stairs.

Rene' stepped gracefully from the last step and, taking a small piece of bread from the bar, swept past the table toward the two elves.

"Huntsmaster." She nodded as she passed him.

"M'lady," he replied as he came to his feet and caught the mage girl's arm. She stopped and looked at him questioningly as he continued, "Are you sure about this? I know you feel that you must go with us, but it will be dangerous. Are you certain you wish to put yourself in that position?"

Her eyes fell for a moment. Then, as she tilted her head slightly and grinned, she replied, "But if you are all going with me, what have I to fear? I am not worried, Huntsmaster. Besides, how else am I to learn more of my chosen craft?"

She stepped to the two elves and took Solothon's arm.

"Are you off to the Mage's Guild?"

"Yes, m'lady, though we have other stops before that. We search for our property, and it may take us to several different shops before we get a lead, but you are very welcome to accompany us."

"Thank you, sir. I would be delighted." Then, to Arantar, "I will return shortly, Huntsmaster. Will I see you here?"

"I have errands of my own, m'lady, but I will most certainly be here later."

"Good, then," she said with a smile. "We shall all meet back here, say, at the stroke of noon?"

"That sounds reasonable," answered the Huntsmaster. "Gentlemen?"

"Sure, Arantar," replied the young elf. "Me and Solothon will look after her."

As the three turned to leave, Arantar called after them. "For your safety, stay together."

The knight glanced back with a frown, but continued toward the door with Rene' and Bonaire.

As they passed the bulletin board, Bonaire stepped over quickly and tacked the parchment to it. Arantar shook his head with a grin and, as he stood, addressed his table companions.

"I too have errands. Where can I find a weapons shop? I need to have my weapons professionally serviced."

Savon'el rose carefully from his chair and waited for his eyes to focus.

"If you'll wait just a bit, I'll join you."

"Well," replied the Huntsmaster a bit hesitantly, "I do need to check on the horses. I can wait."

"Good. I need to get back to my room and see what I have in my pack. Then I'll know what to get while I'm out."

Arantar looked at the blond half elf strangely.

Red Wolf noted the look and added with a chuckle, "If you saw the way he packs, you'd understand."

Arantar looked long at the barbarian before he nodded and headed toward the side door and the stables. Red Wolf watched as Savon'el stumbled and caught himself on the bar.

"Maybe you should go with him."

Melisande gazed after the blond half elf and nodded.

"Maybe you're right," she stated. She rose and caught up with Savon'el and, taking his arm, helped him up the stairs.

Red Wolf watched their slow progress and shook his head with a grin.

"Great One," he mumbled, "what have you gotten me into this time?"

Chapter Twenty-one

"It looks as though we shall all be off on adventure together."
Rene' walked between the Elvin knight and Bonaire, a dainty hand placed on the arm of each.

"I have need of supplies. Where do we go first?"

"We were planning to go to the shop next to the Platinum Dragon," answered the knight. "What was that name..."

"The 'Shoppe Arcane', Sol."

Bonaire had been deep in plots this morning, and now a grin formed on his lips.

"I've got a great idea!"

"I know I shall regret asking this, Bonaire," said the knight with a sigh, "but what is it?"

"Look. Suppose we find the shop where that..." Bonaire looked toward the girl and then continued, "daku sold our stuff. What are we gonna do? Just walk in, say, 'Excuse me, my good man, but that stuff is ours'? How are we gonna do it?"

Solothon frowned in thought before he responded, "I suppose we will have to buy them back. I am low on funds, as we are all. However, we need not worry about that until the time comes."

Thinking the discussion was at an end, Solothon stepped up the pace.

Soon the three saw the silver building with the silver and black sign that proclaimed this establishment to be the famed "Platinum Dragon".

"According to the barbarian," said Solothon, "the shop we seek is just around the corner from here."

"Yeah, but you still haven't answered my question."

"Which question, Bonaire?" asked the knight sternly.

"What are we gonna do when we find our stuff?"

"I believe I gave you the only answer that would serve, and unless you've another idea…"

"But I do!"

The knight stopped a few paces from the Platinum Dragon and, knowing full well he wasn't going to like this, turned his full attention to the excited Bonaire.

Rene' looked from the knight to the young elf. She was stuck in the middle, and she was impatient.

"What is it?" she sighed.

"Well, we all know how much pride Sir Jake takes in his own worth, right?"

Rene' folded her arms and tapped her foot impatiently while Solothon looked skyward.

"Well," continued Bonaire. "When we find our stuff, what we do is we go back and tell Sir Jake that the shop owner called him some names or something. Then, after Sir Jake tears the place up, we waltz in, pick up our stuff, and waltz out again. What do you think?"

"Bonaire," said Rene' in a shocked tone, "Sir Jake tends to make a mess when riled. Do you really want that on your head?"

"Why not?"

"Life in Catlorian is expensive at best. Most shopkeepers, with a few exceptions, make but a modest living. Should your plan work, some shopkeeper's livelihood would be disrupted. He, or she, could very easily lose the business, their children would go hungry, and their employees go out of work."

"So what? They shouldn't be trafficking in stolen goods."

Solothon placed his free hand on the hand Lady Rene' rested on his arm and, using that leverage, gently moved the lady behind him. Then he grabbed a handful of the brightly colored cloak at Bonaire's throat and drew the elf's nose to meet his own. In a very low and lethal tone, the knight explained.

"If you dare to lie to a fellow knight, I shall denounce you as liar and scoundrel. On my honor, I will not allow you to lure him into your web of lies to further your ends. As much as those shirakens mean to me, I would rather never see them again as to win them back through treachery."

"But, Sol—"

"That is my last word," said the knight as he released the cloak. He took the lady's hand once again and moved toward the Platinum Dragon.

"Okay," said the detected Bonaire. Then, brightening, "But, what about a small lie?"

Solothon turned a frown on the young elf without stopping. They passed the door to the luxurious restaurant and turned the corner beyond it.

"Look. If we tell the shopkeeper we are looking for stolen goods, what do you think will happen?"

The knight's frown turned to thoughtfulness.

"That's what I thought too. But if we say that you loaned the shirakens to a 'friend,' but the 'friend' wasn't supposed to sell them. We just want them back. How does that sound?"

"I...don't know..."

"Look, Sol. We refer to that...thing as 'friend' when we talk about it, right? And, should we regain our possessions, a loose connotation could be 'borrowed,' couldn't it?"

"Well..." said the Elvin knight slowly. "If taken in that context, I will not be too proud to push forward an avenue that may end in success. Just be careful of your wording, Bonaire. I can only stretch my honor so far."

Bonaire glanced at the golden-garbed girl.

"Did all that mean yes?"

"Yes, Bonaire," she answered. "Just remember, a knight's honor is a very tricky thing. Be careful."

The sign above the door proclaimed the store to be "The Shoppe Arcane".

When she stepped through the door, Rene' saw shelf upon shelf of jars, all filled with a different condiment of the practitioner's art or the alchemist's pestle. There were baskets of odds and ends, scrolls and rings, staffs and runes, books, pens, and clothing. All were under one roof, and all were for the express use of the practitioner of magiks or the study of the same.

An elderly Elvin gentleman sat behind the long counter on the right. He looked up from his book over his spectacles as the tiny silver bells tinkled their arrival at the door.

"Yes?" he asked. "May I help you?"

Solothon walked among the shelves, perusing the contents carefully. He knew that, should Bonaire say something wrong, he would be bound to object. He decided that what he didn't hear wouldn't bother him.

Bonaire and Rene' walked over to where the man sat on his stool behind the counter, and it was Bonaire who took the lead in the investigation.

"Good day to you, sir. I am looking for several items that may have been sold here within the past few days. A friend borrowed these items, and instead of returning them he sold them. We are simply looking to purchase them back."

"I've had good business all week. I may have bought these items. What were they?"

"There were two black crystal shirakens and two black crystal daggers. Have you seen them?"

"Why, yes. A daku by the name of Arendel sold the shirakens to me just yesterday. He wanted—"

"He?"

"Yes, he. If this is a friend, how is it you don't know his gender?" asked the gentleman.

"Well, he has a talent for illusion. He has been known to travel in the guise of a woman, but, please, go on."

The explanation seemed to be acceptable, so the Elvin shopkeeper continued.

"Anyway, *he* wanted to sell the daggers, but I told him I had no use for them. Then I told him to take them to the Guild of the Rangers across the street."

"Do you still have the shirakens?"

"Of course. They're in the back being magiked at this very moment."

"Magiked?"

"Well, they're actually being prepared to be magiked. It's quite costly and time consuming, but some of my customers are patient."

"Then they haven't been magiked yet?"

"No, not yet. Why?"

"I'd like to purchase them in the condition they were in when sold. How much?"

"Without the magiks? Hmmm. I'll let you have them for a mere twenty-five hundred gold."

"Twenty-five hun...!"

"I paid your friend well. They are worth every coin. Besides, I already have a buyer."

"A buyer? Who?"

"I shouldn't tell you, but he's a human fellow with silver eyes. His name is...Yaki? Yobra? Anyway, he put the price at twenty-five hundred."

"Then there is no chance now to buy them?"

"I didn't say that. I figure that the first person to put gold into my hand is the person who wants them the most."

"We are not carrying that amount with us at the moment. Is there a time limit?"

"Well, this Yaki fellow said he would be in tomorrow—"

"We shall be back today. Please hold them for me."

"I will unless someone else enters after you with the price at hand."

"Fair enough," said Bonaire. He looked toward the door and asked, "Where did you say this guild is?"

"Is your hearing gone the way of your sight? First, you can't tell whether your 'friend' is a male or female. Now, you can't remember that I said the Guild of the Ranger is just across the street. You seem to be falling apart, young man!"

"Maybe," said Rene' in her soft voice, "he was just overwhelmed by all of the wonderful goods you have here."

"I suppose so," said the gentleman in a voice that said he didn't. "Anyway, the guild is across the street. You probably should speak with the Guild Master there. He would know if those daggers were sold there or not."

"Thank you for your patience, sir," said the girl as she took Bonaire's arm and headed for the door.

Solothon joined them at the door. "Well?"

"He's got the shirakens," answered Rene', "but he's asking twenty-five hundred for them."

"And if we don't get them today, they will not be here tomorrow," Bonaire added.

"Twenty-five hundred? It may as well be twenty-five thousand! Where am I to get that amount today?"

Solothon walked back toward the Adventurer's Guild to check on his horse and think. He'd come too far to let the only evidence he had to the murder of his friends escape him.

Bonaire and Rene' watched him walk slowly down the street until he disappeared around the corner. Then they walked across the street to the open doors of what seemed to be a large warehouse.

When they stepped through the doors, however, they found a huge arena covered with sand. Several men trained with practice weapons of all types. Others perfected their accuracy with bow and spear while more chased each other around with all manner of capture weapons. One of the men passed them with another on his heels. That one swung a bola about his head, the three steel balls singing. As the pursuer ran past, Rene' called out.

"Excuse me, sir."

"Huh? What?" he blurted as he slid to a stop.

He looked from Rene' to his "prey," then back again. With a sigh, he let the bola spin to a stop. "What kin ah do fer ya?"

Rene' tossed back an errant tress.

"Where may I find the Guild Master?" she asked in her soft, little girl voice.

"Well," he said as he looked about. He spied the answer and pointed toward the archery range. "Stone's over thar. He's the Master here."

"Oh, how delightful!" exclaimed the mage girl. "I didn't think to see him again so soon."

The fellow's eyebrows went up at that, but he didn't comment on his thoughts. "Now, if ya don't mind, ah hafta git back ta mah practicin'," he said with a quick nod. He ran off in the direction his "prey" had taken only a moment before.

"Well, Bonaire," Rene' breathed as she took the young elf's arm, "I suppose we ought to pay our respects."

"I'm with you, Rene'."

The two walked the fifty or so yards to the archery area and waited until Stone had finished instructing a young ranger in the finer points of the fletcher's art. When the big ranger caught sight of the girl dressed in gold, a smile came to his lips. He said something quickly to an older man dressed in green livery, and, as that one took over the instruction, he ambled over to Rene'. He took her proffered hand and kissed it.

"Lady Rene'. How can Ah be of service this day?"

Bonaire stepped back slightly, pleased to have Rene' direct this leg of their investigation. She seemed to have a better grasp on how to glean information from people than he. He watched closely.

"Ah, Stone, my friend, I'm sorry to take you away from your duties, but I'm afraid I shall again need your advice."

"What ah can do, m'lady, I will."

"Thank you," she said with a coquettish tilt to her head. "My friend Bonaire and I have been following some leads on the objects taken from he and his companions. We've located two on sale in the shop across the street.

We still, however, haven't found the two black crystal daggers. Do you have any idea where we can look?"

"Look no farther, m'lady."

He reached behind his back to hidden sheaths and withdrew the two daggers, each shining black in the sunlight. Bonaire fought with himself to keep from reaching out to those weapons. He'd never thought to see them again, yet here they were.

"Where did you get them?" he asked breathlessly.

"From Arendel, of course. Ah paid four hunnerd for 'em just this morning."

"Would you care to sell them?"

"If the price is right, sure."

"Bonaire," interrupted Rene', "did you ever think to report the theft to the town guards? There may be provisions set for retrieving your stolen property."

"Yeah," said Stone, "but do ya have a bill of sale or anything else to prove yer ownership?"

Bonaire hung his head and the big ranger sighed and continued.

"Ah thought not. Ah knew you wanted 'em, so, beside the fact that they are marvelous weapons, Ah decided Ah would purchase 'em. If you can come up with the right amount, Ah'll sell 'em back to you."

"Well, Stone," said the girl, "I suppose we shall have to find a way to get the money."

"Yes, I suppose so," Bonaire added. "I guess we ought to return to the tavern now. There doesn't seem to be any help for it, nor anything I can do."

"Wait," said Stone as he held Rene's hand to prevent her from turning. "If yer lookin' to buy somethin' made of crystal, ya might stop by the Crystal Guild. See if one of them miners has returned. They have some interestin' stuff there that might interest you, m'lady."

Rene's ears perked up. She glanced at the dejected Bonaire and received a shrug.

"That sounds interesting, Bonaire, and you might even find some information on your sword."

"What sword?" queried the Guild Master.

"This one," said Bonaire as he drew the green crystal sword from its sheath. "Do you think I might find someone there with some knowledge of this weapon?"

"Any weapon of the quality that that one possesses, made of crystal, are all made by one gnome. He's kind of a loner and is a bit balmy."

"Balmy?" asked the girl.

"He lives in the Crystal Ranges, and during certain times of the day the sound levels reach intensities high enough to turn yer bones to puddin'. It takes a certain mindset to exist there. Ah'm in command of that sector, yet, Ah try not to stay there very long. His home is there, and Ah still haven't found, other than he must be nuts, how he exists there."

Bonaire took Rene's hand and with a polite "Thank you" to Stone, asked her, "Do you wish to see the Crystal Guild?"

"It could be interesting," she answered. "I've managed to learn a good deal about crystal since coming to Catlorian. Where better to find the answers to my queries as to the different properties of crystal than the place it is mined, cut, and polished?" Then, to Stone, "Thank you. I hope to see you again before I depart. Travel far."

"Travel safe, Lady Rene', and may the blessings of the Mother be yer's."

The Guild Master turned back to his apprentices as Bonaire led the girl from the exercise yard.

Solothon brushed the black warhorse's coat until it shined. He talked to the noble mount now, as he had in the past, as a friend.

"Well, we've come full circle and are right back where we began. Our friends are dead, and I'm no closer to the culprit than I was in the beginning."

The big black warhorse felt the dejection in his master and nudged Solothon in the side with his nose.

"Yes, Enare, I know. Would that you could speak to tell me what to do now. Without those shirakens, I shall be severally hampered in finding those responsible for our friend's deaths. I barely have the funds for—" Then he stopped. "Wait! Am I not a knight worthy of trust? All that I need is a loan, to be paid back, of course, in full at some later date."

He stroked the horse's neck and smiled. Then he replaced the brush on the shelf within the stall, poured a good helping of fresh oats into the bin, and headed back to the Adventurer's Guild.

He found Sir Jake at a table in a posture that proclaimed, "Yes, I am here, and this world would definitely be a better place were there more men like myself about."

Solothon walked straight up to the table. "Sir Jake? May I have a moment to speak to you of a matter of utmost importance?"

"Why, of course, good sir."

"Thank you," said the Elvin knight as he took a seat opposite the large knight. "To get right to the point—"

"Yes. Please do. I like that approach, really, in that there is no 'beating about the bush,' so to speak, and all one's cards will be laid out nicely on the table for all the world to see, for a knight must always be straightforward as well as courteous to all and sundry, as one must uphold—"

"Sir Jake?"

The big knight stopped as Solothon reached forward and grasped his arm.

"Please. This is very hard for me, as you have already been very generous in our cause."

"Certainly. Please. I apologize. Continue."

"I would ask for a loan, to be repaid at your convenience. I have found the items stolen from me, and I must purchase them anew. They are now located in the Shoppe Arcane and are, at this moment, being prepared for some arcane magiks to be cast upon them."

"Well, tell me. Are the items yours?"

"Yes. I've said as much."

"Then I see no problem. Simply enter there and take them back!"

"I couldn't. You see, I've no way to prove—"

"Prove? Hell! You've told me they are yours. I believe you. Go and take them back." Then the big knight's lips drew back into a lethal grin. "Better still, wait until the blaggard is in the middle of his magiks and nudge him. If he's far enough along in the casting, he should blow up!"

"Would you do a thing like that?"

"What? Do you think I'm balmy? I could be reduced to a cinder! Besides, the items in question are not mine. Therefore, the question is moot."

"I couldn't either, which leaves only one alternative. I must repurchase them. I haven't the asking price, and that is why, with humble apologies, I ask for this loan."

"Well," said the big knight thoughtfully, "though I'm not a lending institution, I could not, in good conscience, refuse what aid I may give. How much do you need?"

"Five thousand, if you have it to spare."

"Five thousand gold? Well! And when would you be able to repay?"

"As I have said, your discretion."

Sir Jake reached into his cloak and withdrew a small pouch. He held it gently in his hand. "You find me in a strange position. All I have on me is seven thousand in gems. All the rest is tied up in other things at the moment or in the bank."

"Then, I apologize for the request," said Solothon as he began to rise from his chair.

"Wait!" said the big knight as he grasped Solothon's arm and slipped the pouch into his hand. "Do this. Use what you must, but return all you don't use to me. Keep an accounting, for I shall not check. Your honor is my collateral and, let us say, you shall repay me in full one year from this date, here at this table. Agreed?"

"Yes, Sir Jake, and I thank you. I shall return momentarily with all unused funds. Though one year marks our agreement, I shall be forever in your debt. Thank you."

As Solothon rose to leave, Sir Jake smiled and raised a gauntleted finger into the air.

"No. Thank you, sir knight, for giving me the opportunity...nay, the honor to help another noble knight to get back on his feet, so that, once again, he may smite, with the cold steel of truth and honor, those denizens of evil..."

Solothon walked away softly as to not interrupt the knight's dissertation. He stopped at the bulletin board to again peruse the advertisement left by the sage, Terillion. He nodded his head with a small grin and went out the door. He walked purposefully up the street toward the Mage's Shoppe.

The sign above the door proclaimed this building as the "Crystal Guild," but the small sign next to a pull-rope intrigued Rene' more. It read, "Don't just enter. Ring the Bell."

"Well," said Bonaire as he rocked back and forth on his heels, "here we are. What do we do now?"

"I suppose we follow directions," said the golden cleric.

She reached out a small hand and tugged gently on the rope. The response wasn't quite what the two were expecting, as a great horn sounded from inside the building and rattled the windowpanes in the shops across the street. The door opened and a gnome, three feet tall and dressed in a course brown tunic, trousers, and boots, appeared.

"WHAT DO YA WANT?" he shouted.

Rene' noted the fine sparkling dust of crystal on his arms and chest. This small fellow, in the typical pointed cap, was a gem cutter. He would be the best person from whom to get her answers. However, before she could open her mouth, Bonaire stepped forward.

"I've a sword here—" he began.

"WHAT?" shouted the gnomish fellow.

"I SAID!" returned Bonaire louder. "I'VE A SWORD HERE AND I—"

"A SWORD? WE AIN'T GOT NO SWORDS TA SELL."

"NO!" shouted the elf. He drew the sword from its sheath and, with the sun glistening from its green length, handed it to the crystal cutter.

"OH!" shouted the gnome as he turned the length of green crystal in his hands appraisingly. He looked up at Bonaire and shouted, "WHAT ABOUT IT?"

"I'D LIKE TO KNOW SOMETHING ABOUT IT. THE CUTTER WHO MADE IT AND ANY HISTORY SURROUNDING IT!"

"WHAT? AH..." The little man gazed again at the perfect cut of the crystal. "YOU JIST WANNA KNOW WHO MADE IT?"

"THAT, AND ITS HISTORY TOO, IF I CAN!"

Rene' had watched this shouting match with amusement. Now she passed her small hand before her to draw the small man's attention. As he looked into her eyes, she said softly, "If your records have its full history, I believe that's what he's asking for."

"AH! WELL! I DON'T KNOW IF HE'S IN! WE DON'T JIST GIVE STUFF OUT ON STUFF 'LESS THE GUY'S HERE WHAT MADE IT." Then, with another glance at the green crystal in his hands, he added, "WELL, COM'ON IN." He stumped through the open door.

"How did you...?" asked Bonaire of the girl, only to be told, "Shush!"

They entered the room and found themselves in the fragile world of crystal. A chandelier hung in the center of the room, each of the thirty-five pendants a different hue. A glass case, six feet by six feet, and a foot deep, rested against the wall on the right. It was divided into thirty-six cubes. Each cube contained a different cut and color of crystal mounted on a pedestal of gold, silver, platinum, velvet, silk-lined platforms, or bone.

There, at the base of each cube, save the very first on the top left, was a small brass plate engraved with the description, rank, and uses for the contents.

Rene' noted that the ranking went from the highest, at the second cube to the right of top left, a crystal almost black with an almost clear center on an ebony bone stand, to a pale pink mounted on a satin base in the bottom right. She pulled her small notebook from her pouch and, while she perused the content of the cubes in turn, wrote her notes.

"JIST WAIT RIGHT HERE!" shouted the little gnome, as he marched to a door in the back with the green crystal sword. "I'LL SEE IF...HE'S IN!"

They were left alone in that room for most of half an hour. Rene' completed her notes on the pink crystal and snapped her book closed. She saw that Bonaire had been walking aimlessly about, attempting, or pretending, to be interested in all of this. He was impatient, and the little stonecutter had disappeared with his sword.

Rene' heard the door open in the back of the room and smiled at the little gnome who pattered across the floor toward them. He was dressed in furry slippers and bathrobe, and his gray beard glistened with water as if he'd just stepped out of his bath. He carried the green sword lovingly in his hands as he looked from one guest to the other.

"WHICH ONE OF YOU OWNS THIS SWORD?" he shouted.

Bonaire stepped next to Rene' and whispered, "Are all of these guys deaf?"

"Probably. The Crystal Ranges, remember?"

"WHAT?"

"OH! I DO!" shouted Bonaire.

"WHAT DO YA WANNA KNOW?"

"I WISH TO KNOW WHO CRAFTED IT!"

The gnome, seemingly over four hundred years old, turned the sword in his hands. He glared at Bonaire.

"YES, I MADE IT! SO?"

"I'D LIKE TO KNOW MORE ABOUT IT!"

"IT WORKS, DON'T IT?"

"YES. BUT I DON'T KNOW WHAT IT'S SUPPOSED TO DO!"

"KILL THINGS! THAT'S WHAT A SWORD'S FOR, AIN'T IT?"

Again, Rene' passed her hand before her, and the old gnome locked his eyes onto hers.

"What the impetuous young one wishes," she said softly, "is to know the sword's history, the reason for its crafting, the primary owner—"

"I FELT LIKE MAKIN' IT, THAT'S ALL!"

"Did you give it any special powers?"

"HMM...NOT REALLY! IT WON'T CHIP OR BREAK, AND IT'LL STAY SHARP FOREVER! IT'S MADE OF THE EMERALD GREEN, THE HARDEST GREEN THERE IS! IT'S ALSO THE LOUDEST!"

"The loudest green, or the loudest crystal?" she asked.

"THE LOUDEST CRYSTAL! IT AMPLIFIES SOUND! NOISY STUFF!"

Bonaire jumped in and asked, "What can it be used for?"

"WHAT?"

"I SAID, WHAT CAN IT BE USED FOR?"

Bonaire was getting discouraged. Rene' could talk to these people in a normal tone and they understood her. He, on the other hand, had to strain his voice yelling...

"KILLIN' THINGS, DUMMY!"

...And was insulted.

"BESIDES THAT?"

"OH, I SUPPOSE YOU MIGHT USE IT TO CUT DOWN TREES!"

"I MEAN, POWER WISE!"

The old gnome looked down at the sword again, obviously reluctant to return this beautiful weapon to this stupid youth.

"WELL!" the gnome shouted. "A SORCERER COULD CAST A SHOUT SPELL THROUGH IT! THAT WOULD DO ALL KINDS OF WONDERFUL THINGS!"

"BUT WHAT POWER COULD I USE THROUGH IT?"

"I DON'T KNOW, BOY! I MADE IT FOR A SORCERER! ARE YOU A SORCERER?"

"I AM A PRACTITIONER OF THE ARTS, THOUGH NOT THOR-OUGHLY SCHOOLED!"

"WHAT?"

"He said," said the lady softly, the old gnome's eyes locked to hers, "He is a student in magic."

"OH! WELL! IT DEPENDS ON THE SPELLS YOU USE! ANYTHING THAT MAKES NOISE, BUT DON'T BE SENDIN' FIRE DOWN IT! YOU WON'T BE ABLE TO HANG ON TO IT! THE GREEN TRANSFERS HEAT LIKE CRAZY!"

"WOULD YOU MIND FINDING THE HISTORY FOR ME?"

"WHAT DO YOU WANT TA KNOW? HOW I CUT IT? HOW I MADE IT?"

"NO! I—"

"GOOD! I WOULDN'T TELL YA, NOHOW! IT'S A HUNDERD AN' TWO YEAR OLD!"

"Who was the original owner?" asked Rene'.

The old gnome smiled at the beautiful girl, then frowned and put his hand to his beard.

"LE'SEE NOW! THE FELLA I MADE IT FOR DIED AND ANOTHER FELLA WANTED IT JUST RECENTLY! HIS NAME IS...UH...OH, YES! YAVOSH! YEAH! YAVOSH! HE WAS ONE O' THEM CLERIC AND SORCERER MIXED TYPES FROM DRAGON'S TEETH! DON'T KNOW IF THAT'LL DO YA ANY GOOD, BUT I'LL TELL YA THIS! IF IT EVER BREAKS, BRING IT BACK AN' I'LL GIVE YA TEN THOUSAND GOLD! THE GREEN WON'T BREAK NO MATTER WHAT! BUT," he continued, as he pointed a finger at Bonaire, "IF YA MISTREAT IT, I'LL HAVE YA FER SUPPER! YA MAY'VE BOUGHT IT, BUT IT'S GOT MY HEART AN' SOUL IN IT!"

Another movement of a dainty hand brought the old gnome's eyes back to the girl's.

"You don't magic your own crafts, do you?"

"NO! I AIN'T GOT THAT SKILL! USUALLY I JIST SEND THEM TO THE MAGE'S GUILD MADE TO ORDER! I ONCE MADE A COUPLE OF THINGS FER THE MYRLIN OUTTA THE BLACK, BUT THEY WASN'T 'ZACKLY WHAT HE WANTED! HE NEVER COMES IN HERE! SAYS HE CAN'T TALK LOUD ENOUGH! THAT AIN'T THE KEY TA TALKIN', BUT I GUESS HE FIGGERS US GNOMES IS DEEF OR SOMETHIN'!"

The end of his statement was obviously meant for the young elf, for he looked straight into that one's eyes as he returned the sword. The old man's beard and hair had dried as he talked, and after he brushed back the errant locks and smoothed his beard, he brought a ringlet out of one of his deep pockets and placed it on his head. The crystal that set over his brow was black as midnight, but the center was almost clear.

Rene' looked at the board and then back to the old one.

"You are the Guild Master here, aren't you?"

"Yes, m'Lady," he said in a normal tone. His smile was deep with the lines of years in his trade. "Name's Miner. Don't remember the name my Momma give me, but names is such temporary things, ain't they?"

Bonaire noted the change in voice in the old gnome. He was no longer shouting, as he was no longer looking at Bonaire but at the golden-eyed girl.

"I have but one last question, if you will?" she asked. He nodded and she continued, "I've talked with the Myrlin recently on the subject of crystal and his studies of the properties of the shades, and it peaked my interest. He spoke of some of the inherent powers of the different crystals, and I was wondering, does the Guild keep records dealing with the known powers of each of the different shades?"

"No," he answered slowly. "We just cut the stuff to order. We're not mages here, but I do know that when yer workin' with the black, don't light nothin' with magic. We brought three of them mages back dead jist recently. They didn't listen."

"Is there a way that I might set up an account with you so that I may purchase samples of the different hues of crystal for my studies?"

"Why don't you just look in the bins back in the back? That's where you'll find shards of castoffs. They're useless ta us and if ya want 'em, you can have 'em. Jist be careful what ya carry 'em in. They can be terrible sharp and even leather wouldn't last a day."

"So, sir," said Bonaire, "you're saying that if I—"

"WHAT?"

"DID YOU SAY THAT IF I HIT MY SWORD REAL HARD IT WILL MAKE A LOUD NOISE?" shouted the perturbed elf.

"NO! THAT'S NOT WHAT I SAID AT ALL! WHAT'S THE MATTER? YOU DEEF?"

Rene' giggled at the comment and received a glare from the ruffled Bonaire.

"What I said," continued the gnome in a normal tone, "was if you put *magical* sound through it, it makes it louder. It's a tunin' fork. If you tap it, it will vibrate. If you smack it against a building or somethin', it'll vibrate right outta your hands."

Rene' felt the time was right for them to leave. She didn't know Bonaire well, but he seemed to have become embarrassed. She reached out a small hand and gripped the old gnome's arm gently. He looked up at her and grinned.

"We must leave now," she said. "I would like to come back later, if I may, to collect those shards?"

"Sure! There's always shards. Yer welcome anytime."

Bonaire took Rene's hand on his arm and with a sigh walked her to the door.

"You be careful now," said the old gnome as they went through the door and out onto the street.

Rene' gripped the elf's arm excitedly.

"Oh! Isn't this wonderful? Where to next, good sir."

Bonaire puffed up visibly at that address.

"The Mage's Guild, m'lady," he replied and walked proudly up the street with—if you asked him—the most beautiful woman in Catlorian on his arm.

Along the way, they passed a street flanked by temples. Rene' turned there, though Bonaire began to falter.

"Bonaire," she said. "Come on. We must give offering to our deities before we set out."

"I...uh..." stammered the elf as he looked at his boots.

"You do worship, don't you?"

"Well, Uh... Not really. I mean...uh...I've never had much experience in it."

"How do you function in this world without a higher power to guide and comfort you?"

"I just never... You know!"

"No, I don't!" she countered. "And it scares me to think you've walked through this world so long without guidance. Come. We will see someone about that."

With that, she set off down the street toward the temple marked with the sign of the tree, the symbol of the Mother of all Elvin deities.

Just inside the door, an acolyte, a young blond elf dressed in green robes, ran up to them excitedly.

"What may I do for you? State your sins? Test the church?"

"No, friend," answered Rene' softly. "I wish to speak with a priestess of my order, but my friend here needs guidance in the deities of our race. He has, at this moment, no god or goddess to follow. Can you help?"

"Why, yes! Yes, of course!"

He took Bonaire by the hand and led him down the corridor. As he did so, he began a long and involved discourse on each of the deities worshipped by those of the Elvin race.

Rene' smiled as Bonaire looked back at her obviously looking for help. Then she turned toward the tall door marked with the golden heart. She knocked once, then stepped back and assumed the pious stance of the priestess asking for absolution.

"Rene'?"

The familiar voice jolted her head up. There in the doorway stood Sl'everin, a smile on her face so bright it made her eyes sparkle. "It *is* you, Rene'!"

The girl found herself engulfed in the priestess's warm embrace.

After a moment stolen for their mutual happiness, Sl'everin held the girl at arm's length.

"My, my! Just look at you. You're more beautiful than ever!"

"You also, my sister" said the girl in gold. "However, I've come for reasons other than this welcome reunion."

Sl'everin placed her arm about the girl's shoulders and started for the door. Bonaire saw this and in a panic shouted, "RENE'!"

"Wait, my sister," she said. She turned and called, "Come, Bonaire. We shall find you a deity yet."

Bonaire thanked the acolyte and ran to Rene's side.

"I think I'd like to know more of Celeste, if you don't mind?"

"Certainly," answered Sl'everin. She clapped her hands once and a beautiful Elvin girl approached them. "Celestia, would you mind speaking with this young wanderer on the subject of our Lady?"

"Of course, Priestess," said the blonde girl softly.

She gracefully fell in beside Bonaire, took his arm, and led him toward one of the cubicles inside the temple. Bonaire's smile showed Rene' that he would be safe and, very possibly, saved.

Sl'everin took Rene's arm and led her toward a cubicle on the other side of the auditorium. Rene' draped herself on the settee as Sl'everin poured them both a glass of wine.

"Now, Rene', what is this all about?"

"Well, I'm going on adventure and there are some things I wish to take care of before I go. I need some supplies from here of things I shall need."

"You shall have them! Just give me your list."

"I also need to pray and tithe. I have little money left, but I must do what I must."

"It shall be done, Rene'."

"I understand that the place where we, that is my companions and I, will be going is populated with creatures of evil and darkness, undead and the like. What do we have, my sister, other than our holy symbol that will serve to battle these?"

"Why, water blessed by the goddess! I have five vials here. Take them," she said as she loosened a pouch from her sash and placed it gently on the girl's lap. "It's the least I can do for a dear, dear friend. But, Rene', are you sure about this? Adventure of this type is dangerous."

"I love you for worrying, my dear, but I shall be quite safe. My companions are all staunch men and I shall come to no harm. Besides, how else am I to learn?"

"I suppose you know what's best. You always did." Then, with a grin, she said, "Come. Let's see about the other provisions."

She and Rene' moved gracefully toward the back of the temple talking excitedly.

Chapter Twenty-two

Sir Solothon stepped from the shop with a feeling that he was once more in control of his destiny. He had his shirakens back in the leather pouch at his waist, though it had cost him two hundred fifty gold pieces extra. The shopkeeper had charged him ten percent to convert the precious stones, lent to him by Sir Jake, in this, the center of commerce called Catlorian.

Now that this part of his mission was complete, he decided to find the sage of the advertisement and formally introduce himself. However, where to look for a single person in such a vast city?

Simple. Ask.

"Excuse me, sir," he said of a passing citizen.

The man, dressed in passable garments of a nondescript nature, stopped at the summons and looked the knight over from head to toe.

"Yes, good sir?"

"Could you possibly direct me to the apartments wherein I might find one Sage Terillion?"

"Of course! Of course!" said the man quickly. He rubbed his chin as he looked up and down the street. Then he pointed up the street away from the Adventurer's Guild. "Go up two... no, three streets. Turn right. Go another two, turn left, and his house will be the third on the left. Got it?"

"Yes," said the knight. "Thank you. It's good to know there are those within a large city who will take the time to help a stranger."

"No thanks needed, sir. I'll be on my way now. You can find the place now, right?"

"Of course. Your directions are very distinct."

"Good. Good. Take care now," said the man as he moved a bit quicker down the street and around the corner.

Solothon stepped off in the direction he'd been told with renewed vigor. He turned right at the third street after passing several small shops, went up two, and turned left, but it seemed that the farther he went, the seamier the surroundings.

"A great sage wouldn't live in this area," he thought. "I must have taken a wrong turn."

He turned to retrace his step and found three burly gentlemen blocking the end of the street some thirty paces away. One stopped a pedestrian who wished to enter the street and sent him away. They all stood, smiled, and watched the Elvin knight with what seemed to be amusement.

Solothon looked to either side of the street, but he found all doors and windows shut, and no other person was to be seen.

One of the three walked toward him, a smile on his face, though the smile was obviously not with amusement.

"Looks like you're lost, sonny. Need some help?"

"No, thank you," replied the knight.

"Well," said the man, still moving slowly toward him, "for a little jingle, my friends and I will show you where to go."

Solothon looked back up the street in the direction he had been going and found two more men there, their swords bared in their hands. As he came forward, the brigand's hand found his sword hilt. The smile became malignant and his intent was clear. His sword came free and the smiling villain attacked.

The Song Sword screamed as it left the sheath, though its music was not there. The Elvin knight parried the sweeping stroke and aimed a feint at the man's head. As that one brought his sword up to parry the half-hearted stroke, the sword abruptly changed direction. In the hands of the well-trained and, now, seasoned warrior, the sword plunged deep into the brigand's chest and caused the smile to vanish in disbelief. The man died on his feet, his heart pinned to his backbone.

Solothon pulled the sword free and ignored the man as he slumped to his knees. The knight moved down the street toward the remaining two. One of those two uncovered a crossbow, cocked it, and placed a barbed bolt in the slot. The other brigand nocked an arrow in his bow, but he held the bow slack. He would wait until his accomplices from the other end of the street had dealt with their prey.

Those two had broken into a run toward the knight as their friend died. Solothon turned toward them and met them as they attacked. The elf carried the fight to them, not from any false bravado, but from the sure knowledge that given his back to shoot at, the others would let fly their quarrels.

The two attacked him from either side. The knight would have liked to have had a solid wall to his back, increasing his chances of survival, but he had no hope of attaining one. Yet, though the swords struck him and caused minor cuts when the mail failed, he fought on. He parried the thrust aimed at his heart, spun, and drove his sword through the other attacker's throat. He felt the wind as two arrows passed his body and looked up the street in time to see the bolt leap from the crossbow. The barbed quarrel pierced the mail at his shoulder and came to rest with the point protruding from his back. He felt the pain, but, as any warrior could explain, he used that pain as power. He turned on the other brigand and spun his sword.

The look of amusement faded from that one's face as he attacked. Solothon was a precise machine as his weapon closed with that of his attacker, parried it, and carried through his neck. The brigand's hand went to his neck in a vain hope to stem the flow of blood from his severed jugular.

Solothon turned from this last villain toward the two at the end of the street. The one with the crossbow had dropped that weapon and taken up his sword, but halfway there he witnessed Solothon's prowess and thought better of direct conflict. He ran back to his downed weapon and began cocking it. The other man, however, launched two more arrows from his bow in hope of a quick kill. The first passed close, but the second embedded itself into the knight's right leg.

"Where are the town's guards when they are needed?" he yelled as he took cover behind several wooden casks at the side of the street.

"Yeah? What do you want?"

"Are you with the guards?"

"Sure. What seems to be the trouble?"

Solothon looked from around the cask and saw that the man with the bow had disappeared, and a man in leather had appeared in the middle of the street. He pushed himself away from his cover and limped up the street toward the man. His eyes were blurred from the pain, but as he moved toward the blur that should be a guard, his eyes cleared. Before him stood the man who had used the crossbow. In that one's hand was a sword, and Solothon was too weak from loss of blood to adequately defend himself.

He stopped but three steps away and lifted his sword with a shaky hand. "Come and be finished, bandit."

The brigand smiled and was about to accommodate the knight when, from behind the crowd that had gathered at the end of the street to watch, a deep, melodic voice reverberated from the very walls.

"I believe his soul is reserved for me."

Solothon looked past the brigand who had suddenly gone stiff before him to see the crowd disappear into doors and alleyways. One figure stood in the street, his great black sword placed point down before him, and gazed down the street through the slits in his helm. His flat black armor sported but one relief: the bone white skull upon his left breast.

The brigand before Solothon again found his feet and began moving, not toward but past him. As that one drew abreast of the Elvin knight, fear gave his faltering feet wings. He ran like a man from a demon.

Solothon looked back down the street where the man had lifted his sword, sheathed it soundlessly without looking, and began walking toward him. The young knight tried to draw up all of his remaining strength for this coming conflict, but he was weak and his sword hung limply in his numb hand.

"Is your name Solothon Calendera?" intoned the giant in black as he moved relentlessly toward the knight.

"Yes, I am."

"Good. I shall help you," said the black knight, ignoring the look of desperation as Solothon dug deeply into his reserves of strength only to find enough to keep upright.

The black knight removed his gauntlets as he came and hung them on his belt. He ignored the knight's sword as he knelt and took hold of the arrow protruding from Solothon's leg.

"This will hurt a bit, I'm afraid," he said matter-of-factly as he pushed the arrow through the leg, snapped off the barbed end, and yanked it out, all in one swift motion.

The pain caused the knight to lose consciousness. The man in black caught him as he fell, tapped the crossbow bolt through, and pulled it out the knight's back. He then picked up Solothon and carried him from the street like a child.

Solothon woke a short while later with his back against the sidewall of the Adventurer's Guild. He felt his body, but he found no wounds. He was still weak, but if it weren't for the blood-encrusted hole in the mail covering his shoulder and leg, he would have thought he'd dreamed everything that had happened. Then, in panic, his hands went to the pouch at his waist. He sighed when his hands found the two shirakens still there wrapped in black cloth.

Then, as his hands closed on something else that shouldn't have been there, he frowned. He brought it out of the pouch and found it to be a tightly rolled scroll. He unrolled it and read:

"To: Sir Solothon Calendera.

Greetings. We will meet again when you are worthy. In the meanwhile, don't ask for directions from a stranger in Catlorian.

Cartellion, Lord Saladin"

Solothon rerolled the scroll, stood unsteadily, and returned the scroll to his pouch. He took a deep breath to settle his nerves and stepped up on the walkway and into the tavern.

Sir Jake saw him as he came through the doorway and leaped to his feet. "Ye gods, man! You've had a fight and didn't call for my assistance?"

Solothon looked down and saw that he was covered in blood and grinned. "There wasn't time, but I made out well, nonetheless."

"Well, if they lost, they must look frightful, indeed."

"I got what I was after and, as was our arrangement," Solothon stated as he handed the astonished knight a pouch filled with gems, "here is what was left."

Sir Jake took the pouch and, after depositing it within his cloak, waved Solothon to a chair.

"Tell me what happened, good sir. Was it a good fight?"

"I suppose. I was attacked as I attempted to find the quarters of Sage Terillion. Were it not for the timely intervention of one Lord Cartellion, you might have had to read my tale posted above my tomb."

"Cartellion? Worthy fighter he, though a bit on the evil side. Why did he assist you, I wonder?"

"I know not, yet I am in his debt."

"Well, my friend, you need a drink. Sit there. I shall fetch for you. You're indeed a fighter to be reckoned with, what with incurring the favor of Lord Cartellion, one of the most honorable foes known..."

Sir Jake carried on this way until he came to the bar.

"Blegral, a stiff drink for yon staunch knight, if you please. He has this day acquitted himself most handsomely and at great peril against a horde of brigands, yet without a cry for succor..."

Arantar came in the door from the stable and heard the knight's ramblings. He looked over to where Solothon, covered with blood, sat cleaning his blade. If half of what Sir Jake was saying were true...

"Solothon?" he said as he walked over to that worthy's table. "Are you all right?"

"Yes, friend, but I wish he wouldn't go on so. It was really but a skirmish and I came very close to losing."

Savon'el came down the stairs as Jake continued, "...and at the very peak of the battle, with scores of the dead lying about, and showing no quarter, who should step in, though unbidden by our staunch and fearless knight, but Lord Cartellion, himself a fearless and..."

Savon'el looked in the direction Sir Jake, with wide sweeping gestures, had indicated. There he saw his acquaintances of the morning, Solothon and Arantar, deep in conversation. The Elvin knight was covered in blood, yet, from the look of him, he had suffered no hurt. But this reference to Cartellion...

"Excuse me, Sir Jake?"

"Yes?" he said to the inquiring Savon'el. "What may I do for you?"

"Did you say that Lord Cartellion helped that knight?"

"Of course! Why?"

"That is my question. Why?"

"Why? Why would Lord Cartellion help a knight in distress? A Saladin, and one of Cartellion's rank especially, is a knight, though of a wholly unsavory belief, and as such stands firmly on their own honor, as any knight should. A Saladin's word is his bond, and Cartellion's is chiseled in granite! I have no love for the man, but speak not any dishonor."

"I would not, sir knight. I too have had some dealings with Cartellion, and I am relieved to find he is a man of honor. Thank you for your attention."

"You are very welcome, sir," answered Sir Jake as the blond half elf moved away toward the table at which Solothon sat.

"May I join you?" Savon'el asked as he came to Solothon's table.

The knight waved him to a chair across the table from him.

Savon'el sat and, between sips of Kaff, appraised both the knight and the Huntsmaster with, though he knew not where this talent came, nor that he used it now, a practiced eye for the sizing up of his friends and enemies.

"You seem to be feeling better, friend," said Arantar.

"Yes, I do," said the blond half elf, "but I am more interested in your friend." Solothon glanced at Savon'el as that one continued, "Did I hear Sir Jake correctly? Did you have a run-in with Lord Cartellion?"

"No. Not a 'run-in'. He pulled my arse out of a no-win situation. I am, though it may sound strange, beholden to him for my life. I'm not sure what that portends, but—"

"It seems we may have something in common then. I bumped into him yesterday, and he challenged me, at some unspecified later date, to honor combat."

"Good!" boomed Sir Jake.

He'd made his way back to the table and had heard the blond half elf's last statement.

"It is an honor to fight one of Cartellion's caliber. He only fights those of high station. Use the time wisely to develop your skills. You needn't worry until you've attained such."

With that, the knight placed a glass of wine before Solothon and strutted back to the bar to order another drink.

"Well," said the blond half elf, more to himself than to anyone else, "there's not much hope of that."

"Why not?" asked the Huntsmaster. "Surely anyone can attain whatever status we wish, given time, determination, and trained skill? You or I may, in the fullness of time, become Lords in our own right. Is that not true?"

"I suppose you are correct, Huntsmaster, but with my history—"

"Savon'el?" came the call from across the room.

The blond half elf turned in that direction and saw first the smiling Melisande coming toward him with another steaming mug of Kaff. Then he saw the frown on Red Wolf's face as the barbarian heard the name.

Savon'el took the proffered cup and turned back to Arantar, only to be riveted by the Huntsmaster's eyes.

"You are Savon'el?" asked that warrior, his eyes locked on the amber of the blond half elf.

The Elvin knight leaned forward in his chair, the sword forgotten in his lap.

"That is what I am called," answered the half elf as he slid his chair back, his eyes darting from one to the other.

"Wait," said Arantar quickly. "We mean you no harm. It's just that we have searched for you for a very long time."

"For what purpose?" asked the still-wary half elf.

"Is there a problem, pup?"

Red Wolf had crossed to the table and now stood behind Savon'el. When Melisande let slip the name, he'd risen from his chair and moved quietly to the half elf's aid.

"There is no problem, barbarian," said Arantar, "just questions."

His eyes never left those of the blond half elf, but his tone carried a question unasked of the barbarian.

"We were visited last night by one known as Wanderer. He told us that our fate and that of one known as 'Savon'el' are linked. Also, Landra Brea removed a vile curse from my friend here, one that could have caused his death saying that his friend, again named 'Savon'el,' wished it so. Now, I ask, are you this Savon'el? And if so, who are you?"

Red Wolf's hand found Savon'el's shoulder and squeezed gently. The grip said, "Careful." Savon'el never looked away from Arantar as he answered.

"I may be. I'm not sure."

He reached into his pocket and pulled forth the piece of black plate upon which was painted a red spider. He placed it on the table before him, but before he could speak, Solothon grimaced in pain and his right hand shot to his left shoulder.

"Gods, the pain!" he said through clenched teeth. His shoulder seemed to have been branded with demon fire.

"Put it away!" said Arantar. "Please!"

Savon'el returned the plate to his pouch quickly, and, just as quickly, the look of pain disappeared from the knight's face.

"I'm sorry," said the blond half elf. "I didn't mean to..."

"It's all right," said the knight. "You had no way to know. There is some devilment tormenting my very existence, and it is very probable that you and I are bound to the same fate, whatever that may be."

"Besides," took up the Huntsmaster, "though I saw only a glimpse, I did see the emblem of a red spider. We have a common enemy, friend." Then, to Red Wolf, "But you know that, don't you."

The look was not lost on the barbarian. It stated, in no uncertain terms, that there was a question of trust here, and one that needed to be answered.

"That may be, but I don't wish to bring my curse down upon others," replied the blond half elf.

"We were marked for death long before we knew of your existence. Fear not that you will bring doom on us, but together we might turn the tables on our common enemy, whoever that may be."

The Huntsmaster's voice was low steel with a promise just as hard and sharp. "The question is, where do we go from here? Do we trust one another?"

That question was for Red Wolf's benefit.

"The first thing we shall do," said the barbarian, "is rid ourselves of that plate."

Savon'el handed Red Wolf the pouch, not willing to have a reoccurrence of the same scene of a moment before. The barbarian took the pouch into the kitchen and a moment later returned the empty pouch to the blond half elf.

"It now burns in hell with its owner. Now, what do you know of red spiders?"

Arantar recounted the attack in the woods, leaving out nothing that could be of assistance, and the visit last night by their enemy. When he told of the visit by Wanderer, Savon'el interrupted.

"In peril of your soul?" he asked of the knight. "Why?"

"I believe it has something to do with these," answered Solothon as he pulled the wrapped shirakens from his pouch and handed them to the blond half elf.

Savon'el unwrapped the weapons and gazed at the dragons pierced through with lances. These were familiar to his hidden memory.

"Here, pup," came the deep voice of his friend from behind.

Red Wolf held the silver shiraken in front of Savon'el from behind.

"You seem well enough now to focus on this. It was left by another last night."

The blond half elf's memory took a leap. The dragon on the silver weapon had no lance through it, and his spurious memory showed him using weapons very much like the one he now held, though with little accuracy. With closer observation, he saw a difference from what he remembered and this sharp weapon. The blades were uniformly bent for some obscure reason, as were the blades on the black crystal shirakens.

"Where did you get this, friend?"

"I told you. Last night a fellow by the name of Yokura gave me that and told me to tell you that he sought you. I told him nothing, but—"

Red Wolf felt the half elf stiffen. His big hand gripped Savon'el's shoulder in concern as he asked quickly, "What is it, pup?"

Savon'el heard the name, but the pictures it conjured in his tormented mind held little comfort. He "saw" Yokura, somewhere, some-when, laughing, smiling, and talking with one easily a head taller and armored in silver plate, as he told others to attack him, beat him, and punish him. There was a feeling of respect there, but it was tinged with fear and the notion that this one had done this to him quite often.

He shook his head to free himself of the vision.

Red Wolf felt the tension subside and released his hold as he looked into the faces of those at the table. He saw their concern, from the hardy Huntsmaster and the surly knight to the soft concern on the face of Melisande, whose hand found the half elf's arm.

Savon'el glanced at the black-haired cleric, grinned, and turned his attention once again to the weapons before him. Here were opposites. Though the silver shiraken held unpleasant memories, the blacks gave him the feeling of dread.

The dragons pierced? That was not right in his mind. He looked up into the face of the Elvin knight and found that one's hand again caressing his left arm, a grimace of pain on his face.

"Why, may I ask, are you carrying these around?" he asked as he rewrapped the black weapons in the cloth and handed them back to Solothon.

"I...found them."

"It is my opinion," said the blond half elf, "that if someone left these, they were meant to be found."

"Precisely," answered the knight.

He returned the shirakens to his pouch and sipped from his glass. Savon'el knew that there was more and it rankled, though he didn't know why, that this one would lie. If they were to live through this, he knew there must be no mistrust. Yet he felt he himself should not give more than was absolutely necessary of his own circumstances. He placed the silver shiraken into his pouch and turned to his friend, Red Wolf.

"If we are to survive this…whatever this is that has robbed me of my memories, we must have faith with our companions." Red Wolf looked from the blond half elf to the Huntsmaster and nodded as Savon'el continued. "Brea guided them to us and I trust her judgment, but the inclusion of Wanderer worries me. There is something about him…"

"He seemed helpful, yet unhelpful at the same time, I thought," stated the Huntsmaster. "However, he was right about one thing. If any of us is to survive these machinations, we must do so together. What is it you said about your memories?"

Red Wolf nodded at Savon'el and watched the reaction on the Huntsmaster's face and that of the knight as the story was told.

"My companions and I have determined that Catlorian is not the battlefield we need if we are once again attacked," stated the Huntsmaster. "We have determined that if whoever this is that wants our lives, wants to find us, we should make it difficult enough to allow us an advantage. This mission, this venture to the Lost Souls River, may give us that advantage." Then, to Savon'el, "If the Landra Brea says that our destinies are intertwined, I believe her. If you will allow it, my sword is yours."

"As is mine," stated the knight.

"We shall probably need all the help we can get to see us to the hold and back again."

"Where is this hold?" asked the Huntsmaster.

"We will find it close to the source of the river," answered the barbarian. "It is a keep built by those who traffic with demons. I will be looking to destroy it when we have found what we seek. I have no love for those who dabble with demon power and am bound by my beliefs to destroy those who do."

Bonaire fingered the bit of gold leaf carefully. It was a heart made of wood and covered with fine-beaten gold. He knew it was cheap, but to him it was more precious than a wagonload of jewels. It was a gift from the beautiful girl who walked beside him.

He was in awe of her. She held the meat pie they'd bought from a street vendor as daintily as grapes, her flowing steps pure grace. He found he couldn't keep his eyes from her, try as he might. He placed the heart on the silver chain and linked it about his neck. Then he slipped it under his tunic for protection, knowing that the leafing wouldn't last long, but he hoped it would last long enough.

"Well, Bonaire," came the lilting voice from beside him, "here we are."

Bonaire hadn't been watching, his concentration only for the lovely golden girl. At her words, however, he looked before him and found several buildings set in the middle of a courtyard. There was a sign above the door of the largest proclaiming this to be the Mage's Guild.

Rene' took his arm and with a sweet "Shall we?" proceeded into the alcove at the base.

A man in the light blue robes of apprentice confronted them.

"What may I do for you?"

"We seek for basic supplies for those of our profession for a trip of unknown duration. Quills, ink, supplies of that sort."

"Basic supplies? Those you will find in the supply room two buildings down. Just follow the path around and you will find it."

As the man made to lead them from the main building, Bonaire gripped his arm.

"Wait. I have a request."

The man stopped and looked askance.

"I have a sword that, I was told, could be used by those in our profession to channel magical power."

"May I see this artifact?" asked the man in light blue.

Bonaire unsheathed the emerald crystal sword and handed it to him. The man looked it over, from the hilt to the sharp point.

"I shall see what we have in the library concerning this. I shall bring it to you at the supply room once I have the information. Will that be acceptable?"

Bonaire obviously didn't like the idea at all, but with some prodding from Rene' he allowed that it would be so, and he took the girl's hand as they left the main building and followed the path to the storeroom.

The old gentleman at the counter carried on an animated argument with what appeared to be a small dragon in what sounded like a dialect of Wurmish. Rene' smiled as she swept toward it. She'd seen Faerie Dragons before, and she was always drawn to them.

"You always lie through your teeth anyway," the old gentleman growled. Then, as he noted the two elves, continued, "Hi! What may I help you with?"

The dragonet saw the girl coming toward it and addressed her in a high singsong voice. "I'd watch him. He'll cheat ya! He's a crook you kno—"

The old man's hand clamped the small jaws together as the dragonet tried desperately to get free.

"Don't pay him any mind. Age, you know."

"Please!" said Rene'. "Do let him go. You're hurting him!"

She swept up to the dragonet and, as the man released his hold, stroked the scales between the tiny horns set above its eyes. The dragonet snarled at the man, nuzzled the girl's hand, and then placed his snout under a tiny wing and promptly went to sleep.

"There," said Rene' quietly. "That's better." Then, to the astounded shopkeeper, "My mentor had a device he used to write with that seemed to have an unending supply of ink. Do you know of such?"

"Yes, of course. Would you like one with normal or magical ink?"

"Normal will have to do, as my funds are a bit low. Daddy seems to have forgotten my allowance."

"Why don't you set up an account?" said the shopkeeper. "Some of the things you find on your encounters could be used to barter. An account with us is the normal way to conduct business. However, you must first return from your first adventure. It is not cost effective for me to offer credit to a potential risk. You understand."

"Of course, though I am awfully low on currency."

"I can help!"

Rene' turned to Bonaire in astonishment.

"Bonaire, you must save your funds for your own supplies. Thank you for the offer, but I'm afraid I must decline. I can't be under that obligation."

Bonaire's face fell and the Elvin girl continued.

"Really, Bonaire, I thank you, but you must understand. I must do what I can on my own." She placed a small hand on his cheek and smiled her prettiest smile. "Don't feel bad. It will make me feel the same. Please understand."

Bonaire's face lit up at the sight of that smile.

"Now, I think we should do our shopping and return to our fellows."

"Good idea, m'lady," said he. Then, to the shopkeeper, "Now, sir, do you have..."

"Solothon, my friend, pardon my observation, but you are a mess!"

The knight looked down at his armor and, for the first time in a very long time, laughed. His chain mail was rent in numerous places and most of it was encrusted in dried blood, though it was his own.

"You may be right, Huntsmaster. I need an armorer badly!"

"Savon'el and I were going down to a weaponsmith to see to our arms.

You are definitely invited." Then, to the barbarian, "What are the wages for this excursion to be?"

"That," said Red Wolf, "is up to the crazy old man, our employer."

"We shall need supplies and, as you know, we have little in the way of capital," stated Arantar.

"That seems to be in the area of expenses, though we will be restricted to trail bread until we find game on the way. The old man said he'd pay all expenses, right, pup?"

Savon'el had been thinking his own thoughts after his encounter with the shirakens and had been paying only slight attention to the conversation at the table. However, two tables away, another conversation was under way that, strangely, had drawn his total concentration. It was between two men in the Catlorian border guards.

"Yeah, they been havin' some real problems down around the southern provinces, in Dragon's Teeth especially. The chancellor, man, he's a real bastard from what I hear. My brother had been down there for the past four years, took a thousand gold investment into a business, and made it worth ten...twenty thousand. When the trouble started, he sold out and came up here. The bastard gave him only two thou."

"Yeah!" said the other. "I hear tell the chancellor burned ever'thang anyway! That's what I hear. Did it durin' the takeover, I hear."

Savon'el listened closely without knowing anything of what they were saying. When Red Wolf called, it took a moment to get his thoughts together. There was more of his memory floating about, subjects he needed to know, yet without a link to why they were important. He jerked his head up.

"Wha... Oh. Yes, the old man said all expenses, though your arms, as ours, are your own responsibility."

"You might get someone in one of the inns to fix yours for a meal or a drink," continued the barbarian, "unless you want a perfect repair. Frankly, I don't know why you need armor anyway."

Savon'el grinned.

"He doesn't have your skills, friend," he said, then continued to the knight, "though most of the damage you could repair yourself."

"I haven't the skill, so it would be better for my own safety to have it done by someone who knows what they are about."

"Well then, my friends," said the blond half elf as he stood. "As we are in this together, what say we find an armorer and take care of our business together?"

The Huntsmaster stood and, with a comradely slap on the knight's shoulder, answered. "Why not?"

Savon'el turned to the barbarian, who shook his head.

"I'm fine for now. I'll see you there later."

"Lady Melisande?"

The black-haired cleric placed a hand on her breast and felt the shiny new chain mail beneath her short tunic. She smiled and shook her head.

"Well then," said Savon'el to his two new companions, "shall we?"

He cast a meaningful look at the barbarian, then at Melisande, and back again. He received a nod, and he strode out the door of the Adventurer's Guild.

Melisande stood and without taking her eyes from the doorway sighed. "I too have errands."

Red Wolf shrugged, smiled, and took a long pull from his mug.

"Lady Rene'," said Bonaire as he placed his purchases in a small bag he had purchased from the shopkeeper, "I think it is time we were getting back. I do wish to see someone at the weapons shop before I finish, but that shouldn't take long."

"Ah, there you are."

The man from the tower came through the door with Bonaire's sword casually draped over his shoulder.

"I've looked everywhere for you." he said with a smile.

"You said you'd bring it here," answered Bonaire nastily. "You can't have searched long."

"True. True. Well, one of our more astute has come up with some information on this."

With that, the man handed both the sword and a rolled-up parchment to the young elf. Bonaire looked the sword over carefully. Though the sword was supposed to be totally impervious to damage, the young elf was not taking chances. Satisfied, he sheathed the sword and unrolled the parchment.

There was the history of the sword and not much more. Certainly not the information he'd hoped to find, such as its uses with power.

"What do I owe?" he asked.

The man rubbed his chin for a moment. "Nothing. The scribe has had that information for quite some time and, for some reason, deems that you have done him a favor. Call it a gift, for lack of a better explanation."

The man turned toward the door and, with a quizzical look, glanced back.

"The Myrlin mentioned you, Lady Iaprene', and said he would be leaving this afternoon and the tower was to be closed. There was no explanation save for some confusing mission he had to see about."

Then he turned and with a final salute disappeared through the door.

"That was strange," said the shopkeeper. "I've never known them to give anything away."

Rene' and Bonaire looked at each other for a moment. Then, with a shrug, Bonaire shouldered his bag and, the golden cleric in tow, went through the door into the late morning sunshine.

"Bonaire, we said we'd be back before noon, yet I still have one stop to make."

"I too have one more place to go. Shall I join you?"

"No. If we stay together, we will both be late. However, if you run your errand and I run mine, we should meet at the tavern at the same time, right?"

"I suppose so," answered the young elf in a surly voice.

"What's the matter, Bonaire?"

"It's just that I promised Arantar that I'd look after you."

"I shall be fine. Just fine. Look," she said gently, "I'll take a carriage there, have it wait, and then go to the Adventurer's Guild. I shall be quite safe."

"If you really think so."

"I do. Now, off with you," she said with a gentle squeeze of his hand.

She flagged down one of the two-wheeled carriages pulled by a stout man, stepped in, and gave directions to the Crystal Guild.

Bonaire watched as she rolled away, sighed, and then turned for the street he'd passed that held the armorer's shop. As he entered the shop, the tinkling of the small bell at the top of the door signaled his presence.

The old wrinkled dwarf at the counter looked up from the dagger he'd been honing.

"Just look around. I'll be with ya in a minute."

The shop was filled with all types and sizes of weapons, from pikes and hammers to swords of all types in racks lining the floor. Against the walls were racks of armor and shields of varying sizes and makes.

Bonaire took in the place quickly, but his aim was for more information on the emerald green crystal strapped to his back. The dwarf looked up at him.

"What can I do for you, elf?"

The words, though delivered smoothly, reeked of racial overtones.

"I need daggers."

"Daggers? Made of what? Steel? Alloy? What?"

"Elvin silver."

"Elvin silver? Whatever for? Well, no matter. How many?"

"Do you have a set?"

"Matched of five or three?"

"Three."

"Thirty gold for the set."

"Done."

The tiny bell rang in the shop and Bonaire turned to see Arantar, Savon'el, and Solothon enter.

"Bloody hells!" exclaimed the dwarf. "I'm being besieged with elves and half breeds. Oh well, what is it, your lordships?"

The phrase "half breed" wasn't lost on the sturdy Arantar. He'd lived his life under bigotry, but he knew that no one man could change the minds of those whose bigotry had set in as cold steel. Instead of getting angry, he, on these occasions, used a different ploy.

"This," he said as he presented his old sword to the dwarf, "needs the servicing of a professional, my good dwarf."

"Ah, yes," said the little man.

The words were perfect. This one may insult others that came through the door, but this customer knew a professional when he saw him; therefore, he was different.

"This will not be a problem, sir, as you have cared for it very well."

"I thank you, sir, for the compliment. I know that one with your skills could teach a poor warrior a thing or two about the care of weapons."

"Ah, that I could, but in a moment. Let me first see to this one. YAGRO! Come here!"

Steam rose from a stairway that led down beyond the counter. From this came a beast that was part dragon, part man, and part unknown demon. The heat of his body was felt throughout the room as he gained the floor. Arantar gazed at the demon and then at the dwarf.

The dwarf grinned at the look of dismay.

"Don't worry! He's the best damn metalsmith in Catlorian. He'll take care of your sword as if it were," then with a scathing look at the beast, "*my* own."

"Coming from one of your reputation," said the Huntsmaster, "I shall have no fear. Could I ask that you look upon these items," he continued, "while I look about?"

Then he produced a scimitar and a pair of standard daggers. Somehow the daku had felt they were of no worth and had left them behind. If Arantar could get a good price for them, they could help defray some of the expense of repairing the knight's armor.

"Please, sir. Be my guest," said he. "I shall assess these while you do."

"Oh!" said Arantar, as if the thought just that moment came to him. "My friend here," motioning to the surly Solothon, "is in need of someone to repair his mail. It is in a terrible state, and we shall be leaving shortly on adventure. Would you, in your professional opinion, recommend repair or replacement?"

The dwarf stroked his beard as a gentle smile played about his lips. The Huntsmaster was playing this one so deftly that he was totally off guard.

"Oh. I'd replace it, were it mine," said he. "I can take that in trade on mail of better quality and...hmmm...one hundred forty gold. And, by the way, these weapons of yours are worth...oh, forty gold."

"That, good sir, is very fair. He'll take the trade. Could you please fit him? I know that only a true professional can do the job right. And if you don't mind, give him my forty gold credit to use toward this purchase."

"I shall indeed, and I see that my assistant has returned with your sword, and a fine one it is, I might add."

The demon came out of the cellar, laid the sword on the counter, and turned away toward the stairway.

Arantar picked up the sword, beamed a smile at the dwarf, and sheathed it. He stepped over to Solothon and placed fifty gold pieces into the knight's hand.

"Keep up this ploy," he whispered. "I shall see to our saddles."

Solothon nodded and then beamed a smile at the small man. "I am at your disposal, my expert friend."

"Right this way, sir," beamed the dwarf. He'd take credit where credit was due. He was, after all, a professional.

Arantar walked to the door, but Bonaire grasped him by the arm before he could go through.

"Who is that?" he asked, motioning at the blond half elf.

Savon'el looked through the armor with a faraway look on his face.

"I'll tell you later," said the Huntsmaster. "Right now I'm going to the livery to get tack for our horses. The barbarian said the sage has taken credit there for our provisioning. I plan to take advantage of that."

"Oh, gods!" said the elf as he placed a hand to his forehead. "I forgot! I'll go with you. Lucky for me one of us knows what to do."

"Well, come along then," replied Arantar as he held the door open.

Savon'el, meanwhile, stood before a rack upon which was displayed full silver dragon plate. He reached out a shaking hand and touched it. Instantly the memories began.

A large man, Father, but not Father, wore this. He knew...*knew* that he'd watched this man die. Die in wailing, writhing demon fire. He shivered in pain at the recollection. He couldn't stop. He was in pain, internal pain. Anger, despair, sorrow—all mixed—vied with his mind for recognition.

The dwarf saw this and, as he tightened the last strap on Solothon's mail, asked. "Is that one with you?"

"Who?" asked Solothon. Then he turned and saw the half elf as that one shook before the plate armor. "Arantar," he called softly.

The Huntsmaster heard the call just as he'd stepped out of the door. He waved Bonaire on and reentered the shop. Solothon pointed at the blond half elf and Arantar stepped quickly to that one's side to lay a firm hand on his shoulder.

The half elf cast a blurry gaze at the Huntsmaster as that one caught the anguish, the pain, the look of hopeless distress displayed openly on the young man's face.

"What is it, friend?"

Savon'el shook himself and sighed. "Sorry, my friend. I was just...Never mind. It's just that at times my mind sees something that will trigger a memory or vision or..." He placed a hand on the Huntsmaster's hand where it gripped his shoulder and continued. "I hope that one day I shall be able to explain everything to you, my friend, but for now I may only give you my thanks."

"T'was not needed. You would do the same for me, I know." Arantar slapped the half elf on the shoulder and left the shop.

Savon'el nodded, stepped up to the counter, and unsheathed his sword. "Good dwarf, could you see to the temper and sharpness of this?"

The dwarf took the weapon and turned it over in his calloused hands. He glanced up with a look of askance of this half elf. Did this one not know the properties of this? Obviously not! Well, the casing could use a bit of tempering at that.

"Yagro!"

The demon took the sword, looked at the dwarf, and, after receiving a shrug, opened his mouth and engulfed the sword in his demon breath.

Savon'el was in pain. He couldn't look away. The demon fire had him rooted to the floor. He would have run, though he knew not where, if he could have. Pain, anguish, despair, death—all blazed in his torment while the demon tempered the sword with his breath.

Finally, with a shrug, Yagro returned the sword to the dwarf and made his way down the stairway. The dwarf turned back to Savon'el to present him the weapon, but he found a terrified visage gazing back at him.

"What's wrong with your friend?" he asked.

"Savon'el," said the knight softly as he ignored the dwarf, "I, too, have demons, but now is not the time to give in to them. Come back, friend, and we will face them together."

The half elf was in a cold sweat. When he looked up into the eyes of the Elvin knight, he seemed to remember where he was, and with that he lost some of his strength and leaned a hand on the knight's sturdy chest.

He sheathed the bastard sword and, after tossing the price of the tempering to the dwarf and with a hand on the knight's shoulder, made his way to the door.

Melisande stepped out of a shop behind them as they passed and followed, as she had since they'd left the Adventurer's Guild. She would not allow the blond half elf out of her sight, partly from her need to accompany him and this troop to wherever and partly from a feeling she had that all was not well with this one. She followed.

Savon'el, however, had seen the yellow cloak, as he'd known she'd followed him all morning.

"Sir Solothon," he said, "you go on ahead. I'll be right behind you."

Solothon shrugged and moved on as Savon'el cast his glance back up the street the way they'd come. The girl in the yellow cloak stood at a shop window, seemingly perusing the displayed wares. He stepped up behind the girl and laid a hand softly on her back.

"It would be far easier, m'lady," he said as she turned to meet his eyes, "if you would walk beside me. I need no looking after, though I am flattered by the attention. I am famished and, I wager, you are also. Shall we?"

He held his arm out to the astonished cleric and smiled. She regained her composure quickly, flashed him a smile, took his arm, and they followed the knight back to the tavern.

Bonaire left Arantar on the street and entered the tavern. He saw the barbarian sitting at the table where they'd left him drinking wine, and Sir

Jake was in an animated argument with two of the Catlorian Border Guards on the subject of a usurped monarchy in Dragon's Teeth.

Bonaire, knowing Sir Jake to be rather unstable, skirted that table on his way to the bar.

"What'll ye have, my boy?" asked the barman.

"Beer," replied the elf. The sound of Sir Solothon coming through the door brought a glance and he continued. "And wine for my friend. This could be our last chance to party."

The blond half elf led Melisande into the Adventurer's Guild and, after lifting a hand in greeting to Solothon and receiving the same, seated the young cleric at a table close to the bar. The sound of a mug being slammed down on a table brought his gaze back to the knight's table.

Sitting opposite Sir Solothon was the elf that had sat briefly with them that morning, now garbed in a colorful tunic and cloak. He was well on his way to intoxication as he called for another beer.

"Bonaire," said the knight, "I wouldn't get too far gone at this point."

"Why not?" he asked. "Eat, drink, and be merry and all that."

"We may need to leave in a hurry."

"And we might not. Besides," continued the haughty elf as he covered his mouth with his hand to stifle a belch, "this stuff doesn't affect me anyway."

He took the fresh beer and drank half of it at once.

Solothon looked over at the half elf, shrugged, and picked up his glass of wine. Savon'el caught his eye and waved him over to his table. The knight glanced once at the elf in disgust, rose, and seated himself at Savon'el's table.

"We were just about to order food. Will you join us?"

"If the lady doesn't mind?"

"Please," replied Melisande. "We would be grateful for the company."

"Tell me, Sir Solothon," said Savon'el as his gaze raked the elf at the next table, "is he always like this?"

"I know not, having but recently met him. However, he is a good arm when it comes to battle, as I have witnessed with my own eyes."

"As tentative as our positions are, I believe he should slow down before his drinking kills him or us," the girl said softly.

"I leave his care and feeding in the hands of Arantar. He seems to have more control over that one than I."

Then he saw the Huntsmaster come through the door and, with a frown on his face, approach Bonaire's table. "I believe you will soon see what I mean."

Savon'el watched the Huntsmaster stalk to the table, place both fists down in front of the elf, and lean forward until his face was all Bonaire could see.

"What in the name of the seven hells do you think you are doing?"

Bonaire raised his bleary gaze to meet the steel in the Huntsmaster's eyes.

"Here we are," continued Arantar, "surrounded on all sides by danger, and you, though you are needed to protect your friends' flanks, are deep in your cups! You have a responsibility, a duty, Bonaire, to us all, and you've let me down!"

"Uh! Wha…?" said the elf as he attempted to rise. He was too unstable and all but fell back into his chair.

"I need you sober!" shouted the Huntsmaster as his hand came down smartly on the table. "Kaff won't help, but sleep will. Go up and sleep this off, and, if you are able to understand, I hope to the gods that we won't need you before you wake! Now, *go!*"

The last words were so sharp that the elf was on his feet and moving before he realized what he was doing. He managed to get to the stairway under his own power, but the stairs looked to be impossible to negotiate in his condition. He looked back at the Huntsmaster, only to find that one's stern gaze burning into his soul. He climbed the staircase carefully on his hands and knees.

As the elf disappeared from the top of the stairs, Arantar hung his head. The knight stood and walked over to rest his hand on the Huntsmaster's shoulder.

"You can't be there for him all the time, Arantar."

"I understand that," he answered. "It's just that I thought that by now he'd have a better grasp of the responsibilities shared by companions. I was wrong."

"How can you possibly change what has taken his whole lifetime to develop? You can't do it all for him, my friend. He must be taught to do for himself. In reality, we know not what the Fates portend. You and I may well be dead by morning. Who will watch for him then?"

The knight gripped his friend's shoulder, bringing the Huntsmaster's head up.

"No, friend Arantar, you have done more than I would have, and you will no doubt do more. The guilt, however, must be laid at the proper doorstep: his father and mother, but mostly himself. He is the cause of his worst situations. I only hope his lack of training will not speak doom on us all."

"You're right, I know, but—"

"No 'buts,' my friend. Now, join us. We must plan well. It will not do to run helter-skelter toward our doom, if doom does indeed await us. At least let us approach it with some planned dignity."

Though the words sounded pessimistic, the grin on the knight's lips brought Arantar back to himself.

"You are right, sir knight. I will see to our mounts and return. Then we may see a way to turn our situation to our advantage."

The knight nodded and the Huntsmaster stalked from the tavern.

Chapter Twenty-three

"You guyth want somethin' ta eat?"

Solothon watched as the Huntsmaster left by the side door to the stables, shook his head, and turned toward where the half ogre stood at the kitchen door.

"If you please, Grek."

He walked back to Savon'el's table and picked up his wine glass.

"We got thome meat 'n bread?"

"That, and cheese as well, Grek. Thank you," replied the blond half elf.

"What'll you have, mith?"

"Just bring a platter," Melisande said as she looked across at the mountain of mottled flesh and muscle. With a gentle smile, she added, "We'll fend for ourselves."

"Okay. It'll take a coupl'a minuteth."

"That's fine, Grek. There's no great hurry," said Savon'el. Then, to Solothon, "Where has the Huntsmaster gone off to?"

"He's seeing to our horses. We need saddles and the like since ours has been taken." Then the knight turned to the half elf and asked, "How did you know he was Huntsmaster?"

"What? He...I don't know. It just seemed that he...It just felt right. He could be nothing else!"

Solothon frowned at Savon'el for but a moment and then relaxed.

"I suppose you are right. He is a soldier, tempered in battle, yet his soul is pure. He's saved my life and soul several times in the few days we've been together. One could not ask for better on his flank."

The knight took a slow sip from his wine glass before he continued.

"However, he feels, as every soldier should, a deep commitment to his companions. That, unfortunately, means Bonaire."

"Why do you say 'unfortunately'?" asked Melisande.

"You must understand, I have known that young elf for but a very few, though eventful, days. My opinions are based solely on my observations."

Both Melisande and Savon'el nodded.

"I have seen the result of pampered youth and over-tolerance in my time, but young Bonaire is worse than any I have seen. He seems to believe that the world is his plaything. If it doesn't please him, revolve around him, or meet with his taste, it simply cannot be worthwhile.

"This last escapade is but a culmination, I feel, of his irresponsibility. Is it his fault for being the way he is? Possibly, but there is enough blame to go around, in my opinion. There are those whose life work it was to train him to take care of himself, treat people with courtesy, and share the load. Are we to reap the questionable benefits of his lack of training at the expense of our very lives?"

"I can understand your dislike for the man, Sir Solothon, but I care not for your insinuation of blame for those not here to defend themselves."

The blond half elf's words were harsh and brought the knight's eyes up quickly to find the molten amber in Savon'el's.

"One cannot always 'Go to the source,' as they say," continued the blond half elf sharply. "Let us say that a man and woman had a child and tried their very best to instill in that child the right and wrong way to think, do things, to live. Yet in the end they were defeated by the stubbornness of youthful knowledge. It is said that children should be employed before they reach adulthood, before they forget that they know everything.

"This may very well be the case with Bonaire. If so, we must share the burden carried by the parents of this young elf and, in doing so, relieve the Huntsmaster of some of the burden he's taken on. It is in our best interest to help mold Bonaire, else we may all pay dearly. If we are not willing to do this, we may as well leave him to fend for himself. How long do you think he would survive on his own?"

"Not long, I suppose. You may be right, friend, though in my travels I've never had to depend on such as he."

"Well, my friend, you won't have to depend entirely on him, though I am depending on you for assistance in his training. You never can tell, he may be the one to save us all e'er this thing is done."

"That won't happen for at least the next few hours, anyway," laughed the knight.

But the laugh was cut short.

Just above the table, a swirling shadow took shape. It spun faster as the three rose and backed away, increasing in substance until, with a crash, a knight in rusted armor landed upon the table and crushed it to the floor. Upon his left breast was painted a crimson spider. To that one's left and right rear, two more swirls of darkness became rusted knights. The smell of putrefied flesh permeated the room in short order as the first raised his sword to strike.

Savon'el's actions were instinctive as, in one motion, he pushed the black-haired cleric behind him and swept the dull gray sword from the sheath at his back. The blade in the hands of the young half elf came alive. He parried the down swept blade aimed at his head, then swept the sword back to deflect the blade that came from the leader's companion on his left.

Though the sword missed him by a good margin, Savon'el knew that these were not in the same category as the ones he and Red Wolf had faced in the forest. They moved better, smoother, and faster. He also knew that they were here for him and him alone.

"Run!" he shouted at the cleric as he continued to fend off the two ringing blades.

His words were lost on her. She was angry and no longer reasonable to any suggestion of flight. These larger knights were attacking her charge and, by the goddess, they would not go unpunished! From that special pocket in her cloak came the maul. She'd trained with this weapon and was proficient and willing, perhaps too willing, to use it.

Solothon wasted no time as his sword sang from its sheath. His shoulder was on fire, but his anger pushed the pain aside as he attacked.

"He stands not alone, brigands! For Laranthia and the Laurel!"

From somewhere upstairs, his shout was answered.

"Brigands? *Brigands?* By the Lords of Light!"

Sir Jake appeared at the top of the stairs, his great blade in his hands. He saw, first, the two warriors fighting for their lives, then the cleric. A quick glance down showed him that he was dressed only in the padding he wore under his armor and his feet were bare. Whether the cleric was in danger or not was irrelevant; he couldn't let a lady see him so disrobed. Quickly he repaired to his room and began the tedious task of donning his armor.

Meanwhile, Savon'el ducked under the sweep of the sword wielded by the death knight to the leader's left and swept his blade toward the juncture of the armor at the demon's midsection. That one's suppleness proved protective as it dodged back.

Solothon took advantage of that death knight's position and aimed another blow to the same spot with his backswing. Again the demon lurched back, but this time it countered with a sweeping stroke to the knight's left side. The new mail served as the sword failed to penetrate, yet, if he survived, the bruise would stay with him for a long time.

With a chilling scream of rage, Melisande swept around the half elf's left and swung the heavy maul, with practiced precision and with the strength of her anger, at the knight to Savon'el's left. The demon dodged backward as the maul's steel banded head raked across its armor and struck a chair. The force of the blow was evidenced by the flying splinters of wood as the chair exploded on impact.

"What'th goin' on here?"

Savon'el caught a glimpse of the half ogre as that one dropped the platter and set his four hundred plus pounds into motion. He only had time to yell, "Solothon!" and leap to the side carrying the cleric with him.

Solothon glanced quickly behind, understood what was about to happen, lunged at his opponent to force him back into his companions, and then jumped out of the way.

Grouch roared past moving at full tilt and slammed into the three death knights. The force of his heavy massed muscle carried the demons to the wall, where they were crushed between the proverbial unstoppable force and immovable object.

Unfortunately, Grouch's head also made solid contact with the wall. He stood, stepped back from the crushed armor, nodded with a big grin, and fell back unconscious.

Melisande rushed to the half ogre's side and caressed his still-grinning face. Sounds from the pile of crushed armor caused her to turn.

As the three companions watched, the dented and crushed armor popped out whole. Dislocated limbs reattached themselves to their owners and the green sludge that was once human flesh seemed to suck back through the seams of the armor it had squirted through a moment before.

The three death knights rose again and came for Savon'el's head.

As the half elf brought his sword up to parry a blow from the first to reach him, another brought his sword hard into Savon'el's side. Though it did not penetrate the scale, the force propelled him into one of the posts. He came hard into the post and brought his sword up to engage another slash intended to split his skull.

Melisande brought her maul up forcefully and deflected that slash amid sparks of ringing steel. Her follow through caused the thrust by the death knight's companion to miss, and as it lunged past she slammed the shaft of her maul into its back.

The demon attacking Savon'el recovered and swung its sword at the half elf's head yet again. The blond ducked under the sweep of the blade, and it slammed into the post and exploded. The sound of shattering metal rang in his ears as Savon'el put both feet into the demon's chest and pushed.

Solothon swept his moaning sword in an arc toward his attacker's head, but dodged back as that one ducked under the stroke and slashed at his middle. The knight countered with a slash of his own, but the demon dodged backward.

Arantar came out of the stables, drawn by the strange sounds coming from the tavern. His eyes caught the figure wrapped in darkness and the bone white skin on the arms of the daku as it stood before the closed doors of the Adventurer's Guild and traced red lines of power into the air before it.

The Huntsmaster's hand went to his back as he sprinted toward the daku, the rage in his heart riding him into recklessness. His hand found the hilt of his Grey Wolf and, at a dead run, snatched it from its sheath.

Red Wolf had just turned the corner toward the tavern when he saw the Huntsmaster with his sword in hand and the daku in the middle of casting, red speckles of power sparkling about its head and dripping from the patterns before it, and he heard the sounds of conflict within the tavern.

At a single step, the barbarian was at full speed. He saw the stroke as it screamed toward the daku's back and knew that it would be enough to disrupt the spell. He exploded through the door and, seeing the one death knight bringing the broken sword down again and again on Savon'el's upheld sword, leaped.

His hand slammed with the force of ten broadswords into the juncture of helm and shoulders. As the demon's head snapped back, Savon'el brought his pommel up and into its chin, spinning its head about. Then the half elf saw the barbarian's hand form the claw and his eyes scream cold hate. He ducked.

The force of the blow lifted the demon's head from its shoulders and sent it thudding to the floor some twenty feet away. The barbarian, without losing momentum, spun to his right and within a heartbeat assessed the situation.

The yellow-robed cleric swung her maul in a crushing blow meant to drive her foe into the floor. Her attacker saw it coming and dodged back. As the maul struck the floor, the death knight stepped in and plunged his sword into the girl's abdomen. Solothon parried a stroke from his attacker and with his free hand grabbed the sword arm of Melisande's foe. That one had pulled the sword free of her body and brought it up to deliver a killing blow. The Elvin knight used that sword, in the hand of the demon, to deflect yet another slash by his attacker.

Red Wolf's hands hardened into claws as he moved with alarming grace and speed between the remaining two death knights. His right hand removed Melisande's attacker's head from his shoulders while Solothon drove his sword through the breastplate of the remaining death knight. That foe struck the floor and shattered.

Arantar's stroke swept through the daku without resistance. For a moment he thought this to be yet another illusion. Then the sorcerer turned, screamed, and a bolt of pure energy leaped from its fingertips to impact the warehouse across the street with a ball of wailing demon fire. The Huntsmaster could see the look of astonishment on its face.

"This time," said the Huntsmaster through gritted teeth, "you die." He drove the length of his blade through the daku's chest and twisted it.

The shocked look turned to a lethal grin as the traced lines of power began to change color. They began to swirl faster and faster until, finally, they leaped into the daku's eyes, and with an evil cackle it exploded.

Tattered pieces of darkness blew in every direction. One piece slapped wetly on Arantar's forehead and disappeared. The Huntsmaster was knocked back by the force and landed on his back, the leather-wrapped hilt of his sword still in his hand. The blade was gone, dissolved in the body of a sorcerer whose spell had been interrupted.

Arantar sat up, shook his head, and stood on shaken legs. The hilt fell from numbed fingers as he staggered against the wall. He heard the sounds of fighting within and, skirting the pool of darkness where the daku had stood, went through the door.

He tried to ignore the weakness and feverishness he felt as he moved into the tavern. He saw the shattered armor strewn about on the floor and the barbarian, Savon'el, and Solothon kneeling by the bleeding Melisande.

"What happened?" he asked as he stumbled toward them.

Savon'el and Solothon looked toward him and instantly they were on their feet, hands filled with steel.

The Huntsmaster stopped and asked, "What are you doing?"

Savon'el looked confused and placed a hand on the knight's sword arm. That one glanced quickly at the blond half elf, then looked closer at the confused Arantar.

Savon'el placed himself between Arantar and the downed cleric, his sword held point down before him. He opened his mouth to address the Huntsmaster, but before he could make a sound there was a loud crash at the bottom of the stairway.

Sir Jake, resplendent in his armor, had run halfway down the stairs and leaped to the floor of the tavern. He glanced about the room at the chaos left after the battle and, as his eyes found Arantar, he charged. His sword was in both hands and it screamed in holy anger. A bright silver light surrounded the knight as he advanced.

Arantar was in pain. The light surrounding the knight caused his eyes to burn and he fell back against the wall. He couldn't focus on the sword and knew, if something didn't happen quickly, that blade would be driven through his body. He raised his hands in a vain effort to block the blow, but he knew it would not be enough.

"Hold, sir!"

The command brought the knight to an abrupt halt, his sword raised to deliver the killing blow. The hands trembled but returned the sword to its sheath, and the holy knight turned toward the blond half elf, unable to move. His eyes looked into molten amber and the power he could not resist. Solothon and Red Wolf were rooted where they stood, the power of that command still reverberating through the large room.

Savon'el turned his gaze from the knight to Arantar and, as he did so, Sir Jake relaxed. He stood still, awaiting his next command.

"Why was he attacking me?" asked a shaken Arantar.

"Look at your hands."

Arantar glanced down to see the ebony skin and, as he stumbled past the knight to the mirror on the wall, he drew in his breath. His skin was black and his hair silver. His eyes blazed red from his barely recognizable countenance.

"What the hells happened?" he asked in a strangled voice.

Then, as he watched, his skin paled, his hair darkened, and his eyes slowly dimmed. In moments his appearance was back to normal. He turned his icy blue eyes on his friends as they stood in shocked silence. Suddenly that silence was broken.

"Come to me, Lord of Water! Come to me in my need!"

The power reached into the tavern and, though those who were transfixed by the half elf's command were released from it, they still felt it in their bones. Bonaire, who until then had lain in drunken stupor, sat straight up in the bed, wide awake and sober. He rose and went quickly to the window.

Outside the warehouse was ablaze. What seemed to be a hundred-foot tall column of water with eyes stood next to the fire and seemed to gaze at the flames. From somewhere near the top of the being, a stream of water gushed forth, drowning the flames in clouds of steam.

Bonaire watched as the being seemed to nod at its handiwork, then turn to the wizard who had called. The old man with the white beard and hair floated a hundred feet above the city streets and twenty behind the towering entity of water. Silent words were exchanged and the being vanished in a mist.

Then the old man turned to the young elf, winked, and disappeared.

Meanwhile, Red Wolf knelt beside the bleeding cleric and began dressing her wound as he sent the blond half elf to check on the half ogre.

Savon'el grabbed Grek's huge arm and tried to pull him away from the carnage.

"Arantar," he yelled, "come help me! Quickly!"

Arantar ran to his side, but he asked, "Why?"

"Catlorian," came the reply, "is built mostly of wood. Should the fire find this place—"

"It will go up in seconds!" finished the Huntsmaster as he leaped to the other side of the heavy Grouch and grabbed the other arm. He was too massive for both of them.

Red Wolf finished his bandaging, looked at the two struggling half elves, smiled, and grabbed his wineskin.

"Here, pup, try this," he said as he tossed the skin into Savon'el's arms.

The blond half elf released Grouch's arm to catch the wineskin and told Arantar to step away. He uncorked the stopper, held the open port under the half ogre's nose, and jumped back.

Grouch's eyes flew open and he sat up, completely awake.

"Whew!" he exclaimed. "What happened? Did we win?"

"Yes, my friend," answered the barbarian as he scooped up Melisande and headed for the door. "The city is on fire. Let's get outside."

"Good idea!" stated the half ogre as he rose on shaky legs.

As they filed through the door, Arantar noticed the flakes of darkness that once had been the daku had gathered about the hilt of his destroyed sword to form a blade of darkness. He stopped and watched as that darkness solidified into a blade of shifting shade.

As Solothon moved to pass him through the door, he screamed and, holding his right hand to his left shoulder, passed out onto the street. Savon'el knelt beside him and glanced about for any attackers. However, as his hand touched the knight's shoulder, he felt the searing heat under the mail.

Arantar, his attention only for the strange sword that once was his, noticed none of this. He was afraid of this weapon. He knew that to touch it would be to give himself to that darkness. He moved to that weapon, looking about to ensure none other would come close.

"You are correct, young man, not to touch it."

The voice had come from above and drew the Huntsmaster's eyes.

The old man with the flowing white beard floated down to land next to the dark sword. He took the end of his staff and ran it through the blade as if it were not there. The darkness moved away from the staff and rejoined behind it as it passed.

"What is it?" asked the Huntsmaster softly.

"Oh," came the response, "it looks to be 'Elf Bane,' or a cheap form of it. How did it come to be defiling my streets?"

Arantar quickly related the events that led to the destruction of his sword. While the story was being told, Red Wolf handed his burden to the blond half elf standing next to the door with the fallen knight. He moved to the old man's side, but he stopped and emitted a low growl when he saw the writhing blade on the ground.

"Hello, Myrlin. What do you know of this?"

"Oh, this one was clever," stated the old one, ignoring the lethal tone in the barbarian's voice. "Clever indeed."

He reached down and grasped the hilt over the Huntsmaster's quick protest.

"Don't worry, young man. This one's simple magic cannot harm me. Yes…" He turned the sword in his hand as if assessing it for purchase. "Obviously he borrowed power to do this, somewhat in the fashion of Mage's Wrath, if I don't miss my guess. He was caught in the middle of his spell and, when he knew his spell would destroy him, he blew up. However, he made sure that whatever was left of him would align itself with the youth's sword. He was fairly thorough."

"No!" growled the barbarian. "He should have reconstituted himself elsewhere. Now he will see what Red Wolf thinks of daku demon-traffickers!"

"What do you intend?" asked the old man as the barbarian reached for the club at his belt. The Myrlin knew this sword could not harm him and probably not the barbarian, but the others?

"I intend to destroy it."

The old man held the sword away, but at Red Wolf's growl he grinned. "Mind if I help?"

"How?"

"Well, Wolf," he began as he waved the others away from the area, "you obviously mean to smash it with that bloody club of yours. You will need something substantial to crush it against, I'll wager, therefore…" With a wave of his hand, a three-foot cube of granite appeared. He laid the sword upon it and backed away. "Have at it," he stated as he moved to the others and ushered them even farther back.

He grasped Arantar's shoulder and whispered, "Help me get them all back. This could get rather messy."

"What do you mean? I thought only magic could destroy magic."

"Not always, my boy, but this time it is true enough. Now, we know that Red Wolf has no love for magic—quite the contrary, though he, in his own fashion, respects it. The trick is, that club is almost pure magic, though he is not aware of it. I should know. I made it many, many years ago, but don't tell him. Let it be our little secret."

Arantar looked at the old man and saw, as that one watched the barbarian focus his power, the mischievous grin take form under the white of his beard. The Huntsmaster shook his head in disbelief and locked his attention on Red Wolf.

That one laid the club head gently on the crosspiece then raised it slowly above his head. The growl began deep in his chest and, as the club moved farther back and the barbarian's head fell back, the growl ranged into a crescendo that saw the club head scream down toward the dark sword's hilt. The muscles in his arms and back bunched and strained with the power he exerted. The head of the club struck the crosspiece and an incredible explosion broke the quiet of a few moments before.

When the dust settled, the barbarian stood over a hole easily five feet deep. There was no evidence of the sword, the granite block, or the cobblestone upon which it had rested.

"Pull yourself together this time, daku," growled the barbarian.

The knight jerked to consciousness at that moment and felt the burning pain in his arm subside. He shook his head to clear it and stood up cautiously. Savon'el laid the girl on the walkway, her back to the wall of the Adventurer's Guild, and stepped over to help the knight steady himself.

"Nice work, my friend," stated the old man. "Tell me, did you have to hit it that hard?"

"I wished to make certain that that sword wouldn't survive. Besides," Red Wolf added a bit sheepishly, "I got a bit carried away."

Arantar peered into the hole and saw that nothing, save sparkling dust, was left to show that a sword ever existed.

"You seem to have taken care of that problem handsomely, my friend," he said as he slapped the barbarian on the shoulder.

Red Wolf grinned at that as the old Mage turned to go. Myrlin glanced back at the Huntsmaster and he frowned.

"What's that?" he asked as he pointed at Arantar's head.

"What's what?"

"Why, the smudge on your forehead."

Red Wolf looked, but saw nothing.

"What smudge?" he asked.

"Why that...Oh, never mind. You can't see it anyway. Only one such as I can, and I doubt that it will do him any harm, but I'd see to it just the same, were I you."

"Who do you suggest I see?" asked the Huntsmaster, a bit flustered.

"Well, the Master of the Mage's Guild could probably take care of it, though it probably won't affect you for several years. I wouldn't worry about it."

"What is it?"

The Huntsmaster rubbed at the spot with the back of his hand and looked, but could see nothing on his hand.

"Oh, probably just some sort of death curse, but I really wouldn't worry. You'd need someone of power to dispel it. A cleric couldn't even begin to touch it."

"Then by all means," said the panicked Huntsmaster, "I will see to it immediately!"

The old man grinned, tilted his head, said, "Just kidding," and disappeared.

"Gods!" shouted the duped Arantar. "What a despicable thing to do to a man!"

"Despicable?" answered the barbarian with a grin. "Yeah, I guess that fits."

Arantar shook his head, sighed, and turned back to his companions. Solothon was assisting Savon'el in his attempt to slow the bleeding from the girl's belly. He thought back over the past few days and the newly found power of mind he'd discovered.

Then he realized he'd used this power before, this power of will. His friend Taofey had been wounded, and as he tended the deep wound, he felt the power grow.

They'd been under attack almost continuously for days with no relief in sight. They could not afford to lose a single soldier, much less the small man he'd tended.

While he tried to stem the flow of blood, his desperation released that power and, suddenly, the bleeding stopped. He lifted the bandage and found it knit into a fresh scar and his friend resting peacefully. He'd thought this to be Tao's doing, but now...

"Savon'el," he said as he moved toward them.

The blond half elf glanced up at the oncoming Huntsmaster.

"Let me help. I believe I may be able to..."

Then he saw the look in Savon'el's eyes, and it spoke volumes of distrust: distrust for all who could possibly bring harm to those he did trust.

Arantar hung his head as the blond waved him away.

"Wolf? The lady needs binding," said Savon'el. "Your skills are needed, my friend."

"Take her inside, pup," he stated as he kicked a clump of dirt and watched as it fell into the gaping hole.

Savon'el picked Melisande up and carried her into the tavern and up the stairs to his room with the barbarian at his heels. Arantar followed the barbarian up the stairs, but stopped at the door to Savon'el's room to wait and watch. He understood the reasoning for their mistrust, but it chaffed. He saw Bonaire come out of their room and waved him away when he tried to look into the room. The young elf shrugged and went down the stairway while the Huntsmaster turned his attention to the activity within the room.

The Elvin knight came through the door to the tavern and felt the birthmark again begin to warm. He looked about the room and saw the red spider emblems glowing from the strewn armor. Then he backed out of the tavern and stood beside the doorway, watching for anything that could be considered a threat.

Savon'el laid the girl gently on the bed and stood back. Red Wolf ripped the girl's tunic away from her wound and saw the hole punched through the shiny mail beneath.

"This will have to come off," he said, "and there are shards of metal in the wound that must be removed."

He began unbuckling the mail as Savon'el turned his head. The barbarian glanced up and growled. "Have you never seen blood before, pup? I need your help."

"Yes, but she's…I mean…"

"Your modesty has no place here. She is a warrior who has been wounded in combat. Dispense with your stupidity and help me!"

Savon'el knelt quickly beside the girl and with shaking hands began unbuckling the armor from her body.

"That will do," stated the barbarian as he lifted the armor away from the wound.

Savon'el noted the smooth skin and the ragged wound in her belly.

"Do you think the blade was poisoned?" he asked, his eyes never leaving her body.

"I don't know, but I'll take no chances."

Red Wolf opened his wineskin and poured some of its contents into the wound.

"If there were poison," he said, "this should dispel it."

The girl moaned softly as the barbarian went to his pouch to mix the herbs for the healing poultice. Savon'el laid a gentle hand to her forehead and she stilled.

"Will she recover, Wolf?"

"I don't know, pup," he replied as he placed half of his poultice on the girl's stomach. "I can only do what I can. Now help me turn her over. The exit wound must also be tended. Here, hold this."

He placed the blond half elf's hand over the poultice and gently turned the girl onto her side. The wound on her back was washed with the wine and the other half of the poultice was applied. Red Wolf ripped the bottom away from her tunic and used it to bind the poultices in place, then gently rolled the girl onto her back.

"Now we wait. If my healing arts haven't failed me, she should wake in a few hours. If not…" He sat back on his haunches and sighed.

Hours later, Solothon heard the banging of steel on steel from within the tavern. Thinking the worst, he drew his sword and came through the door only to find Bonaire hammering on one of the breastplates with a hammer. He watched, while his arm grew warm, as the young elf beat on the metal until the emblem fell away. Then he slipped the shard into one of the many pouches at his waist and moved toward the others.

"Wait, Bonaire," said the knight as he strode toward the grinning elf. "These are not yours."

"But, I—"

"Back away from them I said. They are *not yours*!"

The young elf rose and backed away from the angry knight, not knowing that the close proximity to these emblems was causing considerable pain.

Solothon closed his eyes and when he reopened them, desperate determination was evident. He stepped to the closest pile of armor.

"In the name of the Mother," he gritted through his teeth, "I damn you!"

Then he drove the sword through the glowing emblem of the spider. The red glow sparkled and disappeared as the sword slid through, and Solothon could feel the song from the sword as it sang to him. He also felt the pain in his birthmark recede. He withdrew his blade and stepped to the next pile of shattered armor.

Again his blade slid through the emblem with the same result, but the pain was gone. He sighed.

"Gods, Sol," exclaimed the young elf, "that was weird! I need a drink!"

"A drink?!" roared the knight as he stalked toward the elf. "If you had been sober, we might have used your help! Yet in your stupidity, you decided to have a drink when all knew the danger! Why can you not see your responsibilities? Why must you always put yourself above your fellows? Why... DAMN! You'll not listen, so why bother!"

Solothon ended his tirade by passing his sword through a small arc, sheathing it, and stalking past the startled Bonaire for the stairs.

Bonaire found a chair and sat with a jolt, as if his legs would no longer hold him.

In the room above, Melisande's eyes fluttered open to find the blond half elf beside her, her hand in his. Savon'el had pulled what was left of her tunic over her nudity and a blanket up to her breasts. Her mail shirt was folded and lay on the floor next to the bed.

"What happened?" she asked weakly.

"Never mind," replied Savon'el softly. "I'll tell you later. Rest now."

"Oh, my Lady!" she exclaimed softly as she attempted to sit up.

The sharp pain in her stomach brought painful memories to the fore and she laid back. "I remember! I was—"

"You suffered a wound, nothing more," said the barbarian. "It could have been worse, but it wasn't." He brought the wineskin to her mouth. "Drink. It will help."

Before Savon'el could stop her, she took a long drink from the wineskin and, to the half elf's surprise, licked her lips.

"That's good!" she stated a bit stronger. "What's it made of?"

"You don't really want to know," said Savon'el with a grin.

The barbarian replaced the stopper in the wineskin and, as he rose and moved toward the door, slung it onto his shoulder.

"The herbs in the poultice and those in my wine should have you up in no time," he said from the door. "Pup, when she feels stronger, help her downstairs. We have some planning to do."

He placed a hand on the Huntsmaster's shoulder and pulled him toward the stairway, Arantar following without resistance.

The barbarian's wine warmed the girl's stomach as the herbs coursed through her body, bringing their healing properties to her aid. She looked deep into the amber eyes of the youth who still held her hand.

"Don't worry, Savon'el, I'll be fine," she said softly.

"Why didn't you run when you had the chance?" he asked.

"Would you have?" she countered as she squeezed his hand. "I could not—would not—leave you to defend me. I have had training, though not as thorough as I should have had, obviously. It is my duty as companion on this quest to stand by you and the others, even at the cost of my life. I could do no less."

"Well," he replied as he returned the squeeze, "I shall have to keep you near me to keep you out of trouble."

"Good luck with that!" she replied as her smile matched his.

Red Wolf and Arantar met Solothon on the stairway.

"How is the girl?" asked the knight.

"She will be all right, I think," replied the barbarian. "She's strong, as strong as I've ever seen. She'll heal."

"Good. I was worried that we'd lose one of our number, though there is one—"

"Bonaire?" interrupted the Huntsmaster.

"Bonaire."

"What did he do this time?"

"Nothing out of the ordinary, I suppose," came the reply. "Though if I am to rely on him, I'd like to see that his attitude changes."

"That, I'm afraid," responded the Huntsmaster, "may take some time."

"Time we don't have, Huntsmaster," replied the knight.

"True," stated the barbarian as the three moved to the table where Bonaire sat with his head bowed.

Arantar slapped the young elf on the shoulder.

"Buck up, friend. It could have been worse."

"Yeah!" came the surly reply. "I could have been here and really screwed things up!"

"Save your wallowing," said the Huntsmaster sternly. "We have not the time nor desire to watch. We are in the midst of a crisis. Okay, so you made a mistake—"

"So what's new?" replied Bonaire dejectedly.

"So you learned a valuable lesson! Were I you, I'd file it away. We may not be as lucky next time."

"I suggest," interjected the barbarian, "we get some food and discuss our options. Grouch!"

The half ogre had dragged the shattered armor into a pile and now stood over it, obviously trying to decide what to do with it.

"Yeth?"

"Leave that for a moment. We need food, and I must see to that before you take it away."

Grek shrugged and headed for the kitchen as Red Wolf rose and moved to the pile of armor. He took one of the helmets and held it as a bucket beneath the opening of one of the breastplates and poured what was left of the death knight into it. He did the same to the other and picked up the two helms and started for the side door.

"Where are you off to, barbarian?" asked Arantar.

"To offer a gift to Huan-Ti."

"Who?" asked the Huntsmaster to the departing barbarian's back.

"Never mind," came Savon'el's voice from the stairway. "You don't want to know."

The blond half elf led the young cleric down the stairs gently, her wounds still tender, though, amazingly, they had begun to knit. The miracle was in the healing properties in the barbarian's herbs. Melisande made a mental note to learn what she could from the barbarian of these herbs.

Red Wolf stepped back into the tavern and tossed his wineskin to Savon'el.

"Here, pup. Give her some if she begins to feel any pain."

Then he turned and left with the helmets under his arm. The sun had disappeared beyond the west wall and the lamplighters were making their rounds as the barbarian walked into the stable.

Savon'el caught the wineskin and looked into the girl's eyes. They were concentrated on the wineskin and they sparkled. Then he remembered that she liked this stuff! He shook his head with a smile and led her down the stairs, over to the table and carefully helped her sit. Then he pulled another chair slightly away from the table and sat next to her. He watched Arantar out of the corner of his eye as he unsheathed his sword to examine it for any sign of bluntness or damage.

Blegral came out of the kitchen, took one look at the tenants at the table and the pile of rusty armor on the floor, reached under the bar, and as Grouch came out of the kitchen, placed a crystal decanter and four small goblets on the platter the half ogre carried. He whispered something into the half ogre's ear and, as that one proceeded toward the table, began wiping his bar dry.

When he reached the table, Grouch set the platter down and placed a goblet before each except Bonaire.

"Blegral thayth that you look like you need thith thtuff," he said as he poured each goblet half full of the rich amber Sylvan wine. Then he turned and strode back toward the kitchen.

"Hey! What about me?" cried the young elf, but as four sets of eyes riveted him, "No, never mind. I don't believe I need any."

"I do," came a soft voice from the doorway.

Rene' swept into the room, skirting the pile of armor, and stepped lightly to the table.

"What's been going on here," she asked, "and where is my wine?"

"You can have mine," said the cleric as she unstopped the wineskin and raised it to her lips.

"Careful, girl," stated Savon'el as he grabbed her arm gently and brought the wineskin down. "That stuff is potent."

"But it's good for me. Wolf said," she replied petulantly.

As she leaned toward the half elf, her eyes sparkling with the wine, he leaned away.

"That may be so, but your breath is dangerous to the rest of us."

"What?!"

"Ravagar Wine from Red Wolf's lands has a nasty habit of turning fetid on one's breath. I'd suggest," he added with a grin, "you use it sparingly and rinse your mouth with the Sylvan."

"Damn!" she mumbled as she reached for the goblet. "And it's so good too."

Savon'el's face turned from the grin to grave as he related, in short order, the events as he'd seen it to Rene'. Then, as the Huntsmaster held his piece, he turned to address the table at large.

"Now you know what I face. I said it once before that I wished not to bring my doom upon others. I very nearly did this afternoon and I won't risk it again. We were lucky this time. Knowing that I am a lodestone for this sort of danger, I must ask you all to reconsider associating yourselves with me."

"I cannot speak for the others," replied Arantar. Savon'el's quick glance of caution wasn't lost on him as he continued, "but I have a different theory. You were the target this time, and I repeat: *this* time! We have all been marked by whoever is sending these enemies. If we part now, they will hunt us down singly and we won't have a chance."

"Not necessarily."

The soft baritone voice came from the shadows and all eyes turned there. A tall figure in a robe so black it shined stepped from that darkness and tossed back his hood. His blond hair shone in the sunlight that streamed through the windows and his silver eyes assessed each as his glance fell upon them. As his eyes met Melisande's, he noted the secret smile she gave him and returned it.

He passed a chair on the way to their table and it followed to stop just behind him. He sat.

"Hey, you're just the guy we need!" exclaimed Bonaire.

He stood and, as he moved toward the man, he pulled the piece of metal he'd taken from the death knight's breastplate from his pouch. The birthmark on Solothon's arm flared and brought instant pain and a soft moan from his lips.

Bonaire heard the moan and turned on Solothon petulantly. "What are you moaning about?"

This was just too much for Savon'el. His left hand tightened on the hilt of the sword on his lap and he tried to stand. A large hand caught his shoulder and held him firm.

"Sit down, youth!"

The power of that sharp command rippled through the tavern and, as Bonaire stepped back and sunk into his chair, the blond man gripped him with his eyes.

"You obviously have learned nothing on this quest. Had you been with the others, or even a bit interested, you would know that the magiks used to emblazon that..." The man opened his hand toward the startled Bonaire and the piece of metal flew to it. Without wasted motion, he flipped it to Red Wolf. The barbarian had to lift his hand from where it held Savon'el in place to catch it. "...causes a definite and painful response in Sir Solothon."

"Now that I have it, Anteroe," asked the barbarian casually, "what do I do with it?"

"It seems to me," answered the immortal with a tiny grin, "the youth wishes to carry it with him. Now, if it had a hole in it..." With a stiff forefinger, the barbarian drove a hole through the very center of the spider symbol. As he did so, the pain in the Elvin knight's arm disappeared.

Red Wolf flipped the metal piece back to the startled Bonaire and nailed him with his eyes.

Wanderer removed his gaze from the young elf and cast it about the room. When it fell on the blond half elf, he began.

"Some of you should know that while you battled these within, the real battle was being waged outside. You who fought these puppets of magic knew not that Arantar Adenedhel destroyed the puppeteer. The price he's paid is far greater than any you have had to pay, for, because of his reckless attempt to save you all, he has been marked by Death."

The words were grave and the tone deadly.

Savon'el looked from Wanderer to Arantar and dropped his gaze. When he brought it up again, he brought his right hand toward the Huntsmaster and, as he clinched his fist, brought it sharply to his chest. Arantar knew he had gained a friend as well as sword-brother and, the apology accepted, he nodded.

Maxim waited for this to finish, then sat forward in his chair and riveted the Huntsmaster with his eyes.

"The mage you slew was a high-order necromancer. By entering and possessing the body of another, he could have extended his life. However, with the taint of Elvin blood, as well as…"

Here, the druid paused. The pause was very short, but Arantar felt the question.

"Your bloodline would not allow him to hold you, and you threw him out. This was a good thing. However, the aftereffects of this encounter will make your next encounter your last."

"What do you mean?" asked the Huntsmaster as he sat forward in his chair.

"Any dark magiks cast against you, Huntsmaster, will cause your death. That is not a prediction, but fact!"

"What might I do to forestall this curse?"

"Stop. Divest yourself of this company and go no farther! Leave Catlorian and seek anonymity for five years. After that time the curse will lift and you will be safe."

Arantar looked about the table and his smile was grim. When he answered, his words were low steel.

"I cannot and will not. These are my companions, my friends. Were I to hide myself away now, could I live with myself? No! I have been hounded, my friends and I attacked with no obvious reason visible, and my life threatened time and time again."

He picked up his goblet and drank. When he put it back down again his voice was filled with steely conviction.

"No, my friend, I'll not leave this company until I have no breath in my body. My fate is tied to that of my friends. I believe that someone thinks it important to separate us. Therefore, it shall not be! Some things are more important than a nondescript half breed's need to live." Then, with a nasty grin, "Beside that, I have a score to settle with someone, and how better to find out who that someone is?"

"Is that your final word?" asked the Wanderer of Ta'el.

"It is."

"So be it!" Then Wanderer turned to the others at the table. "What of the rest of you? Will you stay or go?"

He needed no answer from Solothon. His look alone spoke volumes on his opinion of the question. Melisande wrapped her arms about the blond half elf's arm and laid her cheek on his shoulder. Her look told the druid that she would not leave his side unless he, or she, was dead.

His mirrored eyes fell on the young elf, Bonaire, and saw that one's fall.

"What of you?"

"Me?" he shrugged still looking at his hands in his lap. "I...uh...Well... I guess I'm going, too."

"Why?"

"Because..."

"You can leave now and not share this danger. Why?"

"Because...Because..." He sighed raggedly and sobbed softly, "Because I have nowhere else to go."

"You have us, my friend," said the Huntsmaster softly. "For now, let that be enough."

Maxim never looked toward Rene' and she knew then that he knew she had to go. But, what of the blond half elf?

That, Rene', was a foregone conclusion.

She took a quick breath when the thought struck her mind and quickly threw up her walls.

"Much better," he sighed. Then he smiled.

"You must have questions. I will attempt to answer all that I may."

"What is the meaning behind the red spider?" Arantar asked quickly.

"It is the symbol for the cult of the Spider God, Yavi, of which Arendel was High Priest. His lieutenant sits now in the palace at Dragon's Teeth. They are aligned with a terrible evil and they will sow chaos wherever they can."

"Why all of the subterfuge?"

"Why not?"

Solothon removed one of the shirakens from his pouch and, as he handed it to the immortal, gritted his teeth against the burning pain.

"What do you know of this?"

As Wanderer's hand touched the weapon, the pain in the knight's arm ceased. The druid turned the weapon over in his hands.

"This was made recently, within the past three thousand years. This was the battle standard for the mages called 'Wormslayers', of which Banshe'e was chief. During the Mage Wars, he was the most powerful of the Hazard Class sorcerers. His power was then far greater than that the Myrlin himself wields now. He waged war on everyone, but especially on dragons, killing them out of hand, thus the lance through the dragon symbol. He was considered insane by friend and foe alike."

"Insane?" asked Rene'.

"Evil and crazy."

"How so?" Rene' leaned forward to look into the druid's silver eyes.

"He would rip the hearts from children to feed his hounds," he replied. "He planted trees in the deserts of the continent below this one just to see how long they would last before they withered and died. If one does evil for a purpose, it is called evil. When one does evil for no purpose or remorse, but just because they wish to, it is called insanity. Banshe'e was insane."

"But why would this Banshe'e be after me?" asked the blond half elf. "I am not a threat to him, save to battle his evil as all others must do. Why me?"

"What I said was he *was* insane. Banshe'e is dead."

"Some are not as certain of that as you."

"True, Rene'," replied Wanderer as he returned the probing glare. "I suppose one should not count a sorcerer as dead unless they kick the dirt over his face themselves."

"All I know for certain," stated the knight, "is that I saw a dark figure in the woods as I stood over the bodies of my dead friends. Who else would use weapons marked thusly?"

"That I cannot say."

"Cannot or will not?" This from Savon'el.

"Possibilities come to mind, yet they would be but conjecture and would possibly lead you in the wrong direction. I can, however, say with certainty that if you stay true to your friends, the villain will become apparent."

Savon'el sat quietly, his mind trying to fit all of this information into some logical sense. The complexity of this task was compounded by his own lack of information, yet what had happened to him and these, his friends, could not be coincidental. The only conclusion...

"If," interjected the Huntsmaster, "that standard is again rising, whether by Banshe'e or another—"

"We should tell someone," finished the blond half elf. "Red Wolf, who do we tell?"

The barbarian shrugged and sipped his wine as Rene' answered for him.

"The Myrlin would be the most logical, would he not? If Banshe'e is alive and is behind everything, it would affect Ta'el. Taking this information to the local magistrates, or even to the king, would be a waste."

"Myrlin would be the best choice, Rene', except that he has traveled far from this realm. None have the capability to reach him, save myself."

"He is still the most logical one," insisted Rene'. "He has shown a great interest in Banshe'e, from the conversations I have had with him."

"That, my dear, is because of the vow Banshe'e made at his supposed death. Should the sorcerer live, Myrlin's life, as well as this entire world, is forfeit. Banshe'e, if he lives, would destroy the world in his insanity just to smile amid the ashes." Maxim glanced about the group and smiled. "However, you are quite correct. The Myrlin must be informed of the possibility and, since none of you have the capability to travel to the realms he has, I suppose I must play messenger."

Wanderer placed the shiraken into the knight's hand and sighed. "There is faerie blood on this."

At Solothon's shocked look, he continued.

"Banshe'e despised those of Elvin blood. He used the dark elves— daku—to do his bidding, promising grand boons for their service, yet at his whim they died as well.

"Though few of you would agree," he said as his eyes raked those before him, "daku are as Elvin as these three." He pointed a finger at Rene', Solothon, and Bonaire in turn. "They were misguided, seduced, and then betrayed in the end. Yet those misguided prejudices still run free."

The druid looked pointedly at the Huntsmaster.

"My dislike stems from years of battle and seeing the aftermath of their raids."

"I never said your feelings were groundless, Huntsmaster, just that your preconceived hatred may be. The fact is, daku still believe in their cause, though they don't recall who designed it for them. They were taught that they deserved to own what was theirs in the first place. The dewlok, or dark dwarves, were seduced by his evil as well and for the same reason: ownership of the great halls of the dwarves.

"The gods of this world have restrictions, yet provide what is needed for each of you to survive in your day-to-day lives. You must admit that there are those who seem to own vast portions of this world, yet you never ask from whom they procured it."

"What do you mean?" asked the Huntsmaster.

"Think about it, ranger. Do you own anything?"

"Just what I have with me and what currency I earn."

"And your horse?"

"I don't own Browen. He is my friend and companion. He allows me transportation in exchange for my friendship and some few edible trinkets I can afford, that is all."

"Exactly. You hunt the wide forests and fields of this world and aid the inhabitants as you pass. However, with your talents," this with a tilt of his head to indicate he knows of his saola familiars, "you could take what you wished—within reason, of course."

"Why would I do that? I have all that I need in my friends and companions. What need I for more?"

"Good question, but one that has been answered badly throughout the lifetime of this planet. That which was freely given has been taken possession of by those gifted with the bounty of this realm."

"Wait, now!" interjected Savon'el. "What of those who till the land and raise the animals for others to consume? Do they not have the right to own and protect their livelihood? And what of the kingdoms that are there to aid in their protection? Do they not deserve the taxes exacted to fund that protection?"

"Of course! However, how many of those you have mentioned actually own the land they till? How many of those are basically indentured servants to others, possibly those who head the kingdoms you mentioned? Most of these have banded together to aid one another to protect the land from predators—both animal and human—help each other in tilling, seeding, and reaping, in milking, herding, and slaughtering. Fishermen aid one another in the catch. This is as it should be.

"Yet there are those who, by dent of 'purchase' or conquest, 'allow' for that land, ship, or range to be worked. They reap the grander harvest without lifting a helping hand."

"I have seen this," stated the Elvin knight, "in my father's lands, yet they are few and are called to account should they become complacent in their duty to their, as you say, indentured workers. Most are allowed to work the land for a modest return to the landowner. That is proper recompense for raising and feeding one's family. I have seen very little abuse that is allowed."

"Yeah!" added Bonaire. "My father owns the land that Borderlend sits on, but he doesn't lord it over the people he rents to. He coulda been very rich, but he always treats everybody with respect and takes only what he needs. Is it wrong for him to own the whole thing?"

"Good point!" replied the druid with a grin. "Yet it has ever been that there are those who, in their desire or greed for more, have caused strife and war to erupt. What do you know of the Elvin-Dwarven War?"

"Not much," acknowledged the Huntsmaster. "Most of what I know is of the devastation of the Mage War, though I believe the earlier war brought on the latter."

"So it would seem. However, evil only needs an excuse to breed. The elves and dwarves fought over the ownership of the lands, the dwarves claiming the lands above their great halls and the elves, jealous of the riches brought out of the mines, claiming them as their right through the Mother. Humans, swayed to one side or the other, joined in the fight with more vigor and power than was needed. The human mages were the ones who created the Mage War, and the reason for the war was forgotten in the vastness of the devastation. The greed for the land was overshadowed by the greed for power."

"Banshe'e?"

"Yes, Huntsmaster. Banshe'e. He and his followers didn't want to own anything but the hearts and minds of the world. Banshe'e convinced otherwise intelligent beings that under his rule peace would prevail. His insanity was seductive in that fashion, though his true desire was the destruction itself."

"Then if it is evil we face, in its purest form, why would one such as Cartellion take an interest in me?" asked the knight.

The druid looked deep into the eyes of the Elvin knight and sighed. "It seems you need a lesson." As the knight bristled at the comment, Wanderer continued. "Lord Cartellion has, arguably, evil beliefs, but he himself is not evil. He is first and foremost a knight. Yet he is also the 'Right Hand of Death'."

At Solothon's questioning look, he continued.

"Death visits all eventually, though he claims precious few souls as his own. He seems to have taken an interest in you and your companions for a reason.

"You see, Death has yet to claim an Elvin soul and, with the first he gathers, his power will increase. With that power, he will be able to claim more Elvin souls until, finally, the bright race would no longer be allowed to pass on to the Bright Lands. He doesn't actively seek that, of course, for it is not part of the bargain he made with the Creator. Yet it is something he would not turn from should it be presented to him."

The druid waited a moment until the knight nodded grimly. Then he leaned back in his chair and glanced toward the bar.

"Blegral, I'd like some of your good herbal tea, if you please."

Then, as the barman disappeared into the kitchen, Wanderer turned to Savon'el. "Would you take tea with me, youth?"

"No!" came the instant reply.

Suddenly, some part of the barriers that had kept the blond half elf in the dark for so long dropped away. He felt the pain, anger, and despair, yet without the answer to their cause. He remembered the tea and the drugged stupor and his anger was instant. His hand tightened on the hilt of the bastard sword, but Red Wolf's hand gripped his shoulder anew, cautioning him to stillness. He relented to the barbarian's warning, but his eyes flared molten amber.

Wanderer smiled and rose from his chair.

"Never mind the tea, Blegral," he called to the barman as he stood and turned to go. Then, as if in afterthought, he turned back to the table. "One more bit of unasked for information," he said softly. "You must be far from Catlorian within two days. Otherwise, you will all die."

As the light swirled about him, his words drifted to their ears.

"Seek not the souls within the Well of Darkness. Necromancers grow as Death grows."

And he was gone.

Chapter Twenty-four

"First things first. Blegral?"

The barbarian's words brought everyone's attention away from the spot, from which Wanderer had vanished, toward the bar. As Red Wolf turned back with a strange look on his face, Melisande put the situation into words.

"It seems as if we are alone."

It was true. Sir Jake, Blegral, and the half ogre were nowhere to be found. All was quiet within and without the tavern. A strange stillness had come to Catlorian and with it, a marked sense of dread.

"Well," stated the barbarian, "I suppose I'll have to get my own drink."

"No more drink!" shouted the knight. "It is a time for action!"

"But," exclaimed the young Bonaire, "Wanderer said we have two days! What's the rush?"

The Huntsmaster turned his steely gaze on the young elf.

"Had you been listening, you would have heard what the rest of us heard. We were not given two days, but a deadline—"

"And," continued Savon'el, "if we don't meet it, we shall all be dead."

His eyes took in those at the table as he sighed.

"I honor you all for your determination to stay, yet I wish—"

"You have no guilt in our decision, friend," interrupted the Huntsmaster. "As I said in the beginning, our choices were made for us long before we met. Now, we must plan our next move, and I suggest we do so on the move."

"Good thinking," said the barbarian. "Pup, go tell Terillion that we are off. I have a few loose ends to tie up here before we leave, so I will meet you here as quickly as I can."

The blond half elf nodded and rose as Bonaire started for the door.

"Well," stated the young elf, "I don't know about you, but I'm going to the temple. I'd hate to leave without letting my new goddess know how rotten I feel. Lady Rene', will you go with me?"

"There is no need for me to go, as I've already paid my respects to the Lady."

"But there is need!"

Lady Rene' glanced toward the knight as that one continued.

"I suggest that none of us travel anywhere alone. Now, more than ever, safety in numbers should be our guide."

"I agree," said the Huntsmaster. "If you, Savon'el, are going to the sage's apartments, allow me to accompany."

"Welcome, Huntsmaster. Lady Rene', if you will accompany Bonaire?"

"Of course! I hadn't reasoned the implications as fully as I should have. We shall make our mounts ready, then the tem—"

A clap of displaced air marked the appearance of a dense gray cloud that seemed to roil and drip from the table at which they sat. Savon'el, as before, though gentler this time, brought Melisande to her feet and placed his body between her and the table, as the full length of dull gray steel filled his left hand.

The others, save Red Wolf, responded in kind, knocking their chairs backward to get to their feet, their hands to the hilts of their swords.

Red Wolf leaned back in his chair and watched. Though to onlookers he seemed unconcerned, every fiber in his being was alive. At the first sign of trouble, the full weight of his awesome skills would, at the speed of thought, come to bear. But for now he watched.

Bonaire backed against the bulletin board to the side of the door and shook as the cloud began to dissipate.

"Will this never end?" shouted the blond half elf as he stood in battle crouch and waited for attack.

"Hold your sword."

The Huntsmaster's soft voice came as the cloud disappeared and a sword was revealed. Its length was five feet of gray steel with a hilt of leather-wrapped bone. A rose as black as midnight rested across the blade and, to Rene's sight, radiated of power of an unknown origin.

Arantar also saw the power radiating, as if in a smooth pond, from the petals of the flower. He knew that this was another byproduct of his newly embraced power of will, as he knew, *knew*, that the ripples of power were attuned to him and him alone. He reached a tentative hand to the rose and picked it up.

"Arantar!" shouted Savon'el, his eyes wide with concern. "Put it down! It may be bane for you and conceal a danger to us all!"

"Fear not, friend," said he as the rose turned from black to deep blue, to light blue, and then the steel blue of the Huntsmaster's eyes.

"Have you not heard of the 'Brotherhood of Steel', the Order of the Black Rose? No?"

The rose wilted in the Huntsmaster's fingers and, as he dropped it on the table, it turned to dust. Arantar grasped the hilt of the great sword and lifted it. It was similar to, yet not the same as, his Grey Wolf.

"When I bought the sword that was this one's twin, I felt that there was something special about it. It felt like it had been made for me and was mine from its creation. The merchant said that should the sword ever break, the craftsman would take his own life. That sounds a bit extreme to guarantee a useful bit of merchandise, isn't it? However," he continued as he turned the sword in his hand to admire the balance and grace of the blade, "if one were to remember the stories of the smiths of old, this was a common thing. The smith would take the death of the wielder as his responsibility since it was his responsibility to make a perfect weapon.

"Now, whether the original craftsman still lives or not, the Brotherhood maintains the oath and has replaced my steel with an almost exact twin. Though I feel this one is attuned for me in its balance and strength, I can feel the slight differences, just enough to prove this one is not a reincarnation of the last."

He swept the blade in a small arc and sheathed it without looking. He glanced at the rafters and mouthed a silent "Thank you," then looked about the table at his companions. He noted the look on the blond half elf's face and recognized it as fear, not for himself, but the Huntsmaster.

"It is all right, friend Savon'el. It is mine and not a threat to me or my fellows. The Brotherhood has but returned Grey Wolf to me for use against our enemies. Trust me to know this."

Savon'el nodded and the sword disappeared into the sheath at his back.

"I'll...I'll get our horses, Lady Rene'," stammered Bonaire as he slipped out of the door and moved down the dark alley toward the stables.

"I believe we were on our way to Terillion's apartments?"

Savon'el nodded again and turned to Melisande.

"M'lady, if you would stay with Red Wol—"

"ARANTAR!"

The shout came from outside, and as all eyes turned toward the door it banged open. Bonaire ran in, slammed the door, and stood with his back against it, eyes wide with fear. His whole body shook and the smell of raw fear touched the barbarian's nostrils.

"Easy, Bonaire," said the Huntsmaster softly as he and Savon'el moved toward the frightened youth.

"You...you don't understand!" he stammered. "It's...the people...Everything alive in the city is gone!"

"What do you mean by gone?"

"Gone! All of them! Even the horses! There's feed in the manger, oats in the bins, but no horses! There's nobody on the streets. The city is deserted!"

Savon'el moved the young elf from in front of the door, opened it, and looked out. The warehouse across from the tavern, from which smoke and steam billowed a few moments before, stood with that same smoke and steam frozen motionless above it.

"What the hells?"

A loud pop sounded behind him and the smoke began to rise anew as people appeared, as if by magic, on the street. He turned to see a very large red squirrel sitting upon the table they'd just vacated, scrubbing at its tail and mumbling to itself.

"What—"

"Hi, yourself," mumbled the squirrel as it glanced at the blond half elf. "Oh! How'd you like my present?"

"Present?"

"Yeah! I heard ol' silver eyes tell you that you had only two days to live so I stopped time for you. Thought you needed it."

"You did that?"

"Sure! I can do a lot more stuff too! Wanna see?"

"Uh...not right now," responded the blond half elf as he and Arantar cast questioning looks at each other.

"Well, the big guy sent me to get some information for you that you might need. Cost me a singed tail too! Boy, that hurts!"

"Sorry, but—"

"Yeah, I know," sighed the animal. "Now, about Arendel, right?"

"Arendel?"

"Yeah. Seems he was gathering a lot of money to hire somebody named Clover to do a job. There are some people Arendel doesn't like and Clover was supposed to...'disappear' them. Know what I mean?"

"No. Not precisely," stated Bonaire as he moved to the table with the others.

"Well, precisely," said the squirrel softly as it scampered over, reached up and grasped Bonaire's cloak, and pulled the young elf's face down to its level, "when Clover disappears somebody, they stay disappeared. Now do you know what I mean?"

As the reality struck him, Bonaire blurted out, "Clover is an assassin?"

"Oh, I don't know. What do you think?" replied the beast, its mouth drawn up in a squirrel's version of a grin.

Arantar looked again at the blond half elf.

"If Arendel hired an assassin to kill someone—"

"That someone is us!" finished Savon'el. "We'd better move faster!"

Bonaire heard this and turned to the squirrel. "Could...could you do me a favor?"

"Why? You're nobody." Then, as he pointed toward Savon'el, "He's somebody, or was, or will be, or something, but," he pointed back at Bonaire and reiterated, "you are nobody!"

"But...but I'd do something for you!"

"How? You'll be dead in two days!"

Bonaire paled and backed away.

The squirrel saw Red Wolf and scampered over to perch on the top rung of a chair close to him.

"Hey! You smell just like those wolves out front of the Eastern Gate!"

"What?" growled the barbarian as he brought his chair forward and glared at the beast.

"Yeah! They're howling and carrying on something terrible! They've got the guards all worked up!"

Red Wolf came to his feet and started toward the door. It would have to be something important to bring his pack to the gates of this city and it deserved his immediate attention. As he opened the door, he shouted back.

"Pup, there is something wrong with my pack and I must go. You must handle the details of our departure. Don't worry about Terillion. Just get everything ready to move."

"I will, friend, but when do I expect you to return?"

"When you see me," responded the barbarian as he went through the door.

"What kind of trouble, Wolf?" asked Arantar as he followed him out.

"I know not, but I will soon find out!"

"I'd like to accompany you."

"If you can keep up," stated the barbarian as he turned and ran.

Arantar started off a split second after the barbarian, but watched as the big man disappeared through the gates before the Huntsmaster was halfway there. As he came through the gates, he saw Red Wolf on one knee growling at a black furred wolf. He turned his mind to his wolf familiar.

Fang?

Here, Arantar-sao,

The ruddy silver wolf loped to the Huntsmaster from the darkness and sat.

What has happened, friend?

Bitches and pups gone. Need Grrirr Gya help to find. I go, Arantar-sao?

If you must. responded the half elf. *I wish I could keep up with you for I too wish to help.*

Arantar caught the movement as Red Wolf stood, sighed, and reached into his large pouch. He removed a pelt of whitish silver and, after removing and storing his cloak, donned the wolf pelt. The barbarian turned north and ran.

As he ran, he fell forward onto his hands and flipped back the hood on the pelt. Instantly he transformed into a very large wolf, over two hundred pounds of muscle and sinew, with a coat of copper red.

Arantar-sao, you come.

I cannot, friend. I'd only slow you.

Not if you are same.

What?

Arantar-sao, you know much, but little. You can be same if wish strong.

How?!

Inside you, saola. Inside power make you same. Try.

But, how can I...

Arantar-sao, look my eye.

The Huntsmaster obeyed.

Feel earth under feet, wind in hair. Smell scent in air, come down, feel ground on paws, feel muscles in body, make self...

Suddenly, as the Huntsmaster placed his hands to the green grass, his senses jumped to new heights of awareness. His sense of smell, his hearing, his vision—all became so much clearer. He glanced down at his hands and found them gone, replaced by black fur covered paws.

<I have waited so many seasons for this, my saola, that you and I would run together as pack-mates. Come, my brother, we must catch up.>

Arantar glanced at his friend and caught the wolf grin as the ruddy silver wolf loped off toward the moving pack. The Huntsmaster stretched his new form and felt the power and the wonder as he ran after his friend.

Red Wolf followed the black wolf to a clearing on a knoll, about which was a stand of elms. At the very center of this clearing, a silver lance had been plunged into the earth. The smell of death was about this weapon, new death. He commanded the pack leaders to send out scouts on a sweep to pick up any scent available, of the pups, bitches, or those who were responsible. As they moved to comply, the barbarian shifted.

<My saola, you must return to your true form.> said the ruddy silver wolf. <To stay in this form for very long is to risk losing yourself to it. I cannot allow that for I would lose you as well. Concentrate on what it feels like to be a man, Arantar-sao. Concentrate...>

As the wolf's words droned in his mind, the Huntsmaster shifted. He found himself standing next to his friend with the largest gathering of wolves he had ever seen.

Thank you, my friend.

The thought was answered softly in his mind, but the words seemed solemn.

Arantar not just friend. Love as brother. Always be brother.

Before the Huntsmaster could ask about the feeling, the barbarian called.

"Over here, Huntsmaster. What do you make of this?"

Arantar stepped through the elms and found the barbarian, arms akimbo, staring at the silver weapon. The Huntsmaster made a complete circuit of the lance before he spoke.

"This is not like any lance I've seen. Notice the size of it? It is half again the girth of a normal lance, yet unless it has been driven into the earth a good ten feet, it is shorter. What is to be done?"

"For now, nothing," sighed the barbarian. "I must find the answers, and only I know where they may be found."

The large black loped up to the barbarian and began growling in that familiar singsong. Arantar felt the loss, for in this form he could no longer understand. The wolf backed away, turned, and ran back to its pack.

"He has said," stated Red Wolf in a very low voice, "the bitches and pups were forced here, yet there is no scent of their leaving. They have seemingly vanished into thin air. This is disturbing." He sat then in lotus, his right foot over his left leg and added, "Very disturbing."

The Huntsmaster stepped away and sat. Fang appeared at his knee, lay down, and propped his head on his friend's leg. With this new power of mind, Arantar saw the magic ripple from the lance. This time, however, he knew that the magic was...wrong somehow, twisted, different from what it should be. He glanced at the barbarian who sat, eyes closed and as still as death.

At that moment, Red Wolf was far away in his place of solitude where the grass was always green and a brook burbled in eternal peace. He sought for his name brother, yet that proved fruitless. He steadied his mind for what he must do next and sent the call.

Across the brook, light sparkled in the air in swirls of color. It grew brighter until, with a soundless explosion, it flashed stark white and vanished. In the light of his own power strode a great white wolf. Over the brook he trod with no ripple or disturbance to its flow until he stood before the young barbarian.

Red Wolf felt the question grow, not in words, but a feeling of askance that went through his senses.

Why had he called the Spirit?

"I need your guidance Great One."

Why?

Red Wolf related all that had come to pass and when he finished it seemed that the great wolf sighed.

A vision began to form in the barbarian's mind then, a vision so stark that he felt he could reach out and touch the objects he passed. In that vision he walked in a place of eternal twilight. The sky above was filled with stars, yet the patterns were not familiar.

There were walls sixty or seventy feet high completely surrounding the place where he stood and seemed to go on for miles in both directions. Upon the walls, lit by the dim light of those stars, were dragons, dragons of every color imaginable from gold to black and all metals and pastels between, all watching, all guarding this place. They seemed not to notice Red Wolf as he stood amongst the huge formations of bone and stone.

Scattered here and there among the bones were lances, much the same as the one driven into the ground. The colors of these lances were reflected in the colors of the dragons guarding this place with marked exceptions. The platinum, silver, and the one that would match the multicolored hues of Tiamet were not here.

It came to him that these lances belonged there and should never be removed and the three that were missing should be found and brought here as soon as could be done. He knew where the silver lance was, but the others? He leaned as close as he could to one of the lances without touching it. Embossed on the hand guard was a dragon pierced by a lance. The low growl in his throat brought a slight stir from the guardians and he stopped. Then the name of the lances came to him.

Wormslayers.

"Why have you shown me this? Has it anything to do with my pack's loss?"

The vision faded and as he returned to his place of peace, the feeling came through to him. He watched as the great white wolf stepped back over the brook and glanced back at him.

North-northeast.

He drifted up from his trance and found, just to his right, a young wolf standing, as stone, and facing north-northeast. As the barbarian watched, the wolf's gray coat changed to white.

He growled and the large black returned to face him.

<Follow the white one, for he knows the direction we must take. Gather the packs as you go. Tell them Grrirr Gya has spoken of battle and their help is needed. Follow him in caution. I shall join you when I may. Good hunting.>

<It shall be.> growled the leader and turned to the pack with a growl.

The white wolf loped in a straight line in the direction he was pointed without waiting. The pack assembled and began to flow after him with the large black in the lead.

Arantar stood and moved toward the barbarian, but he stopped when the growling thought rippled through his mind.

Arantar-sao, I go too.

Why? he shot back quickly. *They are not of your pack. Why?*

Of my blood, Arantar-sao. If not stop now, maybe my pack next.

But I must stay. Our friends need me now more than ever, and I've given my word.

Then you must go. Air Brother go with you, but I must follow pack.

What will I do without you, my friend?

Not without, saola. Never without. Must go. Need you say okay.

Arantar knelt before his friend, wrapped his arms about the thick neck, and felt the tears well up in those steel blue eyes. He knew the only answer he could give.

Go then, my brother, and come back to me safe. We, your brothers, need you.

Travel safe, brother. came the colorful ripple as the wolf bounded after the pack.

Red Wolf's hand rested on the Huntsmaster's shoulder.

"We shall care for him as if he were our own. Worry not, Huntsmaster. He will be safe, as safe as any of us can be now."

Then the barbarian turned back to the puzzle of the lance.

"This thing must be removed from this place and taken to those who know its meaning. I am afraid of the possibilities its presence conjures, but am more afraid of what they mean to my pack and my people."

"I understand you must follow them, Red Wolf, but what of us?"

The barbarian smiled.

"I think you may find that my companion will be more than capable of leading you on this quest."

"Quest? With all that's happened, why should we go to that tower?"

"Why not? If they who wish us ill find you in Catlorian, you will die. Hope lies in moving forward, ever hopeful, ever vigilant to the path that will cheat the Fates once again. Besides, you might find our enemy there and be better able, for the hardships, to defeat him.

"Now," he continued as he wrapped his arms about the lance and heaved, "we must...Ugh!...Take this...Ugh!...Damned thing to...GR-RRRAHHH!" The lance slid out of the ground and was allowed to fall as he completed his statement with, "...Someone knowledgeable in its history."

The thing was heavy, twice as heavy as its mass gave evidence. Why this was so was unknown to the barbarian as he struggled to lift it to his shoulder. The Huntsmaster saw that the lance weighed heavy on the barbarian, but knew that before he could lay a hand to help he would have to ask.

"May I give my shoulder for assistance? I'll not touch it until you've given me leave."

"Most honorable and noble, Huntsmaster," grunted Red Wolf. "How-ever, if you don't help me I shall be driven into the ground!"

Arantar chuckled as he took the barbed end onto his shoulder. Red Wolf slid the thing down until it rested on his shoulder at the hand guard. He felt the pressure ease a bit, but at its great weight it would take their combined strength to carry it back to Catlorian. Then the two set out for the gate, Red Wolf in front and the Huntsmaster trying to keep pace with the single-minded barbarian.

Meanwhile, the red squirrel returned to the table and turned his attention to the frightened Bonaire.

"Hey! Don't worry about it! Clover is quick! You won't feel a thing, you'll see. Well, maybe."

Then with a small "pop" of displaced air, the squirrel was gone.

Bonaire ran for the door in a panic, but the strong hand of the Elvin knight gripped his cloak and brought him up short.

"Where are you going?" Solothon asked softly.

"Away! Quickly! Let me go!"

"Where is 'away,' Bonaire?" asked the knight calmly.

Bonaire stopped struggling and looked up into the knight's eyes. He knew then there was no longer a safe haven to run to. He was trapped.

"Bonaire?" came the voice from behind him.

He turned his head and saw the concern on the blond half elf's face.

"Whatever the danger is out there, do not face it alone."

"Besides," came the lilting voice of the golden mage girl as she swept toward him, "we are your friends, and we depend on you as much as you depend on us. Your faith will also help."

"I think my faith has deserted me," he said softly as he relaxed in the knight's iron grip. "What good has it done me to believe in anything?"

"You should ask the Lady, Bonaire," said the girl as she touched the knight's arm and he released the young elf gently. "I will go with you if you wish."

"That would be the best idea," stated Solothon. "We should never be without one of our own. I count on you, for better or worse, as one of us, Bonaire. We will need all of us to find our way e'er this thing is done."

"Well," said the young elf as he looked at his feet, "at least I belong. I guess that beats nothing." Then he lifted his eyes to Rene'. "Would you really go with me?"

"Go saddle our horses and we shall go together," she answered, her fingertips brushing the hair from his eyes.

"I can saddle yours, but I'll have to ride bareback. That's okay though. I'm kinda used to it now."

Savon'el watched him leave and move with purpose around the corner to the stables.

"I'm sorry," he whispered as he hung his head.

"He'll be alright, Savon'el," said the girl as she stepped out onto the porch to wait. "He's stronger than even he thinks."

Melisande had moved from the table, but had stayed back during the confrontation with Bonaire. Things were moving too fast, yet not quickly enough. The contradiction confused her.

She felt the need to be away from the city, but under more controlled circumstances. She needed to go quickly so she could return as quickly to see her son, if Cartellion's word was as good as everyone had said.

Now they were embarking on this trek helter-skelter and there was little time to prepare.

She felt drawn to the blond half elf, though it could be because of his situation. He too seemed to have lost control of his life, as well as the things he held dear. They were as skiffs cast adrift in turbulent seas.

Now she felt his pain and guilt for thinking he had brought danger into their midst. Through it all, however, his smile helped her face her own pain. She needed him, as much as she hated to admit it, and he needed her as well as these others. He would not survive alone, and she vowed that, until they were all safe, he would never be alone. She heard Bonaire outside with the horses, moved to the blond half elf's side, and took his arm.

"Red Wolf has said we need not see Terillion," he was saying to the knight, "but I feel we must know where we should go for our provisioning."

"In this you are correct," the knight answered. "I will go with you."

"What of me?" asked the cleric.

"You must remain, Melisande," Savon'el answered as he covered her hand with his. "You are still weak and we know not what we will find once on these streets. I would have you safe."

"Safe?" she replied. "Alone? Here?"

"Here Blegral and Grek will look after you until our return."

"Just why would they do that?" she asked angrily. "Will you tell them that Banshe'e has risen to destroy the world? How long before we are stoned for lunatics?"

"What you are saying is—"

"What I'm saying is that we cannot tell anyone save the Myrlin, or at least one of great power who might, and I mean *might*, believe us! And about leaving me here?" she continued as she removed her hand from his arm and placed her fists on her hips. "If you try, I'll just follow! T'would be safer to take me along!"

Savon'el had to chuckle at her determination. She smiled at his response, knowing she had won, and she was glad he could still laugh.

"Well," stated the knight, "I see that Bonaire and Rene' are on their way. She said she would meet us here within the hour, so if we are going we should be about it."

Savon'el reached out a hand to the black-haired cleric and smiled. She grinned, took the offered hand, and followed them out into the street. They stopped and watched as Bonaire and Rene' guided their mounts down the street and around the corner.

"I think that we should stop first at Myrlin's tower and leave a message, just in case Wanderer misses him," said the blond half elf.

The knight nodded and led the way, his eyes darting to either side in search of danger.

He could have saved the trouble, for no one was about this evening. Not one soul stirred the calm of the night.

Melisande thought she heard a baby cry and again her pain returned.

They arrived finally at the door to the tower and Savon'el knocked. The door opened wide, yet there seemed to be no one there.

"Yes?" came a voice from within.

It was deep and lethargic and carried with it a threatening lack of concern.

"We seek the Myrlin," stated Savon'el.

"He is not...here."

"Where is he?"

"Why?"

"I must leave a message," said Savon'el, his patience running thin. "It is important."

"He is not here."

"I know that, dammit," he said angrily as he made to step into the door-way.

A hand—at least it felt like a hand—stopped him before he could step inside.

"You must not enter. I am the guardian. Leave your message and go."

Savon'el backed away from the door angrier than...well, angrier than he could remember. He was being kept out by force! He could go where he wished, by the gods! Was he not...

What? Who was he?

The anger was there still, but now confusion was added.

"Tell your master that the banner of Banshe'e flies," said the Elvin knight.

"I shall." The door closed with finality.

Melisande noted the strain on the blond half elf and took his hand. His eyes found hers and he relaxed.

At least here was reality, he thought. This girl was special and for some reason she wished to stay with him. Though his life might be a mystery and his mind jumbled confusion, there was no confusion in her eyes. He smiled and kissed the hand he held lightly.

"Shall we proceed to Sage Terillion's apartments?" asked the knight.

"I think not," replied the half elf thoughtfully. "It would be pointless at this juncture. I think our best course is to return to the tavern, gather our gear and what provisions we can find there, and leave with all due haste. We must make do with what we have. Melisande and I need mounts, and I believe we can get them there. What is your counsel, Sir Solothon?"

"You are probably right," he answered as he turned and led the way back.

Arantar and the barbarian jogged back toward the gate with the heavy lance upon their shoulders. When they reached the gate, they didn't stop, nor did the guard attempt to stop them. One of their number recognized Red Wolf and the look in that one's eyes. He waved his companions out of the path and let them pass.

Red Wolf looked neither right nor left, but moved straight ahead for the Myrlin's tower with Arantar gasping along behind.

Solothon saw them as they came up the street and hailed them, but though Arantar raised a tired hand in greeting, the barbarian acknowledged nothing save his mission. Solothon had to run beside them to stay up with the stubborn barbarian, the panting Huntsmaster, and their shared burden.

"This is beautiful!" he exclaimed to Arantar. "Where did you find it?"

Arantar had to take a breath. The lance was heavy, far heavier than its size should have made it. It was all he could do to keep up with the large barbarian's megalomania. He started to explain the situation when the knight reached out and touched the silver smoothness.

The weight on the Huntsmaster's shoulder lifted! The bloody thing felt light as a feather for no obvious reason.

Then the "reason" removed his hand and the weight again drove into the Huntsmaster's shoulder. He grimaced under the weight and grunted.

"Stay with them, sir knight. I will be back momentarily."

"Where are you going?"

"To the Myrlin's."

"But he is not there."

"Try telling him that!" grunted the Huntsmaster as he tilted his head sharply toward Red Wolf.

The knight stopped, and as he watched the lance and its bearers disappeared down the lamp lit street he was joined by Melisande and Savon'el.

"What sort of lance is that, Solothon?" asked the blond half elf. "It seems a bit out of proportion."

"I know not, but it is beautiful and seemed to call to me." Then the knight shook his head and grinned sheepishly. "Or maybe I just wished it. No matter. Arantar said he'd return in a moment. I feel a long involved explanation will be required e'er this mystery is revealed."

Then the three turned back toward the tavern.

The two bearing the lance arrived at the tower, and though a note had been placed on the door stating, "Out of town. Myrlin," the barbarian ignored it. He couldn't read well anyway so it was a waste of paper and ink. He jogged straight up to the door and pounded his fist into it.

"Yes?" came the deep, lethargic voice as the door opened wide.

"Tell Myrlin to come *now*!"

"He is not here."

"There is something here he should know, something not seen in an age. He must be told!"

"He is not here."

"Do you know what this is?" asked the barbarian as he tapped the lance with his off hand.

"It is a Wormslayer."

"When was the last one seen?"

"Over eighteen hundred years."

"This one has been used within the past few days."

"No dragon has died within that period."

The voice was dead, rather nonchalant, as it responded with ill-concealed contempt.

"This was left in the forest north of the city as a sign," growled the barbarian. "The Myrlin must be told."

"He is not here."

"Send a message."

"I cannot."

"Surely someone within the tower can!"

"There are none here but us, the Protectors."

Red Wolf growled deep within his chest. He knew of the Protectors and, since their only function was protecting, he knew any more conversation would be but a waste.

There was only one place he could go to get the answers he needed and he grinned at the thought.

"Will you guard this for the Myrlin?"

"Of course."

Both Arantar and the barbarian felt the entity move from the doorway and the lance, lifted by unseen hands, disappeared into the tower doorway.

The door closed with a solid click of finality.

The barbarian took a deep breath and turned to the Huntsmaster. His voice was grave.

"Return to the others. I must have answers and must go alone. I will come if I can or send word of how I fared. If I don't return, trust the savon'el."

Arantar nodded. The barbarian turned and, in a step, was moving faster, according to the Huntsmaster, than anyone should be capable. When he realized in what direction the barbarian was going, he knew what Red Wolf had meant.

The barbarian was on his way to the Guild of Mages. A barbarian of Red Wolf's skill and power, with the beliefs he held, was about to enter the center of magic to ask for help. If there wasn't an explosion in the city this day, it would be due to the extreme caution both sides exerted.

Savon'el saw the streak of red cross the intersection a block from where they stood. Then the Huntsmaster rounded the corner walking slowly and looking down the street after the barbarian. From somewhere in the direction Red Wolf had gone, the howl of a hunting wolf floated back.

"I wonder where he's going now?" mumbled the blond half elf.

Red Wolf's howl was for two reasons: First, he wanted a clear running field for speed. His voiced warning would clear the streets of all but the very hardy of hearts. Second, he wished to alert those "demon traffickers" to his approach. To show up on their doorstep without warning was to increase the chance of wrong conclusions being drawn.

The door to the Mage's Guild was closed and barred from within. Red Wolf grinned and tapped on the door gently. A small caged window in the door opened and a somewhat nervous voice addressed him.

"Yes?"

"I wish to speak to someone of power."

"Why?"

"I have a problem."

"We know of you."

"I know, and I would not be here if I could handle this on my own. On my honor, I wish you no harm. I only wish for aid."

The door opened slowly and a man in dark blue robes stood in the doorway. His cowl was pulled forward so that the barbarian could not see his features. The voice was tight with the tension of the moment and the barbarian's nose sensed the fear.

"I must ask," stated the man carefully, "that you allow me to transport you to a room set aside for this type of meeting. On *my* honor, you shall not be harmed or restrained."

Red Wolf nodded and allowed the man to touch his shoulder.

Instantly, it seemed, the barbarian found himself standing in a brightly lit room with no furnishings save the carpet underfoot and the greenish brown bars of endlibar steel separating the room in half. He sat upon the floor and waited.

A shape took form on the other side of the bars. The shape swirled and a man sat in a heavy chair facing the barbarian. He was dressed in Elvin gray clothing and a deep blue robe. His silver-white beard was neatly trimmed and a circlet of star iron rested upon his brow. A staff of ancient dark wood rested on the arms of the chair and the man rested his hands upon it.

"I need help," stated Red Wolf in a matter-of-fact voice.

"What help could one such as I give to one such as you?"

"I must contact the Myrlin quickly. It is very important."

"Myrlin has gone and there is no way to contact him as far as I know. None at all. The planes through which he travels are so far from the standard, it is beyond most magiks to reach him. I know of but one who, if he chose, could find him now."

"Anteroe?"

"Precisely."

"So you cannot contact him yourself?"

"I could try, but the percentages are low for success."

The man lifted the staff from the chair and stood. He moved closer to the bars and looked deep into the barbarian's eyes.

"Why must you seek him?"

"There is a...problem dealing with my wolf pups and possibly the continuance of this world."

"Sounds ominous. I could attempt an ancient spell that has not been used since the Mage Wars, but I'm afraid should I attempt it now during the tidal turn the response could be devastating."

"Are you of great power and knowledge then?"

"I have been called such. I am Gre'sharr, brother to the Myrlin."

"Then I ask: What would it mean to you should you find an ancient Wormslayer driven into the earth at a location where you've lost...something of value?"

The mage's brows knit. He'd not heard that term in many centuries, and it was curious that the term came from this barbarian's lips.

"A sign," he responded softly, "a symbol, a challenge of some sort."

"This is what I found less than an hour ago in a place where the females and pups of my pack have disappeared from this world."

"You have been challenged."

"I have no knowledge of these Wormslayers, and if this challenge is mine, then I need as much knowledge as possible to arm myself for the conflict."

The mage looked deep within those eyes and found not fear, but determination. He felt pity, not for this one, but for whoever dared to challenge him. Now he understood what his brother had known concerning this particular barbarian. He was a force to be reckoned with and he was not happy! Gre'sharr was glad he was not the one this one hunted!

"The Wormslayer Lances were created during the Mage Wars by Banshe'e and his talon of multi-talented warriors. The power they had then will not function at the level they once had, though they would still retain much of it. Magic doesn't work now as it did then."

"Who would wield one of these things in this day?"

"Only those skilled in the use of a lance and a vengeance against someone, or a dragon, would be able to carry one in comfort. The dragon guardian gathered all she could find after the war, but three were not to be found: the silver, platinum, and the multihued designed for Tiamet."

"This one was of silver and smelt of death."

"They all do."

Red Wolf related his vision to the Mage, and that one scowled and cupped his bearded chin in one hand.

"Is this where my challenge lay?" the barbarian asked.

"What you describe is the Dragon's Graveyard. None but dragonkind may set foot upon this plane. If this is where your challenge has directed you, you have failed already."

A lethal growl rumbled in the barbarian's chest, but it quickly subsided. This one was only stating what he knew was truth.

"What you say may be true," replied the barbarian softly, "but there is a challenge here, and as long as there is breath in my body, there are still possibilities."

"The odds, and possibly the Fates, are against you."

"They have been before, Mage, yet here I sit before you."

"True," said the mage with a grin.

After a moment, "When, Mage, have you ever thought to have one such as I sitting across from you passing idle conversation?"

Gre'sharr looked at the barbarian quizzically as that one continued.

"All things are possible."

The mage waved a hand and the bars disappeared. Red Wolf rose as the Master Mage came toward him.

"What I can do, Red Wolf, I shall do. I wish you safety and success in your quest, but is there naught else I can do?"

"If you could, with your power, place me before my pack to the northeast, I will take it from there."

"You realize how unusual your request is to one such as I?"

The barbarian grinned.

"Besides," continued the mage, a faraway look in his eyes, "there are those thinking of you at this moment. Those you name friends are worried."

"The pup with them has power. He will see to them. There are other pups that need me more."

"I see," stated the mage, his brow furrowed once again. "You speak of the blond one. You are probably right. His blood is that of…"

He glanced quickly at the barbarian and smiled.

"No matter. I shall set you on your road, say, two hours of your travel, north and east?"

"My thanks, friend, and if you contact your brother, say that Red Wolf needs him. Can you get a message to the savon'el?"

"I shall. Trust in me, Red Wolf. Travel far…"

As the mage touched the barbarian's shoulder, the world twisted away in colors and swirls of light. Red Wolf came back to himself on a plain of grass, the smell of the wolf pack drifting toward him from the south.

He grinned.

Chapter Twenty-five

"Arantar, what news?"

The Huntsmaster glanced over at his companions and asked himself again how he would tell these friends that the barbarian would probably not be with them as they fled the city. Red Wolf had said that Savon'el was more than capable to lead them to their goal, though at this juncture that goal was self-preservation.

"You won't like it," he responded to the blond half elf's question. He took Savon'el's offered hand and continued. "The barbarian will join us if he can. Until then we wait."

"If he can? Where has he gone?"

"I'm afraid he's gone to seek help from the very people he despises most. I've heard no commotion from the Mage Guild so—"

"In the meanwhile," interrupted Melisande, "we should be getting our supplies together. I don't have to tell you that our time is short."

"True," responded Savon'el, "and we need horses. Who else, save Melisande and I, need mounts?"

"None," stated the Huntsmaster. "All but you two have what we need except for saddles."

"Rene' and Bonaire should return shortly," stated the blonde half elf, "and when they arrive, I believe the safest place to wait would be here in front of the tavern. If there are any more surprises, we should have an open field to defend. Melisande and I will see what we can procure in the stables and join you here."

The Huntsmaster placed a hand on the savon'el's shoulder and wondered again at the feeling he had for this man. He seemed to know what he was doing, yet without the memories that would tell him from where he learned it. Arantar's new brother would bear watching.

"I must see to my horse as well, friend," he stated as he stepped toward the tavern door, "but first I think I should collect all of our belongings. Afterward I'll meet you in the stable."

"I will accompany these two," said the knight as he stepped to Savon'el's side. "Once we have the wherewithal to ride, I will prepare our mounts for a long journey. I do, however, worry that you go alone."

"You should hear if I find trouble." At Solothon's nod, he added, "I will meet you there in but a moment. Savon'el, your key."

With the blond half elf's key in hand, he strode to the door and, after settling his swords on his back, disappeared into the empty tavern.

The knight followed Savon'el and Melisande to the stables set aside for the patrons of the tavern and moved quickly to the stall wherein his black was stabled. Enare nuzzled his friend as Solothon stroked his nose. The well-trained warhorse seemed excited at the prospect of movement.

Savon'el heard the ring of steel on an anvil in the back of the shop and, with Melisande firmly on his arm, followed the sound. An old man worked at the forge forming shoes for a rather large warhorse. He was so intent on his work he didn't notice the spectators until Savon'el cleared his throat.

"What can I do you out of?" he asked with a grin as he turned from his toils.

"We need mounts," replied the blond half elf as he too grinned.

"Well, do you want a heavy or light horse? Maybe a dog and cart for the missus?"

Melisande grinned at the man's attempt at setting them into good spirits. It would be a long time before they would see good people again, she feared. Savon'el chuckled and took the man's strong hand in his.

"Nothing quite so simple, I'm afraid. We need two mounts capable of carrying us and several days of supplies on a long journey."

"Off on adventure, aye? You look like you need horses trained for this kind of action. For you," he said as he scratched at the stubble on his chin, "a light warhorse would be right. You as well, little lady. Two, with tack and the proper barding, three hundred twelve...Let's say three hundred even?"

"Let us say two hundred?"

"Sorry, son, I don't barter. I have to feed my family and a no good son-in-law. Three hundred is my best deal."

"I understand," sighed Melisande. "Is there no way to strike a deal then? We are extremely low on funds and must be away within the hour. It is a matter of—"

"Sorry, missy, but I can't. I know of your order and what you could do for a poor old blacksmith, but I am very happy in my misery."

"I wouldn't dream of it, sir," she replied softly, still grinning, "but is there anything we could possibly use for barter?"

"No. Sorry," he said after a moment of thought. "You don't have much that I might want and not near enough to reach the price I need to stay afloat."

After another moment of scratching his chin and seeing the cleric's smile begin to fade, he smiled. "You might try the stable just two doors down. He might be able to help."

"Thank you, sir," she answered as she tugged Savon'el back toward the door.

"Solothon!" he called.

The knight looked out of the stall to see Savon'el being pulled toward the door and had to smile.

"We'll be back in a moment!"

Solothon nodded and went back to brushing the big black's coat.

"Wonder why they're in such a hurry?"

Solothon turned from his work to see the old blacksmith walk to the stable door and look after the two.

"We must be out of the city very shortly on business sponsored by a sage."

"Terillion?"

"The same. Why?"

"He's contracted with all of the stables here to supply whatever you need to get you on your way. Didn't they know that?"

"Obviously not." The knight grinned. "So you say you have been contracted as well?"

"Just sign the chit, sonny, and what I have is yours."

Solothon nodded and followed the man to his tack room.

"Slow down, girl!" said the half elf. "I know there is need for haste, but you needn't hurry! I'm with you!"

"Sorry," she answered as she slowed to walk beside him. "It's just that I don't want to be the cause of a tardy departure even for a moment."

"Well," he said as he opened the side door to the mentioned stable, "we can't leave until we hear from Red Wolf anyway. Take your time. Remember you are still healing. If you keep this up, you'll open your wound."

"Strange that," she replied, paling just a bit at the remembrance. "Whatever was in that poultice has all but healed me. All I have left is a tight tenderness where I was—"

She stopped and Savon'el saw her pale further. He squeezed the hand he held and lifted her eyes to his.

"You are safe now, Melisande. You won through."

She smiled. He was right, she thought. Whoever was out to stop them... kill them, had failed. Her color returned as they stepped through the door.

"And what might I do for you?" came a voice from one of the many stalls.

A young man came out of one of those stalls and stood before them. He was very muscular and, to the young cleric, very handsome.

"We need mounts," stated Savon'el. "Light, well-trained horses capable of a long hard journey. Also, tack for them."

"Barding?"

"Yes. Chain if it's not too expensive."

"Leather then. If you have to ask, the chain is too expensive. Let's see now..." he continued as he gazed at the young cleric. "That could run upward of four hundred gold. You have that much?"

"Just a moment."

Savon'el pulled Melisande back to the door.

"How much gold do you have? I have but one hundred forty-seven."

"Then," she replied softly, "we have one hundred forty-seven between us."

She looked back at the stable master and grinned.

"Let me talk to him."

"Why?"

"Maybe a bit of female persuasion could bring his price down."

"We haven't much time or money," he said tightly. "All right, but be careful."

"Oh," she grinned, "I shall be very, very careful."

Savon'el wondered at her comment until she slinked up to the man, took his arm, and in a soft voice said, "Let's take a walk to your...office."

The man smiled and, looking back at the half elf, said, "I'd get a drink if I were you. This may take a while."

"I think not," Savon'el replied tightly.

"Suit yourself," he said with a chuckle as he followed the girl upstairs.

Sir Solothon mounted the new padded chain barding and saddles on his and Arantar's horses and rigged them for rough travel. Then he set aside a saddle and halter for Bonaire's pony. He took only that which was functional and new, nothing gaudy. He took a bag of grain for each and signed the blacksmith's receipt. The blacksmith thanked him and went back to his metalwork.

The knight had but one thing more to do before he committed himself entirely to this company.

He pulled at the silver chain about his neck until the small silver leaves of the forest laurel came from beneath his mail. Cupping the leaves gently in the palm of one hand, he drew his sword. He planted the sword before him and dropped to one knee, his head bowed and his eyes closed.

"Mother of us all," he whispered, "I ask your guidance in this time of great peril and ask for a sign that I have chosen rightly."

A warm feeling came over him as if a mother had enveloped him in a loving embrace. He felt the calm reassurance from that embrace would be with him until the end of his journey and he sighed.

"Thank you."

As he carefully replaced the laurel leaves beneath his armor, he felt and heard a sound as if someone were tapping on silver. He withdrew his sword and inspected it.

Upon the cross guard, three small laurel leaves had been embossed. He kissed the hilt, swung the sword in a small arc, and sheathed it.

"Enare, I will return shortly."

He left both his and Arantar's mounts unfettered and with their stalls open. Should they be needed, the well-trained warhorses would be there for them. He walked down toward the stable where Savon'el stood in the doorway, a frown of anger on his face.

"Where is the girl, Savon'el?" he asked.

The half elf pointed at the stairs.

"Negotiating our transportation," he said in a deadly voice.

"Why so angry?"

"Are you not aware of what she is doing?" he grated.

"No, and neither are you," the knight responded softly.

"I'm not blind, Solothon. I saw the way she looked at him!"

"Then you must be blind, for I have seen the way she looks at you." The knight stepped in front of the half elf and gripped him by the shoulders. "If the girl is doing everything you imagine, or more, it is her choice to do so. I can only say that she is doing nothing more than the rest of us would do in a similar situation. She is a cleric of Freya, by the gods. She sees what she is or is not doing as her duty for her goddess, her friends, and maybe even for herself. Can you not accept her for who and what she is? Or is she supposed to live up to some vague ideal you have designed in your head?"

Savon'el glared at the knight, but as the words struck home, his eyes dropped.

"You are right, my friend," he replied softly. "I just wish that—"

"I know. You care for her, but you must understand that though she may care for you as well, she must also be her own person. Besides, how do you know that there is anything to worry about?"

"Whether there is or is not, she comes."

Solothon turned and looked up the stairs. Melisande strolled down the stairway with a self-satisfied grin on her face. She stopped at the bottom and turned that grin on the two warriors.

"I told him of our mission for Sage Terillion and he said he and others had been contracted for our provisioning. Before he passed out, he said to take what I wanted. Just mark it down. I think that was a pretty good deal, don't you?"

Then she threw the empty wineskin she had been given by Red Wolf to the shocked Savon'el.

"You mean you didn't...He didn't..."

"You thought..." She drew herself up, and in a voice both soft and deadly aimed her response at the blond half elf. "I may be a priestess of the Temple of the goddess of Love and Fertility, Savon'el, but I do not prostitute myself for anyone!"

She paled and almost fell. She grabbed the banister and Savon'el rushed to her and held her.

"What is it? Are you all right?"

"It's just that I had to pretend to take drink for drink with him," she lied, as she had lied before.

Of course she had been prostituted—by her own mother and for the pleasure of Lord Cartellion! She regained her composure as quickly as she could and leaned on the half elf's arm.

"He hated the stuff, I could tell," she continued, "but as long as I could drink it, he felt he could do no less. Men! Oh, I didn't mean you two!" she amended quickly.

"I believe we understand, m'lady," chuckled the knight as he turned to leave. "Now hurry. Arantar will be down soon and we must be ready to leave as soon as our companions arrive."

"We'll be right there," stated the half elf. Then, softly, "I'm sorry, Melisande. I shouldn't—"

"Don't worry. He thought so as well. The dreams he'll have will be magnificent! Well, at least I hope so." She grinned. "Now, let us get our horses and get out of here."

"Well, m'lady, you've paid the price! I suppose we should match worth for worth!"

He picked out the best saddles and bridles, leaving the gaudy stuff and taking only what was of new leather. He found new padded chain barding for the chestnut and sorrel he picked out, as well as supply packs for a small sturdy packhorse. He did not know how he knew their worth, but he accepted what he knew as more proof of what he was.

Once the horses were properly garbed and saddled and the packs had been secured to the packhorse, Savon'el helped the girl onto the sorrel. After helping himself to two large sacks of grain for the new packs, he walked the horses from the stable.

Solothon waited for them at the tavern's stable and grinned at the quality of horseflesh and accessories the blond half elf had chosen. Savon'el had to hold the girl's thigh to keep her seated and talked her through the rudiments of horsemanship on the walk over. Then he began adjusting her stirrups for utility and comfort.

"I see you have a good eye for quality, friend," commented the knight. "I'd say you got your money's worth, m'lady."

She grinned sheepishly.

Arantar rounded the corner of the tavern carrying what they'd left in their rooms.

"Is this all you had?" he asked as he tossed the small pack to the blond half elf. "I found nothing in your room, Melisande, but your mail."

Savon'el took that as well and placed it into one of the bags on her sorrel. His pack he tied to the cantle of his saddle. He'd not thought of its contents since arriving in the city, and now was not the time to check it for lingering memories.

"I procured some supplies from Blegral, enough for now, I hope," continued the Huntsmaster. "We will be on short rations, I'm afraid. We will have to live mostly off the land."

Savon'el nodded to the Huntsmaster, took the bag of supplies, and secured it into one of the packs on the packhorse. Then he gave voice to their final concern.

"I'm a bit worried about Rene' and Bonaire. Shouldn't they be here by now?"

"If they are not here shortly..." the knight began. Then, "Ah! Here they are."

Bonaire rounded the corner leading the two horses, Rene' perched sidesaddle on her palomino.

"Bonaire," called the knight, "let's get your pony saddled and stand ready. Then we can safely wait for Red Wolf's arrival."

"What did he tell you, Arantar?" asked the blond half elf.

Before the Huntsmaster could answer, a small man in the light blue robes of Mage's Apprentice came up behind Rene'.

"Is there one among you known as Savon'el?"

"Why do you ask?" said the knight guardedly.

"I have a message."

"I am he," replied the blond half elf.

"Then, 'North and east marks the trail and trial of the wolf.' I know not what it means, but he who sent me said you would."

"Indeed I do, and thank you."

The knight tossed a gold coin to the messenger and, as that one left, turned to the savon'el.

"What *did* he mean?"

"Red Wolf has gone on ahead, for reasons I know not. He wanted to make sure that I know this." He seemed to be lost in thought for a moment as he gazed after the messenger. Then he continued. "We must leave now. He will meet us on the trail if he can, but if not, we must do what we can on our own."

He turned to his companions.

"Are we ready?" Without waiting for reply, he continued, "Mount up. We must be far from here come daybreak."

As they cantered through the eastern gate in the dark of late evening, they all noted that no guards were present. Why was unknown, though Arantar felt this to be fortunate, for they would not be observed. The lack of guards gave an ominous feeling in its total lack of security for the city.

"Huntsmaster, take the lead."

So commanding was the bearing of the blond half elf, Arantar almost respond with "Yes, sir." He caught himself in time and nodded.

"Sir Solothon," continued Savon'el, "flank his left. You," he added to Bonaire, "guard position to Lady Rene' and trail the supply horse behind you. I shall take rear guard with Lady Melisande. Northeast, Huntsmaster."

All was said in that quiet command voice Arantar knew well. It was the voice of authority, of one who understands the stakes and takes responsibility for the decisions he makes. He looked back at Savon'el and caught the quick look of confusion that traveled across the half elf's face.

"'Tis a good plan of march, friend. The barbarian has chosen wisely." He touched heels to his mount and led the way.

They rode from the city in double column formation at a canter. The warning they'd received gave spur to the importance of distance from this place. They were locked into this expedition, and there was naught they could do save move in dreadful silence along a path chosen for them. All were linked by word, name, or association into whatever devilment had been wrought. Worse, they could not put a face to their shared enemy, nor could they say why they were sought.

Solothon joined the Huntsmaster in the lead, though slightly behind and to his left. He wished to give Arantar room should the need to draw that great sword arise.

The raven, after informing the Huntsmaster that he'd followed his "earth brother" for a great distance before being asked to return to look after their saola, flew high overhead. Its keen eyes were ever watchful for any sign of potential enemies, and it kept practiced contact with the man at the fore of this small column.

Melisande rode left of the introspective Savon'el. She had never ridden before and had to hang onto the pommel to keep from falling off. She vowed to learn this function as soon as possible to keep from being a burden. She glanced once more at Catlorian, the only home she'd ever known, and wondered if she would see it again.

"Of course you will, stupid!" she scolded herself. "You have a very good reason to return so get it together, girl!"

Rene' stroked the sleek neck of the palomino and thought on what destiny had placed her in the company of these fugitives. Doing what she must would have been difficult alone, but now, with this threat hanging over their heads, it seemed an almost impossible task.

"Impossible is what I do in my off time," she muttered with a grin.

Should she tell them? She glanced about her at her companions and decided, again, maybe later.

Bonaire glanced again at the beautiful girl he adored when he thought she wouldn't see. He heard her muttering and glanced her way yet again.

"What is it, m'lady?"

"Oh, it's nothing, Bonaire. I'm just going over some logistics in my head. No use going blindly toward our goal. We will probably stop soon to get our bearings."

"Good! My butt hurts!"

The barriers she'd built about her strong empathy were leaking. She'd worked long and hard crafting them against the constant touch of the multitudes of souls. Now, however, the taut emotions of her companions threatened to tear them away, so strongly did they manifest themselves. It took more control than she wished to expend to keep them out.

She had just begun the meditation ritual that was her daily restorative to those barriers when she was all but unseated by a pulse of magic, followed closely by a blast of stark anger. The pulse was soft, a passing thing, but the anger, along with the residual of fear, exploded in her mind!

She recovered as quickly as she could, her mount mincing a bit at the tightness of the reins, and turned in her saddle to face Melisande. That one was looking to their rear and talking softly to the blond half elf and, as the black-haired cleric glanced at Rene', the mage girl found the source of the emotional assault.

Melisande had made that last look at the city when a figure wrapped in darkness stepped out of the shadows. He was too far away for the girl to determine any details, but the intricate patterns that his hands made were unmistakable.

Before the girl could shout a warning, one hand stretched forth and a cone of soft white spun out to envelope the savon'el's head. Her heart leaped to her throat as he stiffened. Then, strangely, Savon'el resumed his normal demeanor as if nothing out of the ordinary had occurred.

Melisande glanced back in time to see the black figure disappear.

"Savon'el," she whispered, "are you alright?"

Savon'el had been closed within his own thoughts this day. He'd not chosen the path or this position as leader. He was no better than the others that the barbarian had thrust into his care. How could he, in all good conscience, attempt to guide them, keep them together and going forward, when he had no idea from where he'd learned the things his mind blurts out! At least they knew whom they were and from whence they'd come! All he had were vague memories of dreams that haunted him constantly.

Suddenly, calmness seemed to come over him. He had been entrusted with their safety and the completion of this mission, if not their lives! The barbarian would not have chosen him had he not the wherewithal to carry it out. He should stop beating himself up, lean on the skills and advice of this group, and get on with it! He grinned. He glanced over at the cleric and noted the worry in her question.

"Yes, m'lady. I've a slight headache, but those come and go." He touched the scar behind his left ear and added, "I suppose it's the cost one must pay for using one's head once too often."

The humor was lost on the girl as she glanced, again angrily, to their rear and back to the savon'el. If not for…

"Are you sure you're all right?"

"Yes, Melisande. Why? Is there something wrong?"

He too looked to their rear, but found empty plain in the starlight. His grin disappeared as the girl looked once again to their rear.

Melisande noted no change in the half elf's demeanor to indicate that an attack had happened at all! She began to wonder if perhaps she were seeing but the shades of her own fear.

"No!" she told herself, the anger stark in her mind. "It *was* real!"

Something strange was at work here, and the answers seemed to center on her companion. She'd watch and wait. In the meanwhile, she would keep this to herself.

"No. I'm just worried about you." Then, quickly, "As I worry about us all."

"I too worry, but please, m'lady, I'm fine."

Melisande glanced at the half elf once more and sighed. Maybe it was her imagination after all. With all they had been through, and what they have yet to do, maybe…

She looked forward and found the mage girl's eyes locked on hers.

"She felt it!" she thought as she nodded at Rene'.

Rene' acknowledged the nod with one of her own. The nod told her that the explanation would come later, but the eye contact had opened more. In her power, Rene' felt the strong emotions that radiated from the black-haired cleric and those emotions told the mage girl a great many things about

Melisande. First: Though she was afraid, as they all were, she feared more for her companions. The fear came not only from a deep caring nature but from some deeply buried, still bleeding, emotional wound. Second: Melisande was to be trusted. Once set into motion, the girl would see any situation through, even to her own death. Third: The cleric was volatile. She holds a seething fury at bay by sheer will, yet would unleash it at any who would dare to harm her companions. It was an animal anger, Rene' sensed, that would set loyalty and friendship above all else.

Rene' liked her, though the feeling was muted a bit because of the girl's deity.

"After all," she mused, "she is a priestess of that goddess of sex and depravity. Maybe I can teach her the error of her ways, she is pretty enough. There is time, and it seems we are locked into this thing as companions until the end."

Rene' turned her gaze on the savon'el as his eyes reached for hers. She felt hopelessness, but strength, sadness without reason. Barriers.

Barriers?

She reached, as she had done many times in the past, for that power and locked it to her sight. As her sight took in the blond half elf, she closed her eyes with a sharp intake of breath.

He glowed with an aura not of his own, as if...

"Cursed!" was the only word that she thought would fit.

She glanced again at Melisande, then faced forward.

"This is going to be one interesting explanation," she thought.

They rode on in silence at a ground-eating trot through the false dawn into early morning. They each pulled their cloaks about them to stave off the chill of late fall and followed the dirt road toward the King's Way east of Catlorian. The day broke bright and clear, the light and warmth of the sun welcome, though it too failed to lift their spirits more than slightly.

Several hours of riding through the calm sunshine had some of the companions doubting the tensions of the past few days. The threats and curses seemed left in another world. Then the reality of their plight would show itself, and they would again ride on in a tense silence.

It was early afternoon when they reached the bridge that spanned the Lost Souls River. Here, the King's Way stretched due east, its white expanse a straight line to Seaborne.

Arantar led them across the bridge and found the tracks of a great number of wolves just to the other side. They led off toward the northeast moving away from the shores of that cursed river. He reined in, turned, and waited for the rest of his companions to catch up.

Solothon continued off of the road to the wood line and dismounted.

"This is sore work, Huntsmaster," he stated as he arched his back to stretch the soreness and cramps there.

"Yes, my friend, but it seems our companions are not as disposed as we to riding."

Arantar assessed his companions as they dismounted, with the exception of Rene', and walked their mounts toward him over the bridge.

Savon'el knew that riding, though a skill his body seemed to remember, must not have been his favorite pastime. His body was so sore, he'd long since allowed it to become numb. Add the incessant pounding behind his eyes to the miles and there was no joy, even in the sunny calm.

Melisande, unlike Rene', rode astride the sorrel and was feeling the hours of travel more acutely that the others. Though Savon'el had tried to find the most padded saddle in the stable's inventory, she quickly understood why men wore sturdy pants.

Her soft boots covered her feet and calves, but her thin undergarments were not enough to protect her bottom from the jostling gait of the warhorse and her legs were becoming raw to the knees. She tried to walk the tightness in her thighs away, but the rawness made her walk a bit awkward.

Rene', though still elegant in her composure, also felt the strain of sustained riding. Only the fact that she was used to riding sidesaddle for extended periods kept her from falling prey to the soreness that would otherwise have all but crippled her. She stayed in her saddle because she knew that when they did stop for the night, she would not like to return to the saddle for a while.

Bonaire was in terrible distress! His back, legs, and butt ached. If anyone had asked, he would have said he was unable to find a single part of his body that did not hurt!

"We have need for a stop, but from the looks of these, once stopped it could be damned hard to get them going again."

Solothon acknowledged the Huntsmaster's words with a nod and remounted.

Arantar waited until the companions came close enough to hear what he must say.

"I know that you're tired, but we cannot afford to stop now. We must put some distance between us and Catlorian for obvious reasons. Trust me when I say that it will become a bit easier. As we progress, we will be stopping earlier, but for now we must continue. Mount up."

While the others struggled into their saddles, he continued.

"We will be traveling slower through the woods there. I will take point with Sir Solothon taking up position to watch my back." He turned to Solothon and stated, "Give me some room, maybe twenty to thirty feet of space in case there is something wrong. Watch for my hand signals. The rest of you stay, where room allows, in the same order as before, and Savon'el, you will be our rearguard. Any questions?"

He reined his mount around and kneed it along the way the wolves had taken. His military experience came to the fore as he settled in at a fast walk seeking for hidden danger as he went. He'd faced death more than once in his life, but with a military unit, not like this! He had been cursed, his friends attacked, and they had been driven from the city in fear. If they were to regain control of their fate, they first must put some distance between them and pursuit. Then they needed to stop and assess their next move.

We have need for a safe nest, my friend. Find a nest far from here.

Aye, Arantar-sao. came the trilling wind-song in answer.

Arantar saw the black speck in the blue and watched it disappear to the northeast.

Two hours later, the Huntsmaster heard the bird's song in his head again.

Clear place, Arantar-sao. Drink clear. Burn stuff. No uglies. No bads.

Arantar saw the black speck in the blue circling about thirty miles ahead. He dropped back and called to Solothon.

"There is a clearing about three hours ahead," he said as the knight joined him at the head of the formation. "We need to reorganize and we need answers. We need to know what to do next."

Solothon nodded and reined in to let the others pass. As Savon'el came up, the knight fell in beside him. "Arantar says there is a safe area ahead, Savon'el. We should stop for the night and look at our options."

"How far?"

"Three hours."

Savon'el looked ahead into the forest. With Arantar, a Huntsmaster, in the lead there would be no surprises. Huntsmasters were the pride of any army, and this one was no exception.

"Tell the Huntsmaster to proceed, Sir Solothon."

The Elvin knight gave a respectful nod and spurred his horse forward. As he passed Rene', he realized what he'd done and glanced back at the half elf. That one frowned and looked a bit confused.

Solothon drew abreast of Arantar and again glanced back. "Something is strange here and I am at a loss to describe what it is."

"I think I know what you mean, Solothon," replied the Huntsmaster as he glanced back toward the savon'el.

Savon'el was now totally confused. He had no name or history, yet he knew the value of a Huntsmaster. Then he presumes to give curt orders as if he'd done it all of his life? He didn't think about it, he just did it! Red Wolf placed the lives of these companions in his hands and left on a mission of his own. How could he expect them to follow him? Yet they did so without a word.

How did he know so much, but know so little, and why does all of it make his head hurt?

"Just accept what comes, pup."

Sure. Easy for you to say, Red Wolf. Then he laughed softly.

"What is it, Savon'el?"

"Nothing, m'lady," he replied, glancing over at the young cleric. "It's just that this excursion has begun on somewhat of a sour note and I've no doubt that none of us knows why. It just struck me as humorous in a strange sort of way. I apologize."

He nodded and turned once again inward.

Melisande felt the mage girl's eyes on her and, facing front, found Rene' looking askance. All Melisande could do is shrug. Rene' glanced at the savon'el and frowned.

"This is not acceptable," she thought. "If we are to survive out here, we need all of the information we can get to include our companion's problems. We shall talk and I will get to the bottom of this!"

They rode on through the day. The forest promised peace and safety, but though he too felt the calm, Arantar knew that sometimes self-preservation depended on disbelief.

The Huntsmaster had but to move fifty yards into the forest on his right to find the youth in full arm gauntlet paralleling the party. He moved at a silent run, the tawny puma marking the way.

Nothing disturbed the riders as they traveled. The forest seemed to welcome them with song and the buzzing of life. The peace here reminded Melisande of a glade and a promise made.

"If this is the only beauty I find on this trek, Lord Anteroe," she thought with a secret smile, "I can say that the advice was well-founded."

Two hours from sunset, Arantar rode into the small clearing. A brook of clear water bubbled out of the forest on one side and disappeared along the trail they would travel come morning. The raven perched on a small pile of windfall that would serve the travelers this night. He cawed a welcome and took wing.

Solothon rode to the opening on the far side and dismounted. Through the trees he could see the mountains in the distance maybe three or four days away, and he could hear the rushing of the Lost Souls River several miles to his left.

The name of that river was as much a mystery as the source of the poison that plagued its waters. It was said that the further one followed the river to its source, the closer they came to death. That concerned the knight more than he wished as he turned and walked back into the clearing that was slowly becoming a camp. Enare followed unfettered.

Solothon had to grin, though, as he watched young Bonaire limp about picking up dry wood and stacking it next to the Huntsmaster. Seems the hard ride on a new saddle had rubbed a few blisters on the wrong part of his anatomy. He shook his head and moved to stand a casual rearguard at the opening they had just passed through. Enare joined the Huntsmaster's roan just next to the brook and, it seemed, kept a watchful eye on the other horses.

Arantar drew the silver dagger and thrust it into a piece of the wood he'd stacked carefully within a stone fire ring. He whispered, "On" and the dagger and branch burst into greenish yellow flame. A whispered, "Off" and a gloved hand brought the dagger back to its sheath. Not wanting a large fire, he fed branches sparingly until its glow reached only to the edge of the small darkening clearing.

Savon'el sat on a stump close to the fire with his head in his hands, feeling as if every muscle in his body had been violated. He lifted his gaze and surveyed the camp. The horses would need to be unsaddled and rubbed down after the long ride, but that would have to wait until the camp was secure. Besides, the dark-haired clerk walked among them stroking and murmuring softly to them. He rose and moved to Solothon, and the two talked softly about the potential of anyone following their trail.

Arantar took his detection kit to the brook and tested the waters there. After the test proved the water as untainted as it looked, he filled a small leather pail and returned to the fire. He poured some of the water into a kettle, placed it on a set of rocks within the fire ring, and added some barley and crushed Kaff beans.

"We shall have warm drink shortly," he stated softly as he glanced toward the knight and Savon'el. He saw the fleeting anger cross the half elf's face and wondered at it.

Savon'el, however, was remembering another kettle and the anger seethed.

"I'll see to our mounts," he said tightly as he moved in that direction.

Bonaire rose to help, but Melisande waved him off. She saw the anger as well and saw no reason to burden the blond half elf with Bonaire's prattling.

"We'll see to the horses, Bonaire," she said softly. "You need to see to the blisters you must have."

Bonaire gave the cleric a weak smile, sat back down as softly as he could, and sighed.

Savon'el and Melisande unsaddled the horses, rubbed them down with dry grass, and tethered them, save Arantar's and the knight's, on long tethers to allow them to reach water and good grass. Arantar's roan and the knight's black were left free, as the Huntsmaster explained, to come at need to their master's call.

The smell of hot Kaff reached the blond half elf as he and Melisande returned to the fire. Arantar cut slices of cheese and meat he'd procured in Catlorian to go with the brew and it was a welcome treat after the hard travel of the day. The Huntsmaster knew that they would be on short rations soon enough and, though this supply would not last long, it would ease them into the hardships ahead.

"We must post guard," he stated as he poured a cup of the sustaining brew for Rene'. "Solothon and I don't believe we've been followed, but…"

"I'll take the first watch, Huntsmaster," said Savon'el as he looked into the forest in the direction they'd come. "It seems safe enough, but I am too edgy to rest just now."

Arantar nodded and continued distributing the food to the rest.

"I'll stand the next," stated the black-haired cleric as she took a cup of the steaming brew from the Huntsmaster.

Each of the others took a voluntary share of the guard, with Arantar relieving Rene' for the last watch.

"I suggest we make ready to leave just before the dawn," said the Hunts-master with a glance at the blond half elf. "I feel unsafe as long as we are this close to Catlorian and whatever, whoever, dogs our trail."

"Agreed," said Savon'el. Then, to the camp at large, "We must be vigilant from here on. If you feel you cannot stay alert during your shift at guard, wake your replacement and they will stand with you. We are all weary, yet we cannot afford to let down our guard at any time, for we don't know if or when the next attack will come. We can only depend on each other and the skills each of us holds to sustain us. We cannot afford to become complacent."

"True enough, friend," stated the knight. "You all know that both Savon'el and myself have been targeted for, as of yet, unknown reasons and the place to which we travel...this 'Dark Keep,' may hold answers to the rid-dle. I know for certain if the two of us attempted this alone, we would fail. You're assistance, though at this point not voluntary, is welcome, though I wished it were not necessary. I pledge my sword, my honor, and my life to you all."

"As do I," added the blond half elf. "Get some rest. Tomorrow will bring more hard travel, I fear, and we must take rest where we can get it."

As each retrieved their saddles and belongings and bought them closer to the small fire, Savon'el moved to the edge of the clearing at the point where they'd entered. He placed the cup of Kaff on a stump, lifted the bow case and backpack from his shoulder, and retrieved a cloth to clean his sword. There was a feeling here, not of threat, but of watching, and it was unsettling. He sat down on the ground and reached for the sword strapped to his back.

Arantar lay back against his saddle and wrapped himself in his cloak. He felt uneasy as if they were being watched. He would not sleep well this night.

Blacky, is all safe?

Sleep, Arantar-sao. No uglies here. I watch.

Just rest, my friend. It's probably just my nerves.

No, Arantar-sao, smart. Safe nowhere, but here safe maybe.

Wake me if maybe becomes no.

As Savon'el's hand went to withdraw the sword, he touched the pommel and felt it move ever so slightly. He closed his hand on the hilt and pulled.

The hilt came away from the sheath without its blade and, as Savon'el watched in dismay, the cross guard snapped forward and down to form a two-bladed dagger!

"What in the Seven Hells?!"

The curse exploded from his lips and he ripped the sheath from his back. He looked into the opening only to find the sheath filled with a strange configuration of metal, the end facing him smooth and level. A thin layer of dull gray metal surrounded a core of hard greenish brown.

"What is it, Savon'el?" asked the knight as his head came up from his saddle. "Is everything all right?"

The exclamation also brought the Huntsmaster to full wakefulness. He glanced toward Savon'el and found that one looking angrily into the opening of his sheath. In the blond's hand was the hilt, though strangely modified.

"What is it, my friend?" he asked as he rose and crossed to where the half elf sat.

"My...my sword just fell apart! I just pulled on the hilt and it came apart!"

The Huntsmaster laid a hand on the astonished Savon'el's shoulder.

"Come nearer the fire and we'll try to figure this riddle together."

Melisande sat up from her blanket and watched as the Huntsmaster led the half elf to the fire. She looked over at Bonaire as that one slept blissfully wrapped in his colorful cloak, glanced at Rene', sighed, and returned to her blanket.

Rene' came up from her trance just long enough to know that there was no real threat. She looked about the camp, saw the two men and the sword, murmured something about men and their toys, and slipped back into the comfort of her meditation.

Savon'el sat with the sheath across his lap and brought the hilt into the light of the fire to examine it. The hilt was wrapped in strange leather that seemed to conform to the wielder's hand and was topped with an artistically engraved and filigreed pommel. The cross guards were about four inches long and, normally, curved down slightly. Now, however, they had snapped down, and in the process the mechanism within had twisted both until they formed a twin-bladed dagger whose blades curved in graceful representation of a claw. There was a slot in the base in the exact shape of the blade that now rested in the sheath.

"Gods, Savon'el!" exclaimed the Huntsmaster softly. "It's a Grace Blade, but I've only seen those with one blade, not two!"

"A graced blade?"

"No, my friend, a 'Grace Blade'. My father had one. An old friend, before his death, gave it to my father along with its history and uses." The

Huntsmaster took the hilt from the blond half elf and examined it. "It was used in the Games to give a quick end to a vanquished opponent."

"Games?"

"*The* Games," amended Arantar as he looked fondly at the weapon. "Old Balcazar used to tell stories of his days as a gladiator in Seaborne and the bright cities beyond the sea. He told of heroes and battles. Zarok 'The Whip,' Barnak of the Twin Blades, the Red Avenger..."

Savon'el heard no more. The pounding in his ears and the pain in his head were too intense. He remembered...remembered...and it was gone.

Arantar was concentrating on the weapon and didn't see the pained grimace on the half elf's face. He gripped one of the cross pieces and began moving it into its original position. To his surprise, not only did it move back smoothly, but the other blade slid back simultaneously until he felt a slight "click."

"Savon'el, see if you can get the blade out of the sheath. Then we'll try to put it back together."

"All right," responded the blond half elf as he tilted the sheath toward the large flat rock next to the fire.

However, the blade slid free quickly and struck the rock in two equal pieces. Both ends of one piece were smooth, but the other had one smooth end with the sword point on the other. Savon'el now had a sword in three pieces!

"Damn!"

Something about the way the sword now looked jogged Arantar's memory.

"Here," he said as he handed the hilt back to the half elf, "try putting it back together."

Savon'el looked at the Huntsmaster strangely, then nodded. He picked up the non-pointed piece, thinking to slide it into the recess in the base of the hilt. However, as he picked it up, the brownish-green metal slid free of the gray and imbedded itself two inches into the solid stone. Savon'el was left holding a thin tube of hard dull gray metal.

"Wait, Savon'el! Don't—"

The Huntsmaster's warning came too late as the blond half elf set the tube to the side and reached for the greenish brown piece of his puzzle. As his hand closed on it, the ultra sharpness of that blade, apparent from the way it had sunk into the rock, reasserted respect by way of the young half elf's palm.

Savon'el jerked his hand away, the blood trailing down his palm.

"It's endlibar," stated the Huntsmaster, "one of the hardest and sharpest metals known."

Savon'el turned an ironic gaze on the Huntsmaster with his palm to his mouth. He responded with a muffled, "Thanks."

"Here, Savon'el, let me try."

Arantar took the hilt and slid the end of the imbedded endlibar into the slot at its base. When he felt the click, he pulled. The piece of blade came free of the rock smoothly, still attached to the hilt.

"Now, watch," he said as he dropped the blade into the earth.

To Savon'el's surprise, though the end of the blade was flat, it sunk into the hard earth to the crosspiece.

"If you had dropped that piece of the blade here on the ground instead of the rock, it would still be slicing its way through the earth," stated the Huntsmaster as he pulled the blade free. "That's the advantage of endlibar. It will cut through most anything."

He handed the hilt and attached piece to Savon'el.

"I've seen but one other like this. It was strange in make, I was told. Noja…Nanja? Well, something like that. Anyway, it was designed to break down into smaller pieces for concealment. The question I have is: who in this world would have reason to do that to a bastard sword?"

"I have no answer, Huntsmaster, as you know. With my memory in disarray, all I know is what comes to me now and nothing more."

This was said softly. It would do no good to allow the rest to know his condition, especially when they needed confidence to follow him.

"I've had this sword," he continued, a pause at the last word to regain his composure, "for as long as I can remember."

Arantar nodded and laid a hand on the half elf's arm. Savon'el grinned and nodded as well. Then he looked at his puzzle anew.

Savon'el slid the sleeve of gray over the endlibar and felt the click as it touched the hilt. He then picked up the pointed piece and, ensuring not to tilt it to allow the endlibar to come free, lined up the ends of the pieces. As the two flat ends touched, he again felt the click and the sword was once again whole.

Well…almost. When Savon'el lined up the blades, he didn't quite get it right. Whatever the forces were that bound the pieces together, they were powerful. Now, though he tried with sheer force to straighten it, the blade was canted slightly where the two pieces met.

"Damn!" he exclaimed, again softly, as his strength proved fruitless.

"The swords I've heard of, like this one, always had some kind of catch in the hilt." commented the Huntsmaster. "A button, lever, or something of that nature. Maybe you should try to remember what it was you did just before the bloody thing fell apart."

"If I knew what I did," gritted the half elf, "I wouldn't have done it in the first place."

Then, after a deep sigh and a quick glance at the grinning Huntsmaster, he too had to grin.

"Well," he said softly, "the pommel did feel a bit loose. Maybe…"

He gripped the pommel and pulled. The blades fell apart onto the rock and the hilt once again snapped down into the twin-bladed dagger.

"Well," he mused with a grin, "at least we know how to take it apart."

He tinkered with the hilt and found that if he pushed in on the pommel and twisted it to the right, it would lock in place.

"That looks promising," he stated as he looked at his handiwork.

Now, however, with the pommel locked in place, the blades on the dagger would not move at all.

"Let me try this one more time, Arantar," he said as he released the pommel from the locked position and moved the blades back to the original position. "If I can't get it right this time I may need to borrow one of yours."

Arantar grinned at the proposition of this half elf with his great blade in his hands.

This time Savon'el fitted the first piece into the hilt, being careful not to release the endlibar, and was rewarded with the quick click. Then, as he lifted the other piece to the end of the first, a memory took over. His left thumb slipped to the pommel and maneuvered it to full unlock, while the other hand fitted the piece into place, its thumb feeling for the telltale line that should not be there. When his body felt the perfection in the mating, the thumb on the pommel released it. He spun the sword in his left hand and his right deftly locked the pommel in place.

"You've done this before."

Arantar's statement brought the savon'el out of the shock of the precision at which his body knew how to do that. He stood on shaking legs and ran his thumb along the entire length of the blade and felt no seam. He glanced down at the Huntsmaster and saw the concern.

"You may be right. It feels familiar and at least I still have a sword."

As the Huntsmaster rose, the blond half elf sheathed the sword and placed a hand on his friend's shoulder.

"Red Wolf said to accept what I learn or relearn, my friend," he said softly. "Considering the day we've had, that seems to be wise."

"That is true, friend," replied Arantar, "but it seems you've succeeded in burying the endlibar. It would be nice to have that edge to draw from."

"True, but I'll not take this thing apart now that I have it back together again. I'll just have to live with it until we get somewhere safer to study it."

"Granted. Well, if you've finished disrupting my night, I'm for bed."

Savon'el slapped the grinning Huntsmaster on the shoulder and watched as that worthy wrapped his cloak about him and dropped into the "awake-sleep" of his profession. Then he moved back to his guard position at the edge of the clearing. He found his cup and drank from it.

He drew the sword and again wondered where it might have come from. He felt it was his but not, and that confused him even more.

"Where did you come from, my friend?" he asked as he ran his off hand over the blade and sighed.

The same question crossed the mind of the man who watched him sheath the blade and raise the cup to his lips. The tawny puma warmed his side as he lay watching the camp of this uncommon group.

"At the right time, I will confront that one," he thought, "and I will have answers. Else..."

Chapter Twenty-six

The night passed peacefully and each took their turn at guard. Arantar woke them just before daybreak to break camp and move on.

Melisande rose from her blanket, rolled it up, and placed it into one of the bags on her saddle. Though the rawness had mostly healed during the night, the pain of riding was still in her legs and bottom and made it a bit difficult to walk casually to the brook to wash.

"Sore, my dear?" came a lilting voice. "Why, I thought that the followers of Freya had calluses there. You know: sex, wantonness, and all—"

The instant rage slapped the mage girl firmly in the face as Melisande turned on her. It smashed against the walls of the girl's empathy so hard that it almost drove her to her knees.

"We of the goddess Freya believe in love and caring to all and in bringing happiness and peace!" the cleric spat in a lethal whisper. "Unfortunately there are those of other faiths who feel that teasing is an acceptable replacement for *real* love. Those are so stuck in their own vanity and self-worth that they miss the living of life in all of its hardship, pain, pleasure, and gain and blame their loss on their piety and faith!"

"Well, I *never*—"

"That is quite obvious from where I stand!" countered the angry cleric.

She pointed a menacing finger at Rene', and as she advanced the words came out as controlled heat.

"I have no quarrel with you, woman, and I believe that before we are done we shall have need for each other. I'll not damn you for your beliefs if you can contain your comments on mine! Agreed?"

Without waiting for comment, Melisande turned and walked as stately as she could manage down to the brook.

"I hadn't meant to sound like that," thought Rene' as she watched Melisande disappear behind the bushes along the edge of the brook. "I only meant..."

Well, what had she meant? Was she so vain in her power that she could not spare the feelings of those about her? Had she learned nothing of suffering?

"Obviously not," she thought. "I have never really suffered, at least not like she must have. Or is it still?"

She walked toward the brook to apologize, but stopped short when she met the wall of undirected fury that seethed from the black-haired cleric. Rene' lost partial control of that power that made her special and was washed in wave after wave of black anger.

"Such malice!" she thought as she regained control and backed away. "Something devastating must have occurred to cause a cleric of her or any other order to be so cold! Would that I had the talent to ease this suffering, for I know it is suffering. This lesson I have yet to learn."

She turned and walked back the way she'd come, her head down and her mind lost in thought.

Arantar moved about the camp with Bonaire doing his best to remove all traces that anyone had rested there. When Bonaire saw Rene', he realized the mage girl's horse had not been saddled. He scampered to correct that as fast as he was able. His rear was still tender and he favored it by walking rather bowlegged.

Rene' resisted the impulse to aid him with a touch. The word "tease" came quickly to mind, and she wasn't sure now that it wasn't true.

Savon'el tightened the cinch to Melisande's saddle, his own already prepared for travel, and laid a blanket over it to aid the girl in her comfort. He noticed the mage girl and called. "Lady Rene', have you seen Melisande?"

"She's down by the brook...washing up. She'll return in a moment."

The tone in her voice spoke of embarrassment to the half elf, and a moment later Melisande walked back toward him from the brook. The blond half elf noted the tension and that the cleric notably ignored Rene', but he chalked it up to his own paranoia.

"You needn't cater to me, Savon'el," she said crossly as she came up to him. "I can see after myself."

"That I don't doubt," he responded as he backed away and watched as she checked the cinch herself.

A day ago she knew nothing of horses. Now her sure hands checked her mount with practiced ease. She mounted, took a quick glance about the camp, and threw an angry frown at Rene'.

"Shall we go?" she queried a bit sharper than necessary.

Rene' wanted desperately to apologize to the black-haired cleric, but as the days went by, there was not a time when they could be alone.

Three days of slow travel put them into the foothills of the mountains. The forest below was thinning and it made for easier travel. They fell into a comfortable pattern after a while. Savon'el noticed this and warned again about complacency, but there seemed to be no danger. The Huntsmaster found nothing that would tell of friend or enemy passage the way they were traveling, and the wolf sign had long since turned eastward. Game was plentiful, though it would not do to take large game at this time. A week and a day of travel found them tired of rabbit and tubers.

The sun had approached midday when they found the low hut. The raven perched above the door waiting.

Is stone nest good, Arantar-sao?

I don't know, my friend. We'll have to check.

The design of the small hut was interesting. Its sides bulged slightly, all corners were rounded, and the door was small and round with the doorknob in its center. It sat in a small glade, a tiny stream flowing within twenty feet of the east wall. The lawn was wild, but it was obvious that it had been well cared for at one time, from the bordered plant beds to the stone walkways. It seemed that there was a sense of waiting about the glade, as if it waited for the owner to return.

Rene' felt the serenity of the glade and let it wash over her in soothing torrents. There was something about this place that seemed to mute the constant demands on her empathy and it was welcome.

Arantar slid from his horse and approached the door warily. He was too much the soldier to accept anything at face value. Too often it was the undoing of a good soldier.

"All of you stay mounted. Sir Solothon, watch our flank."

The knight nodded and cantered away from the group, aware that his mission was to cover their escape should the need arise.

"Wait, Arantar!"

The Huntsmaster turned to find the blond half elf on the ground and moving toward him.

"Savon'el—"

"You shouldn't go first this time, Huntsmaster." At Arantar's frown, Savon'el continued, "Yes, I know you are the logical scout for most encounters, but we don't know what we'll find in there."

"Which is precisely why I should—"

"I said most encounters, my friend. Not this one. I know we've been traveling for a while, but you and I know it hasn't been five years! You don't know what you'll find once inside, and I don't think I want to lose you should we find your bane in there."

"You might have a point, but I'll not sit on my hands and watch at a distance."

"And I would not ask you to. Let me take the fore on this and you back me. If there is anything within, I believe I can hold it until you get through the door, better able to defend from the curse that follows you. Agreed?"

"Agreed."

"Now, you open the door and I'll enter and take position to cover your entrance."

"What about traps?"

Both men turned to Melisande as that one stepped down from her sorrel.

"My lady, please—"

"You've checked for traps?" she continued.

"It does not seem to be trapped. I worry more about what we may find on the other side. Now, please stay back until we find whether 'tis safe."

Melisande frowned and backed away from the door. "Safe?" she thought. "I didn't come on this trek to be safe!"

She raised her forefingers to her lips and, after saying the words softly, kissed them. Then she brought them to the corners of her eyes. After a moment, she grinned and backed farther away.

Arantar turned the knob slowly, the creaking of the old mechanism vibrating in his hand. When he could turn it no more, he planted his feet and pulled. With the crack of splintering wood, the knob and the surrounding center of the door came free in his hand. The rest of the door crumbled to splinters and sawdust.

Savon'el's body memory snapped into place as the hand that gripped the sheathed sword at his back twisted the hilt ever so slightly and pulled the blade from its sheath. The movement was so quick that, as Arantar fell away from the crumbling doorway and groped for his blade, he felt the wind from the blade that leveled itself in the dusty doorway. The Huntsmaster was stunned at the sight of dull greenish brown steel from hilt to point.

"How did you do that?" he exclaimed as he came to his feet and looked into the amber eyes of a confused Savon'el.

"I...I don't know!" he stammered, shocked at the length of endlibar in his hands. "It just...felt right!"

"Well, no matter," Arantar replied as he began recovering his wits. "At least you know that, now at need, you can bring the strength of that steel to bear." Then, with a glance at the blade that remained unmoved from the dusty opening, added, "And rather quickly too."

Melisande backed away in surprise, but not in reaction to the way the door disintegrated, for she, in her sight, had seen that the only danger was in the sheer age of the wood. She was not prepared for the reaction of the blond half elf or the speed at which the blade appeared in the doorway.

Who is he? If his memory is gone, where did his talents, his bearing, and his trained reactions come from?

These questions would have to wait until the proper time, she knew, but as a soft hand found her shoulder, she knew with whom she could discuss them.

She turned and found the golden mage's eyes locked on Savon'el with something akin to awe. Then Rene' turned her eyes on the cleric and the eyes softened.

"Melisande, I..." she began but could not finish. Her eyes dropped to her feet.

Melisande saw the look of apology and confusion and placed a hand on her shoulder.

"We must talk, sister." she said softly as she led Rene' away from the door.

Savon'el peered through the dusty doorway to the stairs that led down. The stairway was four feet across and five high, and a tight fit if one had to fight his way back up. He glanced back at the Huntsmaster, then beyond to the black clouds building on the horizon.

"Looks like this is the best shelter we are likely to find and none too soon."

Arantar looked in that direction in time to see the jagged streak of lightning dance among the darkening clouds, the roll of the thunder in his bones, but not yet reaching his ears.

"We'd better check this place quickly, my friend," he replied.

"Follow me down, Arantar. See if anyone has a torch or candle."

"Bonaire!"

Bonaire had helped the mage girl dismount and was watching the approaching storm. At Arantar's call, he returned his attention to the two at the door.

"Yeah?"

"Did you bring a torch or candle?"

He smirked. A torch? Of course he had a torch, but with the wave of his hand...if only he could remember how.

"Oh well," he thought as he rummaged through his pack. "It'll come to me."

He found two short torches and brought them to the Huntsmaster.

"Don't wander off, Bonaire," said Arantar as he set to work with his tinderbox. "We may need to leave in a hurry."

"I won't," he replied over his shoulder as he moved away from the doorway. "I'm just going down to the stream and around back to see what I can find."

"Just be careful," stated the Huntsmaster to the young elf's back.

He shook his head and handed one of the lit torches to Savon'el.

"Solothon," said the blond half elf as his eyes turned toward that worthy, "the Huntsmaster and I will search out this dwelling for safety. You, as well as Bonaire, are charged with the safety of the ladies and our mounts, and with covering our withdrawal if necessary."

The knight nodded, cantered his black to the others, and dismounted. He felt uneasy, as if they were being watched. He drew his sword and gazed toward the wood line, seeking anything out of place.

Arantar had been having that feeling for some time, the feeling that they were not alone out here. With a quick look toward the tree line, he followed the blond half elf down the narrow stairway.

<They sense us, my friend.> growled the youth softly.

His brown eyes left the group that stood before the doorway of a halfling hovel and gazed back at the darkening sky.

<Let's withdraw and find shelter. They won't be going anywhere for a while.>

He left off scratching the tawny puma between the ears with his right hand and, still at a crouch, moved deeper into the forest. He moved silent as the breeze that now built up from the direction of the coming storm.

The cat purred softly as it followed.

Savon'el moved down the stairway at a crouch. The blade of his sword swept ahead of him in his left hand as he held the torch low and forward with his right. He felt, more than heard, the soft movement of the Huntsmaster behind him.

When he reached the bottom, he stepped quickly to his left and raised the torch. The smell of scorched cobwebs greeted Arantar as he moved into the room to the right. As he entered, he unsheathed the great sword of gray metal and looked about.

In the light of the torch, they saw a cavernous room, thirty feet across and wide with a twenty or twenty-five foot domed ceiling. The corners were rounded like the outside of the hut.

"Seems our landlord used the hut above as a diversion."

Arantar nodded at the blond half elf's observation and looked about this great room with an eye for defensibility.

There were three doors other than the one they'd entered. One door was situated on the left with a roll-topped desk flanking it to its right with a heavy chair before it, one door to the right, and one large door directly across from the doorway where they stood. A small hearth was built into the wall to the large door's right and there was a crumbling bed frame to its left.

Between them and the large door stood a metal statue situated in the very center of the domed room. All of nine foot tall, the statue was of a fighter complete with "Y" slit helm, ornately carved breastplate, leggings, greaves, and bracers.

The Huntsmaster seemed to remember carvings like this, but he couldn't remember the when or where. He knew they were some type of rune, very ancient and in a language lost in time. To him, they were beautiful in their design and workmanship.

The only deviation in proportion to the statue's design was the number of arms. There were six, three to each side. There were two arms at the top, held up on bent elbows with the hands facing the ceiling; two in the middle held outward with the palms of those hands facing forward toward the two intruders; and two at the bottom again bent at the elbows with the palms facing down. It was placed facing the doorway, possibly to deter trespassers. As the savon'el looked it over, however, he felt as if it watched him as well. He shook his head and smiled at his paranoia.

He glanced toward the Huntsmaster and followed him as Arantar approached the door on the right. As the ranger leaned his back against the wall to the door's right, he glanced from the floor to the savon'el.

"Do you notice something strange in the dust all over everything?"

"Other than its depth? No."

"No? Look closer. What do you see?"

"Everything is covered by at least half an inch of fine dust as if nothing has been here in ages. So?"

"Exactly." At Savon'el's confused glance, he added, "What's missing?"

Savon'el held the torch a bit higher and looked at the thick, smooth layer of dust on everything. Suddenly his quick intake of breath caused the Huntsmaster to grin.

"Ah, now you see what we don't see," he whispered. "Every house, old and deserted as this one seems, always has some small visitors from time to time. Yet here there is no sign. Why not?"

"That, my dear Huntsmaster, is a question we may not wish answered. However," Savon'el continued as a peal of thunder found its way into the room, "we may have to find the answer quickly before that storm drives everyone down here. I'd not like to bring them into danger, so shall we proceed?"

Using the same tactics as before, Arantar gripped the ornate door handle and pulled. This time, the handle came off in his hand with a weak *crack*.

"Damn."

He dropped the handle, gripped his sword in both hands, and planted his foot forcefully into the center of the door. It burst into the next room in a shower of splintered wood and dust.

Savon'el went through the door at a crouch and slipped to the left. He held the torch high as Arantar followed with his great sword sweeping from side to side.

They found themselves in a neat, though incredibly dusty, kitchen. It was complete with a pump, a sink, a wood stove, and cabinets. Pots, pans, and cutlery were hung in racks as if they'd been put away just yesterday and were waiting for the occupant to begin his or her supper.

The chuckle to his left caused the Huntsmaster to glance at his friend.

"Arantar, do you feel as foolish as I?"

The grin was contagious as the savon'el continued through his quiet laughter.

"I think we've just attacked someone's kitchen."

"Come," the ranger replied, his grin as big as Savon'el's. "Let's check the other rooms and get everyone down here before the storm breaks." Then, with a glance at the grinning half elf, "Let's just keep this a secret, shall we?"

"Absolutely!" chuckled the savon'el.

They stepped through the destroyed doorway and crossed to the door that had been on their left when they'd entered. Dust fell from the statue as they passed and they waved the dusty cloud away.

Melisande led the mage girl beneath the eaves of the hut as the small drops of rain began to fall, but they were a distance away from where the knight guarded the door. She turned to Rene' and waited until Bonaire passed by toward the back of the hut.

"Watch the horses, Bonaire," he muttered. "Guard the ladies, Bonaire. Fetch the firewood, Bonaire. They just want to get to the treasure first."

Melisande waited until he disappeared around the corner of the hut and then turned to Rene'.

"First, let me apologize for my outburst at our last conversation. I don't know why it's taken so long to just come to you and—"

"Melisande, there is nothing to forgive. My comments were uncalled for and, frankly, your retort had too much of the truth in it for my liking. Forgive me?"

Melisande squeezed the hand she still held and accepted the return squeeze. She smiled.

"Now," asked Rene' softly, "what is it? Does it have anything to do with the confusion our leader seems to be under?"

"Exactly. I didn't want to say anything before because it didn't seem to matter, but..."

Then Melisande began. She related what she'd heard at the Adventurer's Guild, the nightmare she'd eavesdropped on, and the black-cloaked figure and the spell. When she finished, Rene' brought one hand up to her chin and cupped that elbow in the other hand. One finger tapped her chin as she looked down and thought.

"I felt the spell you mentioned," she mused, "but since it hasn't affected him as far as we know, we can only assume that it was either a delayed spell or he resisted the effects entirely. The latter I doubt and the former frightens me. If it is a delayed spell sent to cause him, or us, harm, when will it take effect and with what result? No, sister, I think we'd best watch and be on guard. He will no doubt show signs and soon. We must be prepared to help counteract whatever—"

"We will, Rene', but carefully. Whoever is haunting Savon'el," the cleric ticked each off on her fingers, "Solothon, Arantar, and—with all probability—Red Wolf, seems to be powerful and have many powerful friends."

"Yes, but we have friends just as powerful, sister. And they have us."

Melisande smiled and looked back toward Solothon.

"Come, Rene'. Let's see what our boys are up to."

She took the mage girl's hand and they moved back to the doorway.

Arantar gripped the door handle as before, but Savon'el laid a hand on that arm to stop him.

"Wait. This time, just to prevent any undue embarrassment, once you open the door, I will stick the torch through to light the way. Then we shall see what's there before we leap."

Arantar nodded and pulled.

This time, half of the door came away with the handle. The Huntsmaster sheathed his sword and ripped the rest of the door away with both hands.

Savon'el extended the torch through the door cautiously, but he felt a resistance as he pushed his hand through. The two half elves gazed into a room that was entirely dust-free. It was a study, it seemed, with a desk, chairs, and bookcases.

Arantar looked down and nudged the blond. "The dust stops right in the middle of the doorway."

The savon'el looked down and then at the Huntsmaster as he withdrew the torch.

"There is a barrier of some type here, Arantar. I felt it. If it is magic or clerical—"

"We need Lady Rene'."

Savon'el nodded and crossed to the stairway.

"It seems safe enough down here," he said, still softly, "and from the sound of things up there, it will be much drier. You agree?"

At Arantar's nod he looked up the stairway.

"Solothon, is Lady Rene' there with you?"

"Yes, just a moment."

Two heads appeared at the head of the stairs and the girl's soft voice floated down. "Yes?"

"We've found something down here that requires your talents to define. I believe it to be magiked. It's safe enough down here, and you all need to get out of the coming storm."

"Surely you jest? I can see the dirt on the stairs and there are bound to be cobwebs and spiders and"—shuddering—"all sorts of nasty things down there."

"Lady, I've not the time or patience. We need your skills here and *now*!"

"Oh all right!" she snapped as she lifted her skirts and started down the stairway carefully and daintily. "I want you to know, sir," she muttered as she came down, "that you are a very rude man to speak to a lady so. Yuck! Cobwebs! See? I told you!"

"Please, Rene'!" said the flustered Savon'el. "It's starting to rain outside and we must hurry!"

"All right. All *right*!" she exclaimed as she reached the bottom of the stairway. "Now, just where is this…'something' you just *must* have my talents to figure out?"

"Here, Rene'," called Arantar from the door to the study.

Melisande had followed the mage girl and now followed her across the dusty chamber to the door. So far she'd managed to hold in the laughter that threatened to explode from her mouth. However, if Rene' continued in this vein much longer, she knew she'd lose the battle.

"Solothon?" Savon'el called up the stairway. As the knight's form filled the opening at the top of the stairs, he continued, "Find a safe place for the horses and bring Bonaire with you down here."

The knight nodded and turned to his mount.

"Enare, you and Browen must watch over these others. Keep them safe and together."

The black nodded his great head while Arantar's roan snorted. The two warhorses herded the others together and followed the Elvin knight around the corner of the building.

Bonaire had made a remarkable discovery. A stable was dug into the back of the hut and there was room for all seven horses and dry racks for the saddles. Then he noticed the small room, possibly the tack room, that seemed to be a part of the stone hut.

He looked about inside, but apart from the small statue of a horse, which quickly disappeared into a pocket, there was nothing left but dust, bits of old decayed bridles, and a leather pail that was old and cracked.

"Bonaire?"

The young elf heard Solothon's call and rushed up the ramp to meet him.

"Hey, Sol! Over here!" As the knight responded with a wave and moved toward him, he continued, "There's room for all of them down there and it's safe. I checked."

"You won't mind if I double-check, do you?" replied the knight sardonically as he led the horses down the ramp.

Between the two of them, the mounts were unsaddled, rubbed down with some dry grass, and furnished with a small ration of grain. Bonaire took the pail to the brook, amid large drops of rain, and partially filled a trough for the horses. Then they both headed for the stairway down.

Rene' stood in the doorway and peered in while Melisande hung back. The cleric had felt the age and dead clerical power that at one time must have permeated the entire area. Her hand went to the surface of the statue and jumped at the vibration that seemed to come from it.

"Melisande, look!" called the golden mage.

Melisande shrugged off the vibration as her imagination and moved to the mage girl's side.

"What is taking so long?" mumbled the blond half elf as he stood looking up the stairway.

Arantar moved to the stairway and sent a call to his friend.

Blacky?

Arantar-sao, find four leg house. Will watch. No uglies. Sky bad. Dry here. All man go dry place with Arantar-sao.

Thanks, my friend. Then, to Savon'el, "They found a stable and will be here shortly."

"How do you...?" the blond half elf began, a look of askance on his face.

"Don't ask," responded the Huntsmaster as he returned to the doorway where Rene' stood.

Bonaire came down the stairway first, a bit clumsily, followed by the knight.

Solothon stopped at the head of the stairway to cover the opening with an old blanket he'd found in the stable. He came down the stairs and replaced Savon'el at the bottom to guard the way as that one crossed to join Arantar.

"What's happening?" he whispered to the Huntsmaster.

Arantar raised a hand, not willing to take his sight from the girl at the doorway.

Rene' closed her eyes and felt the power within the room, once strong but now waning. Once, this power, she felt, had encompassed the entire house and possibly the glade in which it sat. The ages of disuse had seen the decline of that power, reducing it to the point that this room was all that was maintained in cleanliness. She reached toward the opening with a timid hand.

As her hand touched the invisible barrier between the ages, the ward sparkled and dropped away. The ceiling began to glow and bathed the room in soft light. She opened her eyes.

"Melisande, look," she breathed as she stepped through the doorway. "It's a study."

The black-haired cleric followed Rene' into the room and, as Rene' went to the small desk, Melisande moved along the bookcase that flanked the door to its left and completely occupied the left wall. She looked at the leather-bound tomes and the papers that seemed to have been stuck between books. Then she turned her attention to the rest of the room.

It was small and uncluttered. There was a small desk that sat in the middle of the room facing the door, and the far wall had, with the exception of what seemed to be a green crystal wardrobe close to the door, no furniture. A wall hanging depicting the area in which the hut resided hung in the center of that wall. There were several black X's marked, but there was no clue as to the reason for the markings.

The back wall was bare save for the great chest of dark wood banded in bronze. It seemed, to the cleric's sight, to glow.

At the juncture of the bookcases, sitting catty-corner facing the desk, was a heavily wooden-framed full length mirror. Runes of gold had been carved into that frame, and the mirror's surface had a very clear depth. It seemed to ride off the floor by a fraction of an inch as if mounted on a rolling mechanism. When Melisande touched it, it moved freely.

There were two small chairs of stuffed leather that sat before the desk. Melisande tested the comfort of one by dropping into it.

Rene' took in the meticulous way everything on the desk had been placed. It looked as if the previous occupant had set everything in order, possibly to do some work here, but had been called away never to return. There were sixteen sheets of blank parchment in a neat stack in the very center of the desk. Several inkwells and sharpened quills lined the right hand side, each inkwell marked with the same rune, but with a different glyph below each rune.

The mage girl found the small book that stood next to the inkwell stand and opened it. It was a recipe book, written in a small tight hand, for the making and use of the inks, with a description of the power each inkwell contained. She picked up one of the inkwells and found it dried and empty.

Rene' noticed something written in the same tight hand at the top of the first piece of parchment.

"MW 935," she mused.

Then her eyes grew large as her agile mind took in the evidence about her. "Mage War 935?" she breathed.

"What?" Melisande had leaned forward in the chair to look over the desk at the excited mage girl. "What was that?"

"Melisande, it looks like our host was a mage of some kind and, from the size of the furnishings, a small person, maybe a dwarf or halfling. From the note here at the top of this page, he left here in MW 935. The Mage War ended in MW 968, and it is now 1832 of the Empire Reckoning. He left here almost 1900 years ago!"

"That could account for the dust, but what about this room?"

"I think our little occupant was powerful in his craft and at one time cast a spell of sorts to keep things clean around here. I think I dropped the last of the spell when I touched the doorway."

At Melisande's questioning look, she continued.

"You saw the decay in the other room and outside? Well, it seemed to stop right at the door, so—"

"So it probably took a long time for the spell to wane as it did."

"Yes, my dear. It took almost 1900 years for the path of time to reach this room. Imagine it, Melisande!"

"I am, Rene'! I'm imagining the trouble we could be into from some Mage War mage's traps!"

"I don't think he or she would trap their own house, Melisande," chastised the mage girl as she rose from the desk chair and crossed to the green crystal cabinet.

"You never know," quipped the black-haired cleric as she took Rene's place at the desk and began carefully going through the drawers.

Rene' could make out, through the deep translucence of the crystal door, several objects within the cabinet and the glyph that glowed dimly above the handle. She reached out a timid hand and, as her hand came close, the glyph flared with a snap and winked out.

Melisande found the green crystal key in the bottom right hand drawer of the desk and was about to tell Rene' when she heard the sharp crackle and watched as Rene' took two quick steps back and put two of her tiny fingers in her mouth.

"Will this help?" she asked as she dangled the key on its chain toward the startled mage girl.

"Yes, thank you," she mumbled around her fingers.

She took the key and turned back to the wardrobe, stopped, and turned her head toward the cleric.

"Sorry. I tend to get so one-minded sometimes that I ignore anyone and anything else."

"Don't worry about it, Rene'. You're doing fine. Just be careful, okay?"

The mage girl nodded and grinned while Melisande rose and came to her side.

"I know little about the power of mages," the cleric continued, "but I'll be here to help if I can."

"I am not as knowledgeable as I thought I was," Rene' said as she turned back to the wardrobe and inserted the key into the small lock. "Most of this is new to me and maybe you will be able to see what I miss."

The mechanism was old and creaked a bit when she turned the key, but it gave with little force. Rene' glanced back at the cleric as she reached for the handle.

"From what I've seen so far, our little host was a cleric, mage, or druid, or possibly all three. Some of the writings I can read, but most are beyond me. Plus, he or she wrote so small!"

The handle clicked and both girls paused to take a breath. Rene' gently pulled the door open and they both looked inside.

Along the back wall of the wardrobe was a rack intended, obviously, to hold canes or wands, as there were four rods, two wands covered in runes, and a cane resting there. Above the rack were several pigeonholes that contained four or five sheets of the parchment in each. Along the right wall were several hooks, neatly placed in rows. A ring of fourteen keys hung from one, and four small silver and gold rings were spaced out along others.

Rene' curbed her desire to take one of the rings, so dainty and pretty they seemed, by remembering some of the tales she'd heard concerning novices who touched things out of curiosity and the deadly results.

"Maybe," she said as she stepped back, "we shouldn't mess until we know more about what is here."

"You're probably right, Rene', though I, for one, would like nothing better than to place some of these things to good use in our cause. However, I agree that study and investigation will probably ensure these things won't bite us!"

"Okay then, my dear."

Rene' closed the door and turned the small key in the lock. Then she dropped the key into her bodice for safe keeping.

Melisande moved to the chest and ran her hand over the polished dark wood.

"Are you going to open this?"

"No, sister," Rene's replied as she walked to Melisande's side, "we are."

With that, the golden mage joined Melisande in an attempt to lift the lid. It wouldn't budge. Rene' ran her fingers across the front of the chest and found the three recesses there that marked the keyholes.

"Oh, bother," she mumbled as she straightened up and glared at the chest. "Well, we could probably find the keys in the wardrobe, but there is no hurry. Maybe we should find more information before we meddle."

"I agree, Rene'. Our little friend may have left gifts we may not want."

Rene' nodded and grinned as she glanced about the small study.

"It's clean here, at least, and though small, the furnishings look sturdy. Maybe we should start with the writings and papers in the bookcase and desk."

"Okay, you handle the desk, Rene'. I'll look through the stuff on these bookshelves. If we find something, I believe we should look at it together, just to be safe."

"Granted. Just be—"

"Lady Rene'?"

Both turned to the door to find Savon'el and Arantar standing just outside of the doorway. Bonaire stood behind them trying to peak in between the two warriors.

"Sorry, gentlemen," said Rene' with a slight blush. "There seems to be nothing of obvious danger here, though we believe it to be in our best interest if none of the rest of you meddles until we've investigated further."

The last was directed at the young elf who Rene' felt was a problem. She'd felt the waxing and waning of untrained mage power within the youth and felt nervous in the presence of such uncontrolled power.

"Melisande and I would like the opportunity to search through these papers, if you please. They might contain something we can use."

"Of course, if you think that best," responded Savon'el. "We will leave all magical and clerical investigation to you two. However, notify us should you wish to try anything potentially dangerous."

"We will," said the black-haired cleric as she returned to the papers and books in the bookcase.

The Huntsmaster took the young elf by the arm and led him toward the kitchen.

"See what you can find in there, Bonaire, while we look around out here."

Savon'el found the woodbin next to the small hearth and busied himself with a fire while Arantar crossed to the roll-top desk.

When the Huntsmaster tried to lift the cover, the old wood disintegrated into dust and splinters. He brushed at the debris and found more dust in the pigeonholes at the back of the desk. Probably, he guessed, more parchment that had not withstood the passage of time.

There were also several wax-sealed clay vials with markings on them. Though some of the markings were familiar and fairly legible, most were not. He left them alone, not knowing what the contents were nor the danger possible, and began going through the small drawers on the left and right of the pedestal.

He found small clothing, an empty sheath of some unknown leather, ancient quills, and dust. That is, until he opened the bottom right hand drawer.

It was a dagger, thin and of black bone, though the strange absence of an edge was puzzling. He drew the dagger along the edge of the desk and it left no imprint. Yet when he grinned and drew it down his arm as if to shave it, it did. The hair fell away as if shorn with a sharp razor!

He remembered the empty sheath and, as he held the dagger carefully, he found the sheath and slipped the blade into it. It slid perfectly into the leather as if they were a mated pair. When he tried to remove the blade again, however, the blade would not come free. He tried for just a moment more, shrugged, and tossed the sheathed dagger onto the desk. He turned toward the ancient small bedstead.

There, just under the foot of the bed, he could see a small metal box. He crossed to the bed and drew the box from beneath it. It was about the size of a small music box with a keyhole on top, one to either side, and three across the front just below the latch.

He carried it carefully to the study, picking up the dagger from the desk as he went.

"Lady Rene'?"

The mage girl looked up from the scroll she was reading and saw the Huntsmaster.

"Yes?"

"I've found some things that you two should probably see."

He set the box and sheathed dagger on the floor just inside of the door, told Rene' where he'd found them, and withdrew into the main chamber.

Arantar-sao?

The breezy thought drew a grin from the Huntsmaster.

Yes, Blacky?

Stones and water fall. Dry here, but long face nervous.

Thanks, friend. I'll be with you in a moment.

"Savon'el," he called as he crossed to the stairway, "I'm going to check on the horses. I'll return shortly."

"Be careful," the savon'el responded from the area before the hearth. "We still don't know how safe we are."

The Huntsmaster nodded and, after laying a hand on the knight's shoulder and receiving a nod, he went up the stairs.

Bonaire opened the cupboards in the kitchen and found neat stacks of earthenware dishes and mugs, crystal goblets, fine china, and racks of wine bottles. He checked the wood stove and the woodbin. He fed kindling into the stove's hopper, lit it, and added wood to feed the fire.

The pump was situated over an ivory or porcelain sink. He pumped sludge from it for a short while, but soon clear water washed the sludge from the sink. The water tasted sweet, and the young elf felt better. If nothing else, they had water.

An ivory chest, six feet long and three wide and deep, sat in the far corner of the kitchen, the layer of dust hiding the strange runes carved into the silver handle on its lid. As Bonaire gripped the handle, he felt the vibrations. The lid opened easily and, through some mechanism inside, it stayed open.

The young elf found, to his astonishment, packages of meat and vegetables in some type of clear packaging. He picked up one of the packages of vegetables and found it to be a block of ice!

"Now this is strange!" he muttered.

He shrugged and removed several packets of frozen meat and vegetables, closed the lid, and moved with his burden to the sink. He rinsed a large pot he'd found hanging on the wall, put a bit of water into it, unwrapped and dropped the blocks of frozen food into it, and placed it on the stove. He added more wood to the stove's firebox and went in search of spices.

Rene' was reading from one of the scrolls Melisande had found on one of the shelves lining the walls.

Bonaire slumped into one of the small chairs before the desk and felt the pressure of the small arm pressing something into his side. He reached into one of the pockets on that side of his cloak, removed the statuette of the horse he'd found in the stables, and set it on the desk.

"I put some stew on, m'lady," he said as he slumped back into the chair. "That's a well-stocked kitchen in there, but the food bin has me baffled."

"Food bin?" asked Melisande.

She stood next to the mirror in the corner looking over one of the small books she'd taken from the shelf. Bonaire's comment had drawn her curiosity.

"What do you mean?"

"Well, it seems that whoever lived here trapped winter into a white box in the kitchen. Whatever is put in there freezes. Weird, huh?" Then, at Rene's glare, he continued, "I checked the stuff I got out of it. It was as fresh as if it had just been killed or taken from the garden! I'm not griping; it's just weird!"

"I'll look into it later," said the mage girl.

As she started to go back to reading her scroll, she noticed the horse statuette. She glanced back at the scroll she was reading to find the passage there she'd read before. She reread it, grinned, and looked closely at the statuette.

It was flawless from the dimensions and physical attributes of the horse to the saddle, with the buckles and straps shining black in the light. Even the great sword, strapped to the cantle, was proportioned perfectly.

She placed the statuette and the scroll to one side, grinned, and opened the bottom left-hand drawer of the desk.

There was only a book there, bound in soft leather and banded with silver. Across the front, just below a small picture of a key, were the words "Rairy's Book of Power." Rene' felt the magiks as she picked up the book and placed it on the desk in front of her. This could be what they searched for.

"Melisande?" she called softly. "Would you get that ring of keys we found in the wardrobe, please?"

The black-haired cleric sent a cross glance at the mage girl. Then, as she saw the way Rene' was concentrating on the small book on the desk, she grinned.

"Sure. Give me the key."

She placed the book back on the shelf, took the key from a distracted Rene', and crossed to the wardrobe.

Bonaire squirmed around in his chair to see inside the wardrobe as Melisande opened it, took the key ring, closed and locked the door, and dropped the keys on the small desk. She started back to her book, but stopped when she saw what Rene' had found.

"What have you?"

"Wha...?" answered the mage girl as she glanced up from her find.

Melisande had seen the same distracted look on the faces of interrupted scholars intent on their studies. She grinned.

"Oh! Sorry!" said Rene' as she seemed to come back to herself. "It's a book of magiks written by our host, it seems. His name was... Rairy, or so the title states. The name seems familiar, but...Do you have any memories of that name?"

"No," responded the cleric, "but my studies didn't include magic."

"It's just...Anyway, this has been locked with a ward of some kind for protection, but maybe one of these keys—"

"I don't see a keyhole, Rene'," stated the cleric as she leaned on the desk with both hands and watched the mage girl check each key for a match to the one depicted on the cover.

"I know," she replied distractedly, "but I've seen these things before in Yarda's library. You need...the right key...and a word or phrase to...open it."

Rene' paused at each key, comparing it to the one pictured on the book cover as she talked. Finally...

"Ah!" she exclaimed as she took a small key from the key ring, placed it over the emblem on the book cover, dropped the key ring next to the book, and sat back in her chair with a sigh.

"Okay, now what?" queried Melisande' as she looked at the mage girl.

"Now," she replied softly, "we need to see if I can open it."

She leaned close to the book and concentrated on the key covered picture.

"Well," she whispered, "here goes nothing."

She began with the normal words of opening. "Open!" Nothing. "Unlock!" Still nothing.

"Oh, bother!" she exclaimed. Then she rested her hands to either side of the book and sighed softly. "Would you be so kind as to unlock yourself that I might peruse your contents?"

Somewhere in the comment the key phrase hid, and by complete accident Rene' stumbled upon it. The key glowed dimly and turned itself over. As it did so, the picture also reversed itself, and the mage girl heard the tiny click as the wards dropped. She grinned.

"That was a cute trick, Rene', but now what?"

Rene' looked up to see the sardonic look on the cleric's face, frowned, and opened the book to its first page. It was a neatly printed index to the contents of the small book. It was also strange in that, listed together, spells of both clerical and mage sciences were listed. It seemed they had been jumbled haphazardly throughout the pages in a rather confusing and random fashion.

Rene' looked closer, then sat back abruptly with a sharp intake of breath.

"My lady!" she breathed softly. "Melisande, you must look!"

The black-haired cleric frowned and stepped around the desk to look over Rene's shoulder at the proffered page. It was written in the common tongue, which was strange in itself. Anyone, it seemed, would be able to release any spell written and avail themselves with the power there.

Or would they?

As she looked closer, her mouth opened involuntarily as she saw what had shocked Rene'. Not only were the two sciences jumbled in the index, but the levels required to use the spells were as well! Seven spells down the list was a clerical spell every young cleric is taught within two weeks of entering the temple service. Yet third from the top was a reincarnation spell used only by the most capable of high priest and priestess!

"Oh my!"

"Yes, Melisande, it seems our little benefactor was more disorganized in his writings than he was in the organization of his study, unless—"

"Unless by design, Rene'. You don't suppose—"

"Yes, I do!" the mage girl breathed. "We'd better figure his pattern, if any, before we try any of this. If I turned to the wrong page and began forming the spell there, there is a good chance that the power required would devastate me!"

"A nice trap for the curious-minded," commented Melisande. "Let me look through this one," she continued as she took the book from in front of the mage girl. "Maybe I can figure out his pattern while you check the rest of this stuff."

She glanced through the content page and sighed.

"Most of these are way beyond my capabilities, but it won't hurt to go through them at least."

"Just be careful, my dear," said Rene' softly as Melisande crossed to the chair next to Bonaire and dropped into it.

As the cleric sat, she allowed her right leg to dangle over the arm of the chair while she studied each page with frowning intensity.

Bonaire leaned toward her, trying to get a look at the contents of the book, but Melisande waved him away impatiently without looking up at him. He snorted and left the room mumbling.

Rene' was deeply engrossed in the scrolls when Solothon entered. He looked from one girl to the other, glanced about the room, and crossed to the great chest.

"What's in here?" he asked as he fingered the three keyholes in the brass banding.

"What?" replied the mage girl distractedly. Then she said, "Oh. According to this, that contains armor, weapons, staffs, and such, all of which are cursed."

Solothon backed away from the chest, wiping his hands on his cloak.

Melisande glanced up from the book and grinned at the knight's distress. Then as she returned to her book, something caught her eye.

"That's odd."

Rene' glanced up at the cleric. "What, Melisande?"

"That wall. It's not right."

The cleric dropped the book on the chair and crossed to the wall just to the right of the chest.

"Notice the absence of anything here, like pictures, tapestries, and the like."

Rene' looked from the wall to the cleric and frowned. "So?"

"So, Rene', look at the rest of this study. Everything is in balance. The mirror is set just so-so in the corner, the bookcases are all about this other wall, and the wardrobe and tapestry are placed just perfectly within the spaces provided. However, this wall is just not...it's not anything."

As Melisande ran her hands over the surface of the wall, Rene' crossed to stand just behind her and also looked at the wall intently. Melisande's right hand moved close to the tapestry and with a whispered "Ah!" from the cleric, she pressed a small invisible panel. They both heard the click and watched as a panel in the wall opened slightly.

"Careful, m'lady," said the knight softly as Melisande pushed the hidden doorway open.

Dim light bathed the interior of the room beyond and showed the girl tiled floors, walls, and ceiling. She passed a small closet that contained robes of fur, satin, silk, and other rich material, and large, soft white towels as she entered. Just beyond the closet was a white toilet of porcelain or granite with a seat of some soft pliable material. Just to the right of that was a sight that brought a grin to her face.

It was a sunken tub of white tiles. Water poured in slowly through the mouth of a small silver dragon whose tail seemed to wrap itself about the chimney of the small hearth set into the far wall.

Rene' had followed the black-haired girl into the small room, her mouth open slightly in awe at the comfort depicted here.

"Do you know what this is, Rene'?" asked Melisande excitedly as she stroked the dragon's tail. Then, without waiting for an answer, continued, "It's a water heater! The bath must be fed from the brook outside, the water coming in through these pipes. If we build a fire—" she added as she picked up two small logs from the stocked wood bin.

"We can bathe in hot water!" exclaimed the mage girl.

Melisande built a small fire and soon hot water poured from the dragon's mouth. She tossed off her cloak and reached for the hem of her tunic.

"Harrumph!"

She stopped and glanced over to find that the knight had followed them into the room.

"Solothon," said Rene' as she tested the water with a small hand, "we ladies will be in here bathing. See that no one enters, please."

"As you wish, m'lady," he said as he backed out of the room and closed the door behind him.

"I'll bathe first, Rene'," said the black-haired cleric as she resumed her disrobing.

"Together. You wash my hair and I'll wash yours."

Melisande thought for a moment and grinned.

Soon they were splashing about in the warm water like little girls. Rene' found some soft soaps in jars beside the tub, along with perfumes, combs, and a small mirror.

"Seems our little benefactor had all sorts of visitors," commented Rene'.

"Thank goodness!" sighed Melisande. "My clothes are starting to reek!"

Solothon stood for a moment by the hidden door to make certain that the ladies were safe. Then, with a grin, he walked to the door of the study and leaned against the jamb. He saw Savon'el leaning against the wall next to the stairway door with one foot up and placed flat against the wall. Bonaire came out of the kitchen with a steaming bowl and crossed to the study.

"Hey, Sol. There's some stew in the kitchen on the stove. Help yourself."

"Thanks," he replied as Bonaire stepped past him into the study. "The ladies are in the bath."

"Bath?"

"Yes, there is a secret door there in the wall."

The knight pointed a finger at the wall mentioned, then laid a hand on the young elf's shoulder.

"They do not wish to be disturbed."

"Oh!"

Solothon grinned as he walked toward the kitchen. He glanced at the large door in the far wall next to the small hearth, but shrugged and continued into the kitchen.

Rene' felt the draft from the door and reached out with her empathy. She felt childlike curiosity.

"Bonaire! Close the door or I'll turn you into a toad!"

She grinned as she heard the door click shut and returned to washing the cleric's black tresses. After she rinsed the hair thoroughly, she began running a thick-toothed comb through the hair to relieve the tangles there.

Melisande stroked the borders of the small mirror that sat at the side of the bath as she watched the mage girl work the comb slowly through her hair.

"Our men are a strange amalgam, Rene'. I wonder what they think..."

She gasped as her reflection in the mirror swirled and was replaced by the vision of the main room. She saw Savon'el leaning against the wall, Solothon come out of the kitchen, and Arantar returning through the stairway door.

Rene' left off combing and watched over the cleric's shoulder as Solothon crossed to the large door and turned the knob.

Dust drifted from the statue's shoulders as it seemed to stretch itself up, shift its arms, and turn it's now-lit "Y" slit helm toward the knight.

The sound of metal grinding shook Savon'el from his mental retreat and into action. As the statue shifted to face the knight, the endlibar blade appeared in the half elf's hands.

"Solothon! 'Ware the statue!" he shouted as he swept around to the statue's left front.

Arantar's blade was in his hands at an instant and he ran to the statue's right flank.

"What in the bloody hells!" he breathed through clinched teeth.

Solothon hadn't needed the warning, for he had heard the grinding from his rear and turned, sword in hand to face the now-mobile statue. While the statue shook his arms and legs, seemingly to relieve the ages of inactivity, Solothon spun his sword and rested it on the back of his other hand, up and ready.

Strangely, though noted only in a distant part of the knight's awareness, the Song Sword had no familiar vibration. No song came from the blade that rested on Solothon's hand.

The statue noticed its flankers and, with a flip of all six of its arms, filled the hands with scimitars. It assumed a defensive stance, its head turning from warrior to warrior as it awaited attack.

Rene' had seen all she needed.

"Stay here!" she snapped as she leaped from the bath, water spraying everywhere.

Melisande could only nod in open-mouthed astonishment as she continued to watch the drama unfold in the mirror.

Rene' grabbed a robe and drew it around her as she threw the door open and ran through the study. Bonaire was jerked from his doze as the girl ran by him and into the main room.

Savon'el swept his sword in a small arc and, as he slipped into a combat crouch, tucked it up next to his left forearm. He did it smoothly as if the movement were common to him. Yet, had he thought on it, he would not be able to remember where he'd learned it. Now, however, his mind was turned off and his body ran the show. It knew. It would respond.

Rene' stopped in the middle of the room, placed her small hands on her hips, and stamped her foot.

"YOU STOP THAT!" she screamed.

The statue turned its head toward the girl, then cocked its head to the side.

"I am the new mistress of this house," she continued in a petulant voice, "and I said *stop*!"

The statue turned toward the golden-haired girl, cocked its head to the other side, and swept its arms up. The blades disappeared back into its arms. It looked down at the girl and seemed to sigh.

"Can't a lady take a bath without being interrupted?" she yelled at the three warriors as their swords fell slack in their hands. "And you!" She turned her attention back to the metal giant before her and slapped a small hand on the hard breast piece. "When was the last time you were serviced? You scare my guests half to death and have the nerve to squeak as well?" Then, with a light shove on that breastplate, "Go fix yourself!"

The statue stumbled back from the girl as if it had been slapped and glanced about the room. That look seemed to take in Arantar, Solothon, and Savon'el in turn before it returned to the mage girl. Then, with a stiff bow toward the girl, it turned and walked toward Solothon and the large door.

The knight thought an attack was coming and returned his sword to the ready.

Oddly, the statue stopped before the Elvin knight and looked toward Rene'. Rene' understood.

"Solothon, do get out of his way, please."

Solothon, his sword still up, slipped carefully to his right and out from in front of the large door.

The statue nodded toward the mage girl and, ignoring the knight, opened and stepped through the door. Once the door closed, three sets of eyes turned toward Rene'.

"That's what I thought," she sighed raggedly.

She glanced around at the warriors whose faces held both concern and question.

"It is a golem, though in my studies I've not seen one of metal before. It was obviously designed to protect and guard this place. Please, leave that door alone until I at least finish my bath."

"Yes, m'lady," came three voices as the girl turned on her heel and marched back into the study.

Savon'el sheathed his sword as his eyes followed the girl's path into the study. "I wonder what in all the hells that was all about?"

Arantar joined him and, after placing the great sword point down before him, leaned on the pommel. His answer had the ring of amusement to the blond half elf.

"I don't know, my friend, but we'd best leave that door alone."

Chapter Twenty-seven

"What was that?" asked the cleric as the mage girl came through the door, tossed her robe into the closet with shaking hands, and returned to the comfort of the warm water.

Melisande had watched everything that had transpired in the great hall in the mirror and gasped out the question as the mirror returned to normal.

Rene' sighed as the warm water enveloped her and, as she felt the cleric's emotions, grinned.

"Come here and I'll explain while I comb the rest of the tangles from that mess of black hair."

She picked up the comb again and began on Melisande's long tresses.

"I just had a terrible thought!" exclaimed the cleric as she turned to face Rene' with an impish grin. "What would your mother say if she knew her daughter was bathing with a priestess of the goddess of Lust and Depravity?"

"Quiet, you!" grinned Rene' as she pushed Melisande's head beneath the soothing waters.

An hour later, Rene', in a gold satin robe, and Melisande, wrapped in deep brown fur, sat in the two easy chairs in the study. Solothon stood by the door occasionally glancing toward the large door through which the golem had disappeared. Arantar sat on the corner of the desk while Savon'el sat cross-legged on the floor before the two ladies, his sword across his lap and the hilt to his left hand. Between off-key renditions of some unintelligible song Bonaire was rendering from the bath, Rene' attempted to explain what had happened.

"We saw what was happening out there through a 'Mirror of Looking'. My mother had one like it, and when Melisande touched it, she must have been thinking of you fellows in the main hall. Lucky for you she did, it seems!"

"What *was* that?" asked the blond half elf as his right thumb nervously released the blade from its sheath and his left hand reseated it.

"As I said, it is a golem. I've read many passages concerning their development, creation, and purpose, though I've not read of one made of steel. They are reputed to being very dangerous unless you are either the creator or the appointed master. I just gambled that its inactivity for several centuries would give credence to my claim of ownership, but there is something else that puzzles me. All of those I've read about have a very low intelligence, one step up from a frog, so to speak. If this fellow were normal, he would have attacked you three out of hand and, Solothon, he would have walked over you to get to that door. Instead, he looked to me for assistance, obviously not wishing to do undue harm. Strange."

"Not so strange if one truly knows my master."

All eyes in the room snapped to the door as the deep voice resonated through the room. There the steel warrior knelt, a faint yellow light glowing from his eye slits.

Rene' stood quickly and, as she laid a hand on Savon'el's arm, she turned toward the door. The blond half elf's was on his feet, his hands filled, as if by magic, with the endlibar sword, the sheath clattering to the ground before him.

Melisande slipped gracefully over the arm of the chair and crouched, her hand buried in the dirty yellow cloak and gripping the shaft of her secreted chosen weapon. She grinned.

Arantar sidestepped left and forward to place himself between this threat and the ladies, his hand to the hilt at his back. Solothon backed away from the door, his hand caressing the hilt of his sword.

"Know him, friend?"

"'Friend' may not be the correct term, m'lady," he answered. "I've yet to decide. My master will return shortly. Thou may not leave until he does. Meantime, be comfortable. I shall serve thee. Seems the dwelling has become incredibly dirty in a short space of time. Please, thou may call me Maxim."

Rene' gripped the blond half elf's arm.

"It will do you no good," she whispered. "Please, put it away."

Savon'el glanced at the girl, saw the look in her eyes, and returned the sword to its sheath. He stood at a slight crouch, ready to retrieve the blade if necessary in her defense.

Rene' stepped around him and walked slowly past the Huntsmaster until she came to the door. She looked up at the golem and tilted her head slightly to one side.

"What year is it, Maxim, to your recollection?"

"Why, 'tis the nine hundred thirty-fifth year of the war, of course."

Rene' caught the look of frowning disbelief on the face of the cleric as that one moved slowly to Solothon's side.

"And where is your master?" Rene' continued.

"He has gone to meet another. He should be along soon. He said he'd not be long."

"Maxim," said the girl softly as she took a small step forward, "feel your joints. See the dust and decay about you. How long has your master been gone?"

"Why...?"

The steel warrior seemed to be in a bit of confusion as he looked about the main hall.

"He just left but a moment—"

"Maxim?"

The girl's soft voice brought the golem's attention back to the occupants of the study.

"It is now the year 1832 by the reckoning of the Empire. The Mage War ended on the 968th year of its reckoning. Your master went out to meet someone some 1900 years ago." Rene' paused long enough for that to sink in. "Could your master live that long?"

"It is possible, m'lady," answered he after a short thoughtful pause. "He was in possession of the Crystal of Immortality."

Nineteen hundred years? Rene' shook her head at the attempt to fathom living that long. Elves were long-lived, but even their lives normally didn't last beyond five centuries. She shook her head again and looked up at the warrior.

"Is there no way to know whether your master survived?"

"There is," stated the golem slowly. "Within the weapons case is secreted his soul gem. If it glows, he lives. If not..."

Rene' glanced at the green crystal wardrobe toward which the golem had nodded.

"I saw no gem in there earlier."

"As I said," he said, "it is secreted. There is a small panel revealed only if one pulls down on the very last key hook in the back."

Rene' glanced over at Melisande, who now leaned against the back of the chair, her hands still buried within the dirty yellow cloak. The cleric nodded and Rene' stepped back to the desk.

She picked up the crystal key, crossed to the wardrobe, and unlocked it. She found the described hook and gently pulled it down. A small panel above the rack of wands and rods slid back to reveal a silver chain to which a pendant had been attached. Rene' lifted it gently from its peg and brought it out, relocking the locker and slipping the key into one of the pockets of her robe. She held the chain, pendant dangling, out toward the golem.

"If the pendant is glowing…"

The stone within the silver mounting would never glow again. It was cracked in several places and its center, normally clear crystal, was smoky black.

"Maxim," she asked softly, "do you really believe he will return?"

In a voice soft with loss came the answer.

"No, m'lady. For the crystal to have cracked, my master has met a particularly nasty end."

He stood and moved back into the cavernous main room and stopped with his head down. Rene' stepped to the doorway to watch him, a touch of pity in her eyes at the golem's strange countenance.

"What can I do, Maxim?" she asked softly.

"Nothing," came the sad reply. "This means that I must now do that which I was directed to do these many years ago."

He turned and, with a sigh, moved toward the large door.

"What were you directed to do?"

Maxim stopped, cocked his head toward the girl, and then lowered his gaze.

"I must destroy certain artifacts to keep them from falling into the hands of novices, rendering them dangerous. Then I must return here and recite the spell taught me by my master. It will destroy this dwelling and me."

His eyes came back to the girl and he sighed again.

"My master was a good man, m'lady, and he wished not to have his home ransacked by thieves and the power of some of his creations to fall into evil hands."

"Do I appear to be a thief or evil, Maxim? Do my companions?"

The metal warrior seemed to ponder the girl's question as the companions filed from the study into the main hall. He seemed to look them over individually as if an answer would present itself by merely gazing at them.

"I may be able to offer an alternative," continued the girl as she crossed to stand before him. "Destroy those things you must, but stay as guardian for me. I have a need to learn the skills of your master. You can judge my worthiness as compared and aid me in my study. Your master gave you above normal intelligence for a reason, Maxim. Would he sacrifice you and the possible good his creations could bring on a vow taken over 1900 years ago amidst a terrible war?"

The golem's helm dropped again, but this time it looked, to Rene', that he was weighing her words. Rene' moved to his side, placed a small hand on his lower arm, and his head turned toward her. She spoke softly, a sad intensity in her voice.

"I think not but, please, should you decide to fulfill those vows, warn us first. I offer only a logical alternative, nothing more. I haven't the power to stop you, as you well know. The decision, as it always has been, is yours."

She stepped back and waited as the golem looked, first at her and then the companions, the large door, and then her again. He walked slowly toward the large door again, but stopped and looked back at the girl.

"I must ponder this. In the meanwhile, I must do what must be done with certain items in my master's armory."

He strode to the door and opened it, but turned back as Rene's soft voice again reached him.

"May I watch?"

He turned his head toward her as he seemed to consider the question.

"Yes, but be warned! Attempt to touch anything without my leave and I am bound to destroy thee, sad as I will be at thy passing. It has been many years—more than I can remember, I'm finding—since kind words have passed these ears and beauty such as thee and thy companion's have graced this household."

"I shall—" Rene' began, but amended her statement as Melisande stepped up beside her. "We shall merely watch and, if you please, question."

"At thy pleasure, m'lady," he answered as he led the way through the door in the far wall.

Melisande stopped in the doorway and turned an impish grin on the three men as they stood by the study door.

"Now, you boys behave," she remarked in a motherly voice, punctuating her comment with a pointed finger.

She heard Bonaire hit an awkward note in his song and she frowned.

"And please get Bonaire out of the bath before he harms himself."

Then she closed the door behind her.

She trotted down the short hall to catch up with Rene' and the golem, only to draw up short as she entered the room at the end.

Here was an extensive armory filled with rack upon rack of swords, daggers, and archery equipment, all made of highly polished bone of various colors. There were red, green, gold—all of the colors the young cleric had heard of in relation to dragonkind. On a rack beside the huge wardrobe at the end stood a stand that bore armor of an elaborate nature, but it was sized to fit a halfling's body. On the wall above hung a shield of equal proportions with a gold, rampant dragon pierced with a lance on a field of blue.

"Yes, Melisande, I see it," whispered Rene' as the cleric tugged at her robe. "Isn't that—"

"Shhh," the mage girl whispered. Then, to the metal warrior, "Maxim, is this the crest of your former master?"

"Yes, m'lady," he answered as he looked at the shield, then at Rene'. "My master was of a group known as Wormslayers. In ranking of Mage power, there was Banshe'e, Moredan Raden, my master, Radagast, and Torval."

"What about clerical?" asked Melisande softly. "From our studies, we've found that your master was multi-talented."

"Yes, indeed he was," Maxim answered thoughtfully. "By the ranking of godly power they wielded, they would be ranked a bit differently with my master as first."

Maxim opened the double doors to the large wardrobe and stepped within its emptiness. He pressed a panel in the back wall and a click sounded softly. Then the metal warrior turned back to the ladies.

Melisande had wandered over to one of the racks of bone daggers and was about to touch one of the blades. Maxim's deep voice changed her mind.

"DO NOT TOUCH!"

The cleric jerked her hand back and looked with embarrassment at the warrior.

"I'm sorry! I—"

"These are not a part of my earlier caution, m'lady, and I apologize if I frightened you. It is just that, though they look dull, these weapons about thee will cut at a thought. They were specifically made to rend living tissue. I apologize for alarming thee, m'lady, and thou may study these later if thou wilt. Just please be careful."

He turned his attention to the back wall of the wardrobe and pushed a secreted door open. It was small for him, but negotiable. He stood aside within the room beyond and allowed the ladies to follow.

"I must, in good conscience, repeat my last warning. This is...was...my former master's private armory. These items are more powerful than you can know, and I cannot allow you to touch any of them. I am bound by unbreakable vows to defend them from all who would enter here. Allowing entrance is stretching those vows to their very limit, and I fear for thy safety should thy curiosity overwhelm thee."

"Fear not, Maxim," stated the mage girl. "One warning is enough."

Melisande nodded her assent and buried her hands in the soft clinging fur. She stood off to one side with Rene' as the guardian entered the small private armory of their absent host.

Here were not the extensive racks of weapons and armor seen in a normal armory. Here, a multi-talented warrior placed his most prized and powerful weapons.

On a rack by a small chest on the far wall, platinum chainmail rested in opulent splendor, a shield of smaller proportions across it. A sheathed sword, sparkling in jeweled radiance, hung just to the right of it, and a small bookcase, containing seven small books and a folded piece of silvery cloth, finished the furnishings along the back wall of the small room.

Above the bookcase, a panel divided into squares of many colors glowed dimly. On the left wall stood a small rack with two small staffs the only residents.

Maxim moved to the bookcase and retrieved the cloth. As he began to unfold it, it seemed to grow until it was a very large bag with a silken drawstring. He stepped to the rack containing the mail and shield and stopped. He turned his helm toward the women and sighed again.

"Please do not be alarmed at what thou wilt see, but stay where thou art. This bag is a special device. Anything I place within will be transported to a place of negative energy where it shall be destroyed. I shall be careful to control the devastation to within this bag."

He turned back to the rack of splendid armor and sighed again.

He took the bag into the hands of his lower arms and picked up the shield. He broke it in two and dropped it into the bag, instantly closing the opening. Muffled thunder followed the spasmodic expansion of the bag and the guardian reopened it.

He lifted the platinum chainmail from the rack, ripped it to shreds, and dropped it as well into the bag, repeating the instantaneous closing with the hands that held the bag. Again there was muffled thunder and expansion, and again he reopened it.

Maxim lifted the sheathed sword from the wall and cradled it gently in his hands.

Rene' felt the emotions that should not have been part of this creature's makeup.

"Maxim, must you?"

"I'm afraid so, m'lady," he replied sadly. "This weapon is much too powerful for any save my master. I shall miss him greatly."

The huge warrior unsheathed the sword, broke it, and it followed the other things into the bag. The sheath followed it as well. He stepped to the bookcase, went through the seven books there, took six, and dropped them into the bag. He picked up the seventh, thumbed through it quickly, and with what seemed to be a meaningful glance at the two women, returned it to the bookcase.

"I shall keep this one...for now."

He passed the small chest and caressed it with one of his middle hands. Then he stood before the rack that contained the two small staffs. As if in one motion, he broke both staffs together, threw them into the bag, pulled it closed, and threw the bag into the far corner of the small room.

The thunder vibrated the walls of the room and the bag seemed to expand to twice its size. Then it disintegrated into dust.

"I have carried out the first directive given me by my former master," said Maxim, "save this."

He stepped back to the small chest, opened it, and removed a pair of leather bracers etched with silver runes. He opened his breastplate and hung them within.

"What are those?" asked the black-haired cleric.

"They contain power, m'lady." Then, as he turned his attention to Rene', he continued, "Since I have decided that thy alternative holds a merit for which my former master would approve, these will go to one of sufficient power and need as to...win them."

He stepped to the multicolored panel and said, "There is but one thing more."

He touched several of the colored panels in a special sequence and the panel slid back into the wall with a *snick*. The cabinet within contained a book and a silver ring. He removed these and closed the panel.

"As thou hast shown a desire," he said as he returned to the entrance of the armory where the ladies waited, "despite the obvious danger, to study my master's arts, and with the exception of one of your companions, thee two hold the closest skill to be apprenticed to my master, I have decided to entrust thee, Lady Rene', with this key."

The large warrior placed the ring gently on Rene's right little finger.

"The key grants entrance to this dwelling within three miles. Think of the main hall and thou wilt be transported here. Also, thou may summon me if within but a mile."

He handed the small book to Melisande.

"This book lists all of the items and the uses for each within this domain," and with a glance at the pile of ash in the corner, "with notable exceptions.

"This was Lord Rairy's summer home. There are two more listed: his winter dwelling and the castle. Each was crafted individually and with its own defenses. Please be wary, ladies, for there is nothing here to tell of those defenses. This was by design, for should they still exist, each holds powerful artifacts that could, should they fall into the wrong hands, be devastating."

"I see," mused the mage girl as she glanced at Melisande.

The cleric thumbed through the book, shrugged, and handed it to Rene'. The blonde girl wondered at the cleric's lack of curiosity, then remembered that they were cut from two very different bolts of cloth.

Maxim led the women back to the door into the wardrobe and, as they emerged, locked the door. He turned his attention to Melisande.

"Lady Rene', thy companion looks comfortable in the robe gifted by an Elvin princess."

He placed the key to the wardrobe within his chest plate and, at Melisande's look of askance, continued.

"'Tis the coat of the Mimic, of which many stories are told, long extinct from the Southern Reaches. 'Tis to thy liking?"

Melisande snuggled into the robe and replied, "I'd like it even better were it the color of my calling: yellow. However—"

The words had no sooner left her mouth when the fur color changed in a shimmer. It became tawny beige.

"I'm afraid that that is the best it can do, m'lady. Speak of an animal and the robe will attempt to duplicate its color and texture. I believe it is now the color of the western puma."

The robe seemed to mold itself to the cleric's body, trying to please its new mistress. Melisande, after the first shock, grinned and the sparkle of youth seemed to come from her eyes.

"I love it!" she exclaimed.

If a robe could purr, it would have.

Melisande walked down the short hall to the door to the main room, stroking the fur and smiling. Maxim stopped Rene' at the door with a gentle touch of his hand on her arm.

"Lady Rene', I must ask that, upon thy departure, thee return the keys thou hast to the place wherein thee acquired them. The crystal key must be returned to me for safekeeping."

"As you wish, Maxim."

As they stepped through the door, Maxim sighed. "I must see to the cleanliness of this house!"

Melisande touched the warrior gently and he seemed to look down into her green eyes.

"Yes, m'lady?"

"Maxim, where did you get that name?"

"Why, from one who assisted my master in my creation. T'was his name first."

He strode through the door, leaving Melisande to stare after him, her mouth agape.

Chapter Twenty-eight

"I was created as a defense and sparring partner for my former master."
Arantar sweated as he attempted to bring the great sword into contact with the colored plates Maxim had attached to his breastplate, legs, and arms. The metal warrior had allowed that he needed practice as much as they but, to keep the game even, used blunted scimitars in only his two middle arms. He held the others behind his back.

Savon'el leaned against the wall next to the stairway and grinned. His head still hurt, but not as much as it would have were he not concentrating on the skill of the Huntsmaster and golem. He carried on the conversation with the guardian as that one pushed Arantar through the training session.

"Was he ever as good as you?"

"Not at first, but later he could if he concentrated. Most of the time, in the latter days, he would use me as a distraction, allowing his mind to work out some deep problem while his body reacted to my pressing."

There was a final parry by the great sword and it slid in to strike the red panel on the guardian's breastplate. That one stepped back and slid the blunted blades back into his forearms.

"Well struck, young sir! With more practice thou couldest strike me even at normal speed!"

Arantar caught the cloth tossed him by the blond half elf as that one strolled toward him. He looked up from the cloth incredulously.

"Normal speed?"

Six scimitars flashed into being in the steel guardians hands and, in a blinding display of speed and dexterity, the winds from the blades whipped the Huntsmaster's hair. A second or so later, the blades disappeared.

"Normal speed," commented the golem.

"I could only dream of being that good!" gasped the Huntsmaster.

"Come, Maxim," said the grinning Savon'el as he drew his broad-bladed sword. "My turn."

Four arms disappeared behind the guardian's back as two blunt scimitars appeared in his other two hands.

The sound of swordplay from the main room invaded the concentration of the girl in the gold robe. She looked up from the book Maxim had given her and frowned.

"I wish those boys would stop playing."

"They're not playing, Rene'," came the cleric's voice from before her. "They must practice to stay sharp. We may well need their skills before we are done."

Melisande leaned against the bookcase just next to the full-length mirror and studied the spell book Rene' had found. She still hadn't found a pattern that would allow for its use, but at least the reading was interesting.

"You are probably right," Rene' replied, "but it's so hard to concentrate with all of that going on." She sighed. "We've been here but two days and I've just barely brushed the surface of the information here."

She sighed again and turned her attention back to the book.

"No matter," she said as she read a short passage. "Wait!"

Melisande looked up from Rairy's spell book and watched the mage girl reread the passage she'd found.

"The chest Arantar found, the small one, it's listed here."

"Oh?" replied the cleric as she closed the book, laid it on the bookcase, and with a glance at the mirror in passing, moved toward the desk. "This place is full of—"

The mirror shimmered and, as Melisande stopped in wide-eyed wonder, it showed an older Melisande staring back. There was a light touch of white in her black tresses and she was dressed in black leather and cloak, the latter embroidered with a gold sunburst at her left breast. Her gasp brought Rene's head up.

"What is it?" she asked.

"This mirror! Look!"

Rene' rose from her chair and, skirting the desk, came to Melisande's side. As she came within the purview of the mirror, it shimmered and showed an older Rene' in flowing white robes with the same...no, just a slightly different sunburst over her heart. Her hair, strangely, was a deep auburn with gray streaks, but there was one wide white streak from the front of her auburn locks to her right shoulder.

She smiled and touched a small-silvered rune on the frame and the mirror shimmered again. When it came clear again, it became a mirror once more.

"It's a Mirror of Possibilities," explained the mage girl. "It shows possible futures relating to the viewer's past or possible choices that may be made. It is possible to show a past that leads to their present and can explain the reason for one's existence based on their choices. I just hope my choices don't include dyed hair!" she added with a grin.

Rene' moved back to her chair, an interested Melisande in tow.

"I've seen but one other like it. Yarda, my mentor, had one in his study. He used it sometimes to show me how his choices had brought him to be what and who he was. It was sometimes entertaining in the possibilities determined by choice.

"Now, back to this book Maxim lent..."

Melisande's thoughts drifted to another who could possibly benefit from the information this mirror might be able to present. She walked to the door of the study, barely listening to the mage girl as that one went on about the objects listed in the book.

Savon'el stepped down from the stairway dressed in soft leather from his pack. The salt smell of the clothing tugged at his memory, but it was washed away by the nagging headache that seemed to be his constant companion. He'd bathed and entrusted his armor to the guardian for its repair, as well as Melisande's Elvin chain mail, and he had gone outside for a bit of fresh air.

Maxim had vowed that the house and surroundings were well-protected now that he was awake, yet Savon'el could not shake the feeling of dread with each passing day. He'd come back down, leaned against the wall to the side of the stairway, and dropped his head into his hands, hoping for some relief. He vaguely overheard Maxim and Arantar in an animated discussion next to the hearth.

"The one calling himself Myrlin and his brother, Gre'sharr," Maxim was saying, "dealt with the balance of all things, whereas my master and his companions within the Order believed that chaos was necessary to prompt choice and add spice to life."

Melisande shook her head and grinned at the irony. The Huntsmaster and knight were engaged in a friendly discussion with a creature that, days ago, could have killed them. She turned her attention to the blond half elf.

She could almost feel his pain and distrust brought by his memory loss. His was a life with no grounding save the here and now. Who he was could be boon or bane to this group's existence, yet she, as the others, would follow him to the gates of the hells and beyond if necessary. She glanced back at the now-quiet mage girl.

"Rene'," she asked as she allowed her eyes to turn back to the savon'el, "what do you know of Savon'el?"

"Apart from what you've told me, as much as I know of any of us. I was thrust into this as much as anyone else, although 'thrust' was not the initial force that brought me. Originally I was to accompany a group to the keep at the source of the Lost Souls River and search for certain records and artifacts pertaining to—"

"BANSHE'E?"

Maxim's deep voice cut into the conversation accompanied by a long resounding laugh.

"All I can say about that one is…he is totally insane!"

Melisande turned back to Rene' as the mage girl continued.

"Banshe'e. The Myrlin of Ta'el himself gave me this charge. However, I don't believe he could have known that…" She shrugged hopelessly. "Who knows?"

"Unfortunately, no one," stated the cleric as she stepped out of the study and moved softly to the blond half elf.

"Savon'el," she said quietly, "I think it is time for honesty."

The blond half elf raised red-rimmed eyes to those of the cleric as she laid a soft hand to his cheek.

"All of us have been compelled in one way or another to take up this expedition. You, for good or ill, were chosen as leader, but you should not attempt to puzzle everything out on your own. Let us help. We are the only companions any of us are likely to have for quite a while."

Savon'el glanced at the study door, the three by the hearth, and then up the stairway indecisively.

Maxim heard Melisande's words, though she'd spoken in a low voice, and turned toward Savon'el.

"Thou hast a need to confer with thy companions, young master?"

Melisande cocked her head to the side, her frown a question at the title given.

"Yes, Maxim, I do. There is much my companions should know, but safety prevents active discussion."

"I understand, young master, but fear not, for this household is defended. Thou may rest in safety within and speak with openness."

"In that I agree, my friend," he replied, though the pain behind his eyes was evident. "Thank you."

To Melisande, he said, "'Tis time at that, m'lady."

Savon'el paced the floor in front of the tapestry while he related all that he knew of himself and how he'd arrived in Catlorian. Rene' sat behind the desk with Arantar perched on the edge of the desk while Bonaire and Melisande occupied the two cushioned chairs. Solothon stood, arms akimbo, at the door to the study, occasionally glancing out at the golem. That one had placed himself in the middle of the great room and stood, still as death, facing the stairway.

"That is all," Savon'el stated. "Though I have been dogged by trial every step of the way, I have no idea who I am, where I'm from, or why Red Wolf appointed me as leader. The responsibility is honorable, but I would be remiss if I did not confide everything. Trust is important, especially now when all seems to be against us. Now, though your choices have brought you to this place, you must stay and I must lead. I am sorry."

The pain was getting worse. The only time it lessened was when physically occupied in battle or practice. Once still and capable of thought, the pounding came back with a vengeance.

The black-haired cleric leaned forward in her chair and watched the savon'el's brow furrow with each word.

"It still hurts?"

"Aye, Melisande, but not as much as before," he responded with a small grin.

"I, for one," stated the Huntsmaster as he sat his wine cup on the desk, "am happy with your leadership, friend. You may not know exactly how you know, but so far your judgments and tactical knowledge have been flawless. I feel that when you find the answers you seek, they will account for all. I'll follow you, no question."

"As will I," stated the knight from the doorway. "You have a regal bearing, friend Savon'el. 'Twould be interesting and rewarding to find from whence it stems."

Rene' looked up from her fingers where they drummed aimlessly on the desktop. She looked at Melisande and, after getting a look of askance, glanced at the mirror in the corner. The cleric looked at it, at Savon'el, and nodded to the mage girl. Then the cleric rose and moved to the blond half elf's side.

"Savon'el, would you mind an experiment of sorts?" Rene' asked.

"An experiment?"

"It may help with your problem, or maybe not. Indulge me, please?"

"As you wish, m'lady."

As Rene' rose from her chair and stepped around the desk to the mirror, Melisande took the blond half elf's arm and led him in front of the silver surface. Arantar followed and stood behind the savon'el as that one glanced from the mage girl to the mirror.

"Relax your thoughts, my friend," Rene' said softly. "Then gaze into the mirror."

Savon'el closed his eyes, sighed, and looked.

The image in the mirror swirled, shifted through numerous distorted scenes, and then cleared.

He saw himself, though older and dressed in fine clothing, with a thin circle of gold on his brow and a sheathed bastard sword in his hands. Strangely, he knew the sword had meaning. Obviously, from the design of the sheath and the hilt protruding from it, it was not the one he now carried, but it had a familiar feel...

The pounding in his head threatened to blind him as it increased with the effort to remember why...

Rene' felt it as well through her empathic wall.

The image distorted again and returned to the present and the image of the savon'el with both hands pressed to his temples.

"I'm sorry," said the golden mage girl softly. "I only meant..."

The mirror swirled again. When the image cleared, a man stared back. He was grim-faced and of huge proportions, dressed in black buckskin with eight silver shirakens mounted on a leather sash across his body. He held a pair of bared katanas in his hands.

Melisande could have sworn she'd seen this man in Catlorian, but she couldn't remember where or when.

"Is this the enemy, Savon'el?" she asked without looking from the image in the mirror.

He lifted his head from his hands and looked. The pain in his temples increased with the effort to break through to those elusive memories.

"This is an image from your past, I think, Savon'el," Rene' said. "Something you need to remember, but it seems every time something is tried to restore your memories, the pain increases to defend the block placed there." She pursed her lips and tapped a finger on her chin. "May I try something else?"

"If you think it will help, yes. I feel that I should know him, the fellow there in the mirror, but…" he sighed and brought his hands back to his temples. "Anything you can do will be welcome. I feel that everything is just there out of reach and is taunting me."

He sighed again.

"Do what you will. What must I do?"

"Trust me," she said as she cupped his chin in her small hand and raised his eyes to meet hers. "Blank your mind. Try to think of nothing at all. Empty your mind of all…"

She droned on as Savon'el's eyes began to droop. When she felt he was ready, she gathered her talent and molded it into a thin beam. She'd used this method many times before to enter the minds of the suffering and empathically pull soothing healing from within. Sl'everin called it "self-reparation".

Rene' probed that barrier, found resistance, and pushed.

Whatever guarded the savon'el's mind pushed back hard! Rene' reacted as if she'd been slapped. Savon'el moaned and slumped as the pain almost crippled him. Melisande steadied Rene' as the Huntsmaster caught Savon'el before he collapsed.

"Melisande," said the mage girl in a shaken voice as she grasped the cleric's arm, "I've caused him more pain. Please, if you can, give him some peace."

"But what of you? You've gone pale."

"See to him first. Then we will talk."

She helped Rene' to the chair behind the desk while Arantar led the blond half elf to the chair vacated by the cleric.

After assuring herself that Rene' was all right, Melisande came to Savon'el and sat on the arm of his chair to rub his temples softly with her fingertips.

A light tap on her bottom and a slurred "I got somethin' here might help" brought her attention to the occupant of the other chair.

Bonaire held a small silver flask out toward her in a wavering hand, the grin on his face proof that the contents were not poison.

"What is this?" she asked. "Where did you get it?"

"I foun' a bottle an' that flask tucked away inna wine cab'net inna kitchen," he said, his eyes drooping a bit. "It's good stuff too, but it's kinda strong."

Then, with a grin, he fell out of the chair onto the floor unconscious. Arantar picked him up and carried him into the great room to the newly rebuilt bed and dropped him onto it. The Huntsmaster shook his head with a frown and returned to the study.

Melisande opened the flask and was rewarded with the bloom of two-thousand-year-old brandy. It enveloped her in soothing calm and she placed the open flask in Savon'el's hand.

"Sip this. It will definitely help."

The blond half elf lifted the flask to his lips and drank. The brandy slid smoothly down his throat to his stomach where its warmth radiated out to his limbs and head immediately.

"I see a boat...a fishing boat," he murmured, "a leather flask and a big red-headed fisherman."

Melisande lifted the savon'el's head with her hand and watched the calm flow through him.

"Does anyone know of any fishing villages," she asked without looking away, "or of anyone matching his description?"

The Huntsmaster frowned.

"We brought a contingent of elves when we heard of a band of slavers working the eastern coastline south of Seaborne. Let's see..."

He ticked off the names of the villages through which he'd tracked the slavers until...

"Seafoam."

"Seafoam?" asked Savon'el as he turned his head toward the Huntsmaster, the name screaming at him for recognition.

"Yes, my friend. It was one of the last the slavers hit. It was populated with ex-gladiators and their families, but it seems most of the men were at sea when the slavers came. By the signs we read, they killed all of the old men and boys and took all of the girls and women." He looked at Savon'el. "Do you know the place?"

"I know I should, but..." Savon'el winced at the pain and shook his head. "It's hopeless."

"Nothing is hopeless, my friend," said Melisande as she took his face in her hands and gazed into those amber eyes. "May the peace of Freya grant you rest," she whispered.

Then she kissed him. The power of her calling flowed within that kiss and the half elf drifted into soft, painless slumber.

"Your powers are extraordinary, Melisande."

"As are yours, Rene'," she replied as she glanced over at the golden mage. "How do you fare?"

"Better now," the mage girl sighed. "I've never run into this type and power of resistance before, and what's more, it seems to have been induced."

"Induced, Rene'?" asked the Huntsmaster.

"Yes." Then Rene' told the knight and Huntsmaster about the spell cast as they left Catlorian.

"I don't believe that this was caused by that instance, but was rather thwarted by it, if you get my meaning?" At the quizzical looks she received, she continued, "His memories, from what he told us, were removed long before he arrived in Catlorian. The power I felt when I tried to probe his memories is very strong, maybe strong enough to beat off a weaker casting, I don't know. I do know, however, that he was robbed of his memories for a reason, though I cannot fathom it."

"If he knows of that destiny too soon..." whispered the cleric.

"What's that?"

"Oh! Sorry, Rene'. It's just something Brea said. She said something about him not knowing his destiny too soon, for whatever that's worth. I don't know if it's pertinent but..." She sighed and looked back at the sleeping half elf. "It seems we must wait for whatever or whoever caused this to remove it."

"I believe you are correct," Rene' mused, her fingertips again tapping at her chin. "Whatever drives him and whatever is locked in his mind will no doubt affect our lives. Unfortunately, or fortunately, depending on how each of us sees it, our fate is irrevocably tied to his."

"That may be true, Rene'," said the Huntsmaster, a frown of anger just tingeing his voice, "but this is the first I've heard of a spell being cast on our friend. Just when were you going to tell us of this?"

"We, Melisande and I, just—"

"You must not assume, Rene'. There is just too much danger not to give us whatever tactical advantage we can get. I don't know that we could have done anything about it, but it should have been our choice. If we are to go forward, there must be trust. We depend on you two for answers so that Savon'el, Solothon, and I can properly defend your efforts. Please don't leave us out."

"I'm sorry, Arantar. It won't happen again, I promise."

"I believe you, m'lady, but I cannot stress enough that we all must do our part at keeping each other informed."

Rene' nodded at the Huntsmaster and her eyes sought her hands as they rested on the desk. Arantar's frown softened as he took in her sad visage.

"I'm sorry, m'lady, but you must understand. We are all in this together. You and Melisande are important to us for the talents each of you holds. We also need the savon'el, though not one of us can tell why at this time. Even now I see the strain on you and our cleric as you try to do everything yourself."

He stopped and crossed to the desk and lifted the girl's face to his eyes with a finger.

"Remember when I told Savon'el that he shouldn't take on everything himself? I say the same to you. Do not try to solve this puzzle by yourself. We are here and we can help."

He stood and looked from Rene' to Melisande.

"You look tired and you both need rest."

"I am," she sighed as she placed both hands on the desk and rose from the chair, "and if one of you gentlemen would please remove young Bonaire from the only bed this house offers, Melisande and I would like very much to use it."

Arantar grinned as he moved to the study door.

"Allow me, dear ladies."

Eton rolled into his cloak beside the small fire and was soon in the "awake-sleep" of the ranger. The tawny puma slipped silently from the forest and lay beside the large youth with its head on his ankles.

A wrinkle in the fabric of the air brought the cat's attention to the edge of the small clearing. A figure appeared there, placed a forefinger to his lips, and smiled.

Fleet watched as the figure disappeared again, began to purr, and closed his eyes.

Chapter Twenty-nine

Try as she might, Rene' couldn't force herself into her healing trance. She was surrounded by eons of information and history just waiting for her to scoop it into her hungry mind. She sighed softly and, moving carefully not to wake the black-haired cleric next to her, rose from the warmth of the bed.

She glanced about the room in the dim firelight. Her eyes stopped at the bundle that was Bonaire, who lay before the hearth covered with a blanket from the house stores. She wondered again how one of her race could sleep, but she shrugged it off as a bad habit the young elf had picked up.

She picked up a small piece of wood from the woodbin and placed it on the andirons. Autumn was turning to winter and it invaded the warmth of this house. She knew that the chill she felt was not only from the cold. All that had happened on this trek fell heavily on her sensibilities as she pulled the satin robe she wore closer about her.

Her movement caused the Huntsmaster to stir; his eyes opened and his mind was totally alert. He glanced about, nothing missing his quick assessment, and when he saw it was Rene', he slipped back into his half-sleep.

The girl saw the way the knight sat with his back against the wall beside the doorway, his resting trance obvious to her. She heard the sound of soft tapping and knew that somewhere in the house Maxim was repairing her companion's armor. She smiled and stepped into the study.

Light still glowed dimly from the ceiling and came up a bit at her command. She'd found the commands to control it from the book Maxim had provided. She softly stepped by the chair where the savon'el slept with a blanket tucked about him, no doubt by Melisande. He murmured softly as the girl took the chair at the desk and picked up the book she'd been reading earlier.

"Autumn? Can't be."

Rene' looked up to see the blond half elf's brows knitted in confusion, though his eyes were still closed in sleep.

"I must find...wood elves are not...Cully?"

A glimmer behind the half elf brought her eyes to the swirling mirror. The distorted visions that flowed across it reminded her of the one in Yarda's study and the results when the old mage would wander too far from it during one of his lessons.

She hurriedly but quietly rose and pulled the mirror closer to the sleeping half elf.

The images grew clearer. There was a village on the coast upon a white cliff above a blue bay. The images flickered through images of smiling fishermen, women, and children. It seemed to linger on a small fishing boat with a huge red-headed fisherman at the helm. He smiled and motioned toward her to come.

Then the image shifted to the same village, now decimated with bodies laying about in grotesque abandon. The same redhead filled the mirror, but he was no longer smiling. He was looking out to sea and speaking. Though Rene' could hear nothing, she felt the anger seething and when the figure faced the mirror she felt the hatred, not for the listener but for the cause of the destruction.

"Seafoam..."

The sad murmur told her everything, yet the image shifted again. Trees! She saw trees whisking by, and it seemed the farther she went with Savon'el through this journey, the older the trees became. She began to recognize the kind only found within the Eldewood Vales and wondered.

She saw the white surface of the King's Way. Then a tall figure in a dark cloak with mirrored eyes and Red Wolf whisked across the mirror in short order. She saw something cover part of the vision of Wanderer and the barbarian, but she was not prepared for the visions that followed.

A huge man sat astride a large black warhorse, his armor and his mount's were shining silver. His red beard was lined with gray as it spilt from his silver helm. His blue eyes were hard as was his visage. On his breast there was a rearing dragon rampant on a field of red and, noted the golden mage girl, no lance pierced the dragon's heart. The sword in the saddle sheath was of the wide-bladed Bastard two-handed style with a well-worn leather hilt.

The scene shifted again to show the smiling face of a pretty Elvin woman dressed in garments usually worn in court. That face was replaced and Rene' took an involuntary step back.

The leering grin and the red-rimmed eyes of the daku in black screamed hatred for the savon'el. The staff he held bore a crystal, a red crystal carved in the image of a spider. The daku laughed as red fire sprang up behind him. The scene shifted to the silver armor on the floor engulfed in that same red fire.

Rene' glanced at the savon'el and saw the tear as it trickled down the side of his face. The scene swirled to show two mirrored silver eyes and suddenly herself sitting on the arm of the chair, her mouth agape at the horror she'd witnessed.

"Princess Dorvair...Mother..."

Rene' looked down at the half elf and, after just a few more incoherent mumbles, his face softened and he slept dreamless.

She rose, swallowed, and pushed the mirror against the wall, partially covering the tapestry map that hung there. She looked back at the savon'el and shook her head.

"I don't know what to do, friend," she whispered. "I could help, but I'm almost afraid of the answers."

"What answers, Rene'?"

"Wha...?" she gasped as her eyes found the Huntsmaster in the doorway.

"I sleep only lightly, m'lady. I heard you move the mirror and the words he spoke. Do you have an explanation?"

"I'm not sure I..." she began. Then, as she felt the fear this warrior had for his companion and friend, as well as his deep responsibility for all of them, she sighed. "I'll tell you what I know, but as for telling him or the rest..."

Arantar sat on the edge of the desk while Rene' returned to her chair. She folded her hands over the book she'd left and began. After the telling, Arantar's look turned stern.

"I don't know, Huntsmaster. Melisande was told by Brea that it could be destructive should our friend know his past too soon. If we show him what we found, would it help or harm? Do we keep this from him and the others, and would that be fair? I just don't know."

The Huntsmaster saw the indecision on the girl's face and sighed. Then he smiled.

"Rene', I don't have an answer, but I do know that most clarity comes from a rested mind. Let us take this up again in the morning. If it is to be, we will reason it then."

Later, after Arantar had returned to his blanket, Rene' sat and thumbed through some of the books from the bookcase. She opened one on the crafting of weapons from bone and read.

"Each will only cause damage to living tissue. Caution: Any used against the donor will result in damage to the wielder."

She closed that book and opened another, this one a book of potions. From the table of contents, all listed were offensive in nature.

"Potion of diseases," she read. "Liquid fire. Potion of withering manhood..."

She closed the book quickly and took a deep breath. Offensive and disgusting, she decided.

The third book she opened had but "Goals" as a title.

Under the heading "Marked for Termination," Prince LeMand and Lady Galen led the list, with the four Lord Rangers next. The knight captains of the Order of the Laurel were followed by several names of dragons, both metallic and pastel, many of which were crossed out. Rene' deduced that "termination" had removed those names.

Cashme're's name was numbered in the top, but still below the knight captains. She'd known the ranger for many years, but it was strange to see his name on this ancient document. How could her ranger live so long? He was not Elvin with the life span a thing of legend to some. Then she remembered the crystal he wore about his neck and wondered. She shook her head and read on.

There were several names listed under the title "Sylvan," but she was puzzled at the question mark placed next to the name "Tensor." What was the meaning of this singling out of the legendary Elvin Lord?

"Canst thou not sleep, mistress?"

The soft deep voice from the doorway roused her from her musings and she closed the book. She looked toward the doorway where Maxim knelt and again wondered at this gentle warrior.

"My kind have no need for sleep as others do, Maxim," she said as she rose and crossed to the doorway. "Though my body craves rest, there is just too much here that calls to me and far too little time allowed."

"Time, mistress?"

"I've a feeling that our time here will soon come to a close. Whatever is after us," she began, then knitted her brow, "or before us, won't wait on our convenience, and I will not have it find us here. Each of us, my companions and I, have given up our individuality to find answers to unasked questions, the answers at our journey's end."

"Where wilt thou go, mistress? If evil chases thee, here would be the best place to fight it."

"I know, Maxim, but we have a mission...well, at least I do."

She sighed and looked to the warrior's helm slits hoping, maybe, to find kind eyes.

"We must travel to the source of the Lost Souls River to an abandoned keep to remove some items, much as you have done here, to keep them from the hand of evil."

"You travel to Radagast's Rest, mistress?" said the guardian softly. "This is a very dangerous place, a place where Radagast trained others in his dark arts. My master spoke of a Well of Darkness"—Rene' gasped as she remembered Wanderer's words in Catlorian—"from whence Radagast called up demons of incredible evil."

Rene' had to control her heart, so loudly did it pound in her ears.

"The keep belonged to Radagast?"

"Yes, mistress, but Radagast is no more, dust e'er my master departed. Yet even if his keep were abandoned as thou has stated, his dark power may still reside within that evil place. I fear thou travel toward thy doom, mistress. All of my master's former Talon are long dead. I see no reasoning that would drive thee toward that evil place."

She paused and hung her head for a moment. When she looked back at the warrior, she knew she would have to tell him.

"Maxim, I think...we think that Banshe'e is still alive and has returned here to wreak havoc upon this world. Some of us have been asked to travel to dangerous places to secure some of the more powerful artifacts to keep them from him or others who serve his evil. I know your master served him—"

"Yes, mistress, but he confided that he wished to end the evil that had been wrought with his handiwork. The lances, for instance, my master worked with a...girl to hide them from Banshe'e. I think that that was why my master is no longer..."

The great head bowed and he seemed to sigh.

"Maxim, my friend, I could stay here for years attempting to absorb but a small part of the knowledge of your master, but I'm afraid centuries would not be enough."

"Mistress," began the golem in a deep, soft tone, his head coming up, "this household has lasted these many centuries and will still be here when thou hast completed thy mission...answered the unasked. I shall remember thee and thine, mistress, and on mine honor, thou shalt have a place here when thee return."

The tears ran freely now as the golden mage girl placed a small hand on the gentle guardian's arm.

"Thank you, my friend."

She recovered quickly and, after brushing the tears away with the back of her hand, grinned.

"I believe I would enjoy a tour, if that is permissible? I believe you've shown but a small part of the makeup of this household. If I'm not mistaken, there is much more to this place than we've seen."

"You are quite correct, mistress. I should be pleased to show thee all there is to show, yet again I must caution thee not to touch lest I explain. What I would show are restricted areas, and though I am bound by my vows, those bonds slacken at each meeting. As thee become more proficient, I feel the bonds will unravel entire."

Maxim rose and allowed the girl to follow him to the large door to the armory. They moved quietly so as not to wake those sleeping next to the hearth and the girl sleeping in the bed. As the steel guardian opened the door, the Huntsmaster shifted in his blanket and his eyes opened for a moment. Rene' smiled and those steel blue eyes closed once more. The mage girl was comforted in the knowledge that once they left this place, his talents would help to maintain the security she felt here.

Maxim closed the door carefully behind them and moved halfway down the small hallway. When he stopped, a hand went to a panel high on the wall, and as he pressed it, a secret door slid silently away. He stepped through the rather large opening and the ceiling began to glow softly, much as the one in the study had done.

Rene' stepped into a room devoid of furnishings, save the small pentacle with its five small pillars placed in the very center of the room. It was a miniature of the Druid's Pentacles she'd used for most of her young life, but something was different.

"This," explained the golem, "is my master's...my former master's Room of Summoning. Lord Rairy used it to summon those whose council he required."

He watched the girl as she concentrated on the runes of the small pillars.

"I see that thou hast found the strangeness in the patterns upon the pillars."

Rene' saw that the runes were not exactly those that she was used to seeing. She'd used this method of travel for years, yet she had never really studied the runes that appeared on those larger portals. Now she looked harder and finally she saw it. When it came to her, it was obvious, so obvious that her mouth dropped open in shock.

"If someone were in there, they couldn't get out!"

"Exactly, mistress! Lord Rairy was a very powerful man, yet some of those with whom he conversed were more powerful even than he. Thus, the Runes of Containment were added. My master was powerful and honorable, but he wasn't careless, though..."

"I'm beginning to have more and more respect for your late master's talents." the girl said softly as she watched the guardian's head bow in sadness. "I am certain that he was as proud of you as you were him, my friend."

"Come," Maxim said softly as he glanced at the girl and stepped around the pentacle to the door in the opposite wall. "There is more."

Rene' followed to the door of brass-studded oak. The golem lifted the bar from the iron and brass fittings and pushed the door open. Again the ceiling began to glow softly within.

The light revealed a vast laboratory filled with much more complicated paraphernalia than she'd used as a student in Yarda's alchemy room.

"Maxim," she breathed, "this is incredible!"

She moved toward the rows of vials and the glass plumbing mounted on the low counter.

"Please, mistress!" said the guardian sternly. "Let not thy curiosity cause thee harm!"

She stopped, returned her hands to the pockets in the robe, and turned to the golem. The glow in Maxim's helmet slit had grown much brighter, and she knew she'd come close to straying too far from safety.

"I'm sorry, Maxim. I will try to be more careful. I assure you, I don't wish to have you take up your weapons against me."

"It is not that I would stop thee here, mistress. I would not have to."

Rene' waited while the guardian seemed to sigh.

"Mistress, note how well-preserved everything is within this room as compared to the study."

Rene' looked up at the guardian, then to the room at large. Though a bit cleaner, she could see not much difference. Maybe the lack of a tenant over the past centuries had helped to keep everything in this room so neat and...

Then it struck her. This house was old. The study, even though it was kept clean through the use of the halfling's magic, felt old. Here, there was no such feeling. Only timelessness. Timelessness and power...

"I can see that thou hast come to the correct conclusion, mistress. As thou canst see, this place is exactly as it was left, held in time and warded. The wards are not so obvious as they are within the rest of this household. T'was my master's work, mistress. This place has a special significance for my Lord Rairy. Though the rest of this household contains powerful objects that could be used for evil, his workshop could cause irreplaceable destruction, and in the wrong hands—"

"Or in the hands of a novice. Yes, I see," sighed the girl. She laid a small hand on the guardian's arm. "Thank you."

"Unnecessary, mistress," he said softly as he strolled carefully between the workbenches toward the archway beyond. "There is but one more room that thou shouldest see."

Rene' followed, her hands firmly in the pockets of her robe, but her eyes poured over all of the curious plumbing and containers of alchemy condiments.

Through the archway was another room, but this room contained no furnishings at all, save the swaying curtain on the far wall. It was flanked to either side with a short pedestal crowned with the likeness of a rearing silver dragon. Runes in a language unknown to the mage girl adorned the archway. The graceful writing in platinum splendor rose from behind the dragon on the left, over the curtain to disappear behind the dragon on the right. Rene' stepped closer.

"Lady Rene', please!"

The golem's voice brought her eyes around to him, the voice whispered in the solemn tones of respect for something unseen.

"I'm always saying 'I'm sorry,' aren't I, Maxim?" she said softly, her eyes finding the floor.

"It is not that, exactly, mistress. Look closely at the portal, but do not dare to touch it."

"Portal?" thought the girl as she turned once more to the curtain.

She drew in a sharp breath when it became apparent that what she thought was a swaying purple curtain was in reality the warping of time and space. This portal was not to another room, but another "when" or "where"!

"My Lady!" she breathed.

"Maxim," she asked after a moment to allow for a certain amount of calmness to return to her heart, "where does it go?"

"T'was once the gate through which my master...my former master went in search of the items he required for his brand of weaponry. 'Tis the only portal, in my limited knowledge, that directly links this world to that of dragonkind."

Rene' couldn't breathe. The words she heard went to her heart in the cold realization of the depth of power wielded within this household. After a moment, she shook her head to rid her mind of the shock and turned to the golem.

"You mean that anyone who has access to this room could simply walk through that curtain and be in that most protected of realms? Do the Dragon Lords know of this?"

"They do, mistress, and the portal was sealed from the other side, at Lord Rairy's request, by the Guardian. As my former master explained it, to destroy this portal could unleash power enough to destroy both realms."

The steel guardian seemed to stare into the curtain for a moment and sigh.

"Dragonkind hated my master and his companions for obvious reasons. In the weeks before he left, he was attempting to make some sort of...reparation."

Sadness crept into his words as he continued.

"I would sometimes step through this gate and speak with those upon that plane. I miss those times and the stories the Dragon Lords would tell. I had, and still have, no animosity toward them. Strangely, I could call them friend."

"Maxim, is it common practice to give one such as myself a tour of this magnitude? It would seem that the things you've shown could be considered extremely dangerous if placed in the wrong hands."

His one hand caressed the silver dragon on the right as he sighed.

"My master seemed a bit sad the last day I saw him. He said he would return shortly, though he did not know when. He said that I was to maintain our—and he said 'our', mistress— home while he was away."

Rene' felt the sadness in the steel guardian's heart—strange that emotion, too, should not have been part of his creation.

"Then he told me this: 'Knowledge and power for its own sake is not enough. It is not enough to know thou can do a thing, but rather that thou should or should not. Knowledge should be dispensed only at the level that it can be reasonably and safely received. Some knowledge is hurtful and must be tempered with good sense. Power should be used only in humility and only for the good of the many.'"

His helm turned toward her and she thought she "heard" him smile.

"It seems that my former master had knowledge of thy coming, mistress."

He brushed at the silver statue once more and walked toward the laboratory.

"About the tour, mistress. It was 'common practice,' as thou hast said, for Lord Rairy to allow his visitors to view his accomplishments. Yet they could never remember how they arrived here."

"A mind wipe?" asked the girl as she followed him through the laboratory to the door beyond.

"Selective, mistress. When thou and thy companions leave here, all memories of this location will disappear. Thee, as key holder, wilt remember, but only when thou art resting in safety. 'Tis the best I can do, mistress. I have given thee my trust in the hope of seeing thee again."

He led her through the door to the pentagram room, but stopped at her next question.

"Suppose we don't succeed in this quest, Maxim? Suppose I..."

The steel guardian went to one knee and the light within his helm dimmed.

"It would greave me greatly, mistress, but thou may name another who may gain entrance without thee...should the need arise."

The girl thought for only a moment before replying.

"Melisande only, my friend."

"What of the others?"

"If possible, some will no doubt wish to come here to rest, study, or just to see you once more." She laid a small hand on his knee and added, "You've made friends, Maxim."

Her smile was rewarded by the renewed brightness within that helm.

"Melisande or I will bring them here when the time comes. Until then..."

"What of the princeling?"

"The what?"

"The youth who e'en now sleeps within the study in fitfulness?"

"Why do you say 'princeling'?"

"I smell royal blood flowing in his veins. Have I spoken wrongly, mistress?"

The girl's brow furrowed as the realization caught her. All of the evidence of the past weeks leapt to her agile mind. His bearing, his tactical knowledge, and his power of presence all brought to mind those with whom she'd moved in the past—those of the court!

"You may be right, Maxim," she said after a moment, "though even he doesn't seem to realize it." After a moment longer in thought, she added, "I think that with all we've learned about his condition thus far, it could be wrong at this point to allow him this knowledge. There are those who feel that to give him too much information may be his undoing. I just don't know."

She shook her head softly and smiled at the golem.

"Lord Rairy is correct, my friend. Some knowledge should be dispensed with care. If possible, Savon'el will want, I believe, to return here. If so, and if I survive, I will bring him."

"I will look forward to that day, mistress," said the guardian as he rose and opened the secret door.

They walked softly through the main hall to the door to the study. Maxim knelt as the mage girl continued into the study. She saw that the half elf still slept soundly, sighed, and turned again to Maxim.

"May I have the use of some of the books and scrolls to take with me for study?"

"Of course, mistress. I would have suggested it if thou had not."

Her hand fell on the small chest Arantar had pulled from beneath the bed. The cool feel of the metal brought a frown and the question softly from her lips.

"What is in here?"

"In where, mistress?"

"Oh, I'm sorry, Maxim," she replied, her smile bringing softness back to her face. "I was wondering, aloud it seems, what was locked so tightly into this chest. I've not seen this many locks on anything this small before."

"If thou wilt," he said as he opened his breastplate and removed a small key, "I will show thee. Bring it and the key ring within the weapons chest to me for, as thou may know, I cannot come within the confines of this study."

The girl placed the small chest on the floor in the doorway and, after unlocking the wardrobe, brought the ring of keys to the steel guardian.

He inserted his key into the top keyhole, turned it to the right and then the left, and left it there as he inserted certain of the keys from the key ring into each of the other five keyholes. Rene' heard a small click and Maxim lifted the lid from the box.

There, in a soft bed of blue satin, lay eight small stones of different sizes and shapes. There were two in the shape of a small spindle, cylindrical and tapered on each end, and they were a bit over one inch long and one half inch in diameter. They were white and glistened as if made of the finest pearl.

Next to them lay two strangely shaped stones of translucent pink. The base of these stones was one inch by a half inch, but the other sides were cut in rather haphazard rhomboidal shapes.

The last four of the stones were prisms, five sided on the two opposing sides and about an inch and a half long. The color was a cloudy pink tinge, the color of a rose in bloom, yet dusty in its translucence.

Rene' refrained from touching these stones. Her studies of the legendary "Ioun Stones" of legend told her that to touch one of these could make it unusable for others. She knew the value of these for, outside of its soft bed, each of these would float, neither rising nor falling, until retrieved by its owner. If she were to be able to distribute these to her companions, she would have to take great care in their handling.

Once launched, these stones would orbit the owner's head supplying whatever magical supplement the user required. The spindles, for example, would tend to increase the mage girl's power to heal her own hurts, while the strange rhomboidal stones would increase her stamina and ability to sustain in desperate situations.

"Maxim," she asked as she pointed at the dusty rose prisms, "do you know the properties of these prisms?"

"Yes, mistress," he responded softly. "Those would provide an extra layer of protection to the bearer, as if armor were added to their person."

"They could help protect them in combat?"

"Yes, mistress. My master used these frequently, he being of small stature, to great avail."

"I see." Rene' tapped a finger to her chin before she continued. "Maxim, would you have any objections to my taking these for our use?"

"No, mistress, though I would ask that you leave something behind as replacement that you would deem valuable."

The girl thought for a moment.

"My clothing is missing. I assume that you have taken them for cleaning?"

"Yes, mistress."

"In one of the pockets you will find several gold pieces and a few small jewels. Take them as payment for these."

"I said nothing of payment, mistress. I spoke only of replacement with something thee values. It would seem to me that should thou leave something thee prizes, thy return will be of a certainty."

Rene' thought for only a moment before she slowly reached behind her neck and unclasped the chain that bore the delicate golden heart about her throat. She held it toward the guardian and, with a small catch in her voice, explained.

"This was a gift from a special person in my life. I thought I would never see the day that I would willingly part with it." Then, as she laid it into the guardian's open hand, she added, "I would be honored if you would hold this until my return, my friend."

"I shall keep it here within me and safe until thou come to claim it, mistress."

Rene' watched as he opened his breastplate, removed a small velvet pouch into which the golden heart was placed, and placed it within his chest.

"Maxim," she asked softly, "is there anything I can do for you?"

The deep soft voice of the steel guardian floated through the doorway.

"Only that thee say naught of good-bye when thee and thy companions depart. Say only 'Until I return,' if you please. I've not had this much comfort from any in a very long time. Do not forget me, mistress, for I'll not forget thee."

Then he stood and moved quietly through the door to the armory. Moments later, the soft hammering began again.

Rene' sighed and, after stepping softly past the resting knight at the stairwell, went up into the night air. The chirping of night insects greeted her and she felt safe and at home.

It was bright, this night, so bright that the stars were only barely visible. The moons, the "Lords of Light" as they were called in her childhood, were, all three, in the night sky, two traveling from east to west and one from west to east.

She frowned. According to her studies of lore, only a few months were left before these moons would align themselves with Ta'el with unknown consequences.

A new chill invaded her body with the thought and she pulled her robe about her and went back inside.

Chapter Thirty

Melisande found the mage girl at the desk the next morning, still reading. She tucked the blanket about the savon'el and sat in the other easy chair.

"Don't you ever sleep?"

"No real need, Melisande," Rene' responded as she closed the book and clasped her hands on top of it. "Things...happened here last night. Things we must discuss before Savon'el awakes."

"He won't wake until I wake him."

"Good! Now..." she began, and the golden mage girl told Melisande all that had happened, from the mirror to the tour.

"Now," she continued with a sigh, "we have to make a decision. Do we try and help him by replaying the visions stored in the mirror, or do we keep this to ourselves in the hope that he may remember on his own? The former may bring more pain, maybe more than he can withstand, but the latter may mean that we will not succeed nor survive. We don't know who or what hunts him so passionately, and if it catches him, are we powerful enough together to stop it?"

"I believe he should be told here and now," came a voice from the study door.

Arantar leaned against the doorjamb and, as green and golden eyes fell on him, he continued.

"You are correct in your assessment of our foe's power, but I would want to know, were I in Savon'el's boots, all there is to know. To keep any information that might help from him and hope he finds it on his own at some later time would be wrong and, I believe, dangerous. Besides," he continued, a small grin warming his stern visage, "where better to seek what answers we can but in a place of power as this is with a friend as powerful as Maxim?"

Melisande moved to the arm of the chair occupied by the blond half elf and stroked his hair softly.

"But what if the pain is too great and it kills him? I can feel the pain he is in almost incessantly. I can't see how he bears it now. What of after?"

"I understand, m'lady, but I still would want to know. You and Lady Rene' are gifted in your arts. If it gets to be too much, will you be aware of it?"

He stepped away from the door and stood behind the sleeping savon'el.

"I have seen both of you working hard together for this fellowship, and I have faith that you will monitor his condition closely and will know when too much is too much. I will be here to do whatever you recommend and will bow to your expertise. You must choose whether to proceed or not, for I am not skilled in your disciplines."

Rene' stood, stepped around the desk, and leaned on the front of it facing the savon'el and cleric. Her eyes dropped and she sighed.

"The way I see it, we really have no choice," she said softly, her voice filled with dread. "If we show him and it cannot help, we may be lost. If we do nothing, we may still be lost. Frankly, if we are successful and he regains his entire memory, we could still be walking to our deaths."

She stood and as she folded her arms in front of her, she turned hard golden eyes on the blond half elf and then the cleric.

"Arantar is right. I would want to know. What say you?"

Melisande turned to the Huntsmaster and received a curt nod. Then, as the mage girl repositioned the mirror before the savon'el, the cleric brushed an errant hair from Savon'el's brow and kissed it.

"Awaken to the new day," she whispered.

Savon'el's eyes fluttered open, and as he saw Melisande, he smiled.

"Good morning, m'lady," he stated in a sleepy voice.

"That has yet to be determined," replied the mage girl from behind Melisande. "Savon'el, we must talk."

"What is it?" he asked a bit panicked as he strained to look beyond the cleric. "Have I done something in my sleep to—"

"Nothing like that, my friend," replied the Huntsmaster as he laid a strong hand on his friend's shoulder.

"Why would you ask that, Savon'el?" asked the mage girl with a frown.

"Why? Because my memory begins a scant few weeks ago and I am... frightened to death of who I might be, as you should! What could I have been or done to warrant this much malicious hatred and from an unknown quarter? I've been afraid to sleep lest I return to that person and bring harm to you all!"

"I don't fear that, friend, because I have a...talent that allows me to read a person's character. It is not a part of his memory, but his very being. You, on your worst day, could never be whom you fear. It's not in your makeup."

"Yes, Rene', but suppose I am but a pawn to this evil and have drawn you here for it to take you? I know you all have stated that you were cast here before you met me. Suppose I am the 'Judas Goat' intended to bring you to my...master?"

Arantar's hand tightened softly on Savon'el's shoulder as the mage girl replied. "That too is not possible. You have shown a...let us say a regal bearing, my friend, and knowledge of tactics that can only have come from training at the hands of a master. Again, your makeup would not allow you to be duped into being used. Of this I am certain."

She looked deep into those amber eyes and again marveled as they went from molten to calm at her words.

"Now," she continued as she moved toward the mirror, "there may be a way to help you to regain some or all of your memory, but it may come with a price."

Rene' angled the mirror so that they might all see what it displayed. She tapped Melisande on the arm, and as the cleric moved from the arm of the chair to kneel next to it, she gave the mage girl a look that read, "Don't harm him." Rene' gave her a slight nod and turned her attention to the blond half elf.

"During last evening as you slept, the Mirror of Probabilities remained linked to your mind. I've seen this happen more than once in my former master's study when he forgot to release his mirror, and I recognized the signs. I brought the mirror close to you and as you spoke in your sleep, the images you saw in your dreams were recorded into this mirror. After last evening's pain-filled session, I am not sure what will happen, but I have the talent to call these images back for you, but only if you wish it."

The constant pain he'd been under was returning slowly upon his awakening. At the mage girl's words, the pain increased behind his eyes and he closed them for a moment. It seemed that the closer he came to the truth, the greater the pain became.

The hand on his shoulder gently squeezed it again and he knew. Arantar would protect them should he become what he feared. He nodded and raised his eyes to the mirror.

"Please, m'lady, I must know."

Rene' smiled softly and, as she stroked a certain rune on the mirror's border, she whispered the words she'd learned many years before in the house of Yarda.

The images flashed across the mirror's surface, much in the way they'd done the night before, but nothing registered until the image of the man in silver plate came into view.

"Father?" he said softly, the word coming unbidden to his lips.

Through his pain, he knew, even before the image of the armor engulfed in demon fire, that "Father" was dead.

"Mother" was the Elvin woman displayed, though "Royal Concubine" was the title more readily associated in his mind.

His hands were to his temples now, the pain almost intolerable, yet he refused to turn his gaze away.

"Please, Rene'," said the cleric. "Enough!"

"No!" Savon'el shouted. "I need—"

The memories came on; the trawler, the fisherman.

"Cully?" he said softly. "I should know more than a name! Damn!"

The mirror ran rampant now, following the half elf's mind through its turmoil. The figure of a man in black cloak with mirrored silver eyes sat at a campsite close to the King's Way, then the image later in the forest brought a gasp from Melisande.

"Damned Meddler!" came from the tormented half elf as the vision turned to his nightmare.

"He did this?" asked Melisande as she glanced at the savon'el. "Wanderer is the enemy?"

"No, m'lady," he rasped through his pain, "he is!"

The leering grin of the half daku brought instant anger to the Huntsmaster as he stood behind his friend, and his grip on the savon'el's shoulder tightened. He saw the emblem on this evil one's staff, the emblem of a glowing red spider.

"Who is he, Savon'el?" he asked through gritted teeth.

"That is the problem, Huntsmaster. I have no name to go with the face. I know not what he's done, nor why he is the enemy. I only know that he is the cause of my loss, whether intentional or inadvertent. He is the reason for all of this, but I just don't know..."

He dropped his gaze to his hands. The pain was lessening slowly as the memories came, but his confusion increased with every image. Who he was, was still up for discussion. It seemed he could be royalty, but he could as well be a guard or just a soldier. His skill at arms could give evidence of either. He shook his head.

A sudden grip on his shoulder caused him to look up into the granite face displayed in the mirror. The big man wore black leather with a sash of silver shirakens across his chest. In his hands he held two bared katanas.

"Yokura."

As before, the name registered as one he knew, but the mixed feelings confused the memory. He knew he'd had many disagreements with the big warrior, though he had no memory of them. He respected this man, but...

He grinned in his pain as the word "asshole" came through to be impressed on the big warrior. The pain that had seemed to be waning suddenly jumped to full strength, and the savon'el closed his eyes and moaned.

"Please, Rene'," said Melisande as she returned to her place on the arm of the chair and placed her hands over his at his temples. "Enough. Please!"

Rene' spoke a word and the link was severed. The mirror was a mirror no longer. The images were gone, but a dull sheen now rested upon its surface. She pushed the mirror away and knelt in front of the chair.

"How do you fare?" she asked. "And more importantly, am I still a friend?"

Savon'el opened one eye and grinned at the mage girl through his pain.

"Yes, Lady Rene', a friend and a thankful one. I know more now than I did yesterday, thanks to you, and if I read the images correctly, that daku hates me as much as I hate him. 'Why' eludes me, but at least I know I am not that one's lackey. It may not seem like much, but every small victory is at least a victory. I am in your debt."

"Believe me, Savon'el," she said as she rose and pushed the now-dull mirror back against the wall, "this was a joint decision. I could not have done this on my own, nor would I have."

"Then," he said, his right hand going to Melisande's cheek and his left to the hand resting on his shoulder, "thank you all."

Rene' glanced though the doorway and noted that the knight was no longer sitting next to the stairway.

"Where is Solothon?"

The youth scratched between the puma's ears as he watched the hut through the brush. There was enough cover between him and the hut to keep him and his companion hidden, even from the elf in chain mail who appeared a moment ago at the door and disappeared around the back. He had decided to move to a better vantage point to see both the front and side of the hut.

"The blond one will pay for his betrayal, Fleet." he whispered through his ruined throat as he crouched ready to move.

The light cough behind him threw the youth's body into action as he turned and his hands filled with steel.

The man stood casually, his arms folded, and smiled. He was tall, six feet plus, and his smile was of reassured tolerance. He wore his black, shoulder-length hair tied back with a strip of leather as a headband. His eyes danced in amusement as the youth before him swept the large blade in his gauntleted left hand from side to side and waited. The broadsword at the man's right shoulder was ignored as his smile broadened.

"Would you fight me, youth?"

"Only at need, sir," came the whispered reply.

The man looked over the youth's head toward the hut.

"The one you stalk has no family blood on him."

"Yet he has my father's blade?"

Eton settled into his fighting crouch as his angry eyes surveyed this possible opponent. The man's smile was beginning to wane as he looked into the youth's stormy eyes.

"You should take more heed to your companion," he said softly as he went to one knee. "He knows a friend, even if you don't."

Eton glanced down at the puma and grinned. Fleet lay with his head on his front paws and purred deep in his chest.

The young warrior straightened up and returned the long sword to the sheath at his back. The Bourjon blade remained in his gauntleted hand out of caution, but the man seemed to accept that.

"Now," said the man as the puma padded to him and received the petting he knew he would receive, "you say he has your father's sword?"

"Yes. My father would never let that sword out of his hands unless it were stolen."

"Even at need? Culligan Vandergast—"

As the name rippled from the stranger's mouth, Eton's mouth dropped open.

"Oh yes, I know him, and he knows me," stated the man as he watched Eton sit. "I will tell you this. Culligan gave the youth his sword, not as 'booty,' but to be used to identify him to the wood elves. Unfortunately, those wary souls only watched."

"Do you know where my father is?" whispered the youth.

"He is...where he is, and he doesn't need your help. These, however, do."

"I would rather go to my father. It seems I've wasted time enough on that one."

"The blond one? Yes, I suppose tracking and watching him and his companions from hiding could be considered waste, but joining them would not be. Your talents are needed, Nethan."

"How do you know that name?"

"I know a great deal, Nethan DeBurge, but I believe you will find more answers with them if I don't tell you all that I know of you."

"What do you want of me?"

The man sighed. "As I said before, join them, but protect the blond half elf especially. It is imperative that that one come through this ordeal alive."

"I don't understand—"

"Don't try," came the quick reply. "You may be able to turn the tide for them. Maybe not, but they will fare better with you along and not skulking in the brush."

The man removed a ring from his finger and tossed it to the young warrior. The youth caught it and looked from it to the stranger.

"If you need my help, simply dash it on the surface of one of the Druid's Pentacles. I will come at once."

"Thank you, lord," whispered the youth as he slipped the ring on his right little finger and stood.

"Don't thank me too soon, Nethan," stated the man as he too rose. "There are terrible enemies tracking your charge and great danger from being at his side, but there is where you and your companion must be."

The man reached down and scratched the puma between the ears and looked toward the hut. Eton looked the man over, noting the way his clothing seemed to reflect everything around him in perfect camouflage.

"Who are you, lord?" asked the youth in his perpetual whisper.

The man looked back at Eton and smiled.

"I serve the Lords of Light, my friend. Now, we must go."

"Lady Rene'?"

The mage girl turned toward the doorway. Solothon stood outside of that portal, again armored in his tight chain mail, and held a thin box, about a half a foot square, toward her.

"I found this in the stable under some molded straw as I checked on our mounts. It does not seem to be locked, yet I felt the need to have you look into it first. I have not the talent to say whether it is magiked or no."

All Bonaire heard was "treasure in stables." As quietly as he was able, he slipped up the stairway and disappeared around the hut.

The knight laid the box into Rene's tiny hands. Then he surveyed the room as the golden mage girl moved to the desk and set the box next to the one already there.

Solothon noted a change in the blond half elf and in those around him. Arantar stood behind him, his hand on the savon'el's shoulder, while Melisande sat on the arm of the chair, her hand firmly clasped in his.

His usual stern countenance slipped ever so slightly into a small grin. He didn't know what had happened to warrant this new bond displayed by his companions and didn't care. He'd vowed to follow this one no matter the consequences and was heartened that he would not be alone.

He heard the large door in the main hall open, stepped through the study door, and watched as Maxim moved toward him and the study. The guardian carried Savon'el's scale on one arm and Melisande's silver mail shirt upon another.

"I've repaired these for thy companions, sir knight, as I did thine," he said as he knelt short of the doorway.

"Thank you, Maxim," the knight responded as he turned toward the door.

He stopped and looked back at the guardian for a moment, then turned to him.

"Maxim, do you have a moment?"

"Of course, sir. What is it?"

"I have with me a... weapon. I am looking for its wielder and, with your knowledge of Wormslayers, I thought you might be able to aid me in my search."

"May I see this weapon?"

Solothon removed one of the shirakens from his pouch and began to cautiously unwrap it from the soft leather.

"I have a...link of sorts to this thing. When not tucked away, it brings me pain. Please study it in haste, for e'en now the pain has begun."

Indeed it had. The birthmark on his left arm flared, the pain goading a grimace.

Maxim saw this, took the weapon quickly, examined it, and returned it to its wrappings. He was pleased when the grimace faded from the knight's face.

"It looks to be gnomish in origin and, from the embossing, made for one of my master's companions."

"Do you know who would have used these?"

After a slight hesitation, Maxim stated, "Of the five, only Radagast would have the talent in its use, but he was dust before my master left. During the war, black crystal was the medium for casting necromancy. Only Radagast would have contracted these, as far as I can remember, and I know not what became of that one's armory. I am sorry, my friend."

"Do you know of any who could use these at this time?"

"If he survived..." The golem stopped and seemed to think. "No, I think not."

Solothon felt that there was more, but decided not to push. He nodded and grinned.

"Thank you again, Maxim," he said and stepped away from the doorway.

Maxim stooped to look through that portal and, as Savon'el turned his head toward him, the guardian addressed him.

"I have repaired the rents in thy and thy companion's armor, young master, but have a query."

Solothon took the Elvin mail shirt on one arm and laid the shining links on Melisande's lap. The girl held the garment out at arm's length and inspected it. There was no hint that a sword had penetrated it at all. She looked up at Maxim with a grin and saw that he held the scale armor by the shoulders.

"Upon the leather of the collar piece," he continued, "I've found the initials 'RA.' 'Tis thine?" At Savon'el's quizzical look, he added, "If thee wish, I can remove them."

The pain in the blond half elf's head had increased. The initials meant something, but what he could not remember. His left hand massaged his forehead as he fought for the fleeting answer.

"No, Maxim," he finally replied. "It, as well as this sword, have much to do with my past. It must stay until I have the answers that I seek."

"As thee wish, young master."

Savon'el rose slowly and crossed to the doorway. Maxim laid the armor over the half elf's arms with a composed nod.

"Thank you, my friend," the half elf said as he turned back toward the others.

He sighed and glanced at his companions. They'd been there too long, he felt, and it was getting harder and harder to justify staying. He sighed again.

"I wish we could stay longer," he began, "but though we all could use the rest and safety of this place, we must remind ourselves of the dangers. We should be prepared to leave at a moment's notice. I would not like to be the cause of violence falling upon this house and upon our new friend."

He sighed again as several of his friends nodded, the frowns of worry now upon their faces.

"I plan to don my armor, as the rest of you must, and begin packing for our withdrawal. Agreed?"

Solothon and the Huntsmaster nodded, and as the savon'el moved toward the bath, they started toward the door to the main room. Maxim stood and allowed them to pass, then he knelt once more. He saw Melisande caress the robe with one hand while the other held the mail shirt on her lap.

"May I be of assistance, m'lady?"

"Well," she replied sheepishly, "it seems that my clothing has taken quite a beating on this trek. I didn't have time to pack a change, and now I find that I have need of trousers and a sturdy blouse. My cloak has disappeared as well, but that, I believe, was your doing."

"Thou art correct, m'lady. Thy cloak has been cleaned and thy weapon repaired and placed within."

He said the last part softly to let the girl know that he knew of the secret of her cloak.

"As for clothing," he continued, "there is little to choose from here. However, I shall seek for thee. Rest while I do, m'lady. Though I wish thee to remain, I'll not restrain thee." He turned to the mage girl as that one returned to the chair behind the desk. "Mistress, thy clothing has been cleaned as well, and I shall return it to thee momentarily. Please wait while I search the closets in the armory for fitting attire for Lady Melisande."

"As you wish, Maxim," replied the mage girl.

She watched as the steel warrior rose and moved toward the door to the armory.

"I'm going to miss him."

Melisande turned her attention to the mage girl. A quizzical look came over her face as Rene' sighed and pulled the thin box Solothon had brought before her on the desk.

"Why so sad Rene'?" she asked. "Maxim said we would be welcome here when we return."

"Return? Really?" said the mage girl as she frowned at the cleric. "The past weeks have seen us run out of Catlorian by a powerful necromancer and the place we *must* go is the former fortress of a powerful and evil necromancer! Let's face it, Melisande, this is not a spring outing we are on! There is a good chance that few of us, if any at all, will survive to go anywhere after this!"

Instant fury slapped the mage girl as the black-haired cleric's rage riveted her to her chair.

"You think I don't know this? Do you think that this is a worry only you have privy to? The difference between us, Rene', is that I cannot and will not allow that consequence to linger in my mind! I will survive, and I will do everything in my power to ensure that all of my friends survive as well! I will not die and allow that..." Melisande's hands clenched and unclenched as she fought with her anger. She took a deep breath and glared at the mage girl. "I will survive." she said softly and strode from the study.

Rene' had to remind herself to breathe, so powerful was the rage that followed the cleric.

"This one has much too much hate for what she is," she thought as she gazed after her friend. "I pray to the goddess that she survives this, if for no other reason than to cure herself."

She sighed and turned her attention to the thin box.

Melisande stopped in the middle of the main hall and took a deep breath. Her rage was upon her, though she knew that it was not directed at the mage girl. It was just the thought that...

"How could she even suggest..." she thought. "I must survive for my son's sake!"

She again felt the weakness of loss begin to rise and fought it down.

"No time for that!" she thought angrily. "I've a job to do. Then—"

The door to the armory opened and Maxim motioned her to him. She walked through that door after the guardian, her mind returning to the forced steel of her existence.

Arantar watched the girl disappear into the armory and turned to the knight.

"Solothon, we should make up two extra packs of provisions just in case we are separated."

"Right you are," he stated as he picked up his saddlebag and moved toward the kitchen. "I'll see what can be found to replenish what we've used."

Before he reached the kitchen door, however, the sound of heavy footfalls came to him from the stairway.

He and Arantar turned to see Bonaire almost make it to the bottom of the stairs before he tripped. He sprawled at the foot of the stairway with an "ummf!" The Huntsmaster, with a grin, ran to him and helped him to his feet.

"Are you all right?" he asked, barely able to refrain from laughing at the wobbly way the young elf stood.

"Hey! I'm fine! Really!"

Bonaire tried to take a step and almost fell again.

"Why don't you just sit?" grinned the Huntsmaster as he helped the elf to the stairs.

Solothon shook his head sadly and continued into the kitchen. Arantar moved back to their belongings and, between worried, grinning glances at the young elf, returned to his packing.

Bonaire sat for a moment. Then he remembered the parchment he held crumpled in his hand.

"Uh...Arantar?"

"Just relax, Bonaire. We haven't the time right now. We must pack for our departure."

"But Arantar—"

"Not now, Bonaire."

Bonaire shrugged and sat back to wait until they *did* have time. Until then, he'd just keep his news to himself. "Serve 'em right!" he thought.

Maxim came from the armory carrying Rene's folded garments. He knelt by the door, as was his habit.

"Lady Rene'?" he called softly.

"Yes?" she replied, looking up from the box opened before her.

"I've thy clothing, mistress."

"Thank you, Maxim," she said softly as she stepped to the doorway to receive the bundle. She looked around him into the main hall and asked, "Where is Melisande?"

"Dressing in the armory, mistress. I've found garments that may serve to replace hers."

"That should be interesting," she mused as she moved back to the desk.

She looked up at the sound of the door to the bath opening. Savon'el stepped out, again clothed neck down in the tight fitting scale, his hands still working the buckle at his neck.

"We will have a meeting here within the next twenty minutes, m'lady. I will tell the others." He sighed as he completed the connection at his neck and picked up his sword from the side of the chair where he'd been sleeping. "We shall be relying heavily on what you and Melisande have discovered."

He nodded a short bow and walked out of the study, nodding to Maxim as he passed.

"Excuse me, Maxim," Rene' said as she took her clothing toward the bath. "It seems I have little time left."

"'Tis my loss, mistress," he whispered as Rene' disappeared through the door.

Chapter Thirty-one

"We must be prepared for any happenstance on our journey. That is why I've asked for this time to go over the tactics of our withdrawal from here and the method of travel toward our goal."

The blond half elf addressed his assembled friends solemnly in the study. He paced before the tapestry, his head down and his visage one of thoughtful concern.

Rene' sat at her now-familiar chair behind the desk. Melisande, wrapped in the floor-length fur robe, had taken one of the chairs before it and Bonaire slumped in the other folding and unfolding a small piece of parchment.

Arantar sat on the edge of the desk and cupped his chin in his hand while Solothon leaned against the tapestry next to the device that was once a mirror. The knight held his arms akimbo as his mind raced over similar meetings he'd attended in his young life.

"We must be away from here soon, maybe sooner than we wish, for I don't wish our fate to fall on this place. With that in mind, I believe that an order of march is appropriate. There are but four of us who are fighters—"

"Five!" corrected Melisande sharply as she sat forward in her chair.

"Granted, m'lady," responded Savon'el softly. "I meant no slight. I simply meant that the four of us will be called upon for the heavier fighting should the need arise. You, though warrior trained, are of more use to this party as a healer," he continued as his eyes softened toward the cleric. Then, as his glance took in the rest of his companions, "I will not attempt to deceive anyone here. There is great danger ahead and we will all, at one time or another, have to take up weapons in our defense."

Melisande nodded and sat back into the plush softness of the chair. She knew her worth as a fighter, but she also understood the blond's planning. It would do them no good to fight their way free only to succumb from the lack of the touch of a cleric. She and Rene' were the only ones, save maybe the ranger, with that power.

That did not mean, however, that she would allow herself to be "kept safe." That, she felt, would place too heavy a burden on the rest. No, she vowed, she would carry her own weight in any situation. Her pride and her calling would accept no less.

Savon'el went through the "order of march": Arantar would be in the lead, his talents as Huntsmaster serving to break the trail and keep them out of trouble; himself and Melisande next; and Bonaire would serve as right guard to Lady Rene' with the pack horse trailing behind.

When Savon'el told the knight that he would be acting as rear guard, Solothon took offense.

"A knight in the rear? Not likely! My place is to the fore, first into battle center on line!"

"That is true, normally," stated the blond half elf, "but our situation is far from normal. We are not merely going forward on a quest, my friend. We are, in actuality, going in two directions at once: forward in the hope of finding Red Wolf and maybe some answers that will hold us in good stead when we reach our destination, and away from the dangers that I fear follow us even now.

"No, my friend," he continued, a hand to the knight's shoulder, "I would never relegate you to a position where you are not needed. Since we have no idea from which direction our enemy will strike, we need your skill to protect our backs and, at need, lead us away to safety."

Solothon looked into those amber eyes and knew the truth. Savon'el was arranging the strength of this group strategically to protect all sides. He saw the wisdom and tactical advantage in this to allow for safe change of direction, strength always to the fore.

"I see," he replied slowly. "Of course you are right, my friend. In our situation, yours is a sound solution. Know that I shall do what must be done. Depend on it!"

"I do, sir. I do."

Then, with a sigh, Savon'el turned to the others.

"I feel that now is the time for information. Ladies?"

Rene' glanced at Melisande and, when that one waved her on, she stood up behind the desk, her hand resting on the thin box Solothon had retrieved.

"So far Melisande and I have made some rather unique discoveries about this place and some of the items you've found throughout this household. Most of those items, at Maxim's insistence, will have to remain, but we have been given leave to take certain books that may contain needed information toward our endeavor. Also, the Ioun Stones—"

"The what?" asked the blond half elf.

"Cut crystals with magical properties," she replied as she lifted the lid to the thin case. "Solothon found this case in the stables and Arantar this other in the main hall. They contain a total of twelve stones, some of which may be useful in our quest. I've been able, with some study here and my past studies with the mages in Catlorian, to determine the properties of most of them, but there are two here that may serve your needs, Savon'el, more than others."

Savon'el stepped to the desk as the mage girl lifted a small translucent pale blue crystal from the thin box. She used great care in lifting the stone from its bed of green satin by holding it at either end with thumb and forefinger. All six of its sides were rhomboidal, though not extreme in its cutting. The half elf held out his hand and the girl released it, but instead of falling into Savon'el's hand, it floated just above it.

"Wha—"

"You'll have to take it, Savon'el," said the mage girl softly. "Don't worry. It won't fall. Just take it and toss it above your head with a little spin."

He closed his hand around the stone and, as he opened it again, it seemed to nestle into his palm. He looked from the crystal to the mage girl with a strange askance.

"Really," the girl prodded, "just toss it with a spin above your head. It's all right. It won't fall, I promise."

The strangeness was almost too much for the confused half elf, but as Rene's tolerant smile goaded him, he did as instructed.

The stone rose slowly to a close orbit within two inches of the half elf's head and rotated there just out of his sight.

"Very pretty, Rene'," he commented as he tried to see it by moving his head back and forth. "I can't see it up there. Is it still there?"

"Yes, my friend, but it is staying out of your sight. The stones are designed to aid you without being a distraction."

"Aid me? How?"

"Young master?" came a voice from the door.

Savon'el turned in time to see the heavy chair from the main hall sailing toward him.

"What?" he gasped as his hands sought to fend it off.

However, as his hands closed on the chair, its momentum was interrupted. He'd caught it! He was stunned that the weight he thought should be there simply wasn't. It was heavy, certainly, but he held the chair much easier than its bulk supposed.

"'Tis a strength amplifier, young master," came Maxim's voice again from the doorway. "As long as the stone encircles thy head, thy strength will be far greater than its norm."

"That is all well and good, my friend," said Savon'el as he carefully set the chair on the floor, "but what is to keep someone from simply snatching it from its flight?"

"Arantar," said the mage girl in answer, "try and catch it."

The Huntsmaster stepped around the chair and raised a hand to interrupt the flight of the slowly rotating stone. As the stone neared his hand, it abruptly changed course to bypass the hand and continue its slow rotation. Arantar frowned and grabbed at it only to watch the stone jerk out of his reach and regain its close orbit.

"You see, Savon'el," said the girl as the Huntsmaster let that hand fall on the savon'el's shoulder, "unless one is possessed of an obscene amount of speed and dexterity, only you can catch it."

"Only I?" whispered the blond half elf as he raised a cupped hand toward his brow.

He was just a bit startled when the stone floated softly into his hand to nestle as if it knew exactly where it belonged. He closed his fingers about the fragile stone and placed it into a small pouch at his waist.

"I shall keep it here and safe until needed," he said softly. "Rene', you said two?"

"Yes," she replied as she opened the large case.

She lifted one of the four dusty rose-colored prisms from its bed of blue satin, again holding it on either end between thumb and forefinger, and waited until the half elf's hand was cupped below it. She released it and it too floated waiting for Savon'el to close his hand around it.

"That stone will afford you more protection, should you need it," she continued as Savon'el placed it with the other stone, "but be careful not to try to use more than two of these stones at the same time, for they will avoid everything but each other, unfortunately.

"I will distribute others as required," she continued to the rest of her companions, "but with your permission, I will maintain them with me to keep them safe until we return."

Savon'el looked from one to the other of the companions as he gently stroked the pouch.

"There are several things we know," he said softly. "First, someone or something pursues us for reasons unknown or unremembered. From what Rene' has been able to ascertain, our stumbling upon this cottage was either incredible luck, or we've been guided here. I'd prefer the former seeing that the latter implies more manipulation of our movements. Second, Red Wolf has no way to know where we've gone, save toward the source of the river, nor we him. I believe, however, if there is the slightest chance, he will try to find and rejoin us. With that in mind, I suggest that we continue toward the Black Sorcerer's Keep as intended."

"Radagast's Rest, mistress?" came the guardian's voice from the doorway.

"Yes, Maxim," replied the mage girl. "and the rest of you should know..."

She sighed and hung her head. What right did she have to...

"What is it Rene'?"

"Savon'el," she said softly. Then, louder and to all of them, "I have to go to that keep."

"Why?" from the Huntsmaster. "For some artifacts Myrlin said you might find there?"

"No, Arantar, for some artifacts I *know* are there." She stopped and took a breath. "I've said before that there are some who believe that Banshe'e is alive. I am one of those and the Myrlin is another. Everything that has happened—the fall of Dragon's Teeth, the blockade of Heartstone, the rumblings of evil coming from the deep southern reaches—all are portends of what we believe is a resurgence of Banshe'e's ill-favor.

"Now, it is said that Banshe'e and some of his thralls are searching for powerful weapons, like those Wormslayers, Savon'el, and Radagast's armory. That black keep once belonged to Radagast! If his armory is there, it is my fate to go there and attempt to destroy or remove those weapons to a place of safety, at least until Banshe'e and his ilk are defeated. There are also two very powerful items that I must..."

She stopped as the tears began forming behind her eyes. Melisande came to her feet.

"Rene', if that place is so dangerous, maybe we should wait—"

"I cannot, sister, and—"

She looked at her feet.

"She cannot go alone."

They all turned toward the doorway where Maxim knelt.

"My mistress will go alone if necessary, for that is her mission. There is evil there that, even at this late date, still exists and will try her skills beyond their limits. I cannot attend her, for it is my fate to stay here and maintain this household, nor can I dissuade her."

"She will not go alone, Maxim," stated the blond half elf. "If Rene' says we must enter that keep, that is exactly what we shall do."

"Why?" exclaimed Bonaire as he sat forward in his chair. "We are safe here. I, for one, don't feel any need to go further. You do as you will. I'm staying here!"

With that, he sat back in his chair and folded his arms in defiance.

"That, of course," said the blond half elf softly, "is your choice. However, the chances are great that whoever or whatever pursues us will find this place. If any of us are here, for remember they know all of us, they will stop at nothing to secure the direction of travel of the rest by whatever means presents itself."

Bonaire's arms unfolded slowly as his face went pale.

"Besides, Bonaire," added the Huntsmaster, "there is the treasure."

"Treasure?"

"Why of course. Didn't you know that a sorcerer's tower is generally a safe repository for his great wealth? It's too bad that you won't be with us to share that."

"Well," stammered the elf as his color began to return, "if you need me, I suppose I can't let my friends down now, can I?"

"Of course not, my friend," said the Huntsmaster.

He grinned as he looked about the room and his companions. The grin disappeared when he saw the look of pain on the mage girl's face.

"What is it, m'lady?"

"I now know how Savon'el feels. If I allow you to accompany me, I've placed you within the reach of death. If not, I shall fail. I cannot ask—"

"Then don't!" stated the cleric. "I sought this out and all but demanded to be here and now! I felt that I needed the experience, the adventure, if I'm to ply my craft properly. Besides," she added in a voice laced with a small amount of venom, "I've a score to settle and this outing should give me some of what I need to accomplish my personal ends."

"Revenge?" Rene' asked softly.

"Of a sort."

"I see," said Savon'el. "It's a pity that your first quest is not so much going to somewhere as it is running *from* somewhere. I'm sorry."

"No need," she replied as she folded the yellow cloak and, as she returned to her chair, placed it upon her lap.

Savon'el nodded and turned toward the Huntsmaster.

"Don't ask, my friend," said he. "If Lady Rene' says it is important that we continue, that is all I need to know."

The knight punctuated the Huntsmaster's comment with a curt nod.

"It looks to me, Rene'," stated the savon'el with a grin, "that we've decided to accompany you. When you find what you are looking for there, please let us know that we might aid you."

"I shall and...and thank you all."

Rene' was feeling very uncomfortable, and it wasn't from the guilt alone. Melisande's controlled fury beat at her empathic walls and her eyes sought the cleric's. As if by command, those green orbs came about and met the golden ones of the mage girl.

After a moment, the fury receded and a small grin played at the black-haired cleric's lips.

"Savon'el," asked the Huntsmaster, "does anyone here know exactly where this keep is?"

"That question has worried me since we arrived," the savon'el replied. "I'd hoped that Red Wolf would have returned by now, but since that has not occurred, I thought to go on what we know. We know, for instance, that the Keep stands north-northwest of Catlorian and is either at or near the source of the Lost Souls River. Beyond that..." He shrugged. "If we go in that direction, whether we find it sooner rather than later matters little as long as we find it. If Red Wolf does return, he will no doubt follow the same path we take. Either way, we still have a good chance of eluding pursuit."

"Unless *they* are aware of our destination as well," stated the knight. "I, for one, have no desire to travel in any direction without at least a grasp as to which direction. In keeping with those other knights-errant before me,

I've sought to lay our trek to pen. I've taken council with Maxim, and he has stated that Lady Rene' has the answers needed to complete my map."

"Me?" whispered the girl. "But where would I…"

Then, her eyes found the tapestry.

"Wait," she breathed as she rose and walked stiffly toward the wall hanging.

Solothon noted the look of deep concentration as the mage girl moved toward him and he stepped aside.

"What is it?" he asked as she drew near.

"Shhh!" whispered Melisande. "Leave her alone and watch."

Rene' emptied her mind of all but her need for the keep. It filled her mind as she gazed at the map that was the tapestry. She demanded to know where…where…*where!*

It seemed to leap from the map, a place marked discretely, but now unmasked.

"It is here!" she said as she stabbed her finger to the tapestry. "It stands just east of the source of the river. The river flows southeast from the source several hundred miles south of the Northern Shelf. Then, it turns ever so slightly to the south. Here, just before this range of mountains, maybe four or five days travel, is a Druid's Pentacle. If we can get there, we can jump to here," she stabbed at a place just north of the keep, "where another Pentacle stands. Then we can approach the Keep from the north and bypass any who may lay in wait."

Solothon quickly transferred this information to his map he held rested upon the covered shiraken in his hand. Arantar looked closely at the map and found the small writing just below the mark where the keep should be.

"Is that the name of the keep, Rene'?"

"Radagast's Rest? No, it seems that Lord Rairy named it 'Den of Nightmares'."

Arantar's blood ran cold and his hand, unbidden, caressed the hilt of the great sword strapped to his back.

"I've heard of that before, Rene'. Is that—"

"Yes, my dear Huntsmaster, it is an ancient temple used for training the Necromantic Lords of the race of Daku."

Instantly, Rene' was slammed back into the tapestry by a sudden and incredibly strong tide of pure rage. She fought to hold her walls in place as she sought for the source. She found it.

Solothon stood in a crouch, his silver sword in his hand. The shiraken he'd held wrapped but a moment before was now imbedded a good inch into the wood floor at his feet. The map he'd been working on fluttered to the floor next to it.

But it was his visage that brought terror to his companions. His lips had drawn back baring his tightly clinched teeth and his eyes pulsed blood red, the glow emanating a good inch from the eyeballs. Those eyes darted back and forth searching for a target and the animal mind that was left searched for prey.

Melisande slipped from her chair over the arm and crouched behind it, her fur robe clinging to her as a second skin. Strangely the robe was no longer a tawny brown; it was jet black. Her hands were concealed in the yellow robe and held the weapon concealed there. Though her frown spoke of reluctance to fight a friend, the green glint in her eyes spoke of another need.

Arantar began speaking softly to him, the words unimportant and the tone of his voice even and calm. He'd done this before with wild dangerous animals and, without thinking, knew this to be the only approach to take with this one. He'd begun to take a slow step toward the knight when Rene's ragged voice reached him.

"Stay where you are."

Her voice was soft, but her mind was screaming through the talents she'd learned, trained, and perfected. She reached softly into Solothon's mind and found savage, unrelenting rage. She reached deeper and nudged his sedated consciousness.

As that part of the knight's mind came slowly awake, Rene' revealed what was happening as it slept. The steel that was the honor this knight held sacred came forth, then, to pull back on the reins of the beast.

Rene' stayed with him as the rage was beaten back inch by inch as the knight drove the demon down. She stayed until she was certain that he controlled the rage and withdrew.

As she came back, she looked about to see if any had been harmed. Arantar stood behind the knight now with a look that meant, though he would hate himself forever, he would kill this man, this friend, to save her. Arantar sheathed the dagger, and she knew the look he gave her was real.

Pain was mixed with the anger surging toward Rene', anger and self-reproach. Solothon fought on, unmoving, but his eyes betrayed the shame that threatened to overtake him.

"It's all right, Sir Solothon," she said softly.

"No, m'lady," he replied gravely, "it is not. It will not be well until this demon is ripped from my soul or I am dead."

"No, Sir Solothon," answered the girl softly as the Huntsmaster's hand gently fell on the knight's shoulder. "Friends do not desert friends in need, no matter the cost. As for the other," she continued as her face took on a frown, the slim fingers from her right hand tapping gently at her chin, "I can only give an educated guess."

"Please, m'lady, if you know something—"

"I said a guess," she interrupted. "If what I fear is true, you will have to remain ever vigilant." She took a deep breath, let it out slowly, and continued, "When I ventured within your mind, I found a…darkness. The ragged edges of a mental wall fluttered about it and it seethed of pure rage. Add that to the pain centered in your hereditary birthmark and the answer, to my mind anyway, is quite clear. The curse placed upon you did not work quite as intended. Instead of causing your rage, it ripped the walls from your inherited curse and, in doing so, was reduced to ash long before Brea removed its residual."

"But why did the mere mentioning of the word 'daku' cause this?"

The girl looked askance. Then she realized that he'd said the word that a moment before had almost cost her life. She pursed her lips and her brow wrinkled in concentration as the answer came to her.

"It must deal with the hereditary, Sir Solothon. It is possible that the close proximity of your shirakens weakened your control and all your rage needed was a catalyst. Your birthmark is a family trait, as is your rage. When we find who passed it to you, we may find the way to remove, or at least control, it."

"Until then, my friend," came the blond half elf's voice from the knight's right, "we will face this together. So say we all?"

The room echoed with soft "Ayes," with the notable exception of Bonaire. He was still huddled behind his chair, the parchment crumpled in his hand.

The knight's head fell forward into his hands, his palms to his eyes. He felt it then, the deep-seated, patient anger held in check for eons, waiting. He knew his curse then, though he knew not from whom it was cast. He was the descendent of one whom the mere mention of the word "daku" was anathema. He would have to concentrate on that and try to repair those walls. He could not allow that terrible demon free again, not here among his friends.

He took his hands from his face and, as his vision cleared, he saw the shiraken embedded in the floor. He knelt and retrieved it and, after wrapping it in the soft leather, he returned it to the pouch with its twin and handed the pouch to Rene'.

"Would you keep these? It may well be easier to leave them here, but before this is finished, I may have need for them. I wouldn't ask were it not important to me."

"I will do what I can, but—"

"If they become a problem to us, use your own discretion," he said soberly. "I'll not have you harmed through my insistence."

"Have no fear of that, friend," said Savon'el as he glanced about the room. "If we are in accord, it will not happen."

The frown on Savon'el's face deepened.

"Where is Bonaire?"

Melisande stepped around the chairs, grabbed a handful of cloak, and lifted. Bonaire came to his feet, his eyes closed and his hands pressed against his ears as if to shut out the danger his fear and panic fed upon. He opened one eye and glanced around the room.

"Is it over?" he asked in a small voice.

"Yes, Bonaire," answered Melisande. Then, in afterthought, she added, "For now." She wiped her hands on the robe as she made her way to the green crystal wall locker. She leaned against its coolness and surveyed her companions.

"Good!" said he as he instantaneously returned to his former composure, stepped around the chair, and dropped into it.

Arantar reached out and snatched the parchment from his fingers without warning.

"What's this?"

"What? Oh, that," he answered casually. "I found it tied to the black's mane."

"You found it *where?*" shouted the knight as he stalked to Bonaire's chair.

"Tied to your horse's mane. He didn't like it, so he shook it free. I picked it up and came down here, but you guys didn't seem to be interested so... URK!"

The knight's gauntleted hand closed about the cloak at the youth's neck and Bonaire found himself being lifted bodily from his chair to hang suspended a good foot above the floor.

Bonaire's eyes caught the pulsing tinge of red in the knight's eyes and for a fleeting moment wondered what being dead was going to be like.

"Enough, Sir Solothon."

The quiet voice that carried so much latent power held the knight's anger in check. The blond half elf laid a gentle hand on the arm suspending Bonaire and repeated, "Enough."

The knight glanced at Savon'el and that act returned him to control. The half elf's amber eyes didn't demand obedience, but the power, now somehow gone, had turned the trick. The anger that had threatened to overtake him receded into the shadows of his mind once more.

He lowered the shaken Bonaire to the floor and, as the young elf collapsed back into the chair, looked at the offending hand as if it were not his.

The blond half elf turned toward the shocked Huntsmaster.

"Though a note tied to the mane of one of our horses is cause for concern, I don't…"

Arantar shook his head as if to push away sleep for he too had felt the power. Then, as his agile mind grasped the implications, he replied.

"On all but Solothon and mine it would be but cause for concern. Our mounts, however, will not allow a strange hand to come near without our permission. Even with that, it would still be their choice."

That said, he headed for the stairway, handing the parchment to Melisande' and slapping Solothon's shoulder in passing as an indication that he should follow.

Blacky, what's going on out there? queried the Huntsmaster as he took two steps at a time.

All is well, Arantar-sao. All is well.

"Melisande, dear," said the mage girl softly, "may I see that?"

Melisande passed the parchment to Rene' as Savon'el buckled his sword to his back.

"You two should be safe here until we return. Maxim will protect you."

"Protect, my ass!" exclaimed Melisande as she snatched up her cloak and ran past the half elf for the stairs.

Rene' shrugged at the look Savon'el gave her, smoothed out the parchment on her desk, and began to study it. With a peculiar glance at the shaken Bonaire, the blond half elf followed the others out of the study and up the stairway.

Blacky?

The Huntsmaster's call went unanswered as he moved swiftly but cautiously around the hut toward the stables. That feeling of being watched was strong again, and when he made quick mention of it to the knight who was right on his heels, Solothon answered that he too felt the eyes.

When the Huntsmaster reached the down ramp to the stables, he stopped and faced toward the brook and the forest beyond. Solothon continued down into the stables, but he reemerged a moment later.

The hair on Arantar's nape bristled. The feeling that they were watched was keen, and now he felt it from two distinct directions.

"Enare was but perturbed. The others were calm as ice."

"I can't shake this feeling, Solothon, that..." Both men whirled as Melisande rounded the hut, her right hand wrapped in the folds of that yellow cloak.

Her green eyes darted about like those of a predator and, stranger still, a grin of anticipation turned the corners of her mouth up displaying tightly clinched teeth.

Arantar-sao, why fear?

Blacky?

The Huntsmaster's mind feverishly sought the direction of the communication.

Where in blazes are you?

Above on nest.

Arantar turned in time to raise his arm to receive the weight of the large raven.

"What befalls?" came the blond half elf's voice as he rounded the side of the hut.

"I'm not sure," replied Arantar distractedly. "Give me a moment."

What's happened?

Nothing, saola.

Did you see a man or something with big four-legs?

Only friends, Arantar-sao.

No strange four-legs?

One hand of and same as legs more. That all.

Arantar had to pause to consider what the bird was trying to convey. One "hand," the term the bird had learned from Arantar, meant "five," but...

Blacky. thought the Huntsmaster, a gnawing doubt eating at his insides. *This many four-legs?*

He held one hand out, the fingers splayed, while he held the other with but two fingers displayed.

Yes. Same.

No other rider, but...

Only friends here, Arantar-sao.

Then the smell reached his hypersensitive nostrils. An oily, metallic smell lingered on the currents. The smell of steel, but that was all. There was no sign that anyone or anything had been in this vicinity in quite awhile. But that feeling...

"Something is wrong. Someone tied that note, but there is no one here."

"How do you know..." began Savon'el.

Then the raven's black eyes seemed to lock onto his.

"The bird!" he almost whispered. "You can talk to the bird!"

"In a way," replied the Huntsmaster, his eyes now locked on those of the blond half elf.

Savon'el shook his head with a grin and then sobered.

"One day you must tell me of this, my friend, but for now we will have to see to the immediate. Seek further for sign while Melisande and I return to the study. Sir Solothon?"

"Yes, Lo...friend?"

"You will act as companion to Arantar?"

"Done."

Savon'el made his way back to the stairway and started down, Melisande reluctantly following. They found Rene' studying the parchment with ill-concealed excitement.

"Look!" she breathed, waving Melisande to her side. "It's written in the 'Runes of Landre'a'!"

"Can you decipher it?" asked the black-haired cleric as she moved to look over the girl's shoulder.

"Oddly enough, I just finished a study of these runes but a week before we left. I've got most of it done. Just a moment."

She continued with her study for a bit, then, "This doesn't make much sense to me but..."

Then, she read aloud. "'By dragon's teeth and dragon's wing, the Talon shall not fall. Truly born of Moshar, Raven of Seventh Talon.' Dated the twenty-first day of the eleventh month, MW 133."

"'Tis the reckoning of a birth, mistress."

None of them had heard Maxim approach the doorway and kneel.

Rene' recovered from the shock quickly and asked, "A birth? You know of Moshar, Maxim?"

"Of the house Moshar of Dragon's Teeth, a seaport city on the lower east end of Catlor."

There was a twinge of recognition, but that was all. Savon'el had no knowledge of that city or that area, and he had alarmingly just now learned the name of the continent upon which he stood. The depth of his loss finally sunk in. As far as he was concerned, he was a newborn with the power of speech. That was all. He would have to learn everything from the beginning, should his memory recede beyond reach.

"Arantar and Solothon come from close by that area," said Rene', noting the concern on the half elf's face. "They will know more of this. Meanwhile, if I've read the date rightly, this note references a date over 2500 years past. Eight weeks from now will be the anniversary of that to which this refers. I just wish I knew more…"

"I had hoped that we might have lingered here, recouping our strength a few more days, but in view of this message…"

Savon'el's voice trailed off.

"I don't feel evil in this. It seems to be but a notice," said Rene' distractedly.

"From whom, and why dated so long ago?"

"The question isn't 'from whom.' It should be 'to whom' that our thoughts should entertain. Why to this party?"

"Nevertheless," sighed the blond half elf, "I believe we should be away from here as soon as possible."

He started for the door, stopped, and added, "Gather what you think we shall need of the maps and references, m'ladies. We need all the help we can get."

Then he continued through the main hall and up the stairway.

Nothing moved in the morning sunlight, but Arantar still felt the awareness on his skin. Someone was watching, waiting.

"Huntsmaster?"

Arantar turned from his musing on the tree line to see the blond half elf come around the hut.

"Rene' has deciphered the writing on the parchment."

"What does it say?"

Savon'el was silent for a moment, then answered, "Should I not get the message right, it may not sound as it should. Lady Rene' will be here momentarily, but I suggest that you and Bonaire gather our gear. Solothon and I will make our mounts ready for travel."

"As you will," answered the Huntsmaster as he headed for the stairway.

Melisande met him at the top of the stairs and stood aside to let him enter. As the Huntsmaster disappeared into the hut, Melisande felt for the day. The calm relaxed her, the warmth sang to her, and the peace filled her. All the power that was hers as a gift of her goddess was aligned with what was this day. This day was perfect.

As the thought passed through her mind, it jolted her back to reality. Perfect? Too perfect! Ten feet from her, a squirrel sat casually ignoring her as it gnawed on an acorn. She frowned and moved swiftly to the stables.

She moved as closely as she could to Solothon's mount, with Solothon in attendance, and called on the power of her clergy while scanning the confines of the stable for residuals. Still, all felt perfect. Her frown deepened as she walked back up the ramp. She felt that Rene' should know of this even if it were only her imagination.

"What's wrong, m'lady?"

Melisande glanced at the blond half elf in passing and replied a bit crossly, "Nothing." Then added, "Not a damn thing," and continued around the hut.

"Something is wrong, Rene'."

Melisande heard the Huntsmaster's statement just before she reentered the study and amended it for him as she stepped through the door.

"No, Arantar, something feels right. Too right!"

Rene' sat for a moment, her hands cupped together before her and her thumbs absently tapping her teeth. Then she abruptly stood up, gathered her books from the desktop into a shoulder satchel, and went out of the door.

Arantar and Melisande watched her leave, looked at each other, and then jumped up quickly to follow.

"Where you going?" asked Bonaire absently.

Arantar stopped at the door while Melisande continued up the stairway and turned to the elf.

"Are you going to stay down here alone?"

"What? Alone?" The elf was on his feet and following the Huntsmaster.

Arantar's went to their packs and, between the two of them, gathered all of their possessions, placed the packs next to the stairway, and moved up the stairs.

Rene' marched right into the stable and up to the big black warhorse. Before Solothon could say, "Don't!" she reached up and scratched the big mount between the eyes with her dainty fingers, all the while a look of stern concentration held her face taut.

Solothon didn't move. If the trained war mount went for her, there was nothing he could do.

Strangely, the horse didn't seem to mind and seemed not to care as the girl retrieved the pouch containing the shirakens and tied it into the flowing black mane. Solothon held his breath as the girl reached back into her pouch and brought forth some dried fruit for the big horse. After the fruit disappeared into the great mount's mouth, Rene' smiled, kissed it on the nose, and walked out.

Solothon couldn't believe what he had just witnessed and, after remembering to breathe, followed the girl out.

"What..."

"I'll explain in a moment, Sir Solothon," Rene' replied. Then, to Melisande, "You are correct, my dear. Everything is too perfect, but did you notice that this perfection stops but fifty feet from the house?"

"Do you think it a problem, m'lady?" asked Savon'el.

"If it is," came an answer from the Huntsmaster as he rounded the hut, an embarrassed looking Bonaire slinking behind him, "it just got worse."

"Worse?"

"Bonaire just closed the new door and, if my senses haven't deserted me, it locked."

"What?" exclaimed the knight.

"Rene'?" asked Savon'el as he turned toward her. "Are we locked ou—"

Melisande caught the pale girl before she fainted. Rene' shook with her weakness from her expenditure of magic. Solothon recognized the problem immediately, for he had seen his mother weakened in this matter after casting some powerful spell in the defense of the keep.

"She needs sleep, Savon'el," he said as he moved to help Melisande escort Rene' into the stable. "Without it, she will be incapable of recouping her strength."

He picked the girl up into his arms and, as her black-rimmed eyes met his, he asked softly, "What have you done, m'lady?"

"I've made your shirakens his, sir," she murmured weakly. "None may now make off with them, not even you, and one cannot barter with a horse."

Her weak smile held a self-satisfied amusement that was reflected in the slight upturn at the corners of the knight's mouth.

"Before you sleep, m'lady," asked the Savon'el, "what is the meaning of 'talon' in that message?"

Solothon turned to allow Rene' an unobstructed view of the blond half elf.

"I'm not sure," she said softly. "It could be the title of an outpost of the city of Dragon's Teeth, or a ship, or—"

"It was also used to describe a fighting group numbering five."

The soft baritone came from the direction of the hut and from above.

Arantar spun, his hands filling with the dull gray steel. Solothon placed the girl's feet on the ground gently and, just as gently, moved her behind him where she, in her weakened condition, held to him for support. The ring of Elvin silver clearing its sheath was echoed in the brownish-green blade now in the hands of the blond half elf.

Bonaire had slipped down the ramp into the stables, his hand on his undrawn sword.

Melisande had moved a bit to the left of Solothon and had dropped into a fighting crouch, both hands now wrapped in the gaudy yellow cloak with her back to the stable wall.

The man, for this one appeared human, stood on the edge of the roof his arms akimbo as if he were having a casual conversation in a tavern. He was over six-feet tall, his black hair was tied back with a leather thong, and his blue black eyes seemed to dance with amusement. His clothing, if such is the proper word, was very dull, glinting silver down to his boots and conformed to every ripple of his body. The only weapon visible to the six below was the broadsword strapped to his back, its hilt raised above the level of his right shoulder.

As Arantar spun, the raven, of long practice, lifted in flight to give his saola room, but he didn't stay aloft. Arantar watched incredulously as his winged friend dropped to the man's shoulder. Then, as the man scratched under the bird's beak absently, those blue black eyes locked on his.

He's told you that all is well, young ranger. Do you not believe him?

The thought rippled in velvet tones and soft reds through the Huntsmaster's mind and, knowing from whence came the thought, caused his mouth to drop open in shock and the great blade to drop slowly until its tip touched the turf.

"Who are you, sir?" demanded the knight softly, the sword still in his right hand as his left helped to support and protect the mage girl. "Was it you who left that note and if so, what is the meaning of its reference to a talon?"

"It was," came Arantar's voice from his right, "a group of fighters whose talents, when added together, were unbeatable. Such was the Talon of Wormslayers."

Solothon glanced at his friend concerned at the softness and incredulousness of his voice.

"They used the talon in the games at Seaborne," Arantar continued, "but they date as far back as the Mage Wars. I've heard Prince LeMand speak of them."

Savon'el's head was pounding. There was something...

"You are correct, young ranger," said the man in his melodic baritone. Then he smiled.

All were captivated by the man's presence. It would seem, from his stance and bearing, that the sun rose and set at his whim. This feeling surrounded and flowed through those looking up from the ground.

"As for who I am, that is unimportant. What is important is your quest."

"You know of us?" asked the savon'el, the anger of more manipulation tingeing his words. "Whom do you serve, sir?"

A whisper, soft yet stern, came from behind Melisande.

"He serves the Lords of Light."

Melisande whirled, all pretense gone. Her hands came from within that cloak filled with five feet of seasoned wood, capped at one end with steel and topped with a large steel-banded head.

The voice had come from close behind her. Too close, she thought. The maul whirled as the thought became action.

The whisperer saw the blow coming and stepped back out of the path of that explosive weapon.

Melisande allowed the maul to pass through the air where this foe had recently held his head and, spinning the great maul about, crouched to face this threat head-on. She quickly surveyed him.

He stood there, his scarred face sporting a gentle smile and his right hand up and empty. The only weapon the black-haired cleric, and the eyes of the rest of them, could see was the heavy, nasty-looking blade the young warrior cradled in his gauntleted hand. Strangely, he only wore one gauntlet and, stranger still, it extended to his shoulder.

"To help you to succeed," came that baritone again, "I bring you assistance."

"Hold, Melisande," said the Huntsmaster abruptly.

The black-haired cleric had spun the maul again in preparation for her attack, but she stopped at Arantar's voice.

"Are you not Surfr'el the whisperer?"

The young warrior's right hand moved in Elvin sign.

<I am he.>

<Welcome to my fire, Surfr'el of the cat.> signed the Huntsmaster.

"What is going on? Who are you?" asked Melisande tightly, her eyes missing nothing in the signing except its meaning.

The youth returned his Bourjon blade to its sheath and replied in his whisper.

"I am Eton DeBurge. Your companion remembers me from long ago. I am no enemy. I wish to join you."

"Why?"

"Because," came the reply from the man on the hut as he seemed to step off and float to the ground, "you need all of the help you can get."

As the man walked toward Melisande, Solothon watched Arantar's great blade disappear into its sheath and, trusting to his judgment, the knight did likewise. He then turned and lifted the weak mage girl back into his arms and followed the man to Melisande's side.

Savon'el hung back a bit, wary of treachery. He spun the large blade and tucked it up against his left forearm, a move not lost on Eton who knew from whom he'd learned that move. He smiled a grim smile.

The man looked down at Melisande, whose eyes sought his. She felt he could see into her very soul.

"There are forces moving in this world far greater than any you have imagined. The danger is great and the rewards few. Yet what you must do must be done. Do not refuse assistance where it can be had."

The Huntsmaster moved to Eton's side and placed one hand on the youth's un-gauntleted shoulder.

"I vouch for him with my life. In view of our past ordeals, I can see that trust is hard to find, but until he proves that trust to you, my word will have to do."

"Well said, Adenedhel," stated the man in an amused voice, "but there is another among you who, in vouchsafing me, will vouchsafe for him."

His blue-black eyes sought those of the knight.

"I knew your great uncle, Solothon Calendera."

"Yes?" queried the young knight. "Lord Bonif'el was first of the Seventh Talon under Paladin during the war. How did you know him? Were you a friend?"

A softness came to his voice as the man in dull silver answered.

"I knew him. He fought and died well, but a commander cannot be friends to those sworn to him."

Still holding his golden burden, Sir Solothon, knight errant in the New Order of the Laurel, went to one knee and in a small shaken voice made his reply.

"Lord Paladin?"

The man nodded and smiled. Then he turned his attention to the rest of the companions.

"Have any of you met one called Yokura?"

"Can you describe him?" queried Melisande in answer.

Lord Paladin smiled at the girl's stern visage.

"He seems to be Elvin, though closer observation would show the contrary. He uses little or no armor. His chosen weapons are the katana and sai daggers. He wears leather, though his arms are free. On a sash of leather he carries several silver shirakens. All in all, with or without his weapons, he is extremely deadly."

They'd all seen this one in the Mirror of Probabilities, yet Savon'el couldn't snap the memory into place. The description caused pain, but no memory. He knew there was something here to remember.

The man glanced about the group and with a smile said, "I see you know of him." Then, to Savon'el, "You most of all."

The blond fought with the blinding pain to reach into his pouch and retrieved the shiraken Red Wolf had given him—how long ago?— and, now stepping up before Paladin, laid it gently into the proffered hand.

"This was left by the one you describe with...a friend. Do you know what it portends?"

"This is the house emblem of Moshar, the Rearing Dragon. Other than that..."

The man stopped when he saw the knight glance over his shoulder toward the stable.

"Is it the youth who"—the pause for thought—"protects your flank by remaining hidden in the stables? Or is it the question you have concerning the crystal laced into your mount's mane?"

"How do you know of—"

"The question you wish answered isn't mine to ensure, but…" The man paused and his eyes caught and held Solothon's as if gripped in steel. "Hear me, Solothon Calendera. You will come into your own…much as your forefathers did. *Neither friend nor foe can stand before the rage of Shan'troa.*"

Rene's mouth dropped open. The language was ancient, the archaic tongue of dragons and its meaning explained everything. Strangely, all that heard the uttering understood.

"Help me, Lady!" she whispered, for the word this man had uttered was the family name of the legendary berserker, Lord Bonif'el Shan'troa. The name was used in some circles instead of the word "berserker." Since this man who seemed to know everything about everyone used this in reference to Solothon, Shan'troa must be that distant relative whose curse was passed to an unsuspecting knight.

"I see that I must reserve my strength," she thought.

"You would be better off with a more powerful shield."

The man had said this directly to Rene' as if he read her very thoughts.

"If it were mine to have," she replied weakly, "I would have it."

Paladin smiled softly at the girl, then sighed.

"You must be in the mountains by nightfall tomorrow. It is imperative." He continued, aiming the statement at the blond half elf, "You have a task."

"Our task, it seems," answered he, "would have been simpler had not chance locked the door behind us."

His voice was tight. The pain in his head fueled the anger at the young elf's bungling.

"Most of our supplies are below in the hut and, frankly, I've no wish to break in again. The…protections might not be as hospitable the second time."

"Maxim?" asked Lord Paladin. "One among you has the capability to call that one," his eyes lingered on Rene's drawn face, "if she will."

The golden mage girl glanced down at the ring Maxim had placed on her finger. A tiny touch to that circle of gold, a thought of the big guardian, and the silent call was all that was necessary.

With a rush of displaced air, the metal golem appeared carrying all of their belongings, plus a pouch of papers he felt his "mistress" would need.

"When I heard the lock close, I thought never to see thee again. I saw thy belongings in the hall and realized it was by mistake. I thought to follow thee, but sensing no danger, I felt the need to allow thee to test thy key. Please forgive me, mistress."

A gentle smile played on the girl's lips.

"I thank you, Maxim, for allowing me this time of learning. I sincerely hope to see you again, goddess willing." Then, to the rest, "Now, if we are to depart soon, I must rest. I cannot be a burden at this time."

The guardian gave her a curt bow and then glanced at the companions. His gaze stopped on the black-haired cleric and the robe of the mimic.

"Wouldst thou take the robe with thee, m'lady?"

"I...I don't know."

"In thy travels, thee may cause it harm. 'Twould be better to leave it here for thy return, would it not?"

"I suppose," answered Melisande.

She sighed softly, ran her hands over its softness for a moment, and then removed it.

"You, as always, are correct Maxim," she said as she handed the robe to him.

As she turned the robe over to the metal guardian, she felt all eyes on her and she grinned.

Skin tight, though strangely flexible, black leather britches covered her lower body, legs and continued into her boots. Her tunic had been repaired and now covered the newly repaired chain mail, but over that she wore a black leather vest laced over her breasts. She tossed her yellow cloak about her shoulders and grinned.

"Thank you, Maxim, for your hospitality and the loan of clothing."

He nodded. Then, saying, "Mistress?" to Rene' and receiving a nod in return, he stepped away and disappeared.

"The Fates," commented Arantar, "are dealing this hand. I suppose one must play—"

"Think not, young ranger," stated Paladin sternly, "that being here is coincidence. What you do here, you and the Lady Rene' serve the Prince and Lady Galen."

Paladin turned then and, as if strolling through a safe park, ambled toward the forest. He stopped and with a strange look turned back towards the Huntsmaster.

"Beware the wielder of Arapel'ho."

Then he turned and with a smile was swallowed up in the shadows of the trees.

Savon'el, now slowly sheathing his blade, looked cautiously at the large warrior.

"Rene' must rest, but we must make ready to move."

With that, Savon'el followed the knight and his burden into the stable.

Melisande cast a frown after him and softly, as if to herself, asked, "What's gotten into him?"

"It's my presence," whispered Eton.

Arantar noted the look of big youth gave the blond half elf's back and signed, <*What is it?*>

<*Nothing worth noting, my friend. As of yet anyway.*> answered Eton as he threw a quick smile at the Huntsmaster. <*I must see to Fleet. I shall return.*>

Arantar watched the big warrior lope toward the wood line.

"Where is *he* going?"

Arantar glanced down at the cleric and took in the concern on her face, as well as the distrust. He followed her gaze to the strong back as Eton disappeared into the wood line.

"He's going to make ready, as we are," he answered. "He has a...companion, but fear not. They are both gentle of nature, yet deadly at need. I trust him at my back for good reason. You can also."

"Can I *really*?" she snorted as she made for the stable.

Arantar grinned, shook his head, and followed.

Chapter Thirty-two

"He said that we must be in the mountains by tomorrow evening," mused the blond half elf. "From what you have said, that is at least four or five days of hard riding."

"That is my reckoning from Rene's map," responded Solothon.

Arantar nodded agreement and for the first time on this quest felt the hopelessness.

Bonaire stood guard outside while they sat on the straw in the stable, close to the small tack room where Rene' rested, to plan for their next move.

The Huntsmaster glanced at the door to the tack room and again marveled at Melisande and her loyalty. Somehow the cleric knew that for an elf to sleep, a serious drain to her health must have occurred. The black-haired cleric sat beside the sleeping mage girl and held her hand.

Arantar's gaze passed to the doorway where Eton crouched.

Where had he come from, and why was he casting sidelong glances at Savon'el? These were questions for which he wasn't sure he wanted answers. He'd met Eton long ago and, as a point of honor, knew that no matter the reason for the looks, this large youth would never dishonor Arantar's vouchsafe.

"However," continued the knight, "there is a Pentacle but a half day's ride from here according to my map. It is, however, behind us to the southeast. If we could make it there by nightfall, we could transport to the one... here, just below the foothills." His finger touched the map at a mark next to the words "Lady of the Woods." "It is our best bet, but we must move soon one way or another."

"Are you sure that Pentacle even exists?" asked Savon'el.

"How can I be sure?" replied the knight. "I am no more familiar with this area that any. If it is there, we will reach it. If not…"

"Rene' may have been told more about where we are going then she's said." Melisande stepped lightly to Savon'el and continued, "She's poured over those books and maps in the study since we've been here."

"Yes," replied Savon'el, "but she is sleeping off the effects of her conjuring. Until she wakes, we must wait. Though I know the need, I chafe at the delay."

A thoughtful expression came to Arantar's face.

"Lady Melisande," he asked, "from where do you get your power?"

"Some say it is bartered from our souls, but the truth is our deities allow us to channel life from ourselves to the ailing. Why do you ask?"

The Huntsmaster stood, the look still in place, and looked toward the tack room.

"We have a need for haste and I just recently found I have a talent that may help." Then, with a glance at the black-haired cleric, he added, "With your permission?"

"If I may attend?"

He nodded and headed for the tack room, Melisande in tow.

Rene' slept deeply, a dreamless stupor brought on by the massive drain to her life force. Suddenly, a sense of wellness found its way into her consciousness that seemed to say that all would be well soon. She sensed, more than felt, the Huntsmaster's gentle hand on her forehead and a small smile played at her sleeping lips.

Arantar concentrated. He felt for the need and, with his newfound talent, began the conscious manipulation of the girl's very cells. Without knowing how he knew, he provided energy to those cells that were lacking. Those damaged were mended. He felt the loss to his own constitution as he went, and something inside tutored him in the careful transference of that force to the one before him.

Rene', still in a dream state, felt the power of the earth envelop her. After a moment, with her eyes still closed in sleep, the girl lifted her hand to his, drew it down to her lips, and kissed his palm. Then she turned onto her side and drifted into a more natural sleep. She was whole, but it would be a while longer before she would come back to them.

The Huntsmaster sat back on his heels and raised a hand to his forehead. He'd expended a great amount of his life energy to do this, and the throb of a headache centered behind his eyes as evidence.

"She will awaken soon," he said softly to Melisande. "Call when she does."

He stretched and left the tack room for the stable, snatching up his blanket.

"It will be a little while before she will be ready to join us," he said to his companions as he walked toward his horse. "I suggest we all get some rest. We don't know how long it will be before we will rest again."

He caught the glance from Eton.

<I will watch.> he signed. <I am rested. I will send the other down to join you.>

Arantar nodded and the youth disappeared up the ramp. A moment later, Bonaire came through the stable door, occasionally glancing up the ramp.

"Hey!" he said softly. "Who is that guy?"

"A friend," stated the Huntsmaster, who then laid down next to his roan, rolled into his blanket, and dozed.

It was late morning when Rene' woke. Melisande sat next to her, her green eyes filled with concern. Rene' reached a hand to the girl's arm and patted it.

"I'm well, sister."

She sat up and stretched.

"I must do this more often. Sleep does do a body good. Now," she said as she gripped the girl's hand, "what are our boys up to?"

"From what you've told me and from what I've read in the study, Solothon's suggestion is the best. There is another Pentacle in the direction we're going. However, as I said before, it is too far from here and no good for our necessity."

Rene' sat next to the Huntsmaster, her elbow cradled in the palm of one hand and her fingers of the other tapped her chin.

"We do have one problem," she continued. "Does our new companion have a horse?"

"He doesn't ride for…reasons you will learn of later," replied Arantar. "Even if he did, we have none to spare."

"Worry not about me," came a whisper from the doorway. "I will keep up."

Eton stood inside and leaned on the door joist. His spirit ached for motion and his mind cried out for answers as his eyes glanced once again at the blond half elf who wore his father's sword.

"I'm not worried about you keeping up," said Rene', "but let's be practical. We will be riding hard and fast. As Paladin says, we have little time to waste and, frankly, we've wasted enough. It would be ridiculous for you to run as hard as we must ride and still be fresh enough to fend off any enemies we might meet."

"The question, as I've already stated, is moot," commented Arantar. "We have no mount for him."

"Don't be too certain, Huntsmaster," she responded with a slight smile.

She brought the statuette of the horse from her shoulder bag, the same one Bonaire had found two days before, and handed it to the big youth.

"What am I to do with this toy, girl?" he whispered.

"Just place it in the middle of the stable and watch."

As Eton complied, Rene reached back into her bag for the scroll she sought. A grin marked the end of her search, and with a flourish she swept the scroll out and began to read it while her free hand drew small incantations in the air before her.

At the end of her reading, the sound of a small bell came to their ears and the statuette began to take on size. It grew until it was all of seventeen hands at the shoulder and stood as if still a statue. Then it snorted.

All eyes beheld the jet-black warhorse whose muscles stood as if chiseled from stone, yet rippled with power. Its bridle, saddle, and lattice barding were of fine-tooled leather, dyed black and shined to a high luster. From the pommel hung a sheathed great sword, a match for the one on Arantar's back save for the color of the hilt. It too was black as pitch.

He, for it was an uncut stallion, looked at Eton with eyes filled with a strange intelligence. The big youth felt something strange in his mind. A tug, a feeling of...

"How do you like him?" asked the mage girl.

Eton's hands flashed in sign.

<Arantar, I would do almost anything for you, but this?>

"You must apply yourself," replied the Huntsmaster. "We haven't a moment to waste, Eton. You must let him know you."

"May I help?" asked the black-haired cleric as she moved to the warrior's side. "Two weeks ago I had never ridden. Necessity is a cruel teacher, but the rewards are worth it."

Strangely, as the cleric neared the magnificent warhorse, he stepped away. Not away from her, but closer to the warrior in studded leather. She stopped and, glancing at the youth and then to the mount, backed away.

"There is something strange here, Rene'," she whispered.

"What is it, my dear?" replied Rene' as she made her way to the girl.

"Look at the tack!"

Rene' looked closer, all eyes following hers, and found that what they had all thought were bronze rivets binding the bridle, saddle, and barding together, where in actuality small bronze skulls.

"The rider of this horse was short," commented the knight. "Look at the height of the stirrups."

"Not so," replied the Huntsmaster. "Many who wield a sword that large cinch the stirrups up high. If you stand in the stirrups—"

"Quiet!" whispered the mage girl.

The big black mount eyed the mage girl as she carefully and slowly stepped toward the sheathed sword. Before she came within reach, she felt it.

The hunger. The eons long sleep had given it a ravenous thirst and need to be fed. It fed on...

The mage girl, without taking her eyes from that dark weapon, removed a golden silk ribbon from her hair and laid it across the cross guard.

"Bind!" she said softly.

The power of her cantrip rippled from the ribbon, and after several spasmodic jerks it looped itself about the hilt and sheath, effectively binding the sword in place. She took a ragged breath and backed away from it.

"Whatever you do," she said, her eyes still on the black hilt, "don't touch that blade. It is an unknown that I wish to remain unknown."

Eton looked at the girl's face and knew that there was a touch of fear, yet a dangerous curiosity.

"Don't worry," he replied as he gently and cautiously raised his ungauntleted hand to stroke the huge beast between the eyes. "A blade of that size is not to my liking," he whispered, "though my friend here..."

Arantar imagined the blade that could only have been wielded by a powerful lord. It would have to be something special. If only he could...

"No!" he cautioned himself. "I know not the power, or the danger to us all, that I would bring to bear if I took that weapon."

He shook his head to remove the desire that resided there.

"If we are to make of the Pentacle by nightfall," commented the blond half elf, "we must be leaving now."

<What of Fleet?> signed Eton.

<I will warn them, but you should take your new mount out to meet him.> replied the Huntsmaster in sign.

Eton nodded and, gently taking up the reins, led the big black toward the door. Before he got there, however, the horse nudged him in the back and shook the reins from the startled youth's hands.

"He may resent being led," commented the knight, who then returned to tightening the cinch on his own well-trained warhorse. "Mounts such as he are trained in their craft. You may find that he will carry you with ease, protect you with his life, and comfort you in your loneliness. It all depends on how you respond to him, as a horse or a companion." He glanced at the warhorse again and added, "If I were you, I wouldn't treat him as a horse."

Then he turned his attention away and stroked his black's neck.

Eton looked from the knight into the blue...This horse had blue eyes! The big warhorse snorted, nuzzled the warrior's chest, and then pushed him toward the door.

Eton gained the sunlight, followed closely by the warhorse, and felt for the cat. He found him at the edge of the forest. In the universal language of felines, Eton growled.

<Come. Meet friend.>

The puma padded out slowly and glided to a stop before the black warhorse. When Fleet raised his muzzle to sniff at the mount, the big black brought his own nostrils down to the cat. Eton marveled that the horse had no fear of the puma and wondered.

<Friend.> growled Fleet.

Then the cat turned and padded back into the wood line.

Bonaire had to work to control his pony as the companions traveled toward the southeast and the Pentacle. Eton had thought to bring the puma into the group, but after Bonaire's horse shied so violently, thought it better that Fleet range wide flank.

Only Rene', Arantar, and Solothon's mounts showed no sign of fear at the sight of the cat, the two warhorses by training and Rene's by her will alone. The two warhorses ridden by Savon'el and Melisande had settled down quickly with a gentle word.

Now, though the cat moved quietly and out of sight, Bonaire's horse still knew it was out there and was not pleased. The small packhorse, however, didn't seem to care whether the cat was there or not.

Blacky, called the Huntsmaster, **how far to shiny place?**

Not far, Arantar-sao. Not far.

Arantar cut the trail for the companions, Savon'el riding a bit to the left and rear in support. Bonaire struggled with his horse and the packhorse next to the mage girl just twenty feet behind them. Next came Melisande, with the big warrior on the black warhorse on her flank. Solothon ranged as rearguard.

"I wish I knew your name," whispered Eton as he stroked the warhorse's mane.

"If you wish," said Melisande, "I can ask."

"Who?"

"The horse," she replied with a grin.

"You can do that?" asked the quiet man incredulously.

"Of course, just as you can speak with your cat. I learned the language of horses because until recently I was afraid of them." Then, with a tilt of her head she asked, "Shall I?"

"I would like to know…" he whispered as Melisande's grin broadened.

She closed her eyes and, as she mentally recited the words, touched both index fingers to her lips were they received a light kiss. Then she placed those fingers to either side of her mouth and felt the power surge.

<I address thee.> came the equine greeting from her lips.

<I address thee.> responded the black as he tossed his head.

<Thy shape is of equine, but thou move as a shadow. Art thou equine?>

<Yes…and no.>

<Which?>

The big black brought his head about and his blue eyes to those of the cleric's.

<Wouldst thou know?>

<He, who sits astride thee, wouldst know.>

<He could ask if he wishes it.>

Now it was Melisande's turn to look. She gazed upon the man in studded leather, the strange infinity scars adorning his cheeks, and wondered.

<He hasn't that knowledge?>

<He has the birthright.> After a slight pause, added, <He will not, or knows not how to use it, therefore, thee may translate.>

<I thank thee. Thou hast a name?>

<'Twas given by my former companion. "Hellshadow" it is.>

The girl appraised the horse from nose to flank.

<Why Hellshadow?>

<Heredity and grace. Though my companion was of darkness, he, though he knew it not, bred my heredity within. My father was "Hellspawn" of the breed of Nightmare, whereas I was foal to "Moonshadow," a Unicorne mare. Though I am warrior bred, my mother's grace and compassion lie within me.>

<Who was your companion?>

<Pantor.>

"Melisande?" whispered Eton to the now-pale girl.

She shook her head and caught his worried look.

"It's nothing," she sighed. "Just the strain, I suppose."

<What of your new companion?> Melisande asked of the horse.

<I like this one, for he has the gift.>

Eton watched the strange look come over the cleric's face.

"Melisande? What is it?"

"He has quite a history," the cleric said softly. Then, with a grin, "He has a most colorful ancestry. His name is…" She frowned, then quickly continued, "'Shadow.' He likes you."

"Strangely, I like him," responded the warrior. "I've never liked horses, mostly because they don't like Fleet. But this one, Shadow, is different. I feel a certain…something in him that I've only felt with Fleet. Besides," he whispered with a grin, "Fleet says that this one is a friend, and that is enough for me."

"I hope so," she mumbled.

"What?" asked the youth.

Melisande caught motion in the corner of her eye and turned quickly to the front.

"Look!" she exclaimed. "The raven is back! That must mean we are close to the Pentacle."

Blacky glided in to land on Arantar's outstretched arm.

Will find shiny place when dark not full, Arantar-sao.

The Huntsmaster brought his roan to a stop and waited until all of his companions were close.

"We'll arrive just before dark," he said softly. "Keep close and quiet."

Quiet earth brother say uglies here before, but gone now.

Quiet earth…?

The raven took wing toward the "shiny place."

Two of Ta'el's moons were high and the third had moved up to greet them when Arantar broke into the clearing. There, strangely, a small stand of tall elms rose shimmering in the moonlight.

"I think we've found it," he cast softly over his shoulder to the blond half elf.

Savon'el quickly took in the clearing and drew up on his reins next to the Huntsmaster. The others came in behind and slowed to a stop as well, save Eton.

He rode to the Huntsmaster's side and cast a suspicious eye at the wood line that surrounded the clearing. He glanced at the Huntsmaster and received a nod, but it was Savon'el who put words to the obvious.

"I like not the openness of this place. Arantar and I will go forward and check for our safety. The rest of you stay within the woods."

He tossed a meaningful glance at the knight, who still rode at the rear of the party.

"Sir Solothon, should you hear fighting, take this group to safety. Don't risk all to save us. We will be better able to retreat if we do not have your safety to worry about."

The knight nodded and, though he scowled, Eton joined him in finding a space in the trees to dismount.

Arantar followed Savon'el as that one set his horse slowly toward the stand of elms. Off to his right, Arantar noted the silent movement of the sleek cat padding slowly toward the elms.

Arantar-sao. came the wind song to the Huntsmaster's mind.

Blacky?

Same. No uglies here. Once was, now not. Come quick.

We are on our way.

Then, to the blond half elf, he said, "Be careful. There seems to have been activity here recently, though there is none now."

"The bird, Huntsmaster?"

Arantar caught the grin as the blond stepped up his mount's pace. They made it to the elms without incident and dismounted. Savon'el's sword slipped silently out of its sheath as he moved through the trees. Arantar released his great blade a moment later and flanked the young blond half elf to his right.

The Pentacle was there, its pillars tall at the points of the Druid's pentagram. From the warmth of the three campfires just off of the shiny surface, both knew it had been used recently.

Just as the two half elves were about to split up and move in opposite directions around the Pentacle, the puma padded out of the elms and, after moving to the center of the silvery pentagram and sniffing the air, mewled softly and sat.

Arantar smiled and relaxed.

"That's Eton's companion," he whispered to the tense Savon'el. "I think he's trying to tell us that it's all right to bring the rest here."

The Huntsmaster caught the quick grin.

"Looks that way, doesn't it?" said the blond softly. "But that cat sets up a new problem. How are we to transport us, our horses, and him at the same time?"

"Good question," responded the Huntsmaster as he followed Savon'el toward their horses. "We'll have to ask Eton."

"What do you know of him, Arantar?" asked Savon'el as he gathered the reins to his mount and stepped into the stirrup.

"I know," replied he, "that he is different, yet the same as we. I've served with him many times in the skirmishes on the borders and I trust him. More than that..." He shrugged.

"That, my friend," commented the blond as he drew his mount about, "is good enough for me." He tapped the chestnut gently in the ribs.

Once all the companions arrived at the Pentacle, the question of the cat returned.

"I cannot see how we will be able to control our mounts on that thing with your puma in residence."

Rene' felt the quick anger that rose from the big warrior at Savon'el's statement and marveled at the attempt to remain calm. Eton looked to the mage girl and nodded.

"There are only two horses among us that need extra care," she said. "That would be Bonaire's and possibly the packhorse. The rest are either trained or respond to command."

"Then what are our options?" asked Savon'el.

"The packhorse may only need a strong hand to maintain its calm. Bonaire's is another problem. I can probably lock its fears away long enough to pass, through I won't be able to hold the concentration long through the transition."

The knight stepped forward and took the reins to the packhorse.

"Worry not, m'lady," he said. "I shall hold him through all."

"Do what you must, Lady Rene', and let us mount the Pentacle."

Rene' smiled at the blond half elf and moved softly before the untrained black. She closed her eyes and reached deep. As she touched the horse's fear, she threw a mental wall over it, effectively blocking it, though for only as long as she held it in place. Holding her concentration intact, she took the reins and stepped toward the pentagram and the puma.

"Eton, will you please move your cat to the edge?" she asked stiffly.

At a quick growl from the big warrior, the puma padded to the far side and lay down. Solothon, his hand wrapped in the reins to the packhorse, led the way onto the pentagram. The others followed suit, save Eton.

Eton's black pranced over to the cat, snorted, and placed himself as if a shield before Fleet. Eton followed Shadow and leaned back against the big horse's rump, his arms folded akimbo.

"Are we ready?"

Savon'el glanced around the Pentacle. He knew he should remember how to use the Pentacle, but that memory eluded him.

"Solothon, you know of our destination. As Rene' is indisposed, would you..."

The knight nodded and stepped to a pillar and touched two runes in turn. At the last, he took a firm grip on the reins he held, closed his eyes, and saw, again, the words "Lady of the Woods."

He concentrated on that as he touched the last rune.

There was a drifting, a lightness. They rode a breeze through time and space.

However, just as they were to emerged on the other side, Rene' felt a jolt, a wrenching that seemed to wrapped her insides into knots. When it hit, she lost concentration, and as the companions appeared on the other side, her charge's fear came up. She might have been able to reestablish that protective wall, save for the way they all arrived.

They appeared two to three feet above their destination and fell to the broken surface below.

The silver Pentacle that had been placed there so many centuries ago that it was lost to historians was, impossibly, shattered. The pillars were cast down all about in disarray and a six-foot high wall of stone a meter thick surrounded the desecrated surface.

The puma landed, let out a snarl of confusion, and leapt for the wall as the mounts and companions fell to the broken surface.

Shadow was the first horse on his feet and he placed himself directly in front of Eton. While Bonaire's pony and the packhorse kicked, bucked, and bit at everyone around them, the other horses, Rene's palomino especially, fidgeted wide-eyed and frightened. Though the companions tried to calm the two out-of-control horses and their own, they were in danger of being crushed or crippled in the small confines of the pentagram.

Rene' shook off the effects of their passage and saw that not even the knight could bring order to the frightened horses. She threw back the mantles that concealed her power and, in a single blast of "Peace," expended all of her remaining strength and collapsed to the broken surface.

Suddenly, all was still. The horses stopped and stood as calm as if in stables. The companions felt the peace wash over them. Then Savon'el saw the prone mage girl.

He'd knelt quickly and lifted the girl's head. He felt her breath come in ragged gasps and, as Melisande joined him beside the girl, glanced at that the others.

"Arantar, Solothon," he stated in a sharp command voice. "Check the perimeter. Bonaire, watch the horses. Eton?"

The big warrior had already leapt to the top of the wall. He watched as the puma, which had cleared the wall and landed on the narrow strip of land between the wall and a foul-smelling, twenty-foot wide moat that completely surrounded the walled Pentacle, sniffed at the sludge and snorted.

On the other side of the moat, the grass was green and the land fertile. On this side, the brown grass, what little there was of it, had grown in strange deformation.

Eton looked down at the outside wall. It was studded with two-foot long steel spikes spaced every six to eight inches over the entire surface.

Eton knew of these Pentacles, but he never had a reason to use them until now. His knowledge was a sense of history and beauty in the construction of these platforms. Now, he felt the desecration that invaded his soul. He growled.

"What could have happened to cause this?"

Eton cast a quick glance at the Huntsmaster as that one knelt at his side. Then he turned his attention back to the puma as it moved silently along the banks of the churning ooze.

"I cannot think of the power brought to bear here, friend," Eton whispered. "To have destroyed this sacred place in this way…"

"I know," responded Arantar softly as he glanced up at the sun as it fell, unmistakably, toward nightfall. "We must find a way out of here for our horses. Then we can worry about that open sewer."

"What of the lady?"

That comment brought Arantar's eyes back to where the blond half elf held Rene's head on his lap.

"Come," he said as he stepped to the inner side of the wall, "we've seen enough."

He dropped back onto the broken silver of the destroyed pentagram and crossed to the savon'el while Eton went to check the big warhorse.

"What did you see, Huntsmaster?" asked the blond half elf as Arantar knelt next to him.

Arantar glanced at the cleric where she sat holding the mage girl's hand. He sighed.

"I don't know how we even made it here with the Pentacle destroyed so absolutely," he said as he sat. "The wall is thick, about four foot, and it is studded with spikes all over the outside, as if to dissuade anyone from getting in. Beyond the wall, about twenty to thirty feet out, a twenty-foot moat filled with something foul-smelling and evil."

He laid a hand on Rene's forehead and felt for damage. Finding little, he sighed again.

"She'll be out for quite a while," he stated as he took his hand away. Then, "Savon'el, the thing that bothers me the most isn't the devastation, though it feels more like sacrilege than anything else. It's more…Is all of this meant to keep something out, or to keep something in?"

"I haven't a clue," he replied as he brushed golden hair from the girl's closed eyes. "We can do nothing until Rene' is ready to travel and I feel our time is running short," The savon'el looked at the sky as it turned toward dusk. "If this were done specifically to stop us, it seems someone succeeded. If not…"

Arantar could see the concern and turmoil in those amber eyes and it hurt.

"My friend," he said, drawing those eyes to him, "you must not take this blame upon yourself. I believe that there are no coincidences in this universe. Therefore, we were meant to be here, now, with you."

Then he returned his hand to the mage girl's forehead.

"As for Rene', she did what she thought she must. That is all. Now," he continued distractedly, his eyes for the girl in gold, "if you will join Eton on the wall, you might see something we missed. Meanwhile, between Lady Melisande and myself, we will attempt to rouse Rene'. Somehow we've lost time, probably through the broken portal. I don't know whether 'tis but a day or several, but I do know that we must move."

"Then do what you must," replied Savon'el as he stood and allowed Melisande to take his place at Rene's head. "Your counsel, as always Huntsmaster, is welcome," he stated as he moved toward the wall.

Chapter Thirty-three

"The wall was not built," stated the golden-haired mage. "It was conjured."

Savon'el paced before the girl as she sat on the blanket Arantar had provided. She sipped at the watered wine Melisande carried.

"Notice the lack of joints, mortar, and trowel marks. This wall was thrown up by a powerful wielder of magiks in seconds, probably as a defense. Whatever happened here used an amazing amount of power. The question is, why?"

"If a great mage did this, is it fair to say that he or she is in front of us, possibly hunting us?" asked the blond half elf.

"Not likely," she replied, "though it would help to know if there were any tracks on the outside of the wall."

"We found none, m'lady," said Arantar. "As far as we can see, there are tracks beyond the moat, but they seem to bypass this place altogether."

"Then I can see nothing that tells me what or why this happened."

"Wait, Rene'," the cleric broke in, "do you still have Rairy's spell book?"

"Yes. Why?"

"I remember some of the spells that you and I both dodged because they were just so far beyond us. There were many, of course, but these dealt with conjuring great blocks of granite into existence and walls many feet high. Remember?"

"If it were…conjured, as you say," asked Savon'el, "can you take it down with another spell, maybe one from that book?"

"I wouldn't begin to know how, nor would I try it," Rene' responded. "The spell itself is so far beyond my capabilities that the reversal spell would be even worse. I am...vain in some things, as my friends so thoughtfully bring to my attention," this with a secret grin at Melisande, "but I am not given to self-immolation. I'm finding that my limited talents are more limited than I thought."

"Rene', stop asking for compliments," said the cleric with a faked stern wag of her finger. After she received the smile she was looking for, she said, "Look about this place."

"What are you talking about?" this from the blond half elf.

"Just look at the way this place has been destroyed. The surface has been buckled and broken, but nothing but heat, and a lot of it, could cause the edges of the blocks to melt so."

The mage girl noticed the melting, not charring, of the broken pieces about her, but she looked back at Melisande with a question in her eyes.

"Remember when Maxim said that Lord Rairy must have faced a horrible end?" the cleric continued. "He said that Rairy was going out to meet someone. We know that Radagast was...now, how did our friend put it... 'dust' before Rairy left, so who was he going out to meet and where?"

"What you are saying, my dear," said Rene', her fingers again tapping her chin, "is that we may now be occupying the last stand of our little benefactor?"

"Yes. The evidence is all about us. Is there anyone in your mind who could, or would, attempt to destroy a Pentacle? They have been here longer than...than we have as a species. They don't rust or corrode, and they are not eroded by weather or the passage of time. Many swords have been driven into the surface as a traveler touches the last rune and shouts his destination, yet there is no mar on the surface at all. The only way this surface could have been destroyed, and I admit to having limited knowledge, is if a Mage War mage cast a very powerful spell. Now," she continued, "I am not too certain of my facts, but here is what I think happened. Lord Rairy, who, as Maxim told you, was working to help end the war on dragons, accepted an invitation from, or was ordered to report to, someone like Banshe'e. Fire Gap Keep or Radagast's keep would have been an appropriate destination and this location the perfect ambush."

"So," added the mage girl, "when Rairy popped out upon the Pentacle, Banshe'e was waiting, and as Rairy cast the protective spell that erected the wall and moat—"

"Banshe'e cast a more powerful spell, destroying the Pentacle and everything, and specifically everyone, within the Pentacle," finished Melisande. "But the Pentacles were created with a ward, I've been told, that won't allow anyone standing within to be harmed."

"That may be, Melisande, but if you are powerful enough to destroy a thing—"

"All of this is interesting conjecture, m'lady," broke in Savon'el, "but it still doesn't answer the immediate questions. How do we get out of here and where do we go from here? Solothon, does your map show this area and our direction of travel?"

"Yes, Savon'el, it does," stated the knight as he pulled his map case from his saddlebags and removed the parchment from it.

He spread the map out on a piece of the broken surface and frowned at it for a moment.

"From what I can make of the surrounding landmarks, we are here." A gauntleted finger stabbed at a point on the map many leagues from the last Pentacle. "Exactly where we were supposed to be. Obviously, we cannot use our planned jump to the Pentacle north of the Keep, as this Pentacle is no longer operative. So, our route must then be along the edge of the woods we saw on the other side of the moat, through what seems to be a valley or canyon. Beyond that is Fire Gap Keep and the road to our destination."

"I believe we will find more than a 'Keep' at the end of our journey."

"Why do you say that?" Savon'el asked as his eyes swung quickly to the Huntsmaster.

"If this place is, or was, what we believe it to be, it would almost have to be more extensive." After a short pause he continued, "With the kind of power we are speculating still exists, it is probably well-defended, even at this late date."

"That would stand to reason," replied the blond half elf, his eyes now blank with introspection. "If Rairy's cottage could last so long..."

Then, he shook his head.

"But the question is moot. We will never know what waits before us unless we can get out of here. Now, I see this problem in two stages: First, if we climb the wall and jump to the other side, which is within our power to accomplish, we will never be able to jump the moat. For that, we need our mounts. Yet, second, our mounts, though maybe Eton's could be different, cannot leap the wall. Without luck and answers, we have come as far as we can."

"You sound as though we are already defeated," stated the Huntsmaster as he wiped his great sword one last time with the oiled rag from his kit and returned it to its sheath.

"Not so," responded Savon'el slowly, his face taut with thought. "There is just...there must be something we missed, something..."

His eyebrows shot up and he turned his attention to the mage girl.

"Rene', where would you stand if you conjured a wall such as this?"

"I've told you that I cannot—"

"Yes, of course, but if you could?"

"Then," replied Rene', her fingers tapping her concentration on her chin, "given the dimensions of this enclosure and the almost perfect dimensions of this wall, I would have to stand directly in the center..."

Rene's mouth dropped open.

"So," said the blond half elf slowly as a grin crept to his lips, "if you did this—"

"I would have left a *door!*" she finished.

"Arantar," he barked, "you and Solothon start at that point where Eton stands watch and go in opposite directions until you find something out of place. Eton and I will do the same on the top of the wall. Just be careful."

Eton nodded from his vantage point and moved to the edge to help Savon'el climb up.

"Bonaire, you stay with the ladies and our mounts. Now, if you find something—"

"Wait!" said Rene' as she rose from her blanket.

Melisande stood close, for she feared that the girl had not rested enough to sustain long activity. The Huntsmaster's hand stayed the knight and they turned back toward the mage girl.

"Don't look for something out of place, for you won't find it. *Feel* for it, but carefully."

Savon'el nodded and followed the two to the wall. Arantar gave him a hand up while Eton aided with a hand of his own.

"As Rene' suggested, move slowly," said the savon'el as he began moving slowly along the wall.

He tested each step before he put weight on it. Eton turned and mimicked the blond's movement while Arantar and Solothon moved slowly along the wall in opposite directions, feeling for whatever they could find with their hands.

Arantar, who moved in the same direction the blond had taken, found what they were looking for just feet from where they started. He had been running his hands up and down the wall when his right hand abruptly seemed to sink into the stone.

Automatically, his tongue clicked the warrior's signal for stop. The savon'el froze with one foot in the air. He brought that foot back until it was next to the other and knelt carefully.

"What is it, Arantar?"

"I think I found it!" he replied as he again passed his hand into the stone.

He moved the hand through the stone as he walked slowly along the wall until he met an obstruction.

"The opening is about four feet wide, just wide enough for the horses," he stated. Then, "Watch for me on the other side."

He walked slowly into the wall and moments later he appeared on the other side, the spikes there seeming to penetrate his body. He continued walking slowly until he was free of the illusion before he turned back to his friends.

Solothon had joined Eton and Savon'el on the wall by then and all looked down at the grinning Huntsmaster.

"It's like walking through deep water, but it's passable. Before anyone else attempts this, let me see if I can return."

The Huntsmaster walked slowly back toward the spikes until they seemed to touch his body. Then, with a grin, he stepped forward.

The spikes looked as if they passed through his body as if he were a wraith. A few steps and Arantar was once again within the enclosure and was joined on the ground by his companions from the wall.

"Solothon and I, being more familiar with the horses," said the Huntsmaster as he and the knight moved quickly to ready the mounts, "will take them through. It will be difficult to convince them that that is not a wall, so we will blindfold them."

The last was said as he looked toward the knight and received a nod. However, as the knight approached the big black warhorse in the black livery, that one snorted and tossed its head.

"I don't think he wants to be led," came the whisper from behind.

Solothon turned to find the big warrior stepping toward the wall, his eyes only for the massive mount. The horse tossed his head again and followed Eton through to the other side.

"It's amazing," said the Huntsmaster as they all watched the black tail disappeared through the wall. "A day ago he couldn't ride. Now those two are almost inseparable."

Then he picked up the reins to Bonaire's black and the palomino of the mage girl and moved to the wall.

The knight followed with Savon'el and Melisande's mounts with Bonaire at his side. A moment later, Solothon and Arantar returned for their own mounts and the packhorse.

Savon'el and Melisande aided the mage girl through the wall by lending an arm apiece until they were clear of the wall on the other side. Then Savon'el turned back toward the wall while the black-haired cleric led Rene' to a blanket Eton had thrown onto the twisted grass. A moment passed and the two fighters appeared through the wall with the packhorse and their own mounts in tow.

"Our only problem now," exclaimed the blond as he quickly surveyed the moat, "is negotiating that foul-smelling mess. Our friend back there said something about us being in the mountains by late tomorrow. Hopefully, since he expressed the importance of that, it is now tomorrow."

"Do you think there may be a bridge here hidden by illusion?" asked the Huntsmaster of the golden girl.

"If there were," replied the blond half elf for her, "we haven't the time to search. We have less than an hour, by my reckoning, to get to yon mountains. The question we should be asking is: can our mounts leap beyond the moat carrying us and our possessions? And what of the packhorse?"

Savon'el looked from Arantar to the knight for that answer.

"All but that one," responded the knight, his finger pointing directly at Bonaire's black, "should be capable of it. The packhorse should be able to make it without a problem. We may have to share its load between the larger horses to aid it, but—"

"Wait a minute!" shouted the young elf. "If you think I'm gonna leave him here, you're mistaken. Just like you must be balmy to think I'm gonna try and jump him across that!"

"There's no other way," said the mage girl softly.

"There better be!" came the stubborn reply.

"You discuss it with him," said Melisande crossly as she turned toward her mount and, in a gentle leap, was seated in the saddle. "I'm going over," She touched heels to the sorrel's ribs.

They all watched as that well-trained mount burst into motion and, at the very edge of the roiling sludge, lunged into a leap that cleared the other edge by better than a yard. The black-haired cleric slid from her mount's back and, as she stroked its neck, faced back toward her companions.

"We haven't got all day, and I don't really wish to continue on my own."

The Huntsmaster grinned at the knight and turned to face Bonaire. Behind the young elf, Arantar noticed that Eton's black had followed the young warrior as that one aided the mage girl into her saddle. As the palomino minced, the big mount snorted. Eton looked at Shadow as that one tossed his head.

"I think," he whispered, "that Shadow would rather you jumped with him."

"What about my horse?"

It was Arantar's turn.

"I think she will follow you over without a rider. Believe me," he continued as Rene's hand brushed the palomino's neck, "that black will carry you over better than yours could. Besides, without your weight and its instincts to keep you in the saddle, your mount will more easily clear the foul-smelling stuff."

Rene' nodded, gave the golden horse a last pat on the neck, and allowed Eton to lift her into the big black saddle. No sooner was the girl seated than Shadow was in motion. At two quick steps he was in the air, sailing gracefully over the brown sludge to land gently on the other side. The big black war mount turned, the mage girl unruffled on his back, and snorted.

The palomino responded in kind and lurched for the moat, clearing it by mere inches.

"You two next," said Savon'el to the Huntsmaster and knight.

Once they had safely made it to the green grass on the other side, the blond turned to Eton.

"You can call your mount back and he will take you to safety. I will remain here and attempt to convince our young friend to join us. Besides, I may need you on the other side to coax the packhorse over."

"Not so," answered Eton as he looked across at the black warhorse.

Shadow snorted again and the packhorse was in motion. It leaped scant inches from the edge of the moat and landed scant inches from the moat on the other side.

As soon as the packhorse landed, Shadow, as if on signal, again leapt the moat. As that animal pranced to Eton's side, the big warrior turned back to Savon'el.

"They need you," he whispered. "I will handle this one."

Savon'el glanced at the recalcitrant Bonaire, nodded to Eton, and mounted. As the blond half elf cleared the moat with room to spare, Eton approached the young elf.

"I don't know what game you think you are playing," he began in a lethal whisper, "but those others are concerned for you. Frankly, I don't give a damn. Stay here and rot. There is no other way off but the way they've gone. Now, get mounted!"

The entire time the big warrior spoke, he backed Bonaire toward his horse. At the last word, he grabbed the elf by the belt and lifted him bodily into the saddle.

Unfortunately, that only tended to make the smaller black more nervous and it jerked about skittishly. Eton had his right hand on the saddle and looked up at the elf while Bonaire grasped the reins and the pommel of his saddle for support.

The young elf had just looked down at the warrior when the black screamed and ran for the moat. It went into the air inches from the edge of the sludge and landed a foot to the other side.

What neither of them had seen, nor had the others watching from the other side noticed, was the strange visage that had greeted Bonaire's mount as it looked past Eton to Shadow.

That great mount had simply parted its lips. Lips that, once parted, displayed its birthright: the three-inch fangs of the Nightmare! The fear that had caused the poor horse to bolt made it difficult for both Arantar and the knight to stop it when it reached the other shore.

Eton was nudged out of his shock by a warm nose on his back. He turned, stroked the big black's jaw line, mounted, and was quickly carried to his new companions. The tawny puma followed them in a graceful, almost effortless leap. Then it disappeared into the woods that seemed to reach toward the valley and the mountains beyond.

"He has the right idea," commented the blond half elf as he watched the puma go. "Huntsmaster, if you please."

They made camp at the mouth of the valley as the sun went down. Savon'el sat across the small fire from Melisande and Rene' and cleaned the length of brownish-green blade carefully. The two women entered into a friendly discussion of the differences between their faiths.

Bonaire sat away from the group, his back to them as he mumbled to himself.

"Just wait and see. I'll get to the treasure first and then they'll see."

Sir Solothon had taken his sword and, after seeing to Enare's comfort, walked into the woods to pray. His soul was troubled by the knowledge of his inheritance and he needed a sign from the Mother to continue with these friends.

Savon'el returned his sword to its sheath and looked about the small camp. The horses, with the notable exception of Eton's big black and the two well-trained warhorses, were picketed away from the mouth of the small valley. The small smokeless fire was too small for anything save heating the small bits of smoked meat on the end of sticks. The worry lines gracing his brow, however, were due to the absence of the Huntsmaster and the big warrior, Eton.

He could have saved his worrying for himself and this party. At that moment, Eton knelt to read the sign closer. He and Arantar had moved farther down the valley to the point where it became a lengthy ravine. Here, the warrior's keen senses detected the path taken days ago by a large group, but it was the Huntsmaster who found the greatest threat.

"These were made by gualu boots, my friend," whispered Arantar. "But these over here are much larger and cause me more concern. What do you make of this?"

"Fifteen to twenty on foot and in full battle dress. Those you found are not like any I've ever seen. The wearer of those boots is either laden with stores and armor, which I doubt due to the speed at which they are traveling, or is a very large warrior, not one of these. If I hadn't seen those tracks, I would have looked for the smaller footprints of daku. Yet now…"

"I agree. I've seen boots like these before worn by a mountain of a gualu. Those we call Habuk-ha. I met one on the way to Catlorian dressed as a human, not in the stinking leathers of these other fouled beasts. That one, like this one, was in charge. The difference is, that one had daku leadership. I haven't seen sign of daku, just these, and that worries me."

"I say, 'where there is smoke'…We must be careful from here on. Ambush is their weapon and we must guard against it."

"Let's get back to the others. Savon'el must be warned," said the Huntsmaster as he and the big warrior slipped back toward the camp silently.

Less than fifty meters from the small fire, Eton growled deep in his throat and a small flutter of brush was all that the Huntsmaster heard as the puma stole into the night deeper into the valley.

"Who is this Savon'el, Arantar?"

The whispered question was one that the Huntsmaster had expected long ago. He knew this man's reputation and his eccentricities. He knew that Eton never asked about anything unless there was a reason. To withhold any information from the big warrior, in light of the past day's events, would be dishonorable and foolish. The Huntsmaster slowed his steps and began.

It was much later when the two men of the forest returned to the camp, slipping noiselessly through the brush and stepping into the small clearing.

Savon'el sat with his head in his hands; the pain behind his eyes gave him no rest.

Rene', however, slept beneath the blanket from her saddle, while Melisande sat cross legged beside her wrapped in her bright yellow cloak.

"You should get some sleep," said the Huntsmaster softly.

Melisande's eyes left the fire and took in the two men at the edge of the clearing.

"Rene's just dropped off," she whispered. "She's not strong enough to protect herself right now. She's spent much of her strength and it will take time for her to regain it. I will watch over her until she wakes."

"It is not necessary," whispered the warrior with the brand of the infinite upon his cheeks. "Fleet watches this night. His senses are far better than ours and, frankly, whatever rest we get now will probably be the only good rest we get from here on."

"What do you mean?" asked the blond, his head coming slowly from the cradle of his hands.

Arantar didn't like the weariness he detected in the amber eyes or the haunted look he also found there. He also wasn't prepared to see Eton, who'd never seemed to get close to anyone, lay a hand on Savon'el shoulder as he crouched before him.

"You must rest also," he whispered through his ruined throat. "There is much to be done on the morrow and we need you at your best."

Then the warrior stood and glanced about the campsite.

"Where is Shadow?"

"He left shortly after the knight slipped away for his nightly prayers," answered Melisande.

"Worry not for me, m'lady," came the knight's voice from beyond the flickering firelight. As Solothon stepped out of the wood line, he continued, "I'm cursed, but in good spirits."

The big black warhorse stepped from the wood line farther down from where the knight had appeared and, after catching Eton's eye, snorted and disappeared again. The warrior knew that with that steed on this side and Fleet at the other, they would be relatively safe this night.

"Don't speak so, Solothon," the black-haired girl chastised softly. "You are not cursed and we will soon find a way to rid to you of your malady. Rene' and I have been discussing that very thing this night. I'm sure that with time we will find the answer. You must have faith."

"I have faith, dear lady, but I'm a realist. If I should lose myself again, mayhap one of you will be forced to stop me. I pray that it will not come to that, but if it does, stay not your blade. It would be far better to die by the hand of a friend then to have friendly blood upon my sword."

With that, the knight stepped quickly to his black, removed his bedding from behind the saddle, and came to the fireside.

"What news?" he asked as he spread his bedding on the ground.

"Gualu," replied the Huntsmaster.

<I will sleep with Fleet this night.> signed in the warrior.

Arantar acknowledged this with a nod and Eton slipped cat-like into the brush.

"Where is he going?" asked Savon'el softly.

"Where he will do the most good," replied Arantar. "Now, as to what we found..."

A few hours before dawn, the blond half elf came up from his nightmare drenched in cold sweat. He sat up from his bedroll and, with the end of a stick, poked new life into the coals of the fire. He added two small pieces of wood and as they caught he rubbed at his temple in a vain attempt to ease the pain there.

"Do you need help?" came the query from across the flickering flames.

The light danced in the green pools of the cleric's eyes as she gazed across at the troubled savon'el.

"No, m'lady," he replied. "I have slept enough, though I feel I haven't rested since—"

"Since your life began?" she finished as she sat up on her blanket. "You are troubled, and rightly so. I do not know if I could bear your pain with as much strength."

"We all have burdens. Mine is not as great as others."

"Perhaps," she replied. Savon'el thought he saw a flash in those eyes as some secret thought went through the girl's mind. Rene' turned in her sleep, a frown on her face. As Melisande's face softened, so too did the frown lines on the golden mage girl's face.

"Each of us has seen sadness, but we've known at the time who we were. You have been stripped of your youth, your memories of friends and enemies, of your birthright. I would much rather face my demons than yours, my friend. Know this: I am here should you have need."

The eyes softened further and Savon'el nodded. As the cleric lay down once again and drifted back to sleep, he gazed into the flicker of the fire to let his few memories assemble themselves. Each was scrutinized until the light of dawn seeped across the land about him.

It did not take long for the companions to be up and about. After all of their mounts were prepared for travel, Arantar and Eton took the time to ensure that the signs of their campsite were as hidden as possible.

They rode slowly through the ravine at the end of the small valley, the light of morning full across the cliffs above.

Arantar led with the quiet warrior on the great black to his left rear. The puma ranged left and even with the Huntsmaster, each stealthy pad at full alert.

Bonaire rode solemnly at guard to Melisande, as she glanced back occasionally at the blond half elf. Savon'el and the knight rode to left and right of the sleep renewed mage girl.

Both had strung their bows that morning as they prepare to leave. Solothon carried his in his left hand while his right gripped his reins firmly and his eyes raked the cliff tops for danger. Savon'el had opened the case and draped the short bow over it. It seemed natural to him and he had long ago decided to let his body dictate his hidden talents.

Arantar-sao! the breeze screamed through the Huntsmaster's mind. *Big ugly! Uglies all place!*

"Wagagoon, combagya!"

The deep, guttural gualu command chased the raven's thought to the Huntsmaster. His sword cleared his sheath as the first gualu burst from the surrounding brush.

Then, as he parried that one's thrust, more enemies leapt into the fray. Arantar had no time to see how his companions fared and prayed they would live through this.

He needn't have bothered.

The smell of his hated enemy caused Eton to slide immediately from the big black's back. The basket hilt of the Bourjon blade slid comfortably into his gauntleted left hand, and the long sword flashed from the sheath at his back. As the gualu crashed through the brush, the big warrior smiled and moved though them.

Melisande followed Eton's lead as she too dropped to the ground. She had no training from horseback, but once on firm ground she was in her element. The pent up rage in her heart burst through now to be displayed in the angry visage her face had become and the spinning destruction of the great maul in her hands.

She felt sheer joy as the steel-banded head of her weapon crushed the chest of the first unlucky creature to reach her. She spun the weapon and drove the steel capped shank into the forehead of the next. The crushed skull and crossed eyes fueled her savagery as three more of the beasts surrounded her. Her green eyes flashed fire as she spun the great weapon over her head and grinned.

Savon'el, as the Huntsmaster drew his sword, lifted the bow from his quiver with his right hand while his left deftly plucked a silver-tipped arrow. The arrow was nocked in an instant, but before he could draw it to his ear, he felt the pain in his right leg. He spun in his saddle and, ignoring the arrow that protruded from his armor, released the shaft at the movement on the edge of the cliff. The arrow careened off of the stones and past the enemy archer's ear with little room to spare. That gualu dropped to the ground as the half elf nocked another arrow.

The knight felt the arrow drive through his mail as it narrowly missed his kidney and protruded from the other side. He kneed his mount around and saw his target: a gualu archer on the left side of the ravine. As the archer placed another shaft into its bow, Solothon ground his teeth in anger, drew the shaft on his long bow to his ear, and released it. It sped toward the enemy, yet missed its mark by mere inches. The knight had used too much control, wishing not to drop into madness, and his aim was affected.

The gualu jumped up as the knight's arrow screamed over its head. It drew back on its bow only to watch helplessly as three spears of blinding light drove through its chest. Its eyes rolled up as it died, and Solothon glanced over at the mage girl.

Rene' wiped her still-smoking fingers on her cloak as she looked from the fallen gualu to the melee to the front. She watched as Eton danced through four of the luckless gualu, both blades screaming through air, flesh, and bone.

As two others join the battle, those four crumbled to the ground, dead where they stood. The Bourjon blade parried the down swept blade as the long sword in the warrior's right hand slipped under the parry to pin the wielder's heart to its backbone. Eton turned in time to see a brown blur hit the other gualu in the back. One swipe of the great cat's paw ripped that one's throat away.

The maul was a living thing in the hands of the black-haired cleric and she seemed to be enjoying herself. The three surrounded her and tried in vain to penetrate the spinning defense she wove with the iron-hard maul. She parried stroke after stroke, apparently toying with them.

Finally, one of her attackers came too close to skewering her and her anger flared brighter than ever. That unlucky gualu caught the steel-banded head of the great maul directly on top of his head. The irresistible force of that blow drove his head down into his chest while the furious cleric reversed the maul and without looking drove the steel-capped end into the chest of the foe attacking from the rear, crushing ribs and bursting its heart.

A third gualu burst through the brush and, seeing the speed at which its companions had met their end, backed away, eyes wide with fear.

Melisande was having none of that.

In two quick steps she came within striking distance and strike she did. The gualu's kneecaps shattered as the great maul screamed through the dusty air. Unable to move, it could only lie there and watch as the grinning cleric brought the maul down upon his head with enough force to drive it into the ground.

Her green eyes flashed as she spun the maul, blood and brains from its head spraying the ground all about her.

The Huntsmaster stood in his stirrups, the great gray blade wreaking destruction on both sides of his mount. There were seven in the beginning; now there were three. He leaped from his saddle as one of the surviving attackers yanked on Bonaire's mount's bridle, pulling that animal to the ground.

Bonaire was on his feet in an instant and drew his sword just in time to deflect the blow aimed at removing his head. The sword once again came alive in the youth's hand as it danced down the length of the foe's blade to imbed itself in its chest.

As the green crystal sword slid smoothly into the foe, Bonaire's power waxed to full. A strange tingling streaked down the elf's arm and into the blade. The gualu screamed as its bones ceased to be. It collapsed in a mound of throbbing flesh with no substance to hang its muscles upon.

Bonaire was in a state of shock. His sword left his hands and he backed away from the still-living puddle of flesh.

Arantar watched as that gualu's companion gripped its sword tighter and ran toward Bonaire. The Huntsmaster made short work of the gualu before him. Then, as Bonaire's new enemy jumped over the fallen horse to attack him, Arantar leaped. He crashed into the gualu's side and, spinning hard to his left, swept the great blade around and through that enemy's chest. Then, as three more gualu burst through the brush, the Huntsmaster's right hand landed smartly on the young elf's cheek.

"Wake up, you fool!" he screamed as he turned to face the new on-slaught. "Pick up your sword and defend yourself, or die!"

Bonaire looked down at the green crystal blade with loathing, but as the Huntsmaster's blade clashed with the blades of the others, he knew that death was waiting for the fainthearted.

He scooped up the weapon and, taking a stand to the Huntsmaster's left, returned blow for blow with the enemy.

Great Wolf drank deep as the Huntsmaster sliced through one of the at-tackers, but now another was behind him. Without pause, Arantar spun the great blade and drove it backward under his armpit. The gualu had thought it would have its kill with no chance of retaliation. The surprise of that great blade thrust through its heart went with it to the next world. The Huntsmaster twisted the sword and withdrew it without looking, his eyes on Bonaire.

The young elf was hesitant in this fight. He'd almost retched when his crystal sword had rendered that gualu to a mass of quivering flesh. Now, though he knew his life depended on it, he didn't seem willing to drive that damnable blade through the remaining attacker. There were many chances to do so, as the Huntsmaster saw, but each time the elf let the chance to go by.

"Kill him, or you kill us all!" shouted the Huntsmaster.

That was enough. The sword came back to life in the hands of the blooded youth. It danced against the steel of the attacker's blade and slid through the gualu, not once but twice.

As that enemy died on its feet, Bonaire returned his sword up and cra-dled on the back of his free hand. He waited. The gualu crumpled to the dirt and shuddered. It never moved again.

Arantar started to move to the elf's side when he heard the gurgle behind him. He turned toward the sound and found, at the feet of Bonaire's now-standing pony, the mass of flesh looking up at him. The eyes held something strange for the Huntsmaster. Instead of loathing, which was something Arantar expected, he found only a look of pleading. The Huntsmaster nodded and drove the great blade down between the thing's eyes. It's shuddered momentarily and lay still.

Solothon had taken in the tide of battle and how, though outnumbered, this group fought with daring and finality. He saw in a quick glance the outcome even before the black-haired cleric spun the maul and looked to the only other resistance.

Savon'el had the gualu effectively pinned down. Every time it raised its head, the blond half elf launched another shaft. Savon'el knew that soon something would have to be done. He couldn't afford to have this archer at their back, yet he couldn't get a decent shot.

As he released his fourth arrow and plucked another from his quiver, he caught the movement of the knight's black mount racing for the cliff. Savon'el prepared to defend the knight's assault, for he thought that Solothon would dismount and attempt to scale the almost sheer obstruction to get to this enemy.

To Savon'el's surprise, though it didn't take him from his task as he released yet another shaft, the knight never slowed the horse. Instead, Solothon brought the trained mount at a full gallop parallel to the cliff and spoke but a word.

Instantly the black Joshua Cantrell dug its hooves into the light rock surface of the cliff wall and at a gallop ran up the cliff side! The knight had to use both hands and soothing words of encouragement to get this well-trained warhorse to do the almost impossible. Once at the top of the fissure, his gauntleted hand once again filled with shining Elvin silver.

The sword's sweet song trilled in his bones as it left the sheath and made quick work of the flabbergasted gualu archer. But the song was not finished.

"Sogh! Sibagraph jibah?"

The guttural language rasped off of the Elvin knight's ear. He pulled his mount to a stop and turned. There, but twenty meters from the edge of the ravine, stood the largest gualu he'd ever seen.

Over seven feet tall and dressed in scale armor, the beast stood with what resembled a smile, applauding sardonically. Before it, standing on its great double-bitted head, was a battle-axe, the heavy handle laced in leather up to the loose strap. The Habuk-ha's breastplate, the only alteration to the full-scale armor, had been scrubbed, seemingly to remove an emblem. The colors—green, red and blue—could be seen, but not the design.

The knight cantered toward the grinning enemy and, less than five meters away, drew rein.

Below, Savon'el watched as the knight ran down the remaining archer and turned to see the end of this battle. He watched as Arantar laid a hand on the young elf's shoulder to gave it a gentle shake, and a grinning Eton stride back toward Melisande, his puma at his side.

Lady Rene' cast her eyes about the battlefield, then leveled them at the half elf.

"Where is Solothon?" she asked softly.

"He's..." he began as his eyes followed his pointing hand toward the edge of the ravine, only to find the knight missing.

Then he heard the guttural voice.

He spurred his mount toward the side of the ravine and leaped from the saddle, but his wounded leg collapsed before he could begin the climb to the top. His face went white as the pain shot through his leg.

"Savon'el!" shouted the mage girl as she drew rein on her own mount and slipped from the saddle.

But the half elf was too one-minded to stop. As he tried to crawl up the side of the cliff, the shaft of the arrow caught on the rocks. This brought a grown of pain and a reluctant cessation of movement.

"Savon'el, you must stop!" said the girl as she came to him. "You will cause yourself more—"

"That matters not!" he gritted. "Solothon is..."

Then, as he caught the Huntsmaster's eye, Rene' watched the irises of the half elf's eyes turned molten, like brass in a smelter.

"Huntsmaster, I need you!"

The power rippled in the air as Arantar's feet set into motion. He had been called and he had to answer. As his feet stopped before the blond half elf, Arantar shook his head.

Savon'el came to his feet and leaned heavily on the Huntsmaster's shoulder.

"Solothon has ridden to the top and I'm afraid that I heard the sound of gualu voices. We must help him!"

All of this time, Eton, feeling the backwash of the voice that had demanded Arantar's presence, had been watching the group below the cliff. He watched as Savon'el motioned toward the top of the ravine as Arantar's eyes followed the movement. He heard the clash of metal from somewhere atop the cliff and knew with a quick glance which of their number was missing.

<Fleet!> he growled. *<Find!>* He pointed up the side of the ravine.

The big cat wasted no time racing up that obstacle. He let out a yowl that could only mean danger and settled, his ears back and bristling, on his belly.

Arantar glanced at the big warrior and caught the sign.

<Danger from above.>

Then the Huntsmaster watched Eton scale, with remarkable ease, the nearly vertical wall.

A moment later, he followed.

Chapter Thirty-four

The Habuk-ha pointed a gauntleted finger at the knight, then at himself. He spun the great axe up and patted the blade.

"You ask for battle?" asked Solothon, his anger under control, but just barely.

The great gualu drew a big circle in the air before him with that same finger and looked askance of the mounted knight.

"Honor Combat?"

Solothon looked upon his opponent now, and noticed how the gualu stood. This one had no fear and obviously knew more about honor than most men. To challenge Honor Combat was to surrender to the strict rules of the code of honor. He'd never heard of Honor Combat in relation to gualu before, but that didn't mean that it couldn't happen. Hell! It was happening right here and now.

The knight nodded and brought the hilt of his sword to his lips. The Habuk-ha acknowledged this sign with a slight bow and then crouched in readiness for the first onslaught.

It was not long in coming as the furious knight touched heels to his war-trained mount.

The initial clash resounded through the ravine below. The knight drew his mount away, a gash opening on his fore quarters. It wasn't deep, but Solothon wouldn't allow his companion to be harmed further. He dismounted and turned to face this enemy.

The Habuk-ha had drawn away and now stood crouched, the axe cradled ready in its big hands. It looked at the horse, then at the knight, and shrugged.

A strange feeling rippled through Solothon's very being. If he had listened, he would have heard the light singing, as if a breeze blew through the trees, emanating from the blade he held in his right hand. But he was not listening. He was angry. Angry at the hurt his friend and companion had taken from the cruel axe in this monster's hands. Angry that he could have avoided that, yet attacked anyway. Angry because...because he was angry, and as his anger built, so sang the silver blade. The knight grinned.

"Pray to your gods, you filth," he said in a very low and lethal voice. "Your blood will soon stain this field."

Then he attacked.

The huge gualu bellowed an unintelligible war cry and returned blow for blow delivered by the skilled knight.

Finally, after trading parries and glancing blows, the Habuk-ha spun through a feinted stroke and brought the seasoned handle into the knight's helm.

Solothon, now at the very edge of reason, reeled back and brought the song sword before him, hoping to buy time to regain his footing, but the big gualu backed away grinning, obviously enjoying this and, just as obviously, not wanting to rush the outcome.

That is when it noticed the two men stalking toward it, weapons up and ready.

Once Arantar and Eton had made it to the top of the cliff, Eton had growled, <Protect> at the cat without looking. The puma disappeared over the edge of the ravine as both Huntsmaster and warrior drew steel and moved into the field of battle.

The big gualu growled something that sounded like an insult to Solothon, spun his blade down, and rested it in the dirt before it.

Solothon was caught between the song of the sword, the blood screaming in his veins for escape, and the honor of his strong will that cautioned him to wait. The gualu shook its head and, with one large hand, pointed toward the two warriors.

Solothon turned and shouted as he caught sight of Arantar and Eton.

"What are you doing?"

Arantar had no way to know that this battle was anything other than a continuation of the battle below them in.

"Don't kill this one, Solothon," he said sternly, his eyes and sword blade trained on that huge enemy. "We'd need information."

"This is none of your affair!" the knight roared, his anger just barely under control.

Arantar ignored that comment and, his great blade floating menacingly before him, stepped past the angry knight. Eton moved around to the knight's left, both blades out at the ready and a grin of willingness distorting the scars on his cheeks.

<*I wish to talk.*> said the Huntsmaster in the gualu tongue.

The Habuk-ha seemed both startled and amused at his language coming from the Huntsmaster's lips.

<*Talk.*> it responded without moving.

<*Give us information and we may let you live.*>

That comment seemed to amuse the big gualu even more.

<*My name is Ched'rah.*>

<*Where are you camped?*>

The look on the gualu's face changed. He was no longer amused.

<*My name is Ched'rah.*> It replied with a bit more growl than before.

Arantar had no love for gualu kind and this one had stretched his patience to far. These beasts, he knew, were deceitful, arrogant, and merciless, and they would sell out their own mother.

<*What is your price?*>

Anger flared from the gualu's eyes as it looked first at the Huntsmaster and then at the knight. He took the strap of his great axe in his hand, lifted it, and turned his back to them.

Arantar stared in shock at the meaning behind this move. This gualu had as much as said he and his companions were beneath it for some reason. His teeth ground together as he stepped toward the huge gualu, his sword swung back for a blow at the nape of his hated enemy's neck.

A strong gauntleted hand gripped his arm and stopped him.

"What in the name of the Mother are you doing?" roared the knight, his eyes showing his anger and disgrace. "How dare you!"

"What in the hells are you talking about?"

"You interrupt Honor Combat and then have the audacity to strike from the rear? How were you raised, man?"

"Honor Combat?" asked the Huntsmaster incredulously. "You challenged the gualu to—"

"No!" roared Solothon. "He challenged me! Now, back away or, by my honor, we shall cross swords!"

The point of Arantar's dull gray sword dropped to the dirt.

"You are joking, aren't you? You wish to continue Honor Combat with…*that*?"

"He shows more concern for my honor then you do!"

"Well, then," rasped the Huntsmaster as he raised his sword and backed away. "As long as you realize that, should he win, I am bound to let him leave without restraint."

"I do."

The Huntsmaster looked deep into the knight's hazel eyes and noted the slight glow. Then he turned his gaze to the gualu's broad back.

<*Resume your combat. We shall not interfere.*>

<*You have already.*> growled the Habuk-ha over his shoulder.

Then he ran his hand down the shaft of his great axe and, taking a firm hold just above the blade, straightened up and began walking away toward the woods several hundred meters distance.

"Hey there, you!" roared the knight. "Turn and fight!"

But the gualu seemed not to hear as it continued strolling away.

The knight turned his angry gaze back on the Huntsmaster and rasped, "Tell him to stop! Tell him to…Damn it!"

<*This knight is not at fault here.*> Arantar yelled. <*He wishes to continue this combat according to the code. Do you accept?*>

The Habuk-ha stopped and looked back at them over his shoulder.

<*According to the code?*>

The Huntsmaster replied to this question by stepping back and, as Eton watched in shock, sheathing his great blade. He glanced over at the big warrior and nodded, then turned and walked back to the edge of the ravine where he stood facing the combatants with arms folded.

Eton sheathed his sword, but he kept a firm hold on the Bourjon blade as he joined the Huntsmaster. He didn't understand, but he trusted Arantar to know what he was doing.

The great gualu turned and placed the axe head on the ground. Then, with the shaft leaning on his massive leg, he spit into his palms and rubbed his hands together. With a grin, he lifted his weapon to the ready and strode toward the Elvin knight.

The silver sword had quieted during the pause, but as the knight again lifted it into action, it resumed its moaning song. Solothon's felt the racing in his blood and the anger in his heart. He attacked.

Steel rang on steel as the two came together.

The gualu was good, very good. He handled the great axe as if it were but a dagger. The thrusts of the Elvin blade were parried as deftly as the knight parried the return strokes.

But the knight's blood ran true. As the blade of the great axe raked across his mail chest, the red haze that had been floating before his eyes turned blood red. Solothon no longer cared that this was honor combat. He saw only an enemy that was meant to die!

As the gualu stepped back, as was the custom during this type of combat, to allow one's foe to regain his composure before continuing, the knight grinned and attacked.

It was hack and slash now rather than thrust and parry. The gualu's eyes grew large as it backed away, striking at will upon the elf's armor. Then the axe's blade severed the shaft of the arrow still protruding from the knight's hip.

With a roar of pure rage, Solothon slashed the gualu's left hand from its wrist. Then he brought his singing sword up and through the Habuk-ha's thick neck. The blood gushed from the gash as the gualu dropped its weapon and, trying to stanch the flow of blood with both hands, backed away.

Arantar and Eton both thought that the combat was complete and moved to join their companion, but both stopped in shock as the knight roared in animal hate and systematically hacked the Habuk-ha to pieces! In no time at all, the great gualu was reduced to hacked strips of slashed flesh and bloody pulp, and still the knight would not stop.

"What are you doing, Solothon?" yelled the Huntsmaster as he shook himself from his shock and ran toward the knight.

His answer came as a shock when Solothon turned, the sword still in both hands over his head. Lips were drawn back from teeth set in a leering grin, and the pulsing red glow of the berserker reached out toward a new victim. Thick drool spilled from his mouth as he roared and attacked. All pretext of style was gone from the knight's mode of attack. He saw only a foe that needed to die.

Arantar had just enough time to draw his sword and spin away from the approaching blade. As he spun, he brought the heavy hilt of the great blade hard against the knight's left ear. Solothon dropped to the dirt unconscious, the song of the sword dying as it left his hands.

"By all the gods, Arantar," whispered Eton as he joined the shaking Huntsmaster at Solothon's side, "what is wrong with him?"

Arantar knelt and rolled the knight over.

"It would take too long to explain now."

Then, as he felt for a pulse at the knight's jugular, he sighed.

"He'll be all right now, but when he learns what he has done..."

He looked up at the warrior with a sad look.

"Arantar, we must return to the others."

"Yes," he replied as he brushed the black hair from the knight's brow. "Give me a hand and we'll carry him."

"Never mind," replied the big youth.

Eton sheathed the Bourjon blade and, after removing the knight's helm and handing it to Arantar, lifted the knight as one would carry a wounded child.

He slid down the steep embankment with the Huntsmaster in front of him to break his fall should the need arise, and soon he lay his burden next to Savon'el.

The blond half elf had been tended by both clerics moments earlier. Melisande had removed the shaft from the half elf's leg, but it was Rene' who had administered the anesthetic. She'd rested Savon'el's head in her lap and rubbed his temples until the black-haired cleric had gently, but firmly, gripped the arrow shaft.

As Melisande yanked the arrow from the blond's leg, Rene' empathically dumped all of the fatigue she had endured for the past two days directly into their patient. Savon'el never felt the pain. He'd just felt overwhelmingly tired.

By the time Arantar, Eton, and the warrior's burden joined them, Savon'el had returned to consciousness and, though the effects of Rene's ministrations hadn't worn off completely, he was lucid enough to know that something of consequence had happened on the bluff above.

"Rest, Savon'el," cooed the black-haired cleric as she took Rene's place at his head. "It is over."

Her statement, though intended to calm her charge, came as a question to the Huntsmaster. It was answered with a nod and a small smile. Then Melisande looked to where Rene' worked to remove the piece of arrow still embedded in the knight's side.

"It is not serious," said the mage girl as she glanced up at the Huntsmaster and then back to her patient. "It could have been worse, I suppose."

"It was," responded the sad-eyed Huntsmaster softly. He began…

Arantar and Eton moved through the battlefield checking each body to ensure each was dead.

When they returned to their companions, Solothon's eyes were open. He sat up on his blanket, fear displayed openly to his companions.

"The last thing I remember was the gualu's axe striking me. It hurt, but then I remember nothing but red nightmares. Tell me, Huntsmaster, were the nightmares true? Is what I believe happened real?"

"Yes, Solothon, it's true, but before you start blaming yourself," he replied as the knight's eyes dropped to gaze at his hands, "know that this is not your fault."

Arantar faced the knight squarely, having seen the look of pain, dishonor, and grief in those hazel eyes. Though he had been witness to the savage butchery, he spoke with his soul.

"Listen to him, Sir Solothon," came the blond half elf's voice from the blanket next to where they sat.

He raised his head from Melisande's lap and propped himself up on one elbow. "It was the blood, not you, who turned into an animal. Don't blame yourself for the consequences of birth. And," he added quickly, "I say this not in pity, but in friendship. I don't envy you your demon, friend, but would gladly take it from you if I could."

"As would I," said the mage girl as she knelt behind him and laid a hand on the mail covering his left arm.

She felt the heat beneath the armor and frowned. "I think your birthmark is a clue to this inherited curse, Solothon. Do you mind if I examined it?"

"No, m'lady," he replied distractedly. "Do what you will."

It took a moment to unbuckle the mail sleeve from the knight's shoulder harness, but once removed Rene' took one look and cast a worried look at Melisande. The black-haired cleric didn't like the feeling she'd received from the look and slipped over beside Rene' to see what had caused it.

There, within one of the points of the pentagram birthmark, a red dot had appeared. It hadn't been there earlier, both women knew, and the reason for its being there now escaped them both. Rene', however, put her conjectures to voice. "I believe that this birthmark, and the response it makes to certain stimuli, is the key to your problem."

"Then," stated the knight in a voice that sounded too serious for the mage girl's liking, "I shall remove the arm."

"Nothing quite so drastic as that need be a attempted," said the blond half elf as he gently flexed his wounded leg. "If you will be patient with us, we will help contain your fury, and hopefully together we will find a cure."

Savon'el's eyes caught sight of the big warrior and Bonaire as they crossed the ravine toward them. Eton kept his senses flared at peak as his eyes raked the area for any sign of more enemies. He tossed a small pouch into the knight's lap as he crouched beside the Huntsmaster. Solothon glanced up at the big warrior and then down at the pouch.

"What is this?"

"Spoils of war," was the whispered reply.

Then, from beneath the strap of his long sword, Eton drew forth the Elvin blade.

"This is yours too, but it's the strangest thing..."

"What is?" asked Solothon as he took the silver blade lovingly in his hands.

"It seemed...it seemed to call to me, to beckon me to where it lay. Then when I retrieved it, I felt that though it knew I would return it to you, it had no love for my hand. As I said, strange."

"It was probably your imagination," replied the knight softly as he checked the length of the blade. Then he returned it to the sheath that lay beside him.

Eton glanced at the Huntsmaster and signed, <Not so>, but he whispered, "Possibly."

The knight untied the cord holding the pouch closed and poured the contents into his palm. There, glittering in the late afternoon sunshine, were twelve pieces of gold, twenty-seven pieces of silver, nine electrum coins, five coppers, a small ruby of poor quality, and three keys. He lifted his hand slightly as if weighing its contents, then gently poured his treasure back into the pouch.

Eton noted the keys, the wealth having little meaning to him, and logged them into his agile mind for future reference.

"We must move," he whispered. "Bonaire and I have hidden the bodies of those beyond the brush, but I fear that we have stayed here much too long."

His words were for the blond half elf, and he stared into those amber eyes as if waiting for his orders. Arantar noticed this and, though he had never seen this warrior speak so to a stranger, allowed that Eton saw Savon'el as the leader of this party and as such had last say over all decisions. But still...

"Can you ride, Solothon?" asked Savon'el.

"Yes, but Enare has been—"

"Don't worry," interrupted Rene'. "Arantar has...helped your animal to heal himself. Enare will be completely healed in a day or so and has no pain. He has been chomping at his bit for the past hour. Moving for him would be therapeutic at this point."

The knight turned a slight grin to the Huntsmaster.

"It seems there is much I am grateful to you for, Arantar Adenedhel. I will not forget it."

"Then you won't mind that I took the liberty of taking the Habuk-ha's battle-axe?" Arantar returned with a grin.

"No," said the knight slowly. Then, "But what do you want with it?"

"It may come in handy. Do you mind?"

"Of course not," replied Solothon with a frown. "Besides, I couldn't use it anyway. It is not within my skill. It is yours."

Savon'el felt uneasy. The pain had returned behind his eyes, and it seemed only combat and movement eased it. He looked toward the end of the ravine.

"Eton is right. We must move on. We need safer surroundings before nightfall."

"What?" exclaimed Bonaire as he placed both hands on his hips and turned a stubborn glare upon the blond half elf. "We have just fought a battle for our very lives. Yet you say we must go! I, for one, am tired! I think a little rest, some wine, and a snack or two is called for!"

The clouded look upon the blond half elf's face was one Arantar had seen before. It was the same look Prince LeMand was famous for, as was the power that rippled from Savon'el's lips.

"I haven't the time for your struttings, youth. *You will get to your horse and mount up now!*"

After the last word, Bonaire found himself moving quickly to the small black horse and stepping into the saddle to sit stiffly, as if waiting for other orders.

The power reached out to the others, though Eton and Arantar came out of it once mounted. Rene' stood beside the blond, her lips parted in amazement, while Melisande's anger at the driving order stirred her to disregard it entirely. She turned molten green eyes on the blond half elf, only to have them soften at the confusion registered on his face.

The ravine narrowed as the walls became less high until it spilled out at the beginning of a rutted trail. Arantar, again in the lead, turned in his saddle and motioned for the half elf to join him. Savon'el held his hand up to halt the others and joined the Huntsmaster at the edge of the road.

"Fire Gap Keep?" whispered the ranger as he pointed across the tops of the trees toward a structure visible upon a hill in the distance. "If Solothon's map is correct, our destination is five or six days beyond that."

Savon'el glanced at the distant building that rose above the trees and then studied the road that wound through those trees toward it.

"I think not, Huntsmaster," he said softly. "It's too close. Fire Gap Keep is well over half a day's ride from here, but we all need rest. I hope that that is vacant, but we must be ready to continue beyond it if necessary."

Arantar nodded and set his mount in motion, his battle-hardened senses reaching out to both sides of the road seeking danger.

Savon'el fell in at a discreet distance behind him and the rest followed in order. Eton took up the rear with the puma ranging wide flank as was its custom.

This road seemed to have been at one time well-traveled. The Huntsmaster read this as a sign that there were others, not necessarily friendly others, who used this road frequently. It passed through a rolling wooded hillside, deep in its turn to winter, but with uncommon warmth for the season.

He communicated with the raven almost constantly, but the sharp-eyed bird could report nothing, for all was silent.

It was late afternoon when the group came to a bend in the road flanked on both sides by small hills cut away to afford the easement. Beyond this small pass, the pathway took a sharp turn to the left. At the apex of that curve, a smaller trail led over a wide bridge to the structure they'd seen from a distance.

It was about eighty feet square and at least thirty tall, a sheer block in the middle of nowhere. There was one large door that faced the road. To either side of the door and along the side they could see, arrow slits had been cut to afford a wide, though protected, view of the road and the surrounding landscape. All about the building the land been cleared, obviously to make for unobstructed view and little protective cover for those who wished to approach unseen.

"Damn!" exclaimed the blond half elf softly as he, Arantar, and Eton watched their objective from the cover of brush at the top of the hill on the right. The others waited in the woods back from the bend.

"The only way we are apt to pass here is to be invisible," sighed Savon'el. "Whoever constructed that, and he that is in charge, knows his business."

"The clearing is fresh too," commented the Huntsmaster.

"Eton, can you see a way around to the woods on this side?" asked Savon'el.

The big warrior had been thinking the same thing, but while seeking a path with his sharp eyes, he had seen the bridge just twenty or so meters ahead. It spanned a wide and deep gorge, and the sound of swiftly flowing water told him that there was no other way to cross it.

"The only way," he responded, "is straight ahead, either across or under that bridge."

"Whoever tries that will be seen immediately by those inside," said Savon'el. "The risk is too great for any to attempt. Suppose we follow the gorge south?"

"We could ask Solothon," replied the Huntsmaster, "but a glance at his map earlier showed me that this gorge travels far south of here. It may take as much as a week to find a crossing point. I'm not certain we have that kind of time."

Savon'el sighed again and hung his head. They were again stopped. They could not turn back because they did not know whether their pursuers were behind or before them. He shook his head and looked again at the bridge and the building beyond.

"I can see no other way. Somehow we have to get to the other side of that bridge without being seen," he said softly as he rubbed his temple against the pain there. "Gentlemen, I am open to suggestions."

"I will try it."

Savon'el glanced at Eton. The statement was whispered with conviction and the set of the young warrior's jaw line was something he'd seen before, though he could not remember when or where.

"Sorry, friend, but you are just too large to go unnoticed. Our best hope is to try this after nightfall."

"I'm not one to disagree, Savon'el," said Arantar softly, "but we haven't got until nightfall. There is no place on this side of the gorge to hide our party or our horses against another group like the one we just faced. Besides, if this is where they originated, chances are they will soon send out search parties. If there are reinforcements within that building, I would rather take my chances there than in open battle."

"Let's get back to the others," the blond said softly as he slid on his stomach back away from their vantage point.

Once everything was explained to the other companions, it was Rene' who questioned the logic of their approach.

"This plan is not a plan at all! Do you think they will just let you walk up to the front door and knock? This is insane!"

"Not necessarily," replied Eton as he stroked the big black stallion's neck. "One person on foot might be able to make it without drawing too much attention. By myself, they may not simply shoot me out of hand. If all goes well, those within that building will open the doors and come out to face me. Gualu bravado is predicated upon safety in numbers. In my experience, if one comes out, they will all come out."

"Then what?" asked Rene' petulantly.

"Then," responded the Huntsmaster, "the rest of us will ride out and meet them. Surprise is our best weapon. If they think there is but one of us, they may become brazen. If so, our mounted attack will give Eton time to fight his way to the door and hold it for us."

"Eton," said the mage girl softly, her eyes hard, "I've seen your prowess on the battlefield, but if there are as many as twenty within, even with surprise on our side, I just can't see you holding them off until the rest of us join you."

"It's a risk I'm willing to take," he whispered as his fingers laced themselves into the big black's mane. "The only other option is to somehow appear at the corner of the building. It's the only blind spot I can..."

The world writhed away.

Suddenly Eton found himself standing at the corner of the building, the big black next to him. It took the warrior a second to realize what had happened, and he shook himself at the thought.

His hand was still laced into the flowing mane and, as the horse pushed him gently with its muzzle, he released his hand and drew his long sword, the Bourjon blade already in his left. He slipped noiselessly toward the arrow slit that occupied the wall on this side of the large door.

Rene's sharp intake of breath and her wide eyes caused the rest to look to where Eton had been.

"What the—"

"It's the horse!" Rene' responded to Savon'el's outburst.

"Then where is he?"

"I think I know," stated Arantar as he rose and moved to his horse. "Remember the last thing he said? I think he's at the building now."

Eton glanced quickly through the arrow slit and just as quickly pulled back and flattened himself against the wall. It was dimly lit. He waited but a moment listening, but no sound came from within. He risked another look though that thin portal and saw what looked to be a deserted stable. He slipped silently below the arrow slit to check the door, but he found it locked.

He moved back to Shadow's side and, after running his hand over the muscled neck, laced his fingers into its black mane once again.

"If you can understand me, my friend, take us just beyond the bend in the road."

The black warhorse nodded and again the world writhed away. Seconds later Arantar watched as the big warrior and his horse appeared before him just below their earlier vantage point. The Huntsmaster dropped the reins to his roan and silently moved to Eton's side.

"What the seven hells was that?"

"I'm not sure," replied the big warrior. "Let's get back to the others."

They walked back toward their makeshift campsite, the roan and black warhorse trailing behind.

"If what I believe to be true is true, Shadow is the war mount Hellshadow that I read about years ago in Yarda's library."

Rene' sat, her left elbow cupped in her right hand and the fingers of her left hand tapping nervously at her chin. Arantar watched as the big warrior shot a sharp look at the mage girl while he stroked the big black horse's neck.

"He said that that was his name," Melisande said as she looked at Eton. "I'm sorry, my friend, but I thought that if you knew—"

"Knew what?" Eton asked a bit more sharply than he wished.

"Remember when I told you that his heritage dictated his name? Well, he is...he is half Unicorne and half...Nightmare."

"That explains it then."

"Explains *what*, Rene'?"

Eton felt that his friends were somehow...insulting his new friend. This animal had touched a place in his soul where only Fleet had existed. He stroked Shadow's neck and felt again the chiseled power resting there.

"In my studies," Rene' began, "Hellshadow was the warhorse of Pantor, one of a talon of the...the other side. He was killed early on in the Mage Wars, around the third or fourth century, but his legend was made during those early years. It was said that his sword, Arapel'ho, was a soul drinker, though there are few stories that alluded to the truth in that."

"What has that to do with—"

"I'm getting to that, Eton," responded the mage girl sharply. Then she sighed. "Unicornes can…phase from one location to the next, but only as long as they can see their destination. Nightmares travel using portals they've opened, it is said, through the pathways of…well… hell. They also are gifted with mind touch, if trained properly. If they are somehow…connected to their rider mentally, they can get a…picture of their destination."

"So you're saying that Shadow looked inside my mind—"

"Shadow is far more intelligent than any I've seen," Rene' interrupted. "I think that if he knows that you want or if you need to be somewhere you've never been, but he has…" Rene' shrugged.

"Breeding and grace," mumbled the cleric.

"What was that?" Rene' asked with a sidelong glance.

"When I was talking to Shadow, he said that he loved his companion, but didn't necessarily like his choices. He said that Pantor provided grace with his breeding. I don't know what that means, but—"

"It means that Pantor was never aware of that beautiful animal's talents," stated Rene'. "Did he say anything else?"

"Just that Eton could talk to him if he tried." Then it was Melisande's turn to shrug.

"I don't have the talent for horse speech."

The whispered reply brought a frown to Melisande's face.

"I don't think I misheard…"

"We will have to puzzle this out later in safety perhaps," interrupted Savon'el. "What news of the building, Eton?"

"It looks recently deserted," he replied, a frown settling on his face. "I think our friends from earlier lived there, though I cannot be certain. I suggest caution. Besides, the door seems to be locked."

"Is there no way to compromise the door, much as we did at Rairy's cottage?" asked the blond half elf.

"Possibly, but we might not have to." Eton turned to the knight and continued, "Was it my imagination, or was there keys in the pouch I gave you?"

"Yes, there were," Solothon said as his pulled the pouch from his saddlebag. "I believe there were…" He poured the contents of the bag on the blanket and stated, "Yes. Three."

The knight handed the keys to Savon'el and returned the treasure and pouch to his saddlebag.

"Gentlemen," said Rene' as she gazed at the old map spread on the blanket before her, "I don't know if it means anything now, but…"

"Go on," responded Savon'el to the mage girl's pause. "What is it?"

"It's just that the script here is faded, but I believe it says 'dewlok' in the legend right here next to 'Fire Gap Keep'. If this is an outpost of the keep—"

"Then the keep may be inhabited with dark dwarves as well," stated the Huntsmaster. "Eton and I have not looked for sign in that direction, but I think it prudent to do so before venturing into that outpost."

"Yes, Arantar, but it could mean something else entirely," said the mage girl softly. "Tell me, how would you change the guard here if you controlled it from the keep? Ride down the road, or—"

"Or would they have a way to travel unnoticed from without?" finished the Huntsmaster. "Eton, did you see anything within the outpost that could be a way down, maybe to a tunnel beneath?"

"I couldn't see much, but it is possible."

"It doesn't matter at this point," said the savon'el as he rubbed his temples. "We'll have to risk it. We are losing the light and it has gotten colder."

The temperature had dropped sharply and the companion's breath now came in small puffs of white. Savon'el pulled his cloak closer about him and rose.

"Arantar, Eton, and I will enter and check it out. Solothon and Bonaire will serve as rearguard here with Melisande and Rene', as well as our mounts and belongings. If anything out of the ordinary…" At this, he chuckled. "If anything happens, protect the ladies and find a way out of here."

"Lady Melisande needs no protection, Savon'el," came the taut response from the knight, "and I believe that the Lady Rene' may surprise you." As Solothon caught the quick look from the blond half elf, he continued, "They are both, in their own way, very capable, though they may need our backing from time to time. I believe that at this juncture, it would be unwise to separate us. If one of us is encountered, we may need all of us to survive."

"I'm sorry, my friend," replied Savon'el softly as he again rubbed at his temples. "You are, of course, correct. It would do no good for us to be separated now."

"I suggest," whispered the big warrior, "you all wait here while Arantar and I scout the road to Fire Gap Keep, to ensure no surprises. Then we will come back here to get you and hopefully get somewhere warm and safe."

"I think not," replied Savon'el. "As you said, it would not be prudent to separate now. I suggest that we all go, and while you and the ranger seek for sign on that road, we wait at the pass. Then we will all cross that bridge. Agreed?"

"I don't see why we don't just walk up there and knock!"

All eyes turned to Bonaire. He stood wrapped in his cloak, so cold that his teeth chattered.

"You never can tell. There might be good people in there who would open their door to us."

"Where have you been, Bonaire?" asked the Huntsmaster tersely as he moved toward the gaudily cloaked elf. "We are in enemy territory. Everyone and everything we meet here is likely to want our heads on a pike! Damn, man, I'm not even sure in what territory we stand! There are no friendlies here save us, and you had better get that through your thick skull!"

All was said in a tight, quiet voice, but the effect it had on the young elf was as if the Huntsmaster had screamed in his face. He backed up and dropped his eyes as the Huntsmaster shook his head and moved after Eton.

"Well, it was just a suggestion," he muttered as he lowered his ears into the cloak and turned away from the others.

They packed quickly and moved up the road to the cut in the hill before the bridge. There, Eton and Arantar left them to scout the road toward Fire Gap Keep, while Savon'el and Solothon watched from their earlier observation point.

Eton and the Huntsmaster crept silently along the left side of the road to the Keep while the tawny puma padded softly to the other side and kept abreast. Less than fifty feet from the crossroad, the road became overgrown with grass and brush.

"There hasn't been any traffic here in a very long time," whispered the big warrior.

"And that makes me wonder if the Keep is occupied at all," replied the Huntsmaster, also in a whisper, "and with what."

"Let's cross over and get back to the crossroad."

Arantar nodded and they moved, still low and silently, to the puma's side of the long dormant trail and made their way back. Once at the crossroad, Arantar waved to the two on watch to come and moved with Eton across the bridge and toward the large double door of the outpost.

Soon the other companions appeared beyond the pass and made their way over the bridge. Savon'el led the way, sword drawn, with the two ladies just behind him. Bonaire led the packhorse and four horses, while the Huntsmaster, the knight and the big warrior's mounts followed. Solothon took up the rear, his eyes watching behind them and to either side.

Savon'el had just moved toward the door when Eton clicked his tongue. He didn't know where he'd learned the meaning of that sound, but he responded correctly by freezing where he stood and looking toward the big warrior.

Eton motioned around the outpost with one hand while pointing at himself and the Huntsmaster with the other. Savon'el nodded and took Arantar's place next to the door.

The big warrior and ranger lost no time in doing a quick circuit of the building. They found that though there were two to three arrow slits per wall with more in the wall above where the second and third floor should be, there was but the one door. They could hear nothing from within the outpost. When they arrived back at the front of the building, Eton nodded to the blond half elf and motioned toward the door.

Savon'el pulled the greenish brown blade from its sheath as he twisted the larger of the keys in the lock. The muffled snap within the mechanism told him the way was open and he nodded to the three warriors as they arrayed themselves about him, weapons drawn.

Savon'el pulled down on the handle and the door swung silently open. The dim light from the dying fire in the large hearth in the center of the room illuminated the four warriors as they entered. The knight slipped quickly to the right of the doorway with Eton just behind and to his left, while Savon'el and the Huntsmaster moved quickly to the left to survey the room.

It was a stable, warm and dry. From the smell of new wood and the fresh straw on the dirt floor, the stalls had been recently rebuilt.

The large open hearth in the center of the room had a large flue that disappeared into the ceiling just ten feet above. Along the wall to the right, a stairway ran up to a trap door in that ceiling, probably the entrance to the second floor.

However, it was the mechanism beneath the stairway that surprised them the most.

It was a trap door in the floor, barred and bolted into its frame with strange catches and thin wires mounted upon it. The wires led from the thick wood of the trapdoor, up the wall and across the ceiling to a large square box mounted on the opposite wall. It was tilted at a strange angle, its top pointed toward the secured entryway in the floor.

"Don't touch that."

Savon'el turned and caught the green glow in Melisande's eyes as she swept past them toward the trapdoor. She turned and looked back into his eyes.

"It's trapped. The box up there contains multiple crossbows all primed to fire if the door is lifted, as is the one at the top of the stairway."

"How do you—"

"She knows, Savon'el," said the mage girl softly as she stepped into the light, "because it is her talent to know. Clerics not only bind hurts, but sometimes they have the power to prevent them as well." At his confused look, she added, "Trust her. She knows."

"Then, what of the rest of this room?" he asked, his eyes on the black-haired cleric.

"It is quite safe. As long as those wires are not disturbed, we will be fine."

"Then let's get the horses inside quickly and close that door. I don't want prying eyes to find us here. We will check the floors above, but we may as well do that in relative comfort."

The horses were quickly quartered in the stalls, the door was closed, and the small band turned their attention to the trap door at the top of the stairs.

"Melisande," said the blond half elf as he strung his bow, "you said that there was a similar trap on the door above. Do you know how to disarm it?"

The girl's eyes still glowed with the power she directed there earlier. She looked and saw not only the trap, but also the mechanism behind it.

"The door is locked," she said. "If you lift it eight inches, you will set off the mechanism, but if you lift less than that and reach inside carefully at the left hand corner, you will feel a lever. Pull it toward the center until it catches and the trap will be disarmed."

"Good," said the blond as he studied the stairway. "Arantar, Solothon, and I will cover you from here. Take these," he continued as he handed the Huntsmaster the remaining keys. "One of these should open the lock. Then..." he explained how the trap was devised and how to disarm it.

"Check the steps, Arantar," said the cleric softly. "There is something—"

"Bonaire, watch the door."

"Why?" he demanded as he glanced at the blond half elf. "Why can't I go up there with them?"

"Because I need you here to guard our escape if the need arises."

"Well," replied the elf, "okay, but throw me the key."

"I don't want the door locked, Bonaire," said the blond softly, the pain behind his eyes reaching toward the unbearable. "If we have to run, we won't have time to stop and unlock the door."

"Besides," whispered Eton, "Fleet will let us know if something comes from out there."

"Okay, then why do you need me to watch the door?"

Savon'el sighed.

"I need you there to cover our withdrawal if the cat finds enemies or if we find nasties on the floors above."

"But—"

"Just do it!" rasped the blond half elf.

"Sure! No problem!" responded the elf sarcastically as he sauntered over toward the door. Melisande heard him mumble, "They just don't want me to find anything useful or anything." as he passed her.

"One day I'm going to—" she began softly.

"Never mind him, dear," said Rene. "Just concentrate on our boys. They need your talents more."

Arantar moved cautiously up the stairway while Solothon and Savon'el watched from below, an arrow nocked in each bow. There were twelve steps leading to a small landing four feet below the door. He checked each step carefully before trusting his foot to it and found that the seventh, eighth, and ninth step were wrong.

Eton followed him up the stairs to lend him support, but stopped when he caught the sign.

<Trapped!>

The Huntsmaster used his dagger to scrape the dirt from the center of the seventh step. It had a hairline separation that, should someone step upon it, would send that someone crashing through to the floor below. The other two steps were done the same way so there was nothing solid to hold onto as one fell.

Arantar looked beneath those steps and found the trap door and the wires. If the fall didn't kill the intruder, the crossbow bolts from the far wall would.

Eton watched the Huntsmaster investigate the three steps and, as his friend looked back, he smiled. The big warrior laced his fingers together to make a cup of his two palms and looked askance of Arantar. It was Arantar's turn to smile and nod.

Eton set his back against the wall, Arantar stepped into that cup, and when Eton counted to three in his hoarse whisper, he launched the Huntsmaster up the stairs to the landing.

Arantar landed softly, the big warrior's strength and accuracy lending control to the exact strength required for the function. Then Eton made his way up the trapped steps, one at a time, placing his feet, cat soft, over the risers.

He joined Arantar on the landing and watched as the Huntsmaster first listened at the door, then inserted one of the keys into the lock. The Bourjon blade was cupped in the big warrior's gauntleted hand while the long dagger rested in the other.

Arantar turned the key slowly until he heard a muffled click. He rested the gray sword against the wall as he placed both hands on the wood door and lifted. It moved easily until he could peer into the room above. It was black as pitch, so he lifted the door a bit more, short of the eight inches, and found the lever. He felt the safeguard snap into place and waved Eton back.

The big warrior shook his head and stood waiting for the Huntsmaster to get on with it.

The ranger lifted the door slowly until it was out of the way and lifted himself into the darkness. Then he reached back down and took his sword from Eton. That warrior followed him easily, stood to the side, and waited for his eyes to adjust to the dark.

The faint light from the doorway showed a torch resting in a sconce mounted on the wall above the trapdoor and he motioned toward it. Arantar caught the sign and, while Eton replaced the dagger with his sword, the Huntsmaster set about lighting the torch with the tinderbox he carried.

Soon the flickering torch showed a row of bunks along the far wall beyond a second open hearth. The flue from the hearth below came up through the floor behind it and joined that flue toward the ceiling, but turned toward the far corner, then up.

A table and several chairs sat close to the stairway. Playing cards were arrayed on the table as if a game had been interrupted. Just beyond the trapdoor opening, another stairway began.

The whole of this room was strangely clean and orderly. It was a barracks for soldiers, disciplined ones, if the Huntsmaster's senses had not totally deserted him, but the soldiers were gone.

Eton moved softly to the hearth and held his hand over the ashes. <Still warm.> he signed. <Probably from the morning fire.>

"I think we met these soldiers this morning," said Arantar softly. "Watch that stairway while I get us some help."

Eton nodded and moved to the foot of the steps, his body poised against a surprise attack. Arantar returned to the trap door and saw, just behind the open door, three thick wooden slats. He slipped down the opening with the wood and, as he approached each compromised step, laid one of the slats over it. Then he waved for Savon'el to join them.

"Solothon, Melisande, and I will go up," said the blond half elf. "I will meet you on that landing." Then, turning to Rene', "Will you be all right?"

"I'll be fine," she answered. "After all, Bonaire is here to protect me." At Savon'el's frown, she continued, "Don't worry, just be careful."

Solothon had already moved up the staircase to the landing and waited for Melisande and Savon'el.

Moments later the blond half elf had levered himself through the opening to the second floor and turned to help Arantar lift the lady through. Solothon stood on the landing to watch both floors and to come if necessary.

Arantar went up the stairs to the third floor carefully, each step a challenge. The steps, however, were solid and, strangely, did not creak when his weight was put on them.

"M'lady?" said the Huntsmaster as he looked up at the trap door above. "Is this one trapped as well?"

Melisande looked back at the door they just came through and saw what the trap there was meant to do. Had the Huntsmaster lifted the door over eight inches, the mechanism would have been released, the door would have been flung open, and from a box mounted on the ceiling above, twenty crossbow bolts would have been loosed down the stairway.

She shivered and cast her still-glowing eyes toward the trapdoor above.

"That one is a bit different," she said softly. "The lever you want is to the right this time. Watch out for the poison on the spikes."

Arantar didn't like the sound of that, but as he took the last key in hand and inserted it into the keyhole, he planned to move as cautiously as he possibly could. He turned the key and lifted. The door swung up easily until he could slip his dagger through to engage the lever. He felt the snap as the lever reached its farthest point and looked back at the cleric.

"It is disarmed," she said.

Then she visibly relaxed. She'd pressed hard at her power to make sure everything was safe and, seeing no other traps, let the tension leave her.

Arantar lifted the door slowly until it reached its top. All was dark here, yet the smell of the barracks was not to be found.

"Pass up a torch," he said without turning.

Eton took another torch from the wall and, after lighting it from the one Solothon now held, moved quickly up the stairs to Arantar's side. The Huntsmaster took the torch and held it up through the door. He looked about the large room and found it unoccupied. He would have been less cautious of entering here had it not been for the mechanism he saw hinged to the opening of the trap door.

It was another door, but it was not friendly. It was made of steel, and every inch or two, a steel spike at least ten inches long was placed. Once tripped, it would snap down over the opening and lock itself there. The Huntsmaster looked closer and saw the strange discoloration on the sharp tips.

"Poison," he breathed.

"What?" whispered Eton who stood two steps down from him on the stairway.

"There is a panel of spikes up here," he replied. "Be careful of them, for they look poisoned."

Then he lifted himself through the hole.

The torchlight showed him a bedroom, but not any bedroom he'd ever seen in any outposts he'd served. It was luxurious, to say the least, from the large four-poster bedstead, to the comfortable hearth in the corner. A large banded chest sat at the foot of the bed, a small emblem, or crest, imbedded in the dark wood above the keyhole.

Only half of the room was used as a bedroom. As the Huntsmaster cast the light of the flickering torch about the large room, he found an area obviously used for the former occupant's exercise.

Racks of weighted rods were set against the far wall, and at the edge of the large sandy area in the center, a worn post had been banded securely to the floor.

"I saw arrow slits from the outside," came the whisper behind him.

The Huntsmaster glanced at the big warrior and raised the torch slightly. Where the arrow slits would be, as they had seen them from outside, dark heavy cloth hung down from the ceiling to the floor.

"He's covered them," said Arantar softly. "He's covered the slits to allow for light in his sanctum. I saw the same thing in the barracks room below."

"In that case..." replied Eton as he moved from sconce to sconce lighting each in turn.

As he lit the third torch, the armor rack in the corner of the bedroom became visible. It was full-scale mail, save for the dark breastplate. An axe, double-bitted and sharp, leaned against the wall next to it. Arantar had seen this armor earlier this day, though somewhat larger, and the axe was a twin to the one that now rode strapped to the cantle of his saddle.

The emblem that had been scrubbed off of the armor worn by the Habuk-ha stood out clearly on the breastplate before him. This armor was worn by a large man, not a gualu. It was the armor of a soldier, a knight.

"I'll be damned!" whispered Eton as he passed the Huntsmaster to look closer at the armor. "Our welcoming committee left us a warm place to sleep tonight."

"So it seems," responded the Huntsmaster. "So it seems."

"Is all well?" came the knight's voice from the trap door.

"Yes. We're coming down now," responded the ranger.

Then he nodded to the warrior, crossed to the trap door, and dropped down onto the landing.

"It seems that this was the barracks used by those we met earlier today. That room upstairs belonged to your Habuk-ha, Solothon."

Rene', Melisande, and Savon'el sat at the small table while Arantar spoke. Solothon stood at the open trap door to the stable below, listening, while Eton prowled about looking through the small chests at the foot of each bed on this floor. Bonaire had been left below to guard the door.

"It looks safe enough," continued the Huntsmaster as he resumed his pacing, "but it seems extraordinary precautions have been taken to assure our departed host's health."

"What do you mean?" asked the blond half elf.

"All the traps, for one. Though his soldiers seem to have been well-trained, this from the cleanliness of this barracks and the disciplined tactics they attempted this morning, he didn't trust them. Why?"

"He didn't seem to be like any gualu I've seen or heard of," said the knight softly without turning. "He seemed..." He paused with a frown. Then, "He was more chivalrous and more concerned with my honor than any I can remember. There was more to him than we see." Then, in a very soft voice, "He deserved better."

"That may be, Solothon," said the Huntsmaster as he crossed to the knight, "but let's be clear about what happened. You gave him Honor Combat, but your birthright took it away, not you. Were I you, I would be angry and not drowned in self-pity." Then, as the knight's eyes met his, he added with a grin, "But not too angry, if you please."

Solothon returned the grin and walked to the hearth to get a cup of Kaff from the pot Arantar left there.

"That reminds me," continued the Huntsmaster, "there is a suit of armor on a rack upstairs. On the breastplate is a family crest of some sort. Maybe you can tell us the origin."

"I'll look after we've seen to the security of this keep and our mounts."

"The keep!" said the Savon'el with a grin. "I don't think it was his own soldiers he didn't trust. Remember the trapdoor in the stable? He didn't trust the dewlok at Fire Gap Keep!"

He leaned forward and looked from one face to the other as he explained.

"With the security our host has put in place, I think he trained his own soldiers, as any good captain would, and from the description of the training area above, he required them to train every day with him. I believe that he trusted those he trained and the respect they gave him. Look at this barracks, for instance. Only soldiers with respect and discipline would keep it so."

"Eton and I found no sign from the crossroad toward the Keep. In fact, it looked as if it has been disused for a long time," stated the Huntsmaster softly. "It seems that these...elite soldiers were sent here to guard the way, but why? Does someone know we are on our way here? If so, can we expect more along the road?"

"I think not," stated the mage girl, her fingers once again tapping at her chin. "Banshe'e, if he is behind all of this, is looking for weapons, I believe. The objects I have been asked to retrieve and Radagast's armory are powerful temptations for him. It is possible that he is setting up outposts to keep anyone from venturing too close to the possible locations of objects of power. I hope I'm right in this, for if not, someone does know of our quest and has set events in motion to stop and possibly kill us."

"I agree with your first premise, Rene'," said Savon'el softly as his brow furrowed. "We know that someone wants us dead and the reasoning behind it is sketchy at best. I want to believe...I really, really want to believe that we are a nuisance, nothing more. Were we more than that, I believe that that someone would have thrown a heavier net about us. As it is, we've escaped Catlorian, and we have arrived here—granted with help—but arrived here essentially unscathed. That, coupled with the seeming lack of pursuit, gives me hope."

"Hope, Savon'el?"

"Yes, Huntsmaster, hope. Yes, someone of power sent our albino daku and his ill-trained retinue to kill us—Solothon and I—but he failed. Yet there were no further attempts as far as we can see. No chase was given and no ambushes that we can definitely say were meant for us alone.

"I can see someone like Banshe'e going after Red Wolf, Cartellion, or even the Myrlin, but an amnesiac and a young knight of a far away order? It doesn't make sense. No offense intended, Solothon."

"None taken, friend. So, if we have eluded our pursuers, what then?"

"Then if Rene's premise is correct, we can safely lock the door downstairs and move everyone up here for the night," said the blond half elf as he rose from the chair and followed the knight toward the doorway down. "If there are dewlok or worse in Fire Gap Keep, the former occupants of this outpost have done better than we could have at keeping this place safe. I say we take advantage of that."

Savon'el went to the trap door and followed Solothon through.

"Lady Melisande," said the Huntsmaster as Eton dropped through the trap door, "would you and Lady Rene' please stay here until we can render the spikes up there"—he pointed up the stairs—"ineffective?"

"I'm not moving," said Rene'. "Besides, Melisande and I have some notes that need matching."

Arantar grinned as the two ladies fell into a soft discussion of the differences in their practice. He marveled at the golden mage girl's stamina. She didn't seem to be someone who could bear up well under continual hardships, but there she was, knowing that they were in danger at every turn, calmly discussing some discovery or other.

Melisande came to his mind as he dropped through the trap door and negotiated the stairway. He'd noted the subtle changes in her on this trek. She'd begun this trip a girl, but now she seemed more barbaric then Red Wolf! There was more at work here, he knew, than just the hard road they traveled. Her transformation had started long before they'd set foot in

Catlorian. She was a puzzle and, with his ranger's curiosity, he'd like to be there when the whole story was told and the transformation was complete.

"I can't believe it!"

Savon'el's soft exclamation reached him as he took the last step to the stable floor and looked toward the cause. Bonaire sat with his back against the door and his head lolled forward, obviously fast asleep.

Arantar joined the blond and Solothon as Eton moved to his mount to remove the saddle, a look of disgust on his face.

"I'll handle this, Savon'el," said the Huntsmaster. "You two go ahead and see to the horses. This won't take long."

Savon'el didn't like the anger in the Huntsmaster's voice, but tapped the knight on the shoulder and moved to the stalls.

Arantar squatted next to the sleeping elf and poked him softly on the shoulder.

"Bonaire," he said softly.

The elf didn't move.

"Bonaire," he said a bit louder.

Still no movement. The Huntsmaster's patience was gone now, and he grabbed a handful of colored cloak and shook it vigorously.

"Bonaire! Get your ass up!"

Bonaire leaped straight up from the floor and stood, his eyes blinking as he tried to remember where he was, clawing for his sword. When he saw Arantar, he stopped and frowned.

"What did you do that for?" he whined.

"What are you supposed to be doing?" came the terse reply.

"Guarding the door, like you said. I was! If any bad guys had come, they would have had to push the door and me out of the way. I would've woke up and defended us all!"

"Of all the…" Arantar stopped and took a breath. "Bonaire, if you don't understand the importance of each of us doing what we can for the whole—"

"But, I do!"

"If you do, then why were you asleep on guard?"

"Me? Asleep? No! I was just…resting my eyes. I was really awake."

"Look," said the Huntsmaster in a very controlled voice, "I don't have time to go into it right now. See to your horse and go to the second floor."

As the young elf frowned and started past him, Arantar's soft voice followed him.

"Think on this, my friend. If you were in the guard, I'd have killed you on the spot."

The expression on the elf's face as he glanced back at the Huntsmaster was one of fear and disbelief.

"Would you really?"

"Damn right! In a dangerous position, the danger within is generally... removed. It's much safer for the rest that way."

Bonaire stopped for a minute, his forehead wrinkled in thought at the ramifications, then moved smartly to his black's stall.

Eton couldn't understand it. After all the miles they'd ridden, the other horses had their noses buried in the portion of grain that had been spilled into the feeders in every stall. Shadow, however, hadn't touched his, and looked instead at the other mounts. As his blue eyes passed from one to another, the horses seemed to get a bit skittish.

"What is it, my friend?" he whispered as he brushed the blue-black coat with a brush from Solothon's bag. "Are you well?"

He was answered, in a way, when the big black's head came up suddenly and he looked at the door. Seconds later, Eton heard the soft scratching on the hard dark wood.

"It's all right. It's Fleet," he said as he passed Solothon's mount and heard the half-drawn silver sword slide back into its sheath.

Eton moved from one arrow slit to the other before opening the door. The tawny puma lay just outside the door cleaning his paws. Before him, just to the left of the door, lay the freshly killed carcass of a small deer. Eton scratched the big cat between the ears for a moment, then, with the Bourjon blade, gutted the deer and carved the right front haunch from it.

<For you and friend.> growled the cat.

<Thanks.> responded the warrior as he gave the cat a last pat and the haunch.

As the cat loped toward the woods, the haunch firmly in its teeth, Eton dragged the rest of the carcass through the door. As he turned from closing and locking the door, he was surprised by Shadow. The big black mount had moved silently to the carcass and sniffed at it. Shadow lifted his big head until his eyes met Eton's and snapped his teeth together.

"You are joking!" exclaimed the warrior in a shocked whisper that seemed to carry through the room.

"I'm afraid not," came Melisande's soft voice from the top of the stairs.

"You mean…" whispered the shocked warrior as he looked up at the girl.

"I mean, he is not your normal horse," she said as she came down the stairway. "He was bred, after all, for a specific purpose from two opposites. Just believe me when I tell you that, though he won't hurt any of us, he eats only meat, the fresher, the better."

Eton shook his head and, after carving the other haunch from the deer and dropping it in front of the big black horse, grinned as he followed the black-haired cleric up to the barracks room with the remainder.

With the outpost secured for the night and a meal of roast venison and trail bread eaten, the companions settled in. The Huntsmaster ground the Kaff beans and, with a bit of barley, brewed another small pot of the steaming drink for his companions and the guard they would set for the evening.

"A week from now, barring any more delays, will find us at our destination, for whatever that's worth," said the mage girl as she rose from one of the chairs at the table.

What was left of the deer meat roasted slowly over the low fire in the barrack's hearth. Bonaire snored in one of the cots while Solothon and Arantar sat on the edge of a bunk close to the table where the rest of the companions finished their meal.

"Be careful of those spikes," whispered Eton as he watched the mage girl approach the stairs to the upstairs bedroom. "Melisande and I have tried to render them harmless, but…"

"Caution is ever my watchword," she responded with a grin. "Melisande?"

"I'll be with you in a bit."

As the golden-haired mage disappeared up the stairs, Melisande turned to Savon'el.

"What is the plan for tomorrow?"

"I'm not really certain," he replied as he again rubbed at his temples. "Solothon, may I see your map?"

The knight pulled the parchment from the saddlebag at his feet and passed it to the blond half elf. Savon'el cleared a place on the table and unrolled the sheet before him.

"If we continue along the road, we will have to pass Fire Gap Keep. The commander of this outpost set traps for the occupants of that keep, if what we've seen downstairs is any indication. I suggest that we bypass the road and cut directly across country. It may slow us a bit, but it may also cut more than a day from our travel and put us where we wish to be that much sooner. Besides," he continued, "anything we can do to thwart possible pursuit is in our best interest. Comments?"

"How do we know that there is a way through?" asked Solothon softly.

"In the morning, a means will be found," replied the blond as he looked pointedly at the Huntsmaster. "In the meantime, I suggest we get some rest. We will take guard in shifts until morning."

"No need," whispered Eton as he stood. "I will sleep in the stable this night. If something comes, Fleet will alert me and I will, in turn, send the alarm."

He slapped Arantar lightly on the back as he passed.

"I need to see after my...horse anyway."

"Arantar?" asked Savon'el, his eyes on the route the warrior had taken.

"Believe him, my friend. He knows what he is doing."

Eton noticed that Shadow had not returned to his stall, but instead stood next to the door. The bone of the deer haunch gleamed white at his feet.

The big warrior glanced about the stable to see if the other mounts were affected by the black's eating habits. Bonaire's seemed to be a bit skittish, but the rest seemed not to notice. Eton grinned and moved softly to the big mount's side. He combed the black mane with his fingers as the horse sighed in obvious contentment.

"You feel as closed in as I do, my friend?" he whispered. "If only we could go out, if but for a moment..."

The room blurred. In a second the walls vanished and Eton found himself, his fingers still laced in the black mane, standing in a small clearing just within the wood line that surrounded the blockhouse. Fleet padded out of the brush toward him.

<Friend come.> growled the cat as he came to a stop before the big horse.

Eton grinned in embarrassment as he rubbed the big black's neck.

"Sorry friend, I forgot," he whispered. Then, to the cat, <Can ride friend?>

Fleet raised his muzzle to the big mount's nose for a moment, then replied, <Can ride.> He leaped softly to the big black's broad haunches.

Eton saw that the cat kept its claws sheathed, though the leather barding would protect the mount's hide. It was strange. All of his adult life Eton had stayed afoot because of the way horses responded to Fleet. To find a mount that had no fear, one that actually liked the big cat…

He locked his right hand in the horse's mane and, as he thought of the area just outside of the door to the blockhouse, his sight blurred once again.

When it cleared, the youth found that he, the horse ,and the cat were now standing exactly where his thoughts had willed. He grinned and rubbed the strong neck with his bare right hand.

<It is good?> he asked the cat as it dropped silently to the ground next to him.

<Is good.> came the growled reply. <Safe inside. Go.>

Eton's hand was still on the black neck as the puma growled his farewell and the warrior watched as the tawny cat blurred. A second later, he stood next to the mount, again within the stable. He rubbed his strong hand along the mount's neck until it reached the apron of the barding.

Then he remembered that he had removed the saddle and barding earlier to brush the big horse down.

"How…" he began, but the big horse brought his warm nose into the warrior's chest and pushed him toward a stack of hay next to the stairs.

"You're right, my friend," whispered the youth. "What does it matter 'how'?"

He wrapped his cloak about him and lay down. Answers would come when they came. For now…

He drifted into the awake-sleep of the woodland ranger.

Chapter Thirty-five

Melisande left the bed softly, not wishing to rouse the mage girl from her trance-like sleep. It was dark in the big room, yet the girl's eyes could make out most of the furnishings using the small beam of light that slipped past the dark curtains over the arrow slits. It was morning, and the first light came straight into the slits on the eastern wall.

The smell of boiling Kaff and roasted meat greeted her as she walked to the trapdoor. She found the tinderbox she'd brought with her and struck fire into one of the torches in the sconces along the wall.

The chest intrigued her. Her power of the day before had shown no protection on the banded container, and as tired as she was, her curiosity had been left on hold. Now, however, she was rested and it was a new day.

She slipped the torch she held into a sconce that had been mounted on the left post of the footboard and looked to see if the chest was locked. The catch was oiled and had seen much use. As she touched the release, a small snap inside the mechanism told her that it had been left unsecured.

As the lid lifted on silent hinges, the contents of the chest were displayed to the girl, all folded and laid out neatly within.

"That's strange," she mumbled as she lifted a silken shirt from the chest.

She shrugged and refolded it. As she returned it to the chest, her eyes caught the folded, soft blue leather in the bottom left corner under other garments. She lifted it out carefully and unfolded it.

Something had been folded within and fell back into the chest.

Melisande draped the leather over her arm and reached back into the chest for the shining object. As she brought it into the light, her indrawn breath described her awe at the workmanship of the object.

The dagger.

The sheath was of Elvin silver, as was the pommel and the light chain that was wrapped about the hilt. She drew the blade slowly from the sheath.

Rene' tossed suddenly in her sleep, a pained look on her soft features. Melisande slid the blade back into the sheath, and the mage girl settled back into a dreamless trance.

The black-haired cleric laid the sheathed dagger on top of the neat pile of clothing in the chest and stood to shake the blue leather out. It was a tabard, she saw, as the last fold slipped softly away. This was something she'd seen knights wear over their armor as they moved about Catlorian. It displayed their rank and to whom they owed allegiance.

The symbols on this tabard, however, were new to her. Over the left breast, below two silver-colored parallel stripes, was a crest. The shield was divided into three sections with red, green, and blue fields. Superimposed over all three was the head of a great black panther, its outlined features displayed in an open-mouth growl.

She folded the tabard over her arm, retrieved the dagger, and closed the lid to the chest. She glanced once more at Rene' and moved to the trap door.

"Good morn, m'lady," greeted Solothon as the girl made her way down the stairway.

He poured two cups of the steaming Kaff, placed one before Savon'el on the table, and crossed to the girl with the other. Savon'el looked over the map again while his right hand rubbed at his temple.

"How is he today?" asked the girl softly as she took the warm cup.

"He says he is all right, but I feel his pain is still with him," he responded softly. "Is there naught you can do?"

"I've tried, Solothon, as has Rene. Whatever this ailment, it is not something either of us may heal. We decided to wait and be here for him. It's all we can do."

"Call on me if I might help," he said as he laid a hand on the girl's arm. His hand touched the blue leather. "What have you?"

"Oh!" she said as she handed the tabard to the knight. "I found this in the chest upstairs. Do you recognize the emblem?"

The knight unfolded the tabard and studied the emblem. The name came to his lips. "Shedran, I think."

"What?"

"Shedran, as written in *The Book of Battle*, is described with this pattern and standard, I believe. My father keeps the book in the Keep library at home in Laranthia. I don't remember where this land lies, but I do know that it is not on this continent. I will know more once we are home." His fingers touched the silver stripes above the crest. "This belonged to a captain or high ranking officer. These stripes declare this to be so. Where did that beast get them?"

"He earned them."

Both turned at the sound of the Huntsmaster's soft voice and watched as the ranger pulled himself up into the room through the trap door. He crossed to the pot of Kaff and, as he poured himself a cup, the knight asked the obvious question.

"What do you mean?"

Arantar glanced at the blond half elf as that one concentrated on the map. He answered the knight softly while he gazed at the displayed crest.

"There is a suit of armor upstairs," he stated, with a nod from Melisande, "that is identical to the suit worn by the Habuk-ha, save for the size. I didn't understand at the time, but as Eton and I reconnoitered the possible path from here to our objective, all of the pieces came together for me."

He glanced again at the blond half elf.

"I've heard many stories of men who, for reasons unknown, wished to be more than they were. They were second sons, passed over officers or others who thought they deserved more, who would strike bargains with those of power to bring this about. I believe that our host did the same and, in the bargain, lost his humanity."

Solothon frowned.

"I thought it strange that he would wish for Honor Combat. Maybe—"

"Maybe he'd had enough," interjected the Huntsmaster. "Maybe, when he saw a knight of honor, he found his way out. His challenge could have been his way to die with the honor he'd lost long ago."

"Are you saying that once that gualu was human?" asked Melisande in a low, shocked voice.

"From what you found, the discipline of his troops and from his actions—all uncommon for a gualu—I would say yes. It might also explain the absence of a daku master here. Possibly he lusted after more and, in striking a bargain with some powerful evil, was changed. The histories I've read speak of this being the case during the Mage Wars, but who could be so powerful as to do this today?"

Melisande glanced quickly up the stairs to the room in which Rene' slept. Short of the Myrlin of Catlorian, only one possibility came to mind.

"It doesn't matter now, however," continued the Huntsmaster. "What's done is done."

His gaze rested on the blond half elf at the table.

"The pain still persists?" he asked softly.

"Yes," answered the knight. "He works through it somehow. I've never seen a man so driven."

"I have," said the Huntsmaster as his mind returned to the court of Prince LeMand.

"That Kaff is good," he said a bit more cherry. "I'll have another cup and tell you what we've discovered."

Arantar took his and Solothon's cup, filled them, and returned to the table to sit across from Savon'el.

"According to my sources," he said with a grin at the blond, "the road turns here, west-northwest, and turns again northeast just before the walls of Fire Gap Keep. But if we crossed the bridge and move down the unused road to this point and turned to the north, there is a good chance that we can bypass that Keep and cut twenty to thirty miles off of our travel."

Savon'el looked at the map and made mental notes from the Huntsmaster's report.

"What of the terrain?" he asked.

"Rough, but passable. The horses should have no trouble negotiating it and there seems to be game trails throughout. We can use the cover of the woods to our best advantage by this path and maybe arrive unannounced."

"Good. Let's get the others here for a briefing. Then I suggest we move out with all due haste." As the blond glanced about the room, he asked, "Where is Eton?"

"He's down with the horses. He said he'd be up in a moment."

"Would someone please help me down?"

Rene's soft voice drifted down the stairs and caused the knight to come swiftly to his feet. He went up the stairs and, with his strong hands on her tiny waist, lifted the girl to the landing.

"Thank you, Sir Solothon," she said graciously as she stepped lightly down the stairs.

"How are you this morning?" asked the black-haired cleric. "I know that you expended much over the past several days."

"I'm fine, really. That beautiful bed has done wonders for me. Strange, though," she added with a frown, "just before I woke, a pinch of fear entered my trance. I can't quite seem to put my finger on it."

"Maybe I can," replied Melisande.

She pulled the sheathed dagger from her belt and laid it on the table. Solothon's stretched his hand toward it, but as it neared a feeling of sickness passed through him. He withdrew the hand and the sickness left.

"What is this?" he asked.

"I found it in the chest upstairs," she replied as she again picked up the dagger and drew the blade.

Chairs were thrown back as everyone with Elvin blood around her dodged back in panic.

"What's wrong?" she asked as she looked upon the pained faces of her friends.

Bonaire's snores ceased as he turned fitfully in his sleep.

"Put it away, Melisande."

The voice was Savon'el's, but the tone was of someone else. She looked toward him and found the amber eyes molten. She slid the blade quickly into the silver sheath and dropped it on the table.

Bonaire resumed snoring while the rest sighed in collective relief.

"What did I do?" asked the distressed girl.

"Nothing, my dear," answered the mage girl. "It's just that you had no way to know what it was you held."

"Enlighten me then!"

"It is an honor blade," responded Savon'el in a dreamy voice. "It was obviously given to a knight of consequence by royalty."

"However," added Solothon, "not to one of Elvin blood."

Rene' laid a soft hand on the black-haired cleric's arm and explained. "The blade is cold-wrought steel, and obviously of Dwarven make, which is soul-searing poison for us. You, being of human stock, are unaffected, but we cannot even get close to it."

"That answers one question then," commented Arantar.

"What's that?" asked the blond.

"Whatever our enemy of yesterday was, he was definitely not Elvin."

"Of course not," said Savon'el, a look of question on his face. "He was Habuk-ha, a gualu, nothing more."

"He was Habuk-ha, but..." Arantar related the discussion he'd had earlier as Savon'el and Rene' listened intently.

"Be that as it may," said Savon'el softly, "why did they come here? They were all well-trained, and the repairs to this outpost have been recent. What are they guarding? We know that we were probably not worth their trouble, so why this outpost?"

"Possibly to guard the way to Fire Gap Keep or Radagast's Rest, or both, as we discussed last night," said the mage girl.

"Who has the power to reopen the Den of Nightmares?" asked Arantar. "I don't mean just enter, but open it to the terrors it contains and release them?"

"Cartellion might," replied Melisande as he cast a quick glance at Rene, "but I don't think he'd bother."

"You *know* who I think it is," said the mage girl softly, "and if I'm right, we have to move fast because, were I him, I'd open that keep as soon as I could to retrieve what power I could."

"These objects we are after," asked Savon'el softly, "you believe them to be that powerful?"

"In the wrong hands, devastating. I promise I will tell you everything before we get there. Right now there is no time. We must move!"

"What of this?" asked Melisande as she displayed the tabard and dagger.

"If Arantar's conjectures are correct," answered Savon'el, "it is our duty to try to return them to his family." At Solothon's frown, he continued, "Though he may have lost himself to greed for whatever reason, he was still a knight. The honor weapon shows that somewhere there are those who remember him in honor. We must try, on *our* honor."

Solothon's frown softened. "I agree."

"Who will carry it?" asked the Huntsmaster. "Though Savon'el and I are but half Elvin, it still affects us as well, even while sheathed."

"I will if I must," replied the blond.

"I'll carry it," said the cleric matter-of-factly. "It doesn't affect me in the least." She rolled the dagger into the tabard and put it under her arm. "If we ever return, I will see that it gets to wherever Shedran exists."

"We will all help," Savon'el replied. "Now, let's make ready to depart. Check weapons and rations, then pack quickly."

A great snort resounded through the room.

"Someone wake Bonaire," added Savon'el. Then he moved for the trap-door to the stable.

The raven guided the party through the game trails and brought them out of the wild country some miles beyond Fire Gap Keep. There was a river between their objective and the Keep behind them that had but one bridge. The only way to cross it was on the road.

They spent the night at a cold camp on the Keep side of the bridge and within the woods. In the morning they crossed the bridge and returned to the game trails for safety.

It was cold in the late afternoon of the fourth day when Arantar topped a small rise. He raised a hand to halt the party and waved Savon'el to him as the rest of the party drew rein.

The ground fell away in a gentle slope to a wide plain. In the middle of that plain sat their objective.

It was a large block of bleached stone, over two hundred feet square and over forty feet high. The road ended at the large stone doors—forty feet wide by twenty feet tall—that were closed with no obvious way to open them. With the exception of the road that led directly to those doors, the land was blasted all about the stone citadel and the earth razed in ragged destruction.

The road leading to those doors was puzzling as well. It was gleaming white and smooth. It came from the stone doors to just twenty or so yards past the devastated earth and stopped, perfectly square and straight. It looked, from Arantar's vantage point, to be of the same material as the King's Way.

"Blacky says he can't see any movement on or around that," he said to the blond half elf.

"I don't like it," replied the blond as he turned away from the distant fortress and sat. "It's too easy. We've seen no one on the road and no sign of life anywhere about that keep. Yet our reception of a few days ago would say the contrary. If this is someone's objective and they wished to keep it safe..."

"What do you suggest?"

"We need more information. Take Bonaire and scout about. The rest of us will wait for you there, just this side of the destruction, off the side of that road."

"Eton will want to join me and frankly—"

"Eton will scout too, but I feel that Bonaire needs the experience." At Arantar's frown, the blond half elf continued, "I can't go into it now,

Huntsmaster. Just suffice it to say that, for some reason, I feel it's our duty to try to bring that youth around. He must be trained in more than his own self indulgence."

"At what cost?"

"I understand, but—"

"You are probably right," interrupted the Huntsmaster with a shrug, "though I wish I could trust him more."

They moved back down the hill to join the rest of the companions. Savon'el left it in the Huntsmaster's hands to explain to Bonaire what was required. The companions stopped short of the devastation, moved off to the right of the white road, and set up camp to wait for word from the scouts.

Arantar and Bonaire moved swiftly down the left side of the white road while Eton followed on the right. There, around the base of the tower, was a clear area of dead flat dirt. Dead in that there was nothing growing on or around the stark white walls, as if by design.

As they came to the edge of the devastated ground outside of the dead soil, Arantar flashed a quick sign and Eton disappeared behind a jagged boulder on the other side of the white road.

"Bonaire," said the Huntsmaster softly, "I need you to go left down the wall to the end. I'll go right. Eton will be here to help if you need it. Just be careful."

"Okay, but what exactly am I looking for?"

"A way in. Look for windows, doors, and footholds in the stone that might allow us to climb up and into that building. I don't like the look of this. Just stay alert and be careful. If something feels wrong—"

"You worry too much," came the youth's response.

"And you too little," Arantar replied sharply as Bonaire eyed the doors with a grin. "Why would someone put armed and well-trained soldiers to guard the only road to this place and then leave it unprotected?"

"Just careless, I guess," grinned the elf.

"Just you don't be careless!" snapped the Huntsmaster. "Move!"

Arantar moved toward the doors slowly and stepped off of the white roadway to the right. He scanned the ground as he moved, but he found no signs of passage or tracks near the door and none, as far as he could see, along the twenty-foot wide path of smooth dirt about the base of that white building.

The hair on the back of his neck prickled. Something was wrong. He turned back toward the road and began running.

Bonaire walked casually down the wall to the left of the doorway. This was a piece of cake, he reckoned. If there was something out here, maybe it was treasure of some kind. He caught the gleam of white farther along the flat ground and grinned as he sauntered over and crouched to inspect it. It was a set of bones of a small bird, bleached white in the sun. The bones weren't broken, and the young elf reasoned that it must have died and rotted where it fell.

To his left rear, the ground slowly and softly slipped away. Antennae mounted above multiple eyes felt the heat of food, and its mandibles clicked in preparation of its meal.

The clicking noise brought Bonaire around in a spin. There, coming for him out of the very ground, was a five-foot-long and four-foot-wide black beetle, it's maw opened wide and its sharp mandibles quivering in anticipation.

"Arantar!" Bonaire yelled.

The young elf's hand found the hilt of the green sword and drew it from its sheath, but he was trying to run backward away from the beast.

It was too late. The beetle was on him, its mandibles sinking into the soft flesh of the youth's thigh. Bonaire screamed and slashed at the creature, but other than a crack in the carapace, the beetle was unharmed. The young elf lost consciousness as the venom entered his bloodstream.

The Huntsmaster's great sword was out as he ran, and he watched as the beast sunk its mandibles into the youth's leg. As the creature released its jaws to take a better grip, the Huntsmaster roared his challenge.

The beetle thought only of food and, though there had been precious little for a great many years, found these warm meals gratifying. It didn't even have to chase them. They ran toward its hungry mouth of their own desire. It turned toward the charging Huntsmaster and attacked.

The gray sword sunk into the carapace above the beast's eyes as the mandibles sunk into the leather over the Huntsmaster's thigh. Burning poison coursed up Arantar's leg, but he wouldn't quit.

He drove the gray blade deeper into the cracked shell and, with both hands, ripped it back and forth into the soft green flesh beneath.

The mandibles released their grip as the creature shuddered in death.

Arantar ripped the blade from the beetle and drove it into the ground to remove the green slime that clung to it. Then he limped toward Eton as that one knelt next to the fallen Bonaire.

As Arantar knelt next to the youth and laid his hands on the youth's forehead, Eton crouched next to him, both blades in his hands and his sharp eyes darting all about.

Arantar had shaken off the poison before it could do any damage. His strong will caused his body to attack the venom as it would a virus and, in doing so, had rendered it harmless.

Now he cast his will to this boy's body, repairing what he could. He could do nothing for the poison, however, and had to chase after it repairing what he could as the poison raged through the elf's body.

"We must get him back to the clerics," said the Huntsmaster tightly as he attempted to lift the youth.

He was weak from his own battle and the added burden of the willed cellular manipulation he constantly passed into the youth, but he got the youth into his arms and began the long trek back to the white road.

"These," he said to the warrior as they passed beetle, "come from beneath the ground. Watch where you walk."

Eton yanked Arantar's sword from the ground and walked ahead, his eyes searching for any movement of the ground that would tell of another attack. Arantar walked slowly carrying his burden as one would a child.

Savon'el saw them as they mounted the white road and correctly deduced the Huntsmaster's colorful burden.

"Bonaire has been hurt," he shouted to Solothon. "Stay with our clerics and help them prepare for our wounded." Then he ran.

Though the Huntsmaster was reluctant to release the youth to anyone else, less he lose contact with him, he did allow the blond to help him with the burden.

"There is poison within," he gasped as Savon'el picked up some of the elf's weight and fell into step with him. "I've tried, but I can't stop it."

"Don't worry," replied the blond. "Melisande and Rene' are preparing for our arrival."

Rene' helped Melisande spread her blanket and watched as the cleric lay out the contents of her kit. Although accomplished in her own right, the mage girl acted as Melisande's assistant. It would do no good for them to act in conflict with one another with the life of one of their number in the balance.

It was all the Huntsmaster could do to keep going. By the time they'd reached the makeshift aid camp, his will and strength were close to finished. He'd poured so much of himself into the youth that his body shook with the effort.

"Lay him here, Huntsmaster," said Rene' as she ran to help him and Savon'el with their burden.

"It's poison," he gasped. "I can't seem to stop it."

"Let us try, Arantar. You've done your best. You must rest now."

They laid Bonaire on the blanket and, as Melisande began treatment of the twin gashes on the youth's leg, Rene' pushed Arantar away.

"Go and rest. Savon'el, come and make him rest!"

"Come, Huntsmaster, allow them to ply their trade," said the blond as he gently led Arantar away. "Tell me what happened."

Eton watched the women work, but he saw the youth dying by inches. Bonaire's face and hands were red as if he were burning up. The elf was indeed in a raging fever, the poison eating away at him without rest. The big warrior watched Rene' stiffen as she reached into the youth's mind and Melisande kissed each of the youth's hands in turn, but nothing seemed to work.

Nethan DeBurge knew little of his life before Seaborne, but from some deep memory of a time before the shimmering portal plunged him into this world at the tender age of three, a voice slipped through.

He knelt beside the blanket and, as he took one of the hot hands in his right and placed it on the ground beyond the blanket, he whispered. "Sola chandu' shinoi."

Then he stood and walked back to the road.

Rene' felt the strength that seemed to stretch through the young elf from the very earth. Something in the boy's mind woke, and he began to fight off the effects of the poison. His skin cooled as his victory was made certain.

Melisande bound the gashes on the youth's leg with clean bandaging as Bonaire drifted into soft slumber, his head in the golden mage girl's lap. Rene' looked over at the Huntsmaster and smiled.

The Huntsmaster took a deep breath and let his head fall into his hands.

"Arantar," asked Savon'el as he sat down beside him, "what did this to him?"

"It was a poisonous beast that comes from beneath the dirt."

Arantar was tired, though he was regaining energy quickly. His reconnaissance had yielded nothing save a wounded companion.

"Before the creature attacked, I could find no way into that place. There is no handle on those great doors, nor a smaller portal though which we can enter. It looks hopeless."

"Hopeless or not, Huntsmaster, we must gain entrance," replied Savon'el.

"I agree," said the knight. "We won't find any answers out here."

"We might not find any in there either," Arantar commented. "I agree that we must continue, but how?"

Then Savon'el looked about the campsite.

"Where is Eton?"

"He stayed behind to watch for more of those things," replied the Huntsmaster.

"Don't worry about me," whispered Eton as he stepped off of the white road into the makeshift camp. "How do you fare?"

"Better, and the ladies said earlier that Bonaire's fever was gone. He's stronger than we thought and he should be up and about shortly. According to Rene', they'd almost lost him when he suddenly took on new strength. They can't account for it, but I say that the gods were sitting on his shoulder."

"That may be," said the big warrior with a grin. "It is said that the gods protect drunks and fools. He's a bit of both, isn't he?"

"I suppose," replied Arantar as he returned the grin. "Now, about getting in..."

They took turns at watched that night. Savon'el decided, over Rene's protest of unidentified haste, they should camp where they were and recuperate. He understood the urgency, but with the exception of their exposed position on the road they were still relatively safe. One night wouldn't make much difference if they all collapsed once at their goal.

Bonaire woke hours before dawn and looked about the camp in the bright moonlight. He was chilled to the bone and pulled his cloak closer. He sat up slowly so as not to alarm Rene'. She'd drifted into a trance as she sat beside him and her breath came slowly, white with the cold. As his eyes took in the small encampment, he saw that everyone slept except for Eton.

The big warrior stood next to Shadow and gazed toward the white keep in the middle of the blasted plain. The young elf stood up carefully and quietly moved toward him.

"Up and around?" whispered the warrior. "That's good."

"Yeah, I guess I got lucky," replied the youth in a whisper.

"I suppose."

"Eton?" asked the elf after a moment's pause. "Can you tell me something?"

"If I can."

"I know that Arantar was there for me, and I understand that, more or less. No matter how stupid I act, he's always been there to help."

"Yes?"

"But while I was dreaming that I wouldn't get back...You know, when I was out? I had this feeling that you were there. Were you?"

It was Eton's turn to pause. The elf waited patiently in the chill of the winter morning air while the big warrior looked out over the plain again.

"Yes, in a way."

"Why?" asked Bonaire. "I mean, don't get me wrong, I'm grateful, but you don't know me and what you *do* know can't have made you feel...You know."

"No, I don't," whispered the warrior. At the strange look on Bonaire's face, Eton continued, "We all do what we can for the whole. If it were left up to me, we would all leave here for another destination. It is, however, not up to me, and I will not leave my friends and companions here. There is an old saying from my youth: 'A man who walks alone, dies alone.' I only do for others what I wish could be done for me."

"I see," said the youth reluctantly.

"Do you?" whispered the warrior sharply. "Do you realize the burden you place on this party every day with your prattling and strutting?"

Bonaire jerked under this quiet onslaught.

"What have you done for your supposed friends since you've been with them?" continued Eton. "Were you there when they needed you? When did you ever go out of your way to help them? Yet each would lay down his life to save yours. Yes, even me! That is the way of things in this life."

"I'd never thought about it that way," said the elf softly. "I thought that everyone was out for themselves."

"A great many are, but they are the minority. Even now you think of the treasure that may lie within those white walls."

That comment snapped Bonaire's eyes away from the Keep back to the warrior. He had been thinking about that and how much his share would be.

"You believe that these others feel as you do," continued Eton. "There is more here between them than petty greed. They work together as a team to reach a common objective. I don't believe that any of them has thought past getting in there. That is their objective, their goal, their pact."

"What about you? Why are you here?"

"I have my reasons," answered the warrior. "And," he added as he shot a quick glance at the elf, "they have nothing to do with treasure."

Eton slipped easily into the saddle and looked down at Bonaire.

"Think about what I've said while you guard your friends."

"Where are you going?" whispered the elf in a gasp.

"Don't worry. I'm just going to check out that doorway again. I won't be gone long."

"But—" Bonaire choked.

Where the big warrior once had sat astride the black warhorse there was now emptiness. It was as if Eton had disappeared into thin air. He looked down the road toward the keep and, to his surprise, saw a black figure appear before the door to the white structure.

He looked back over his sleeping companions and shrugged. Maybe the big guy was right. Then he looked back at the warm blanket he'd left and thought about returning to it.

"Why not?" he thought.

Then he answered himself in a way that shocked him.

"They depend on me."

He stepped over to the small campfire, poured himself a cup of the thick Kaff, and stood where he could watch over them and the big warrior down the road.

"I don't know, Shadow," whispered the warrior as he stood next to the stone doors.

His eyes raked the entire surface looking for a handle, lever, or anything that would allow for entrance.

"There doesn't seem to be any way through, though the raven told Arantar that this was the only way in."

He shook his head and returned to his mount.

"I can see no way," he said as he mounted. "Let's get back before they miss us." He turned his mind to the picture of the small campsite in the moonlight.

Rene' came out of her trance to the smell of freshly brewed Kaff. Bonaire sat next to the small fire with his hands wrapped around his cup while Eton stood with the big black warhorse and gazed toward the keep.

"Bonaire," she called quietly.

The youth turned from the fire.

"May I have a cup of that, please?"

"Of course," he replied softly, and he hurriedly poured a cup and brought it to her. "Thanks for what you did yesterday," he said as he looked down at the blanket. "I know I don't—"

"You'd do the same for me," she said, "wouldn't you?"

The youth looked up into her golden eyes, and the mage girl caught the sparkle of a tear as it streaked down a sad face.

They broke camp an hour before dusk and, as the fading light receded over the western horizon, rode slowly to the stone face of the double doors. It hadn't changed from the day before. It was still without keyhole, handle, or entrance. They watched the edge of the road carefully for any sign of movement in the dead dirt there.

"There must be another way in," said Rene'.

She stayed close to the knight for protection and left the others to look over the doors again and again.

"There isn't," said Arantar tightly. "There is not an opening in this entire block of stone, nor anything resembling a door. This is it."

"There must be a way," said the blond half elf softly. He felt his life ending before he even knew what his life was and it ate away at him. The pain behind his eyes was now pounding, unrelenting, and almost unbearable. "It can't end like this."

The Huntsmaster looked at the blond half elf as that one rubbed at his temples yet again. Arantar couldn't help him unless they found the end to this, yet it seemed that circumstances constantly altered their options.

"I know a way!"

They all turned toward Bonaire as he ran toward Eton.

"Get on your horse and pop in there," he said breathlessly as he grabbed the warrior's arm. "Then you can just open the door!"

"What in the seven hells are you talking about?" whispered the warrior as he turned stern eyes on the young elf.

"Your horse, Shadow. You can just hop on and go anywhere, right?"

"Is that possible?" asked Savon'el as he looked up at Eton. "Can Shadow make that kind of a jump?"

"I don't know. I'm not sure," whispered the big warrior. Then, as he looked toward Melisande, "M'lady?"

"Not unless he or Eton have been here before," Rene' answered for her. "Unicornes can only phase where they can see. Shadow, being a half-breed Nightmare, would have to have a picture in his mind—either his own or Eton's—to make that kind of jump."

"Then, Lady Melisande," whispered Eton, his eyes still on the black-haired cleric, "could you ask him?"

Melisande looked from the big warrior to the black warhorse with apprehension and nodded, but before she could bring that power to her lips, the big mount nudged Eton in the chest and brought that warrior's eyes to his.

Thou canst ask for thyself.

The voice in his mind tasted of ozone and brimstone. The shocked look on his face told everyone there that something out of the ordinary was happening. Melisande stopped and stared.

"How did he do that?" thought the warrior, his shock a tangible thing.

How did thou not know thou couldest? Thy companion and I have spoken of thy lack, but the quiet one cautioned patience.

"The quiet one?" Eton whispered softly.

Hast thou not the capacity for mind-speech, Nethan DeBurge?

"I—"

T'is a lesson thee must learn e'er we continue. Thou must concentrate within thy mind. Thy power is dormant, yet I can see that it merely awaits thee. Look into my eyes and cast thy doubts aside.

Eton looked from the horse to the tawny puma lying patiently on the white road some distance from the companions, his head upon his outstretched paws. He recalled the many times he'd thought to tell the puma to do something, only to find that the big cat had either done it or was in the process. Was it possible? Could he...

He concentrated on the puma, his will driving his desire.

Can you hear me, Fleet?

He felt something stir inside his mind, yet it was so quick he thought he'd done something wrong. The cat, however, jerked its head up and looked directly at him.

Not 'Fleet,' Nethan-sao, but Fleret of the western mountains. I have waited many seasons to feel you within my mind.

The thought slid softly through his mind, a quiet purr. Eton sat down hard on the white surface. The tears came quickly to his eyes and rolled across the scars on his cheeks.

"What is it, my friend?" asked the black-haired cleric as she knelt beside him. "What's wrong?"

"My friend of many years has spoken to me," he whispered, a catch in his throat. "I have wasted so much time when I could have gotten closer to my best friend simply by thinking."

"How is that possible?" asked the cleric as she looked towards Rene'.

It is quite simple. came the crackling thought to Eton's mind. *Thou art Cheal.*

"Cheal?" Eton whispered.

"But there haven't been Cheal here for over twenty-five hundred years!" exclaimed the mage girl. "How is that possible?"

Cheal? the big warrior sent to his friend, Fleret.

You need not shout, Nethan-sao, though I think it is but your inexperience with this way of speaking that makes it so. Practice will help.

In answer to thy question: came the ozone-flavored crackle to his mind, *There were few Cheal left when my companion and I rode these lands, some because they waited too long to escape while others stayed because of their love of this place. Some found lives within the races of men while others died in defense of those they loved. My companion, Pantor, loved one of these and changed.*

"He says that there were many here before, but has no answer for my presence here," whispered the big warrior. "He also said that Pantor changed sides."

"That might explain why he died early in the Mage War," said Rene'. "If Pantor changed sides, he would be a threat to Banshe'e and his talon. It might also explain why Rairy had Hellshadow at his house."

"That still doesn't answer the question we need answered."

Melisande looked up at Savon'el as that one moved to kneel beside a big warrior. The pain the half elf felt behind his eyes showed on his face.

"Eton," Savon'el asked, "can your mount take us within this keep or not?"

"Savon'el!" exclaimed the black-haired cleric.

"I'm sorry, m'lady, but we are exposed here. If there is no way to enter here, we must look at alternatives."

"You're right," whispered Eton as he rose to his feet and wiped the tears from his face. "We must press on."

The big warrior turned to the warhorse and sighed.

Can you take me into this keep?

If thou canst picture thy desire, yes.

I've never been here. Can you do it any other way?

Only at great risk.

To you?

No, friend Nethan, to thee and thine.

"He has a way," whispered the warrior, "but he says it involves great risk."

"Then," responded the blond half elf, "ask him if he'll do it."

There was great danger here. The warrior felt it in the marrow of his bones. He wanted to shout at them, scoop them up, and carry them away from here, away from the danger and the hardship. As he looked into each face, however, he knew that it would be a waste of time. He looked back along the road to where the tawny puma lay, its massive head again on its paws.

Wait three suns, no more, Fleret. If I'm not back by then...

I will wait as long as it takes, Nethan-sao, brother, however long that is.

Fleret rose, stretched, and loped back up the road.

Quiet earth brother say will wait until return, Arantar-sao. I too. I too.

The sad breeze blew through Arantar's mind as he watched the raven circle toward the rise.

"My friend said he'll watch after your bird, Arantar," whispered Eton. At the shocked look, he continued with a grin, "Come on, we have work to do."

Eton stroked the black neck of his new friend and sighed.

What must I do, friend?

Where we go, none should be afoot. Thou and thy companions must ride, for walking through the plane I will open will be difficult at best. Tell them that they must stay upon the path. Otherwise, they will perish.

"We need to get mounted," whispered the warrior.

"Then let us proceed," stated the blond as he mounted his warhorse. "We'll go as before, with Arantar and Eton in the fore, Bonaire as guard to our clerics, and Sir Solothon and I serving as rearguard. Bonaire, you have the packhorse."

"Just stay close," said Eton, his whispered caution causing all to look at him as he mounted. "Shadow states that to leave the path he will create will be death."

"Remember," added Rene', "Nightmares travel through the bowels of hell. I trust Eton and Shadow to get us through, but you must control your mounts and keep them on the path."

"Are we ready?" asked the blond half elf. Accepting the nods from most of his companions as a "yes," he continued, "At your convenience, Eton."

They are prepared, my friend. Eton thought to the Nightmare under his knees. *Take us through.*

Chapter Thirty-six

Shadow reared, and as he pawed the air he let out a soul-searing scream that made blood run cold and shivers of ice race up and down spines. Before the half-breed Nightmare, a swirl of blackness began, getting larger and larger until it was the size of a large stable door. The acrid stench of sulfurous brimstone reached them on the winds of heat, as if from a blast furnace, that blew out of the hole in space and time.

Shadow's blue eyes glowed as he trotted into the gaping darkness.

The companions waited but a moment before they too followed the big black into the void. Once through that portal, they saw that they tread on a dark cobblestone walkway. To either side and as far as they could see, a roiling sea of molten rock boiled and bubbled, the heat stifling and the noxious fumes causing their lungs to struggle.

Where are we? the big warrior asked.

In hell. was the only answer he received.

Time meant nothing here. The heat drove at them as they followed Eton along the straight path in single file, each holding the reins to their mount tightly.

Suddenly, just twenty paces away and to the left of the pathway, a great being of molten stone rose from the sea of fire. It was at least twelve feet tall and ugly. Its great maw opened, and a challenge reverberated throughout the openness of the cavernous plane.

Eton instinctively slipped his left hand into the basket hilt of the Bourjon Blade as his right pulled on the reins. He looked upon this creature and knew he would never be able to defeat it, nor could his companions. He set his mind into that cold place reserved for soldiers who know they will not survive, but would still give themselves to protect their brothers.

Then a voice, a deep baritone voice, stopped him. The voice came not from the horse but from somewhere close by. It was a language that tasted of age, and its quiet power filled the hellish space.

Rene' recognized the language. She could not understand it, of course, but she'd heard it spoken before. Yarda had used it on her when she'd become too "pushy" for the old mage. When she'd asked what the words meant, he explained that the language had died long before the Mage War and that the words' meanings would sear her tender ears.

Whatever was said in that long dead language caused the molten beast to step back from the pathway and slip silently back into its fiery pool. Shadow snorted and moved on at a canter.

Whether it was days, weeks, or just seconds was hard to comprehend. The timelessness of that passage weighed heavily on the companions. The oppressive heat and thick, poisonous air left them tired and muted.

Finally the big warhorse stopped and again screamed that soul-rending scream. A portal opened before them to blackness and they all stepped through. The portal closed behind them. It was pitch dark. Eton slipped from the saddle and filled his hands with steel. He felt for the size of the darkness; his battle-honed senses sought possible danger, yet he found none. He waited in his fighting crouch until his companions could ignite a torch and dispel the cloying darkness.

He was relieved when the black's warm nose slipped over his right shoulder. He grinned as he reached up and scratched the great jaw.

A spark was struck and suddenly the room was lit by the torch in the Huntsmaster's hand.

"Where are we?" asked Arantar as he moved to Eton's side.

The big warrior looked behind and past the companions as they dismounted and inspected the room. There, beyond the group, were the same wide stone doors they'd faced on the outside.

"We're in," came the whispered reply.

He looked back at the strange latticework in the large double doors in the wall opposite the stone entrance. Eton moved toward them.

"Stop!" came the soft voice from his right.

Rene' moved toward the doors and, without touching them, looked them over carefully. Her mouth dropped open and she backed away.

"It's made of bone, the rib bones of every known race of being I've ever seen or heard of, and a few I don't recognize."

"Is it safe?"

Melisande answered Savon'el's question by bringing her talent to full and was nearly blinded. The blond half elf caught her as she stumbled back from the doors, her eyes closed tightly.

"It's a trap!" she said breathlessly. "Total magic!"

Rene' looked quickly at the girl and then brought her own talent to bear. The walls floor and ceiling rippled in power, but the stone doors were dark.

"How do we get around it?" asked the savon'el, his voice betraying his concern for their safety.

Melisande opened her eyes slowly and, muting her talent carefully, looked once again at the latticework door. Then she grinned.

"We already have," At Savon'el's look, she continued, "Shadow brought us around it. The door is safe, Rene'. Push it open."

As the mage girl tenderly placed her hands on the bone latticework and pushed, the door opened silently into a hallway that went to the left and right.

"Had we managed to open that door from the outside," explained the cleric as she moved with the others into the large hallway, "we would have been plunged into another plane of existence, probably somewhere less desirable than the place we just visited."

The hallway was at least twenty feet wide and fifteen feet high. Dust and rot littered the floor, though once Rene' swept her foot from side to side, she found that underneath the mess was beautiful marble.

There was a smell of age and decay. Death was here in every pore of every wall and littered about the floor. The cloying mustiness surrounded the group as they led their mounts through the double doors into that hallway.

"Where to from here?"

The question posed by the Huntsmaster was one Savon'el had struggled with the night before.

Yes, what to do and where to go once within the great edifice? Poke about a bit in the hope that Red Wolf might show or that they might stumble upon the items Rene' was sent to collect? Even if they found any of those disgusting teeth Terillion was so interested in, would they now be allowed to return to Catlorian to claim the bounty?

Somewhere in the back of the blond half elf's aching head a stir began. It wasn't a voice, really, but an idea or lesson he knew had been repeated over and over again. Somehow the repetition had made the concept part of his pattern of thought even though he could not remember where or when the lesson was taught.

"In the worse positions you find yourself, the very worst is allowing for inactivity. It makes the even most hardy nervous and the fearful frozen in his fear. Movement for the sake of movement is far better than standing still, though a moment's thought will greatly aid your decision."

"We go right," he said quickly. "I see doorways there that may prove to be rooms where we can stable our mounts. We must see to them before we can continue. Huntsmaster, you will share the lead with Sir Solothon, and I will follow as fore guard to Rene' and Melisande. Bonaire' will come next and will share, if you will, the rearguard with Eton. Comments?"

Arantar answered the question by drawing the great gray blade and moving down the right side of the hallway, his war mount trailing behind him. Solothon stepped over to the left of that hallway and, as he drew the twin to the leaf-etched sword, kept pace with the Huntsmaster. His black mount followed closely behind him.

Bonaire took the reins to Savon'el's mount, his own, and those of the ladies and the packhorse and followed as he watched the blond half elf walk down the center of the hall with the ladies flanking his left and right.

One torch became three as Rene' struck fire to the two she and Melisande had retrieved from the mage girl's saddlebag.

Eton walked softly behind them all, Shadow walking as quiet as a whisper beside him. His senses were at peak. He couldn't see into the darkness behind them and relied on his other senses to tell him where and when to strike.

Arantar approached the closed door of a room at the far corner of the hallway where it turned abruptly to the left. He turned to call to Savon'el but stopped. The distinct sound of bone grating upon bone drew his attention to the hallway to his left.

Solothon heard it as well and stopped by the corner to listen closer. He felt, as he gripped the silver sword in his hand, that the evil that approached was beneath the divine purpose of the blessed sword that rested in its sheath at his left hip.

The grating noise became a rattle and, as Savon'el fell in behind the two warriors as they both faced toward that hallway, the danger came into view of the torchlight.

Once they were men, but now the very flesh of their being was gone. Tattered cloth covered arms of bone that ended in gray bony hands. Rusty blades rested in those hands, and they moved their jaws open in a soundless roar of attack as the red fire glowed from empty eye sockets.

Savon'el moved forward to close the wall of protection while Bonaire stood with the two women just to their rear. The blond drew the endlibar blade as he watched the host of apparitions stumble down the hallway toward them.

Bonaire reached for his sword, but he stopped when he noticed the four-foot piece of wood that rested against the wall at the junction of the hallways just beyond the door where Arantar had stood. He ran quickly and hefted it. It felt solid, though extremely old, and was of sufficient weight for his purposes. He returned to his place behind the savon'el and grinned.

"MAY THE PEACE OF THE GODDESS CELESTE GRANT YOU REST!"

The skeletal warriors stopped in their mad rush as the words traveled the length and breadth of that hallway.

Savon'el turned to see Rene' perched sidesaddle on her horse, her right hand toward the enemy and her eyes bright in clerical indignation.

"TURN NOW OR BE DAMNED!"

Four of the skeletons directly before the three fighters suddenly crumbled to dust at their feet. The others stood for a moment, then, as the red fire in the empty sockets flared, they attacked.

Eton had drawn both blades and crouched facing the darkness behind them. He was a warrior, a soldier, and though he knew where the battle raged he refused to allow for an attack from their rear. He glanced over his shoulder more than once and hoped that his companions would withstand the onslaught.

Shadow moved silently to Eton's side and turned his glowing blue eyes on his new companion.

Join them, friend Nethan. came the crackling thought. *Fear not that any can pass me here. Go now, my friend. Thou art needed elsewhere.*

Then the mount turned his attention back down the dark hallway, his eyes a blue smoldering fire.

The warrior nodded, grinned, and raced into the torchlight as the skeleton warriors broke against the wall of fighting men.

The Huntsmaster's sword was as a scythe. He swept it through the first two to reach him and was pleased at the sight and sound of the skeletons returning to dust. His great blade rang against the rusted blade aimed at his chest, and he slammed the heavy pommel against the skull, shattering it into bony shards.

Strangely, Solothon was at peace. He felt a sorrow for these beings that stemmed from some compassion deep within. He dispatched two in short order and silently wished them peace. There was no anger in him, only sadness that warriors of past battles had not been allowed an earned rest. The third raised its sword, only to have a strong gauntleted hand crush the bones at the wrist and the silver blade drop solemnly upon its skull.

The skeleton before Savon'el had no skill with its blade as the blond half elf brought his endlibar sword down with force. It tried in vain to bring its sword up to protect its head, yet it just didn't matter. The endlibar bit through the rusted blade and continued through the skull to shatter the bones of the skeleton's body in all directions. The blond stepped over the shards to face the next.

Bonaire had decided to use the short staff instead of his sword, the reasoning that the staff would shatter the bones better than the green crystal could cut them. Unfortunately, the young elf had never fought with a staff before and tried to swing it like a club. His first attempt at a sword-swinging skeleton missed and the staff swung him past his target, and it raised its blade to plunge it into Bonaire's unprotected side.

Suddenly its skull exploded into bony gray shards and it dropped the sword. It crumbled to dust at the young elf's feet. He turned to his left rear and saw Melisande grin.

In her hands, the cleric held a five-foot piece of limber wood with a strap of leather that dangled from the Y at the top. She dug into a pouch at her waist and retrieved another pellet of lead the size of the man's thumb. She placed the pellet into the leather pocket, wedged the ground end of the staff against one foot, and placed the other about midway up the shaft. Then she drew the leather pocket to her cheek, took aim, and released. The lead pellet caromed off an upraised sword and ricocheted down the hall.

Bonaire's return swing turned the next skeleton to dust, and its skull bounced against the wall and cracked in two.

Eton surged past Arantar directly for the remaining three attackers. Arantar followed, crushing bone beneath his swiftly moving boots.

As Eton came between the first two, both of the attackers swept their blades toward him. The blades in the big warrior's hands danced as they first parried the sweeping blades and then returned to shatter backbones.

The blades both spun and drove down. Both skulls were split at their passing.

Then the last of the attackers stood before the warrior, raised its sword, and attacked. The Bourjon Blade and long sword, crossed before the big warrior, stopped the down-swept blade.

Arantar struck at that enemy, but he had to pull the sweep of his great sword as the skeleton closed with Eton. The great blade bit air.

Arantar watched as the big warrior ripped both of his blades apart and, as the attacker's blade spun skyward, brought both blades back through the gray bones.

Solothon looked about the bone-littered hallway and down at the shattered skeleton at his feet. Then he noted the pouch it wore on its back. As he turned what was left of the skeleton over and ripped the rotted leather from its shoulders, the skull rolled up to face him. A weak red glow grew in its eye sockets and the jaw dropped open.

"Soul death will you find here," came a weedy voice. A cackling laugh came from those jaws and, as the glow dissipated, the voice continued, "Soul death...for...one...of—"

"Hey! We're pretty good, aren't we?"

All eyes turned to the colorfully clad Bonaire, the piece of wood held over his shoulder as if it were a club.

"Hey, Sol, what did you find?" he continued as he strolled toward the knight.

The knight's frown didn't deter the elf at all, and his grin of relieved fear annoyed the solemn thoughts that floated through Solothon's mind.

"Here these have had to die a second time and this one feels nothing?"

The knight turned away from the elf as if he were not there and opened the pouch. All that he found was a large key of bronze. He brought it out and turned quickly on the elf.

"This is what I've found. Is this what you wish, a treasure? Was this trinket worth the battle?"

"That depends on how much we can get for it," came the offhanded response.

Everyone looked at the bronze key, which was maybe worth a copper to the owner of the door it fit, and then back at Bonaire.

"This?" shouted Solothon. "This wouldn't bring the price to return with it, you fool!"

"Oh, I don't know," said the elf as he watched the knight shake the key toward him. "Platinum is worth more now than it was yesterday."

"Platinum?" The knight was angered. "What you see here, though I don't know why I bother, is—"

Then Solothon stopped and looked at the key in his hand. It seemed to ripple as if underwater. Then it blurred.

When his eyes cleared, the knight beheld rich platinum, and from its weight it was solid!

"How—" began the knight.

"It was an illusion," said Rene' as she walked near. "I glanced at it with my Sight, but magic is not the same as illusion. The mask was good, better than I could detect. Bonaire saw through it right away, though, if the truth were told, he would have to admit luck and the gods had a bit to do with it?"

Bonaire looked at his feet and answered, "Well, yeah, maybe." Then his head jerked up. "What do you think it's worth?"

"That depends on what door it opens," responded Savon'el. "Until we are safe, its function is more important than its makeup." Then he turned to the knight. "You found it. Keep it until we need it or we are safe. If we return to Catlorian, we will place it with anything else we find as treasure and divide it accordingly. Agreed?"

"Agreed," said the knight and he dropped the key into his pouch. "What of the curse?"

"What of it? We have been cursed from the beginning. We must guard against letting our situation deteriorate, otherwise we will not live long enough for the curses to bother us." Savon'el answered. "Now, we need to see to our mounts. One of these rooms should do."

His head dropped for a moment. Then he raised his head and looked at each of his companions.

"There is no reason to believe that anywhere is safe within this evil place, and I regret our bringing these with us."

"Would they have been safer outside?" responded the knight. Without waiting for answer, he continued, "I think not. They are here with us now and we must see to their immediate safety if we are to continue."

"We should check each room until we find one that is safe," said the Huntsmaster as he took his roan's reins.

He moved back to the door he'd investigated before they'd been attacked. His hand went to the handle, but a strong, small hand gripped his wrist before he could turn it.

"It is not wise to take anything here for granted," said Melisande as she lifted the Huntsmaster's hand away. "This place is well-guarded. Who's to say that each and every door here is not trapped?"

"I'm sorry, m'lady," replied Arantar as he backed away, "you are correct. This is not the time for recklessness." He glanced at the knight and Savon'el and continued, "After Melisande checks the door for safety, we should enter ready to fight."

Savon'el joined the Huntsmaster at the door and watched as Melisande brought her power to bear.

"Solothon, you will enter first," said Savon'el without turning, "while Arantar and I enter behind you and flank to left and right. Bonaire will stay outside and help protect our clerics while Eton watches our backs."

"Why do I always have to stay with the women?" asked Bonaire. "I'm as good as anyone else in a fight! I will—"

Melisande turned from the door, her eyes still glowing with the power of her calling. When Bonaire saw the glow coupled with the look of disgust on her face, his mouth snapped shut.

"Bonaire," she said softly as she stalked toward him, "I've had about enough of your whining. If you used your brain instead of your mouth, you would realize that doing it the way proposed would allow for total defense. If we are attacked from outside of the room, those within can come to our rescue and vice versa. By putting fighters on both sides of the door, we allow for time for that to happen."

"It is tactical purity," came the whisper from behind the young elf.

He turned into the quiet gaze of the big warrior and listened as Eton continued.

"We are in this together, are we not?" At the elf's short nod, he added, "Then it is settled. We will each do our part for the whole."

The big warrior took Bonaire's arm and gently led him back toward the horses.

"Now, help me see what we can do for our defense on this side of the doorway."

Melisande turned back to Savon'el with a frown.

"The door is not trapped, but I wish you'd let that little—"

"Enter first? Is he that much of a bother?" asked the blond. "Yes, I agree that he is annoying most of the time, but I can see no good coming from sending him into possible harm alone. Besides, we have to look after each other." He placed a finger under her chin and tilted her eyes up to meet his. "True?"

Melisande's eyes softened a bit and a small smile played at her lips. Savon'el returned the smile and turned back to the problem at hand.

"Rene'," said the blond over his shoulder, "once we get inside and see to the immediate danger, we will need your talents to see if there is magic present. Can you do this from the doorway?"

"Yes, I can, Savon'el," she answered.

She stayed back from the door out of the way. She knew there was not much she could do until they got inside and was content to wait.

"Solothon?" said the blond as he and Arantar stepped away from the door.

The knight drew his sword—the one with the leaves embossed on the hilt this time—and grasped the handle.

Though it was unlocked, as the knight found when he turned the handle, the mechanism was old and it creaked. He looked at Arantar, nodded, and pushed the door open. He took his torch in his left hand and stepped inside. Savon'el slipped into the room and took up his position to the left while Arantar entered to the right and drew the great blade as he came.

The room was empty, save for the half inch of dust on the floor and the musty air. The flickering torchlight showed a room thirty feet by thirty feet with no windows or doors save the one behind them.

"Rene'?"

The golden-haired mage girl stepped forward to the doorway in response to Savon'el's call and gazed inside. Her golden eyes sparkled with the power of the Sight.

"It is dead, Savon'el," she responded. "There is no residual power here. There is nothing."

"Good," he said. "Let's get everyone in here with the horses."

He stepped out of the way to allow the mounts to be led in one at a time. Once all had entered, he closed the door and indicated to Eton that he should stay by the door on watch. The big warrior nodded and stayed close to the door as Savon'el moved back to the center of the room.

"We won't be able to leave anyone with them, so we must see to our horses as best we can now. Loosen the belly straps, grain them, and put what you may need into your bags. We move as soon as we are finished."

Then he moved to his own mount and began the task of making his horse comfortable.

Rene' stood beside her palomino with her face buried in its mane. When Solothon came to assist her, he heard the quiet sobs. He touched her shoulder and she turned. Her eyes were filled with tears and the question she couldn't ask.

"I am sorry, Lady Rene'," he said softly. "It is better to leave them here with the hope that we will return. If we do not..."

Her head dropped to rest on his chest and he held her for a moment while she wept.

"Have faith, m'lady," said the stern knight. "My companion and that of Arantar's will be here to protect them all, and do not forget the stalwart Shadow. He too will remain. All will be well."

"You are correct, my friend," she said finally. She wiped her eyes on her sleeves and gave the knight a small grin. "They will be fine until we return, and if I don't get myself together, I won't be much help to see that that happens."

She reached out a small hand and lightly touched the knight's cheek. "Thank you," she said.

Eton stroked the bluish-black neck of the great horse, then turned to follow the rest into the hallway. Melisande stopped at the door and turned.

"What of light for them?" she asked as the big warrior came to her. "If we leave a torch, chances are it will go out before we return. I do not wish them left in darkness if they are attacked while we are away."

"What is to be done?" he asked in his whisper.

The girl thought for a moment. Then her face brightened.

"Watch!" she said softly with a grin.

She returned to the middle of the room and looked up into one of the corners where the walls met the ceiling. She concentrated on the words she would speak for a moment and closed her eyes. Power flickered at the fingertips of her right hand, manifesting as small flashes of light.

Eton could not hear the mumble of words coming from her smiling and strangely inviting lips.

She drew her fingertips together and, as the sparks of light seemed to join there, kissed them. The light began to pulsate and grow. Melisande smiled and flicked her hand toward the juncture of the walls and ceiling.

Eton watched the now-glowing ball sail slowly toward that intended target. The small ball of light struck and stayed, glowing brighter and brighter until the room was bathed in soft yellow light.

"How did you—" began the warrior as the cleric returned to the door. She smiled sweetly at him and he stopped.

"It is a talent we learn at an early age," she said as she glanced back at the animals. "The light will last as long as I'm alive. At least they will have light while we are gone."

"Melisande," called Savon'el as she and Eton entered the hallway. "We've checked the room for other entrances and found none. Is there a way to secure the door?"

"Not without the use of a key."

"Allow me," said the knight as he stepped past the warrior to the door.

He looked at the keyhole for a moment. Then he retrieved a small leather packet from his pouch. As he unfolded the packet, Melisande recognized the small tools displayed. She had a similar set in her kit.

The knight selected one of the tools, and as he slipped the curved blade of the tempered lock pick into the keyhole he closed his eyes. A second of gentle twists and soft jiggles of the special tool bought a click from the mechanism and a small grin from Solothon.

"I'd thought I'd lost the knack, but—"

"Where did you learn that?" asked Savon'el.

"From others of my order," he replied.

"You have thieves in your order?" asked Bonaire in a gasp.

Instead of the flare-up of anger the others expected, Solothon smiled his stern smile, though, it seemed to Savon'el, it was sharper than required.

"No, the lesson was given with the concept that should an honorable knight find himself in the position to save a damsel, right a wrong, or whatever, yet find a stout door locked before him, the choice is to pound the door to dust or simply manipulate the lock. As the former causes much noise and, frankly, tends to harm the knight as badly as it does the door, the latter is recommended."

"And it is a good thing that you have that talent," said Arantar. "From what I've seen of the key holes in these doors, and the size of the only key we have, your talent may very well save us time and noise." Then, as he turned to the blond half elf, "Should we check each room, and if so, what are we looking for?"

Savon'el looked down the hallway as far as the torchlight Arantar carried would let him before he answered.

"Both questions," he said as his eyes returned to his companions and specifically Rene', "deserve an answer."

Chapter Thirty-seven

The mage girl took a deep breath.

"I don't know if the library or objects would be left in such a haphazard manner, but nothing is certain. It is possible that one of these doors leads to a hidden chamber or a stairway up or down. I believe that if Banshe'e is alive, he or one of his agents will want to look here for an edge. The items we are looking for are part of that, but the information, if we find any, and specifically information on Radagast, may explain everything and help in the coming conflict.

"According to the Myrlin, it is possible that Banshe'e killed Radagast for power as he did Rairy. His talon was in conflict, and Banshe'e wanted Radagast's armory and artifacts. It is entirely possible that Radagast knew of the threat or had turned on Banshe'e, and the wards in this keep were intended for him."

"Oh, great!" said Bonaire with a flutter of arms, his eyes cast skyward. "We get chased out of Catlorian by...whatever. Then, just to be on the safe side, we decide to visit the home of a not-necessarily-dead bad guy who was probably killed by the same guy who's trying to kill us!"

"Shut up, Bonaire," said the Huntsmaster sternly. Then, to Rene, "If these are the agents of this Banshe'e or they were left by Radagast to keep Banshe'e out, how many more can there be?"

"That's hard to say, Huntsmaster, but remember Radagast was the necromancer, not Banshe'e. Banshe'e uses men of power as he did Rairy and possibly Pantor. The agents sent against us in Catlorian were from Arendel, a necromancer priest of Yavi, the spider god, and probably a top lieutenant in Banshe'e's camp. If they were here, we would not have made it through the front door. However, the artifacts may not only help the Myrlin, but us here."

"How so?" asked Savon'el.

"Of the artifacts I was sent to retrieve, the most important to the Myrlin is the *Book of Summoning*. According to my studies, it was used to summon demons from the Well of Darkness. Though I haven't been able to find its location anywhere in my readings, the Myrlin believes it to be here," she replied. "However, the second is a very large crystal. Again, according to my research, large crystals are generally used as a power source. They can be used to amplify magic, either offensive or defensive. If my hypothesis is correct, the crystal I was sent here to collect is being used right now to power this entire keep. If so, once we remove it, the evil that was cast upon this place will cease."

"So, if we can find and remove this crystal, all of these dead things—skeletons, death knights, all of these—will lose their power? Are you certain of this?"

"No, I'm not," Rene' responded softly, "but the logic fits. I believe that we will find that crystal somewhere close to the center of this place. That's where I would put it. If I'm right, it is imperative that we remove that crystal as well as the book from this place and get them into the hands of those who can keep them safe."

"And if you're wrong?" Savon'el asked, his eyes turning molten.

"If I'm wrong, then this whole adventure has been a waste and I have risked your lives for nothing. But if I'm right, we will have removed at least two powerful items from Banshe'e's reach and, with the possible information we might find on Radagast, a powerful armory of weapons as well."

Savon'el's eyes cooled. He rubbed his temples and sighed. "We have trusted you this far, m'lady. I see no reason to distrust you now."

He turned his attention to the rest of his companions.

"Throughout this entire ordeal we have been beset with beings of necromancy and evil. Now, though we have an idea as to what to expect, we cannot be reckless or foolhardy. Each step we take must be done with care. Any written word must be seen by Rene' or Melisande before discarding. Any object or talisman that you run across must be researched by them before it is placed into your belongings or into our service." His eyes found Bonaire. "This is no time for greed to take the upper hand."

Then his amber eyes locked on the mage girl.

"I leave it to you to decipher each and to tell us when enough is enough. There is danger and death here. I can almost taste it."

The girl nodded solemnly and Arantar turned down the hall. All that needed to be said had been said. The search had begun.

The hallway completely encompassed the large doorless center section. It turned left and was littered with the broken bones of the skeletons that had attacked them earlier.

In the outside wall of that hallway were four doors, one of which was placed close to their corner. Arantar headed for that one, his eyes raking the hallway for the telltale sign of undead attackers.

It took but moments after Melisande had scanned the door for the knight to render it unlocked. He stood, returned his lock picks to his pouch, and drew his sword. He glanced at Savon'el on his left, at Arantar on his right, and then turned the handle.

As the door creaked open, the sickening smell of rotting decayed flesh rushed from the long closed room and forced the knight to take several staggering steps back. Try as he might, he couldn't keep the bile from rising to his throat. He turned away and vomited in great gasps.

Though Arantar's stomach churned as well, he was able to control it and stepped away from the door. He threw his arm up to his nose and glanced at the rest of his companions.

Savon'el wasn't so lucky. He spun away from the door and stomped down the hallway, drinking in great gasps of air, but the stench was in every corner of the hall. Finally his stomach won out and his body convulsed as the powerful nausea threw the contents of his stomach to the floor.

Eton had smelled this before in his travels, though it had not been quite so strong. He drew both blades and waited as he watched the door over Bonaire's retching figure.

"Beautiful Lady!" exclaimed Rene' as she pulled a small scented handkerchief from her bosom and held it to her nose. She would have said more if it weren't for the four nightmare figures stalking stiff-legged toward the door before her. Melisande saw them at the same time, her nose wrinkled from the smell but her stomach under control.

Once they were human. Now they were dead things stumbling about in the darkness of limbo seeking the warmth of living people. Melisande knew also that the touch of a zombie was death. Her eyes narrowed in anger as she brought the power of her calling about her as a cloak.

Rene' snapped a dainty hand toward them as she spoke the words softly. From her fingertips, a shaft of blinding light speared the first evil-smelling body to exit the door. Though the mage-powered spell curled the dead skin at the zombie's chest, it did no more than enrage the pitiful creature. She was ready to cast again, but stopped as the black hatred from the black-haired cleric enveloped her with the feeling of empathic loathing.

Melisande stepped toward the creatures then, her hair and cloak billowing in her power. The dull red eyes of the falcon embroidered on her cloak glowed as the words leaped from the girl's lips.

"DENIZENS FROM THE PLANE OF EVIL, BE GONE! BY THE POWER OF THE LADY FREYA AND TWIN SISTER TO THE GOD OF WRATH, FREY, I COMMAND YOU! TURN AND FLEE, OR BE FOREVER DAMNED!"

Her eyes glowed as the power of that goddess flowed through her body. The zombies stopped and, as the girl approached them, backed into the room.

She continued her pursuit until the ghastly beings were backed into a corner. Then, with a curt nod, she turned back toward the door. She saw the small chest in the light of the torch Arantar held as he'd followed her into the room. She pointed to the chest and turned her eyes back to the zombies as they stood quietly in the corner.

Arantar scooped the chest up quickly and led the girl out of the room. As they cleared the portal, Arantar slammed the door and held it.

"Solothon, quick," he yelled. "lock this thing before they change their collective little minds!"

The knight wiped his pale face on his cloak and removed his lock-picking tools from his pouch. He relocked the door with shaking hands and then leaned against it, his eyes closed and his chest heaving.

The smell still permeated the hallway, but it was getting easier to breathe. Savon'el had finally ceased retching and had straightened up, one hand on either hip, to regain his composure. Arantar's hand on his shoulder did little to help.

"Gods, Arantar, I'm sorry! I couldn't get past the smell! I just wasn't ready for that...that..."

"How does one get used to that, my friend?" asked the Huntsmaster with a grin. "Trust me when I say that I wished to be here next to you, but I have seen this before. You never get used to it; you just build a capacity for tolerance that is all."

"I hope you're right, friend, for I've a feeling that this is not the last we will see of such things." Then, as he stretched back and turned, "Come. Let's join the others."

Rene' placed Bonaire's hand on the damp cloth she'd laid on his pale forehead and crossed to the small chest Arantar had abandoned next to the door. With her Sight, she saw the pulsing glow of magic surrounding the small oaken chest. Without touching it, she examined the catch.

"Well, m'lady, is it safe to open?" asked Arantar softly.

"I don't know," she replied.

Something called to her, something from down the hall, from somewhere...She shook her head and continued her examination of the chest.

"I may be mistaken, but it doesn't seem to be locked." Then, as the Huntsmaster reached down for the catch, she exclaimed, "No! Don't use your hand! It's been in there with...*them*!"

Arantar glanced at the black-haired cleric and, after witnessing the angry frown on her face while she watched the door, decided not to ask her to scan the chest for traps. He also noted the distracted way Rene' seemed to glance down the hallway.

"Do you think it safe, Rene'?" he asked softly.

"If you mean do I think it's trapped, possibly, but I doubt it," she replied as she glanced once again down that hallway into the darkness. "Just use something besides your living flesh to open it."

"Right," he said and drew the long dagger from his leg sheath. "Stand back. Trapped or not, it is better to be relatively safe."

The mage girl stood and stepped away, her eyes never leaving the chest except for glances down the corridor. Gauntleted hands gripped her shoulders gently, and she allowed the knight to hold her while she watched.

The Huntsmaster placed the sharp tip of the blade under the lid and, as he stretched himself as far back as he could, flipped the lid open. Save for a light creak in its hinges, the chest held no danger. Arantar let out the air he'd stored in his lungs in one long sigh.

"Savon'el," he called gently, "would you bring a torch closer. There seems to be something here..."

The torchlight glinted off of the two large silver bracelets sitting on their beds of red velvet. Arantar picked up one and gingerly brought it into the light. It seemed to be of the purest silver he'd ever seen, its surface unmarked by rune, design, or time.

"Whoever wore these had a very large wrist," he said softly. Then, as he demonstrated by pushing the bracelet with his sleeve up his bared left arm, "See how this one slides over my hand and elbow as if designed to be held by the muscles of my arm? They may not be bracelets at all!"

He left the one ring of silver on his left arm and reached for the other.

Strangely, however, it moved away until it wedged against the side of the chest. Even then, try as he might, the Huntsmaster could not seem to touch the other armband.

"I guess it doesn't like me," he quipped with a chuckle and raised his right hand to remove the band on his left arm.

It wouldn't move! It had reduced in size until it had become the same shape and size of the Huntsmaster's arm. Then, as he watched, the silver band seemed to sink into his skin to become a part of him.

"Rene'?" he asked in a weak voice.

"Don't worry, Arantar. Maybe the other one will work to remove it," she replied as she reached in to pick up the other silver band. As her hand came in contact with the silver ring, it leaped up her arm and conformed itself to her small right bicep. Arantar reached for her as the ring began to sink into her delicate golden skin, but he was thrown back by an invisible barrier.

Savon'el helped the Huntsmaster to his feet and he again tried to remove the silver ring from his arm. Where the ring had sunk in, there was now a band of silver-colored skin. What alarmed both Arantar and Savon'el more was the skin below the band. It had turned black, and while they watched the black began creeping toward his elbow.

"Do I cut it off, Arantar?" shouted the blond half elf, his amber eyes full of fear for his friend. "Tell me!"

"No," came the mage girl's soft voice.

Savon'el glanced up from the Huntsmaster's arm where the blackness crept past his wrist to his hand. Rene' was watching—no, studying—her arm as it turned white below the now-silver band of flesh.

"Arantar," she asked casually, "do you feel pain?"

"No," he answered in an awed voice, "I feel...strength!"

"What have you done?"

"What do you mean, Savon'el?" asked the girl calmly as she watched her fingers become a soft, creamy white.

"Why didn't you leave those things alone?" he replied, the fear plain in his amber eyes. "I thought you intelligent, yet you insist on...*this*!"

"We are attempting to find whether the power within these will be useful in our cause," replied the girl.

"By submitting yourselves to that power? We could have just as easily studied them at a later time—"

"What later time?" interposed Melisande. "Yes, I agree that it would be wonderful if we had the leisure to study all that we find as we did at Rairy's cottage, but that just is not the case here. Somehow, I believe that if we are to put our lives back into our own hands, some choices...some damned extreme choices will have to be made."

"Savon'el," said the mage girl as she stepped toward the seething blond, "what she says is true. If we are to progress from here, we must be willing to take chances, be bold. Otherwise..."

Suddenly her face brightened. She looked at the Huntsmaster as she placed a small hand on the blond half elf's chest.

"I know what they are!" she exclaimed.

"What?" asked Savon'el, taken aback by her excitement.

"These bands! I know what they are and what they were made for!" Then her brow wrinkled as she seemed to look off into space. "But I don't know for whom." The bright smile returned. "Anyway, these were told of in story long ago when I was but a child. My ranger told it to me as we sat beneath the boughs of an old—"

"Get to the point, Rene'," said the blond, who was still seething at the chance his friends were taking. "If it has something to do with how to rid you of those bands, let us know!"

"I don't think—" came the Huntsmaster's voice.

Savon'el turned his molten eyes on him, but as the look of peace and relief crossed the Huntsmaster's face, the blond frowned in confusion. Arantar looked up from his now-ebony arm and his smile was genuine.

"It's over," he said softly. "I can feel that the curse is over. Whatever this is that has found a home on my arm, it has negated the threat I've been under since Catlorian." Then he turned his eyes on the mage girl. "Why?"

"Because we have found the fabled *Bands of Balance*, Ebony Force and Alabaster Peace. I think Cashme're said something about them being linked to the Lords of Light, but I'm not sure. I remember that he said that they were two opposites forged for one purpose: to bring about balance."

"But why did it not allow me to touch you?"

"For that same reason, Arantar. If what I think is correct, they are opposites: Ebony Force for the fighting side of Balance, and Alabaster Peace for the healing side. They work together but separately." Then in a soft, sad tone, "Always separately."

"We must move on," she said with a sigh.

"I agree," responded the blond half elf, "but to where? If there are more of these things in each room, how are we to combat them? Are you and Lady Melisande strong enough to hold them back while we search the room for that which we seek?"

"They may be, Savon'el," replied the Huntsmaster, his voice low and quiet, "but I don't believe that will be necessary. Do you, Rene'?"

The mage girl looked quickly at Arantar, the question on her face, as the Huntsmaster continued.

"You have been preoccupied with the door at the end of this hall for a bit now. What is it that draws you?"

"But how did you—"

"I seem to know what you know," he said calmly. "No, not what you know exactly, but a sense of...I don't know. I just seem to be attached to you somehow, possibly because of these bands. I just...feel somewhat of what you are feeling."

"It must be that attachment," she said softly. "It will be interesting to see how this plays out." At Savon'el's scowl, she grinned. "Yes, I've felt it ever since we entered this hallway. Some yearning...a drawing of sorts that tells me to enter there, for it is there where our answers may be found."

"Then we are wasting time," stated the knight as he turned to stride down the hall. "It is close to sunrise and we should be moving."

Arantar felt it as well, the subtle change in his sense of time. It was indeed close to sunrise. Any second now the sun would lift up beyond the horizon in the east, bringing warmth to the earth.

"I'll take the lead to the door, Solothon," Arantar said as he rose and moved in that direction.

"Why the far door?" asked Savon'el as he grabbed the Huntsmaster's cloak.

"Rene' has been preoccupied with it, and if she's right I believe it to be the right choice."

Savon'el frowned down the hallway, indecision on his face. Then he turned to the mage girl.

"Rene'…"

Outside the sun rose to strike the white building on its eastern wall. At that exact instant, the girl's now-white arm began to glow. The companions heard three distinct peals of a small bell, its tone rich and silvery. Then the glow dissipated.

"My, that was refreshing!" said the mage girl with a small grin. "I feel as if I've just wakened from a soft bed in a warm hou—"

She saw the startled looks on the faces before her and the open-mouthed surprise on that of the blond half elf.

"It seems," she said, the grin still in place, "at sunrise my new attachment renews me, both physically and spiritually. The side-effect of the glow bothers me a bit, but…" She shrugged.

Arantar grinned, shrugged, and moved down the hallway, the others falling in behind. His right hand drew his sword from its sheath on his back and he brought the new ebony hand toward it.

He stopped in his tracks, his look of astonishment causing the knight to stop and turn to him. The ebony hand wouldn't grip the hilt! Try as he might, he couldn't get the hand to hold that blade.

"What in the—"

"I think I understand now, Arantar," the mage girl interrupted. "I remember that Cashme're said something about not being able to hold a weapon if danger was not imminent."

She reached her white hand to the small dagger at her waist and watched as it moved away.

"What good is this thing," said the startled Huntsmaster, "if I cannot use the weapons I'm used to? Do I need now to learn to use a standard sword?"

"I don't know, my friend," she replied, "but I don't think that the creator of these would leave us defenseless."

"We shall see," said Arantar angrily as he gripped the great sword in his right hand and moved down the hallway.

The door at the end of the hall was different from the ones they passed to get there. It seemed newer somehow.

Solothon felt the wood, then placed his ear to it. He heard soft eerie moaning through the thick door, like wind playing through a haunted woodland.

"What is it?" whispered Savon'el from beside him.

"I don't know," he replied, "but…"

The knight attempted to turn the locked handle and the moaning ceased. He stepped away from the door.

"Something is in there."

Rene' swept past him to the door and laid her tiny hands to the wood. "This is where we must go."

Gauntleted hands closed gently on her shoulders as the knight drew her away from the door.

"Then this is where we shall go," he said as he brought the wrap of lock picks from his pouch.

The tool in the hands of the talented knight did its work and he returned it to his pouch. He drew his sword and placed his left hand on the handle.

"I will enter, as before, with you two"—nodding to Savon'el and Arantar—"on my flank. Once within..."

The handle turned suddenly in his hand and, as the door opened a bit, a clawed, mottled green hand reached out of the room to grasp the knight's mailed arm in a steel grip. He was yanked into and through the door to land, stunned, on the floor several feet within the room. Clawed hands raked at his chain mail as he lay unable to regain his wits.

There was no hesitation in the Huntsmaster's leap through the door. When the knight was yanked through the doorway, Arantar's body exploded into the room. The darkness was expelled as a ball of light screamed into existence on the ceiling. He didn't question; he acted. His right hand gripped the hilt of Grey Wolf close to the crosspiece as he quickly surveyed the room and advanced.

There were eight of them, these dead things, all humanoid in form, but devoid of human thought. Their long claws raked at the knight's armor in a desperate effort to reach the ghastly feast waiting just below his skin. They ate the warm entrails of living men as the victim screamed in terror and pain.

So far the knight's armor had protected him from all but seemingly harmless scratches.

Eton slipped through the door at a crouch and quickly scanned the fight. Two of the ghoulish beasts had turned on the advancing Arantar while the other six clawed at the prone Solothon. One of the six had its back to the big warrior. Eton smiled and attacked.

Melisande had seen enough. She drew her power around her and her eyes flashed.

"TURN AND FLEE, EVIL ONES. YOUR DOOM AT THE HANDS OF THE LADY FREYA AWAITS YOU HERE!"

Four of the beasts stumbled back from the beaten knight in wild panic. They drew up at the wall and tried vainly to claw through. The other two continued their attacks on the knight, and the two approaching Arantar had more than enough to contain their attention.

The great gray blade in the Huntsmaster's right hand screamed through the musty air, striking the beast at the shoulder at a downward angle slicing the ghoul to its waist. It convulsed in death as its green gore poured out of the great gash through its body. The other beast arrived in time to receive the ebony left hand, balled into a fist, in its chest. Bones snapped like twigs as the fist drove hard into that body. The ghoul was lifted into flight by that power and thrown into the far wall. It crumpled to the floor and, as green oozed from its jaws, gave up its death rattle. Its chest had been destroyed and its back broken.

Eton drove both blades in and up into the back of one of the beasts that clawed at the knight. When the blades stopped at the hilts, the warrior lifted the screaming ghoul and flung it away, ripping the blades out in a cascade of green blood. The warrior snarled at the other ghoul as it lifted its attention from the knight and turned on him.

The greenish brown blade in the hands of the blond half elf made no sound as it sliced through that luckless beast. Eton watched as Savon'el spun the blade and drove it through, turned on his toes, and sliced the blade out of the ghoul's body.

As Savon'el pivoted, however, one of the beast's claws raked his boots. It penetrated the soft leather at his ankle and drew a bloody gash in his skin. Ice raced up his leg as the poison rendered it useless.

Solothon had managed to get to his feet and glanced about in anger for a target. His left arm was paralyzed to the shoulder, but the shining silver sword was in his right. He moved to the four beasts cringing against the wall. He stepped before the first and brought his sword up to strike.

Unfortunately the power incumbent in a cleric to cause evil to flee depends on the evil ones seeing her. Solothon broke those fetters and the beast attacked. It leaped on the knight and wrapped its arms about him. Fanged jaws snapped at Solothon's throat as he tried to remove it.

He had no choice. He couldn't strike the beast with the sword, and his left arm was useless. He dropped the blade to the ground and gripped the beast at the throat and squeezed, but it was strong. Too strong.

A black fist struck that beast on the side of its head. It cracked like an egg, the dislocated jaw dangling at a strange angle. It was dead, but its death grip held it snug to the knight's body. The ebony hand gripped the beast at the back of the neck, ripped it from Solothon's body, and tossed it across the room.

The Huntsmaster was in full battle mode now. The black hand gripped the hilt of the great gray blade and lifted it with weightless ease. Arantar moved toward the three cringing ghouls, his mind only for their destruction.

Solothon stumbled, relieved of his extra burden, and passed before the next cringing ghoul. When it snarled and leaped, the knight realized that he was disarmed, his sword on the floor six feet away. He stretched his hand toward the silver blade, his need driving his will. He needed that sword and he needed it *now*!

Strangely, the sword stood up on its point, spun twice, and leaped toward his open hand. As it settled there, the knight turned toward the ghoulish threat.

He need not have bothered, however, for Eton, having seen that the knight was weaponless, had interposed himself between the knight and the threat, both blades out and his eyes screaming hate.

"Down, Arantar!"

The Huntsmaster dropped to the floor and rolled as the blast of white streaked from the mage girl's fingertips to strike one of the two still cringing ghouls in the chest. Smoke curled from the beast's body as the magiks ripped a hole and spilled the creature's heart onto the ground.

Bonaire listened to the words that rippled from Rene's lips, and as she turned her power on the last of the beasts, the young elf joined her chant.

Two shafts of pure white power ripped into that creature's chest, and Arantar rose and moved purposefully toward the wounded beast. Its skin had been ripped apart and it was in screaming pain. The Huntsmaster waited, an angry grin on his face, until the scream was done.

Then, as the black orbs opened, the Huntsmaster raised Grey Wolf and brought it down on the ghoul's head. Such was the power inherent in the ebony arm that the blade sliced through the top of the creature's head and didn't stop until it exited at its crotch. Green gore poured from it as it fell in two separate directions.

Arantar spun the sword, sending showers of the nasty gore in all directions, and looked for survivors.

The long sword, in Eton's hand, caught the ghoul in mid-leap and pinned it to the wall. The creature's right claw swung toward the warrior's head, but it was met by the gauntleted arm. It swung its left claw and the warrior smashed its wrist with the basket hilt, crushing it and ripping a scream from its nasty maw. The Bourjon Blade sliced through the green flesh at its throat and stopped the scream forever.

The warrior backed away, jerked the sword from its body, and watched as it crumpled to the floor. He spun both blades to rid them of green gore and sheathed them.

When the last of the ghouls died, the ebony hand on the hilt of Arantar's sword suddenly snapped away. Arantar looked at it and then remembered that during the fight, he'd used that hand. He realized then that if danger were present, Ebony Force would use whatever weapons were available in his defense. Once safety is assured, the hand would reject all weapons until the next danger appeared. He grinned, sheathed the sword, and stepped over to help Solothon.

Melisande grabbed Bonaire's cloak and moved into the room toward the limping Savon'el.

Rene' stood in the doorway and felt the draw. She looked about the room until her eyes fell on the dust-laden, four-sided pyramid in the far corner of the room. It was approximately five feet tall with an approximate four-foot base. It was constructed of green crystal, she saw as the dust seemed to slip ever so slightly from the sides. She opened her Sight and found the pulsing power buried deep within the structure. She stepped toward it and felt the subtle pull on her empathic senses. As she neared, a low hum began and more clots of dust rolled from its smooth sides. She took another step.

Melisande dabbed at the scratch on the blond half elf's ankle with some clean bandaging. It didn't seem to be deep, or at least not deep enough to cause the paralysis apparent in the savon'el's leg.

"It is asleep, m'lady," he said softly. "It doesn't seem to want to obey me."

Melisande frowned at the savon'el's half smile and the flippancy of his statement. She shook her head and thought. Undead things generally respond negatively to god-blessed action. She retrieved a small vial of her holy water from her pouch and, saying, "This might sting." began pouring it over the scratch.

As the blest water touched the wound, it began to boil and foam. Burning pain shot up the blond's leg and brought a moan from his tightly pressed lips.

The pain receded, but now the leg began to tingle as the nerves came back to life. Soon he was able to move the leg, though painfully, and he stood up to walk the numbness away.

She joined him and suddenly put both hands behind his head and drew him into a deep, lingering kiss.

When he finally broke free of this unasked for, though pleasing, embrace, he felt the power race through his body. The black-haired cleric grinned impishly as the power of her calling, though delivered in a very unorthodox manner, did its work.

"Thank you," he said softly. As her grin became a smile, he continued, "Now, I believe that Sir Solothon could use some of your...time."

She looked down coyly and moved to Solothon.

Arantar had stripped the mail sleeve from the knight's left shoulder and examined the small scratch at the juncture of the mail sleeve and the shoulder flap. It was small, too small to account for the paralysis of that limb.

Melisande joined him and, with another small vial of holy water, washed the scratch as she had Savon'el's. Soon the tingling of feeling began, but as the knight flexed the arm, Melisande saw it.

"M'lady!" she exclaimed as her finger touched the second red dot that had appeared within the next point of the pentagram birthmark. She had no idea what this meant to the knight, but from past experience she was certain that it did not bode well.

"Solothon," she asked, "when did this come to be?"

The knight lifted the tingling arm and looked as Arantar looked on.

"I felt a pinprick earlier. What does it mean, m'lady?"

"I don't know," she replied. "Rene' had better see this."

Arantar felt it then, the calling, the danger, a need. His gray sword slipped into both hands as the room blurred.

Rene' approached within three feet of the pyramid and marveled at the gyrations it presented. It was now vibrating enough that she felt it in her feet. The dust was gone from the green crystal and she could just see the cylindrical darkness within the pyramid. She moved her foot to step even closer and the room blurred.

When her vision cleared, she stood next to Melisande, and she looked into the shocked eyes of the Elvin knight.

Arantar found himself in a fighting crouch less than three feet from the now-calm, green crystal pyramid, his sword in both hands. He turned toward where he should have been and, as the sword snapped away from the ebony hand, found the golden mage girl staring back at him.

"Arantar," she said softly, "come away from there."

He turned back to the pyramid and brought the black hand to the hilt of that sword. It gripped it easily and tightened as if there were danger about. When he turned to walk back to his friends, the sword began to vibrate in that hand. When he released it, the sword recoiled away. He returned the sword to its sheath one-handed and continued toward his companions.

"What was that all about?" asked the knight as he flexed the still-tingling arm.

"Good question," replied Arantar, his eyes on the mage girl. "What happened, and what is so dangerous in that cylinder as to allow my hand to take up the sword?"

"It must be the bands," she replied. "If I am in physical danger, they must know it. I know Arantar's talents as he knows mine. The bands seem to play to those talents and switch us as the need arises. That can be dangerous and annoying if we can't find some way to control it."

"Maybe if you'd just stop placing yourself in danger," stated Savon'el sternly.

"Yes, I know," she said, her head bowed just a bit. "It's just that there is something in there and it calls to me. That pyramid contains—"

"Leave the damned thing alone!"

All eyes turned to be confronted with the molten amber in the half elf's eyes.

"Why do you insist on meddling with everything we come across? We are still recovering from the last onslaught! Arantar says that the object within that...thing is dangerous. I believe him! Just leave it alone for now, please!"

"We can't," Melisande responded softly. "If that cylinder inside can help our cause, we must chance it. Rene' says that it may hold some of the answers that we need. I believe *her* and I don't believe she would put us in danger if it weren't necessary. Do you?"

As his eyes cooled, she saw it: the guilt he still felt for bringing them into this kind of danger. Whether by their choice or not, it still weighed heavy on his soul.

"Listen to me," she continued. "We must take every opportunity as it presents itself, and that includes this one." Then, with a quick look at Rene', "We also should learn to wait a bit for advise before blundering forward."

Rene' grinned and hung her head. Then the black-haired cleric turned back to Savon'el. "We are not being rash. We have no choice any more but to plod forward, in darkness if need be. We are not blind to the risks, but what are our alternatives?"

"She's right, you know," commented the Huntsmaster. "I realize that you feel a responsibility, but it just isn't true.

"If all were honest, I believe you'd find that we have all been maneuvered toward this place from the very beginning: Solothon and the attack at his home, the 'coincidental' meeting in Borderlend, Melisande and her needs, Rene' and her orders. Me and my 'savon,' which, by the way, came at a very opportune moment to place me here, don't you think? Bonaire just happened to be in Borderlend? You get the idea."

He turned to Eton.

"What of you, Eton. What was your reasoning to join this group? Were you just wandering about and just wandered into this?"

"No," he whispered, his arms folded akimbo. "I've followed you for weeks to join you, and my reasons are my own."

"Accepted, but I would warrant that those reasons just happen to coincide with this journey."

"It is possible," Eton replied, his brows lowered in thought, "that I may have been maneuvered here, but that is of no concern. As to whether we proceed, I have no opinion one way or another. Magiks are foreign to me, as Arantar knows. I need only a target, a real target of flesh that can be cut and bleeds, to do what I do best. As to these undead things, they died once and, as we've seen, can die again. As long as that is the way of things, I have no objection."

"Savon'el," said the mage girl, "You have no reason to trust in my judgment, I know. Frankly, we are stumbling about in the dark, but so far we've always managed to land on our feet. Somewhere within these walls, I feel, are the answers to a lot of questions: Who wants us dead? Who wishes us to fail in our quest, whatever it is? Who, especially, wants your head and why?

"I don't believe that the things I've been sent here to collect are laying about waiting to be found. I do believe, however, the more important an item is, the more danger it presents. Keeping that in mind, the thing buried in that green crystal," she said as she pointed a dainty finger at the pyramid without looking, "has been well-protected. I don't know what that protection is, nor what, if anything, will come of it. I only know that it has drawn me to it, for gain or ill, and I cannot walk away without trying. Do you understand?"

"We do not," added the knight, "wish to usurp your position, Savon'el, but—"

"I know that, my friend," the blond replied with a sigh, "and maybe you are all correct. I have no past to draw from, no memories of occult knowledge to impart. My fear, I believe, comes from not knowing," he continued as his eyes met Rene's, "not distrust."

He cast a sad look at his companions.

"I ask your forgiveness, my friends. I have no right to doubt or be angry with you. I just—"

"You just want to protect us, Savon'el," said the black-haired cleric. "We all know that, but we are running out of time. We must be bold now and grasp what we can with both hands. It may destroy us, that may be true, but if we stand still we invite destruction."

"Stay at our lead, my friend," interjected Solothon. "We have need of your solid counsel."

Savon'el looked into their determined faces and knew the truth. If he said no to this dangerous venture, they would follow him out. Melisande, however, had put it all into perspective. What did they have to lose that they wouldn't lose anyway?

"Then, this is my counsel…"

Chapter Thirty-eight

The plan was simple: If Rene' approached the pyramid at some point, the danger, or whatever, would cause her to switch places with Arantar. He could touch, beat, or kick the green crystal all he wished to no avail because he was not a practitioner. The only answer was...

"Bonaire."

"What?" gasped the young elf. "If you think I'm gonna go near that thing, you are nuts!"

"Look, Bonaire," Rene' said sweetly as she laid a dainty hand on his arm, "it only responds to those who are practitioners of magic. I can't go near it—"

"Only because those bands are smarter than you are!" he countered sullenly.

"No. I believe that if one of our calling gets too near, it will break apart. That's all."

"Break apart, or *explode?*"

"Well, to be perfectly honest," she answered carefully, "there is a slight chance of that, but it won't be able to hurt you even if it does happen."

The look of astonishment on Bonaire's face at what he thought to be her obvious loss of reason brought a grin to Rene's lips.

"Look. I was taught a simple spell a long time ago that will shield you from any harm. I'll cast it on you and, as long as you face the danger no matter what happens, you won't be hurt."

"Are you sure?" he asked as he looked at the green crystal pyramid in the corner.

"Absolutely! Would I send you into a possible dangerous situation without total protection? Of course not! You will be just fine," she cajoled as she placed her hand to his cheek. "Of course, if you don't do it"—a gentle sigh and a look of sadness on her face—"I guess we'll just have to do without the possible treasure—"

"Treasure?" he said quickly. Then, in a voice marked with false bravado, "Well, if it needs to be done, I'm just the guy to do it!"

"Good for you, Bonaire!" she said as she gave a quick hug to the startled but pleased elf. Then Rene' turned to the rest of the companions. "We must all wait in the hallway while Bonaire plies his trade."

"What?" the elf said in a shocked voice. "Hey, wait! Why—"

"They, nor I, will have the magical shield I will bestow upon you. Do you wish to cause your companions possible harm?"

"Uh...Of course not!" he replied, the bravado once again tingeing his words. "Go, my friends! Wait in the safety of the corridor while I open this thing!" Then, in a quick aside to Rene', "Uh...After you cast the spell, right?"

The golden mage girl smiled her sweetest smile and, as the others filed out, laid a hand on the young elf's forehead.

The words of power were whispered, but they seemed to fill the room. She lifted her hand away with a flourish and smiled again.

"Go ahead, Bonaire, and do your best. We are counting on you, but remember, always face the pyramid. Don't turn from it no matter what."

"Sure! Sure!" he answered a bit uneasily. "No problem, okay? I'm going now. You'd better join the rest, but be ready to come back in a hurry, okay?"

"I'll be right here with you the whole time, Bonaire. Now don't let me down!" she said as she followed the others through the door.

Solothon had moved through the doorway first and walked down the hallway a distance to watch and guard against any possible attack. Even with his Elvin sight, he could see nothing moving, and he turned back toward the others.

Then he heard the sound. It was of stone grinding against stone farther down the hallway. He glanced back at his friends and then back down the hallway. The stern look returned to his face as he drew the silver sword and walked slowly toward the sound.

Bonaire took a deep breath and, stretching to his full height of five feet, two inches, stepped slowly toward the pyramid. When he arrived at the place where Rene' and Arantar had switched places, the pyramid began to vibrate alarmingly.

"Rene?" he said in a frightened voice as he glanced back at the door.

"It's all right, Bonaire," the girl replied from the doorway. She stood just outside and looked in. "It can't hurt you as long as you face it! Go ahead! You're doing fine!"

"Okay, if you're sure," he said nervously as he brought his eyes back to the madly vibrating green crystal.

He took another small step and the pyramid began bouncing on the marble flooring. Bonaire's courage began to flag at the sight.

"Go on, my friend," the girl called again. "Keep going!"

He took another step.

It exploded and shards of sharp green crystal ripped through the room. Bonaire lifted both arms to cover his face in the sure knowledge that he was dead and wished to look good at his funeral.

Savon'el acted on instinct as he tightened his grip on the small girl's waist and jerked her from the open doorway. Seconds after the shards crashed against the wall and out into the hall, he was through the door, the Elvin war bow in his right hand and a silver-tipped arrow nocked and drawn. What he saw caused him to let down the tension on the bow and allowed a grin to play at the corners of his mouth.

Bonaire stood still as a statue with both arms over his face. Shards of sharp crystal and crystal powder were scattered all around him, but there wasn't a scratch on him. He didn't move until Rene' walked up and placed a small hand on one of his arms.

He parted his arms and, as he spotted the mage girl, asked in a weak voice, "Am I dead?"

"No, Bonaire, you're fine," she responded gently. "I told you that you would be, didn't I? Well, the spell didn't allow any harm to come to you, just as I told you. Right?"

After carefully inspecting himself and reaching the unalterable conclusion that he was indeed still alive, he looked at the mage girl with more strength.

"Of course I'm fine," he said in a shaky voice. "I was just...uh...checking, you know?"

"Sure," said the mage girl a bit distractedly, "I understand."

Then she moved toward the small tube that floated but two feet off of the ground before her.

Arantar followed the mage girl into the room at a distance and stopped some ten feet away. He'd nodded at Savon'el as he passed that doorway and knew that, should the need arise, the silver-tipped arrow nocked in the war bow would scream to their defense.

Eton followed Melisande into the room and stopped next to her a few feet away from the Huntsmaster. He squatted and retrieved a shard of the green crystal with his gauntleted hand and showed it to the cleric. She nodded and turned her attention to the mage girl as that one closely examined the tube.

It was a small black crystal scroll tube, much like the ones Rene' had seen in her Temple's library. This one, however, was capped on both ends, not with a paraffin plug, but Elvin silver.

The mage girl lifted her white hand to the tube without touching it and ran it the length of the tube. A light tingling in her palm told her that there was an incredible amount of power stored here. There were no runes, designs, or markings to deform the smooth black surface. It was so smooth, so inviting. One white finger of her right hand touched the cold black surface.

Blue white fire erupted from that touch. The silver end caps blew off of the tube and roiling black smoke poured out and up from the two ends. The two columns of smoke joined above the tube and, though still roiling with its own power, formed the upper half of what looked to be a large muscular being. He had no facial features save the blood red sparks that served as eyes and the gaping nothingness that served as a mouth.

That mouth moved. Words as old as time rippled out into the room with a power the companions felt rather than heard. No one understood the words save Arantar.

As the words crashed over him, the meaning came clear.

"'Ware the ghouls!" he shouted, his hands filling with steel. "That thing has brought them back again!"

All but Rene' turned toward the corner where they had thrown the lifeless carcasses a few moments before.

The green dead things were moving. Limbs and heads, hacked off during the battle, remolded themselves to the severed stumps. Quickly eight ghouls spread their claws and moved toward the life in the room, aching for the taste of living bowel.

Rene's hesitation at the shock of seeing this thing appear before her almost destroyed them.

She'd retrieved the vial of the precious holy water she'd taken to use in helping Melisande with the knight. It rested now at the top of her medical pouch on her hip and was the first thing her hand closed on as she reached into it in a panic.

She thumbed the stopper from the fragile vial and threw it toward the vile black thing that called up the dead. As the blessed fluid sparkled from the glass, it seemed to suck the blackness to it. The being disappeared in a flash of white sparkles.

Bonaire's fear sparked his powers to full and, though he knew not where he'd learned it, caused the words of the spell to ripple from his lips. He raised his left hand toward the corner from which came the reanimated beasts and tendrils of white silk spun from his extended fingertips. Where the thread struck the beasts, it stuck.

The young elf moved the hand in a pattern he learned long ago at his mother's knee. The tendrils of white formed a web of magical strength. Three of the nasty things fought, to no avail, to break free. The other five had moved faster than their companions and made for the mage girl with death in their eyes.

The floor rumbled, but not enough to throw off the blond's aim. The bow snapped up, the arrow flew, and the silver point sunk deep between the shoulders of one of the beasts and it went down. A fraction of a second later, another was nocked and drawn, the amber eyes seeking a new target.

The floor in the center of the room began to crack as the terrible forces of the being's spell rippled about the room.

The great blade in the ebony hand sliced another of the ghouls into oblivion. Arantar spun the sword to rid it of gore, then he stood in a crouch as the floor buckled into darkness.

Bonaire had run forward and placed himself between the mage girl and the three remaining creatures. The first of these found itself impaled on the green crystal sword. Bonaire felt a slight vibration in his hand as his anger flared. The ghoul died as a sodden pool of green, the power of the sword rendering it boneless.

Rene' was angrier than she'd ever been in her young life. Her friends had been harangued from every side, badgered to distraction, and now after winning free of these vile ugly creatures, something she'd touched had caused them to again come alive. She seethed in clerical indignation and turned her flashing, goddess-filled eyes on the two beasts coming at her. She stretched her hand toward them as Lady Celeste gave vent to her distaste for the ugliness.

"TURN, VILE CREATURES!" came the words of power. "DARE NOT TO SHOW THY UGLY FEATURES IN THE PRESENCE OF THE GODDESS CELESTE! BEAUTIFY THIS PLANE WITH THY ABSENCE!"

The ghouls turned as one and ran from the enraged mage girl toward the door, but the creatures vomiting from the floor had not been touched by the goddess's curse. They made directly for the golden mage girl, caring not what was between them and their goal.

They were large, almost three feet long, and looked to be weasels. They had been dead for quite some time, their bodies mummified in the catacombs beneath the flooring. Their sharp teeth and quick movements were accentuated by the blood-red glow emanating from their empty eye sockets.

They had been called by the Guardian and they responded. They would attack the thief that even now stood before them, the slight glow on her fingertips showing her guilt.

Arantar's indecision caused the great gray sword to falter. The ghouls were going to pass close to him as they fled for the door, but the beasties slithering from the hole in the floor had their eyes glued to Rene's dainty figure.

Finally he brought the sword down at one of the creatures that appeared at the edge of the hole. The sword clanged on stone as that quick beast slipped to one side. Its dull red orbs turned in his direction for but a second. Then it returned its attention to Rene' and it darted toward her.

Eton stepped directly into the path of the two fleeing ghouls, a grin of anticipation stretching the infinity sigils branded to his cheeks. He held the Bourjon blade out to his left side and the long sword to his right. If these creatures passed as close as he wished they would, they would kill themselves on his blades. All he had to do was hold them in his two powerful hands. He gritted his teeth and tightened his grip.

Suddenly the beast passing to his right sprouted a white fletching to its chest. Savon'el's arrow sank deep and rendered the dead thing totally inanimate.

The other, seizing the startled second that Eton lost, ducked under the heavy blade in the gauntleted hand and sped for the door. It never made it.

The big warrior recovered in an instant and, with a flick of his massive arm, sent the long sword sailing into the beast's back, the point protruding in finality from its chest. It fell at Savon'el's feet, twitched once, and lay still.

Savon'el knew that the warrior's expertise was diminished without a blade in each hand. He also knew that there wasn't time for him to try to extract Eton's sword from this creature's back. He only had time to reach the hilt of the sword strapped to his back and, with a twist and jerk, released it from its sheath.

"Eton! Catch!" he yelled as he tossed the greenish brown sword toward the big warrior.

Eton turned and stretched out his hand for his father's sword. The hilt slid easily into the pocket of his right palm and his fingers wrapped themselves around the leather-covered hilt as if coming home.

For another fraction of a second, all of the thoughts and threats he'd leveled against this blond half elf came back to him. He looked into those intent amber eyes as Savon'el's dancing fingers nocked another shaft to the war bow's string and drew the shaft to his ear.

"This one has no family blood on his hands," the man had said.

He knew that it was so. As the thought settled in granite in his mind, he vowed to stand with this one until that day came for explanations. He turned, with both hands filled with steel, on the creatures erupting from the earth.

Melisande stood between the golden mage and the ghastly little creatures, the great maul spinning effortlessly in her strong hands. The steel-banded head suddenly crashed down to squash one of the beasts into a dusty pile of bones, but the other two sped past her intent on Rene'. One outdistanced the other and leaped for the girl's throat.

Rene' started the words to the conjuring as the beastie sailed toward her.

Arantar used the great blade as a scythe, dispatching one or two at a time as they scrambled from the dark pit below. However, for every one of them he killed, another two took its place.

He lifted the blade again, and the room blurred.

For a second he stood where Rene' had stood, then he was back again. Rene' found herself on the other end of a pendulum that swept from danger to danger until, with a stutter in the fabric of magic and the blinding flash of magiks gone awry, both she and Arantar were knocked unconscious and dropped exactly center of the distance between them.

The weasels changed their direction in an instant, turning in midstride to attack the girl lying defenselessly beneath the Huntsmaster.

Savon'el loosed his last arrow at one of the creatures as it scrambled from the hole. Without stopping, he tossed the bow to the ground, yanked the warrior's blade from the ghouls back, and waded through the creatures, slashing with one hand as he approached. He saw Eton on one knee slashing with both hands at the creatures that rose from the pit.

"Arantar and the girl are down!" croaked the warrior as the mottled blade sliced another weasel in half. "We must get to them!"

Savon'el nodded quickly and flipped the long sword toward the warrior.

Eton did likewise, just in time to catch his sword and drop it low to the ground. One of the creatures swallowed it until the tip of the blade protruded from its tail end. The warrior casually lifted the blade and turned it toward the hole. The beast was ripped apart as it left the blade. It struck two more of the creatures and carried them with it as it disappeared over the edge.

Bonaire had his hands full trying to fend off the creatures from his unconscious friends. As soon as he slashed one away from Arantar's back, another would leap through to gnaw at the Huntsmaster's chain mail. The young elf muttered the spell Rene' taught him and burned another of the beasties in mid-leap. He saw the weasel that was trying to get under Arantar to get at the girl and he brought the green crystal sword up for a stroke.

He hesitated when the weasel emerged tugging at the girl's arm with its sharp teeth. If he missed… He opted to crush it beneath the heel of his boot.

Eton missed and one of the creatures scurried between his legs. It found Bonaire between it and its intended target and attacked. Its sharp teeth bit deep into the young elf's unprotected leg, but the young elf slashed at it. He missed, but it was enough to allow the beast to scamper around him toward its true goal. Bonaire tried to stomp on it as it passed, but it was just too fast.

Savon'el, after catching the sword in midstride, strode through the midst of the growling, slobbering beasts, his blade black with their gore. His only hope was to fight his way to the Huntsmaster's side and, hopefully, save his and Rene's life. As his sword flashed again, removing the head of yet another beast, his eyes caught sight of his goal.

There lay the Lady Rene' with Arantar draped across her, both unconscious and both vulnerable. The girl who stood above them, however, was no longer the sweet, innocent Melisande.

The great mall on the five feet of thick, seasoned wood spun in her hands as if its weight were nothing. When the maul stopped, the sound of bones breaking, flesh rending, and howls of pain from some unlucky beast followed.

He recognized the grin spread across the hard lines of her face, hardened by hardship, violence, and battle. It was the grin of the warrior in the throes of battle lust. Somewhere inside his mind, he reasoned that this was good; the other part of him argued the loss of her humanity at the hands of fate.

She was every inch the fighter and nothing, or no one, would get to her charges as long as there was breath in her body. The half elf took no more time for more reflection as more of the beasties erupted from the darkness below.

Solothon was torn between pursuing his present course and returning to the sounds of battle behind him. He felt the danger that was coming, though he couldn't see it. The screeches, growls, and the ringing of metal on stone made the decision for him. He turned and ran for the room where his friends fought with the creatures from hell.

The sound of stone grinding over stone stopped, only to be replaced by the slow stamp of metal boots on marble.

Though their arms grew tired, the companions fought on. All, that is, except Bonaire.

His mage power, somehow passed to him by his mother, again reached full. He was tired and bitten and angry and hungry! As he stomped again at one of the nasty beasties trying to get at Rene', he gave voice to his mother's old cuss words.

He raised the green crystal sword before him, and as his eyes closed, he said the words his mother had used on him when his practice of the arts went sour. The words, old and powerful, ripped from his lips.

The ancient tongue of Mages rippled off of the walls and down into the hole. The creatures twitched as the power engulfed them and then lay still. The magiks used to animate them was sucked up into the ancient spell and dispelled into the nether void of limbo.

Bonaire's eyes jerked open at the sound of the now-powerless scroll tube ringing on the marble floor. He looked around and saw that all of the creatures had simply dropped dead. Everyone's eyes were on him, and he knew he'd done something right. He didn't know what it was, but they didn't know that! He looked up and saw Solothon come through the door, sword in hand.

"Too late, Sol!" he said with just a tinge of scorn. "It's all over."

"I'm afraid not," came the knight's reply as he turned again to the door.

The sound of metal boots in the hallway brought both Eton and Savon'el to their feet.

"I shall hold them as long as I can," said the knight as he stepped through the door. "Try to get everyone to safety."

Bonaire ran for the door as Eton and Savon'el glanced down at their two prone companions.

Arantar bled from the bites on his neck. It wasn't too bad, but neither he nor Rene' seemed to be able to fend for themselves.

"It's the bands," said Melisande as she grabbed the Huntsmaster by the shoulders and lifted him from the mage girl. "They couldn't get Rene' out of danger so they canceled themselves out. If I can get them apart, they might come out of it on their own."

She placed Arantar down several feet from the mage girl and stood up to face the two warriors.

"They can't be moved. I will stay and guard them. You must help Solothon."

Both men nodded and ran for the door as the sound of conflict rang from the hallway. Bonaire stopped at the door and looked out. The light from the ball on the ceiling lit the hallway dimly, but he could see the fully armored beings approach the knight.

"Gods!" he thought. "Old Sol is going to have to be good this time! He's going to have to be vicious, dangerous, and scary! He's going to have to..."

Then he brightened. The words came to him quickly, and just as quickly they were said. With a flick of his hand the spell was cast. He smiled and, after he stepped aside to let Eton and Savon'el through the door, strutted back to where Melisande tended to Arantar's wounds.

Solothon lost all reason. His lips drew back over his teeth and the red glow in his eyes searched for blood. The being directly before him was chosen as his first victim and he attacked. A wailing scream ripped from his throat as he brought his now-screaming sword up to hack at this foe.

Savon'el saw only three, but they were encased in tarnished full plate armor. Each wielded an ancient two-handed broadsword stiffly and with little coordination. The strokes were sure and strong, but left them open to attack. A quick glance showed the embossing on the breast of the one in the center, though the blond half elf couldn't make it out amongst the tarnish.

This was the one at which Solothon threw himself in a mad rush to destroy.

Eton and Savon'el were like two old campaigners as the blond broke left to parry the broadsword aimed at the unprotected back of the Elvin knight, and the warrior blocked the other attacker's blade with his crossed swords.

The silver sword in the hands of the berserker knight sang on, its voice finding its way into the minds of his friends. Swords flashed in the dank air, rang, and chimed as they thwarted every stroke.

Solothon didn't try to defend himself, so deep was he into the battle lust of the Shan'troa. He hacked and hacked at the target before him, oblivious to the damage the broadsword did to his body and armor.

Slowly, ever so slowly, the anger incumbent to that song filled Eton and Savon'el with hate until, finally fully enraged, they both succumbed to the song of the sword. There was nothing then, save the enemy before them.

The endlibar blade rose and fell like an axe, though most strokes missed the target entirely. Savon'el's foe, though dead for many centuries, strangely recalled the red glow in this one's eyes, and instead of attacking out of hand it began to fend off the strokes in strange panic.

Saliva dripped from the lips of the big warrior as his two blades spun in unison as a whirlwind. He too cared not whether this foe touched him. He cared only for the feel of his blades crashing into the armor over and over again.

Melisande heard the sounds of the battle as she tended the wounds on Arantar's neck. The Huntsmaster slept deeply and that worried her. Rene also worried her. The golden mage girl hadn't moved a muscle in all the time Bonaire sat rubbing her hand.

What worried her most were the howling, snarling growls that came from the hallway.

"Bonaire," she said as she repositioned her maul for the third time, making sure it was to hand, "what are they fighting out there? Wolves?"

"No," he replied absently. "Three more of those death knights, but don't worry, I've given old Sol an edge."

"An edge?" Her head jerked up and she stared at the young elf. "What edge, Bonaire? What have you done?"

"Nothing, really," he said nonchalantly. "Just some musty spell my mom kept in her old spell book." He caught the look of anger on the girl's face. "Look!" he added quickly. "I figured the guy would be more dangerous in his nastier state. I just triggered his nastier self, that's all!"

She ran for the door. Even from this distance she could see the red glow in the eyes of the three friends.

She started to ask if the elf had cast that thing on Eton and Savon'el too but stopped. She felt the song of hate and anger emanating from the silver sword that rose and fell as if it were in the hands of a woodchopper.

"Take it off of him, Bonaire! Now!"

"Wha—"

"The spell, stupid!" she shouted. "Take the damned spell off of him before you get them all killed!"

"Uh...Sure, if you think I—"

"Don't think! Just do it!"

The elf shrugged and, as he walked to the doorway, dug into his memory again. The counter spell came to his lips and he spoke the words. When he was finished, he looked back at Melisande.

"Okay. It's canceled. Is that better?"

No, it wasn't. It was too late. The sword had taken over and drove the three warriors into the frenzy of madness.

Savon'el hacked with his sword, each stroke more and more animalistic. His scale armor was cut and torn in several places and he was bleeding. He didn't notice, so intent was he at hacking this foe into nothingness.

Eton howled as his Bourjon blade sunk into a thin area of his foe's leg armor, but instead of pressing that advantage, he brought the long sword crashing into the hard breastplate. The death knight before him kept trying to drive the broadsword into Eton's guts, but the magical properties of the studded leather turned the blade each time.

Melisande retrieved her sling stick from the pocket of her cloak and ground it into a niche in the marble floor. She loaded a heavy pellet of lead into the sling's pocket and watched.

Finally the knight drove the silver sword into the small space between his foe's breastplate and its apron of steel. As that death knight stiffened, the one to its right slashed at Savon'el and missed.

Its blade rebounded from the shoulder piece of his companion and lodged in the junction of the helm and breastplate. Solothon's foe toppled to the ground, but it took two more strokes of Solothon's sword before he got the idea that it wasn't going to get up again.

His target down, the Elvin knight turned to the closest body in the battle. He screamed and raised his sword to strike down the fellow in the single arm gauntlet.

Melisande saw that Solothon had lost his dented helm. She had no choice. If she did nothing, Solothon would kill Eton. If she did what she knew she had to do, she might kill Solothon. She took a deep breath and set her resolve.

She placed her foot to the staff of the sling, drew back on the leather pocket, and released it. The pellet struck the knight hard in the back of his head, and as he went down the song of the sword suddenly stopped.

Unfortunately, the poison of that song still flowed strong in the veins of the other two companions. They hacked on, taking more damage than they dealt, but they refused to go down.

The two remaining death knights continued to fight until suddenly they both stiffened. As Eton and Savon'el struck at them with their weapons, the armored foes fell. Whatever had powered them seemed to have run out.

The two companions gasped for air and turned from their downed foes to face each other. The madness was still with them as Eton's crouch became more pronounced and Savon'el brought the greenish brown sword up to attack.

"Eton! Savon'el! *Don't!*"

The girl's cry snapped them both out of it. Eton wobbled a bit and then dropped to one knee, both blades falling to rest on the marble in tired hands. Savon'el let the blade fall to his left from his numb hands as he returned to normal. The strength drained from his slashed limbs and he abruptly sat down.

Melisande returned the sling to that special pocket in her cloak and ran to her friends. She checked Solothon first to see that she hadn't killed him. He wasn't bleeding too badly, so she turned to Eton.

"I'm fine for now," he whispered. "See to him first."

He raised a shaky sword toward Savon'el and sat.

Savon'el's armor had kept him from receiving mortal wounds, but it was now in tatters. The leather bindings were torn and the metal plates hung from strips were it should have been covering his chest and right arm. He'd lost a lot of blood, but he was still conscious.

"What happened?" he asked in a tired confused voice.

"Don't talk. Relax and let me work."

The girl began the process of binding the many wounds on the half elf's body.

Chapter Thirty-nine

"What in the bloody blue blazes—"

The Huntsmaster came from total unconsciousness to his feet with total awareness, uttering an oath. He glanced about the room in an attempt to reorient himself. The last thing he remembered were the nasty little animals that poured from the darkness below.

His eyes took in the dusty room, the littered bodies of those undead beasts, and his recuperating friends.

Bonaire kicked one of those beasties into the dark hole in the center of the room and moved to another. He plucked a white fletched arrow from it, added that shaft to the six he held in his left hand, and kicked that creature too into the darkness.

Melisande wrapped the bandaging about the blond half elf's now bare chest. All Savon'el wore were the scale armor trousers; the rest of his armor lay in a crumpled heap beside him. His neck knife lay next to the sheathed sword to his left on the floor.

The black-haired cleric turned from Savon'el to check on Rene' where she lay with her head cushioned on the cleric's yellow cloak. Melisande touched the mage girl's cheek with her fingertips, nodded, and turned back to her bandaging.

Solothon squatted next to the door, an ancient helm held gently in his hands. With a finger, he traced the pattern of embossing that completely encompassed the crown of the helm.

"Arantar, sit and rest," said Melisande in a gentle voice. "All is well."

"What of Rene'?" he asked as he crossed to Savon'el's side and sat. "And where is Eton?"

"Rene' is just sleeping, as you were. As for Eton..."

A clatter at the doorway drew the Huntsmaster's attention.

"Ah!" whispered the warrior.

He dropped an armload of armor pieces next to Solothon. Then he crossed to squat before the blond half elf and smiled at Arantar.

"How do you fare?"

"Better, now that I'm awake. What's happened?"

"That story would take too long to tell," answered the blond. "Let's just suffice it to say that we, as Rene' put it, landed on our feet once again."

"Rene'?" asked the Huntsmaster with some concern.

"She'll be fine," said the cleric as she turned to gently caress the mage girl's cheek.

Rene's eyes fluttered open at that touch and she sat up slowly.

"Wha—"

"Easy, Rene'," cautioned Melisande. "You've been out for a while. Take your time."

Eton rose as Solothon walked toward them. He carried a tarnished breastplate in one hand and his other held the helm close against his chest.

"Where did you find this?" he asked Eton, his voice soft and low.

"It was worn by one of those we fought," whispered the warrior. "I thought it prudent to collect what serviceable armor there was."

He turned a quick glance at Savon'el.

"It seems that Savon'el's has taken quite a beating. Maybe we can find something in there to replace that which was destroyed."

"Why do you ask, Solothon?" questioned the blond as he noted the strange look on the knight's face.

"Look upon this," was the knight's reply as he held the breastplate out for them to see.

Amongst the tarnish was something else. Over the heart of the armor piece was a pattern that looked like...

"By the Mother!" exclaimed Arantar in a hushed voice.

"By the Mother, indeed," repeated that knight harshly. "'Tis the emblem of she that you and I follow, Huntsmaster."

It was a tree, raised from the armor by the clever hands of a loving craftsman. Arantar drew a shaking hand across it, and where the tarnish was rubbed away, silver glinted in the light.

"This," said the knight as he shook the breastplate, "and this," he displayed the helm, "were worn by one of the original knights of the Order of the Laurel."

Arantar recognized the pattern of a circle of Laurel raised about the crown of the helm.

"Who?" he asked in a hushed tone.

"I know not," replied the knight sadly. "Were we at home in Laranthia, the Book of Heraldry would say, but here—"

"It is only fitting that you take up the armor of your brother, Sir Solothon."

They all turned to be held in the molten amber of the blond half elf's eyes.

"Who better than he who has risked himself again and again in the service of his friends?" he said. "It is fate that guides us, I believe. You have said that your goal, as well as that of your brothers in the new Order, is to return the honor and glory to its rightful place.

"He who fell here so long ago and who has finally found peace by your hand would want you to carry on in his stead and in his armor."

"Maybe so," the knight said sharply as his right hand released the catches on the mail sleeve covering his left arm, "but what of this?"

He stripped away the armor to display the birthmark. Melisande couldn't quite stifle a sharp intake of breath as she saw the third red dot within the pentagram.

"What will be the result when each point is marked thus and the center as well?" Solothon asked stonily. "Do I then kill my friends? I had hoped to learn to control this thing I've inherited, but that hope has been dashed by this last encounter."

Arantar frowned at these words of self-recrimination, not knowing what they meant, but he knew that something had happened to cause them.

Rene's right arm had begun to throb, not painfully but with power. Her mind floated in the half-dream state of possession. A thought was impressed upon her, oddly, by the alabaster arm. She rose and stepped before the downcast knight.

"May I examine that?" she asked in a dreamy voice.

Her white hand reached toward the pentagram as Solothon looked into her eyes.

Eton stepped around behind him to better see what the mage girl was doing and noted the slight glow from the arm as the hand approached Solothon's shoulder.

"It will do no good, I fear," said the knight sadly. "I am cursed to—"

The girl's dainty white palm pressed over the birthmark, and Rene' felt the pulse of power race down her arm.

Fire and pain ripped through the knight's body. The tendrils of the healing power parted at his neck, and as one tendril burned about his heart, the other scorched upward into his brain.

Eton caught him as he fell and laid him gently to the floor. The big warrior looked up in concern at the startled look on Rene's face.

The mage girl gazed, transfixed, into the palm of her hand. Melisande, standing at the girl's shoulder, saw it too. It was an exact mirror image of the birthmark that was on Solothon's...

It was gone! Melisande saw only smooth skin on the knight's arm. She glanced back into Rene's palm in time to watch as the pentagram with the three red dots slowly faded.

"Rene'!" breathed the girl. "You've healed him!"

"Have I?" asked the mage girl softly. "Or have I removed his birthright? If the latter is the case, how do I now ask for his forgiveness?"

"You don't."

The blond came to her and took her right hand in his. As he raised it to his lips, he felt the pleasant pulse of healing power race up his arm to the wounds there and into his chest to speed up the knitting of the wounds beneath the bandaging.

"Only time will tell if you've rid him of the curse of Shan'troa. If you have, he will thank you, though maybe not at first. He is not one to allow his heart to rule his mind for long."

Rene' nodded, glanced once to where Melisande placed the knight's head on her folded cloak, and returned to her blanket.

"Now," said Savon'el as he flexed his bare right arm, "let us attempt to make a secure camp."

Arantar moved toward the black crystal scroll tube and picked up one of the silver cap ends as he went.

"Bonaire," continued the blond, "secure the door. Then throw the rest of these things"—he kicked a weasel—"into the hole. The ghouls as well." Then he added, "I'll help."

He glanced at Solothon, then at Eton.

"If you will, see if there is armor enough in that pile to outfit him as befits a knight." He glanced down at his bandaged chest and then down at the destroyed pile of scale. "And some for me, if there is any to be had. You may need some as well."

Eton stroked the studded leather on his chest, and Savon'el barely heard the strange whisper.

"I need no more than I have."

Eton began to sort through the armor, inspecting each piece with a practiced eye.

Rene' watched as the Huntsmaster retrieved the crystal tube and walked back toward her.

"There is a sheet of parchment within, Rene'," he said as he stopped a few paces away. "I'm not sure that I wish to put my hand in there to retrieve it."

Rene' scanned the tube but found nothing of magical or clerical power remaining.

"It is safe," she said. "Bring it here, please."

Arantar moved within a few feet of the girl and thrust the end of the tube toward her. She retrieved the ancient sheet of parchment and nodded. The Huntsmaster laid the tube on the floor in front of her with the silver end cap and went back across the room to retrieve the other.

Rene' gently unrolled the strangely well-preserved sheet and began to study the ancient writing. It took her a while to translate the language, one of both age and cryptography, but, save for the signature at the bottom, the words soon began to have meaning.

It read:

> "Beware the darken Sidhe, brothers of evil,
> Servants of evil…but take from them what aid is offered.
> Within the Tower of Dread Masters is power and
> knowledge for the taking.
> Beyond the Lake of Dreams and deep within the
> Mountain of Fire,
> true hearts can prevail.
> Before the door with no escape,
> look for the lock within the dragon's nape.
> Within the stock, find the key

and find the courage to release me."

"What does it say?" came a soft voice over her shoulder.

Rene' answered Melisande's question by reading the message to her.

"I can't read the author's name," she added, "nor am I sure of its meaning."

"Well," said the black-haired cleric as she watched Arantar help Savon'el drag a dead ghoul to the edge of the hole and roll it in, "it might mean something later. Keep it safe."

Rene' rerolled the parchment as Melisande laid a strong hand on her shoulder.

"Help me put something together for our boys to eat. They have worked up quite an appetite, I'd say."

Rene' had to grin in the face of the cleric's smiling observation. She patted the girl's hand and nodded.

Solothon woke an hour later to a sensation that all was well, but with a definite feeling that something of consequence was missing. He lay for a moment with his eyes closed and searched. It took some time, but finally he knew that the rage, which had lain within his mind ready to take over should his guard fail, was gone. He felt at peace with his soul for the first time in many years.

He sat up slowly and opened his eyes. His companions sat and chewed on smoked meat and sipped sparingly from the diminished supply of water. He flexed his bare left arm and glanced down at it.

He jumped to his feet in shock and, not believing what he saw, grabbed his left arm with his right hand and turned it to his startled gaze. The birthmark of his forefathers was gone! The anger shot to his eyes as he stomped to his companions and stared at the golden mage girl.

"What have you done, bitch?" he yelled.

"That is uncalled for!" said the blond as he came to his feet. His eyes were molten and his voice held an edge. "Your tone and your choice of words are not those of a true knight addressing a lady."

"She has taken—" the knight began in a low deadly tone.

"What?" interrupted Savon'el. "Your birthright? The right to fly into a fit of rage so deadly that none near you are safe? The right to become an animal at will to hack and kill indiscriminately?"

The knight's gaze cooled as he looked into the sad eyes of the mage girl. He saw there the indecision that had marked her choice.

"Even if it were not so," continued the blond, "your tone leaves much to be desired!"

"He is correct, Solothon Calendera Shan'troa."

They all came to their feet as all eyes turned to the source of that deep deadly voice. It resonated from the vicinity of the door.

He stood something over seven feet tall, his body glinting in the light as only black crystal could. He leaned his massive crystal hands on the hilt of the great sword, made of the same material, which stood point down before him.

Savon'el, his eyes never leaving the tall being, knelt to retrieve the bastard sword that lay in its sheath next to his crumpled armor. He drew it and dropped the sheath as he stood.

Arantar cross-stepped to his left at a crouch, his right hand to the hilt of his great sword, and Eton stepped between this possible enemy and the women. At a crouch, his gauntleted left hand at the hilt of the heavy blade that rested at the small of his back, he watched the golem with narrowed eyes.

The crystal golem raised his left hand, palm out, before them.

"Please. I do not wish for battle," he said casually. Then, as he let that hand fall back to the other, "Frankly, it has been many years since I have had intelligent company with which to chat. Those within this place are... well...not alive. I've come bearing a greeting and a warning."

"A warning?" said the blond as he rested the endlibar blade in his left hand. "What sort of warning?"

"Only that I am charged with the guardianship of this place, and if you continue I will have no other choice then to destroy you."

"We must go on," said the blond softly. "We too have no choice."

"Then let it be so," replied the golem in a tired voice.

"Is there no other way?" asked the mage girl.

The crystal guardian glanced at Rene'. Then, his head down, he seemed to be deep in thought for a moment. He raised his head, cocked it to the side, and looked at Rene'.

"It has been many centuries since I've been paid. My commander seems to have forgotten that he placed me here. Now, should employment be offered at, say, one thousand gold pieces worth..."

"He might as well have asked for the Court of Catlorian," whispered Bonaire from behind Rene'.

"Shush!" she replied in a sharp whisper. Then, to the golem, "We don't carry that much with us, but if you will accept the down payment of three hundred and a promissory note, my family will honor it if I don't survive."

"I don't doubt your sincerity, Lady Anolin, but, you see, if you don't survive, I could never set foot within the Vale."

"Then it would be in your best interest to see that I do survive." she replied tartly.

"True," he said with a chuckle, "if I were to take your offer."

"I would collect it and bring it to a site that you name," said the Huntsmaster.

"No, Adenedhel. I might, except for the rules that I have made for myself. Meaning no discourtesy, but knights and members of royalty are given credit. All others, cash only."

"Then I shall vouchsafe the funds," said the knight.

"I have a better idea," said the golem as his black orbs locked onto those of the blond half elf. "You can give me employment in return for pointing you in the right direction and seeing to your mounts."

"Me?" asked Savon'el. "I have nothing! Not even a name!"

"Then, may I sweeten the deal?" said the amused crystal being. "I will do all that I have said and prove that you have the capacity to employ me in the style to which I would like to become accustomed."

"Who are you that you know so much of us?" asked the knight tautly.

"I am Kohl, fourth in the line of command under X'hel. I used too much...initiative at one time, and I was sent here to guard this place as punishment."

"Then you have never left here? Never been in the outskirts of Laranthia?"

"Laranthia? Not hardly! I've been here—"

"You will do as you are told!"

The power of those words rippled from the walls and assailed Kohl from all sides. Savon'el had grown impatient and without thought had reached into that hidden place in his soul. His was the power of command so powerful, so irresistible, that all stiffened at the words.

All, that is, save the black crystal golem. There was anger in his words as he lashed out at the blond half elf.

"Don't try your tricks on me, young Prince!"

Savon'el's mouth dropped open.

"Your father tried that on that half-breed cleric, Yavosh, and it did no good. How do you think to affect one of my creation? I care not for your rash outburst, Raven of Moshar! Don't try that again!"

Savon'el heard no more. The sword fell from his hands as he dropped to his knees, his hands to his temples. He saw again the wheeling beasts as they careened through the sky above dragon's teeth, spreading fire, acid, and destruction in their wake. He remembered the honor guard, led by Yokura, who broke into his room and ushered him from the palace. They passed through the great hall where his father's corpse burned in wailing demon fire, though that fire never scorched the silver armor his father wore in death.

Outside the palace wall, running, running. The guard took him on toward the sea as Yokura turned back to fight for time. They were overtaken and all of the guards were destroyed. Fire licked toward him as he ran off of the cliff and fell, head first, into the sea. He remembered the sharp pain behind his ear as he slipped under the water. Then...

"My gods! Culligan!" he said as his head came up from his hands.

The tears ran freely from his eyes as he searched the startled faces of his companions.

Solothon had dropped to one knee before him, his head down and the hilt of his silver sword toward the newly revealed monarch.

"Don't bow the knee to me, Solothon Calendera," he said bitterly. "I have no right to your fealty."

"What do you mean, friend?" asked the Huntsmaster.

"Friend?" The last was bitter as well. "Do friends desert their father in the middle of conflict?"

His head fell. Then he took a deep breath and explained.

"I scorned Bonaire for his spoiled attitude, but I am much worse! I spurned the teachings of my father and his right hand, Yokura. I hated him because he insisted on driving me through my lessons without any regard to my"—more bitterness—"position! My father allowed it! I hated them both.

"I thought that my golden universe would last forever, not knowing how short lived my spoiled existence would be. Then, when I should have stood by my father's side, I ran."

The last was spoken softly as the tears fell to the floor and the young Raven's head fell into his hands.

"What could you have done had you stayed?" asked Kohl in a strangely concerned voice.

"I could have stood by him and—"

"Died, young prince," interrupted the golem. "Your father forced Yokura to take you out to keep you from harm. He knew, he must have known, that his time was through."

"How do you know these things, Kohl?" asked Rene softly.

"There is a mirror of seeing in the catacombs beneath this place. I've had to live my existence vicariously through that medium for many, many years. I have also, through another object in the catacombs, kept in contact with a member of the white legion. A strange friendship at best, but he's kept me informed of the turn of time."

Eton watched the blond half elf closely. The despair and self-loathing was apparent in the downcast head and demeanor. He moved quickly as Raven slid the small neck knife from its sheath and turned it toward his stomach. Eton's right hand clamped the half elf's wrist in an iron grip that allowed for no movement.

"What are you doing?" he whispered sharply.

"Savon'el, stop!" shouted Melisande as she ran to kneel next to him. "What will this solve?"

"You don't understand. It must end this way. I have run in the face of danger and, then, when I could have helped save a magnificent lady, I couldn't."

"What are you saying?" asked the warrior as he lifted the half elf's chin in his gauntleted hand, his other hand never moving from the knife so close to the savon'el's stomach.

"She treated me with kindness, love. It was she who saved me from the waters to treat me as one of her own. I betrayed that trust."

"Whose trust?"

"Lady Megan's!" sobbed Raven.

Then, in tears, he related the whole story of the rescue, the attack on Seafoam and the mission he had failed to complete.

"I suppose," he added stonily through his tears, "I could blame much on Wanderer, but the greatest guilt is still my own."

"Is this how you would repay her trust?" said the warrior in a harsh whisper. "Do you think she would want your blood on her hands? Would Cully want you to end it all here?"

"What do you know of it?" asked the half elf sharply.

"They are my parents."

Raven's head shot up until he looked directly into Eton's eyes. Those eyes held steel as the warrior spoke.

"I have searched for you for a long time, from Seafoam to Catlorian. I followed when you left there and tracked you to where we met. I thought you a thief and an agent of the slavers. You stayed in my room while in Seafoam. Megan took you in because she loved life. Did she waste her time? My gods, man, if Cully were here he would tell you the same! I was wrong and so are you! Besides, what happens to us when you are gone? With one less member, could we survive?"

"Listen to him, young prince," said the golem matter-of-factly. "He makes good sense. Without you, there is no bargain."

"Raven," said Rene' softly from behind, "you have been given a second chance. Don't throw it away."

The blond relaxed his grip on the dagger and let it fall to the floor.

"I will say this, my friend," stated the Huntsmaster. "You are not Prince Raven, spoiled, egotistical, and a self-serving waste of good flesh."

As the blond half elf looked into those steel blue eyes, Arantar continued.

"You are Savon'el. You are a true friend, loyal companion, stalwart fighter, and one of the best tacticians I have had the pleasure to know. You have placed yourself between us and danger as long as I have known you. Would Prince Raven have done that? You stood by us throughout this entire ordeal and never once backed down. You may have been all that you said you were, but that is past. You are now, and always will be, Savon'el, my friend and brother."

"I appreciate that, Arantar, but what do I say to my friend Solothon when I know that the shirakens his mount now protects may have belonged to my teacher, Yokura?"

Solothon stiffened and turned flashing eyes on Raven.

"I know that Yokura would never have killed your friends had he another choice, but that is another death lain at my doorstep."

"And does this Yokura always poison his weapons?" asked the knight through clenched teeth.

"Poison?" replied the half elf. "He'd never use poison. Yokura is Kansai, a master of the arts. He *is* a weapon. He uses no poison."

"Not purple worm poison?" pressed the knight.

"None. He would see it as a weak…" Raven's voice grew harsh. "Yavosh! He boasted of a poison that would kill any living being."

"Yavosh from the mirror?" asked Rene'.

Raven gazed into the golden cleric's eyes. She was in pain at his state of mind, but she was also angry.

"That fits," she said, her anger tingeing each word. "Yavosh usurps Dragon's Teeth after killing the royal family. You escape and he sends assassins after you. He also sends someone for Solothon to cripple the Knights of the Laurel by dishonoring him. He is probably behind the problems they've been having at Heartstone. If he works for Banshe'e—"

"Banshe'e?" came the quick question from Kohl. "My commander used that name when he put me here...What year is it?"

"It's 1832 of the empire reckoning. Why?"

"I was sent here over three centuries ago. My commander used both of those names, Banshe'e and Yavosh, in reference to those with whom he'd aligned himself."

"Yavosh betrayed my father and my house. It will be answered!"

Raven's voice had turned hard. Now, as he rose to his feet, the tears were dried and gone. He stood in anger, the royal blood in his veins boiled with a new mission. He turned molten amber eyes on the crystal golem.

"You will have a place on the palace guard, complete with accommodations and wages befitting my left-hand man. My right is reserved for Yokura, if he desires to continue to teach this spoiled child. In exchange you will obey my commands, keeping in mind that I do, now, except council. Do you accept?"

"I do," said Kohl with a chuckle. "That, of course, must be cleared with my commander, X'hel."

"X'hel is but the commander of the black's. I will take this up personally with Lady Desiree. She commands all legions. Now, I want your word."

"You have it, Prince Raven."

"And mine, lord," intoned Solothon, still on one knee.

"Come, my friend," said the blond as he lifted the knight to his feet, "friends don't bow to friends."

"But, my lord—"

"Save it for if and when I win back my throne. Then, if that is your wish, I will gladly accept your sword in service. For now I would rather have the council of a friend." He turned his attention back to the golem. "Kohl, we are here to find some specific items and Radagast's library. We have little time in which to fulfill this mission."

"What are these items? Describe them."

"Rene?" said the half elf as he looked at the mage girl.

"There is a book of summoning and a large crystal. Both are said to be in this keep, but we don't know exactly where."

"I do. I will show you to the entrance, but I will not be able to join you."

"Why?" asked Savon'el as he strolled with Kohl toward the door.

"The passage has been protected against those of my kind, though for you there is no danger. I shall stay with the horses and care for them while you are away. Have no fear, you have my word-bond."

"You will need a key," said Solothon.

"No, I have access to all but very few rooms here. The only question left is how we are to leave here."

"If all else fails," said Savon'el as he glanced at Eton, "we have a method."

"Savo...Raven, wait!" shouted Melisande. As the blond turned toward her, she continued, "You have forgotten that you have no armor. You can't go further without clothing. Not now!"

The blond half elf grinned and sighed.

"You are correct, as usual." Then, he glanced at the neat pile of armor that Eton had been working on. "There doesn't seem to be anything in that that will fit one of my build."

"Mine can be adjusted for you, my lord," said the knight as he began to unfasten the catches to his chain mail. "I will take your advice and don the armor of my brother Knight of the Laurel, if you please."

"I can think of none better."

The knight nodded with a grin and began to remove the sections of armor. Raven retrieved the endlibar blade, sheathed it, and held it toward the big warrior.

"Your father loaned me this blade to seek help. I failed him and I wish to return the sword to you, his son."

Eton looked deep into those amber eyes before he answered.

"My father would want you to keep it until you can return it to him yourself." Then, with a grin, "Besides, ol' Meg would have my hide if I left you weaponless."

The grin was answered by a smile and two strong hands met.

Chapter Forty

"The heirs to the throne of Moshar have always been crowned on the eleventh day of Passing. That leaves us eighteen days to get what we've come for and return to Dragon's Teeth."

Rene' stood before the blond, her elbow cupped in one hand while the fingers of the other tapped absently on her chin.

"That may be true, Rene', but what I wish is to complete our mission here and, tradition or not, crowned or not, thwart Yavosh's scheme," said Savon'el as Solothon tightened the straps to the mailed shirt he now wore.

The knight wore the armor of a Knight of the Order of the Laurel and, though the armor was tarnished with years of neglect, the companions could see the pride well up in their friend.

"If you are going after that one," the mage girl said thoughtfully, "you're going to need more help then we have now. He is dangerous, as you know, and if what I fear is true, he has a very powerful backer."

"That doesn't matter," he replied. "I have no choice. No Moshar has ever allowed any subject to the crown to be treated as anything but free men. I'm not about to stand idly by and watch it happen now. There is one other thing, however."

"What is that?" asked the girl.

"I owe a debt of honor to Culligan Vandergast. He asked for my help, but circumstances kept me from it. I must do everything in my power to find Megan, yet I can't forget my people in Dragon's Teeth."

"Think of it this way," said the mage girl. "When you seize back your throne and defeat Yavosh, you will have placed a large obstacle before Banshe'e. In so doing, you will be in a far better position to help both Culligan and your people."

"And don't worry too much about Culligan." added the big warrior. "I worry more for the poor souls he is after."

"How does that feel, my lord?" asked the knight as he slapped the half elf's shoulder.

"Good," he said absently. "Good, but I think, until we can get to Dragon's Teeth, I should remain Savon'el. Should we succeed here, we will still be a threat. The less they know of us the better." He returned the knight's stiff nod, looked about the makeshift campsite, and continued, "Now, let's take only what we might need for, say, two days. If we haven't returned by then, we won't be returning."

He picked up the sword, his backpack, and quiver and stepped over to where Arantar and Kohl were in deep conversation. "What have you discovered?" he asked as he secured his weapons to his back.

"Kohl has been telling me of the laboratory, located on the second floor, and the library and treasury on the third...What did you call it?"

"The Tower of Dread Masters," said the golem. "The second floor contains the focus of all studies, but the third is the Point of Summoning."

"'Within the Tower of Dread Masters'..." quoted Rene' softly. Then, her eyes shining in revelation, "That is where we must go! That is where we will find what we are after."

"Then," said Savon'el softly, "that is where we shall go. Are we ready?"

At a nod from the Huntsmaster, he turned to Kohl.

"Which way?"

"One question, m'lo...Savon'el, if you please," said the knight as he moved up behind the new prince. "Is Terillion's business all that important in light of what we now know?"

"It is important if we find the information and artifacts Rene' was sent to retrieve. We must complete this mission, if for no other reason than to be a nuisance to Banshe'e."

"I just wish to see you to Dragon's Teeth. If we could avoid—"

"There are a great many things I've avoided in my life, my friend, most of which could have been beneficial if I'd had the good sense to heed the lesson taught. I will no longer avoid what my honor demands."

Arantar laid a hand on Savon'el's shoulder.

"The sooner we are about this business, the sooner we can seat you on your throne. If that be your fate, I am here to aid you."

"Thank you, Huntsmaster," said the blond half elf. Then, "If we are ready, let us begin."

Bonaire heard nothing past the word treasury. He stayed in the rear of the group and listened, certain that if he failed to hear some small bit of information he might not get his share.

Kohl led them from the room and down the hallway back along the way they had come.

"I heard you speak earlier of crystal shirakens," he commented. "Might I ask if they are black and have the emblem of the pierced dragon upon them?"

"Yes, they do," replied the blond, a bit startled. "What do you know of them?"

"Nothing much, save that they sound like the Crystal Shirakens of Kedah."

"Do you know of any who have the talent to use them? Maybe someone like yourself?"

"Only four have the ability to use those, as far as I know, and only two like myself."

"You?"

"No," the golem chuckled, "I haven't the talent with thrown weapons, sir. No, I speak of Siron, Commander of the White Legions, and my Commander, X'hel."

Raven reached out a hand and stopped him. The golem turned at the touch and looked down into eyes of molten amber.

"Does X'hel have the ability to enter the Eldewood Vales?"

"Yes, Lord, and if you are going to ask if he might use poison or if he might know your Yavosh, the answer to both, as you know, is yes. Shall we proceed?"

The half elf's mind ripped through the evidence that was presented and he came to only one conclusion: X'hel, though sworn to Desiree, was in league with Yavosh and, indirectly or directly, Banshe'e. If he lived, he would take this information to Desiree. She should know of X'hel's treachery.

The golem stopped in front of a blank wall in the center of the hallway and touched a panel high in the wall. Ancient mechanisms ground into motion as a section of the stone moved away to display a rather ornate keyhole of large proportions.

"I believe one of you has found a platinum key, have you not?" he asked without turning.

The knight quickly retrieved the key from his pouch and attempted to hand it to the golem. Kohl suddenly backed away, his eyes on the key as if it were poison.

"Solothon, wait," said the blond softly. He took the key from the knight and continued. "He cannot use this, nor can he enter with us. This portal, as well as the key, has been made a bane to his kind."

"Sorry, Kohl. I didn't know," said the knight, his embarrassment echoing in his words.

"It matters not, but it would do to have one of your number investigate this portal to see if there is danger to other than myself," he replied nonchalantly.

Melisande scanned the wall and found that, should one have tried to pick the lock, the entire wall would have collapsed upon them. She turned a small smile of thanks toward Kohl, then related to the others what she had seen.

"Uh...Solothon," said Bonaire nervously as he backed away. "It's your key. Why don't you open it?"

After giving the young elf a scathing glance, the knight attempted to retrieve the key to make good on the suggestion. However, Savon'el laid a hand on his arm and turned a question to Kohl.

"What can we expect to find once we are inside?"

"This," answered the golem with a sweep of his hand toward the wall, "enters the stairway. Go up the stairs until you arrive at a position on the stairs that is exactly above this doorway. There you will find another secreted door. It is not locked.

"Once through that portal, go directly across the hall to the double doors into the alchemy laboratory. There is another door secreted within the chemical storage closet of the laboratory. This will lead you down into the catacombs to the place where stands the Crystal of Power. It is the power source for all that live here. Remove that and all of these creatures will finally be at rest. Once you have the crystal, place it into one of the bags you will find hanging in the closet. Then return to the secret door and take the stairway up to the third floor. There, you will find the *Book of Summoning* and a Pentagram of strange design. You will also find the library, with all references to its contents in a file by the door, and the treasury."

"This...*Book of Summoning*," asked the Huntsmaster. "Summoning what?"

"I know not. I am not a sorcerer."

"What dangers are we liable to find within, Kohl?" asked the blond half elf.

"None of what you've found here, if you have the crystal, but don't linger. You must move quickly. Once the wards have been removed, others may seize the moment." He turned his gaze to the golden mage girl. "As you look for references to Radagast's armory, seek also in the library for information on Alabaster Peace and its companion. They were crafted here many years ago, I've been told, by Lord Rairy for Lord Pantor and his wife. It is rumored that he had help from another, but of that I am not certain."

"Kohl," said the blond softly, "do you know of the history of this place, its lords and creators? We know that Radagast—"

"This keep, from information I have found throughout this evil place, was here long before Radagast, and later Lord Belmont found it. It was Lord Belmont who had the wards reset many years before I was placed here."

Savon'el nodded.

"There is much of this world that has changed since you were left here, and I will attempt to explain most of it later. For now, know that my offer is my oath and I will see to it once we have returned. I ask that you maintain your vigil here for a bit longer. I also wish to thank you, in advance, for your service to us."

"Not necessary, Prince Raven. As I have sworn, so let it be," was the reply. Then the big golem moved down the hall.

"By your leave, Savon'el?" asked the knight as he held out his hand for the key.

Raven returned the key and the knight inserted it into the lock. The door slipped silently into the wall and a faint blue light rose over a circular stairway to dimly light their way. A cylinder of blue light flickered with power as it rose from deep beneath them to disappear into the heights above.

Solothon stepped through, surveyed the area quickly, and motioned for the others to follow. Arantar took the lead and cautiously mounted the stairs. When the group arrived at the point Kohl had described, Solothon reached out and stopped Savon'el from entering that door first.

"Let us lead the way, m'lord," he said in his stern tone.

But the blond half elf would have none of it.

"Have I changed, Solothon?" he asked.

"Sire?"

"Am I any different than I was a few moments ago that I should now be protected?"

"I just thought—"

"I know, my friend, but you," he turned to the rest of them, "you all must not treat me any differently now that my birthright is known. I'm, above all else, one of the companions on this endeavor and still a savon'el. While it is true that my birthright is of royalty, it is also true that I have you, my friends, to thank for it. If not for you, I could very well have died long ago."

He paused and when he continued, there was determination in his words.

"I started this with you as an equal. I can wish for no more than that, nor do I crave it. I have misspent my youth in folly. Now, let me earn what would be mine as Savon'el."

He drew the endlibar blade and moved to the left of the knight in the position he had taken throughout their travels through this place.

"You've grown, my friend," said Arantar with a grin as he took up his place to the knight's right.

"I hope so," replied the prince tautly.

Solothon pushed the door open and entered with Raven sliding to the left and the Huntsmaster to the right. Before them, in the half-light of the blue flicker from the stairway, stood the double doors as Kohl had said.

Rene' was close, so close. Her enthusiasm bubbled through and she pushed her way past the men to stand before that portal. She looked at the three small keyholes and grew impatient.

"Do we have the keys?" she asked, then without waiting for answer, "Oh, bother!" and raised her hand to the door.

As her tiny fist knocked gently on the door, she whispered the words of power. They were old, those words, old and powerful. Any normal door would have burst asunder had she done this, but this door simply transformed into a shimmering blue opaque curtain.

Rene' was impatient as well as angry at the result of her conjuring. She drew back her small fist to strike the door again, but she found herself standing next to Solothon as they watched Arantar's black fist come down on that powerful field of mage force.

The bands knew and acted. Had Rene's hand touched that force, she would have turned to ash. However, as Arantar's fist smashed into it, a massive jolt of electrical energy leaped from the arm and struck it as well.

Unfortunately, the force within the arm had little effect on the force covering the doorway. The power rebounded from the shimmering blue as a bolt of white and ricocheted through the hallway, just barely missing each of the companions in turn.

When it finally dissipated, a shaken Arantar backed away from the door and turned to Rene'.

"I...I'm sorry," she said in a small voice.

"Are you all right, Arantar?" asked Savon'el as he moved to the Huntsmaster's side.

"I think so," he replied. Then, as he glanced at the mage girl, "It's okay, Rene'. Just be more patient from now on."

"I will try," she said softly. "I just didn't think."

Melisande threw a protective arm about the girl's shoulder and gave her a gentle squeeze.

"What do we do now?" mused the prince absently.

The Huntsmaster, however, had not heard the question. Something within was directing his thoughts. Something from the ebony arm reached into his mind and made him concentrate. What had he been thinking when he struck the door? What should he have been thinking?

"Stand back, Raven," he said in a voice very different from that of his own. "Stand away from this portal and from me. This wishes to contain me and *it shall not be*!"

Savon'el backed away as Arantar moved smoothly toward the shimmering force that barred his way. That new thing within him had calmed him as he directed his concentration to his main desire. The door must come down.

The ebony fist struck the field at its very center and it rang as a deep peel of thunder. Cracks formed at the edges where the field touched the frame.

The Huntsmaster drove the fist again into the shimmering blue, his concentration at its peak. The door *would* come down!

Thunder echoed through the hallway, only this time it sounded ragged as if a bell had been flawed and the vibration of that flaw rang in its voice.

"YOU WILL LET ME PASS!" shouted Arantar as the ebony fist smashed a third time into that field of force.

The shimmer took on a pale blue hue, vibrated strangely, and blew into the next room with such force as to draw dust from the floor of the hallway.

The Huntsmaster stood panting as he looked into an ancient laboratory. He brought the fist up to his eyes and flexed it. Then, as he took a deep breath and let it out, he smiled and turned to the others.

"Shall we?"

Solothon and Raven followed the Huntsmaster into the ancient room, followed by Rene' and Melisande. Bonaire stayed close to the ladies, sure that they would be more likely to find treasure than the others. Eton stayed by the door periodically glancing up and down the hallway outside.

As the two ladies walked between the laboratory benches considering the possible uses of the assorted paraphernalia, the knight found a door in a small anteroom that opened off of the laboratory to the right. He tried the door and found it unlocked.

"Here, Savon'el," he said as he pushed the door open.

The blond half elf followed him into a walk-in storage room. The walls were lined with shelves, mostly empty, but one was neatly arranged with several small vials. Behind the vials were three small jars.

The runes inscribed on the vials and jars were those the young prince had been schooled to decipher. The small vials contained blood: six Elvin, one pegasi, and two of the race of Titans.

In two of the jars, the hearts of demons beat slowly in a bath of glowing pink liquid. The other jar contained, sadly, the severed spiral horn of a small unicorne.

Solothon moved further along the shelves until he caught a glimpse of bone white under a bit of cloth on the bottom shelf. He lifted the cloth and a small chest of smooth ivory was revealed. It was a foot long, six inches wide, and five inches deep.

The knight, sensing the fragility of the chest, lifted it gingerly and looked for a catch that would allow him to open it.

"What have you found?" asked Savon'el as he glanced momentarily over the knight's shoulder, then moved farther down toward the back of the closet.

The knight turned to answer, but stopped as Savon'el began backing toward him.

"What is it?" he asked quietly.

"I don't know," said the blond in a ragged voice. "Something down there on the floor won't let me near it. It causes me pain. It eats at my—"

"Lady Rene'!" shouted the knight as he stepped before the prince. "Attend us, please!"

Rene' and Melisande came through the door in a rush with Bonaire close on their heels. Arantar stood by the door and watched to let them pass and, if need be, hold off any danger with sword at the door.

"What is it?" asked the mage girl as she stopped next to the knight.

"In the corner."

The mage girl stepped toward the pile of fine mesh steel, and the closer she stepped, the more loathing she felt. She stopped and backed away.

"'Tis Urhu Steel, cold wrought!" she breathed.

"What?" said Melisande as she joined the girl in staring at the bundle.

"'Tis a bane, soul death to my kind!"

Melisande moved slowly to the bundle, grasped a handful of the steel mesh, and lifted it. It was a bag with a cable drawstring.

"That must be what Kohl meant," said the mage girl. When Melisande looked at her questioningly, she continued, "Kohl said to take the bag down to the catacombs to get the crystal. I should have known it would have to have been steel. Crystal, especially sharp crystal, would cut through any other material. I didn't know, however," a shudder ran down her spine, "that it would be cold wrought."

"It doesn't seem to affect me," said the cleric softly.

"That is as it should be," commented the mage girl. "You must carry it, my dear, and the crystal once we've gotten it. None of the rest of us has that capability."

"Unfortunately," added Raven, "none of us will be able to stand close to you while you carry it."

Melisande nodded and rolled the fine mesh into a small ball. She placed it under one arm and stood well away from the others as they continued their search of the storeroom.

Arantar read the runes written on the containers and was shocked.

"What are these, Rene'?"

The girl looked at the vials and shuddered again.

"They are potions and chemicals. The potions I see here give the user the attributes of the donor, though I'm not sure how they work. The jars are strange, hearts and the horn of a—"

"Unicorne," said the Huntsmaster as he retrieved that jar gently and held it close to his chest. "How could anyone—"

"Remember in whose fortress you stand," she answered tautly.

"I will take this," said Arantar softly, "and the blood of the pegasi with me. Once free of this mission, if I live, I will endeavor to return them to their kind for proper disposal. Is there any…I mean…"

"I've felt for souls, Arantar," said the girl sadly. "Though I sense that the deaths were painful and long, no life still exists within those vials. The hearts live on, though without souls. I don't think we should take any that we have found here. It serves no purpose."

"We can't just—"

"Yes, we can, and we must," said Raven softly. "If we attempt to add to our burden, we may not succeed. If we survive, I will make it my personal mission to return here for them. For now, let them rest."

The Huntsmaster set the jar back on the shelf gently. He placed two fingers to his lips and used those to touch the jar. He took a deep breath, let it out slowly, and then moved to where Solothon and Savon'el stood.

"I shall carry the ivory chest until Lady Rene' and Melisande can check it out, if you please."

At Savon'el's nod, the knight slipped the fragile box into his pack, making sure it was well-cushioned and snug.

The blond half elf looked past the knight to the far wall and found the thin seam of the hidden door. He remembered the lesson that Yokura had taught so many years ago and was pleased. He moved toward it, keeping well away from Melisande as he went, and after a moment of searching he pressed the hidden panel that would open it.

The door swung silently outward into a stairwell hewn from the living rock.

"This is the way," he said as he stepped halfway through the door. He glanced back and continued, "Get Eton and Bonaire in here. Have Bonaire stand by the door. I see no way to open this from inside once we go through."

They moved down into the dark tunnel. The flickering yellow of the torch Arantar carried cast shadows behind them and reached deep into the gloom ahead. Savon'el followed closely with Rene' at his heels. Melisande hung back a bit because of the steel mesh bag she carried.

Solothon stayed far behind the cleric, though close enough if he were needed. He too could feel the loathing of the Urhu Steel she carried under her arm and, though he realized the necessity, felt a sense of uncleanliness.

Eton took up the rear after warning Bonaire not to let the door close while they were gone.

"What?" the young elf had said. "You're gonna leave me here by myself?"

"We have to," the blond had replied. "We have no way of knowing whether we can get out of here another way. As far as we know, this is our only escape. I need you here."

"Sure!" he'd said to their departing figures. "Leave me here while you guys get to the treasure first. 'Guard the door, Bonaire. Don't get in the way, Bonaire.' If you find something," he shouted down the stairway, "I'd better get my share!"

The tunnel changed to a stairway and then to a walkway as it leveled out deep beneath the fortress. Arantar caught a glimpse of the flickering blue light as it reflected up the tunnel.

They came out of the passage into a rough-hewn chamber. In the center, a column of flickering blue rose from a smooth hole twelve feet across to disappear into the heights above. The spiral stairway they'd used to get to the laboratory began some twelve to fifteen feet above the floor directly across from where they were.

Raven glanced back at the passage and hoped that Bonaire would have the good sense to stay where he'd been put.

"Have you ever seen anything like this?" Melisande whispered.

"Never," replied Rene' as she too gazed though the blue field of force to see the many faceted ball of purple crystal that floated a foot above the level of the floor.

It was larger than any crystal she'd ever seen, over a foot in diameter. It spun gently, and as it caught the rays of yellow light from the torch that filtered through the blue, translated it into the many colors it displayed on the walls of the chamber.

Melisande felt something, something dangerous and explosive. She brought her power to her need and saw the three levels of force that surrounded the crystal ball. All were fields of disintegration, each stronger than the one before. She relayed that information to the rest of the companions as she stepped close to the edge of the smooth sided hole that seemed to reach down into nothingness.

"There is no way that I, with my small talents, can dispel this much power," said the mage girl.

"We must—" began Raven.

"No, Savon'el," said the Huntsmaster, "I must."

Then he gently waved the cleric away from the edge.

The three levels of protection began at the very edge of the hole and were spaced only two inches apart. Arantar flexed the ebony hand and concentrated as he had never before. He focused on bringing this force field down as he drew back the ebony fist.

The first stroke reverberated through the chamber and the second caused the first field to vanish.

The second field was of darker blue and rang deep at the Huntsmaster's stroke. Cracks in its fabric spiraled up the column and sparks seemed to leak through them. Arantar drove the ebony fist forward again and was rewarded as that field shattered into many pieces and fell into the pit.

The final field was a deep translucent purple. Arantar stopped and traced it down into the depths, then up into the blue above. He was tired, so tired, yet he knew he could not stop.

He reached deep for the strength he needed and found it in the steel of his will. The fist rang against the purple field of magical force, causing cracks of black to run from the point of impact and spread throughout the column. He could barely bring his fist up again, but his will refused to let him stop. His body couldn't refuse that will and the fist came forward again.

He'd put every ounce of strength he had left into that final stroke and was rewarded as the field shattered in sparkling purple glitter that fell away into the depths.

Arantar stumbled and felt a hand grab his harness. He all but fell into the arms of the blond half elf as that one pulled him from the edge of the pit. He was pale and tired, bone tired, as if he climbed the tallest peak in the kingdom at a dead run.

"Arantar!" shouted the mage girl as she ran toward him.

The alabaster arm flickered with power as the girl stretched it toward him, her concern driving her will. However, she was stopped three feet away as the power of the bands reasserted themselves.

They could not touch, ever. She stood, concern clouding the beauty of her face, and watched as the Huntsmaster's head came up from his chest.

"I did it," he said weakly, but with a grin.

Rene' smiled sadly and again wondered if she'd made the wrong decision to pick up that silver band.

"He is just tired, Rene'," said Raven. "Driving the power of that arm must take a great deal out of him. With some rest he should be fine in a little while."

Raven helped the Huntsmaster to the side of the chamber and sat him down. He turned to Melisande and nodded.

"It's up to you now, Melisande," he said. "I will help if I can, but I can't see how we shall be able to reach that far with the bag to retrieve that crystal." he added as he pointed to the pulsing purple crystal that floated and spun over six feet away from the edge of the pit.

"Leave that to me," she said.

She found the sling on its five feet of staff in the special pocket of her cloak. She tied the cable drawstring tightly to some rope from her pouch. Then she looped the drawstring about the fork at the end of the staff. She wrapped the end of the rope about her waist and turned to the blond half elf.

"I'll need an anchor," she said as she stepped to the edge of the pit.

"I shall be that anchor, m'lady," offered the knight.

He took the girl's left arm in his hand as she gripped his arm, and he planted his feet.

Melisande stretched the hand that held the end of the staff toward the spinning ball of crystal. The bag slipped over it easily, but as she began to pull it in, she felt a strong resistance. It didn't want to move from where it was and was still spinning within the bag.

"Pull, Solothon! Now!"

That knight heard the haste in her voice and pulled with all of his strength. Melisande felt the strain on her body as if she were a bit of rope tied between two ships in a storm at sea. Slowly, the ball came toward her, the knight pulling against his footing with everything he had.

Finally, at the edge of the pit, the crystal seemed to lose its anchor and fell in the bag toward the floor. Melisande's remaining strength was just enough to stop it before it hit.

The black-haired cleric sighed, and as the knight released her arm and backed away, she turned to him.

"Thanks," she said softly with a grin.

The knight nodded sternly, returned the grin, and moved back toward Arantar. The girl set the bag softly onto the floor and, moving to the fork end at the top of her staff, began untying the steel mesh bag from her sling.

Eton noted the color returning to Arantar's face and he turned to Savon'el.

"I will go to Bonaire," he said and started up the tunnel.

Arantar got to his feet and, though still wobbly, stood by himself.

"Can you make of it?" asked Raven.

"Nothing is wrong that a week's rest wouldn't cure," replied the Hunts-master lightly.

The prince smiled and glanced at his other friends.

"We will go first. Melisande, you follow Rene'. Solothon—"

"I shall guard our backs," he responded without waiting. "Lead on."

They arrived at the top of the stairs to an angry Eton and a recalcitrant Bonaire.

"This fool thinks that we've found treasure and we refuse to share," said the warrior angrily. "I, for one, have no more use for him." He brushed past the elf and out into the laboratory.

"You want treasure, Bonaire?" asked the black-haired cleric as she followed the others up the stairs. "Here!" She thrust the bag toward him.

The loathing crawled over him as if it were scaled. He shuddered and backed away.

"N-no, thank you!" he stuttered and threw up his hands to ward her off.

"Melisande, don't!"

The mage girl's soft words caused the anger within the cleric to recede. She shook her head at Bonaire and followed the others through the storage room.

"You'd better learn, my young friend," said Solothon as he stepped through the door and allowed it to close. "There are things more valuable than treasure. Honor and duty are two. Friendship is the greatest. Don't lose what you have to gain that which is of less value."

Bonaire followed him out of the storage room into the dimly lit labora-tory, his head held low, but his eyes watching Melisande.

"Where to now, Lord Raven?" asked the knight as he joined his friends.

"Please, my friend, Savon'el," stated the blond half elf. "Rene'?"

"To the library," answered Rene'. She closed the drawer she'd been ri-fling and started for the door.

"Eton," asked the young prince, "does the steel of that bag affect you?"

In answer, the warrior stepped over to the cleric and lifted the bag from her shoulder.

"Then," continued Raven, "you will stay by her side. Arantar and I will lead, and Solothon and Rene' will follow. You and Melisande will come after with Bonaire guarding our rear."

"Why do I always have to—" began the elf with a whine.

"Because that is where your duty lies," answered the prince sharply. "We will live or die as a team. No single individual can survive what we've already been through, and there is still more hardship in the offing, I fear. Do your part and we may all live through this."

Bonaire drew back as if he'd been slapped. Then he hung his head and kicked absently at the dust on the floor.

"Arantar, are you well enough?" asked Raven.

The Huntsmaster had been gaining strength at a rapid pace. He'd almost depleted his reserves, but his body, with the help from the power of his ebony arm, was replacing what he'd lost.

"I shall be ready when you say, Savon'el."

"Then I say we take a short break, eat something, and rest for the next leg of this journey."

Chapter Forty-one

Light came in through the dome of clear crystal that was the ceiling of the top floor of the tower.

Arantar led the group through the secret door in the hallway and up the spiral staircase that bordered the great chamber, and he arrived first through the hole in the marble floor above. He held out his hand and the others stopped where they were on the stairs.

He brought his ebony hand toward the hilt of his sword and found that it, again, would not touch the great sword's hilt. That in itself was a good sign, but he would take no chances. He drew the blade with his right hand and continued up to survey this last room.

There was a twelve-foot hole, perfectly smooth, cut into the very center of the floor. If one were to measure, it would perfectly align with the pit at the bottom of the catacombs. Where that pit led, the Huntsmaster was loath to wonder.

Beyond the hole, the Huntsmaster could see a pattern etched into the marble floor. To the left of the etching, near the wall, stood a three-pronged stand of black metal, and to the right a heavy wooden stand held a thick book bound with bronze and leather.

Two doors, six feet apart, stood in the wall to his right. On the wall between the two, a scene had been carved. It was too far away for him to see just what was inscribed there, but he knew that they would probably be here long enough for him to investigate.

"Come," said Arantar softly down the stairs. "There doesn't seem to be any danger, but stay alert."

The companions came up the stairway slowly. While Raven followed Arantar around the hole one way, Solothon moved the other. Rene' followed Solothon closely to the great book. She glanced at the runes carved into the leather.

"As'Modious' Book of Summons," she read.

Then she looked to where Raven knelt to trace the runes cut into the eight-foot circle of silver etched into the marble. Her eyes traced the triangle of gold within that circle and, even without the runes of Law inscribed at each corner, knew what it was.

"Thaumaturgic Triangle!" she breathed in awe.

"Within a Circle of Protection?" asked the prince. "So much protection! Why?"

"I can guess," said Melisande.

Her eyes shone with clerical power as she looked from her vantage point next to the metal stand toward the book on its pedestal.

"That book wreaks of evil. Pure, hateful evil."

Rene's brow was furrowed in consternation. There was something here. Something...

"Hey, guys! Look at this!" came Bonaire's voice from behind her.

She turned to look as Eton walked over to where the young elf traced the carved pattern in the wall.

It was a carving of a dragon swooping over a herd of cattle, sculpted into the white marble of that wall between the two solid wooden doors. The doors had no handle, lock, or markings. They were set flush with the marble facing and there didn't seem to be any way to open them.

Rene' found the link using her empathic talents as she joined them to her mage abilities. Somehow the doors were linked to the protective circle. She looked back down at the book as if it would give her the answers she sought.

It glowed.

Three silken ribbons—red, blue, and black—protruded from the top of the book. Maybe...

"Melisande," she called, "place the crystal on the stand, please."

"Wait!" Rene' glanced down at the prince as he continued, "What are you about to do?"

"I am going to test a theory," she replied. "Those doors are linked to the circle and possibly this book. If we are to pass, we must find how."

"Then I shall stand within the circle," he said as he stood and strode toward the center of the triangle.

"No, my friend," whispered Eton as he passed the mage girl and moved to Raven's side, "if any are to test this, it will be me."

Before Raven could protest, there was a shimmer of black at the head of the stairs. Once solidified, the great black warhorse, Shadow, pranced up to the big warrior and nuzzled him.

"How'd he get here?" asked Bonaire from Rene's elbow.

Eton smiled and whispered, "I had been thinking of him, missing him. I guess he felt it and came."

He scratched at the horse's great jaw and then patted his neck.

"If you are going to test Rene's theory," said Melisande, "maybe it would be better to have him with you."

Her statement was answered as the horse tossed his head and pranced behind the big warrior, his head over Eton's shoulder, as the big warrior took his place in the middle of the triangle.

"I think he likes the idea," whispered the warrior with a grin.

Raven smiled, laid a hand on the warrior's shoulder for a moment, and stepped out of the circle.

"Place the crystal," said Rene' again.

As Melisande did so, the crystal began to glow deep purple and a dome of transparent blue covered the magical Circle of Protection.

From the corner of her eye, Rene' saw the flash of fire from the great horse's saddle just as the crystal was put into place. The golden ribbon that she'd used to bind the sword to its sheath burned. The dark blade began to slide from its sheath slowly.

"Melisande! Remove that crystal!" Rene' shouted as she ran to the side of the dome.

But it was too late. No matter how hard she tried, the black-haired cleric could not remove the crystal from its stand.

Raven stood next to the mage girl, helpless to help his friend.

"Look to Shadow for protection," he shouted. "If his master once wielded that blade, maybe he can keep it from harming you."

"It's worse than that, Raven," said the girl softly. "When I neared the blade earlier, I felt a distinct hunger. I know not for what it hungers, but—"

The dark blade slipped from the sheath and hovered for a moment, its point directed toward the warrior's chest. Eton's left hand slipped into the basket hilt of the Bourjon blade as the sword speared toward him. At the last moment, the sword flipped end for end and the hilt thudded softly against Eton's chest. It hovered there as if waiting.

Eton looked over his shoulder at Rene'.

"What do I do?"

In answer, the crackling thought entered his mind.

My companion's sword must be taken, friend Nethan. Worry not, for thou art in no danger unless thou refuse.

No! he responded stubbornly. Then, to Rene', "He says I must take the sword. I've heard the old stories and their outcomes. I would rather—"

"Take the damned blade, or you risk your life and maybe ours!" Melisande yelled. Then, softer, "Please, Eton, take the blade!"

The big warrior looked from one to the other of his friends, sighed, and slowly brought his hands to the hilt of the sword at his chest. As his hands closed on the strangely wrapped hilt, a flash of white nearly blinded the onlookers. Suddenly Eton was faced with shocked looks from his friends.

He stood in skintight armor, smooth and jet-black. A helm sat upon his head, the face open except for the nosepiece. Though his hands were now gauntleted, he could feel the fabric of the hilt. There was no confinement at all, as if this armor were a part of him.

Then he realized that everything else he'd had on him was gone. He turned toward his friends, the dark blade before him, with a look of confusion on his face.

"I AM ARAPEL'HO, THE HELL RAZOR!" came a voice deep and resonant from the blade. "LET THE BATTLE BEGIN!"

Over Eton's heart, etched in gold, was a sunburst. Solothon recognized it as the symbol he'd seen on Sir Jake's breastplate and was an awe and shock at what that meant.

"Rene'," whispered the warrior, "what do I do now?"

Before the girl could answer, two rays of white light emanated from the blade and completely encircled Eton. He stiffened until the light dissipated. Then he seemed to relax.

"Eton!" shouted the mage girl.

He felt strong and well. He turned a grin to Rene'.

"I'm fine..." he began, but he didn't finish.

After so many years spent without a voice, to hear his words in a deep baritone came as a shock.

"Lady?" he said in a hushed voice, the joy evident in the waiver his new voice took.

Rene' was concentrating. Her mind stretched back to her days in Yarda's hut and the books of lore and, she thought, fantasy. Souls locked into swords of power and might and dragons that gave the swords utterance. She'd been forced to converse in the languages of power. Yarda would accept none less. If this were of those she'd read of...

She reached into her mind for the ancient tongue her mentor had used in referring to those days and brought it to her lips.

"What art thou?" she asked, the words hanging in the air as tangible things.

"I am what I appear to be, a weapon crafted for service to the Lords of Light. What doest thou think that I am?"

"I know not. Friend Eton has fear for thee. Is that fear founded?"

"Not lest he be evil, for on that I feed. Long have I fasted in yon sheath, the souls of demons a dreamy repast of long ages past. I sense that thou art about to bring sustenance to my blade and rejoice. Have I sensed wrongly?"

"Friend Melisande cannot lift the crystal from its base. Thy doing?"

"Yes. Mine is the protection of my wielder. I knew thee not and wished to protect he who loves my porter."

Rene' thought that the big black stallion might take offense at being held at such a lowly position, but...

"Friend Eton, thy wielder, is friend to all here. Please release thy power from the crystal."

Rene' sensed the release of power from within the circle of silver and nodded to Melisande. The cleric again grasped the crystal in her strong hands. This time the crystal rose from the stand and darkened as the shimmering dome of force disappeared from about the warrior.

"Now," echoed the voice of the blade in the common tongue, "bring on the first of the evil one's, that I might slake my thirst."

I shall await thy call, friend Nethan.

The crackle snapped through Eton's mind, leaving a taste of amusement, and the warhorse shimmered away.

"I must...I must address you," said Eton with a quizzical look on his face.

He'd never spoken to a sword before and felt as foolish as one would be addressing a wall. He sensed that the sword was waiting for him to continue, so...

"I am a proficient fighter with my own weapons. I've not had the training in…in your type of weapon. Though I revel in the power I feel running the length of your blade, I must suggest an alternate wielder."

With that, he turned his eyes on the Huntsmaster.

Arantar loosened the straps that held the great gray blade to his back and brought it, sheathed, before him.

"I would accept, but I've seen that when your hilt touches the wielder's hand, all else disappears. I'd not wish to be parted from this blade."

"You needn't be," came the voice. "Let a friend carry it for now. Maybe at a later time you will find that I am more than enough for you."

The Huntsmaster handed the sword to Raven, dropped his pack, and stood ready.

As Eton released the hilt, the sword flashed toward Arantar, point first, until it again flipped end for end to settle into his waiting hands.

Eton found that all of his old armor had returned, as well as his weapons and pack. He breathed a sigh of relief and, with a quick thought, hummed a tune he'd heard long ago. He was pleased when the tune lifted from his throat, the deep baritone still with him.

Even before the flash of power brought the armor to his body, Arantar felt a bonding. Then, as he glanced down, he saw that, though his right hand was now covered with the black gauntlet, his ebony left was bare. Shock came as he realized that the sword rested comfortably in the hollow of the ebony hand with no tangible danger about. Not only that, the feeling of kinship with the sword came from the arm itself.

The sword spun in the palm of that ebony hand as the sheer power welled up inside the Huntsmaster. He grinned and looked at his friends.

"Arantar!" breathed the mage girl. "Your eyes!"

The Huntsmaster's eyes had turned black. There was no white, nor an iris, just ebony beneath the eyelids could be seen.

"Fear not for his visage," said the voice. "They are the eyes of Pantor, the shield bearer. There is power here that will become apparent to him the longer he is my wielder. Now, let the game begin."

"Wait, Arantar," said the prince, "what are you doing?"

"What only I can do to help," said the Huntsmaster softly. "It's all right, Raven. Get our friends into the protection. This is something I must do alone. My fate. Do you understand?"

"No, I don't!" he replied angrily. "What makes you think that fighting, and possibly dying, against whatever evil comes from that pit is helping us in any way?"

"Because Rene' says it is so."

Raven turned on the golden mage girl, his look of anger causing her to take a step back.

"Melisande and I have both come to the conclusion that the Seal of Law, *The Book of Summoning*, and those doors are all somehow interconnected. None of us wish for Arantar to face this evil alone, but if our hypothesis is correct, he is the only one of us who is now powerful enough to see it through."

"But this is insanity! Is it logical that every time the past occupant of this place wished to open one of those doors, he would call up a denizen of hell to fight? I think not! There must be another way!"

"I'm open to suggestions!" she snapped, her eyes blazing. Then, as she looked down at her feet, her eyes cooled. She looked back into those molten amber eyes and continued, "Look, Raven, I've said it before. We are searching in the dark and our choices are limited. I've looked at this from a hundred different directions and if there were another way, I haven't found it."

"Then I shall stay out here and help."

"No, my friend, you won't."

Raven turned to Arantar as that one stepped up to him and placed a strong ebony hand on his shoulder.

"You being here would be a distraction. Even with the intoxicating power I feel coursing through my body from this blade, I will need every bit of concentration I can muster to defeat the evil that might...*might* open the last door to this quest. In this, only I have a say. This is mine, and mine alone, to do. No one else can do this and no one else can help."

Arantar watched as those formidable eyes cooled and the blond head dropped. He squeezed the shoulder he held gently and those amber eyes came up to look into black.

"We have no evidence that this will even work, but we have always, as you know, tried to use the information and items we've found at hand to overcome the threats leveled against us. I believe we have been successful so far because we have been bold." Then, with a grin, "Maybe a bit of luck and the gods helped, but we are still alive and possibly a step ahead of the evil that haunts us."

"But this, Arantar? With none of us to help—"

"Ah, my friend, you underestimate Lady Rene'. If I haven't missed my guess, if there is a spell of summoning, there should be a reversal, yes?"

Those eyes took in the mage girl and he received a nod and grin.

"This is as it should be then, with a Huntsmaster breaking the trail and a King's entourage following closely in support." Arantar got the grin he was looking for and continued, "If this is a mistake, I would hope that I will survive to hear you say it."

Raven nodded and looked at his companions.

"If we are to do this, all must be in order. Rene', what must be done?"

Rene' glanced about the room, her brow knitted in deep thought.

"Eton, can that pedestal be moved within the circle?"

In answer, the big warrior walked over and lifted the heavy stand in his left hand.

"Place it in the upper corner of the triangle," Rene' directed. "If Solothon and Raven will help, I wish this book on its pedestal moved within as well."

"Lady Melisande," Arantar said softly, "if you would, take the mesh bag within also. I'd not like some demon using it as a weapon against me."

The girl nodded, rolled the bag into a tight ball, and stepped onto the pattern holding the crystal in one hand with the mesh bag under her arm. She stood next to Eton and handed him the large ball of crystal.

Rene' had the book and pedestal placed before her at one of the other points of the triangle and told Bonaire to stand at the last.

"Three Points of Power," she muttered as she opened the book to the page marked with a red ribbon.

At the top of the page, a one-line instruction in the language of mages was written. "Speak the true name thrice."

She read the name scrawled on that page in red ink.

"Amon."

The name didn't sound familiar, but the "true name" written below was long and tasted of grit as she read it slowly in her mind.

She closed the book completely, something she'd been taught to do as an apprentice to Yarda, then opened it again to the black ribbon.

The name printed neatly in black ink followed the same instructions as on the previous ribbon.

"Chaktran' Nakot'ish"

The name sounded familiar, though the familiarity escaped her. The long and involved "true name" did nothing to aid her memory. She closed the book again.

Rene' sighed and opened the book at the third ribbon, this one blue.

"Bael."

The name brought a shiver that ran over her skin like ooze. The blue ink of the scrawl seemed to be moving constantly, though remaining on the page as the name. There was a short "true name" for this one, and she closed the book on it without attempting to read it.

"You have a choice of three, Arantar," she called.

She felt, then, the tendril of power touch her mind. When it departed, it was the sword that made the choice.

"There are two over whom I have little power," the voice intoned, "but Chaktran' Nakot'ish, Heart-Render, Child Eater, is one I've wished to rend for eons!"

Rene' shivered.

"Child Eater?" said the Huntsmaster in rising anger. "Bring that vile thing to me!"

"Eton, the crystal," said the mage girl as she turned to the page marked with the black ribbon.

She began to chant the "true name" carefully, each syllable uttered clearly and perfectly. As she did so, she remembered the name. It was one that she'd heard as a child, and it belonged to the demon children checked for in their closets and under their beds before they could sleep at night. Chill bumps crawled on her skin as she began the third recitation.

At the end of the last syllable, black smoke came from the hole and descended upon the marble floor. As the being took form, the crystal changed color. It was now ebony and its shine was gone.

Arantar faced a monster out of children's nightmares that made his teeth clinch in hate and allowed the anger and power that flowed through the sword to invade his very being. His eyes narrowed.

Eight feet tall and hairy, it looked with hate-filled red eyes at the man in black. Drool dripped from its fangs and it wiped its nasty maw with the back of one hairy arm. The other controlled the massive halberd with the gleaming sharp blade at its top.

The sword sighed.

"Now, I feed!"

Anger and disgust drove the Huntsmaster as he brought the great sword up and ran at the beast. The demon spun the great spear and slashed the blade toward the on rushing ranger, only to have Arantar slide under the stroke and drive the screaming blade deep into its stomach. It howled in pain as the Huntsmaster ripped the blade free in a spray of black bile and gore.

The halberd came slicing back and again Arantar ducked under. However, the beast had learned. As the slash swept by his intended target, the demon spun the weapon and drove the shaft into Arantar's side, slamming him to the floor and sliding him toward the edge of the pit.

Raven, watching from the safety of the protective seal of Law, drew the bastard sword and looked to Rene'. She glanced over and shook her head.

"Not yet," she said softly.

The prince frowned and turned back to watch his friend.

As the great beast stomped toward the Huntsmaster to take advantage, the ranger came to his feet and moved to meet it.

This time the stroke of the halberd was low. Had Arantar been there, the blade would have removed his legs at the kneecap, but the Huntsmaster was a seasoned warrior and his instincts in battle were next to none. His senses were at peak, his body operating in the battle fury he knew so well.

He leaped and let the blade pass below him and slashed at the unprotected side as the heavy weapon pulled the demon around. The blade of the wailing sword bit deep. Blood and gore splattered on the marble floor as the angry beast turned red orbs on the cause of its pain. It snarled and brought the heavy weapon up to drive it down onto this terrible thing that had hurt it so badly, but that was not to be.

Arantar roared as he drove the five feet of screaming blade deep into the demon's chest. He felt the blade drink deeply, engorging itself in the evil soul, and with a grin of pure hate, left it there to feast.

The demon was paralyzed, its weapon held up in frozen hands. The pain-filled visage on its face seemed frozen as well as the great sword drank its fill.

Finally, as the great sword's greed sucked the last of the demon's soul, the evil being exploded into sparkling red dust that settled slowly to the marble. The halberd rang as it bounced off the marble floor and down into the pit.

Arantar felt, more than heard, the sated "Ah" from the great blade before him. He grinned and turned to the shimmering blue dome and his friends.

Rene' motioned to Eton and he lifted the crystal from its stand. Raven, once the shimmering field collapsed, ran to his friend and grabbed his shoulders. His worried look was greeted by a wide panting grin.

"How do you fare, Arantar?"

"Bruised but healing, my friend," he responded, the grin of pure wonder on his face. "Gods, Raven, what a feeling! The power! The...the—"

"I know, Huntsmaster, but you need to sit and rest," responded the blond softly.

Rene' saw the glow form around the door on the right of the carved mural. As she watched, it opened slowly and silently. Light from some unknown source came through that door and beckoned.

"What of the demon?" Arantar asked as he sat down on the cold marble floor.

"Gone," said Rene' as she stepped past them toward the open doorway on the other side of the pit. "Solothon will stay with Melisande while we look into—"

Bonaire's colorful cloak passed them at a dead run. He would be first to the treasure this time, he swore!

"Bonaire, stop!"

The words rang in the power the young prince now wielded without hesitation. The young elf skidded to stop just feet from the door and stood paralyzed by the power that enveloped him.

"Rene'," Raven said as he stepped to Bonaire's side and laid a hand on his shoulder, "scan the doorway for any magiks, traps, or...whatever." Then he turned to Bonaire.

The young elf relaxed when the prince's hand touched his shoulder. Now he looked into molten amber and for the first time was afraid of what he saw there.

"You are going to allow your greed to destroy you!" said Raven angrily. "I give you my word that should we find treasure, you will share in it as an equal. That is my solemn promise to you!" Then, softer, "Bonaire, you are a part of us, a necessary part of this mission. We would never steal from you or cause you harm, if it could be avoided. We are your friends and companions. Why can you not see that?"

The young elf hung his head, but he had no answer for the blond half elf. Raven shook his head.

"Raven!" called Rene' as she motioned toward him from the open doorway.

The prince patted the elf on the shoulder and, as he joined Rene', he looked into the room. Tables stood about haphazardly laden with precious gems and ingots of gold and silver. Crowns and scepters lay in and around chests thrown onto the floor with strings of pearl, silver, gold, and platinum.

"This is not what we've come for," he said softly as he turned and walked away.

He looked at Bonaire's pleading face and smiled.

"Take only what you can carry, my young friend," he said softly. "We still have a long way to go before we are done. Remember that."

His last words were lost as the elf skipped into the sparkling room.

Eton joined the two as they moved back toward where Arantar sat next to the protective circle.

"Eton," Raven said as he threw a thumb back toward the open door, "please see that our young friend doesn't take more than he can handle."

Eton nodded with a grin and moved silently back to the door. When Bonaire realized he was being watched, he turned toward the warrior with a guilty look on his face.

"What are you doing?" queried the big warrior.

"Why, taking inventory, of course!" replied the young elf snobbishly.

Eton leaned against the doorpost with a grin and watched.

Chapter Forty-two

"There must be another way."

Raven looked from Arantar to Rene'. He leaned against the wall between the two doors and glanced to where Melisande talked with Solothon next to the Circle of Protection.

"Arapel'ho said he had no power over the other two names marked in the book." he said as his eyes snapped to Arantar. "I'll not have you face something you have no chance against."

Something dug into his back through the mailed shirt. He levered away from the wall and stepped away, his brow furrowed.

"What I don't understand is the sword," he continued.

"What about it?" asked Rene', her head tilted to one side.

"If what we've heard is true, Pantor fought on the other side but switched because of his wife. The histories say nothing of this, but how do you explain Hellshadow and Hell Razor? Were I an evil sorcerer, cleric, or fighter, would I have a mount that is half-breed Unicorne and Nightmare and is seemingly more intelligent than I? Then, would I have a dragon-blest sword that seeks only the souls of evil? It just doesn't make sense!"

Rene' thought about what Raven had said, weighing each anomaly against what she'd studied concerning the Mage War. Her left elbow was cupped in her right hand and the fingers of her left tapped softly against her chin.

"I agree, my friend. It doesn't make much sense. Arapel'ho states that he is linked to the Lords of Light, yet in all I've read, Pantor was not. Was he approached by the Triad? Was it his wife, the Cheal, who somehow changed this? It is an interesting quandary, Raven, but, should the answers not be forthcoming from the library here, I'm afraid those answers will have to wait. Myrlin made no reference to Pantor, only Radagast."

Raven glanced about the large room, his eyes stopping at each of his friends. At a noise from the treasure room, he glanced back at that door. Then his eyes were drawn to the mural.

"If we ever get back to Catlorian," Rene' was saying, "I'll look into—"

"Wait!" interrupted the prince in a hushed tone. He walked to the mural and traced the engraved dragon's head with a finger.

"What is it?" asked the Huntsmaster.

"Rene', what did the scroll say in its poem?" asked Raven in answer.

"What?"

"The scroll you found down in that room with the—"

"Oh, yes!" she said as she dug into her pouch. In a moment she held the piece of parchment up and smoothed it. "Let's see," she whispered. "'Beware the darken—'"

"Not that," Raven interrupted again, "the last part."

"Hmm. Ah! 'Before the door with no escape, look for the lock upon the dragon's nape.'"

"Look here," said the prince as his finger found an oddly shaped hole in the carved neck of the dragon. "What else did it say?"

"'Within the stock, find the key.' What does that mean?"

Arantar now looked at the carving with new interest. The dragon was carved by a master, its claws reaching out for the scampering cattle.

"Cattle?" he said softly. "My father had several farmers he visited from time to time. They have cattle on their farms to subsidize their income, but they never called them cattle. They called them *stock*!"

He and Raven both looked, but they could find nothing in the herd of carved cows that could represent a key.

"Come away from there for a moment, Arantar, that I might look," said the girl.

Arantar gave up his position and watched as the mage girl began to trace the lines of the cattle carved in marble.

She found nothing and almost gave up. Then she thought of who had probably placed this here. Would it be simple? Not likely. Magical? She looked at the carving again, this time with eyes filled with Mage power.

There was a slight glimmer from the udders of one of the cows. She touched it with one small finger and was rewarded as the udder lifted back out of the way. Her finger found a ring secreted within and she withdrew it. It was gold with several small jewels mounted rather haphazardly about it.

Raven looked at it, then at the hole in the dragon's neck.

"Try it here," he said and motioned toward the dragon.

After turning it several times, Rene' found one way that fit perfectly. The ring slipped into the hole, and it clicked into place as the mage girl turned her finger. There was a snap from the direction of the other door and, as they all turned toward it, it opened silently.

Eton leaned against the doorpost of the treasury until he heard the click. He glanced toward his friends casually, but when the far door swept slowly open, he put himself into motion.

"Solothon!" he grated as his hands filled with steel.

The knight looked up from Melisande's face and was instantly galvanized into action. His sword cleared its sheath before he'd taken two steps. He stopped at the ready next to the big warrior as they waited for...

"If anything were coming out of there," said Rene' as she moved up behind the men with Raven, "it would have been at our throats by now."

"That may be true," replied Raven as he drew the bastard sword and moved the mage girl out of the way, "but let us not take chances."

He nodded at both Solothon and Eton, then tapped the door wide open with the point of his blade. Eton put his back to the wall next to the doorway as Raven stepped around in front. There was light inside, but not much else save dust. The prince glanced cautiously inside to left and right of the doorway before he stepped within.

Eton waited only long enough for Raven to clear the door and slid in to the lighted room behind him and to the left. Solothon repeated this move to the prince's right and they all gazed about the totally empty room.

"This cannot be," said Raven softly.

"What is it?" asked Rene' as she followed them in.

She glanced around at the empty shelves and her heart sank. Yet there was something about this room that she couldn't...It felt odd.

"Kohl said we'd find the treasury and the library here," said the prince. "We found the first, but can this be what is left of the last?"

"I suppose they could have taken the books with them when they left," commented the knight, a question in his voice.

"No," said Raven slowly.

There, in the corner, there was something—or something that was supposed to be nothing. His anger boiled. He'd allowed Arantar to risk his life to open these doors, yet there was nothing?

"I don't believe it!" he spat as his anger and will drove the illusion from his eyes.

There it was then, stripped of its illusion. A Pentacle, smaller than those they'd used through their hardships, but a Druid's Pentacle nonetheless. Books lined the shelves in pristine order and in obvious sets.

"There!" he said and moved to stride toward the small pentacle.

"What?" asked the knight as he grabbed Raven's shoulder.

"Don't you see?" said the savon'el as he gestured around the room. Then he stopped and dropped his hand to his side as he saw the confusion on the knight's face.

They didn't see, he found, as he looked from one face to the other. They didn't see at all! He realized that the illusion was an individual spell and each of them was affected independently. He turned to Rene'.

"It is magiked, Rene', but if you look hard in disbelief you will see, in the far right corner, a small pentacle." Then, to the others, "Look hard, all of you."

Then he slipped away from the knight's hand and moved to the pentacle. Rene' followed Raven, but down the left side of the room while Eton flanked his right. Solothon stopped in the middle of the room, his frown displaying his question.

"Melisande! Bonaire!" the Huntsmaster called from the doorway.

Melisande stepped quickly toward him, but Bonaire simply stuck his head out of the treasury with a perturbed look on his face.

"Bonaire," repeated Arantar, "come on!"

"But I'm not finished yet!"

"Yes, you are!" the Huntsmaster replied sharply. "Get over here now! That will wait!"

"Okay! Okay!" complained the elf as he tightened the straps to his overladen pack and walked heavily to the ranger's side. "What's so important?"

The Huntsmaster took in the bulges in the elf's pockets and the obvious weight of the backpack.

"I hope you've left room enough for food," he commented. He received a sidelong glance from Bonaire and continued, "We may need to move quickly. Are you capable?"

"Sure! Sure!" replied the elf as he stepped through the doorway toward the others. "Don't worry about me!"

Arantar heard the telltale rattle at each step the elf made and looked skyward.

"Will he ever learn?" he asked of any deity that bothered to listen.

Raven stepped into the Pentacle and turned to the others.

"I'm standing in the center of a Pentacle," he said. "There are five small pillars. Rene', you are—"

Rene' walked right into one of the hidden pillars. Raven started toward her, but she waved him off. She knew it was there now, and she would be damned if she would let it stay hidden. This isn't magic, she thought to herself. This is merely illusion.

She closed her eyes and remembered the spell that would remove the illusion from her sight. She said the words softly and they rippled throughout the room.

Gradually, like rippling fog, the illusion lifted from their eyes.

"Melisande," she said to the cleric as that one glanced about the huge library with her mouth open, "check the books to see if there's any information in them while I check this. Kohl said something about an index…"

"I've got it," said the cleric as she stepped to the card catalog next to the door.

The Pentacle had but one destination. Three identical runes were etched in silver on each of the ivory pillars. She looked closer and found that though the three runes were repeated exactly on each of four pillars, they were reversed on the fifth.

"It has one destination," she said in a musing tone, her brows knit in concentration. "These runes are the key to that place. See?"

Raven traced the lines of the runes with his eyes, knowing that to touch them meant energizing them. Then he saw the fifth pillar.

"What of that one?" he asked.

"That is the thieves pillar, if I'm not mistaken," she replied. "As with other Pentacles, the thieves' runes are backward, but still lead to the same place."

"Where?"

"I don't know," she replied as she turned toward the door, "but I'm certainly going to find out."

Melisande followed the mage girl out into the main hall and up to the pedestal. They spoke quietly as Rene' retrieved a strip of leather from her pack, looped it about the closed book, and tied it tight. After muttering the words of binding that locked her knot in place, she turned to the cleric.

"Melisande, we will need to take the crystal. Would you bag it, please?"

The mage girl slipped the book into her backpack and lifted it to her shoulders while Melisande crossed to their pile of possessions and placed the crystal in the Urhu bag.

"Where are we going?" asked the cleric as she shouldered the mesh bag and lifted her pack.

"That," said Rene' as she pointed at the open door, "is the door to the library and probably the armory. I think that the Pentacle is the hallway to that place and I'm going to find it. Coming?" she added as she turned on her heel and started for the open door.

Melisande shrugged and followed.

Raven and the others, except Bonaire, were inspecting the shelves of books and the small pentacle when the women arrived. Bonaire stood at the door and, in between angry looks at Arantar, glanced back at the door where his treasure lay.

"I think we should all go through together," said the mage girl as she stepped into the room.

"Through?" asked the prince. "What are you talking about?"

"The real library, of course," she replied. "It must be on the other side of that Pentacle."

"This will take some discussion, Rene'," responded the prince sharply. "The library you seek is right here."

"Not really," she said as she moved toward the Pentacle. "I have the items I was sent to retrieve, but not the information. Melisande has looked at the titles of these books, but—with a few exceptions—these are all reference books found in any temple in Catlorian."

"Listen, Rene, we all want to succeed, but this...this is a blind jump without even Shadow to guide us. We don't even know that the information you seek is there. I'm just not sure of the risk."

"Fine," she replied, "but tell me this: have we come all of this way to give up now? Is this any more difficult than all the other things we've gone through?"

"I can't ask—"

"Nor should you," she interrupted. "I have come this far in the knowledge that somewhere here the task I was set will come to fruition. I am going to the library and I wish you would also."

Raven watched the mage girl step up on to the Pentacle and turn to face him with the black-haired cleric joining her, but standing well to the rear with the steel mesh bag. He looked back into the faces of his other companions and his head fell. He knew she was right, but he hated it.

"I don't know how any of us could leave here if we stayed, nor if we would even be allowed to leave. I will be joining Rene'. Each of you must make your own choice."

Then he turned and stepped up beside Rene'. The others, with the exception of Bonaire, quickly arrayed themselves on the small Pentacle. Melisande stood as far from the rest as she could with her bundle of misery.

"But, uh," stammered the young elf, "who will see to the horses?"

"Kohl will see to them," said the prince. "You must choose. If you choose to stay here and we do not return, you may find yourself very alone. Then again, you might find a way out." He shrugged. "Like I said, it's your choice."

Bonaire hesitated for just a moment before joining them on the Pentacle.

"Besides," he commented as he patted his pockets, "I've got our treasure."

"Good, then," said Prince Raven. "Rene'?"

The mage girl stepped to the pillar that would have been used by mages on other pentacles and touched each of the runes in turn. The room disappeared and they floated in time and space.

While with a normal Pentacle traveling would have taken a fraction of a second, this trip strangely took considerably longer. Finally the murk began to lift beyond the boundaries of the silver platform and it turned a soft blue.

The chamber was blue. Soft, quiet, relaxing blue crystal.

As each of the companions looked about the room, each felt the exhaustion of the past days in every pore of their being. Bonaire was the first to slide to the floor and curl up in sleep.

"This can't be happening," thought Rene' as her eyes began to droop. Then, as she shook her head, she realized their danger.

"Stay awake!" she said sternly, but it was too late.

Somehow the magiks in the room had no effect on Eton. He caught Melisande as she succumbed and laid her gently to the floor. The others slipped slowly to the floor where they stood, unable to combat the spell on their own.

Eton looked from them to Rene'.

The mage girl had thrown off the spell as soon as she'd realized what it was. She looked from her downed friends to Eton, then at the chamber itself.

It was a faceted blue crystal dome over a blue crystal floor. A cabinet of fragile blue crystal sat next to one of the larger facets in the far wall. Inside the cabinet, four books could be seen, all bound in what looked to be leather. Next to the case on a small stand, a tiny silver triangle hung with a small hammer.

Rene' looked closer at the large facet near the cabinet and gasped. It was thin, very thin. It seemed that it would shatter if one were to blow on it, so thin it was, but that was not the worst of it.

Through the translucent crystal, a thick fog roiled in vile contortions.

"Eton?" she whispered. "I fear I've brought us to our deaths." Then she explained the situation.

Eton thought for a long moment before he spoke.

"Would one of those books," he pointed at the case, "possibly hold the answer to our dilemma?"

"Possibly, but how to get to them? There is no door in the cabinet and it seems to be very fragile. The choice is this: Do I break that case to get to the books, at the risk that the vibration would shatter that portal, or do I ring the triangle in the hope that it would shatter the case, but not the portal? Whatever churns on the other side of that crystal portal looks to be poisonous or caustic, or both. How do I choose?"

"If it were a foe before us, I would know what to do, but it is not," he said softly. "In this, I have no experience. I leave it to you to choose. Any way it turns out, know that I've enjoyed your company for the little time we've spent." He turned back to the others.

"Eton?" she called softly. As he turned to her, she continued, "Promise me something?"

"Anything."

"I do not wish to die in pain."

Eton saw the fear in her eyes and knew what she asked.

"You won't," he said.

He drew his long sword and, cradling the blade in his gauntleted left hand, watched as she studied the cabinet and the triangle.

She took the small hammer from the stand and held it to her breasts. The wrong choice would kill them all, she knew, and there was a possibility that there wasn't a right one. There was no more time. Her courage was slipping away as fast as the air in this confined chamber.

Her hand stretched out with the hammer and she tapped the triangle.

It was a sweet sound, high and mellow. Rene' closed her eyes to listen to it. It seemed to sustain itself forever.

Behind her, Eton held the blade of the sword cradled in his left hand. If the wall shattered, he would drive the blade into the back of her neck and into her brain. She would feel very little pain, he hoped. Then he would stand, weapons in hand, and except his fate.

The bookcase began to resonate at the same pitch as the triangle. Small cracks formed in the smooth top as the sweet tone swept through it. Suddenly it turned to dust and the tone faded into nothingness.

With a shaking hand, the big warrior returned his sword to its sheath and stepped away from the mage girl. The wall was still intact.

Rene' knelt and picked up the first of the books while Eton moved back to his sleeping companions and tried to make them, at least, appear more comfortable.

The book was titled *The Rise and Fall of the Lords of Light*. She turned the leather bound book over in her hands and looked at the next. *Celebration of Light* was the title. She laid the first book aside and turned to the table of contents of the second. Here, the listings told her that this book was a textbook of devotions required for the worship of the three Lords: Peace, War, and Knowledge.

She laid that one aside for the moment and picked up the third. *Druid's Pentacles: Use and Divination* was written in blue on the brownish red leather.

People had used the Pentacles for ages without a thought. Here, in her hands, she held the handbook for those, and from the size of the volume, there was much more than travel intended for them.

Rene' almost opened that book in her need for more knowledge, and she would have had it not been for the condition of the last book.

It was old and tattered, yet had no title engraved upon the rich blue leather. She stacked the handbook for the Pentacles on top of the other two books and picked this last one up.

She opened it to the first page, but found it blank. She flipped to the second and found the same. She thumbed through it and, in shock, realized that every page was the same. Blank!

She set it down carefully in her lap, a look of confusion on her face, and lifted the worship book from the pile she'd made of the other three. As she read through the table of contents, she couldn't get the idea out of her head that someone, or many others, had used that blank book. It looked too used and beaten. Something was strange here, and she couldn't put her finger on it.

Under the title chapter for the Lord of Knowledge was written, "Reference: Tairmon's Book of Faith." She turned to the noted the section and read.

"Tairmon's Book of Faith is the life's work of the High Priest Tairmon and is the central source of catechism and rights for the proper study and worship of the Lord Infinitus, Lord of Knowledge.

"It is an old book, studied by many. If you are worthy, the tattered pages will give up its treasure of knowledge and joy to the third of the Triad, Infinitus, and will guide the acolyte to high priest and beyond."

She glanced down at the worn tome in her lap.

"If this were my private book of worship," she thought, "how would I..."

She dug into the beliefs that made her priestess and brought the divining power of that faith to her vision. She had thought to see if some residual power remained that would indicate that a priest of power had formed an illusion about the tattered book, causing all who saw it to see only blank pages.

The book glowed so strongly that she had to shut her eyes to the glare and release the power she'd drawn to her sight.

She closed the book and set it back onto her lap as she leaned back on her heels. She needed answers and a funnel for her guilt.

"If one is worthy," she whispered. But was she?

She felt responsible for the danger in which they now found themselves and was quite prepared to pay any price to save her friends. For her, the only way to find absolution was to call on the goddess who had been the focal point of her life for so many years.

"Eton?" she said softly as she looked over her shoulder at the big warrior.

"Yes?" he replied as he turned from placing a cloak beneath Raven's head.

"I am going to...meditate for a bit. I won't be sleeping, but I will be looking for answers."

"I know the ways of Elvin kind, Rene'."

"I know," she said softly. "I just...I just wanted you to know."

"I'll be here when you return."

She gave him a small grin and nodded. He went back to seeing after Raven and she turned back to her mission.

She closed her eyes and let all of her worries wash away, cleansing her mind for what she hoped would happen. She reached for the small golden heart that had always rested at her throat. She sighed softly as she remembered where it was now. All she could do was try.

"Lady Celeste, goddess of Beauty and Romanc—"

"Yes, my sweet Rene?" came the throaty voice of her fantasies to her mind.

"Is that you?" she gasped in thought. "Is it really—"

"Did you do not call, beautiful child? Yes, it is I."

Rene', now deep in trance, sobered to the confessions she knew she had to make, the confessions she would make to save her friends, even if the penance would be her life.

"I...I've done badly, my lady."

"In what way?"

"I've dragged my friends to certain death."

"Have you?"

"Why, of course—"

"Did they complain?"

"No, but—"

"Then it must have been by their choice."

"No! I was going and I forced—"

"How?"

"By...by—"

"By being a friend?"

"Well, yes, I suppose."

"Would you deny them the right to follow a friend, even to their deaths?"

"If I could avoid it, and I could, yes."

"Could you?"

"I didn't have to come here. I could have stayed away. Maybe if I had—"

"No, you couldn't."

If a thought could have an open-mouth reaction, Rene's would have.

"Listen to me, my sweet child. You could not have kept from this place, or one like it, even if you had tried. It is by your choice and fate that you are here now."

"What do you mean, my Lady?"

"It is strange, I know, but you were never meant to be mine forever. You are too curious for the limitations I've set upon you. You have a hunger, an almost insatiable hunger, for knowledge. If you'd had more patience, you might have become a sage, but your impatience to know now would not have allowed a moment's peace."

"Have I been unfaithful?" asked the girl in anguish. "I've always tried to do my best."

"And you have, Rene'. You have. I have never been served by one with more grace, caring, and beauty before. Your heart is pure."

Rene' felt the goddess pause.

"But, Rene', you have another destiny, one you've been traveling toward ever since you found Cashme're in the forest. You have a calling. Go to it."

"But what of my love and devotion for you?"

"I shall hold that sacred for an eternity, and though I will not be able to help you—"

"Wait! You won't—"

"You were never mine, my beautiful Rene'. Your mind is too precious, too seeking. Mine was to help you attain this point in your growth, nothing more. I shall miss you."

"Please, don't—"

Rene' felt the slight warmth on her forehead as if she had been kissed. Instantly she felt the power she had within her, gained as a priestess of the Lady Celeste, drain from her body.

The loss was indescribable, and as she came out of her trance, the tears of loss and loneliness traced a path down her cheeks and dropped from her eyes to the book she held in her lap. She opened her eyes and, through the tears, saw the blue book in her lap change.

As she watched, silver threads began to appear through the binding. Soon, the words "Tairmon's Book of Faith" became visible on the cover. She dried her eyes on her sleeve and opened the book.

The very first page proclaimed, "To serve the first, seek the last."

This was a test, she thought, and her agile mind solved the riddle in short order. She turned to the very last page. There, a portrait of a necklace was revealed, the drawing so perfect that every detail of the heavy golden chain and pendant could be seen.

The pendant was that of a bright sunburst of gold surrounding the golden leaves of an open book. It seemed that she could touch it, so real did it appear.

Then she read the caption, "Have the courage to release me."

"That was the last thing written on the scroll," she whispered as she moved her hand to touch the pendant in the painting. "I don't..."

Her fingers touched the pendant and it moved! With a shaking hand, she reached into the page. The pendant glowed momentarily as the girl's fingers wrapped lovingly about it and a power, almost the same as what she lost but stronger, more powerful, rushed up her arm to envelop her in loving warmth.

She basked in it, drank of it as if it were an endless fountain. She pulled the necklace from the page and fastened it about her throat. She stood and turned slowly to Eton and her sleeping friends.

The warrior felt her eyes on him and he turned. He saw the large pendant and the sweet smile and grew cautious. He turned at a crouch and started to say her name but stopped.

The pendant began to glow and a tiny flash of light leaped from it into the air before Rene' as if a living thing. It spun and danced for a bit, then began a strange pattern. Faster and faster it went until the pattern was revealed.

It was a shining infinity sigil, held before the golden-haired girl in power older than time itself. Suddenly a cocoon of white light encompassed the mage girl.

Eton started for her, his gauntleted hand within the basket hilt at his back, but stopped as the light dissipated.

Rene' stood before the spinning sigil, her golden hair now a deep auburn with a white streak that flowed from the front of her hair to rest softly on her right shoulder. Her dress was white and layered gossamer. Her Elvin cloak too,had changed. It was now a deep blood red.

Chapter Forty-three

"Do not sleep through the rebirth in power of the Lords of Light." The voice was powerful yet gentle. Eton felt a stirring at his feet and looked down at the prince. The half elf's eyes were open and questioning. The warrior reached down and helped him to his feet while keeping his eyes on the spinning sigil and Rene'.

Arantar went from a dreamless sleep to being wide awake and in one smooth motion was on his feet. He took in everything at a glance and, seeing no alternative or a bona fide threat, waited. The sword in his hands was silent and, to Arantar's senses, reluctant to move. He placed it point down in front of him and rested his hands upon the pommel.

"Wha—" Bonaire came to his feet unsteadily, but he was silenced by the Huntsmaster's hand held toward him.

Solothon was on his feet the moment his eyes opened. His hand went to the hilt of his sword, but he stopped when he saw the Huntsmaster's hand held toward Bonaire. He looked in the direction Arantar was looking as he held a hand down for Melisande.

The black-haired cleric left the bagged crystal where it was and came to her feet. Then she crossed behind the knight to a better vantage point, one that—if she'd thought about it— would also allow her more room if fighting should be the course of the day. She listened as the voice, strangely wise and loving but with power she could feel and beyond any she'd ever felt before, spoke again.

"I am Infinitus, Third of the Triad. I have accepted the first of hopefully many followers this day. It has been many ages since this pleasure has been mine and I revel in it!"

After a moment, the voice spoke again.

"Knowledge is to be dispersed, not hidden away. All questions—"

"Will be answered—" intoned Rene' softly.

"To the best of one's ability, using care and common sense as a guide."

The voice then seemed to turn to the rest of the companions.

"Each of you may gain, each in his own way, in service to the Lords of Light. This is a choice you alone must make, with no coercion allowed, as dictated by the Creator."

"But, Lord," said Arantar slowly, "though three of our number are Elvin, the rest are not. Well, not totally."

"Long ago, we of the Triad kept to our chosen, those of the Sylvan Sha'terra. In coming back, here and now, we sought counsel from the only being here as old as we, and his counsel was pure. We left the last time this evil came upon this world, thinking to follow our chosen to some peaceful paradise. It was not so.

"Now, we come with an understanding that all the races of mankind have those within who, by dint of character, are as worthy as the Sidhe and, according to our counselor, less demanding. Those we now seek."

"To what purpose?" asked the black-haired cleric.

"To aid humanity in its struggle against the coming evil, as you are."

Melisande nodded, but her frown was one of doubt and her hand was still within that secret pocket grasping the maul.

"Melisande Dorn," came the voice, deep and gentle, "you serve a goddess whose main joy is love, caring, and the proliferation of happiness."

Melisande's head jerked up and her frown deepened.

"Yet in your heart there is no forgiveness, no joy, no happiness. There is darkness there, a malice hidden from open view and, though your innate goodness fights to control it, it reveals itself all too readily."

Melisande was taken aback by this accusation, but her anger at this admission came flashing from her eyes.

"I meant no insult," said the voice a bit softer. "Knowledge is to be dispersed, but truth is truth. Peace is a goal that is not always attainable. We of the Triad seek those whose talents and convictions will not faint at hardship, but will harden as steel in the face of danger. You are such a one. Will you serve?"

Melisande's frown softened. Her anger sometimes drove her far beyond the bounds of her faith, her anger and malice a joy in battle. Many times through their trials she'd wondered why her goddess had stayed with her, why Lady Freya hadn't simply withdrawn her power and let the girl drown in her own hate. The Lady of Love and Caring deserved better! But this offer…

"How can I serve, Lord?"

"The Lord of Battle has need of a cleric. Fear not that, to serve, you must lose what compassion you still hold. In war, one has need for compassion, honor, and the comforting touch of a cleric, else battle becomes evil and serves no purpose. One must be chosen who will not flinch at the hardships that war provides, but can still feel compassion even for a downed foe. Are you she?"

"And if I fail?"

"I have searched the minds of your friends, and from what I've seen, in this you could never fail."

Melisande glanced at Rene' and saw the tear that ran down her cheek as the mage girl smiled at her.

"Then," she said as she bowed her head, "I am she."

The Pouncing Falcon embroidered on her cloak faded as the cloak turned jet black. The power that had coursed through her veins receded for but a moment. Then a power older, more powerful, and more attuned with her state of being roared in to fill that void. She breathed deep of her new wholeness and liked it.

"There is much you need to learn, priestess, before you can truly appreciate the faith bestowed upon you. Priestess Iaprene' will show you where to find that knowledge within the Celebrations."

Rene' bent down and retrieved the book. Then, moving around the sigil, she stepped in front of the cleric.

"Is this what you truly wish, my sister?"

"Yes, Rene', it is," Melisande answered softly, certain now that this was what she'd been bred to do.

Rene' grinned and opened the book. It fell open to the beginning of the Celebrations to the Lord of War.

"Then," said the mage girl with a grin, "read the passage below the sigil."

Melisande saw the skull, but it was gold and a softer design. Then she remembered Shadow's barding and smiled.

Below the sigil were the words, "Call the name Thanatos."

The cleric looked back into the mage girl's eyes, now strangely a paler gold than before. Rene' nodded, closed the book, and moved back beyond the symbol of Infinitus.

Melisande felt that this was her moment. The power she would gain was there within her waiting for acceptance. All she had to do…

"Thanatos!" called the cleric, a stern concentration locked into her mind.

Suddenly a small man dressed in gray appeared before her. His smile was framed in the silver-streaked blackness of his close-cropped beard. He removed his floppy hat and bowed.

"You called, cheesa?"

Her instant anger caused the smile to widen as he returned the hat to its place on his head.

"Who are you?" she asked, a bit more forcefully than necessary, thought Rene'.

"I've been called many names, cheesa: Thanatos, the White Horseman." Then, as his black eyes met her green pools, "Death is the name most use though."

"But, I thought…" she began a bit more contrite.

"You thought correctly, child. You will serve the Lord of Battle. I am here only as a courtesy to the Triad. Did you not know that Death and War are cousins?"

He grinned as the girl's lips parted in shock.

"War always begets death, cheesa, though war is not an exclusive commodity. I don't seek for men to die; I am but the gardener of their souls, harvested and delivered to the Creator for judgment. All, save Elvin kind, pass through me eventually."

"Then," Melisande asked, "why are you here?"

"To welcome you to service to the Lords of Light. That is all, cheesa." Then, as if an afterthought, "Oh, yes…and to present you with a gift."

He pulled a scroll, tied with a black ribbon, from the inside pocket of his gray coat and handed it to Melisande.

"Take this and your weapon, with which you are most proficient. Read the words as you hold your weapon before you and I will do the rest." He stepped back and smiled. "I will see you again, cheesa, but hopefully not for a very, very long time."

Then he was gone.

Melisande looked from Rene' to the Huntsmaster and at Arantar's nod she pulled the great maul from its pocket and held it in her left hand. With her right, she flipped the scroll open and, after reading the words slowly to herself, she held the maul out and spoke the words.

The shaft of the maul began to vibrate in her hand. Then slowly it turned white as ivory while the steel band at the top and the cap at the other end turned silver. As the transformation finished, it became almost weightless. She frowned at the weight difference.

"Worry not, daughter of U'Marz! Your weapon is only weightless to you. Others will feel its weigh, sure enough."

The voice was deep and amused. Its owner materialized next to the infinity symbol and grinned.

He was all of eight feet tall, muscled to perfection and dressed in kilt and tartan. His bright red beard was contorted in a smile that showed his strong teeth and flashing green eyes. On his back, a great blade smoldered in perpetual fire. He held his hand out to the black-haired cleric and knelt. It contained a pin of gold, a sunburst in which a soft featured golden skull rested.

As Melisande took the pin and began pinning it to the leather vest, Eton stepped forward and knelt, both blades out and crossed before him.

"You know me, boy?" asked the large being in his clipped tone.

"I've supped with you, drank with you, and fought by your side, Lord."

"Aye, that you have, but what of the token for peace you wear?"

"Peace?"

"Aye, lad, the token for the Lord of Peace and Law. Though you are of another world, I offer you service to me, but first you must cast away that symbol. There is no room for peace in what I do, boy. Battle is what I offer, remorseless war for the sake of balance. Make your choice, boy!"

"He means the ring, Eton."

There, on the other side of the symbol still flashing before Rene', stood the man they'd met at Rairy's cottage. He stood with his arms folded and a grin on his lips.

"You're...But I thought—"

"Yes, I am that Paladin, commander of the Talon of Light during the Mage War. I am also the Lord of Peace and Law, First in the Triad, Lords of Light."

He made a short, grinning bow and stepped over to face Eton as that one stood up.

"Anteroe said you'd come to Raven, and it was important that he survive. I just helped you to put things into a better perspective."

Eton grinned and nodded.

"Now, you wouldn't enjoy following my doctrine, my friend. Too many restrictions. I do not hold with war for war's sake. I believe that if all else fails and war is inevitable, war should be fought to win, but only until the other side quits and reasonable men can sit down and come to a non-violent agreement. Peace.

"I won't insult you by implying that you would rather fight than have peace, for I know that is not the truth. However, the truth is you are a born warrior, bred for fighting. Restrictions would but hamper you in the prosecution of war. That, I would never want."

Paladin held a silver-gloved hand toward the warrior, but was surprised when Eton took the ring from his finger and crossed to Prince Raven. He held out the ring on the palm of his right hand and lowered his head.

"Every warrior of any intelligence knows that he needs direction, my lord."

Raven looked from the ring, to Eton, and then to Paladin. He returned the nod from the latter and took the ring from the warrior's hand. Then he placed his other on Eton's shoulder.

"Every ruler craves peace, my friend," he said softly, "but we depend on warriors to win and hold it. Peace will be my goal, but honoring just warriors will be my life's work."

Raven slipped the ring onto his left little finger and bowed to the Lord of Peace.

Paladin glanced at the knight and cocked his head.

"And what of you, Sir Solothon Calendera Shan'troa?"

"I thank you for your offer, Lord," the knight replied sternly, "but I serve the Mother of Creation. She I will continue to serve."

"As shall I," stated the Huntsmaster softly.

"In you both I see she has worthy followers. I am pleased."

U'Marz caught sight of the great black sword in Arantar's hands and, as he drew his flaming sword, a solid barrier of fire formed about the Huntsmaster.

"Do you wish to take up the banner of Pantor?"

"If that be my fate," replied Arantar sternly.

Lord U'Marz looked deep into those eyes, looking past the black and into the ranger's soul. Then he grinned.

"It is not," he said with a chuckle. "You would try, I can see that, but Arapel'ho would most likely get you killed. Your Grey Wolf, at least, will follow you and not the other way around."

The Lord of Battle raised a hand and the great black sword disappeared.

"Keep the armor, if you will," he continued as Arantar's eyes returned to ice blue, "for services rendered to the Lords of Light."

"I thank you, Lord," replied the Huntsmaster with a short bow. As he took his great sword from Solothon, who had carried it since the summoning, he asked, "What of my clothing?"

"That armor is somewhat special, young ranger. Maybe you've noted the absence of catch and strap. Your will can remove it at a thought and will return it at need. My thanks to you and the Mother."

Then he turned back to Melisande.

"My little priestess, I see that you have the propensity to use that weapon, but you need more. I offer training in the fighting skills you will need in the future, if you desire."

"Maybe later, m'lord. Now I am in the midst of a mission with my friends and haven't the time. I thank you."

"Time means nothing to us, priestess," he said as he reached out and took her hand.

She stiffened and moments later the Lord of Battle released her.

"I shall be watching!" he said.

Then he disappeared.

"To you all, for service in the cause of the Triad, Lords of Light, I thank you," came the deep voice again.

Then the sigil of Infinitus also vanished.

Raven moved to Paladin's side as that Lord watched the friends and companions sort through their packs and make ready to move.

"Lord Paladin," asked the blond, "what can you tell me of the strife around my homeland? I've heard that Heartland is basically blockaded with gualu soldiers and that bands were, at least a month ago, striking at the Western Border."

"I am not at liberty, due to restrictions I have from the Creator, to say all that I wished, but I can tell you this. Laranthia was attacked by a large force," Solothon's head shot up at that, and the Triad Lord looked over as he added, "but they were thrown back time and again by the Prince's Own and the young Knights of the Laurel. They finally gave up and limped away.

However, other smaller villages were sacked and burned, the young women taken, and the men slaughtered."

"What about Borderlend?" asked Bonaire as he walked heavily toward Paladin.

"Sorry, my young friend, but it was raided and burned. Many of the men were killed, the women were killed or taken, and the village burned to the ground. The few survivors were taken to Heartstone by a battalion of rangers."

The tears rolled down the young elf's cheeks.

"Borderlend is essentially gone, my friend. I'm sorry."

Bonaire broke down in great gasping sobs. Melisande ran to him and held him until the young elf quieted.

"We must be on our way, Lord Paladin," said the blond half elf. "If you—"

"Hold that thought, young prince," said the Lord as he moved to Rene' and Arantar. "You have found the Bands of Balance."

"So it seems, Lord," replied Rene'. She looked at the floor while her left hand absently rubbed the white skin.

"I see that you have already run into some of the restrictions as well."

Arantar nodded and then asked, "I don't understand, Lord Paladin, if these were made for Pantor and his bride, why can we not touch?"

"Because these were a cruel joke brought on by Banshe'e. Though Lord Rairy wished to make those for the lovers as a wedding gift, he allowed Banshe'e to aid in their characteristics. I do not believe that Rairy knew of the real reason Banshe'e wanted to help, but I feel it was jealousy. Banshe'e wasn't happy and wanted none else to have that happiness. I've heard that Pantor and Shareen died here, victims of Banshe'e insane paranoia. I also believe that their deaths helped to convince Rairy to change."

"That makes more sense," stated the mage girl. "I suppose Arantar and I will have to work this out in some way."

"Not necessarily," said the Triad Lord as he took Rene's white hand and Arantar's ebony one and brought them together. At their astonished looks, he continued, "As I said, a cruel joke, but one that can be reversed."

Rene' watched as her arm again turned to a golden tan and Arantar's changed to match his color.

"Don't worry, my friends," Paladin said as they looked up at him, shock written upon their faces. "At need, they will come back, your Ebony Force, Arantar, and Alabaster Peace, Lady Rene'. I've simply removed the restrictions.

Had I left them as they were, not only could you never touch, but you would never be greater than one hundred paces from each other. That was Banshe'e's joke. Always together, yet never together.

"Now, if necessary and you, Huntsmaster, are within a mile of the Lady Rene', she can call you, and if *you* wish, you can switch. It is no longer the choice of the bands. You will also find that you still have that...connection."

"Thank you, Lord Paladin," said the Huntsmaster as he took the mage girl's tiny hand in his.

"Lord Paladin," said Raven as the Triad Lord turned back to him. "We now have many things to think about and do. The problem remains, however, how do we leave here?"

"By using the Druid's Pentacle just beyond this wall," said Rene' softly as she pointed toward the thin blue crystal facet. "I remember seeing it on the map at Rairy's cottage, but it is so clear to me that I almost feel that I could read the fine print at the bottom..." She gasped. "I *can* read the fine print and everything else about that map!"

Paladin chuckled.

"The curse of Infinitus, my dear. Any question will have an answer. You have access to all of the knowledge you've touched in your life. If you've seen it, you will remember it. Unless you can somehow learn to control it, it could become tedious."

"Maybe," she answered with a grin, "but I doubt it. Unfortunately, I have no answer for that noxious-looking vapor."

"Simple," he replied as he stepped over to the thin sheet of crystal and rapped once with the ring on his finger.

The shattered crystal tumbled to the ground as all of the companions watching instinctively held their breath. However, instead of cloying, caustic poison, the air without was fresh and clear.

They were inside a cavern in the Northeastern Mountain Range. A rough pathway led to the opening in the mountain face and continued on some distance away to the Druid's Pentacle Rene' had said was there.

As they came closer to the Pentacle, they saw the horses just off of the pathway, looking sleek and well-fed, saddled and provisioned for travel. The raven perched on the cantle of Arantar's roan while the puma lay at the feet of the big black warhorse, Shadow.

Just off of the Pentacle, Kohl was tending a small fire. The smell of fresh-brewed Kaff reached them and began to help them all relax.

Raven came to Bonaire then and, after nodding to both Melisande and Arantar, led the elf to the campfire with an arm about his shoulders. The rest followed.

Paladin took a cup of the Kaff and turned to Raven.

"I will not join you on your journey back. Know that, should you need me, I shall be there. We of the Triad have been long away, though I have stayed with the hope that one day we three would return. You and your friends have made that possible.

"I have but one request, Raven," he said as he set the cup down and turned to go. "To maintain the tenuous balance of the Lords of Light, I will need a priest to carry my banner. The three Lords must remain in balance, so please do this for us all."

"I shall, Lord," Raven replied softly.

Paladin raised a hand, turned, and walked away. Within a few steps, he shimmered and vanished.

"We need to get back to Catlorian," said Rene'. "We have to get the book and crystal to the Myrlin as soon as possible."

"The Myrlin wasn't there when we left. What make you think he will be there now?" Raven asked.

"I suppose we could deliver them to the Mage's Guild, but I think that could be dangerous," said the mage girl softly.

"Why don't we keep them for now until we can determine our next move?"

"I agree," said Solothon. "Now, where do we go?"

"To Borderlend."

They all turned to Bonaire as that one wiped his face on his cloak.

"I don't know what you guys are gonna do, but I have to see if my mom…"

"I agree, Bonaire," said the blond as he dumped his Kaff on the fire and placed his cup with the other cups in the pack for the packhorse. "First we travel to Borderlend, then Laranthia for information, and then to Heartstone. If your mother isn't in the area around Borderlend, she might have made it to Laranthia or Heartstone. Okay, my friend?"

"Okay," he responded a bit more positive than before. "What about the treasure? We can divide it up right here if you want."

"I think not, Bonaire," Raven said slowly. "Why don't you take care of it for us? You will be in charge of the packhorse anyway. Why don't you load the bulk of it to the packhorse, keeping some of it on you for emergencies, of course. That way you can keep an eye on it while we travel."

"Are you sure?" the young elf asked. "I mean, it's ours. All of us."

"We know, my friend, and we trust you to keep it safe and available if and when we need it," said the Huntsmaster.

"Okay!" he said as he stepped over to the packhorse and began unloading his full pockets. "You can count on me!"

Raven moved to his horse and checked the belly strap. Kohl arrived next to him and presented another problem.

"I have no horse, m'lord, nor can I ride. I can move quickly at need, but I will not be able to keep up at a gallop."

"I doubt we will need to gallop anywhere, my friend," replied the blond as he turned to the crystal golem with a grin. "We will be moving by Pentacle for most of our journey anyway, but I do have one question."

"What is that?"

"How did you—"

Kohl grinned and answered.

At one point, in the room with the horses, Shadow had snorted at the Huntsmaster's roan and the knight's black. Those two had backed the rest of the mounts into a corner and they'd taken their places with their sides to those horses and pressed them tightly into that corner. The big black pranced to that corner and, as he brought his eyes to the golem, pressed in close to the roan and snorted again. Kohl moved to the black's side and raised a hand to his neck.

"Then I found myself here with the mounts and your belongings."

"I see," said the prince with a grin.

They arrived at the Catlorian Pentacle as the sun fell toward the Western mountains in mid-winter splendor. Snow was on the ground just off of the Pentacle and crunched as Eton stepped off with the big black following him.

"This is where I leave you," he said.

"Where will you go, brother?" asked Raven.

"I'll start in Seaborne. If I don't find him there..." He shrugged.

"Then I will join you."

"No, Raven!" replied the warrior sternly. "You have a destiny and a mission. You will do more good once Dragon's Teeth is free once more. Get that done and then join me. Between your corsairs and our gladiators, those responsible stand no chance at all." Then, as the big warrior mounted Shadow, he said, "Travel safe, my friends."

The puma leaped to the barding on Shadow's flanks and the big horse whisked them into nothingness.

"He speaks truly, my lord," said Solothon as he moved to Raven's side.

"I know, my friend," he replied, "but I hate it."

"We have no way to know what the date is, Raven," commented Arantar. "If we are going, we'd better be about it."

The prince turned to Rene' and Melisande.

"Do the two of you have a need to stop in Catlorian," he asked, "or will you be traveling with us to Heartstone?"

"One is as dangerous as the other," Rene' responded, "considering what we carry."

"Then leave them with me."

The deep melodic voice came from the man in the black cloak as he stepped through the elms toward them. The cloak seemed to reflect the snow as he walked. He slid the hood from his features, revealing the sun-blond hair tied back and the mirrored silver of his eyes.

"Why would we do that?" asked the young prince, the anger in his voice obvious and his eyes molten amber.

"I know you are angry, Prince Raven, but answer me this. Would you be the man you are today and the leader of these good friends were I to have allowed your memory to return as quickly as you wished?"

The half elf let his anger slide away, and as his eyes cooled, he knew the Wanderer was correct.

"I thought not," continued Maxim Anteroe. "Now, the reason you should leave the items with me is that I can keep them safe, out of the hands of the evil that is attempting to take a foothold on this continent."

"That may be true," said Rene' softly, "but we found nothing of Radagast's armory. I know that the Myrlin wanted desperately to remove that temptation from Banshe'e's grasp."

"I know, Rene', because documents that reveal its former location exists only within Terillion's library."

"What?"

"Don't get excited," Maxim chuckled. "I said former. It has been... moved to a location where even I cannot get to it."

"The only place I know that would be safe from Banshe'e..." the mage girl mused. Then her head jerked up as she stared, wide-eyed, at the grinning Wanderer.

"Yes, daughter of Infinitus, but don't say it. That black-hearted sorcerer might try it anyway. Now, about those items?"

"Leave them with him, Rene'," said Raven softly. "They will be safer with him than with us, and probably safer than the Myrlin."

Rene' nodded and, as she retrieved *The Book of Summoning* from her pack, Melisande pulled the mesh bag from her secret pocket.

"See that these are secreted, Lord Anteroe," the mage girl said with a small amount of trepidation. "I'd not like to see them appear again."

"Trust me, Rene', they won't," he replied as he took both in his hands and they disappeared into his cloak.

"Borderlend is all but gone, Bonaire," said Anteroe to the young elf, "but your father is still there with members of the Western Border Guard searching through the ashes. As far as I've heard, they have not found your mother. There is hope."

"Thanks," said Bonaire, the tears beginning to well up again.

"We are going through there on the way to Laranthia," said Raven as he laid a hand on the young elf's shoulder. "What news?"

"That is a good plan, but don't tarry there. Heartstone is where you need to go. There you will find companions like yourselves who will help in the coming strife in Dragon's Teeth."

"What are we to do once there?"

"That I cannot say. I know only that Heartstone should be your true destination."

Wanderer turned then and walked away.

"Travel safe," floated back to their ears as he disappeared into the trees.

Raven sighed and looked at his companions.

"One problem behind us, one more in our path," Arantar stated.

Rene' thought for a moment, then turned to her friends. "We should travel by Pentacle to the location where we met, Arantar. From there we can ride to Borderlend, then on to Laranthia."

"All agree?" asked the prince. "Then..." He stepped to a pillar and began touching certain runes.

Epilogue

Rene' walked through the hushed streets toward the temples of Elvin kind. Her white robes flowed about her under the blood-red cloak. Her wardrobe contrasted with the black cloak of the black-haired cleric beside her.

Rene's firm step brought them to the steps of the temple to the goddess Celeste and she paused. A priest came from the doorway to greet them with a smile.

"May the grace of Lady Celeste bring you peace, beautiful ladies. How may I be of service?"

Rene' glanced down the street to the empty temple on the end while the man in silken robes turned his smile on Melisande. The smile vanished in fear as the cleric's eyes caught and held them, but it was Rene' who voiced their desire.

"You will take me to the High Priestess at once!"

He glanced from one to the other. Then, while Melisande waited outside, he ushered Rene' into the great hall.

"Doesn't the lady wish to join us?" he asked, his voice trembling a bit.

"I wouldn't bother her, were I you," she replied stonily.

Rene' looked about the symbols of the deities that had sprung up from the ages and shook her head.

The priest left her there and the mage girl looked once more on the golden heart that graced the door to her former temple. There were memories here, good memories, and she smiled.

"What is it you seek?" came the soft voice from behind.

Rene' turned to the sound and confronted Sl'everin. Her gasp was reflected in her friend's gaping awe as she looked the mage girl up and down.

"Rene', my sweet, what has happened to your gown? And your hair? Where have you been for so long? I was sent here to Heartstone to help in the House of Healing, and when I searched for you about the city..."

"Sl'everin!" said the mage girl softly, but with sternness the High Priestess had never heard before. "I have a duty and you must hear me!"

"A duty, Rene'?"

"Sl'everin, my friend, I am priestess to the Third of the Triad, Infinitus, of the Lords of Light and I have work to do."

While the priestess stood in shock trying to soak this in, Rene' continued.

"The Lords of Light have returned."